Visit the 'Alexandra' website: scan this code

Or type: https://xxxalexandra.blogspot.com
[Bing or Firefox recommended.]

"THE ADVENTURES OF ALEXANDRA."

SERIES 2

By STEPHEN J. WILLIAMS

Based on the original internet adventure series:"The amazing adventures of Alexandra" by Stephen J. Williams writing as 'William Alexander Stephens.'

THESE ARE THE ALTERNATIVE ADULT VERSIONS FROM 'THE TEMPORAL DETECTIVES' SERIES. THEY WILL DIFFER FROM THE ORIGINAL STORIES - AS PREVIOUSLY PUBLISHED - IN THAT SERIES. THEY ARE ONLY SUITABLE FOR ADULT AUDIENCES!

Series 2 contains ELEVEN selected episodes of those adventures from 2021. The series is also known as the **'THROUGH THE KEYHOLE'** collection.

IT WOULD GREATLY ASSIST THE READER TO ENJOY THESE STORIES, IF THEY ARE FAMILIAR WITH THE BOOK SERIES: 'THE TEMPORAL DETECTIVES' BY THE SAME AUTHOR.

ISBN-SBN: 9781738487578

NOTE*:* Cover and illustrations on pages 1, 3 & 6 found in the Public Domain with no copyright details apparent. Illustrations on page 155 & 373 and pages 488 to 489 are copyrighted by the author. All silhouette drawings were found in the Public Domain.

—— ⋆★⋆ ——

"INTRODUCTION TO THE TEMPORAL DETECTIVES and DETECTIVE ALEXANDRA CAPPANNI."

Jericho lives in Stark Island's Lighthouse on Heaven's Edge Bay, in the North of Scotland. A wild and desolate place, the now disused lighthouse is his home and office. You see, Jericho actually works for God! Well, his direct Boss is, for now, Angel Margret who is the current Duty Death Angel and runs the Temporal Detectives Department.

The Temporal Detectives police the current Timeline of Humanity on the lookout for people who, for whatever reason, have appeared in the wrong time and place in human history. Their mission is protecting the current human Timeline from unwanted changes.

Jericho is the Inspector currently in charge of TEAM 74. He has three full time assistants to help him: Temporal Detective Sergeant Wilson Franklyn, Temporal Detective Constable Alexandra Cappanni and trainee Temporal Detective Constable Owen Jones. The team has a full support staff at hand [as all Teams have]. The Support Staff provide anything - and I mean anything - that the Team may require to complete a mission successfully.

They can provide 'extras', period clothing, money, carriages and cars. For one mission to Ancient Egypt in 2300BC, they provided camels, servants, and gold - but no sunglasses! Another Department the Temporal Detectives have many dealings with is 'Collections'. These men and women collect the recently deceased souls for processing in the afterlife. They often call upon the detectives when they find no soul to collect and upon occasion; pass on a story that a soul has described to them that may require investigation.

They really are the 'front line' of the afterlife process! The 'Guardian's' Department specialises in vanquishing minor demons of the 'Dark Prince' and is waiting for the call from any of the temporal detectives at any time. Armed with a 'Staff of Mosses' they fearlessly tackle the demons of the underworld. Oscar Le Farge is such a Guardian and is well known to TEAM 74; he was Jericho's sergeant at one time and just loves returning to the lighthouse for dinner with his old colleagues and good friends.

But for the major demons and 'Dark Angels', there are the 'Knights of God' - these are the elite of the afterlife and are handpicked by the 'BOSS' himself [God]. Bestowed with special powers they are referred to as 'little angels' and can cross over into the world of living humans [both Dark Angels and Angels of Light are prohibited to enter the realm of living humans by agreement between the 'Boss' and the 'Dark Prince'.]

These are the naughty adventures of Temporal Detective Constable Alexandra Mary Cappanni [Nee Featherstone] who was born in 1871 in London. She was one of the few qualified female Doctors at the time. Alex worked at the Whitechapel Hospital in London's East End. Her father – Arthur – and her older brother – Charles – were also surgeons. Her younger sister Elizabeth was an aspiring actress on the London stage and married to a young lawyer, a certain Mister Jericho Tibbs!

But in 1901, Alexandra suddenly vanished and no trace of her was ever found, in that time period. But in 1790 there appeared in Italy; an English Countess of Cappanni; newly married to the dashing and handsome young Count of Cappanni; Henri the 16th Count.

Henri was a 'time traveler' and had persuaded Alex to abscond with him back to Cappanni in the 1790's. In 1801; tragedy struck the seemingly happy couple when Alex – in childbirth – almost died. Henri in a desperate bid to save her life; returned her to 1901 and sought her father and brother's assistance. He also knew that – if she died out of her ordained time period – her soul would be lost to the darkness of real death.

Alex could not be saved and died February 28th, 1901. But her soul was collected and processed. Temporal Detective Inspector Jericho Tibbs persuaded the Duty Death Angel – Margret – that she would be a valuable asset to the Department and so Alex joined the temporal detectives.

Having experienced death; Alex decided to grab this chance at 'living' again with both hands.

She certainly did that!"

SJW.

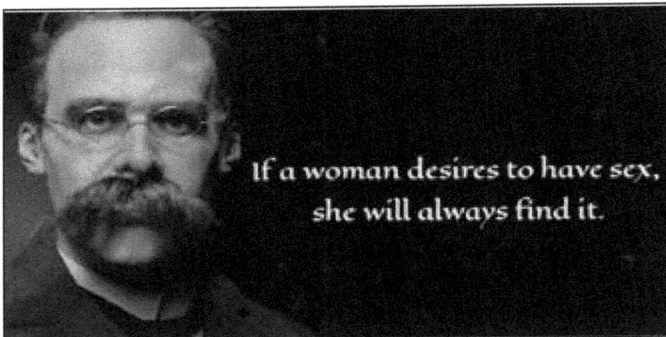

If a woman desires to have sex, she will always find it.

Friedrich Nietzsche

SERIES 2 EPISODES:

NOTE: 'TRIGGER' WARNINGS ARE SHOWN ON THE START PAGE OF EACH EPISODE.

1. ALEXANDRA'S DIRTY WEEKEND IN 1970'S BROOKLYN.
Start page: 13.

PROLOGUE: "Alexandra and Wilson are sent ahead to Brooklyn, New York City in 1972 to scout for a possible mission about ghostly apparitions appearing in a disused subway station. This is Wilson's old 'stamping ground' and he intends to show Alex a good time. What he doesn't know is that Alex also wants to show him a good time! But bloody earth-bound spirits keep getting in the way!"

The original version of this story is published and appears in the **TEMPORAL DETECTIVES:** Series 4 – Episode 9 entitled: ***"THE TROUBLED SPIRITS OF 153rd NORTH STREET SUBWAY STATION."*** This is a special **EXTENDED** episode of the original story.

2. ALEXANDRA, HARRY, TESS & LISA TOO...
Start page: 65.

PROLOGUE: "Ms. Teresa Green - A Human Agent for Jericho Tibbs in England during the early 21st Century - passes a strange story onto Jericho which he may be interested in. Apparently, a local London magazine has reported a story about an unknown young man, who is visiting stores and markets in the city purchasing large quantities of Victorian and Edwardian money. Alex finally meets the handsome and dashing Harry Hadden and with her friend Lisa [from Team 52] they arrange to meet Harry...."

The original version of this story is published and appears in the **TEMPORAL DETECTIVES:** Series 3 – Episode 4 entitled: ***"STRANGER'S MARKET."***

3. ALEXANDRA AND THE ARTIST.
Start page: 105.

PROLOGUE: "An art exhibition being held in a major London gallery, in Summer 2016 is causing quite a stir in the 'Conspiracy Theory Community' and social media is filled with theories about the pictures of a certain Victorian painter; Cranfield Sommers. Some sharp-eyed conspiracy followers have spotted something strange about some of the models; three of the girls shown in the extensive collection are dead ringers for three missing women - from 2016 - and even their family and friends agree that the models are doubles of the missing girls. But the paintings are dated between 1870 and 1872! Jericho is on the scene because not only the girls are missing; but so are their souls. Alex is about to get painted; several times!"

The original version of this story is published and appears in the **TEMPORAL DETECTIVES:** Series 4 – Episode 10 entitled*: "THE MYSTERIOUS PAINTINGS OF CRANFIELD SOMMERS."* This is a special **EXTENDED** episode of the original story.

4. ALEXANDRA AND THE PROFESSOR.
Start page: 156.

PROLOGUE: "Dr. Xavier Tabbert opened his hospital for the chronically sick in the autumn of 1849. It was supposed to be a place of final and peaceful rest for those facing certain death; in modern times it would be referred to as a 'Hospice'. Now in 1999, a team of paranormal students under Professor Alec Sweetman have arrived at the derelict hospital to investigate the many strange happenings that have occurred over the years - are they about to encounter some real evil? Alex finds that that the professor isn't just interested in dead people!"

The original version of this story is published and appears in the **TEMPORAL DETECTIVES:** Series 3 – Episode 7 entitled:
"XAVIER TABBERT'S HOSPITAL FOR THE DEAD, THE DYING AND THE UNFORGIVEN."

5. ALEXANDRA AND THE DARK PHARAOH.
Start page: 194.

PROLOGUE: "Pharaoh Amenhotep V's magician has been ordered to investigate a strange mirror that appears to show alternative versions of the future - apparently, the mirror was robbed from an ancient tomb which belonged to the legendary magician; Tha, who is said to have received it from the God Thoth himself. But the King is known as the 'Dark Pharaoh' and plans to use the device for his own benefit and alter the destiny of his ancient Empire. Mr. Tibbs is dispatched to protect the current Timeline from change. Alex finds out that he's also known as the 'Horny Pharaoh!'"

The original version of this story is published and appears in the **TEMPORAL DETECTIVES:** Series 1 – Episode 9 entitled: ***"PHARAOH AMENHOTEP V AND THE MIRROR OF TIME."***

6. ALEXANDRA ENCOUNTERS THE OTHER NAPOLEON BONAPARTE.
Start page: 240.

PROLOGUE: "Alexandra is with the team in 1814, investigating Napoleon's new mysterious mistress who has jumped back from 1864 and intends to change the great man's fate. The team hatches an audacious plan to trick the emperor and discover his new mistress's plans and thwart them; which means Alexandra has to lure the emperor away from the scheming woman and she certainly has the talent to do that!"

The original version of this story is published and appears in the **TEMPORAL DETECTIVES:** Series 3 – Episode 5 entitled: ***"NAPOLEON'S CHINESE CABINET OF MAGIC – PART 1."***

7. ALEXANDRA AND THE OXFORD SPIRIT CHASERS.
Start page: 278.

PROLGUE: "Britain is basking in an unprecedented heatwave with a drought declared, but a small group of students at Oxford University have other matters on their minds. This group consists of students - who are studying various degrees - that have formed a very special out of study club; 'The Spirit Chasers'. While they do like the 'hard stuff', the spirits they chase don't come in bottles! But it's when they decide to play with an old Ouija board, found in an attic that things start to go wrong. Mr. Tibbs is sent to investigate, and Alex meets a hunky professor and his team..."

The original version of this story is published and appears in the **TEMPORAL DETECTIVES:** Series 4 – Episode 8 entitled: ***"THE OXFORD OUIJA BOARD SESSIONS."***

8. ALEXANDRA AND THE SCHOOL FOR SCANDAL.
Start page: 320.

PROLOGUE: "In the spring 0f 1961 at a very expensive and exclusive girls school there are some very strange happenings occurring and Jericho Tibbs is ordered to investigate after a soul goes missing. So, team 74 must jump back and Alexandra finds herself playing the role of A school Matron, whilst young Owen must appear as his alto ego: 'Jacqueline' and go undercover as a Schoolgirl. They find some very naughty girls and a chef who is better at sex than cooking and some gardeners who look after more than the school grounds!"

The original version of this story is published and appears in the **TEMPORAL DETECTIVES:** Series 5 – Episode 3 entitled: ***"QUEEN CHARLOTTE'S ACADEMY HOSTS THE DEVIL."*** This is a special **EXTENDED** episode of the original story.

9. ALEXANDRA AND THE SNOOKER, STOCKINGS & DEVILISH DECEIT PLOT."
Start page: 374.

PROLOGUE: "Alexandra is under investigation after a saucy picture of her appears in a newspaper in 1985. It appears that she's been on a date with David; the Dark Prince. They apparently attended the famous 'Black Ball' World Snooker Championship Final and Alex was caught flashing her stocking tops and panties to the TV cameras! But Alex gets the opportunity to visit someone she really wanted to see."

The original version of this story is published and appears in the **TEMPORAL DETECTIVES:** Series 3 – Episode 10 entitled: **"SNOOKER, STOCKINGS & DEVILISH DECEIT."**

10. ALEXANDRA AND THE BUFFALO SOLDIERS.
Start page: 411.

PROLOGUE: "In 1864 a small company of African American soldiers – soon to be known to the Arapahos Indians as 'Buffalo Soldiers' because of their bravery and courage - are trekking through the wilds of South Kansas on the North Oklahoma border, heading for the strange town of 'Devil's Dyke' and come upon a band of Arapahos under war Chief Youngblood. What happened when the two groups meet brings Jericho Tibbs on the scene because the timeline is threatened with change. Alex meets some interesting young men who really want to get to know her!"

The original version of this story is published and appears in the **TEMPORAL DETECTIVES:** Series 4 – Episode 7 entitled: **"YOUNGBLOOD AND THE BUFFALO SOLDIERS."** This is a special **EXTENDED** episode of the original story.

11. ALEXANDRA'S TITANIC NIGHT TO REMEMBER."
Start page: 462.

PROLOGUE: "April 1912 - the ill-fated RMS Titanic is sinking: But when Mrs. Lucy Crawford gives up her place in the lifeboat, the services of Mr. Tibbs and his team are required to protect the Time-Line - she should have survived the sinking, but for some reason she abandons her seat to a strange young man and this gesture will change the future - and possibly not for the best! Our Alex gets something to remember when the heating in her cabin goes wrong...."

The original version of this story is published and appears in the **TEMPORAL DETECTIVES:** Series 2 – Episode 10 entitled: ***"MRS. LUCY CRAWFORD LEAVES LIFEBOAT No.13."***

EPISODE 1: "ALEXANDRA'S DIRTY WEEKEND IN 1970'S BROOKLYN."

EPISODE PROLOGUE: "Alexandra and Wilson are sent ahead to Brooklyn, New York City in 1971 to scout for a possible mission about ghostly apparitions appearing in a disused subway station. This is Wilson's old 'stamping ground' and he intends to show Alex a good time. What he doesn't know is that Alex also wants to show him a good time! But bloody earth-bound spirits keep getting in the way!"

75 Minutes approx. Episode Warnings: Smoking – Alcohol – Strong language – Violence [including sexual violence and BDSM] – Strong graphic sexual references – Mild horror – References to death, Devil worship & Witchcraft – Human sacrifice.

NOTES: This is the **ADULT version** of the original story which is published and appears in the **TEMPORAL DETECTIVES:** Series 4 – Episode 9 entitled: *"THE TROUBLED SPIRITS OF 153rd NORTH STREET SUBWAY STATION."* This is a special EXTENDED episode of the original story.

CAUTION: Recommended for **18+** only.

1. THE NEW MISSION.

Alex had actually made up her mind about Wilson some days ago. All that was needed now; was opportunity. She relaxed in her favourite armchair by the fireplace and flicked through the brown paper file that 'little Ivan' the Messenger had delivered for Jericho. She slowly sipped her brandy and read with some interest about the forthcoming assignment.

She peered over the top of the file and saw Mr. Parker sprawled across the coffee table, cleaning his front paws. "This sounds quite interesting Mr. Parker; we could have a trip to New York in the 1970's. Well, 1972 to be exact, investigating some strange happenings in a city subway station."

She leaned across and stroked the big cat with some affection; "That will make Wilson happy, going back to his glory days as a Detective with the NYPD." A naughty thought popped into her head, and she actually giggled a little. "If Wilson and I could get some time together – alone for once – I believe I could pull it off." She slumped back in the chair and placed the file down. Then ran her hands around her breasts and imagined his big hands cupping a tit and pushing it into his warm, wet mouth with his tongue running across her erect nipple.

She was having some delicious thoughts about what would follow that act when the study door swung open and the man himself wandered in. He was clutching a paperback novel and he grinned at Alex, who dropped her hands immediately. "For once, you actually recommended a book that was really good. I loved it. I didn't think a Frenchman could have such imagination; bloody submarines before they were even thought of and a sodding big octopus: marvelous." He dropped into the armchair opposite and grinned.

"What's in the report?" He asked, giving the book to Mr. Parker to play with on the coffee table. "Anything that we may find interesting?" He added, stretching his legs out and relaxing. Alex stirred in her seat and smiled; "Do you want a brandy?" She asked and rose from the chair and headed for the tray of glasses and brandy bottle that Mr. Harris had placed there earlier. Wilson nodded; "Thanks baby sister."

Alex filled a glass and walked back, handing Wilson the brandy.

"You may find this assignment interesting; its back to New York in 1972." She smiled again, slowly resuming her seat. She crossed her legs and straightened her long dress, picking up her own glass of brandy. "Back to your glory days."

Wilson chuckled; "I wouldn't call them glory days – I was killed - if you remember." He sipped his brandy and thought about Alex's long slender legs, under that crappy Edwardian dress and he sneaked a glance at those magnificent tits; hidden under that crisp white blouse. He licked his lips and sipped his brandy again. His thoughts recalled Alex dancing naked around that old tree stump at Hobbs Wood; those large and perfect tits bouncing about – topped with dark erect nipples. He took a little breath, when he remembered the sight of her shaven fanny, coming open and then closing, as she squatted and opened her legs to lure the fucking demon out of its hiding place.

Then, laying on her front and pushing her delightful arse in the air and pulling her cheeks apart. He almost groaned, as he remembered catching a glimpse of her bum hole being opened; what a fucking invitation, little wonder that demon simply could not resist – what a fucking sight! [See the episode **'Alexandra and the Archaeologist'.**]

The memory of those few minutes haunted his sleep and clouded his thoughts when awake. He finished his brandy and tried to drive such memories away – but he couldn't – no matter how hard he tried. The sight of her vagina's beautiful full lips; pink and clearly moist, simply would not depart his thoughts. He smiled at her and visualised her sitting naked, opposite him on that damn armchair, crossing and uncrossing her legs just for him.

"Penny for your thoughts." She smiled at him, as she caught the look upon the big man's face and her own thoughts were about his magnificent, large black cock. They both chuckled, as if they knew each other's erotic thoughts and their smiles betrayed those thoughts, much as they tried to hide them.

"Do you want a refill?" She asked and he nodded; yes. He watched intently as she walked to the drinks tray again. Her perfect peach arse seemed to hypnotize him and he watched the swing of her hips with real passion. She looked over her shoulder and gave a little – almost knowing – smile. "Not a penny, but a bloody pound." Alex actually giggled a little and bent over the tray, pouring another couple of brandies. She knew that his eyes were fixed firmly on her bum and she smoothed the back of her dress; so that he could get a better view.

"Apparently, it all centres's around a subway station that is closed and under refurbishment; 153rd North Street Station, I believe." She could feel the big man watching her and that made her smile; maybe I should drop him a little hint about what's on offer. But he's already seen me stark naked, so it would have to be something a little erotic and naughty – but what? That thought really did make her happy and she walked back with their drinks.

They sat opposite each other; talking softly about what the mission could entail. "I would have to find an appropriate costume for the period, but you could go just as you are." Alex laughed, then added; "You could give me some advice on that front, after all, you must have noticed what girls were wearing back then. So tell me what I should wear." Wilson took a little breath and grinned.

"Well, if you were my white bitch and I was taking you up town. You would be wearing a real short skirt with bare legs and heels. A low-cut top with no bra, a little black leather jacket and small matching bag, your hair would be tied with a ribbon and around your neck would be a black collar; meaning your my bitch." He really did smile, at the thought of Alex dressed like a black man's bitch; he sipped his brandy with some joy.

Alex nodded; "Well, I if you think such an outfit would be appropriate, I will wear it. But what panties would I be wearing? For the sake of authenticity, of course." Wilson shrugged his shoulders; "Little white cotton panties, they were always a favourite of mine. So, if you're pretending to be my bitch, you'd certainly be wearing them." He could feel a slight shift in his cock – Jesus, he thought - she's giving me an erection, just by talking about her damn panties; never mind seeing them, or better still, slowly pulling them off. He swallowed down his brandy and

moved awkwardly in his chair, his swelling cock could be a real problem. He was saved by Owen bouncing into the room; followed by a serious looking Jericho, who picked up the file and read it quite slowly. Owen poured himself a drink and asked if anyone else wanted one. Jericho muttered a 'yes please' and dropped into the chair that Alex had vacated. She stretched by the fire and accepted a refill from Owen. Wilson watched her closely. Her gentle movements, pushing out those wonderful tits and peach shaped arse, he took the brandy from Owen without comment.

Jericho coughed and everyone turned to him; "According to newspaper and television reports coming out of the city in 1972, several people have complained that they saw strange figures about the empty – its being repaired – 153rd North Street Station in the city. It's been derelict for years. One report is particularly interesting for us, it says that a certain construction worker, a Mr. Monroe Jones actually saw a women in strange old-fashioned clothing, walk straight through a wall opposite him; he dropped everything and ran for it."

Everyone chuckled; Earth bound spirits – usually the souls of people who had died and weren't too happy about it and refused to accompany their collectors – for whatever reason. "Why would they be congregating in an old subway station?" Owen asked and stroked Mr. Parker, who threw the book Wilson had given him and kicked it away with his back legs. Owen also stared at the stretching Alex and really did smile; she was a very good friend to him – a very good friend. He slumped in the chair opposite where she stood; talking to Jericho and remembered that quiet afternoon with great fondness and pleasure.

"Maybe all the disturbance of the station has unearthed something that affects them?" Alex offered her opinion and caught the look on Owens's face, as he stared at her, smiling and remembering. He would certainly hold Alex to her promise.

2. SOLOMON COHEN'S HOTEL, JULY 1972, BROOKLYN NYC.

"The room's at the back so it's quiet - very little street noise - and the room's here are clean and well furnished. Solomon does a lot of trade with Jewish businessmen and so he keeps the place up to a good standard." Wilson dangled the key and they walked to the elevator after signing in. He smiled at Alex in her 1970's costume - which was quite respectable - and the pair found Room17 on the fourth floor. "I thought a 'midi-dress' and blouse would be fine with these heels." she explained as Wilson unlocked the door, adding; "Besides, I couldn't wear a short dress with the underwear I'm wearing." Alex giggled a little and Wilson really smiled in anticipation. He absolutely loved being back in NYC in 1972 and on his old stomping grounds. All he had to do was avoid bumping into himself!

He placed the small suitcase down and headed for the mini-bar and found two miniature bottles of brandy and a couple of clean glasses. Alex sat on the huge 'King-sized' bed and bounced up and down for a few seconds; it felt good. He handed her a glass and raised his own; "To Brooklyn." he muttered, and Alex returned the salute saying; "And for what we are about to receive." They both chuckled and sipped their drinks. Alex placed her's on the bedside cabinet and stood. Wilson watched her carefully with a spreading smile. Alex slowly removed her blouse and skirt to reveal a black Basque that simply couldn't restrain her large breasts and her big nipples spilled out over the top. She was wearing sheer black silk stockings and suspender belt with tiny 'see-through' lace panties. She gave Wilson a twirl, bending over to show her magnificent peach shaped bum to him.

Wilson placed his empty glass down and gathered her to him and they kissed passionately for some minutes. Then Alex pulled off his jacket, shirt and tie while he ran his hands over her body. She unbuttoned his bright coloured 'flared' trousers and snapped open his belt. They dropped to the floor and her hands went straight into his shorts and found what she wanted. She eased his big erecting cock out and caressed it gently.

 "I know what you would like." she whispered and knelt down, easing the monster into her mouth. She worked his throbbing shaft with her lips and tongue, pushing her soft wet mouth down upon his erection with some skill. He stoked her hair gently and groaned a little with sheer pleasure.

Alex slipped onto the bed and lay on her back; legs open, slowly removing her Basque and Wilson crept between those long legs and gently pulled down those little black panties. His mouth and fingers went straight on her already wet vagina and with some skill, worked on her clitoris as she groaned stroking his head and whispering encouragement; not that the big man needed any!

Alex reached to the bedside table and pulled her handbag down. Fumbling inside and finding the 'KY' jelly. She knew damn well that she would need plenty of the magic potions to cope with

Wilson's big cock. He knelt over her as she smeared her fanny and his cock with the jelly. He then mounted her and pushed his cock into her willing cunt; gently at first and then started to thrust with some determination and joy. She gripped his shoulders and said softy; "Fuck me hard like a black man's whore." He chuckled and replied; "I can sure do that." And did.

Wilson fucked her hard and fast causing Alex to have a couple of little orgasms quickly. Their mouths came to together and the passion exploded between the two. They were soon rolling about the bed, fucking in various positions and when Alex was astride him riding like a Rodeo rider, her first big orgasm came. It was so powerful that her legs shook, and she screamed with sexual passion, really bouncing up and down. Wilson now gripped her swinging breasts and held on as she fucked him hard. Alex had a couple more -much smaller - spurts and Wilson thrusted upwards, cussing a little as he finally came inside of her. Alex's mouth found his and they lay kissing with some real passion.

They were still locked together when the bedside phone buzzed. Wilson reached over and answered it as Alex kissed his neck and shoulders; he spoke softly to the caller for about two minutes and replaced the receiver. He embraced Alex again and said quietly; "That was the receptionist; he says that witness - Monroe Jones - called and said we could call around this evening after he finishes the afternoon shift. I know the address." Alex sighed and stroked his face; "Yes, but we do have time for some more, don't we?" Wilson just grinned and turned her gently onto her back, pulling open her legs as she giggled. "Damn right we do." was all the big man said.

They fucked for another half hour, and both lay exhausted on the bed, caressing each other and kissing. Their conversions were just whispers and Wilson checked his watch; "Let's grab a shower and get on with the job." Alex nodded and smiled; "I thought we just did." They both chuckled and kissed passionately some more before - reluctantly - departing for the bathroom to share a well-earned shower. Alex's dirty weekend in Brooklyn had started well and she really wanted that to continue.

3. MONROE JONES APPARTMENT - PART 1.

 Alex was wearing a real short skirt with bare legs and heels. A low-cut top with no bra and a little black leather jacket and matching bag. Her hair was tied with a ribbon and around her neck was a black lace collar; meaning she was Wilson's white bitch or 'snow-bunny'. She had followed Wilson's advice to the letter, and he really appreciated it. They walked up two flights of stairs with Alex a few steps in front so that Wilson could really, really appreciate her outfit. He chuckled; "Sweet Jesus Alex; if those little white panties were any smaller, they would be a finger plaster." She just looked over her shoulder and smiled. Wilson banged on the apartment door and they both could hear music coming from behind it. "Monroe has taste; that's Jimi Hendrix's 'Who knows' playing." He said as the door was pulled open. Alex and Wilson stared, and then smiled, refraining from laughing outright. The well-built black man was dressed in a superb white cocktail dress with all the accessories including white heels. He smiled at the pair; "I like to dress comfortably in the evenings after finishing work for the day. Do come in and have a drink. What would you like I have quite a bar." He gestured for them to enter, and they did; still smiling. As Monroe fixed them drinks; Wilson whispered to Alex; "I've dealt with Monroe before; he's a Drag-Queen who does turns at the Apollo Theatre in Harlem and he has quite a following."

Alex nodded looking around the incredibly glamorous apartment which was furnished like - in her modest opinion - a Paris brothel! But she said it was lovely when asked by Monroe as he handed around the drinks.

Alex and Wilson sat on the huge pink, fur covered sofa and sipped their brandies. Monroe confessed he had made himself a 'Manhattan' cocktail. He sipped it with some grace and sat very lady-like on the big pink armchair. Wilson asked him about the subway ghost and Monroe happily recounted his tale of seeing the woman dressed in 1920's clothing disappearing through a solid wall, right in front of him. "I nearly wet my panties because I know fashion and she was dressed like a 'flapper' from the 1920's." He spoke quietly between sips of his large cocktail. He was quite amusing with little 'one-liners' and near the knuckle jokes [for 1972] especially about President Nixon. He re-filled their glasses and Alex asked where the bathroom was; she really needed to pee. He pointed to a vivid red door marked 'LADIES?' and smiled. "Straight in there darling and don't mind Honey Bunny: she's crashed out in the bath."

Alex noticed another door - painted jungle green - was marked with a sign declaring 'CHARLIES ROOM'. Like a lot of New York ers, Monroe must share his apartment to help pay the rent she mused and pushed into the bathroom.

"My God Wilson darling where did you get her from? She's absolutely gorgeous and does your wife know about her?" Monroe asked Wilson quietly and Wilson just smiled, explaining that Alex was his partner for this operation; Detective Alex Cappanni from the 23rd precinct. Monroe grinned and rolled his eyes; "Of course darling. If Lizzie [Wilson's wife] believes that, then so do I!" Wilson just chuckled at that and finished his drink. Monroe leapt up and headed for the kitchen/bar to fetch more. Alex re-joined Wilson and spoke softly; "There's a stark-naked young woman lying in the bath - probably been taking something more than aspirin - covered in feathers; the bloody things are everywhere; she must have busted open a couple of pillows."

Wilson nodded; "Honey Bunny is a part time actress and prostitute who works the hotels around here. Her tricks are normally middle-aged white businessmen and her most popular costume is a Cheerleader. She's OK actually but does smoke a lot of weed and pops some pretty interesting pills." Alex sat and smiled; "You really did have an interesting career, didn't you?" That made Wilson laugh and they were joined by Monroe with more drinks.

They sat talking and drinking until the bathroom door opened and 'Honey bunny' wandered out - still stark naked and with a few feathers in her hair - she smiled at everyone and without a word went in the kitchen. Alex now noticed the thin red stripes across the girls buttocks and Monroe lowered his voice; "One of her best paying and regular tricks likes to cane her on occasion; usually makes her dress in his teenage daughter's cast-offs. He makes her piss on him too. I understand he works on Wall Street."

'Honey-Bunny' joined them clutching a huge glass of Bourbon and coke and sat cross legged on the floor and smiled at everyone again. Finally, she spoke; "I know him, he's a cop and he's alright according to Fingers and the Bear. But that is some high-class white hooker he has there." She spoke directly to Alex: "I bet you make fifty or sixty dollars a trick, don't you?"

Alex just smiled as Wilson explained - again - that Alex was also a detective. 'Honey-Bunny' just laughed and swigged her drink with gusto; "Yeah and I'm President Nixon's bit on the side." Alex said nothing and finished her drink, tapping Wilson's leg as a signal they should go; he had promised to take her to a Disco-club.

Monroe showed them out, insisting they do drop in anytime and pushed several tickets to his show at the Apollo into Wilson's hand. He kissed Alex on the cheek and whispered; "My you are lucky girl. I've heard he's built like a donkey and knows how to use it." Alex smiled and thanked him for his hospitality. Wilson waved down a yellow cab and told the driver to head for the 'Roller-Disco'. He smiled at Alex; "I do hope you can roller skate and dance at the same time." She eased into the cab giving him another close up of her 'sticking plaster' panties and said, "You'll be surprised at what I can do." He climbed in and placed a kiss on her head; "Believe me I know what you can do." The cab pulled away as the dark was closing in and Brooklyn's night life was starting to wake up.

They made it back to the hotel just before midnight and the Night-Porter let them in and Wilson slipped him a couple of dollars for his trouble. They had dived into their room, pulling each other's clothes off almost in frenzy and were soon naked and fucking on the bed and the floor. Wilson whispered to Alex, and she groaned; "Bloody men. But you'll have to take care; even my bloody bum hole isn't that big."

Alex was bent over the big armchair with her knees on the seat and both hands gripping the back. Wilson had his big hands on her shoulders and his big cock pushed into her well lubricated bum hole. He was thrusting gently, but deep and slow. He was groaning with real pleasure; if he was a cat he would be purring right now. Alex took little deep breaths as she felt every inch of his cock pushing into her back passage. "What is it with bloody men and bum love?" she asked quietly between almost gritted teeth. Wilson just chuckled and started to thrust with a little more speed. "I'm in heaven darling, so keep bloody still while I enjoy every inch of your arse."

He fucked her for almost twenty minutes before he came in her arse and then he sat on the chair; still buried in Alex's backside and she pushed an arm around his neck, and they managed to kiss. She stared down between her legs at the big black cock up her arse and with her other hand rubbed her fanny vigorously, soon joined by Wilson's hand and she climaxed groaning loudly. They remained together for some minutes, kissing and soft whispering, then separated and collapsed on the bed and slept well.

4. "I DON'T BELIEVE IN NO GHOSTS......"

Maurice 'Mo' Breckenridge pushed his hard hat back and took a long draw on his cigarette and waved his hand down the steps of the South Entrance of 153rd North Street Subway station; "Get those silly buggers back down there! How the hell can I call the Office and tell bloody Mister Taylor that the bloody crews have walked off site because they saw a bloody ghost! I'm not making that call, we're already five days behind schedule, now get the lazy buggers out the vans and back down there!" The small man gripped his hard hat with both hands and tried to smile; "I've told them that Mo and they just told me to fuck off....I think you should speak to them on this one. Sorry."

Mo grunted and threw his cigarette down and patted little Derek on the shoulder; "Ok my old friend. I will, now get that cement lorry backed up to the Shute; if we don't pour this afternoon, we will be in the shit good and proper." Little Derek smiled and was gone. Mo straightened his jacket and lit another cigarette, then headed for the two vans parked outside the Italian café. He wasn't happy to find the vans empty and his crew sitting in the coffee shop. "Fuck it." Was all he said and strode into the café causing all conversation to cease.

The café owner had to ask him to moderate his language because there were ladies present, but Mo's men got the message alright. Back to work or their wages docked. Slowly and very reluctantly they left the café and walked back to the derelict subway entrance. Little Derek shepherded them back down the stairs and they gathered on the old South platform.

Mo walked back to his Plymouth and eased in, leaving the door open. He removed his hat and jacket, cursing this wonderfully clear but hot day. He lit another cigarette and watched the traffic passing slowly on this warm day. He pulled the blueprints from his battered old briefcase and stared at them. 153rd North Street Subway station had closed in 1929 after the new 14th West Avenue Subway Station opened and lay closed and unvisited since. Well; except for the odd inspection Team from City Hall. It had been one of those teams that found the damage to the South platform and the disused offices. Serious damage warranting immediate action and thus the Cities Emergency Building Team was on scene. The Engineer in charge was Frank Taylor and he was a hard task master. Well, he was an utter bastard actually, but Mo seemed to get on with him.

"Fucking ghosts, I don't believe in no bloody ghosts." He softly muttered to himself and leaned back in his seat and then noticed patrolman Sean Finlay walking towards him. He had known the cop for at least fifteen years around this beat. He held up a hand and shouted; "Sean! What's up man?" Sean had his hat off, wiping his brow and neck. He sauntered over and smiled. "How are your ghosts getting on Mo my friend?" and chuckled shoving his hat back on and leaned on the car door. Mo just sighed and then smiled; "You know what those fuckers are like, they would down tools if a mouse ran up their trouser leg." Sean chuckled again; "So you haven't heard the news about the experts coming from Boston University. Real experts my friend and they will tackle your ghost problem for you!"

Mo groaned and didn't smile; that's all he needed now; bloody ghost hunters from a bloody university! He nodded; "Finding them two dead vagrants down there has fucked up all my schedules. Now my moronic workmen are seeing fucking ghosts. That's all I bloody need. Do we know what killed the mangy old men?" Sean shrugged his shoulders; "I knew both of them; they had been together for years around here. Both liked paint stripper and Budweiser cocktails, so I dare say that didn't help. Feel kinda sorry for them; one was an ex-Ranger who landed at Normandy, the other was some kind of disgraced bank clerk who did time up In Rochester, back in the fifties."

He stood back from the door and slowly tipped his hat back; "Apparently they will be here tomorrow and here's the worse bit; three of them are limey's including the professor in charge and one's a bloody woman." He smiled broadly at his friends face; Mo didn't like anyone who wasn't American, and he certainly didn't like women in positions of authority. "How the fuck can you be a professor of something that don't exist? That doesn't make sense. Shit, what a pile of crap." Mo said and threw his cigarette butt down. Sean just smiled and walked off towards the Italian café: it was time for a coffee and a doughnut.

Mo made his way back to the subway station and descended into the cool dim station. He grunted with satisfaction as the cement pour was under way and stared up at the fantastic roof murals; now they did impress him. They showed famous monuments of New York City; well famous before 1929. He really admired the craftsmanship in them. "Fucking real builders back in the day; not like the fucking cowboys and so-called architects of today." He muttered to himself and lit yet another cigarette. That's when he saw the two men standing on the tracks by the tunnel entrance to the platform. He watched as they threw down their shovels and turned, running like hell towards the platform.

They scrambled up the platform edge screaming; "There's a fucking train coming!" Mo watched in utter disbelieve and horror as the carriages flashed past him and the two men groveling on the platform floor. There was no sound whatsoever and the 'train' passed down the tracks and disappeared south in an instance.
 There was absolute silence for a second or two and then a dozen men ran up the station stairs; screaming and shouting, tools clattering down the steps followed by hard hats.

 Unsurprisingly, Mo was one of them. He had changed his mind about ghosts.

5. "WHO YOU GONNA CALL?"

 'Mo' Breckenridge sat sweating and lit another cigarette; this wasn't going to be pleasant. He stared through the glass door of Frank Taylor's office and saw the big man sitting at his cluttered desk; phone in one hand and huge cigar in the other. Mavis – the secretary – handed Mo a cup of coffee and whispered; "He's been on the phone to the Mayor's Office twice this morning already. Apparently, the Mayor is having kittens about all this; the press is all over the story." She walked back to her desk and continued typing and the keys hitting the ribbon and paper seemed to annoy Mo, who wiped his face slowly.

He sipped his coffee and jumped a little when Mavis's phone rang. She answered it and said 'Yes' a couple of times and placed the receiver down. She actually managed a small smile; "They're here Mo." Was all she said and eased from her chair and walked to the door and opened it, then stood waiting. Mo stood slowly and wiped his face and neck with a gaudy orange hankie. He stared past Mavis into the corridor and saw the lift doors open:

five people slowly walked from the lift, heading towards him and Mavis. One man he knew was Phil DeVine; from the City's Building Works Department. He was actually smiling and talking with a very well-dressed younger man. Mo then noticed the big black man – again, in an expensive suit – and thought he looked like a cop. The other younger man looked like a faggot and Mo sighed; they get everywhere! He then saw the woman walking at the rear and Mo really smiled – for the first time in days – she was an absolute stunner in a dark mini-dress with matching shoes and little hat. She could easily walk a 'catwalk' with that body and beautiful face; so, what the fuck was she wasting her time chasing ghosts for? He straightened his tie and wiped his face again. Mavis showed them in and offered coffee's all round. Phil knocked on Frank's door and stuck his head in. "That team from the Dean's office at Boston University are here Frank." He walked back and sat on the edge of Mavis's desk and admired the lady from Boston.

Frank Taylor appeared in the doorway and stared at his visitors. "Which of you is Professor Tibbs?" he asked, sucking on his cigar and Jericho held out his hand and introduced himself and his team. Frank crushed his hand and smiled; cigar gripped lightly between his teeth. "I'm glad to meet you prof and I really hope you can fucking help; I'm nine days behind schedule and up to my arse in fucking ghosts. The mayor is crawling up my butt and I have newspapers popping out of every hole that ain't already occupied!"

Jericho rubbed his hand and managed a smile; "Thank you Frank. That was quite a succinct appraisal of the situation." Owen couldn't stifle a little giggle and got a strange look from Mo who shrugged his shoulders; I was right about him, another fucking queer. Frank ushered everyone into his much bigger office and turned up the air conditioning. Like Mo and Phil; he couldn't take his eyes off Alex; who he offered a chair immediately and watched – almost memorized – as she sat so gracefully and ladylike despite the short skirt. He noticed her bare legs and realised that she had just panties covering heaven's gateway.

Phil speaking drew his reluctant attention back to the meeting. "I've authorized the professor and his team full access to the old station for them and their equipment. They're keen to get down there. Apparently, they will be joined by a certain Father Adams from the Cardinals office in Boston. He's another expert on these

matters and if the Church is involved, then we're in good hands."
Phil spoke to the group but stared at Alex's long bare legs the
whole time. Like Frank he wasn't too subtle about showing his
appreciation of the female form.

The meeting broke up and Frank stopped Alex as she was last to
leave and suggested a drink at a little Irish bar he knew. She just
smiled at him and joined the team heading in silence to the lift.
The city had placed a hire car – a station wagon – at their
disposal and use. Wilson would be the driver; he obviously knew
the city well. The team picked up the car and threw their
baggage in and headed for their hotel which was just a block
down from the old subway station. Owen suggested they walk
from the hotel and Wilson just sighed; "Walk from the hotel if
you wish my baby brother; but you may not reach the subway
station in one piece." He chuckled and the 'ghost busters' drove
to the 'Plaza Hotel' and booked in. Wilson parked the car in the
basement parking area and chatted with the two 'brothers' who
ran the place. Alex noticed some dollar bills were handed over
and she knew that parking was free for guests.

She asked him about that; "Well, the brothers believe I'm some
rich black dude from Boston and they're now sweet and will take
good care of the car. Their friends can steal someone's car that
isn't as generous as me." He grinned and Alex pushed her arm
through his and they walked into reception and found Jericho was
already signing for keys and arranging the luggage to be taken to
their rooms. He smiled broadly; "Father Adam's should be here
by this afternoon." Everyone smiled at that; they all liked the old
priest. He had assisted the team before and they all knew his
worth.

Jericho and Alex had their own room each and Wilson shared
with Owen. They were on floor twelve and Jericho would share
with Father Adam's when he turned up. Unusually, he didn't mind
sharing with his old friend. He respected the old priest and was
actually looking forward to the conversations the pair would
have. After they settled in their rooms; they met up in the hotel
restaurant for lunch. It was excellent and Owen had two helpings
of everything ordered. After lunch they would meet up with Mo
at the haunted station.

Alex pointed out that her door had two 'Chubb' locks and two
heavy duty chains. She had also noticed that there was a red

'panic' button by the bed's headboard. "They take guest security here quite seriously." She told the others and Wilson chuckled; "They sure do; a few years ago, they had some guests murdered by burglars and the lawsuit nearly broke the place." Strangely enough that didn't make Alex too happy!

Jericho called the briefing to order and outlined what was being reported about the old station. "The two vagrants were found dead by Mo's workmen last week and they appeared to have died of heart attacks. Both were in really poor health and had received no medical care for their conditions, so that wasn't too strange. But what the living didn't realize was that no souls were collected, they are missing souls. The Pathologist who dealt with them believed some kind of immense shock caused the pair's demise. They basically saw something that scared them to death!" Wilson flicked through his notebook and grunted; "Demon Ingress reports that no demons were recorded in this area at the time of their departures. So, it has to be just the earth-bound spirits that apparently infest the place. One may have gone poltergeist."

Owen chuckled; "What about the bloody ghost train that was seen by nearly a dozen workmen, including Mo Breckenridge who admitted to being a lifelong skeptic about the supernatural. Now a manifestation of that strength is really unusual without demonic presence." Everyone nodded their agreement with Owens's deduction. Jericho continued; "The workman downed tools after seeing two men, one in an old-style suit and the other in an old combat uniform cross the platform and walk straight through a wall. Now our two vagrants had been a banker and a soldier. Bit of a co-incidence, don't you think?" Everyone nodded their agreement with that.

Alex sipped her coffee and said quietly; "If that was the souls of the two vagrants, then someone or something is holding their souls in that place. Normally only a demon could do that, but we know that there was no demonic activity about the place. That's really strange." Jericho finished his coffee and tapped the cup with a finger; "Then we're left with only one option in this case. "There must be a witches Coven operating around here under a real Warlock, a warlock with real powers granted by the Dark Prince himself. That makes him a really dangerous foe and he certainly wouldn't show up on Demon Ingresses records of movement. We have to find him and strip him of those powers.

That's where Father Adam's will come in; he knows how to deal with such a man. Good human against bad human."

Alex actually chuckled at the look on Wilson's and Owens's faces. "Come on you two! You know that our Inspector is always several steps ahead of us in all our cases. He already summoned the good Father before we even arrived." She raised her coffee cup to Jericho and smiled broadly; "Yet again Sir; our respect." Both Wilson and Owen muttered their agreement with her salute.

6. "LISTEN. I SMELL SOMETHING."

"I'll stay up here thank you very much." Mo politely declined the team's invitation to show them about the old station and so they descended down the worn steps into 153rd North Street Subway station. They stood on the South Platform, and everyone admired the beautiful ceiling murals. Owen consulted his mirror and pointed towards a rusted metal door by the North bound tunnel entrance. "That leads up to some offices and stores, staff restroom and the like." He wandered over and stared at the heavy door with Alex.

Wilson climbed down and stood on the tracks and shone his mirror down the derelict tunnel. He smiled at the discarded shovels and hard hats lying between the rails. "This must be where Mo's men first saw the bloody ghost train coming at them." The tunnel twisted a little left and right and disappeared into darkness. Jericho stood by the edge and consulted his mirror; "According to my mirror there are no less than five uncollected souls around the place." He saw Owen and Alex gesturing to him.

"This door has been opened recently; it could have been Mo's men." Owen shouted over and he and Alex managed to pull the door open. Owen shone his mirror down the metal stairs and saw several footprints in the dirt and dust. "Yep, someone's been down here recently." That's when he stopped and wiped his face. He stood still and held up a hand; "Listen. I smell something." Alex just sighed and peered down the staircase. She held a hand over her mouth for a few seconds. "Jericho, you best get over here because I think there's a human heart and other bits decomposing at the foot of these stairs."

Jericho didn't argue how she knew that; she was a doctor after al! He helped Wilson back onto the platform and they joined Owen and Alex by the old door. Owen tapped his mirror; "They use to belong to a certain Harold Polanski who died six days ago and is a missing soul. His death was unscheduled and there's been no temporal team assigned to it yet, despite the Collector calling it in." He looked up from his mirror and then sighed; "Correct that. Operations have just assigned us the bloody case!"

"Do a body search and find the rest of him." Was all Jericho said and consulted his own mirror. Owen almost smiled; "He's down here somewhere in one of the rooms. Well, the rest of him I mean." Alex grabbed the stair rail and started to descend with Owen close behind. Jericho and Wilson followed. They found the late Harold Polanski in the old canteen/restroom. His smelly decomposing corpse lay on a big metal table; there were black candles and black sheets scattered about the floor and footprints everywhere in the dust. A bucket caught Alex's eye and she peered in; "I think his stomach and other organs including his penis are dumped in this."

Jericho sighed; "Full on Black Magic ritual with human sacrifice. They cut him up whilst still alive I suspect. A gift for the Dark Prince to savour." She was kneeling by the bucket and didn't look happy. "I can't be sure without a proper examination, but these organs were removed with some skill. A doctor, surgeon or good mortician could be involved…or a very good butcher. Anyway, they were done with some skill, almost like an autopsy. Except as you say Jericho; he was still alive when it was done."

Jericho shouted a couple of times. "Harold Polanski!" and they watched without any emotion or surprise as the little man came through the wall and stood staring at them. Jericho turned to Owen to call a Collector, but saw he was already doing that. He smiled at Harold and asked what happened. The small man wrapped his arms about himself; he was wearing a shabby suit and appeared unwashed and disheveled. He had clearly been a vagrant when alive.

"They promised me some whisky and food; she promised she would take care of my pains. I suffered with terrible pains in my stomach and back. She told the others it was probably cancer. I didn't question them; they were so nice and helpful. I mean you trust the Sally Army and a fucking doctor, don't you?"

Alex rose from the bucket; "She was a doctor you say?" He

nodded and almost smiled; "At the mercy Hospital. She gave me an appointment and some pain killers which were great." He stopped smiling; "Then when I woke up….I was here….they cut me, they were all naked with a big man wearing a goats head. I pleaded and screamed but they just cut me….cut me up…like a piece of beef." He stared at his rotting body and sat quietly on the floor. Suki the Collector appeared, and the team greeted her with some warmth. "One for you Suki, I think." Jericho muttered but had a few more questions before Harold was taken to the light; finally.

The team stood back on the platform and Jericho rubbed his chin; they would have to report the finding of the human remains to the police, but they couldn't explain how they knew the details of his murder or who the murderers actually were.

"So, we have a certain Doctor Pascoe at the Mercy Hospital and an unknown captain from the Salvation Army who is probably the bloody Warlock, I suspect." He spoke quietly and checked his mirror again. Wilson folded his arms; "That hospital is about four blocks away and that's the only place people like Harold could go to get any sort of medical help. I wonder how many of the other lost souls were street people?"

Jericho nodded; "That's a good point. We need to visit the place and get a look at this deadly, Satan loving doctor and her bloody Captain of Salvation. They couldn't have a better cover to pick up people for their gruesome rituals; people who nobody would even miss or know had been killed. Come on." The team in a very subdued mood headed up the stairs to tell Mo that he had bigger problems than just ghosts to deal with.

The young woman watched the team depart and smoothed down her dress, she was joined by the soldier and the disgraced banker who asked her about the four strangers. "I don't know who they were, but they helped Harry and they now know about those evil bastards. They may be able to help you two?" The soldier nodded; "And you Kath." She shook her head and stared at the tracks, "No, I threw everything away and I'm condemned to stay here as punishment. There is no heaven for the likes of me." She stared again at the tracks and could see the stupid young woman running towards the platform edge and the train driver's face as she appeared in front of him. That was in 1925 and she relieved that day over and over again. She now asked herself daily why she didn't go with that nice young man towards that bright light. She sighed and the three lost souls were gone. From the shadows of the old toilets came another figure that stood on the deserted platform and stared up the staircase towards the bright light of day. He shuffled back into the darkness and checked his little fob watch. It was always 5.45pm. He disappeared back into the shadows and was gone, cursing his luck.

Mo almost had a coronary there and then when Jericho informed him of the body and cursing like a banshee, walked quickly to the Italian café to summon the police. The team stood quietly on the deserted pavement, which had been closed off the length of the station frontage. That's when two 'brother's' called out to Wilson from the busy sidewalk opposite. Everyone looked at each other; they had called Wilson by his name!

They came strolling over and stood by the barrier. Wilson actually groaned and ran a hand over his face. "Bloody fingers and the bear! What chance meeting those two here and now!" Alex had her arm through his and smiled; "Friends of yours big man?" Wilson shook his head; "No, they were a couple of brother's that I paid for information about dealers. They shouldn't be here; they never use to leave Queens."

Jericho almost smiled; "That's the chance you take dropping back into a time and place you were active in when alive. See what they want." Wilson nodded and said; "Money probably." and walked over to the barrier. Owen tapped Alex; "He knows some interesting people; I mean bloody fingers and the bear?" Alex smiled; "Just Street names, I'll explain it sometime."

The sound of police sirens could be heard, and Mo was returning to the station, and he certainly wasn't smiling. "Keep your statements short and succinct, we don't want any bloody Shakespeare." Jericho cautioned his team as the first police car came to halt by the barriers.

7. "WE'RE THE GHODST BUSTERS."

The big homicide detective sergeant fascinated Owen, who couldn't understand how the big sweaty man could hold a cigar between his teeth, talk and chew gum all at the same time. "It will be called multi-tasking later on down the century." Alex reassured him. He stood notebook in hand and just shook his head. "So, run that past me again. You say you're Supernatural and paranormal event investigators from Boston University here to study, catalogue and document spectral activity at this old subway station?" Jericho nodded and smiled. The big sergeant just stared at him for nearly a minute. Jericho stopped smiling and sighed; "We're the Ghost Busters employed by the city."

Alex and Owen chuckled openly at that.

"Ah, now I understand." The big sergeant called over to Wilson and wagged his pencil at him; "How the hell did you get over here from 19th precinct so damn quick? I just saw you heading to the Bronx with that little Italian partner of yours." Wilson just nodded and smiled; "Had to stop and see a friend sergeant." Alex held up her hand and smiled; "Sorry sergeant I insisted." The sergeant stared at her and shook his head in disbelieve and turned back to Wilson; "For Christ sake Franklyn! That's some snow-bunny you have there! Does that wife of yours know?" he chuckled and gestured his three uniform colleagues down the subway stairs and followed; still laughing.

"Snow bunny? What the hell is a bloody snow bunny?" Alex asked and Wilson smiled; "Just a slang term for a white woman or girl that likes black men." He shrugged his shoulders and Jericho asked him what his other friends wanted. "Help – for once – finger's cousin 'Honey Bunny' is missing. He wants me to take a look at it. She's been gone a couple of days now." He and Alex exchanged a glance; they had seen her three days ago on their unscheduled and unauthorized dirty weekend. But they had to keep that to themselves.

Owen rubbed his chin; "These people seem obsessed with bloody rabbits." He looked across the road at the billboard advertising the 'Bunny Club'. He shook his head; "Bloody obsessed." He muttered and Wilson continued; "This is the best bit and will certainly get your interest; Honey bunny was complaining about small hives on her back, thought she might be allergic to something and so she had an appointment with a doctor at the Mercy hospital. Guess the name of the doctor?"

Jericho nodded; "If that's the case, we need to find her quickly and so I think a visit to the doctor is on the cards; undercover of course and that's one for you and Alex my friend." Wilson nodded; "We'll get an appointment with the doctor and see what transpires." The team headed for their station wagon and returned to the hotel to find Father Adam's waiting for them. They were all a little shocked to see how much he had aged from their last encounter which was back in 1958 when he was still relatively young. He commented on the fact that they hadn't changed a bit.

He, Jericho and Owen sat in the hotel restaurant whilst Wilson and Alex changed into their disguises and set off for the hospital. "So, I'm dressed like an expensive hooker because that's how 'Snow-Bunny's' dress?" Alex asked as she held onto Wilson's hand, walking towards the hospital. He grinned and said; "Of course and you really look the part!" He smiled at her outfit; very short 'hot pants', white heels and bare legs. A bright red blouse tied around the waist which struggled to retain her magnificent breasts without the assistance of a bra; dark classes and her long dark hair tied in a ponytail. A huge flowery knitted bag was slung over her shoulders.

Several 'brother's' called after the pair shouting at Wilson about his 'Snow Bunny' so Wilson ignored them but took a causal look at her bum in those shorts. He groaned and said, "Alex your bloody arse is like a peach and hanging out those damn shorts. No wonder we're attracting attention."

Alex just grinned; "So you want me cover up?" Wilson now grinned; "Don't go putting words in this brother's mouth…." They both laughed and entered the outpatients. Wilson stopped in his tracks as the young woman ran down the steps and stood staring at him and Alex. "What the fuck are you doing n****r?" she exclaimed and folded her arms. Alex released Wilson's hand and smiled; "Hi, detective Alex Cappanni, it's nice to meet you."

Wilson coughed and said, "Celeste this is my partner for this operation; Detective Alex Cappanni from the 23rd precinct."
The woman held a hand over her mouth and then laughed. "Sweet Jesus Wilson; No wonder you're wearing that honky white dude suit and hanging around with some white bitch. You're playing a pimp and his crack head hooker!" Wilson laughed and nodded; "Spot on Celeste." And held up a finger up to his lips and smiled. She nodded and whispered to Alex; "Shit girl, that's the best disguise I've seen. You really look like a paid white whore. Hell, that's good." She wished them well and ran down

the steps, calling for a cab, which quickly pulled up and she leapt in, shouting and smiling at the dour cabby.

Wilson also didn't smile; "Celeste is my sister-in-law; Lizzie's sister."

Alex patted his shoulder; "Your other self may be a little confused when he gets home tonight." and smiled. Wilson just sighed and they walked in the reception area. He stopped and didn't smile; "Shit! This time travel lark really messes with your head. I now remember Lizzie asking me about some undercover gig with a white officer who really did look like a hooker. I just played along; didn't want to spend hours arguing with her about her daft sister and what she may have seen. Nothing came of it, and I must have forgotten all about it."

8. MONROE'S JONES APPARTMENT - PART 2

Monroe was genuinely concerned about the disappearance of Honey Bunny and made Alex a large brandy and a very large Manhattan for himself. She had called on him to question him about Honey Bunny. Monroe was wearing a loose pink fluffy dressing gown which flapped open, revealing he was wearing a white Basque and stockings with matching garter belt and panties. Alex couldn't stop herself looking a few times at the bulge in those panties. He was probably the best equipped Drag-Queen/Transgender she had ever seen. They sat on the sofa together and recounted what Honey Bunny had told him about meeting a new client on the day she disappeared; some hospital doctor - a white woman - she had dealt with before. Alex didn't smile; she knew exactly who that was.

They sat talking and Monroe produced more drinks and appeared to get more upset with each one over Honey Bunny until finally he cried, and Alex comforted him. He wiped his face and quietly confessed that he was very emotional as a child and a teenager. He blew his nose into his hankie and smiled as he remembered how his mother would comfort him by letting him suckle her big breasts: "It was the only thing that settled me down and oh, how I wish I had a lovely big set of breasts to comfort me now." He sobbed quietly until Alex sighed and pulled up her low-cut T-shirt, allowing her bra-less tits to escape. Monroe just stared at them, then smiled; "Oh, you are really a generous lady." Alex smiled; she had certainly been called that before!

Monroe sucked gently at first, making sure he had a fair amount of Alex's tit in his mouth before working hard on the big nipple. He was delighted and calmed down after just a few minutes. Then at Alex's insistence, he sucked hard; really hard and Alex suddenly found herself with damp panties. She groaned a little as he worked on her big breasts with some skill and real pleasure. She ran a hand up her short skirt and rubbed her fanny through her now moist cotton panties, whispering to Monroe who nodded; but his mouth didn't want to leave the big tit he was enjoying. Alex reached down and eased his cock from those little white panties and caressed it with skilful fingers. It grew in her hand as her eyes widened. She whispered again to Monroe, and he nodded again.

She sat astride him; skirt pulled up, as he sat back on the sofa and feasted on those big tits of hers. Alex eased his big cock into her willing and very wet vagina and began to move slowly up and down and back and forth. Her little panties were around one ankle and they waved like a flag as she started to speed up. She was soon bouncing with some real determination and pleasure, though her tits were now a little sore from the endless suckling of Monroe. Within a few minutes she had a little orgasm and that encouraged her to want more.

Alex couldn't believe Monroe's stamina and staying power; they changed positions several times and he constantly fucked her hard and fast in whatever position she wanted. She had several little orgasms, but it wasn't until Monroe pulled a big white rubber cock from under the sofa and inserted it into her arse as they fucked 'doggy-style' on the carpet, that she really let go. He groaned, thrusting it up her willing anus telling her it was already lubed; he was going to enjoy it himself, but she had turned up and so he hid it under the bloody sofa!

The monster orgasm came quickly now, and Alex groaned, panted and finally screamed as Monroe pulled his cock from her to allow her to spurt, which she did, cussing and crying as the liquid flew from her throbbing vagina and spattered his thighs and cock, before he quickly pushed it back in and fucked her some more. They rolled about the carpet, fucking furiously with the big dildo up her arse and Monroe's still stiff cock buried in her fanny; Alex had another monster orgasm which finished her; and she collapsed on her back and watched through tearful eyes as Monroe continued to fuck her hard. She reached down and pulled the dildo from her bum and just lay there until finally Monroe came. Alex actually screamed a little as she filled with cum; he must have spurted four or five times and she felt every drop. He collapsed on her, and she stroked his face and kissed his cheeks. His mouth went back to her heaving breasts and enjoyed them for another few minutes before Alex slipped from under him and walked - quite awkwardly - to the bathroom; she was busting for a pee now. Monroe called after her, but she was desperate to relieve herself and didn't really listen. She pushed open the bathroom door and sat on the toilet and pissed 'like a horse'. She then looked up and saw the big python uncurling itself from inside the bath which was half filled for him. Its tongue darted out several times quickly; tasting the air and it rose from the bath quickly; it must have been at least seven feet in length. Alex didn't hang around to measure it accurately because she ran screaming hysterically from the room, pulling down her t-shirt and skirt; she really had a thing about snakes and it wasn't a nice phobia.

Monroe watched her disappear through the front door and he quietly called after her, holding up her discarded panties. "It's only old Charlie; I use him in my drag act. He's really quite harmless."He said and lowered the panties; "Oh well, I'll add these to my collection." He walked to his bedroom and opened the bottom drawer of the big dresser by the small window and dropped them it; he now had quite a collection from all the women he had fucked; many of them falling for his 'comfort & suckle' routine.

He sighed and closed the drawer muttering; "I had better finish scrubbing Charlie for tonight's show. I hope her bloody screaming hasn't upset him otherwise the bloody old bugger will have to sleep in my bed tonight." He chuckled and walked slowly to the bathroom and said, "You've done it again Charlie!"

9. "THERE'S SOMETHING VERY STRANGE ABOUT THAT MAN."

In the privacy of Jericho's hotel room, Father Adam's pulled his notebook from his battered old 'Gladstone' bag and a large brown envelope. "I was intrigued when you told me about the earth-bound spirits at the Subway station. So, I've done some bleeding homework. Here's a map of the area with all unusual sightings over the last fifty years. Everything appears to have started soon as contractors broke ground for the station back in 1895." He pulled a Xerox copy from the envelope and showed a red circle drawn around the streets surrounding the station. There were red dots everywhere. "I also think I know why the evil 'Black Goat Witches Coven' operates from there. You go back to a map drawn up in 1710 and you see that the area now covered by the station and a couple of blocks surrounding it were sacred ground to the Lenape Indians. It was a burial ground for them."

Jericho nodded; "Well, that would certainly attract our Devil worshippers to the area. Did the original contractors report finding skeletons and Indian artifacts?" Father Adam's nodded; "Didn't delay the city fathers at that the time; they just slung the remains away at a city landfill site and carried on. That's how they treated native Indians in those days."

"So, what do we have on this 'Black Goat Witches Coven' Father?" Jericho asked and Father Adam's pulled more papers from the envelope and opened his rough old notebook. "The Vatican has quite a record on them. They are one of the oldest covens on the East coast; been in existence since about the 1820's. This particular nasty individual is the known Warlock now."

He slapped a black & white photograph on the coffee table. "Wallace Edward Coalman did seventeen years in Rochester Penitentiary for a sex murder when just eighteen. Apparently in prison he became a born again Christian and a model prisoner. He was released a couple of years ago and is now a captain in the Salvation Army, working amongst the poor and homeless. But he's the local Warlock all right."

Father Adam's pointed to an entry in his notebook; "Whilst in prison he shared a cell for some years with John Abbott; yes, that John Abbot." Jericho sighed and rubbed his chin; "How did Temporal Intelligence miss that cracker?" Owen tapped the photograph: "Who was John Abbott?"

Jericho smiled a little; "A four-time child murderer who died in prison; they would never have released that animal back into society. He was also a practicing black witch and surprise, surprise no soul was collected when he died. He terrorized the other inmates and the staff; he had actually sold his soul for real powers form the Dark Prince and I have no doubt that Coalman has done the same; too much of a co-incidence otherwise." Father Adam's agreed with that assessment and Owen lifted the photograph. "He's probably out there now, amongst the many homeless and destitute, picking his next sacrifice. The fucking arsehole." Owen said quietly, adding; "They're perfect victims. No one will even notice they have vanished, never mind been killed and who would suspect a Salvation Army captain and a bloody doctor?"

It was almost midnight when the team arrived at the subway station and the street was unusually deserted for such a warm summer night. Jericho lifted the 'Police – Do not cross' tape and they descended down the stairs after Wilson had dealt with the padlocks on the old metal gates. "They must have another way into the station, these padlocks are untouched. Well, until now." He said quietly and they gathered on the dark derelict platform, switching on their mirrors to illuminate the place.

Jericho stood right by the Northern Tunnel entrance and shone his mirror down. "Come on, this way I think." They carefully lowered themselves onto the rusted rails and make their way up the tunnel. They walked for at least ten minutes before they saw the carriage, tilting a little to the right, ahead of them. "Probably been down here since the station closed in 1929; would be a museum piece if they could get the damn thing out of here." Owen said quietly. Everyone suddenly stopped as the noise and vibrations came over them; "A subway train passing on the new line." Jericho said and consulted his mirror as Owen and Alex climbed up the rear of the carriage and pulled open the door. They shone their mirrors in and Alex said quietly; "Jericho, I think you best come and see this. There's a passenger sitting here reading a paper!" Jericho just stared at her and then quickly made his way over with Father Adam's and Wilson just behind. They joined Owen and Alex in the carriage and the young man lowered his paper and checked his fob watch; it was 5.45pm of course.

"Good evening, Jericho and I do believe I have the honour – at last – of meeting you Father Adam's." he smiled and pushed his watch back into his waistcoat pocket and slapped the old paper back onto the seat. He stood and thrust both hands into his dark black trousers and smiled at Alex, bowing a little. "You truly are a beautiful woman, Lady Alexandra. It's a privilege to meet you."

He nodded to Wilson and Owen and sighed. "Well, are you going to introduce me to your team Jericho?" Jericho nodded; "People, I would like you to meet Alistair Tibbs, you could say he was my younger brother, but there's only three minutes between us. We are twins, not identical one's so we just call ourselves brothers, not twin brothers."

The young man did an elaborate bow and held up both hands. "I bet my dear brother has never mentioned he had a twin brother in the same field so as to speak." Everyone stood in shocked silence until Alex finally said; "No, he never mentioned you, may I ask why that is?" she directed her question to Jericho who stood clutching his mirror. He sighed loudly; "Alistair works for a special section of the Temporal Investigations Directorate; they report directly to Arch-Angel Michael and really have no rank structure; they are called Special Agents."

Wilson nodded; he had heard of them, but never met one in person. They were legends in the department; they normally received their assignments directly from the big man himself. Strangely enough, he wasn't surprised that a brother of Jericho's had reached such a position. It meant one thing; they were bloody good at their job. No one actually knew what powers himself had bestowed upon his 'Special Agents' – they certainly weren't knights - but probably possessed the divine powers of Guardians. They appeared to be something in-between the two.

"What brings you here Alistair?" Jericho asked and everyone noticed the coldness between the two brothers. "Oh, just paying a flying visit to my dear brother, seeing how he's getting on. It's been a while since we met up." Jericho nodded; "About ninety human years if I remember." Alistair smiled; "I'm flattered you remember brother dear." Jericho gestured to him with his mirror; "So what's the real reason you're here Alistair? Or can't you reveal your mission – like usual – to mere temporal detectives." Alistair didn't smile; "I'm hurt that you think that. But sadly you're right of course, I can't say. What I can say is that you watch your back very carefully on this one. The witch's coven covers something far more sinister than just human sacrifice and worship of Prince David. Coalman's mentor John Abbott was a very special pet project of the prince. All I can say is watch for the dark light my dear bother and keep your little team close, especially Alexandra. Remember our dear Prince Jesus was betrayed by a kiss." He was gone.

There was silence for a few minutes and finally Owen tapped his chin;" "There's something very strange about that man." Jericho nodded; "Amen to that, now let's get on." Alex and Wilson exchanged a glance; they both knew that Jericho had not been pleased to see his brother and what the hell did he mean about Alexandra? The team jumped down from the carriage and continued walking in silence for another few minutes before Jericho stopped them. He shone his mirror at a rusting door marked 'MAINTENCE ONLY' and nodded; "I think we'll find that this leads up into a building at street level. This could be their entrance to the subway station and tunnels from above.

Wilson and Owen eased the big door open and could see that it opened readily. Someone had definitely been using it recently. That's when the tracks beneath their feet started to vibrate and they pressed against the wall and watched in amazement as a train rushed past them, disappearing into the darkness. Owen finally managed to say; "For fuck sake! Did you see that? It had people sitting in the carriages; I mean they looked like real people, reading papers and smoking!"

Jericho grunted; "By the obvious style of their clothes, they were supposed to be from the 1920's. Our Warlock manifest's them to scare off any intruders and keep up the ghost story cover for this place. But it also means he knows we're here."

Father Adam's stepped through the open-door muttering; "Smoke and mirrors will not help you my dark friend." Everyone followed and ascended the stairs very carefully. They came to a dingy corridor lit by a single bulkhead lamp. They could hear voices and music coming from behind a black painted door that had its sign missing.

Wilson gripped the bar and looked at Jericho who just nodded and Wilson leaned down on the bar and pushed the door open; they rushed in and stood in silence. Alex and Owen started to chuckle and were soon joined by Wilson. They were in a packed New York disco with 'Outa Space' by Billy Preston playing. Two young girls passed by them, giggling. They wore very little apart from real short mini-skirts and cotton vests. One grinned at Owen and gestured to the busy dance floor; a glass in one hand and a cigarette in the other. "Let's get it on!" she shouted, and Owen just stared at her. Wilson shoved him hard towards her. "Well, go on baby brother." Both girls grabbed him and dragged him onto the dance floor. Jericho gestured to the bar; "The first one's on me." They gathered around the bar and Jericho ordered drinks and they sat in a booth by the toilets. Father Adam's received a few stares as did Alex and Wilson when they took to the dance floor and strutted their funky stuff! [To quote the commom parlance of these groovy times!]

 Father Adam's leaned over the dirty, glass strewn table and grinned; "May as well make a night of it, before we head back into the fray!" Jericho chuckled and knocked back his bourbon in one hit. "Amen to that father." was all he said.

10. "WE'RE READY TO BELIEVE YOU."

 Alex and Wilson slumped onto their chairs; grinning and laughing. "I didn't think I'd feel over dressed in this outfit." Alex shouted over the throbbing music and Wilson chuckled. "It's the heat in here." He said and stared at two young women dancing right in front them. They were wearing nothing but hot pants and bras. They were giggling and giving each other an occasional kiss and hug. Father Adam's returned from the toilets as Jericho placed down another tray of drinks. The priest smiled; "There's a young couple having sex in a toilet cubicle; they didn't bother to close the door." He accepted his whisky from Jericho and added without smiling; "Two young men are sprawled on the floor shooting dope, sharing the needle. Very stupid." He shrugged his shoulders with some resignation and slowly sipped his whisky

"What happened with Doctor Death? Jericho pulled Wilson close, and he waved a hand around; "She wouldn't see us. The dour receptionist practically told us to bugger off. It appears she only helps the real underprivileged. Probably though I was a pimp or something!" Jericho nodded; "Well your friend's cousin hasn't had her soul collected – yet – so she's still around and alive." Wilson looked up and groaned; "Talk of the bloody devil."

Now that made Jericho sit up until he realized that Wilson had spotted 'Fingers' and 'The Bear' heading to their table. He stood and greeted the grinning pair who squeezed in, and Fingers grinned at Alex; "Hi baby sister, do you move right to the grooves?" Wilson saw the look on her face and whispered in her ear; "He means do you dance?" Alex managed a nod and Fingers grabbed her hand and dragged her onto the dance floor. The bear just sat grinning; he was clearly stoned and actually believed he was at a party in his hometown of Houston, Texas. That probably would explain why he kept slapping his thighs and shouting "Hee-Haw!" every few minutes, waving a non-existent Stetson about. Everyone just ignored him.

Jericho sighed and said to Father Adam's; "Dante knew what he was writing about." And the priest agreed with a smile. That's when they heard the shouting and whistles. Wilson slapped a hand over his face and shouted; "It's a bloody drugs raid! Let's get the fuck out of here; this may take some explaining." Jericho agreed with that, and they headed for the open exit that they had come through earlier, scooping up Owen – and the two drunk girls – then Alex and Fingers. Alex was quite happy about the interruption; she had found out why he was called 'fingers'.

They slipped through the door and Wilson slammed it behind them. They made their way down the dingy corridor and back down into the tunnels. The bear stood in the darkened tunnel – lit only by the teams mirrors – and asked Wilson if Evening Mass had started, grinning at Father Adam's. They made their way back through the tunnels and climbed onto the south bound platform. Both girls had their arms through Owens's and were all over him. Fingers wouldn't let go of Alex despite her protests. They stood on the platform and Jericho gathered them together. He gestured up the stairs and told them to leave quietly, then realized just how clean everything was. Everyone stood looking around; the posters were all new and quite readable and Owen noticed that the peanut machine was full.

Jericho pulled out his mirror and sighed, wiping his face. "It's the 12th of July 1925 and the sun will be up in twenty minutes and this station will be opened for business. We've slipped back in time!" Fingers finally let go of Alex's hand and grinned; "Man, your shitting me, that's some crazy gig right there!"

The Bear just laughed and asked if the Italian Pizza palace was open. The two girls just giggled and wouldn't let go of Owen. Father Adam's tapped Jericho and dourly said; "I think your brother could have warned us about a rouge time portal. Little wonder people have been reporting ghosts around the place for years." Jericho nodded and consulted his mirror again. He didn't have much choice because he could hear the metal station gates being opened and voices of the staff coming on duty.

He activated his mirror, and the morning staff found an empty platform; except they all swore they could smell alcohol and perfume. The group stood on the deserted platform and a couple rats scampered past them. Jericho checked his mirror and found it was 1972. They emerged into the early morning sunlight and found several New York Policemen staring at them, standing around their patrol cars eating doughnuts and drinking coffee. Jericho grinned and said, 'Good morning officers." and started to walk towards the road barriers. A big, uniformed sergeant held up a hand and smiled. "Excuse me sir; but would you mind explaining what the hell you were doing down there, intoxicated and dressed for a bloody party?" Jericho slowly smiled; "Well, actually…" Fingers interrupted the pair. He waved his arms about; "Wow! Sergeant Murphy we all were digging it, you know, grooving and moving, doing our thing. Then Pow! Slap! Bang! We grooved back in time, the old day's man. You know before now. It was unreal man. Crazy! And this dude did all that." The Bear asked the sergeant if he had any pizza on him. The two drunken young girls giggled and shouted at the sergeant that they had been dancing with a naughty novice monk and he was really cool. Apparently similar to a happy version of Donny Osmond!

The sergeant stared at Jericho and Father Adam's who both shrugged their shoulders; "They've had a real good time sergeant." Was all Jericho said and the sergeant just smiled; "We're ready to believe you." He muttered.

11. "YOU DON'T ACT LIKE A SCIENTIST. YOU'RE MORE LIKE A GAME SHOW HOST."

Phil DeVine wasn't impressed about being called to the precinct station at 7am to bail the visitors from Boston out. "We only did it because we got a call from the Cardinal's Office in Boston about the old priest. As for you, you don't act like a scientist. You're more like a game show host." Jericho just nodded and the team trailed into their hotel and made straight for the restaurant. They were serving breakfast and that really pleased Owen. After filling their faces, the team split and grabbed some sleep before meeting up again before lunch. Wilson dropped off Owen couple of blocks away in a downtown area where the vagrants, drunks and homeless hung about. He was disguised as a 'down & out'.

Jericho, Alex and Father Adam's sat in the back of a van supplied by operations, which was parked opposite where Owen was dosed down and settled in. "He's certainly making friends." chuckled Alex as Owen was accosted by other vagrants and drunks trying to get money or drink off him. They must have waited about an hour with Alex constantly moaning about the heat in the van. She was soon sitting just her hot pants and blouse again. The only break in the tedium of the surveillance was when two youngsters tried to force open the front passenger door. Jericho suddenly appeared behind the seat, and they ran off. That's when Alex said quietly; "I think he's here."

Wilson buzzed Jericho to say that Doctor Pascoe had arrived in a black sedan and was parked around the corner. He was sitting in the station wagon and had a good view of Owen and the team's van. He did ask how much moaning Alex had done.

The team watched as a three Salvation Army people decamped from a marked van and opened the doors. The vagrants started to form an orderly queue behind the doors. Jericho jabbed a finger at a small man in uniform who was directing the feeding. "That's our man alright." They watched as Coalman walked amongst the homeless and desperate, talking with each in turn. "Maybe he missed his vocation. He should have been an actor." Grunted Alex who was now perspiring and yes; she was moaning about that too.

"Bingo, we have touched down." Alex muttered as Coalman approached Owen and the pair stood talking. Jericho took a sip from his water bottle and offered it to Alex who declined; she needed something stronger! Alex operated her mirror and read for a minute or two. "He belongs to this time and place and is not scheduled for departure until 1986, when he's killed in a burglary at his home. No suspect was caught or convicted for that one, but Human Records show it was a certain May-Lee Curtis; a troubled teenage girl who stabbed him to death in the bath."

Father Adam's nodded; "Does it say if she was in the bath Alex?" That made Alex chuckle: "You dirty old devil Father, but no it doesn't give us that information; Jericho would have to get permission to view the life record to discover that."

Jericho sat back and rubbed his chin; "Our Owen has already queued twice for the bread and soup and scoffed the lot. Coalman is back talking to him; the bastard is interested; I think he's taken the bait." Jericho pushed the orb back into his jacket pocket; there had been no signals showing any demonic presence. "So, it's just bloody evil humans to deal with; at the moment." He whispered to himself, a little relieved.

 The team watched as the Salvation Army people packed away their mobile kitchen and the van drove off. Wilson reported that the black sedan with the doctor was still parked up. "Owen can't join us until she goes." Father Adam's stated and the team had to wait another fifteen minutes before Doctor Pascoe departed. Wilson picked up Owen and headed back to the hotel. The van followed.

 They gathered in Jericho's rooms and Alex waved a hand over her face; "For heaven's sake Owen, get a shower!" His disguise had been that good. He even ruefully admitted to pissing over his shabby coat for authenticity. Wilson groaned; "I bloody wondered about that awful smell in the damn car." Owen just grinned and made his report; "Coalman told me that they run a hostel over on Grant Square and I should make my way there. It's for young homeless people. He really played it up saying the people there will help me get a job or get me back into education. Funnily enough, he also mentioned I need some clean clothes. The place is an old hall apparently, named after some bleeding general." Wilson nodded; "Grant Square – in this time and place – is a rundown area of the Bronx and the hall he's talking about is called the General Custer. Fifty years ago, the square and surrounding streets were quite affluent; now it's just effluent."

Alex liked that description and stood by the little fan on the floor, cooling down. None of the men complained about the sweet smell of perfume and perspiration that now spread around her. Wilson whispered to Owen; "Now that's a little scent of heaven baby brother." and chuckled at the puzzled look on Owens's face.
 Jericho lowered his mirror and thanked Owen for his efforts. "Well, you are going to take him up on his generous offer and get a bed at the hostel. Stay in character; I'll have your dinner sent up to your room, I don't think a posh hotel like this is quite that charitable." Wilson groaned at that; he was sharing a room with him. "I wonder if the bloody hotel will object to me moving my bed into the corridor." He told Alex and meant it.

That evening Owen was dropped off a block from the hostel. Wilson was right about the state of the local area; derelict shops, old cars, pimps and hookers with numerous vacant and boarded up tenement blocks. The van passed a blazing car surrounded by youngsters who threw anything they could pick up, at them.

 Wilson spotted a big red, brand-new Cadillac driving slowly packed with young black men. "Jesus Christ, that's a local drug dealer called 'General Jackson'. I busted him a couple of times when I was on the drugs squad. He's a clever bastard; his lawyer got him off both times. He also supports the local Black Panther group with money, and it's suspected, with guns too." Wilson said dourly and turned the van into Grant Square, adding; "We need to keep a close eye on Owen; a young white dude around her – a vagrant or not – will be a target for the gangs around here."

 Alex was now concerned and called Owen on his mirror to keep his bloody eyes open and stay alert. Jericho chuckled; "Is that the mother in you coming out our Alex?" She just ignored him. Wilson parked in a quiet alleyway and switched off the engine. They watched as Owen ran up the steps into the hall and Alex sighed with relief. Father Adam's patted her arm; "He'll be fine my dear. He'll know when to yell for help."

They waited for about twenty minutes with Alex constantly checking her mirror for Owen's call. Then she looked up as Wilson cursed and said angrily; "They're never around when you need them but appear when you bloody don't!" She saw the black & white police car pass slowly across the front of the alleyway. A few seconds later it reversed slowly back, and a torch was shone down the alleyway. "Fuck!" was all Wilson said and black & white police car pass slowly across the front of the alleyway. A few seconds later it reversed slowly back, and a torch was shone down the alleyway. "Fuck!" was all Wilson said and gave a couple of flashes on the van's headlamps. "Leave Wilson to do the talking." Was all Jericho muttered as the doors opened on the 'Black & White'.

 One patrol man jumped from the car – his service revolver out – and shouted for them to get out the van: with their hands in full view. The other was cop was leaned on the roof with a pump action scatter gun pointed at them. Wilson slipped from the van; both hands held up and shouted for the patrolman with the pistol on him to stand down. "Detective Wilson Franklyn from homicide OK!" He shouted and gestured into his jacket. The patrolman gestured for him to come forward, but the other cop was already walking around the police car; shotgun now over his shoulder, he shouted; "Wilson you mad bastard; what the hell are you doing here and who are your playmates?"

Wilson laughed; "Fuck me, I thought you retired last year Ernie!" They stood talking just inside the alleyway and both patrolmen were annoyed that they could have blown a stakeout by the Homicide Squad. "Nah, we weren't told anything about a bloody night operation in the square Wilson. Shit! Someone has fucked up." Ernie groaned and Wilson slapped his arm; "You know what that new Inspector is like; couldn't organize a piss up in an Irish pub. He's straight out of city hall. Must know someone in the fucking Commissioners office." The other cop laughed at that.

That's when they heard the shouting and the sounds of glass smashing followed by several shots. The two cops dived for cover behind their car and Wilson ran back to the van. "Keep your heads down!" he yelled as he jumped back in. The patrolmen were shouting into their radio; two gangs were fighting and now spilling into the square. There were multiple shots and a car crashed into an empty shop with three Hispanic boy's crawling from it. The driver was dead behind the wheel. They were firing their guns and screaming. Only the team could see the Collector gathering up the boy's soul.

Flames and smoke were now pouring from an abandoned building as petrol bombs were thrown. "The blacks and Hispanic's are fighting over the drug and prostitution trade!" Wilson shouted to the others who kept low in the van. The two police officers were now firing their guns and sirens could be heard in the distance. "Some quiet surveillance job this turned out to be." Muttered Jericho and buzzed Owen's mirror; there was no answer. "Where the fuck are you boy?" he added, now concerned.

Above in the night sky a bright light was sweeping down, a police helicopter was now hovering over the square and local police reinforcements were arriving in strength. The square and surrounding streets were in riot and uproar. "Time to fuck off!" was all Jericho shouted and operated his mirror. The van was now empty.

The team arrived outside the lighthouse with some relief until they realized that Owen wasn't there. Jericho actually cursed loudly and operated his mirror again. "Where the fuck is he?" he shouted, and the team returned to the van. They immediately noticed the police car across the alley way entrance was ablaze and there was no sign of the two patrolmen. The place was in full riot with the gangs fighting openly in the streets. Jericho operated his mirror again and the team appeared by the doors of the general Custer Hall; Wilson shoved open the big doors and the team fell through; bullets thudding into the woodwork around them.

"You certainly know how to show a lady a good time!" Alex shouted at Wilson who slammed the big doors shut and dragged a large wooden bench across them. Father Adam's stood by the inner door and waved everyone over; the hall was in darkness and completely derelict. There were no beds, no helpers, no vagrants and certainly no Owen.

"This place is no fucking hostel." Wilson shouted and switched his mirror's torch on, sweeping the huge room. It hadn't seen people in a long time. Jericho checked his mirror and did a body check for Owen. "Found him, come on!" Jericho pushed through a big door marked HALL MANAGER ONLY and found a staircase spiraling downwards. "Is he OK?" shouted Alex, now really concerned for her friend. Jericho just gestured to follow him. They found a locker room and Wilson basically knocked the door off its hinges and shone his torch in.

Owen was sprawled across an old table, groaning and holding his head and ribs; he had been given quite a kicking. Alex and Wilson pulled him gently up and Jericho asked; "What the fuck happened?" Alex gave him her hipflask and he took a big swig. "They jumped me soon as I appeared; three of them and bloody dragged me down here. They would have killed me but the big fella with one-eye stopped them, soon as he thought I was a cop. But they stole my mirror. Sorry." Jericho patted his arm; "Why did they think you were a cop?" he asked.

Owen - with a shaking hand - picked up the gold badge from the floor; "Wilson gave me his old detective badge just in case I needed to pretend I was. Thought it might come in handy and it certainly bloody did!" Alex leaned across and kissed Wilson with some force and just smiled. Wilson shrugged his shoulders; "Best idea I've had in a long time." No-one really disagreed with him, especially Owen!

"I take it Coalman wasn't one of them. He's too clever to get his own hands dirty." Jericho sighed and then added; "Come on, our cover's been blown." He operated his mirror and the team arrived back at Jericho's hotel rooms, where Alex patched up Owen and Father Adam's poured brandies and handed them around. "If they think Owen was an undercover cop, then they will close down their evil operations for a while. Maybe even move from the area." Father Adam's concluded. Jericho nodded; he was already informing Operations Control about the loss of the mirror, then he suddenly grinned and chuckled.

Alex and Wilson exchanged a puzzled glance and Jericho rubbed his chin; "Taking the mirror was the worst mistake they could make."

12. FINGERS AND THE BEAR.

The team returned to their hotel rooms to clean up and have a well-earned brandy. Alex took a shower and stood by the large window, wrapped in a towel and read her mirror, then carefully replaced it back in her handbag. That's when there was a knock at the door, and she peered through the security spy hole. Alex pulled open the door of her hotel room, leaving the thick chain on, and smiled; it was Fingers and behind him - as usual - the Bear who smiled broadly and removed his hat. "Evening Madam." was all he said. Fingers grinned and looked about; "I...We have a little proposal for you baby that you should think about really carefully for Wilson's sake otherwise he's in some big shit." Alex nodded, now a little concerned and let the pair in; keeping a hand on her handbag that contained her mirror. They both stood smiling, and Alex asked; "What is it, Fingers?" He grinned - again - and ran both hands through his thick Afro-style hair. "Well, it's like this baby, Wilson owes us for keeping our mouths shut about you, I mean what would his sweet little wife say? And I...We think that deserve a little something don't you? That's only fair ain't it?"

Alex folded her arms and nodded; "What sort of something do you have in mind?"

Fingers chuckled and ran a hand over the crotch of his faded blue jeans; "You let us fuck you, one at a time or both together, we don't mind. Then all this will disappear from our minds and if you throw in fifty dollars, we'll even back up Wilson's story if asked.

Now you can't get fairer than that sweet baby sister, can you?" Alex sighed and stared at the pair, fumbling in her bag, and pulled out forty dollars saying; "That's all I have on me." Fingers quickly took the money and grinned - yet again - chuckling; "That'll do fine darling. We'll take the other ten dollars out of your arse." The Bear smiled; "I can have that, can't I Ma'am?" as he started to pull of his clothes.

The bed was bending and shaking as they fucked. Alex was quite naked with the Bear rammed into her backside; he really was groaning and cussing with pleasure as he trusted hard, gripping her hips with some determination. Underneath her, Fingers had his hands and mouth full of Alex's big tits and thoroughly enjoying them. He thrusted upwards as the Bear pushed down and Alex really could feel the two big cocks inside of her and she moaned: gripping the bed sheets with both hands. Her first orgasm came quite quickly, and she cussed as it ran from her cock filled fanny and down her thighs. Fingers laughed; "You can't shout rape now darling! You're enjoying our big cocks too much!" She told him to 'shut the fuck up' as she squirted again, calling him everything from a pig to a dog. He absolutely loved that abuse and fucked her as hard as he could.

The Bear came in her arse and eased from her, giving her bum cheeks quite a hard slap. He immediately started to jerk his cock to raise another erection. Fingers fucked Alex for a few more minutes and then came too. He pulled her down and whispered into her ear and she called him a cunt and lifted herself off his cock. She pushed his cock into her mouth and started to suck and jerk it, feeling their cum loads running down her legs. The Bear grunted with anticipation and ran a hand between her legs and rubbed her soaking wet fanny quite vigorously as she felt Fingers cock start to erect in her mouth. The Bear lay on his back gripping his now stiff cock and Alex climbed onto him and pushed his slippery erection into her wet fanny. He already had hold of her tits and was squeezing them into his mouth with real delight.

She felt Fingers mounting her arse and his hands gripped her waist and he fucked her butt with real determination, giving her bum cheeks a regular hard slap. He moaned and muttered; "This is certainly worth ten fucking dollars of any fucker's money!" he laughed and really rammed his cock up her back passage. It made her eyes water a little. The Bear was thrusting his hips upwards and gripping a nipple with his teeth and mouth. Alex groaned loudly under the determined and frenzied assault by the two big cocks and had a big orgasm which necessitated her lifting off the Bear for a few seconds to let the juice spurt out. He quickly pushed it back inside of her and she rode him with some sexual passion, having another - smaller - orgasm.

They changed position with Fingers back underneath and Alex sitting on him; his cock still buried in her back passage and still rock hard. The Bear climbed back on her and continued to fuck her hard. This lasted for about another ten minutes before the Bear came in her and stayed to suck and squeeze those big titties he had come to adore. Fingers came with some force in her arse, and she felt every drop flying up her back passage. The threesome lay quietly in the aftermath of their sexual exertions and the two men made no attempt to pull from Alex. Fingers reached to the bedside table and grabbed a whisky glass; telling the Bear to fill it as he pulled his cock from the 'little white whore' who must be thirsty after all that fucking.

The Bear chuckled and did as he was told; easing his cock out and holding the glass under Alex's pouting fanny, where the cum quickly ran out and into the glass. When he had finished, Fingers - still in Alex - lifted her over and then into the kneeling position and took the glass. He gave her bum a hard slap and laughed. He slowly and carefully extracted his cock from her arse and held the glass between her quivering cheeks. The cum slopped from her bum hole and ran into the glass. He raised the glass and then handed it to Alex. "Now down that little cocktail in one and we won't fuck you again." he said and really smiled as Alex sat up and held the glass to her lips and called the pair a cunt each. She knocked the 'cocktail' back in one and threw the glass onto the floor; it's didn't shatter. The two men slipped from the bed, laughing and giving each other a 'high-five' and talking about how easy white whores were to fuck.

Alex pulled herself against the pillows and grabbed a sheet to wrap round her abused body as she watched the pair dress and head for the door. Fingers stopped as the Bear disappeared through it; still laughing softly.

Fingers smiled at Alex and waved a hand; "Goodbye darling, next time we see that cunt Wilson, we'll tell him what a good, dirty fucking, little white whore you are and if we ever bump into that pretty wife of his, she'll find out all about you!"

Alex said nothing but stuck up a single finger which made Fingers laugh out loud as he slammed the door behind him. Then a delicious thought popped into her head, and she smiled; "I wonder if James will do me a favour and wipe the memories of a right pair of bastards; for Wilson's sake of course." She actually giggled a little, then admonished herself for not thinking of it before she let the pair fuck her brains out. Still, the Bear had been quite polite about the whole thing!

She headed for the bathroom and realised this would be her third shower today and cleaned herself up; especially her bum which was a little sore from the two big black cocks that had ravished it. Alex smiled a little and thought about Wilson enjoying his favourite hole. "The things I do to keep secrets and now I'm keeping them for bloody Wilson." she said quietly and chuckled.

13. "I'M FUZZY ON THE WHOLE GOOD/BAD THING. WHAT DO YOU MEAN BAD?"

 They sat in the old van, and it was Wilson's turn to moan; "Bloody Supplies, giving us this piece of junk just because the other van was burnt out in that bloody riot. It wasn't our fault." He folded his arms and stared at the derelict church beyond the wire fencing and the big notices telling people to keep out. "How long has this place been closed up?" Owen asked him, sitting behind the driver. Wilson sighed; "I think the local diocese closed it down in '65. It's been the haunt of vagrants and drunks ever since. I seem to vaguely remember they found a young woman's murdered body in there a few years ago. She was a hooker who met the wrong client." Wilson gripped the wheel and cussed met the wrong client." Wilson gripped the wheel and cussed again; "Bloody old Joe from Supplies doesn't like giving us his precious vans." Jericho lowered his mirror; "Well, the signal is quite strong, Owens's mirror is definitely in the place – somewhere."

Owen sat back and didn't smile; "I feel bloody naked without it." Alex smiled and patted his arm; "We'll get it back baby brother." That made him smile; "You're spending too much time with Wilson; your starting to sound like him."

 Father Adam's was rummaging in his old bag and muttering to himself. Alex smiled at him; "What's up father?" He shook his head and then a smile crept over his face. He pulled out a small glass tube sealed with red wax at one end. Alex peered at it;

"What is that father?" she asked, and the old priest now smiled; "Tears my girl. Tears of an angel." He carefully pushed the little tube into his robes and Alex stared at him; "Do you mean they're actual tears from a angel?" the father nodded and now relaxed a little. Owen rubbed his face; "Can I ask how a living human got hold of angel's tears, when our angels – like the dark prince's – can't enter the realm of humanity?" Father Adam's grinned and jerked a thumb towards Jericho; "He got them for me."

Jericho shrugged his shoulders; "I told angel Margret a sad story and grabbed some; with her permission of course. You don't just go around shoving test tubes under an angel's nose….or rather eyes in this case." Owen grunted and shifted in his seat – the old van was bloody uncomfortable – he rubbed his chin again. "What sad story?" Jericho chuckled; "Well, anyone concerning you actually." Alex and Wilson laughed at that, and Jericho suddenly held up a hand and stared at his mirror. "There are several humans in the old church, and I think they're moving downwards must be a crypt below the church. Now that's unusual for a New York Church, isn't it?"

"Heads up; we have visitors." Wilson said quietly and the team watched a new van pull up at the padlocked gates. A big man jumped from the passenger seat and unlocked the gates for the van to pass. Owen slapped his hand down on the back of Wilson's seat. "That's the big one-eyed bugger that took my mirror!" Jericho tapped his mirror and looked quite grim; "Was the name of that missing friend of yours; Susan Grimes?" he asked Wilson who nodded; "Yeah, her street name is 'Honey bunny'." Jericho lowered his mirror; "Well, she's in the back of the van." They watched the big man padlock the gates behind the van and jump back in. The van disappeared behind the church. "Bloody typical; Devil worshippers and witches get better vans than we do." Owen said softly as he shifted on the seat which was like sitting on stone.

Jericho said quietly; "Set your mirrors to stun, I think we have a damsel in distress to rescue." Alex and Wilson pulled out their mirrors and everyone just stared at Owen who – from under his seat – pulled a baseball bat and slapped a hand against it. Wilson had to ask; "What the fuck are you doing with that?" Owen just grinned; ""It's ok; I've set it stun only." Father Adam's slapped a hand over his face and sighed. Jericho just shook his head;

"Come on people, let's get this done." They left the van and headed for the church. "Nice night for it." Owen told Father Adam's who gripped his old bag close to his chest. "Quite so young Owen, any night is nice, that we go after a bunch of murdering, devil worshipping witches in the name of our Father." They pushed through some fencing at the side of the church that Owen and Wilson had opened earlier and made their way to the rear door. The sun was starting to sink and causing long shadows to be cast around the old gravestones.

Wilson stopped by the door and looked about; "Do you know I remember something about this old church when I was alive. It happened a few years before I was killed in that liquor store. I recall the papers carried a story about it." He shook his head; "Can't recall the details now." and forced the lock on the door.
    They slowly crept into the gloomy church and found the place in an utter state of disrepair. All the pews were missing, and the stone alter lay broken, there where holes in the roof and weather damage everywhere. Jericho gestured towards the alter; "I think my mirror indicates an entrance near there." He said very quietly and a couple of pigeons flew past the team and settled in the eaves. Alex knelt by the broken alter stone and pointed to behind the huge crucifix with the figure of Christ hanging to one side. "There appears to be some sort of doorway there."

Jericho cautiously lead the team into the little dark doorway, and everyone stood in silence; they could hear chanting. "The ritual is on." He whispered and slowly they descended the stone steps and found themselves behind a dark curtain, he peered behind the edge and nodded; "All stark naked and dancing around someone laid upon a big stone table. Looks like it was taken from an old mortuary…." he hesitated and then continued; "The Warlock's here, wearing a goats head and carrying a bloody big knife. There are seven of them; three women and four men."

Jericho checked his mirror and then pulled the orb from his jacket pocket and held it out. It remained clear indicating no demonic presence. He almost smiled; "On my signal we go; stun everyone." He whispered and sighed at Owen slapping his bat on his hand. He took a little breath and said, "Go!"

The temporal detectives crashed the witch's deadly little party with some surprise; they rendered three Satan worshippers unconscious immediately with their mirrors and the goat headed, knife carrying Warlock received Owens's bat over his headdress and he staggered around the room screaming. The elaborate creation had shattered but the remains were forced down over his faceand he couldn't get it off. He ended up crawling around the stone floor, cursing loudly and struggling with it. Owen kicked him up the arse, purely for self-satisfaction. Wilson managed to hit one of the escapers and she fell to the floor, but the last two had gone through a dark little hole in the rear wall.

 Wilson hit the struggling 'Warlock' with his mirror and the man lay still on the floor. Owen really hat to pull to get the mask off; it was the one-eyed man. "So, where the fuck is Coalman?" he asked the others. They checked the one's they had got and Coalman certainly wasn't one of them. Doctor Pascoe wasn't one of the fallen women either. Jericho cursed; the two principal witches appeared to have escaped, if they were actually here in the first place.

 Alex was checking Ms Susan Grimes who lay naked and drugged on the table. She wrapped the girl in her jacket and shouted to the others; "She drugged but untouched, she'll be alright!" Father Adam's had found a suitcase sized chest on a small table by the foot of the table. He was impressed; "Jericho, look at this chest: it appears Ancient Egyptian!" Jericho lowered his mirror and told the priest to step away from it; fast. Father Adam's didn't argue with that order and backed away.

The lid began to shake a little and the chest appeared to be throbbing. Suddenly the lid flew into the air and dark grey smoke started to flood from it. Father Adam's was already scrambling in his old bag and to everyone's surprise, cussing like a Liverpool docker. He gripped the small glass tube in one hand and raised the cross in the other. Through the smoke appeared an Egyptian priest in full robes; dark robes indicating a priest of Seth; the God who manifested evil in the ancient kingdom. It was Coalman and he was smiling; "Hello my friends! But you are not welcome here being the followers of the false God. I serve the true God; the Dark Prince and he command's me to rid you from his sacred place!"

 Jericho sighed loudly; "You really are a very bad person, Wallace."

 Coalman ran a hand over his face; "I'm fuzzy on the whole

good/bad thing. What do you mean bad?" He raised both hands above his head and shouted in Ancient Egyptian. The chest crashed from its table and darkness spread from it like water flooding quickly. Father Adam's shouted; "The Dark Light Jericho! What your brother warned you about!" the light moved like ocean waves and spread around the floor; the team found they couldn't move; it was like being wrapped in cords of tight rope. They couldn't even operate their mirrors. Coalman was laughing and commanded Alex to pick up the huge knife that lay upon the floor. She did so, despite screaming no several times.

Coalman gestured towards Jericho; "Woman! Send this dog back to his master!" Alex lifted the knife and shuffled towards Jericho who was struggling with no success. The old priest suddenly stopped struggling and said quietly; "God give your humble servant strength." He smiled and threw the little glass tube at Coalman; it shattered at his feet and brilliant white light exploded; so much so that everyone closed their eyes. The darkness was swept from the room and Jericho pointed his mirror at the stunned Coalman and rendered him unconscious.

Alex dropped the knife like it was burning hot and breathed deeply. "I couldn't stop myself; it was like someone else was controlling my movements." She said quietly to Owen who leaned over the prostate Coalman and pulled his mirror from the man's waistband. It immediately came to life and Owen patted it like a favourite pet or child. "Nice to have you back Cedric."

Wilson folded his arms; "You call your mirror Cedric?" he asked with some astonishment in his voice. Owen nodded; "He was an old monk at the monastery who was good to me; Father Adam's reminds me of him a lot." Everyone turned to the old priest and smiled. Jericho slapped him on the shoulder; "Father, the drinks are on us tonight. But where did the strength come to break that bastards spell?" The old priest grinned and jerked a thumb upwards; "From a loving power that has never let me down." Wilson chuckled, heaving 'Honey Bunny' into his arms; "Amen to that father. A bloody big amen at that." Everyone chuckled and Jericho ran a hand over his face and stared at the naked witches laid around the floor. "Now what do we do with this bunch?" he asked himself and then smiled.

14. "I LOVE THIS TOWN!"

Wilson held up the paper with his hands shaking with the laughter and Owen joined in. Alex had to find out what they were laughing at and jumped up from her armchair and crossed the room. "Come on boys, what's so funny?" she asked. Jericho and Father Adam's – who were playing chess – already, knew.

Alex took the paper and stared at it in disbelieve; then started to laugh softly. She turned to Jericho; "How the hell do you get away with this?" He just shrugged his shoulders and returned to his game. The paper was full of the strange happening at Rochester Prison; apparently a group of stark-naked witches had set up a 'Black Mass' in the prison canteen and were found by the inmates who had turned up for breakfast! The papers stated that they had been charged with burglary of a federal building, outraging public morals and assisting known felons. The paper also stated that one carried a notebook in his own handwriting giving the details of several bodies buried at an old disused subway station. He would be charged with multiple murders, so Coalman wouldn't be going anywhere soon!

"All in all, not a bad result but we still need to find the evil doctor before she sets up another coven somewhere else." Jericho said as he moved his Queen. Father Adam's nodded; "She has completely disappeared from the Mercy Hospital and her plush apartment in Manhattan with no word to anyone." He moved his castle and muttered; "Check mate." Jericho just slumped in his chair and sighed "Best of five?" he had lost two games already.

Owen looked puzzled; "Where the hell did you get that totally incriminating notebook?" he asked Jericho who just smiled; "Oh I know a really good forger; he can copy your handwriting so well that even you can't tell the difference. He's always willing to help out." Wilson started to laugh, and Alex shook her head; "Jericho Tibbs; you are just too much sometimes!" Wilson jumped from his seat and went to the drinks tray; "Brandies all round?" he asked, and everyone nodded. Jericho picked up his mirror and sat reading.

"Apparently Ms Grimes woke up in the Mercy Hospital and couldn't believe she had been there five days. She has no recollection of her treatment and her time spent there. But her hives have gone so she's very happy with the treatment; especially since it was basically free." Owen had turned a couple of pages and his eye had caught a small article about the Mercy Hospital. Just below it announced the departure of Doctor Pascoe for pastures anew. Jericho lowered his mirror; "Human Records have located our rotten doctor's soul in a small town near Richmond Virginia. Let's go people." Wilson groaned; he hated the thought of driving that old van all the way to Richmond.

That's when there was a knock at the hotel door and Owen answered it. It was Phil DeVine and he wasn't happy. He blamed the 'Ghostbusters' for the total close down of works at the subway station; the place was crawling with police and forensic staff. Not to mention reporters and TV channels. Apparently, the Mayor wasn't happy either; the bill from the construction company was mounting daily and nothing was being done. He called Jericho a useless twat to his face and left.

Jericho just shrugged his shoulders and told everyone to get their gear together. They booked out the hotel and piled into the old van, but Jericho had one last task to complete. He called Operations and asked that a senior Collector – preferably their good friend Herbie – be sent to the subway station and attempt to collect the last remaining missing souls there. His request was approved. "Maybe this time they'll go with the bloody collector." He said and Wilson started the van and turned into the slow-moving traffic. "It will be better when we hit the freeway." He explained as they sat in traffic. They didn't make the freeway for some hours and had to find a motel on route. The one they found made a few eyebrows rise. The van sat in the driveway of the little motel and Owen slapped a hand over his face; "Are we really going to stay at the 'Nathan Bates Motel and Diner'?"

Wilson slapped the wheel a couple of times; "Well, according to the map, the next motel is so far away that we wouldn't reach it before midnight, and I'm knackered driving this bloody heap of shit!" That settled the matter, and they booked in. The motel reception made them stand in utter silence; staring until the proprietor arrived. He did look actually like Norman Bates!

He really made them welcome and even offered them cold beers – for free – from his fridge. Alex still couldn't get over the foyer décor; there was wheelchair by the big window and the curtains were shower curtains. A display cabinet contained various large lethal knives and there posters of the famous movie everywhere.

Jericho signed the team in with a pen shaped like a knife and in red ink. Wilson whispered to a still stunned Alex; "I wonder if our over friendly proprietor knows what 'bad taste' actually means." Alex nodded and whispered back; "I wonder if he actually seen the bloody film!" He showed them their rooms and admitted to Father Adam's that he didn't get many priests staying here. Then with a big smile, added that he actually didn't get too many people staying here. Father Adam's was – of course – very friendly and just muttered; "No! I'm surprised by that."

The proprietor completely missed the sarcasm in his voice. Jericho and Father Adam's shared a twin room, as did Owen and Wilson. Alex was given a single. Everyone settled in for the night and Wilson brought lots of beer cans from the now very happy proprietor and they drunk them in Jericho's room. Then they separated for bed; all was quiet for about an hour and then Alex was banging on Wilson & Owen's door. Wilson opened it yawning in his striped pajamas and Alex pushed in and climbed in his still warm bed. "I took one look at the shower curtains in the bloody bathroom, and I knew I wouldn't sleep a wink." she said and smiled. Wilson just sighed as Owen chuckled. Alex fumbled under the sheets and dropped her nightdress onto the floor and slowly pushed the covers down to reveal she was totally naked. She sat up a little and opened her legs; smiling broadly and said, "Do I need to send an invitation?" She certainly didn't. Wilson went first and fucked her hard for about twenty minutes in the Missionary Position before he had to cum. No sooner than he rolled off, Owen mounted her with some urgency and fucked her like a man possessed; he came in about ten minutes, swearing and groaning. Wilson lay next to them clutching his erecting cock; "Sweet Jesus baby brother, I hope you'll take your time when you have her again." Owen laid the other side of Alex, panting and smiling with sexual relief;"I certainly will big man. Thanks for that Alex, I really needed that." Lying between them, Alex reached her hands down and gripped their cocks, smiling; "Never mind that, are you going to toss a coin for who has my bum while the other uses my fanny? I want you both together at the same time." Wilson groaned; "Come on baby brother, we have our orders." Owen almost panicked; "But I don't have a bloody coin!"

Alex laughed; "Well, alright, you can have my bum. Wilson has already enjoyed it." Now that did make Owen smile and the bed was soon rocking and straining as the 'threesome' got underway.

Wilson was beneath Alex who sat on him and leaned well forward so he could enjoy her big tits while thrusting upwards. Owen was leaned over Alex with his cock crammed into her well lubricated bum hole and thrusting downwards with some joy and utter determination. Sandwiched between the two men and being fucked hard by both, who synchronized their thrusts with Olympic precision, Alex quickly had a couple of small squirts and groaned loudly as the bed rattled and squeaked in protest.

Squirting again, Alex yelled in sexual ecstasy; "I fucking love DP!" Wilson groaned and said quietly; "So do fucking I." Owen grinned, gripping Alex's hips; "Fucking Ditto to that!" They managed to laugh a little as the fucking intensified and both men shot their loads within minutes of each other. Owen first and he collapsed onto the side of the bed panting and groaning. He gave Alex's heaving bum a slap and said 'Thank you' quietly. Wilson and Alex lay kissing quite passionately until she pulled away and remained sitting on him; his big cock still deep inside of her. She took a few breaths and said with a broad smile; "Thank you boys. I really needed a fuck like that. Thank you."

Wilson and Owen gave the thumbs up and both realised they had fucked for nearly an hour! Wilson and Alex shared his small bed and Owen lay - exhausted - on his and everyone slept really well until the morning.

15. WITCH HUNT.

The little man sat back and accepted a bottle of beer from his amazed wife. He switched off the little Video monitor and sat back smiling. "I told you we would get some action with them. After watching the damn priest for an hour [he gestured to another switched off monitor; there was one for each guest room] and the young fellow playing bloody chess. Soon as that young woman stripped off and headed for their room, I knew we would see something good." His wife sipped her beer and nodded; "I knew she was a whore; you can tell you know. I wonder how much she charges for a husband and wife." They both laughed and enjoyed their beers; it would be soon time to feed the two little girls in the cellar cage. They had some serious filming to complete tonight when her brother turned up with his pals.

The breakfast was excellent; the proprietor's wife filled their plates and coffee cups, even Alex enjoyed her breakfast despite the sniggers from Owen and Wilson. That's when a sad looking proprietor shuffled over and apologized profusely about their van being stolen during the night. Jericho waved his apology away and told him not to bother calling the local sheriff. He walked away a little stunned. Then the table burst into laughter and Wilson raised his coffee cup and said: "I love this town!"

The proprietor returned to the kitchens - smiling - and spoke to his wife; "They didn't seem to care about the old van that your brother nicked last night to carry the bodies away. I just hope he gets rid of it for good." His wife lit a cigarette and nodded; "Clint knows what he's doing. Those girls won't ever be found."

Old Joe arrived with the replacement van just over twenty minutes later. He wasn't happy. But did smile as he handed the keys to Wilson and said quietly; "Try not to burn or lose this one Wilson. But no one will be unhappy if you do." He walked away chuckling to himself. The team stood in the car park and Wilson just lowered his head and cussed. Owen sighed; "It could be worse big man; at least it has four wheels and one or two of them must work."

Jericho just said quietly; "Come on people, it's better than Bloody walking." The old, dull grey bus was probably already old when President Roosevelt was first elected. But mechanically it was sound. Owen pointed out the name which had been badly over painted; 'New York State Corrections Department' and they found restraining chains on the passenger seats and all the windows were covered with wire. The driver had his own compartment and Wilson barely fitted inside. The language from the big man would have made a drunken sailor blush, as he drove down the motel driveway. The Motel proprietor just wiped his face and stared in disbelief; "City folk sure are strange." He muttered to his skinny wife who just stood and gripped her apron, staring at the departing bus.

Jericho consulted his mirror and told Wilson to take the next left; a county two lane which ran directly into their destination. They drove past endless corn fields on both sides of the road. There was no other traffic until Owen spotted the little sports car, apparently broken down – the bonnet was up – by the side of the road. The lone woman waved frantically at the bus. It came to a halt next to her and Wilson pulled the lever which made the doors spring open. "Oh, thank heavens! I had given up hope of seeing another vehicle on this damn road and a state corrections bus will do just fine." She stood grinning until she stared at the 'crew'. Jericho grinned; "Well do step aboard Doctor Pascoe, we were just about to pay you a visit!" she turned to run, but Jericho got her with his mirror and Owen, with Alex's help pulled her aboard. Father Adam's looked to the sky and whispered; "Truly Lord you work in wonderful and mysterious ways!"

None of Team 74 could argue with that.

 The two sheriff deputies sauntered up to the little car and stared in. One ran a hand over his face and tipped back his hat; "Floyd, don't she match the description of that doctor wanted as an accessory to several murders up in the big city?" Clyde nodded; "Suppose to be a witch so the bulletin says. Suppose that's why she's naked and parked in the middle of a football pitch. The players said it was real strange; one moment big Eddie was about to kick a field goal and the next this car appears." He sighed and told the crowd gathered around to move back a little. Doctor Pascoe came around and stared at the police officers and crowds of people all staring at her. Her mouth opened to scream, but nothing came out. Floyd opened the door and tipped his hat; "I guess your witching days are over doc." and slapped the handcuffs on. Doctor Pascoe really did scream now, and it could probably be heard in New York City......

NOTES:

[1] Supplies attempted to recover the old van and were surprised to find two bodies in it; the van had been driven into a large ditch in the woods and covered with dirt. 'Clint' had indeed done a good job in hiding the van. Supplies reported the bodies and was told by 'Human Records' that both the girls souls had been collected and processed, so that was the end of the matter as far as they were concerned; they didn't interfere in human injustice: Freewill and all that. But Angel Margret stepped in and ordered that the van [and bodies] remain in situ so human authorities might find the bodies and launch a search for the killers. Supplies wasn't happy with the decision because it meant they had to create a 'paper trail' that showed no Temporal activities. But someone in Supplies had a sense of 'justice' regarding the dead girls and made the last registered owner the motel proprietor!

[2] James - a Knight of God - was more than happy to help Alex out and wiped the memories of Fingers and the Bear, which was lucky for Wilson's marriage at the time because the pair bumped into Lizzie and her sister just two days later!

The End

EPISODE 2: "ALEXANDRA, HARRY, TESS & LISA TOO..."

EPISODE PROLOGUE: "Ms. Teresa Green - A Human Agent for Jericho Tibbs in England, during the early 21st Century - passes a strange story onto Jericho which he may be interested in. Apparently, a local London magazine has reported a story about an unknown young man, who is visiting stores and markets in the city purchasing large quantities of Victorian and Edwardian money. Alex finally meets the handsome and dashing Harry Hadden and with her friend Lisa [from Team 52] they arrange to meet Harry...."

60 Minutes approx. **Episode Warnings:**
Smoking – Alcohol – Strong language – Violence [including some Nazi's!] – Strong graphic sexual references – Horror – References to the Holocaust & Demonic presences.

NOTES: This is the ADULT version of the original story which is published and appears in the **TEMPORAL DETECTIVES:** Series 3 – Episode 4 entitled: **"STRANGER'S MARKET."**

CAUTION: Recommended for **18+** only.

1. THE COIN COLLECTOR.

"Well, I'm really surprised how slow it is this morning, hardly worth getting out of bed at 4am for." Ms Teresa Green folded her arms and stared down the street; there were very few people about and it was almost lunchtime. There appeared to be more stall holders than potential customers. She had been speaking to young Ellen, who helped her out on weekends for pocket money; Ellen was about to sit her exams this summer and hoped to go onto college; she was just sixteen.

Teresa, on the other hand, was nearly thirty, small and slim, with dark hair and eyes - many considered her 'quite pretty' - not that she cared about that anymore. She had taken over her late mother's stall in Portobello Road just last year. It sold old clothes, referred to as 'Antique, Retro or Period' to her loyal customers; mainly women looking for dresses that would be unusual and noticeable in these modern times. Her 'Retro' miniskirts [based on the 1960 fashion icons] were good sellers. Sometimes she really wanted to tell some 'ladies' that the skirt they wanted, would not flatter their legs - but she never did - live and let live came to mind; it made them happy.

When she wasn't working her late mother's stall on the weekend, she worked part-time in the local Library. Her late parents had left their only daughter very well provided for and now Teresa could pick and chose what she did and when she did it. They had left her the house [all paid for] and a substantial bank balance. Her father: Gary, had been a deputy Director of a London Merchant Bank when he died suddenly three years ago - a massive stroke had taken him - just months before his planned retirement. Her mother never recovered from his death and kept in poor health thereafter.

She died last year from complications of influenza and Teresa found herself wealthy, but sad and lonely. She had never married or really dated men after Tom Redding had destroyed her dreams and her heart. Just weeks before the wedding, she had left the library [where she was working full time in those days] early one afternoon with a slight toothache and returned to the flat they shared; he was in bed with their neighbour's son. The young man fled the scene in his underpants and Tom couldn't really offer any explanation, as he pulled the condom from his limp penis; silently standing shocked and naked in their bedroom.

That soured their relationship somewhat and they parted - permanently - just days later. She moved back in with her parents and rarely dated anyone after that. Her broken heart was taking time to recover and none of the men she dated really interested her - even sexually. She had her vibrator to relieve matters and some good friends to talk with. But she was desperately lonely now.

She use to laugh about her two cats being her best friends; 'Clare and Susan' were spoilt like only children, and she loved the crazy pair of felines dearly.

Teresa was in a daydream when Ellen tugged her arm and said quietly; "I think old Rosie wants you Tess." She looked over to the stall opposite and saw Rosie gesturing for her to come over. "Well, there's not much going on now. Can you manage Ellen?" Teresa asked and with Ellen's agreement wandered over to old Rosie's stall.

Before she could say anything, Rosie grabbed her arm and pointed down the street; "That's him, the young man in that story. You know, the one in the local paper, I can't believe he's come to my little stall" Teresa looked down the street where Rosie was pointing and just caught sight of a handsome young man, wearing a classic three-piece suit, walking away; brief case in hand.

Teresa grinned; "For heaven's sake Rosie what story in the local rag?" Big Rosie took a deep breath and started to dig amongst the little pile of papers and magazines that she kept for days like this. ""I'll show you Tess, it's him. I know it's him. His description is in the story." Rosie pulled a copy of the local paper out and flicked quickly to a certain page and thrust it under Teresa's nose. "See, it's all about a well dressed - very good looking - young man who is buying old coins. He's bought so many, that coin and antique shops mentioned it to the local Chamber of Commerce, and it was passed onto the paper as a 'human interest' story. That's what they call stories like this."

Tess glanced at the article with very little interest, but she would keep Rosie happy by showing some attention. "So, a young man in a classic suit has been buying old coins, all around the Borough, where's the story in that?" Rosie looked about and turned her back on the street and dropped her voice to a whisper; "Just look at this - they are all genuine - I checked them with the forgery pen." Rosie pulled a wad of twenty-pound notes from her apron pocket.

Teresa stared at the bundle; there must be five hundred pounds there. That did take her back a little, but she recovered and smiled; "Well done Rosie, I wish someone would spend money like that at my stall." Rosie nodded but didn't smile, she pushed the notes back into her apron pocket and waved a hand over her coin and old token stall; "He purchased every Victorian coin I possessed; everyone. Then he bought all my Edwardian coins, but here's the funny thing - just like what the paper says - he only purchased Edwardian coins that where minted before 1905; he wouldn't accept a single coin after that date, even the rare ones. Now what sort of coin collector is that?"

Teresa admitted it did sound strange; all such collectors would be after rare coins, but this one just wanted everyday Victorian and Edwardian coins minted before 1905 - why 1905 she wondered. "He also asked if I had any notes, the old white five-pound notes that were in circulation before 1905. I said I didn't but refereed him to Rubin Cohen's little shop in Newmarket Street. I know that he has some old notes in his antique shop. I bet that's where he's going now." Rosie said quietly, with a look of happy satisfaction on her face.

Teresa re-read the article with more interest this time. It stated that the young man must have spent thousands on these old coins and notes. But he always insisted that the Edwardian coins were minted before 1905; the Victorian coins could have been produced in any year of Victoria's reign. Then the article went on further to say that the same young man had also purchased Edwardian period clothes from a couple of antique shops - again, insisting - that they should not have been made before 1905!

Teresa looked up from the paper as Rosie tugged her shoulder and pointed back across to her own stall. The young man was talking to Ellen!

"Thank you Rosie, I'll see you in the 'Wagon & Horses' when we close, if I can." She mumbled and made her way back to her stall - quickly. He was just about to walk away when she introduced herself. Now that she was face to face, Teresa could see that Rosie and the paper hadn't exaggerated his appearance; he was a strikingly handsome man, possibly in his late twenties with deep blue eyes and sandy blond hair. He possessed big, well manicured hands and it was obvious that he knew his way around a gym. Fucking gorgeous! She thought to herself.

He smiled and asked if she possessed any authentic period wear from the early Edwardian era. His voice was firm, and he was clearly educated and well spoken. Teresa had to say no - regretfully - but if he left a contact number, she could put the 'feelers' out with her associates in the 'Retro' and 'Period' clothes business.

He stood and thought for a few seconds and broadly smiled; "You would do that for me? That is most kind." Teresa had a rare thought that actually made her blush a little - she desperately hoped he had not noticed - She would do a little more for him than find some bloody old clothes!

She fumbled in her apron's pocket and pulled a little black note book out and a small pencil - nicked from the local bookmakers when she couldn't find one - and offered to write his number down. He slowly took the book and pencil from her hands, as they touched, Teresa actually trembled a little.

He wrote a number down and said quietly; "Just call that; they'll get a message to me. I particularly need a dress frock coat of the early Edwardian period; say before 1905." He handed the book back and gently lifted her hand and kissed the back of it. "I look forward to hearing from you Miss Green." He smiled again and started to walk away but stopped and spoke over his shoulder with a broad smile; "Oh, tell them it's for Mr. Wells; Harry Wells."

Teresa watched him depart; he walked with grace and strength, not to mention a fabulous arse. She gulped and watched him until he disappeared. Both Ellen and her watched him leave and then started to laugh together. "Fuck! Now that's some fucking gorgeous bloke!" Ellen exclaimed and started to phone her friend about the young man she just met. Teresa walked behind the stall and ran a hand over her hair. She stared at the hand he kissed and licked her lips; some truly dirty thoughts were jumping around her head, and she had not suffered the like for some time; for a very long time.

She quickly pulled open the notebook and stared at the number;

it was a local land line number, not a mobile. His home number maybe? She clutched the book closely and allowed herself a big smile. "Harry Wells." She whispered quietly and couldn't stop smiling.

"I think we'll close early Ellen; I need to make some phone calls about an early Edwardian Dress frock coat." She said with real anticipation in her voice. Ellen didn't disagree with that decision and started to pack up the stall. Teresa's delicious dream was interrupted by a strange thought; why was he actually buying coins that most serious collectors wouldn't bother with and why the specific period clothing? She sighed; a handsome, mysterious and clearly wealthy and educated young man had just walked into her life, and all she could think about; was passing the story onto Mr. Jericho Tibbs – well - that's not all she was thinking!

After the stall had been packed up and the goodbyes said to Ellen, Teresa walked to the little private car park at the rear of the shops and sat in her car for some minutes just thinking, mainly about the handsome young man. She sighed and flicked through the contact list on her phone until she came to one marked: 'The Times'. She called the number and finally, after going through the useless 'automated menu', was connected with the Personal Small Adverts' desk and paid for an entry using her credit card.

It was the same advertisement each time:
"In the woodlands of Kent,
 the tree's are green,
 their colours are only lent,
 but visitor's are most welcome,
and some are Heaven sent."

Teresa drove home to Kent House, a little distracted by the events of the day and after feeding her cats, slumped onto the large comfy sofa and watched the news on BBC 1, without any real interest. She must have dozed for a while and lying back on the sofa, stared at the clock above the fireplace; she sat bolt upright; the second hand had stopped. She knew what that meant and smiled as the doorbell sounded; easing up she walked quickly to it and pulled the door open, warmly greeting the couple standing on her steps.

2. JERICHO DROPS BY.

Jericho and Alex stood by the door and Jericho removed his hat and smiled broadly; "Always nice to drop in on you Teresa, I don't think you've met Alexandra yet." Teresa shook the woman's hand and immediately appreciated what a real beauty 'Alexandra' was.

"Jesus Jericho, is she a fashion model or something?" Teresa stared at Alex and admired her lovely clothes and figure; she knew real beauty in other women when she saw it - men would certainly fall at her feet - she grudgingly admitted and offered the pair some tea. Teresa stood in the kitchen waiting for the kettle to boil and could hear Mr. Tibbs explaining to his lovely assistant about Ms. Green and how her father had worked for him since he was a teenager. Teresa had taken over from her father upon his death; Jericho had attended the funeral. It comforted Teresa greatly that she knew her father had moved on. The same feeling of well being had manifested itself when her dear mother passed away.

She carried the tea tray into the lounge and found Alex playing with the two crazy cats. "You like cats Alex?" She asked, smiling. Alex nodded; "Jericho's cat, Mr. Parker is a playful bugger when he wants to be; he would love this mad pair." Jericho chuckled; "Yeah, but you would have to put up with a bucket of kittens." Teresa smiled and said simply; "That would be lovely." They sat drinking tea and Teresa explained about the strange young man collecting Victorian and Edwardian coins; especially that the Edwardian coins couldn't be older than 1905.

Jericho was definitely interested and rubbed his chin; "Any other strange or eccentric behaviour?" Teresa nodded and explained about the young man's desire to purchase Edwardian Period clothing – again - only before 1905.

Now that did really interest Jericho and he consulted his mirror for a certain 'Harry Wells' and rather surprisingly; came up blank for this time period of Human existence. He chuckled to himself; "Bloody H. Wells, he may as well have 'Time Traveler' tattooed on his forehead."

Alex accepted a refill from Tess and tapped the cup gently with an elegant finger; "Why before 1905, what's significant about that year? If it was 1914 or 1939, I could understand that."

Jericho nodded his agreement with that statement. "Well, in 1905 Einstein published his famous papers on Relativity and basically laid the foundations for science to create atomic bombs, finally ending up with them dropping atomic bombs on Japan in 1945. Many refer to 1905 as the 'Year of miracles' - but if he wanted to stop or change that - then an earlier time in Einstein's life would probably be better." Tess refilled his cup and threw some biscuits crumbs down for her cats. "Wasn't that really important big battleship launched in that year: didn't that change the history of warfare?" She spoke quietly and sipped her tea.

"You could be near the point there Tess, the launch of HMS Dreadnought changed navel warfare. Basically, the new ship made every other battleship in the world obsolete. That started the frenzy in building new, similar warships all around the world." Jericho placed his cup down and again, consulted his mirror.

Tess explained to Alex that the ship caused an arms race between Britain and Germany that eventually ended up with the First World War. Alex smiled; "But how do you stop a battleship being designed and built - there must have been thousands of people working in that project - who do you take out and when?"

Tess shrugged her shoulders; she didn't know the answer to that. "Maybe it's an event before 1905 that his interested in?" Tess muttered and finished her tea. Jericho looked up from his mirror and smiled; "Perhaps the Wright brothers first flight in 1903? - but then he would be buying old American currency!" Everyone chuckled at that. Alex sighed; "Well, we're getting nowhere sitting thinking about this, why not just ask the bugger?"

Tess pulled the telephone number out, she had been given by 'Mr. Wells' and said with a little excitement in her voice; "He wants an Edwardian frock coat, and I said I would call him when I found something suitable." Jericho accepted the number and smiled; "Good thinking Tess, I'll have a suitable coat dropped off. I'm sure he'll find a competent Taylor to make any alterations necessary."

Alex nodded; "Tess can arrange a meeting and I can check him against Human Records on my mirror, he won't be too suspicious if she turns up with a female friend in tow. We'll have his real identity then and can investigate him properly." Jericho agreed with that plan and Tessa stroked her cats; she didn't like the idea, but said nothing; she really didn't want him having romantic ideas about a beauty like Alex, then cheered up when Jericho told her to call him now and make the meeting happen. "The coat will be from 1903 that should suit his needs nicely." He added and called Supplies on his mirror.

"How much would a coat like that cost now?" Alex asked Tess, who shrugged her shoulders and thought for a few seconds. "We can't make it cheap; he probably knows how much a genuine one would approximately cost; so about three hundred pounds, I think." Jericho looked up, a little amazed at that figure and chuckled; "I think I paid about two pounds for my first one!" Alex grinned; "Yeah, but that was when dinosaurs still ruled the Earth!" Everyone laughed at that.

Tess called the number on her mobile, whilst Alex poured more tea all round and relaxed back in her chair. The number rang for a few seconds and to Tess's disappointment - but not shown - a woman answered. Tess explained that she had managed to procure a genuine coat made in 1903. The woman said that she would inform Mr. Well's, who would attend her market stall tomorrow afternoon - at about one o'clock. She didn't even ask the price and the call ended.

"That's excellent Tess, Alex can be your assistant on the stall - a very good cover - I'm sure your young lady assistant won't mind a day off, especially if you still pay her." Jericho was definably happy with the arrangements made to acquire the young man's real identity. But his mood changed slightly as he re-read his mirror. "That's really interesting, according to my mirror, that telephone number didn't exist in this time period - it's simply not listed - anywhere for here and now."

"But surely that's not possible, if it can be called, then it must exist here and now?" Alex asked and took the number Jericho offered, she studied it and placed her cup down. "Doesn't it have too few digits for this time?" Tess was annoyed at herself, that she had missed that significant clue. Jericho grunted and checked his mirror, then sat back and rubbed his chin; "Good spot Alex; that number was listed for London, but not in 2020. It's shown as active between 1957 and 1961 and was allocated to...." He sat upright and looked quite bemused. Jericho tapped his mirror and nodded to himself, then smiled slowly; "It was allocated to British

Military Intelligence Department Number Six at their offices in Whitehall; their totally secret offices at the time." There was silence for some seconds and Tess looked quite confused; "How the hell did I just ring a number that was only active between 1957 and 1961 on my mobile phone in 2021; nearly sixty years into the past?"

"Now that is a bloody good question." Muttered Jericho and Alex stared at the number; she knew that their mirrors could call between time periods, but surely there was no human technology existing in the nineteen hundred fifties and sixties that had such a remarkable capability?

"I think, we really do need to investigate Mr. Well's. I'll call the team together and bring Angel Margret up to date. This ladies, has now turned into a real mission." Jericho - unsmiling - said quietly and called Wilson on his mirror.

3. MISTER WELL'S? - I PRESUME.

Despite the warm morning sunshine, a sharp breeze had popped up and lowered the temperature all round. Tess pulled on a bright red cardigan and folded her arms; she glanced across at Alex, who clearly didn't feel the drop in temperature. Tess wondered if it was because the lady standing near her had been dead for over two hundred years. She actually shuddered at that and glanced at her little silver wristwatch. "It's almost one." She said softly to Alex, who checked her mirror and watched down the street - it was another quiet morning, turning into a quiet afternoon - and no sign of 'Mr. Well's'.

Alex checked - again- the black frock coat that had been provided by Supplies and replaced it into the clear plastic bag. "That is a beautiful coat, well worth three hundred pounds of anyone's money." She said to Tess, who was staring down the street and nervously tied up her hair; "He's outside the pub." She whispered but didn't point. Alex looked around the pub entrance and caught sight of a good-looking man. Tall and clearly well built, talking to a couple of elderly ladies who were laughing and chatting. "Blimey, you didn't exaggerate Tess; that is one good looking young man by any standard." She whispered, as if anyone could hear the conversation between the women.

It was clear that the old ladies really didn't want their little conversations to end, but Alex watched as 'Mr. Well's' pointed towards their stall and started to walk towards them. He cheerfully waved goodbye to his lady friends and was stopped again, this time by a very pretty young woman dressed like a catwalk model. "He's clearly popular with the girls." muttered Tess, not hiding the jealousy in her voice. Alex did smile at that. It took a few minutes, but he finally managed to extirpate himself from the woman's persist and obvious attention.

He finally managed to arrive at Tess's stall with a gorgeous smile and an apology for lateness, which the woman waved away instantly. Tess, quite reluctantly it should be said, introduced him to her 'Cousin' Alex, who was helping her out today; her assistant having to revise for an important exam. Now her quarry was close up, Alex could really appreciate what a fine, handsome young man 'Mr. Well's' actually was and he was utterly charming and attentive.

Tess chatted away about the coat that Alex produced, and Mr. Well's examined it carefully; "This looks like it was made yesterday!" He exclaimed and ran his big hands over it with great care. Alex stood a little to one side and operated her mirror with great discretion. Harry Well's pulled a brown envelope from his pocket and produced three hundred pounds in denominations of twenty's; they appeared to be all brand new and unused. Alex made a note of that. "You have served me really well ladies, the coat is excellent and well worth the money. I thank you both." He pushed the envelope back into his pocket and Alex thought she saw something in his shirt pocket but couldn't make it out properly.

Alex really did switch on the feminine charm and asked quietly; "You must be a Production Manager for a film company, scouring the county for props; a new period drama is it?" Mr. Well's chuckled; "You're very close in your deductions Alexandra, but we're called Prop Manager's and we find and supply decent props for films and TV. With a period, drama, it's always best to have the real thing. With the drama I'm working on now, I have a small part which requires a proper coat of the period; 1905, to be exact." He folded the coat over his arm and with another smile; said goodbye and slowly walked away. He seemed to be laughing to himself. Alex thought that was quite strange.

Alex disappeared into the rear of the stall and called Owen on her mirror; "Did Human Records identify our handsome would-be time-traveler?" She smiled broadly as Tess joined her, asking; "Anything yet?" Alex shook her head and Owen called her back saying simply; "Best return to the van ladies, as soon as possible." The girls had the stall packed away in record time and headed for the small private car park that Tess normally parked in.

The team was waiting in a plain white Transit van and Wilson pulled open the side door and the girls jumped in, with some impatience. "Well, who the hell is he?" demanded Alex and settled on a rear seat. Owen held up his mirror and sighed; "Now, now ladies. Your gorgeous young man is a certain Mr. Harry Gordon Well's, who lives locally and works at Shepperton Studio's as a Property Buyer for 'Time-Piece' films of London and New York. He is quite genuine; I'm afraid." He grinned, as Alex slumped back in her seat, but Tess grinned broadly; "You mean he actually belongs here? - In this time period - I mean." Owen did grin; "Oh yes, he's apparently the real deal Tess." The look on her face was priceless and that did make Jericho smile.

Alex was still a little troubled about Mr. Well's and leaned forward - unsmiling - "I thought I caught sight of something in his shirt pocket, a device no bigger than a mobile phone of this time-period. But I don't think it was a phone. I can't be sure what it was." Wilson grunted; "It probably was a phone, Alex. Very few people in this era don't carry one." Alex nodded and then remembered the money or rather the envelope it came in. She tapped Jericho on the shoulder; "Did Supplies give you any money for this mission?"

Owen chuckled; "Careful Boss, I think Alex wants to go shopping." Jericho scratched his chin; "Yes they did." He said quietly. "May I see it please?" Alex held out her hand and Jericho pulled the brown envelope from his pocket and handed it over. "Best count it, when she hands it back." murmured Wilson with quite a smile. Alex pulled open the envelope and showed Tess; "Do you have the money he gave you?" Tess nodded and rummaged in her coat pocket.

Alex held up the money that Supplies had provided Jericho with; a big handful of new twenty-pound notes; all unused. Tess produced the notes that Mr. Well's had given her. All new twenty-pound notes; unused. "That's some bloody co-incidence.

Same envelope and same notes." Owen said and everyone was silent for a few seconds. Alex sighed quite loudly; "The thing in his pocket, I think I know what it was." Everyone turned to her, and she folded her arms; "Our Mr. Well's was carrying a bloody mirror; a temporal detectives bloody mirror!"

Jericho sat up in the front passenger seat and ran both hands through his thick, dark hair. "I do hope we haven't compromised another Team's mission here." He said quietly and pulled out his mirror. Wilson gripped the steering wheel; "This doesn't make sense, if he's on a mission here, then Supplies would have provided anything he needs; including a bloody frock coat." Owen nodded at that deduction, but Alex half smiled; "Not if he was trying to lure someone out...or something like that."

Tess sat unsmiling; she really wasn't happy with this particular turn of events; "If he's a Temporal Detective - like you - then he must be...." Alex gripped her arm and said quietly; "Yes, dead like us." She didn't smile. Tess sighed and folded her arms; today wasn't going well for her.

Jericho had put a call through to Operations Control and was waiting to speak to the duty Controller; an old friend of his; Janet Turnkettle. He sat waiting and stared out the passenger window and saw a plain white Transit van sitting at the rear of the private car park with two people in. They were staring at him.

Jericho ran a hand over his face and groaned; "Unless I'm very much mistaken, Lisa Solomon and Tom Slurburger from Team 52 are sitting opposite us in an identical van - provided by Supplies - and wondering what the hell we're doing here!" His mirror buzzed and he answered it slowly; already knowing what the Controller was about to say.

The conversation was quite brief, and Janet really did laugh. She confirmed that team 52 were on a mission in that time and place - headed by Inspector Harry Hadden - Now that did bring a smile of relief to Jericho, who muttered; "Of all bloody people, I should have recognised a young Harry. What a twat I am." Everyone started to laugh, and Jericho jumped from the van and the team followed; they walked over to their much-amused colleagues, who jumped from their van to greet them.

There were handshakes all round and Lisa was introduced to Tess by Alex. There was one topic of conversation: the dashing Inspector of Team 52. Lisa did smile; "Tell me about it, we've only been here a couple of days and he must have been propositioned by half a dozen women and girls, he's like a bloody girl magnet, but is anyone surprised with that gorgeous old style charm of his. He even opens doors for me and stands up when I enter the bloody room. He's bloody charming and it's real; that's how he is around women. For the first time in two hundred years, I've met a real hunk of a man and I'm bloody dead!"

Alex pointed out that everyone was dead – well - except Tess of course. The girls chuckled about that. But Tess wasn't really too happy about it; if she was honest with herself. She had some delicious daydreams about the young man and now, she knew, that's all they would remain; dreams.

Temporal Detective Sergeant Thomas Slurburger slapped Wilson on the back and really did laugh. "I was actually just saying to Lisa, that the big ugly bugger in the identical van opposite looks a lot like bloody Wilson from Team 74."

They chatted for some minutes and the happy - but unscheduled - reunion split up, with Jericho asking Tom to tell Harry to pop round to Tess's address and catch up on old times. The conversation in the van was lively, as Wilson drove back to Tess's home. The unanimous decision was an Indian take-away and a visit to the local supermarket for brandy.

Alex laughed to herself and pointed out, that when she had met Harry Hadden previously; he was an old man in his late seventies. Little wonder he laughed when walking away; he had certainly recognised her. "He must think we're a right bunch of plonkers." Muttered Owen but cheered up at the prospect of curry and booze.

4. RENDEZVOUS.

Alex and Lisa sat in the bar of the very posh hotel and sipped White wine, for an early afternoon it was a little busy. All the Men's eyes kept drifting to the ladies at the bar. Both dark haired beauties dressed to kill, and they impatiently waited their prey; the dashing, handsome young Harry Hadden. Lisa smoothed her cocktail dress down and tapped her heels against the bar stool leg. She smiled at Alex; "Best bloody idea I've heard in ages. It's not often I get to dress like I want too and not in a bloody costume for a mission."

Alex nodded and sipped her wine; "Well, he can't complain. We're both wearing stockings and Basque's that don't hide much." She dropped her voice and giggled a little, adding: "I'm bloody wet already with anticipation." Lisa really did smile and eased off the bar stool; "Well, you don't have to wait much more. He's here." Both women watched Harry walk up to reception and collect the room keys. He walked straight to the lift foyer and waited. The girls didn't even bother to finish their drinks and joined him quickly.

He grinned and nodded his head; "You two look bloody stunning. Was all that for me?" Both girls nodded and Alex whispered - as the lift doors opened - and a couple walked out; "Everything is for you, and we mean everything." Lisa giggled and the trio stepped in the lift and Harry pressed a button. It took them just minutes to reach the room and Harry inserted the card and opened the door. He chuckled; "Supplies are paying for the room, good of them, isn't it?" Both girls smiled and headed for the mini bar and fixed a drink. Lisa sat on the big bed and bounced a little. "I don't think it seen much action." Alex laughed; "Well, it's bloody going to now!" And she was right!

Harry undressed as the girls finished their drinks and helped unzip each other, both laughing softly. Harry actually whistled and ran both hands through his thick curly dark hair. The girls placed their dresses - carefully - on a chair and walked slowly over to him. They were wearing marching outfits; tiny black lace panties, stockings and identical Basques which only covered half their ample breasts.

Alex didn't waste time and gently pulled his underpants down; both girls were really impressed. Lisa took a deep breath; "For heaven's sake boss, you've been hiding that from me!" Harry grinned and kissed her; "Not anymore." Both girls knelt and took turns eating his big cock. Harry chuckled and finished his drink. Softly he told the girls what he wanted, and they both readily agreed. Alex and Lisa would get themselves in the mood - they really didn't need to - with some light lesbian play.

He watched - sitting in a nearby chair - as they pulled each other's panties down and were soon in the '69' position on the bed. The girls really went for the 'pussy eating'. They certainly weren't playing at lesbian sex. Alex moaned loudly; Lisa really knew how to please another woman. They tried the 'scissor' position and were soon having little orgasms. The bed was creaking under the strain of the detectives, as they went for it with some real determination. Alex squatted over Lisa's face and soon had a bigger climax. Lisa didn't hesitate cleaning that up and Harry rose from the chair, clutching his big erection and joined the pair.

He took Lisa first, doggy style, while Alex pushed under her and feasted on her swinging tits and willing mouth. Then it was Alex's turn and they swapped a couple of times before he fucked her hard in the Missionary position, with Lisa now sitting on her face, having little orgasms of her own. They again swapped and Harry fucked Lisa hard and fast. She had a really big climax and wasn't restrained in her screaming with sexual excitement and real pleasure.

The three of them, rolled about the bed, sweating, groaning, panting and fucking. Harry finally shot his load into Alex and lay back gasping as Lisa went down on Alex and cleaned that mess up. Both girls were then back, sucking his cock with urgent need for him to erect again. He didn't let them down and the fucking started again within minutes. Lisa managed to produce a tube of 'KY' jelly from somewhere and Harry fucked her in the arse whilst Alex paid serious attention to her gaping fanny. Then it was Alex's turn. He was only up her back passage for about ten minutes before she had an enormous climax.

Again - Lisa cleaned that up - and finally, Harry fucked Lisa again in the arse and came again. It was Alex's turn to clean that messy cum load up. The Three lay on the bed and the girls took turns French kissing Harry with some real passion. Lisa fetched some drinks, and they sat on the bed, leaned against a pile of pillows and enjoyed the aftermath of their sexual high jinks.

"This is one of the best missions I've ever been on." confessed Lisa, gently jerking Harry's cock. Alex chuckled and muttered to herself; "You should come on some of mine." She leaned across and whilst Lisa jerked, Alex pushed her mouth over his cock and set to work. Harry and Lisa kissed with some passion as he became erect again. Lisa shouted happily; "Here we fucking go again!" and they certainly did. They spend another hour fucking and fell back, this time exhausted. Harry groaned that his 'balls were bloody empty' having shot his last load over their faces and watched the pair kissing and licking. They didn't waste a drop. He staggered to the toilet whilst the girls had some more lesbian sex - a lot rougher this time - on the floor.

Alex and Lisa lay in the bath and splashed water at each other. Harry stood and sipped a well-earned whisky. He would have joined them, but he was a big man, and the bath wouldn't simply fit three. He smiled at the playful pair and asked; "How can we get together again?" Alex threw a cupped hand of water at him and laughed; "Jericho will invite you to dinner and you'll bring Lisa along to visit me and after dinner we can get some real deserts!" Lisa thought that was brilliant and Harry nodded.

Lisa grinned broadly and whispered; "Maybe we can persuade Wilson to join us for some after dinner games?" Alex really liked the sound of that. "I'll work on that one." She promised. She knew that 'Jacqueline' would certainly be up for some fun and games. But Wilson? She would have to be very careful and discrete with any such proposition put to him!

The happy trio left the hotel and the chambermaid complained to her supervisor that a 'herd of bloody elephants' must have danced on the bloody bed! Alex and Lisa had to rush back; Alex was expected at lunch with Jericho and the team, whilst Lisa was going on a surveillance job with Tom Slurburger. They had a house to watch.

5. HARRY'S MISSION.

"How come your mirrors showed him as genuine and from this time; when he's obviously not?" Tess asked Jericho as she laid warm plates upon the dining table. Jericho tapped his mirror and smiled; "When team members are on an active mission, Control will upload their cover profiles; it's supposed to stop two teams investigating each other; that didn't work today!"

Owen chuckled and pulled the lids off the takeaway containers with some relish. "Does our dashing Inspector like a good curry?" He asked and sniffed at a chicken Madras. Jericho nodded; "Harry loves a good curry and a few beers, his lovely sister Dotty was the same. They were the best human agents I had - in any time period - present company excepted."

Tess really did smile at that compliment form Jericho and fetched her best brandy glasses from the kitchen. "I've heard you mention Dorothy before, she clearly must have impressed you Jericho." Alex opened the brandy bottle and wiped the glasses Tess had given her. Jericho smiled; "She's a lot like you Alexandra; a real beauty - inside and out - with courage and humour. She really had a superb mind and would have made a first-class detective in the time period she lived; had the silly buggers allowed women to join the police!" Wilson handed around several bottles of cold beer and eased into his dinning chair; "Don't know about you bunch, but that beef Jalfrezi is just begging me to eat it."

That's when the doorbell buzzed, and Tess answered; it was Harry. He was shown into the dining room by Tess and given a brandy - immediately - by a smiling Alex. "Thank you, Alexandra." he said quietly and smiled, which gave Alex a few little butterflies in her stomach; Harry Hadden was indeed a handsome young man and utterly charming. He could also fuck like a mad dog in heat. He and Jericho embraced like long lost brothers and sat on the sofa together. Alex and Tess started to dish up the meal and Alex simply could not stop herself glancing over towards the young man. He had almost the stamina and skills of Mr. Babette who Alex ached after with some passion. She often thought of a young Mr. Frederick Babette and had already made her plans regarding him; regardless of the warning Jericho had given her.

Wilson placed more open beer bottles near each plate and whispered to Alex; "Who's the moth now?" He grinned broadly and piled his plate with the Beef Jalfrezi that had tempted his palate so much. Everyone sat around the table eating and chatting. Harry - with a great deal of amusement in his voice - said he had recognised Alexandra immediately; you don't forget beauty like that, even when your old and dead!

He became quietly serious when Jericho asked about his mission; he explained that a time portal had been detected in this area which was locked to May 5th, 1906, and someone was using it. They had made two trips back and Inspector Longstreet's human agent for this time and place had reported that a young man had been purchasing coins and notes from that period. So, Harry believed, if the time traveler thought he had a rival, he would break cover to discover who else may have discovered the portal. Harry added that Angel Margret thought he was the best choice for the mission because he obviously knew the Edwardian Era well. Jericho nodded at that and asked where the time portal was. Harry did smile and sipped his brandy; "The old clock tower near the entrance to the East India Docks, which in this era is now really expensive flats and houses. In 1906 it was a thriving dockyard and most importantly, the Edwardian battleship HMS Dreadnought is docked there."

Owen finished his curry; "That ship was really important; it caused the First World War." Harry placed his fork down; "Your almost correct there Owen, the navel arms race that it started really did contribute to the development of the Great War, but there were other factors that actually kicked it off; like the assignation of Austrian Archduke Franz Ferdinand at Sarajevo in 1914. But your right about the ship being really important to the current human timeline."

Harry continued; "We had to make a few assumptions at first, the time jumper must have gone back once and found that he could do little without proper funds and so returned and purchased the relevant money and notes to cover his second trip. He probably took back some gold and silver trinkets to sell and wouldn't need to purchase old coins and notes anymore; there would be plenty of them back there!" Everyone chuckled at that and Wilson grunted; "So if he reads about some young man doing exactly the same as he did, he would certainly want to know; what the new boy on the time travelling block was up to." Everyone agreed that Harry's plan was really good.

"I think it's working, I'm pretty sure that the same young man has followed me on a couple of occasions already. But I had Tom and Lisa follow the follower! That's where Tom and Lisa are now; sitting outside the address we followed him to. We now just have to wait and see if he makes a move." Harry finished his curry and his brandy. Alex gave him a refill with another big smile. Wilson and Jericho exchanged a humorous glance, they were clearly thinking the same thoughts; Alex was smitten, and she really couldn't hide it!

Tess had to ask about the strange telephone number and the woman at the other end. "Why did you use that old number for British Military Intelligence and who was the woman that answered?" Owen mumbled; "Damn Good question." and accepted a refill of his brandy glass from Alex.

Harry chuckled; "Firstly, the woman was Lisa and secondly I thought a real strange number like that would certainly raise the interest of our time traveler; could he resist someone that had contacts apparently going back to the late 1950's and early 1960's?"

Tess nodded and sipped her brandy. It had certainly got Jericho interested, who admitted that Harry's plan was a good one. That's when Harry's mirror buzzed and he answered it quickly. He jumped up from the table and smiled; "To quote the great Sherlock Holmes; the games a foot!" He shook everyone's hand and particularly thanked Tess for her hospitality, then operated his mirror; he was gone.

"Well, we best follow him; and leave, I mean." Jericho said and thanked Tess for her superb hospitality; as did the rest of the team and a few minutes later; they were gone. Standing alone in her dining room; Tess realised just how lonely, she had become.

The team walked back to the lighthouse in good spirits and Alex's apparent interest in Inspector Harry Hadden was the major source of amusement. She couldn't really put up any honest arguments, about her colleagues deductions, because they were right!

They sat about the study. Wilson and Jericho chatting about Edwardian times and Wilson was most amused about Jericho's comment - which he always said about the era - that 'civilization' actually ended in 1914. Owen waved a pack of playing cards about and asked if anyone wanted to play Bridge. Alex was interested and Jericho agreed to play. Wilson grunted and folded his arms; "What about Poker? That's my favourite." Finally, it was agreed, that a few hands of Poker may be interesting; mainly to keep the big man happy!

They gathered around the card table and Owen started to deal, when Mr. Harris appeared in the doorway - he addressed Jericho directly - Mr. Harris explained that 'Little Ivan'; the Messenger, had just delivered this; He held out a brown paper file marked with big red letters: 'Urgent'.

Jericho accepted the file and broke the seal; he read slowly and didn't smile. Everyone could see the concerned look on his face. "What is it?" Alex asked quietly and Jericho looked up from the file: grim faced. He spoke softly: "The whole team has simply vanished. All their mirrors are off-line, and they are missing. Gone." Jericho lowered the file and stared at the fireplace.

"Who?" Asked Owen and stopped dealing out cards. Jericho sighed; "Harry and his entire team has vanished. We've been tasked to go after them." There was silence for a few seconds and Alex rose from the table; "Well, we had better get going then." She said, with real concern in her voice. The rest of the team followed her to the light room without another word being said.

6. IN THE FOOTSTEPS OF TEAM 52.

Wilson pulled up outside the modest house and wiped his face; the weather couldn't have been better; hot and sunny, with just a gentle breeze. "Supplies have already removed the other van. It was parked outside the Clock Tower with three parking tickets affixed to the windscreen." He said quietly and stared at the silent house. He was already sweating, and it was still only early morning. Owen took a sip of water from the plastic bottle that Alex had handed him. "Nothing is really known about the occupant for this year, a certain Rashid Kamill. Human Records have him born in 1996, so he must be about 24 years old; works as a plumber, apparently for a local Heating Company. No time portals: the house appears clean."

"Well, he must be involved somehow, or Harry wouldn't have staked the house out." Jericho muttered and consulted his mirror yet again. Control informed him that there was still no contact with any member of Team 52. "If we draw a blank here, then, it's off to that damn Clock Tower by the old docks." Jericho grunted and the team decamped from the van into the bright sunshine.

The team gathered under the little porch and Alex - rather cheekily - pressed the doorbell. The others stared at her; "The mirrors record no one inside." Owen said and rolled his eyes in mock despair. That's when they heard the barking and Alex just smiled at them. Jericho chuckled; a little basic stuff and they nearly forgot. But Alex hadn't. Wilson peered through the letterbox and started to laugh; "I think you Brits call it a 'Yorkshire terror'." He let Owen have a look, he laughed too. "It's called a Yorkshire Terrier my big yank friend." Jericho indicated to the door and Wilson pulled his lock pick from a pocket and had the door open in seconds. "You certainly missed your true vocation." Owen muttered as Wilson swung open the door and stepped over the yapping, snarling little dog. "Well, he's certainly cute." said Alex and tried to pat the dog, which went for her with some ferocity. She stopped and sighed; "Not a friendly little bugger is he." She murmured and followed the team into the living room, which was neat and tidy. The TV was on and they watched as the little dog sat down in front of it. "Must keep the goggle box on to keep the miniature Rottweiler happy." Owen said and with Wilson, headed up the stairs, whilst Alex checked the kitchen. Jericho stood at the bottom of the stairs and consulted his mirror; yet again.

A very amused - and very puzzled - Owen stood at the top of the stairs and gestured for Jericho and Alex to join him. He was really trying hard not to laugh. "The fucking spare bedroom ...well, you have to see it for yourself...its fucking unbelievable!" He laughed outright. Intrigued; Alex and Jericho made their way up the stairs and stood in the bedroom doorway, with a very amused Wilson.

It was a shrine to Adolf Hitler and the Nazi party. There were flags and busts of 'Der Fuhrer', pictures of Nazi soldiers and politicians, maps and a big cabinet of Nazi regalia. Owen checked his mirror again and was even more amazed; "Our Nazi loving friend is originally Pakistani in origin. What the fuck is he doing with all this?" Wilson chuckled and jabbed a finger towards the huge portrait of Hitler on the wall opposite. The painter/artist had placed a halo around Adolf's head!

Jericho just stared around the room in total disbelief; "In all my years, not much has really surprised me, but this has to be the mother of all surprises." Alex folded her arms; "This doesn't make any bloody sense. An English born descendant of a Pakistani family is a Neo-Nazi?" That's when she saw the little white packet on the small, ornate table by the door. She picked it up; "Photographs." She said and opened the packet.

Everyone stood around; there were loads of photographs of Hitler and his cronies in what appeared to be old Berlin; the place was draped in Nazi flags. There were old cars from the thirties and everyone in the pictures appeared to be dressed for the period;

including the wearing of 'Swastika' armbands. There were a couple of old men in shabby suits standing on a street corner; they both had yellow stars armbands. "Anyone spot the bloody odd thing out?" She said softly.

Owen picked out a couple of pictures and nodded; "They're all in fucking colour; very unusual for the time." Alex just sighed and held up two photographs that had really caught her eye. Jericho took the pictures and nodded; "It's our Nazi loving little friend; in Berlin in the late 1930's. But look how he's dressed? That clothing is straight out of the Edwardian era." Wilson stared about the room; "So Harry was right; he was onto something. But how the hell did Rashid end up in Nazi Germany, when the portal is set for 1906?" Alex threw the packet back on the little table and whispered; "It still has to be the clock tower next."

But Owen rubbed his face and folded his arms; "Why was the little Nazi prick buying Victorian and Edwardian coins, when he was visiting 1930's fucking Nazi Germany?" No-one had an answer to that intriguing question. "Let's go." Was all Jericho said and they departed for the van.

They were climbing into the van when a nice old lady from next door appeared at her gate clutching a huge ginger and white cat. She beckoned them over. Jericho and Alex smiled and walked across to her. "Have they found him yet?" She asked, sounding quite concerned. They chatted together for a few minutes and Alex stroked the appreciative cat.

Wilson and Owen sat in the van and watched; "I wonder if the dear old girl knows that her neighbour is a fucking Nazi?" Owen asked and swigged from his plastic bottle of water; he handed it to Wilson, who chuckled; "Who would suspect an English Pakistani is a bloody Nazi? That's like finding one of my brothers in the KKK." Jericho and Alex re-joined them in the van.

"It appears our Nazi friend has been missing for about a week. No one has seen or heard from him for days. Nothing; didn't turn up for work or even call his mother, who he's very close to apparently. No sign of him." Jericho told his team.

Alex chuckled; "According to Nan [the old lady] he's a lovely young man, nice and quiet, no noisy parties, no loud music and he's good to his mum - apparently - and of course; an animal lover." Jericho just sighed; "So was Adolf bloody Hitler." Owen grunted; "Who's feeding the bloody dog then?" Alex smiled and gestured towards the old lady; "Apparently 'Rommel' and Osborne are the best of friends; they play together." Owen leaned back in his seat; "The cat is called Osborne and the bloody dog is called Rommel?" Alex nodded and sipped her water bottle. "Well, she certainly hasn't poked her nose into that spare bedroom, or she would have a very different opinion about the nice young man next door." Wilson muttered and started the van.

7. THE TOWER.

It took nearly two hours to reach the clock tower; the traffic was horrendous. It took some time to find a parking space and they had to walk nearly fifteen minutes to the tower. "Too many buildings, too many cars, too many people and far too much noise." Jericho was not impressed with the changes since he last visited in 1901. They passed three local lads, sitting on the curbside drinking cans of beer and smoking dope. Owen just stared at them; coming from a Medieval Monastery in the middle of rural Yorkshire; he was suffering a little 'culture shock'.

They [the lads] swore and stuck up their fingers; asking what the fuck he was looking at? Wilson just stared at them and then went back to fighting amongst themselves and drinking beer. One made an obscene gesture towards Alex and told her what he wanted to do with her arse. They all laughed about that. She just ignored them.

They found that the tower was now part of a small heritage museum on site. The place was almost empty and the young Indian woman running reception told them the tower was open and that would be fifteen pounds each; to view the bloody thing! Jericho slapped the money down without comment.

Alex asked her about Harry and his team; had she seen them? She shrugged her shoulders and sat back down without saying anything. She was reading a Jeffry Archer novel and wasn't really interested in who went up the tower as long as they paid. They climbed the stairs, standing aside, so that a party of Japanese tourists could make their way down. They even photographed themselves on the staircase and at the foot of the stairs. Jericho just shook his head; "See what I mean, about when civilization

really ended?" He muttered to Wilson, who just smiled.
They were the only 'tourists' in the clock room and Jericho
discretely pulled out his mirror and gestured towards the cage
that surrounded the clock mechanism; "It's in there." He said
quietly looking about. "The lock won't prove a problem; will
it?"Owen asked Wilson, who was already examining it. He shook
his head.

Jericho suddenly raised his hand and fumbled in his coat jacket
pocket; he pulled out his orb and everyone could see the red
streaks around its circumference. A powerful demon had passed
this way and recently. "Shit!" said Owen and consulted his mirror
for reports about the place, from Demon Ingress. Jericho was
already contacting control for Knight's assistance, on the hurry
up. "We're going no-where until we get assistance." He said
quietly and Wilson gestured towards the cages lock; "It's open -
someone had already forced the lock - recently."

They heard footsteps coming up the stairs and so the orb and
any mirrors were hastily hidden in pockets. They all sighed with
some relief; it was James - a Knight of God - and he smiled
broadly and shook hands all round. He especially lingered over
Alex's handshake; it was well known that he a 'bit of a thing for
her' - like most males – and it showed. James stood hands on
hips and did not smile; "It's that sneaky bastard Kiri. He's back."
Owen had just received that information via his mirror - but then
- Knights of God didn't need mirrors!

"Harry never called for Knight's assistance, but then the traces
are quite recent." Jericho said, as he and James chatted
together, and Alex was peering through the cage at the clock
mechanism. She turned to Wilson; "What's that on the floor,
right there by the bare brickwork in the corner?" Wilson knelt
down and peered through the bars. "I think it's an old coin. An
old English penny I think." He was just able to reach it and
showed to it to the team. "Victorian. 1898." Owen lowered his
mirror. "Either someone just dropped it or its lain there - unseen
- for over a hundred years and I think I know which is the right
answer."

"Shall we go?" James gestured to the cage and Wilson pulled it
open; they disappeared into the time portal at the very rear of
the small room. They all cloaked themselves in anticipation of
meeting living humans on the other side, sometime in the middle

Edwardian period for the London Docks. They were mistaken about that and several other things. They had appeared in the dirty, grim backroom of a Berlin music shop, coming out from the old fireplace. The walls were covered with posters about records and music; all pre-war [the second one]. The shelves had stacks of boxes, filled with gramophone records. There were books about composers and their music stacked in one corner; they looked like they had not been read in sometime. They could all hear the noise coming from outside the small window.

Jericho had to wipe the dirty window to see out. There was a big parade going on outside; it was passing the top of the alley that the room looked over. "Fucking Nazi's." Was all Wilson said. It was a Nazi parade with flags, uniforms and banners. The crowds appeared to be cheering and shouting enthusiastically. Owen held up his mirror, quite grim faced; "Check your mirrors - mine's offline - no signals, nothing." Everyone agreed with him; their mirrors were not working.

Jericho took a deep breath; "Do you realise that if we didn't have James with us; we would be stuck here." Wilson grunted; "That might explain what happened to Harry and Team 52; they're trapped here."

Alex stared out the window and shouted; "What are those bastards doing?" Everyone squeezed around the window. Four Nazi's in uniform had dragged an old man in a black coat and hat into the alley. They were punching and kicking him. Shouting and laughing, they left him lying on the road. He tried to raise himself a couple of times but couldn't. "Come on!" Alex shouted and pulled at the door; it was locked, frustrated she kicked it and went back to the window. The old man lay ominously still in the quiet alley.

That's when they heard the lock being turned on the door.

8. THE OLD MUSIC SHOP.

James actually smiled as the door swung open; he already knew who was on the other side. The old man peered in, clutching the big key with both hands. He turned and spoke to the person who was behind him; "There is no one here my dear. No one." They heard a woman's voice say, "There is Franz, you just watch." Everyone in the room realised that James had uncloaked them;

yes, Knights really don't need mirrors! The old man jumped but didn't seem really surprised by his small back room being suddenly filled with people. Alex rushed to the door and embraced Temporal Detective Lisa Solomon, who looked like she had just won the National lottery's top prize; without having to buy a damn ticket. "They beat up an old man, he's lying..."Alex frantically told her and pushed past the pair. Lisa gripped her arm; "its ok Alex; Tom and Wolfe are already on their way." Alex sighed with relief. Lisa said quietly; "It's bloody common around here. Harry won't let me go out because, well, I really do look Jewish - which isn't strange - considering I was; when alive." She managed to smile, and the pair held each other again.

Lisa then introduced them to old Franz; "He owns this little shop and over the years has seen a few strange people pop out the fireplace. He's not a Nazi supporter; in fact, he detests the bastards and what they're doing to his country. He's being hiding us here. None of the bloody mirrors will work. The portal is one way only and has apparently changed its destination since we checked it last." Owen rubbed his chin; "Who the hell is Wolfe?" He knew that Team 52's trainee was a small Japanese fellow called Suki. Lisa laughed; "His name is Wolfgang; he's Franz's grandson. I call him Wolfe and he seems to like that."

Jericho stared back at the fireplace; "This is just an exit, the portal back in 2019 is a rotating one - a very dangerous aberration - which means it can send its traveler anywhere in time, provided he or she is holding an object from that period. Our little Nazi friend must have had something from this time period on him; something made here. I wonder if he was surprised by the new destination."

Wilson grunted; "If it's one way, how did he get back to place those photographs in his Hitler Shrine?" James smiled; "There must be at least two of them and the second person must have his own control device or be..." Owen had practically read James's mind; "A bloody demon?" He asked. James nodded; "Kiri often uses humans and just abandon's them; the bastard."

The old man gestured down the stairs and mentioned that the coffee pot was on the stove and he had some Schnapps'; if anyone wanted something stronger. Now that did make Owen smile. They could hear the commotion from downstairs and a young boy shouting for his grandfather to come. "Grandpa, its old Mr. Herron, they've beaten him badly." Alex and Lisa ran down the stairs and the old man followed much more slowly; he spoke to Owen, who was behind him; "My days of running anywhere are long gone. The only time I move quickly is for the toilet and when someone opens' a new brandy bottle." He chuckled to himself, and Wilson exchanged an amused glance with Owen.

Jericho and James stood at the top of the stairs and spoke quietly; "There must be a Judas Stone nearby; that's the only thing the 'Dark Side' has that would close down mirrors. If I recall, the last time we encountered Kiri, the bastard had one." James walked slowly down the stairs, with Jericho behind, who did remember his last encounter with Kiri and how they had been trapped without mirrors. He really was glad that he called James. [Please see the episode: **'Alexandra investigates Cordless, Cordless & Fraser (Solicitors)'.**] It appears Kiri - with some forethought - and secreted a 'Judas Stone' near the time portal exit [the old fireplace] to catch out temporal Detectives on his trail and it had worked. James always said that; 'He [Kiri] was a sneaky bastard!'

Tom and Wolfe had placed old Mr. Herron in the big office chair that sat behind Franz's desk, which was covered in papers, magazines and vinyl records. He was bleeding about the face and couldn't move the fingers on one hand. Alex examined him and realised he needed an x-ray; the cuts and bruises she could easily deal with. Mr. Herron thanks her several times but said he couldn't go to hospital. He pointed to the 'Star of David' on his arm. The local hospital wouldn't take him. They didn't treat Jews.

"Little wonder Harry doesn't let you out. The bastards would really have fun with you." Wilson spoke quietly to Lisa; who just nodded with some sadness. Everyone sat around the little shop and drank coffee and brandy; old Franz was a very good host and clearly had acquired some affection for Lisa. He treated and spoke to her like a much-loved granddaughter. He wasn't Jewish, but many of his old friends were. He pointed out, like him; they had served their country, in the trenches of the last war. [The First World War]. His disgust with Hitler and the Nazi's was really apparent.

Owen sat on the floor with young Wolfe, drinking coffee, and Owen said to Jericho; "We have a real problem. If the time portal is one way and our little Neo-Nazi friend jumped through it; how did he get the pictures of himself back to 2021? If we can find an answer to that, it would certainly help." Everyone in the team nodded at that conundrum. Alex sipped very welcome brandy and checked old Mr. Herron again.

James almost smiled; "Kiri. Like I said that nasty big demon certainly has the power to travel where he likes and we've already picked up traces of him." Jericho sighed; "And the bast...bugger would certainly like this little time period of human history." He had moderated his language because young Wolfe was listening with great interest. His grandfather told the boy to refill the kettle and put more coffee on. He left the room with great reluctance. That's when there were several soft knocks on the front door. Owen carefully lifted the 'closed' shutter and peered out. He smiled broadly; "It's Harry and Suki."

He unlocked the door and the pair squeezed in; carrying shopping bags. Everyone greeted them with some warmth; Especially Alex with Harry; that didn't go un-noticed! They had picked up some supplies; another bottle of Cognac, fresh bread, fruit and cheese, with a huge German sausage. Harry handed the food and the change, from the money Franz had given them, over to Franz and patted the old man. He turned to Jericho - unsmiling - and pulled off his jacket. He said quietly; "The place is crawling with bloody demons. My orb was practically blood red." He pulled the 'Swastika' arm band off his discarded jacket; Suki did the same.

Little Suki did not smile; "The bloody Nazi's kept shaking my hands and offering me booze. Apparently, my people are now their Allies." He said that with some real disgust and like Harry, handed his armband back to Franz. "War makes for some strange bedfellows." Wilson said quietly and sipped his coffee.

They both accepted coffee from Lisa and Harry propped himself on old Franz's desk. "Our strange little, Nazi loving friend won't be going home, and his soul is now in the darkness. He was picked up by the Gestapo and they didn't take kindly to an Indian fellow claiming he was devotee of Adolf. They beat him to death and dumped in body in the local woods. I suspect there are quite a few missing people in there."

"I think that's called Karma." Muttered Wilson and chuckled to himself. But Owen sighed; "Now we'll never know why he was collecting those old notes and coins." Alex sipped her coffee and said quietly; "I suspect that he was heading back to 1905 or around that time and ended up here. Whoever was with him, returned and ditched those photographs at the 'Shrine'. If it's Kiri, then he's probably using the house now for his own ends. He probably has more supporters there, Nazi friends of the dead man. What better proof of his powers, than those photographs? That's bound to recruit the other Neo-Nazi's to his cause."James nodded his agreement and almost smiled; "I think a little raid on the place is in order when we return."

It appears that young Rashid had travelled through the portal - the first time - and ended up in 1906. It was still standing at that date when Harry and Team 52 had checked it. He must have met up with Kiri in that time period [a demon like him, would know when humans cross through time] and they teamed up.

But for whatever reason; Rashid had used the portal again; this time dressed for the period and with lots of money to use there. Except the 'rotating' gateway had thrown him to Nazi Germany in the thirties. He must have been carrying a strong object from that time. He had no demon with him to affect a return; he was stuck here and that ended badly; he couldn't return because he had fallen into the wrong hands and killed.

9. THE UTILITY CUPBOARD!

Alex smiled at Harry who smiled back; Lisa smiled at the pair of them, and Harry headed to the kitchen and after a few seconds Lisa whispered to Alex; "You first. The utility cupboard is next to the back yard door." She smiled and Alex knew what she meant and was quite excited at fucking just yards from all these people. She carefully slipped away as well and found the cupboard quickly and opened the door; Harry already had his trousers down and grabbed her arm; "Hurry up for God sake; I'm stiff as a piece of bloody wood and my nuts feel like their full of cement. Sorry darling, but I really need to dump some cum!"

Alex just smiled and squeezed in, she pulled up her dress as his eager hands tugged down her little pink panties and told her to hold onto them. "One leg against the wall and keep your dress up darling." He said with some urgency and Alex had to smile; she could tell he really was desperate to get inside her and she loved that. With great care he mounted her; pushing her against the brick wall and they kissed passionately as he gripped her arse, while she lifted one leg and placed her foot against the opposite wall. Harry didn't waste time and fucked her hard and quick. Alex held a hand over her mouth as her backside slapped against the cold wall behind her; but she didn't mind one bit. They couldn't change position or even kneel down in the small cupboard but neither seemed to care.

Alex whispered hoarsely; "Hurry up before the other's start to wonder where we've gone!" Harry nodded; really restraining his groans and gripped her wobbling backside firmly. "Talk dirty to me." He repeated a couple of times. Alex smiled – this was a new one – and asked; "Talk dirty about what?"

Harry cussed softly and whispered; "How much you love taking it up the bum..." he never finished his request because he came just thinking about fucking Alex's peach shaped arse that his hands gripped so tightly that Alex was to have finger marks on her arse for a couple days. They both giggled a little and Harry sighed with relief; "Sweet Jesus, I've never needed a fanny so badly. I thought my balls would go so hard I could use them for bloody marbles." He kissed Alex with a big smile and added; "Thank you for that my girl."

Alex ran her hand over his face and kissed him again; "Always glad to help a gentlemen whose balls have turned to marbles!" they laughed quietly together until they heard the soft knock on the cupboard door; it was Lisa whispering about it was her turn.

The door opened and Alex crept out and accepted a clean rag from Lisa to push between her legs before pulling up her panties and smoothing down her dress. She kissed Lisa for a few seconds and the girls parted smiling. Lisa closed the door behind her, and Alex joined the others in time for some hot coffee. She stood sipping her most welcome drink and smiled, the old utility cupboard had proved quite an experience and she actually enjoyed this 'quickie'. She could certainly 'talk dirty' if that's what he wanted, and she certainly didn't mind being used as a 'cum dump' by him; she didn't mind one little bit.

Owen stood next to her and grinned, whispering in her ear; "Can I book an assignation in the utility cupboard as well?" Alex smiled and patted his arm; "Now that may be tricky, but if we can: we will." Chuckling together they headed back to the others.

Everyone had settled down and Alex noticed that Owen was missing, she checked around the shop and found no Harry either. Intrigued she slipped away and made straight for the utility cupboard. To her surprise it was empty. She was now thoroughly intrigued where the pair had gone. She walked further into the small kitchen and saw the door which opens into the small yard at the side of the building. She opened it and stepped out; the yard was empty except a couple of old cycles and numerous boxes stacked up by the single gate. That's when the head appeared around the side of the boxes and smiled at her. It was Owen!

She walked over and was about to say something when she realised Owen wasn't alone. He was gripping his knees and bent over from the waist down. His trousers were around his ankles with his underpants. But what did shock her was the man standing behind him; his trousers at 'half-mast' too and his cock rammed up Owens's arse, fucking him with real power and determination. He was gripping Owens's shoulders and watching his cock pumping in and out of the young man's backside. He looked up and smiled at Alex. "Do you want to join in love?" he gasped and moaned quietly; clearly enjoying what he was getting.

Alex slowly smiled; "I see your enjoying this mission now Tom." He nodded and grinned; not stopping his thrusts until he finally groaned and leaned over Owen and rested his head against his back. "Fucking great." He muttered. Tom was most reluctant to withdrawn, but he did, gripping his cock with his hankie and leaning against the brick wall. "Sweet Jesus thanks Owen. My balls felt like they were full of stones."

Alex chuckled, handing Owen her big red hankie. "There's a lot of that going about Tom; balls like marbles or stones." Tom slowly grinned; "Lisa offered a blow job, but I really needed the real thing and Owen obliged me. Now what's this that Lisa told me about you, her and Harry?" Alex just smiled again and said to Owen; "Like me, you don't mind being a cum dump now and again." He just grinned and cleaned up his arse with the hankie offered. The pair chuckled and then they could hear something, and it didn't sound good.

10. SOME ORIGINS OF EVIL REVEALLED.

The sounds of a commotion in the street could be heard and Franz lifted the door blind a little, he turned with some real sadness on his old face. "They're smashing old Joseph's windows and looting his shop." Mr. Herron just sighed and wiped his bandaged hand over his face; "I sent Ester to her sisters; thank God." He said and sipped some coffee that Wolfe had given him. Owen stared at the date marked on the calendar behind Franz's desk. "Sweet Jesus; it's the first of September 1939 and Germany has just invaded Poland and started the bloody Second World War!"

Everyone looked at the fragile old man, sitting helplessly on the floor of his old friends shop and all thought the same thing; the 'Final Solution' to Germany's 'Jewish problem' would soon be underway; extermination - mass murder on an industrialized, horrific scale - would now start in earnest. Alex saw Lisa wipe her damp face several times and cuddled her friend. The two women were silent; they didn't have to say anything for the others to understand.

Finally, Jericho turned to Franz and asked him, if had had seen a young Indian fellow appear from the fireplace and disappear down the back stairs. Franz nodded; "Young Wolfgang told me that a little brown man had come from the room with another; a big white fellow and they were laughing and joking together. I never saw them." James had to chuckle; "I'm surprised that you take all this so calmly; I mean all those strange people appearing out of the fireplace and disappearing down your back stairs into the street. Have you ever wondered about it?"

Old Franz smiled; "My Father and grandfather always said they were just visiting and would do us no harm. This shop has been in my family since 1790. The rear parts are all original, the rest has been refurbished over the many years that this shop has stood here. I have seen many such people since I was a child." He shrugged his shoulders and started to rummage in the shopping bags that Harry and Suki had returned with.

Jericho rubbed his face and stared at the old man; there was something very familiar about him. "May I ask Franz, what is your family name?" Franz looked up and smiled; "Leitcher."

Jericho and Wilson slowly rose from the floor and then looked at Franz's grandson; "Is young Wolfe named after your father?" Franz seemed a little surprised by that question; "Yes, Wolfgang is a traditional name in our family. My own grandfather was called Wolfgang Franz Leitcher."

Everyone in Team 74 just stared at the gentle old man and remembered their adversary; Wolfgang Leitcher [from two episodes; The man who died in the future to save his past and the Dumore Witch Trials] Jericho asked quietly; "Was your ancestor - the first one in your family - to purchase this shop, was he called Wolfgang Leitcher?" Franz nodded; "Yes, like I said; he bought the shop in 1790. I believe he was some sort of music professor or the like. Probably why music has always been part of my family's life down the generations."

Alex touched the old man's arm: "Are there any strange stories about him, your ancestor, I mean?" Franz nodded; "Family gossip has it, that old Wolfgang was ill - dying apparently – and with his final strength, sought out a healer, who lived in the woods. Well, it is said that he was gone for some time. Then returned home; miraculously cured by the stranger in the woods. But within months; he simply vanished and was never seen or heard of again. But it is just family legend."

Wilson whispered to Jericho; "And we know who the bloody healer in the woods was." Alex folded her arms; "Now that's bloody Karma, his ancestor tries to bump us off and his descendant saves Team 52." Jericho nodded and grunted; "Yes, something about the sins of the father and his children come to mind." James interrupted their quiet discussion; "I think it's time we all went home. I need to close the portal here and the one in the clock tower."

"Hope you got fifteen quid for that one." Owen grunted and finished his brandy watching Lisa and Suki rejoin the little gathering; both smiling.

Everyone said a very warm farewell to their gentle and generous host and his grandson. James closed the portal in the fireplace and then noticed that the door, at the bottom of the rear stairs -- that opened onto the back alley - was swinging open. James stared at the fireplace; "Two humans have passed through here whilst we were downstairs. I really need to close that portal in the tower." Then everyone was gone.

Franz stood in the doorway and ruffled his grandson's dark hair; "Don't worry boy, Old great Uncle Wolfgang will soon have it open again for visitors." The pair returned to the shop, they would have to arrange for poor Mr. Herron to get home, after dark and avoiding the Nazi patrols; that were searching the streets for Jews. That's when the shop bell tinkled and old Franz shouted; "Sorry, we're closed." Owen must have left the damn door unlocked when he let in Harry and Suki.

Franz and Wolfgang stood in the quiet shop and looked about; there was nobody there and Mr. Joseph Herron had gone. Franz sighed; "He's probably worried about Ester; they have been married nearly forty years." He smiled and locked the door. He sent young Wolfe to clean up the kitchen and fetch his coat; Franz would walk the boy home. He sat at his desk and pulled the bottom drawer open; he slowly removed the big money box from the back and placed it on his desk.

He slowly lifted the lid and stared at the pile of Victorian Coins and Edwardian notes. He really didn't like lying to those nice young people, but he and Wolfgang had their plan. He lifted one coin; it was an Edwardian half crown and tossed it in his hand. He was a little sorry about the confused young Rashid; but Franz had warned him about dealing with Nazi's - he didn't listen - and now he was in a shallow grave in the woods. But he had added considerably to the old money that the pair was collecting for the 'Great Plan'.

Young Wolfe appeared in the doorway and grinned at his grandfather. "I'm going to be a very rich young man when I go there Grandpa." The old man nodded; "And you will change everything. No Nazi's and Britain on Imperial Germany's side. Your future will be golden Wolfgang." He smiled and dropped the coin back into the box. Yes indeed, his future would be golden, and the future would be quite different for all Germans.

11. RENDEZVOUS: REDUX.

Alex patted Teresa's hand and said quietly; "Don't worry; he has the stamina of a bull. You'll be well pleased with your share of him." She sipped her brandy and added, with quite a smile; "We could always entertain each other while we are waiting for Harry to be free." Teresa shook her head - which really disappointed Alex - and muttered that she didn't go in for 'lesbian stuff' and would use her big vibrator, while she waited her turn to be fucked by Harry.

Alex just smiled and watched as the naked woman [they were all stark naked] fumbled in a drawer near the small sofa they were sitting on and pulled out a huge black vibrator, that even made Alex's eyes widen. Tess checked the batteries and switched it on.

"Sweet Jesus Teresa, you could beat an elephant to death with that." Teresa just grunted and pulled a tube of 'KY' jelly from the same drawer and smeared the ugly looking thing with it. Alex watched a little amazed as Teresa pulled up and opened her legs and carefully inserted the bloody thing into her vagina. it slipped in easily. It sounded like a road drill and apparently took no less than six batteries!

"Must use the bloody thing on a regular basis." Alex whispered to herself as Teresa really began to fuck herself with it. With a real smile on her face, Alex returned to watching Harry & Lisa on Teresa's bed. They were fucking hard with Lisa riding Harry. Alex thought that Lisa was riding so hard, she could push home a bloody Grand National Winner from the saddle, with such exertions.

Alex turned back to the loudly groaning Teresa, who with both hands was driving the big vibrator into her fanny. Alex took the tube of lubricate and squeezed some onto her fingers and rubbed inside and out of her vagina, inserting her fingers in to spread it around. She was now ready for a real hard fucking session.
Lisa climbed off Harry and walked - with her legs open and quite awkwardly - over to the small sofa and panted; "Your turn Tess and give me that bloody thing." Teresa was quickly off the sofa, shoving her dripping vibrator into Lisa's hands and actually jumped straight on Harry's big erect cock and bounced up and down, groaning and cursing like an angry docker.

Lisa dropped next to Alex and carefully inserted the dildo and said quietly; "I take it she hasn't had a real cock in some time." and thrusted the loud - but apparently effective dildo in and out of her cunt - with some determination. Alex nodded and the pair kissed with tongues everywhere. Alex was really tempted to have a go with the monster piece of vibrating plastic, but her attention was drawn back to Teresa. After a few minutes, Teresa, who was screaming; had some kind of monster climax and Harry had to hold her tight. Her language was quite unbelievable; she was calling Harry everything from a pig to a dog and then some. Finally, she collapsed on top of him and sobbed. He cradled in his arms and gave Lisa and Alex a strange look. He mouthed; "What the fuck just happened?" Alex chuckled, shrugging her shoulders, she turned to Lisa, who was having an orgasm of her own, though not on the scale that Teresa had just suffered and said, "Well, that was quick; couldn't have had a good cock in a long time." Lisa just nodded, groaning loudly.

Alex had to go and lift the sobbing girl off Harry's cock and walk her to the sofa. She gave her some brandy and returned to Harry and climbed on him, inserting the big cock deep inside the wet and willing vagina. Harry pulled her down and the pair kissed with some passion as Alex rode him. She was impressed that he lasted another ten minutes with her on top of him. But nature took it course and he spurted inside of her and groaned loudly They kissed again and Alex slipped off him, pushing one hand between her legs to stop his cum running out. She shouted at the girls on the sofa; "Who wants a fresh cream pie. Just delivered?"

She was a little stunned when Teresa jumped up and ran across to her. Alex squatted on the edge of the bed and Teresa was on her fanny in an instant, forcibly pulling Alex's hand away. Alex groaned as Teresa's tongue and lips set to work. She was so thorough that Alex thought her whole bloody head would disappear into her cunt. She went deep and just didn't stop.

"So much for not liking lesbian stuff." Groaned Alex and squirted into Teresa's mouth. That spurred the young woman to push Alex on her back and she really went to work. Lisa joined them on the bed and sucked Harry's cock, grinning; "I think Alex will want you again when the nymphet has finished eating her out. And I mean really eating her out." Harry chuckled and gently pushed her head back on his cock and laid back.

Lisa was right about that, and Harry fucked Alex on her back, legs around his shoulders and she had another orgasm. Lisa was taking a break and sipping her brandy, watching - with some real amazement - as the part time Liberian Teresa, suck her tongue up Harry's arse, as he fucked Alex hard. Lisa sighed but smiled. "I think we've released a sex monster."

Then she re-joined the three on the creaking bed. Teresa grabbed her and with some hidden strength forced Lisa's legs open and set about having lunch out of Lisa's cunt. The sex session lasted another twenty minutes and Harry came inside wild cat Teresa, fucking her doggy style; she was now eating out Alex again, while Lisa rubbed the big vibrator on Teresa's bum hole. She had another screaming orgasm, as the three worked on her at the same time.

While Harry and Lisa kissed passionately, the now un-sexually repressed Teresa used the big vibrator on Alex. Swearing and cursing, Tess pushed the plastic monster into Alex with some passion, using both hands. Alex had another screaming orgasm and actually, had to tell Teresa to bloody stop; she was exhausted, and her legs wouldn't stay still. She grabbed Teresa and the pair French kissed and then Tess sucked hard on her big nipples, while Alex fingered her now very loose red cunt. Tess whispered for Alex to fist her hard. Alex sighed; Lisa was right, they had created a sexual monster!

Tess squatted over Alex as she rapidly pushed her hand into Tess's dripping fanny. She managed to clench her hand into a fist and Tess screamed with pleasure and used language that was quite unbelievable. Lisa joined in, holding Teresa tightly whilst she licked out the screaming girls trembling arse.

Harry watched the girls on the bed and had to smile; he lay back sipping some brandy and wondered about the transformation of the shy young woman. He chuckled and finished his drink; "Well, she won't be shy coming forward for cock or cunt now."

Finally, the girls collapsed on the bed, panting and sweating. Lisa cleaned up Tess whilst Alex and Harry embraced passionately, whispering to each other. Tess laid back, legs wide open, panting and sweating openly. She managed a smile and said quietly to Harry; "Could you manage one more time. I want you to fuck my dirt box really hard and I'll clean your cock with my tongue soon as you finish. I'm the sure Lisa and Alex will want to watch that."

Harry just stared at her as Lisa and Alex nodded, with Alex muttering; "Now that's putting it bluntly." Harry walked over to the bed and Tess sat up and was on his cock in an instant; sucking and jerking it hard to get the thing erected; yet again. Lisa whispered to Alex with real concern in her voice; "What the hell have we done?" and she meant it.

Harry fucked Tess as she requested; hard and fast up her 'dirt box' as she knelt on the bed. Lisa and Alex were too exhausted to join in as Tess screamed, groaned, and cussed, shouting at Harry to really fuck her, finally the pair ended up with Tess astride Harry, fingering herself as she bounced up and down with his big cock firmly stuck all the way up her arse. She had another massive squirt and collapsed sobbing. Harry just lay back groaning; he had come too. Lisa and Alex actually applauded the pair; Tess was one hell of a fuck partner and Harry had the stamina of a breeding beef bull!

The temporal detectives left the sleeping Teresa, sprawled on the wrecked bed, clutching her big vibrator. Alex turned the damn thing off and said quietly; "Must save the bloody batteries, I think she's going to need it again." They operated their mirrors and were gone. They did leave a hastily written note, thanking Teresa for her 'hospitality'.

Alex walked back to lighthouse with a big smile on her face. For a supposed sexually repressed Victorian/Edwardian Ex-Policeman, young Harry certainly knew how to satisfy women; even three in one go. Alex was impressed with Harry and looking forward to their next rendezvous.

She was already anticipating it; Owen had agreed to join in as 'Jackie' – he admitted that he loved the idea of Harry poking his bum – and would dress for the part. Alex smiled at that; he would look absolutely stunning, and she wondered if Harry would turn that down; she didn't think so!

Then there was Tom, did he swing both ways? Owen believed he did because he asked him – if they could arrange it – to dress as Jackie for him and bring her [Alex] too!

But in the back of her mind was Frederick Babette and was he – in some way – related to the mysterious Jacqueline Babette, the time travelling mum who left her baby with its father and then disappeared. [See episode: **'Alexandra goes beyond the Jerusalem mirror.'**] She smiled at Mr. Harris who told her that a mission file had arrived, and everyone was in the study. Dinner would be on time; of course!

She asked him to bring some brandy and the big man almost smiled; "Already in the study my lady." He replied and closed the big black doors behind her and walked slowly to the kitchen.

Alex headed for the study, eager to speak with Owen/Jackie, giving the ever present 'Mister Parker' a quick pat as he sat watching her from the foot of the stairs. If he wasn't a large domestic cat; you would have thought he had quite a look of disapproval upon his furry face and it wasn't just about the quick pat either………..

EPISODE 3: "ALEXANDRA AND THE ARTIST. "

EPISODE PROLOGUE: "An art exhibition being held in a major London gallery, in Summer 2016 is causing quite a stir in the 'Conspiracy Theory Community' and social media is filled with theories about the pictures of a certain Victorian painter; Cranfield Sommers. Some sharp-eyed conspiracy followers have spotted something strange about some of the models; three of the girls shown in the extensive collection are dead ringers for three missing women - from 2016 - and even their family and friends agree that the models are doubles of the missing girls. But the paintings are dated between 1870 and 1872! Jericho is on the scene because not only the girls are missing; but so are their souls. Alex is about to get painted; several times!"

75 Minutes approx. **Episode Warnings:** Smoking – Alcohol – Strong language – Violence [including sexual violence] – Strong graphic sexual references – Horror – References to death, Devil worship & Demonic presences.

NOTES: This is the **ADULT version** of the original story which is published and appears in the **TEMPORAL DETECTIVES:** Series 4 – Episode 10 entitled: **"THE MYSTERIOUS PAINTINGS OF CRANFIELD SOMMERS."** This is a special EXTENDED episode of the original story.

CAUTION: Recommended for **18+** only.

1. LOURDES ART GALLERY, LONDON 2016.

"I can't believe this bloody queue; it's going to take an hour at least to get in." Owen moaned and sipped his coffee from the 'Starbucks' coffee shop on the corner. "At least the coffee is drinkable." He added and stared at the people in the line before him. Alex gripped her coffee with both hands – gloved – and smiled. "I wish I had worn more clothes; my bloody bum is freezing despite the woolen tights." Owen just chuckled; "You know that woolen tights have to be the biggest turn off in history for men."

Alex nodded; "Don't bleeding care; my butt would be ice without them." She sipped her coffee; at least moaning Owen was right about the damn coffee and turned to Jericho who seemed quite impervious to the cold. His long dark frock coat was open, and he wore no gloves. He was staring at a page of a newspaper, folded in one hand and holding his coffee with the other.

"Couldn't we just have sneaked in during the bloody night or something?" she asked, and he smiled; "No, the queue will start moving in a moment and we'll be in quite quickly. Finish your coffee and tell Owen to stop bleeding moaning; he's been dead for seven hundred years so I should think he'll be used to it by now." That made Alex smile and she turned to Wilson who was reading a copy of the gallery guidebook. She tapped his arm and whispered; "Must be full of naked ladies to get your undivided interest." Wilson just smiled; "There are no pictures of the painting's that contain the supposed missing girls. So, we'll have to wait until we're inside to check the images against Human records." He spoke quietly, close to her ear.

Jericho stuck his head between the two; "We'll soon know if we have a mission or not, so an hour's queuing won't hurt us. This could be the shortest mission we've ever undertaken. I hope it is because we really need to look at that strange happening on that Mar's mission." He went back to his paper and Owen tapped it; "What's so interesting boss?"

Jericho shrugged his shoulders and sipped his coffee; "One of the missing girl's mother's is demanding a private viewing of the painting 'Naked Nymphs in Woodlands' painted in 1870 by Cranfield Sommers. She says' she will be able to put an end to the nonsense of it being her daughter and police can concentrate on the catching the real abductors." He chuckled, adding; "She call's time travel utter nonsense!"

Jericho looked up and smiled; "Head's up people; the doors are finally opening and the queues moving at last. Let's take a look at his main pictures." Alex sighed; "Thank for that; I think my bum cheeks have turned purple." She finished her coffee and shivered a little.

Owen grinned; "Now that's something I would love to see."
"In your bleeding dreams." Muttered Alex but smiled at him. His alter-ego 'Jackie' had seen her naked bum several times. They pushed through the doors and dumped their coffee cups in a nearby recycling bin and Owen moaned again, pulling open his heavy coat. "It's like a bleeding sauna in here!" Wilson slapped his arm; "I told you, if you keep dressing up as a woman; you'll start behaving like one and moan all the time." Owen didn't reply but followed Jericho as he strode towards the gallery's painting hall.

"You have the guidebook, where do we find these damn pictures." Jericho asked Wilson and he indicated down a well-lit corridor. "This way Jericho; the 'Victorian Modern Renaissance' section is just off this corridor." They followed Wilson in silence with Alex stripping off her gloves, hat and coat. Owen took her coat and carried it for her. Several men all turned to admire her chic winter outfit. That made Alex moan about being a 'bloody sex object'. Jericho chuckled; "Well, we're in a gallery filled with beautiful things, so they're just admiring one more." Now that did make her smile a little.

Wilson gestured to a large crowd standing beneath a painting which also had a security guard next to it. "That's one of the paintings; 'The Sheiks Harem' painted in 1871, again by Cranfield Sommers. We'll start there. Mirror at the ready Owen?" Owen nodded and accepted Jericho's newspaper to cover his mirror. They eased through the people and Alex didn't smile; "Loads of naked young girls and a fat Arab. Did this Cranfield bloke paint anything other than naked girls?" A couple of people nearby chuckled and one woman agreed with her.

Owen lowered the newspaper and gestured for the other's to follow him. They gathered about a sculpture of two naked men, entwining with a huge snake. It was painted like an American flag. Wilson just shook his head and muttered; "People have died for that flag." He clearly wasn't impressed by whatever the artist was trying to say. Owen looked around and spoke quietly. "Not an exact match but Human Records gives it an 90% match with Danielle Goldsmith, born in 1997 and is currently missing from the Human Timeline and is also a Missing soul. She's one of the missing girls."

Jericho sighed and folded his arms; "Come on, let's check out the other two paintings." The team wandered back down the corridor and found the painting "Naked Nymphs in Woodlands' painted in 1870, again by Cranfield Sommers. Owen simply nodded his head and whispered; "Another 90% match and yes, one of the missing girls." They found the final painting – again surrounded by a crowd – and Owen checked his mirror. He nodded again and mouthed; "90% match again and one of the girls."

They gathered at the end of the corridor and Jericho suddenly walked off to a painting that had several people beneath it. "What's the bloodhound spotted now?" Owen said, pushing his mirror back into his coat pocket. They stood beneath the painting and Jericho read out the plaque; "The Queen of Fairyland' painted by Granfied Sommers in 1870."

Wilson whistled softly; "If that's not our Alex, then I'm a monkey's uncle." They all agreed – including Alex – that it was her double. The 'Fairy Queen' was stark naked apart from some wings and a flower crown, sprawled across a golden sheet laid upon fallen trees. A well-equipped donkey stood by, with a smile on his face.

Owen operated his mirror under the newspaper and chuckled; "Exact match of Lady Alexandra Cappanni born 1871, died 1901. File now classified. Permission to view must be Angel authorised. He looked up and grinned. "Well, that's our Alex all right, so the mission must be on." Jericho nodded and folded his arms; "Come on, let's get some lunch and get hold of Supplies. We're headed back to 1870 and Alex can get her portrait done." Everyone agreed and they headed for the main doors. Alex had her arm through Owens's and said quietly; "Why the hell a bloody donkey with his dick hanging down? That's almost perversion and I thought the Victorians were dead against such things?"

Wilson chuckled; "They were the ultimate hypocrites; sexually repressed in their daily lives but a total free for all if it was considered a work of art. The wealthy enjoyed promiscuous lives and the poor were sexually repressed."

They headed for a McDonald's opposite and Owen had three burgers with all the trimmings. Alex had some fries and Wilson, and Jericho almost enjoyed a cheeseburger each. They sipped coffee and Jericho outlined the plan. "What I do know; is that yet again, I have to show my bloody bits off!" Alex moaned and Wilson tapped her arm; "Yes, but you do it with such elegance and grace my dear." Now that did make Owen and Jericho chuckle. Alex just nibbled on her fires and didn't smile.

2. GYPSIES ON THE COMMON.

Owen and Alex simply couldn't stop giggling at seeing Jericho and Wilson in their 'costumes'. Jericho was wearing red trousers with a bright yellow waist coat and a frilly white blouse. A red beret lay on the back of his head, but it was the two big gold earrings that really set the pair off. Wilson was wearing check trousers, red shirt and black bowler hat. He also wore a single large, gold earring; he carried a guitar which he strummed with some apparent skill. They both looked like refugees from a 'Village People' concert according to Owen.

He was dressed in black and white stripped trousers, white blouse and black waistcoat. Owen wore small gold earrings and carried a banjo which he could actually play. Alex laughed outright at seeing him; "You look like a bloody negative!" she declared. Nobody thought her costume was funny; a beautiful blue and white knee length dress with lots of frilly white petticoats and black knee-length boots. Her tight bodice pushed up her magnificent breasts and displayed her charms to perfection; she wore a black ribbon around her neck and another holding her hair in a ponytail. She actually did the look the part of a gypsy beauty.

The two caravans headed down Summer Street and pulled onto the common; Jericho was surprised to see another caravan parked near some trees. Two magnificent black horses were tied up nearby and a washing line was strung between two trees. A small fire was burning brightly with a large black pot hanging over it; suspended between three metal sticks. "Looks like we have neighbours." He said to Alex and guided their pair of horses to a quiet part of the common, also near some trees. Wilson driving the caravan behind with Owen followed and they set up camp. Jericho was playing a character called 'Jericho Williams' and Alex was his wife 'Sabina Williams'.

Owen was 'Owen Williams' and was the brother of Jericho. Wilson was their American 'Cousin' Wilson Hearn, travelling with the family after arriving from New York. Part of their cover story was that he had to leave the country pretty quick for an undisclosed reason and was, of course, taken in by his English relatives without question.

Alex was stirring a huge pot of stew, when she saw the two people walking towards to the other caravan. "Jericho dear, we have company." She shouted and stood hands on hips, still clutching the big spoon. Jericho emerged from their caravan, where he had been consulting his mirror for mission updates. He joined 'Sabina' by the fire and slapped a huge round loaf on the small table which also contained plates and spoons.

Owen and Wilson sat by the fire and Wilson strummed his guitar, singing softly. Owen was carefully reading his mirror in his lap and said quietly; "A certain Noah Cooper and his young wife called 'Freedom'. They're 'black blood' gypsies alright." He hid his mirror and stood. The couple walked over, and Noah spoke in the 'Romany' tongue, which of course, the temporal detectives could understand. They naturally spoke and understood any language spoken to them. There was one exception to this; no detectives could speak Welsh! Well, except those who were bloody Welsh when alive.

Jericho invited the pair to join them and break bread together. Noah was a big powerful man dressed as colourfully as Jericho or Wilson and to Alex [and Owen....] was a handsome dark man. He had a stunning deep voice, and the team was to find he could sing like an opera star. His young wife Freedom was a dark eyed beauty and was just a little older than Owen. She was dressed like Alex with knee length skirt and boots. Her bosom wasn't so pronounced, and her raven black hair cascaded around her shoulders. Noah told her to bring whisky, the good stuff they had received from their Irish cousins in Wexford.

Owen – as a sign of respect – gave the big man his chair and sat on the dry grass, cradling his banjo. Noah was immediately interested in Wilson and Jericho came out with the 'cover' story. Wilson added to it by simply saying; "The gorgers didn't want me around anymore." That made Noah chuckle and he accepted a plate of stew from Sabina and broke the loaf with Jericho and they handed each other the piece they had taken. Freedom returned with a bottle of decent whisky and several small glasses in a little decorated wooden box.

 The impromptu little dinner party lasted until the sunset and the party broke up and everyone returned to their caravans. Alex sat brushing her hair as Jericho threw himself on the floor with just a pillow for company. Alex was always amazed by his sheer ability to sleep soundly on anything. She settled in bed and lowered the oil lamp and peered through the curtains. The other caravan was in darkness, and she wondered about the age difference between Noah and Freedom, who had stated that the pair had been married for over a year. "Why no children yet?" Alex muttered to herself and drifted off to sleep.

 Owen and Wilson were playing cards for Victorian pennies and Owen had won nearly a shilling before the pair called it quits and Wilson snored away in the single bed and Owen slept on the floor – not as soundly as Jericho it must be said – but being an ex-novice monk from the fourteen hundreds; he was used to lots of discomfort. He consulted his mirror before trying to sleep and found a message from Jericho; their human agents had been spreading the word in the small town about the arrival of 'Sabina' the true fortune teller. That was the other half of their cover story; Alex could tell fortunes with real accuracy. What would happen of course is that Owen would check the person with his mirror before being shown into her tent and she would know all she needs to about the person!

As Wilson said, "It's not cheating people; she WILL know their future!" The night passed without incident and after breakfast, Jericho and Wilson set up the tent and Owen placed a few chairs outside and sat strumming his banjo. Alex sat in the gaudy tent and practiced her routine. They didn't have to wait long; two elderly women turned up and crossed her palm with 'silver' – sixpence apiece – and she read the cards and her crystal ball. She got it so accurate and true for one woman that the old lady almost fainted and Owen had to give her water and then some brandy for her to recover. She staggered away fanning herself with a folded newspaper and cursing her long dead father for arranging a marriage with her wealthy but obnoxious cousin that had caused her such misery over the years. Alex had 'seen' it all.

Jericho and Wilson headed into the town and found a local publican that would have the girls dance and the gypsy 'band' entertain his customers for half a crown a night. He was particularly interested in the girls – as would his male customers – and asked constantly if they were pretty. Jericho sung their praises and bought the publican a few beers and managed to winkle from the man, that artists from the local 'commune' frequented his pub and one was indeed: the Cranfield Sommers. They returned to the Common with some shopping and a decent bottle of whisky. Alex had done nine readings; all hugely successful of course and persuaded Freedom to dance with her at the pub. They practiced their routine between Alex's customers and Freedom excitedly told Noah that Sabina 'had the gift'. He was skeptical at first until she told him about her own reading with Sabina [for free of course]. He had to sit down; his grandmother had told him about such women of pure black blood, but he never thought he would actually meet one!

The team and their two 'guests' appeared at the 'King's Head' that summer evening and found the place packed. "Well, there's no bleeding TV or nightclubs in 1870 so we are the next best thing." Wilson explained to a surprised Owen. The girls danced barefoot on the small stage whilst Jericho vigorously slapped his tambourine, Wilson and Owen played their guitar and banjo, then Noah sung at the close of the session; his voice was simply incredible. They certainly received lots of appreciative applause from the customers; even the women present.

The big publican was more than pleased to book them again the following Saturday and for three shillings this time. He knew good entertainment that brought the punters in to spend money. The following morning Jericho awoke and went for a piss in the trees and saw several caravans coming down Summer Street. Noah had said that the rest of the family would be joining him and he especially wanted Jericho's family to meet his 'cousin' Samson Cooper; a well-known bare knuckle boxer who had quite a reputation. He confided to Jericho that's why they were here, there was match arranged between Samson and 'Big Dan Thatcher' a local champion. The bets were currently even on both men. But Noah had backed his cousin with a golden guinea at three to one. Noah and Freedom could live well on those winnings through the winter months.

The local magistrate – Sir William Drudge – was a fanatic for the 'Gentleman's Sport and the noble art' and had even agreed to be referee! He was even known in the gypsy communities to be fair and honest and was more than acceptable as Referee and judge of the contest. The family invited Jericho and his family over for dinner which turned into music and dancing. Owen amused the children with some magic tricks and silly songs. Sabina helped the other woman with preparing food and was amazed at some of the gossip between the women. She also found just how much power women commanded in family; especially the revered grandmothers, their words were practically law within the family.

 She met Unity – an elderly woman who was apparently nearly seventy years old [a very good age for the times] – who also was known to have 'the gift'. She gripped Alex's hand and slowly smiled, whispering in her ear; "Your quite beautiful my child and have travelled much and seen many strange things with your family. You will pass over when the new century is but a year old. But you know that already my dear and death won't hold you back in your adventures." The old lady smiled and patted a very shocked Alex's hand. "Go in peace my child. You work for a great power now but beware of the Italian. He speaks falsehoods and will cause you much misery and doesn't weep much at your passing. A clock rules his miserable life and passing time is his torture. If you can; change you time with him and seek out the dark man with true love in his big heart."

 The old lady then retired to her caravan; helped by her numerous granddaughters and Alex returned to the team in quite a state of shock. She had been told about true 'passers' who really did have the gift, but she had never met one like Unity before. The old woman knew exactly who she was now and what had happened to her with Henri the Italian Count. She really did sleep badly that night and her head filled with thoughts of "the dark man with true love in his big heart."

3. AN ENCOUNTER WITH A BIG MAN.

Alex woke just after midnight and groaned; she needed to pee. She climbed from the bed and wrapped her pink bed jacket about herself and stepped over the quietly snoring Jericho and headed for the clump of trees nearby. She squatted down and pulled up her short nightie and started to pee with some relief. That's when she heard the big man chuckle, standing by a huge tree, pissing against it. He was massive [in all respects!] and couldn't be anyone else other than Samson Cooper. He smiled at her; "Do you know that I've never seen one without hair and I do like it. I wouldn't get my chin rubbed like I had ran a bleeding brush over it!" He shook his big cock and wiped his hands on his underpants which were all he had on.

Alex smiled at his muscles; the man didn't have an ounce of fat on him and she had already seen that he was built like an Arabian stallion. She stared at his bulging underpants; he had a bloody erection from watching her piss. She slowly rose and didn't attempt to pull down her nightie. Samson grunted and walked over to her and slowly took hold of her hand, guiding it down to his erection. She gripped it through the soft cotton and stared at his battered face. He slowly smiled and simply pulled down her bed jacket and threw it on the ground. His eyes widened at the sight of her big breasts under the thin nightdress. Alex knelt and slowly pulled down the underpants; gripping his big cock with both hands and guided it into her mouth. Samson groaned quietly as her expert tongue and lips went to work. He stroked her hair and whispered encouragement.

Alex was naked on her back - using her bed jacket as a blanket - legs open as the big man enjoyed licking and fingering her fanny with some skill. She ran her hands over his bare head and groaned a little. He didn't even bother coming up for breath until satisfied that Alex was wet enough to take him. He knelt between her open legs and gently pushed his big cock into her. Alex now really did groan as she was filled up with his massive member. "Christ woman you are tight." he whispered and Alex almost chuckled; no man had said that to her in some time!

He fucked her slowly and gently at first until Alex signaled that he could start thrusting as he wished. She gripped his big shoulders as he fucked her hard and his mouth enjoyed those big tits and large hard nipples. Alex lifted her bum in time with his thrusts and she felt the tightness in her belly as the first little orgasm came. He was dominating her totally, fucking her whilst almost doing press-ups, only his mouth never left those heaving big tits. After a few minutes they changed position with Alex kneeling on her bed jacket and Samson fucking her 'doggy-style' with his big hands pulling at her tits like he was trying to milk them.

They ended up standing against the big tree with Alex's hands pressed against the trunk and Samson behind her, she would swear that she could feel his cock in her stomach at one point and her climax gushed from her vagina like someone had turned on a tap. She really struggled not to scream as he fucked her hard and fast against the rough tree. Finally, he groaned between gritted teeth - to keep the noise down - and came inside her. Alex slapped a hand over her mouth to stop the scream of a really big orgasm. It felt like someone had set a soda siphon off inside her and he just kept coming. They finally slid down the tree, still locked together and sat on the grass with Alex perched on his lap. She was panting and the big man kissed the back of her neck and shoulders. "Thank you, my dear that was lovely and quite unexpected." He chuckled and squeezed her tits with both hands; quite hard.

Alex stared down, in the moonlight, at the huge cock still buried deep in her vagina; she would certainly be 'gaped' after this for a few days. She shifted gently to make herself more comfortable and turned her head, whispering; "I take it you want to stay in me a bit longer." The big man grinned and kissed her shoulder. "I've just started my dear." was all he said, and he meant it. Alex groaned a little and suddenly felt the big cock moving inside of her; it was growing again!

"Now I will really fuck you my dear and believe me you won't walk straight for a few days after I've finished." He quietly murmured and started to thrust upwards again, and Alex gripped the grass with trembling hands, pulling little clumps out. Samson was true to his words, and they fucked for at least another twenty minutes, changing positions several times without his cock ever leaving her fanny. They ended up - again- against the damn tree and Alex had both hands over her mouth to silence her screams of pleasure and pain as she came twice really hard. Her cum running freely down her thighs and the big man groaned with some restraint as he came for the second time. Alex felt every drop spurt into her, and the pair collapsed against the tree, and nothing was said.

Alex walked slowly back to the caravan wrapped in her bed jacket; the big man had been right; she couldn't walk straight and had to walk with her legs open. Her vagina was still hanging open and dribbling cum. She had to pee again before quietly climbing over Jericho and collapsing in her bed. She lay breathing deeply under the blankets and realised the pair hadn't even kissed mouth to mouth - which she always enjoyed with the right man or woman - and drifted off in a deep, satisfying sleep.

4. THE BAIT IS TAKEN.

Cranfield Sommers lay sprawled across his deep sofa and sipped another glass of wine. He was stark naked and scratched his stomach a few times. He stared at the half-finished portrait on its stand by the huge window and was satisfied with its progress. Then he thought about the rumours and gossip concerning the young gypsy woman who had arrived on the common with her tribe. A Venus by any standard of beauty apparently. He grinned and took another sip of wine; probably has the manners of a Piccadilly trollop and ate with her fingers. All wild and loose with little morals; he finished the glass and knew already that he must paint her.

John – his valet - appeared with a vivid red dressing gown and slippers, whispering in his ear that Sir Reginald Palmer was here about the painting of his dogs. Cranfield sighed loudly and eased himself from the sofa and grabbed the dressing gown while John knelt and pushed on his slippers. He hated painting for people with no taste or appreciation of true art, but the stupid old gentleman was prepared to pay fifty guineas for a painting of his two spaniels.

Cranfield stood by the big mirror and checked his hair and teeth. "Absolutely lovely as usual." He muttered to himself and swept through the door as John opened it. "Oh, Reggie how terribly wonderful to see you!" he exclaimed as John now opened the door to the study and the old man followed Cranfield in. John just sighed and returned to the studio and woke the young girl asleep on the chair; also, stark naked and picked up her clothes. "You won't be needed until Thursday Nancy." He pulled ten shillings from his trouser pocket and gave them to the sleepy girl who was pulling on her petticoats.

"Thanks John darling." Was all she said and started to dress while yawning excessively. John sighed again and pulled the curtains, clearing up paint and palettes and stopped to stare at the unfinished 'masterpiece' on the stand. He shook his head; Cranfield had a enormous talent with paint, no would argue with that, it matched his ego perfectly.

Then he thought about the gypsy woman Sabina he had seen dance at the King's Head on Saturday. John smiled; now that was a woman worth bleeding painting and no mistake. He cleaned up the studio and headed for the kitchens where Mrs. Pickle would be brewing tea for the servant's afternoon break; there was fruit cake to accompany it. But first, experience made him wait a few minutes by the study door until he heard Cranfield shouting for him.

He let Sir Reginald out the big front door and watched Cranfield pushing a handful of white fivers into the old biscuit tin and placed it back in the bottom drawer of his desk. "I'll start on the damn dog painting on Monday John. Are you good with dogs?" Cranfield asked and John nodded.

"Marvellous. Splendid. You're a most useful person John and I don't know what I would do without you." Cranfield jumped up and stared at the big clock on the mantelpiece; "Don't I have another guest shortly?" he asked, and John nodded again; "Mister Crawly Sir at six o'clock and your carriage is ordered for seven." Cranfield smiled; "Oh yes, look over the gypsy wench and see if you're right about her. I do hope so, I want a Venus to grace my newest portrait and secure my position at the Academy. A position I have long been denied by jealous and petty rivals. My great talent WILL be acknowledged while I breathe, and I will be exhibited for all to see." John just nodded a third time.

Cranfield swept from the room telling John to run his bath and lay out a decent travelling suit for visiting the gypsy encampment. John followed his master up the stairs and ran his bath; his most desired cup of tea would have to wait.

Jericho and Owen were brushing down the horses when Wilson appeared with a big smile; "He's on his way up from the pub. I posted little Lash [one of the gypsy boys] to warn us and it cost me a penny. The boy's just reported that Sommers is with another man called Thomas Crawly who's stinking rich and the painter's patron." Jericho threw the curry brush to Owen and headed for the caravan he shared with Alex. Owen rubbed the two brushes together; "Did you check out this Thomas Crawly?"

Wilson nodded;"There's only one possible match for this time and place; a certain Sir Thomas Edwin Crawly, born in 1835 and heir to a textile baron. A big strapping handsome bugger – I checked his picture taken in 1874 – who likes beautiful women, good whisky and sport. I assume he's along to check out Samson as well, boxing is a favourite of his. I expect he wants to decide who to bet on."

Owen smiled; "I've never seen this Thatcher fellow but having seen Samson; I'd put my money on him." Wilson chuckled and agreed with him. They had met "Samson Cooper" last night and both had been impressed – very impressed – as the big man sparred under the trees with other gypsy men. Wilson is a big man, but he was outmatched by Samson who was six foot four inches of muscle and anger. It was clear that none of the gypsy men would disrespect him and the only person he listened too [and could actually control him] was his beloved grandmother Queenie who was tiny and frail. She would kick him up the arse and shout, slapping the big man about to do as he's told. And he did without question or argument.

"Can you imagine if some idiot disrespected the old lady?" Owen had whispered to Alex, who actually shuddered at the thought. "I don't think they would find much of him after Samson had finished teaching him respect for his granny."

Alex had replied softly, staring at the big man carrying a wagon wheel under his arm like a stick. Samson smiled at her; he had said nothing about their midnight encounter under the big tree. Alex smiled back; despite the gaping of her vagina and that she now had to walk slowly everywhere; she wanted the big man again.

The elaborate dark carriage rolled up the common road and stopped short of the gypsy encampment; the driver jumped down and opened the door. Cranfield and Sir Thomas stepped from the carriage sharing a hipflask of whisky between them.

Noah and Jericho met them halfway. You didn't just march into a gypsy camp without invitation. Jericho invited the pair to his fire and asked Noah to join him with Samson. The men sat around the blazing fire and Sir Thomas was interested in Wilson and was really interested that Wilson could also box. But when Noah appeared with Samson [and his granny] he lost all interest and it showed.

Samson stood arms folded and said nothing. Queenie did all the talking which made Owen giggle a little and he went to fetch Alex after the look Jericho gave him. Sir Thomas gave Queenie a gold sovereign to show his respect, and that made Samson smile – a little – Sir Thomas had clearly dealt with gypsies before and knew their ways. Cranfield was also interested; he wanted to paint Samson as his original namesake; draped with young naked women of course. Then Alex and Freedom joined them.

Cranfield stood and slowly removed his large cigar and bowed a little. He just stared at Alex and said nothing. Sir Thomas was also very respectful and spoke to Jericho about his young wife. Over whisky they struck an agreement; Alex would pose for Mister Sommer's for the unheard model's fee of five guineas – in gold – and she would be accompanied by Freedom and their husbands.

Sir Thomas was more than happy with that. Finally, Cranfield managed to pull his eyes away from Alex and whispered to Sir Thomas; "Yes, she'll do nicely my friend. Very nicely indeed." He could already imagine the rapturous applause as the sheet was dropped from his masterpiece "The Queen of Fairyland" at the London Academy Exhibition of his work.

Cranfield and Sir Thomas left the encampment after an hour, well satisfied with the arrangements made and Sir Thomas confessed he would have easily paid twice that amount to obtain Alex for the portrait. Cranfield sat nodding; deep in thought about his new model. Then the real eating, singing and drinking started at the gypsy camp.

Owen danced – with her watchful father's permission – with Florence; a very pretty dark-haired girl and they really got on. Wilson and two other men played their guitars to much appreciation by the families. The party broke up at midnight and everyone returned to their caravans. Jericho noted that Noah had posted a couple of young men to keep watch by the fire during the dark hours; accompanied by a couple of large dogs.

Owen peered through the curtains and asked Wilson about the

men by the fire. "They have to keep watch; not everyone likes Gypsies and mobs have been known to form and burn them out. Drive them off common land which they have a right to stop on." Wilson informed him and settled down for the night. Owen lay on the floor and thought about Florence before drifting off to sleep.

Jericho also lay on the floor consulting his mirror while Alex curled up in bed. "At least I know how to pose. I've done it before, but I hope he has some proper heating in his bloody studio." She said to Jericho who just nodded. He knew Alex had modelled before. [See the episode; 'Sir Edward Coleville's French House' Series 4 – Episode 3 of The Temporal Detectives Series.]

"Nothing bad is known about Sir Thomas Crawly at the moment and Sommer's seems to be all ego, so maybe it's someone that the pair know or have dealings with we should be after." Jericho muttered and rubbed his chin, pushing his mirror under the pillow. He lay back and wondered about the next steps to take in the case. He drifted off to sleep and Alex was gone just after midnight.

5. A THREESOME DEEP IN THE TREES.

Alex met Samson - as arranged - under the big tree again. She was stark naked under her hooded cloak and had already lubricated herself in anticipation. She had a big surprise; Samson wasn't alone. He was fucking another young woman 'doggy-style' under the big tree. Alex drew closer and realised it was Freedom, Noah's young wife! The big man looked up and smiled as he thrusted hard and fast into the groaning girl. "Come on darling, join in." He grunted and slapped Freedom's bum a couple of times. She turned her head and managed a smile; "For God sake Sabina get over here, I'm out of my depth here with his big cock!"

They were both stark naked, so Alex dropped her cloak and joined in by kissing and caressing Freedom with some passion. That make Samson chuckle with delight, and he said softly; "So you two ladies like 'touching the velvet', well, I love watching it whilst fucking." He roughly pulled Alex into the same position as Freedom - kneeling on the grass - and pushed their pale bums together. He pulled his cock from Freedom and quickly rammed it straight into Alex's open cunt with some force. She groaned and Freedom grabbed her head and kissed her with some passion as

Samson now fucked Alex hard and fast. He alternated between the two moaning girls for some minutes before he emptied his load into Freedom. He pulled out his cock and took hold of Alex by the hair and guided her mouth to Freedom's trembling crotch. "Clean that mess up darling." He ordered and Alex did as she was told, much to Freedom's surprise and delight. He knelt in front of Freedom and chuckled, pushing his cock into her mouth; "And you can clean this up too."

The big man sat against the tree and watched as the girls took turns with his cock, sucking, licking and caressing the swelling member. He told them to kiss each other between their skilful sucking of his big cock and loved it when their tongues came together over his now erect 'John-Thomas' as he called it. They shared his stiff penis for some minutes before he grunted and told Alex to squat over him, facing Freedom and he carefully inserted his cock into her anus with little consideration. Alex moaned and trembled; her legs shaking a little as he pushed his erection further into her back passage. He ordered Freedom - who was wide eyed at the scene unfolding before her - to "get to bloody work on Sabina's cunt". Freedom knelt down and inserted her fingers into Alex's dripping vagina and joined them with her mouth. Alex gripped the big man's knee's and groaned as he now thrusted upwards, watching his cock moving up and down in Alex's arse. He fucked her for some minutes before she had to call it a day and eased herself off him with some real relief; she hadn't 'tapped out' like that for some time.

He tried it with Freedom who simply refused after a couple of attempts; her anus couldn't take a cock like that. Samson just grunted with disappointment and pushed Alex onto her back and pulled her legs apart. He mounted her quickly and fucked her hard and fast. He dragged Freedom down and made the girls kiss and caress again. He slapped Freedom's arse and told her set about Sabina's big tits, which she did with some enthusiasm and Alex moaned as she had a couple of small orgasms under his brutal fucking and Freedom's wonderful touch of hands and mouth. Samson chuckled at Alex's climaxes and slapped her bum a couple of times; "So you like it rough do you darling." He gripped her around her hips and lifted her from the ground and she quickly grabbed his shoulders and held on tight as her pushed her against the tree and roughly rammed her down on his cock several times.

Alex slapped a hand over her mouth to cut off the screams as a big orgasm came over her and she struggled to squirt with her fanny full of Samson's big cock. It was so powerful that she almost collapsed in his arms, but she held on tight, her bum scrapping against the bark of the tree. Thankfully Samson now finished, emptying a full load into her and she felt every droplet of cum spraying about inside her. The pair slid down and lay panting on the grass with Alex wiping tears away.

Samson made Freedom clean up Alex's trembling and well gaped cunt, while Alex had to clean his cock with her tongue and mouth. He stood over the girls who crouched beneath him and smiled; "Thank you ladies. Until next time." He then walked off without another word leaving the pair to cuddle each other. Freedom kissed Alex's wet face and their tongues came together. They had gentle lesbian sex on the grass for about twenty minutes with Freedom actually having a couple of small orgasm's which seemed to satisfy her greatly. Alex ate her fanny out with some real skill and Freedom loved it. They lay in each other's arms in the moonlight and Freedom finally whispered; "There won't be another next time the bloody brute." She turned and kissed Alex's big breasts with the nipples hard in the chill of the summer evening and smiled; "But I think we should get together again my love." Alex just nodded and kissed Freedom for a minute or so and then grabbed up her cloak. They kissed again and parted.

Alex was just about to slip back into the caravan when she noticed that the two boys' assigned to watch the camp were both asleep in front of the blazing fire and there was no sign of their dogs. She reached the caravan and almost jumped out of her skin. Owen appeared from under it, wrapped in a blanket and looking sleepy; "Bloody Wilson is snoring like a road drill so I'm under here. How did the fuck with Samson go?" He whispered smiling. Alex shrugged her shoulders and didn't smile; "Alright, he's a big brutal man in all respects. You best get back in with Wilson and plug your ears or something. Remember they have dogs out during the night." That removed Owen's smile and he crept back to his caravan at some speed. Alex chuckled a little and slipped quietly into the caravan, then her bed. Jericho didn't even stir on the floor and Alex sighed - but smiled - Owen was right about their Inspector; he could sleep soundly on a pile of bricks!

6. ANOTHER MISSING GIRL?

Loud banging at Jericho's caravan door woke him and Alex sat up in bed and grunted; "For Christ sake it's only just after dawn." Jericho threw his blanket and pillow onto the bed and Alex pushed them to one side. They had to keep the deception of 'husband & wife' up. Jericho – yawning – pulled open the door and found several men from the camp standing there; they didn't look happy.

Noah didn't mince his words; "We need to speak to your boy Owen. Young Florence has gone missing; her bed hasn't been slept in. He was dancing with her last night, and we want to speak with him." Jericho nodded and gestured towards the other caravan; "Certainly Noah. Owen will help all he can." Alex had joined him at the door; wrapped in a sheet asking her 'husband' what was going on. Noah was already banging on the door and Wilson opened it.

Jericho joined the men by the door and shouted for Owen. He staggered to the door and sat on the steps yawning. Noah asked him about Florence and Owen jumped to his feet really concerned. He had said goodnight to her – and her father - at about midnight and him and Wilson had gone to bed.

Florence's father nodded his agreement with that. Wilson yawned and added that Owen hadn't left the caravan after they returned, not even for a piss. Noah and Florence's father nodded and grabbed the two young men who had been standing watch; neither had seen or heard anything except the dogs had barked about two o'clock in the morning at the woods. There was nothing they could see there at the time. The group returned to the fire to discuss further, and the team all squeezed into Jericho's caravan, where Alex had brewed tea and made some toast. She wondered if the departing Florence had seen them in the woods last night; then smiled to herself, the girl wouldn't betray her friend Freedom so she couldn't betray her [Alex] and Samson.

Owen sat on the unmade bed and consulted his mirror; "No breeches of the timeline for this time and place and her soul is still showing in the current human timeline." He informed the others, accepting a big mug of tea from a concerned Alex. Jericho nodded; "So, she's still alive around here somewhere. Noah and her father will head into town and report her missing to the local constabulary; they'll have to do something about it, she's just turned fourteen." Now that revelation shocked Owen; "For Christ sake I thought she was nineteen or twenty!" he exclaimed. Alex handed him some toast and almost smiled; "They grow up quick around here, they have too."

Wilson sipped his tea; "What about a body search? We could start at her caravan and follow what comes up. But we'll have to be bloody discrete with the camp in uproar." Jericho slowly ate his well buttered toast and finally nodded. "I don't think it's a co-incidence that Cranfield turns up on site and yet another girl goes missing." No-one could disagree with that conclusion. He swallowed down some tea and added; "The sooner we get Alex to his studio and house, the better. Let's wash up and get dressed; we can't do much in our bloody night clothes."

The impromptu breakfast meeting broke up with Wilson and Owen returning to their caravan. Jericho washed up outside by their small fire, while Alex had a wash inside and fixed her make-up. She really missed not having a proper bathroom or mirror, but most of all not having a decent bath or shower. She dressed appropriately and joined the others waiting outside. They all moaned at how long she had taken. She just ignored their comments and the little group headed into town with Owen discretely checking his mirror. They reached the crossroads when Owen called them around him. "The trail ends here I'm afraid. She reached the crossroads and must have gained a ride or something. Florence may have met someone with a horse or carriage. We need to find where they went to pick up a signal again." Wilson sighed; "I wonder if we'll pick it up again at Cranfield's house." Jericho gestured that they walk on; the morning was bright and sunny, and they passed through the small town drawing some looks of disapproval from the locals.

They were stopped at the bottom of the High Street by a strapping big Constable who easily matched Wilson in size. Alex really smiled; he could pass for a male model with his rugged good looks and physical presence. Constable [collar number 166D] Gerald 'Jerry' McFarlane was in his late twenties, and he smiled at the group, pushing back his helmet to reveal wavy raven black hair and eyes. Close up Alex realized that he was indeed a very handsome man. Owen whispered to her; "Jackie would agree with your thoughts." That made Alex smile and she patted his arm. The constable spoke quietly; "I'm afraid there's no trace in the town – so far – of young Miss Florence. Our Inspector Mister Letterman is interviewing your Noah Cooper and the girl's father."

Jericho thanked him and asked if they were heading the right way for Cranfield Sommer's house. The constable smiled at Alex and nodded; "Don't let him underpay you, Miss; whatever he offers make him double it. If I could paint, I would pay you what you wanted!" He smiled shyly and Alex murmured a little 'thank you' for his compliment. Wilson just groaned; "There's a lot of bleeding moths around here." The little group walked on and Alex was clearly in a better mood now!

They found Cranfield's big house easily; there was a copperplate sign on his gate which declared "Sommer's House – Beware of the genus." Owen just sighed; "He has a bloody ego the size of Mount Everest." Everyone chuckled at that, and they walked up the path and Jericho pulled the doorbell. John opened the door and didn't smile. "We're here to see Mister Sommer's, we have come with his new model." Jericho removed his hat and smiled. John stared at Alex and a smile crept across his face; "Follow me." Was all he said.

They all stood in the big reception room and Owen had to giggle; there were three self-portraits adorning the walls – all of Cranfield of course – and the one hanging above d of course – and the one hanging above the huge fireplace was the best; Cranfield as Jesus Christ blessing an adorning crowd of followers! Wilson just shook his head in mock despair and even the normally reserved Jericho had to chuckle. "I change that to an ego the size of North America." Owen said quietly and checked his mirror. He grinned and held it up; "The signals back and strong. Florence is in the house somewhere!"

John opened the door and announced his master who swept in wearing a long white fur coat, black trousers and red waistcoat. Upon his head was a bright red Fez and he was smoking a long thin cigarette with a gold cigarette holder. But what caught everyone's attention were the pink slippers with gold tassels. He welcomed everyone warmly, especially Alex. "I am a lucky man my friends to have the opportunity to paint two lovely wild gypsy women!" The team exchanged a glance amongst themselves, and Jericho asked; "Two sir?" Cranfield grinned and sucked on his cigarette with some delicacy; "Oh yes, I will pass between the two of them, separately at first and then paint them together. I think for Alexandra, I will paint her as Queen of the Fairies accompanied by her favourite and loyal servant; Apollo the magic donkey King."

Wilson folded his arms; "I take it you are also painting Miss Florence form the camp?" Cranfield smiled, nodding; "Oh yes, a right little beauty I have spent the morning sketching and painting her. I understand that she and her boyfriend are heading for the bright lights of the big city to seek their fortune."

Owen grunted and said quietly to Alex; "Running off with her boyfriend at fourteen?" Alex smiled; "I told you; they grow up quickly around here. But I will have words with her, not they will do much good if her mind is really made up." Owen just sighed. "I was younger than that when I was dragged off to that bloody monastery; at least she made the call for herself." He didn't sound happy about his past. Cranfield tugged the servant's bell rope and John appeared again.

"Serve the good fellows some tea or something stronger if they wish whilst my lovely model prepares herself for painting in the Constable studio. Tell Reynolds to get his camera ready; I will need several photographs for the final stages." John just nodded and gestured for Alex to follow him. "This way misses, I have aroused the fire to make you more comfortable." Alex followed him out giving the boys a little smile. Cranfield was now staring at Owen, and he slapped his hands together; causing cigarette ash to fall on the carpet. "Now young man, have you done any nude modelling? I can see you naked sitting on a stool with spear and shield waiting to enter the arena!"

Owen just stared at him and mumbled something not very pleasant. Cranfield grinned; "There will be ten pounds for your fee." [That was serious money in these times]. Jericho and Wilson quietly chuckled and Cranfield swept from the room shouting for Reynolds and John.

Owen stood with his arms folded; "If he thinks I'm standing around naked with my wedding tackle hanging out for him to bloody paint, he can think again." Wilson slapped him on the shoulder; "Go on baby brother, you will be immortalized in paint and canvas. Maybe loads of people will come and see you being exhibited at that posh London gallery." Owen didn't smile; "I won't be exhibiting my privates any time soon." Was all he said.

Jericho rubbed his chin; "Now, who is this Reynolds fellow?"

7. THE PAINTING - PART 1.

The studio was quite compact, and the blazing fire certainly helped; the girls stripped down as 'Reynolds' set up his camera. He was a big built man with little conversation except to tell the girls how he wanted them. John gave Alex some 'Fairy' wings and a garland of silk flowers to wear on her head. He then posed young Florence in front of scenery that's represented woodland and a river. Reynolds photographed her first while John sat with the naked Alex on the sofa. He was actually quite funny, and they pair chatted quietly, mainly about Cranfield. "Talk of the devil." muttered Alex as Cranfield swept in [he never just walked in any room] and stood before his big easel and mixed up his palette with some care. John was on hand to clean his brushes and arrange the scenery and props. The donkey would not appear until the next session, so it was quite simple to set up.

Alex was called over in her 'costume' and Cranfield posed her for his painting. The first position was quite 'naughty' for the times and Cranfield [and John] loved it that Alex didn't mind laying back with her legs open and her fanny on full display. They were only interrupted when Reynolds had finished with Florence, and she left to get dressed. He then set up his camera and took several photographs of Alex and then he left too; he had a lot of developing to do so that Cranfield could have the photographs tomorrow. Cranfield was smiling and waving his brushes in the air and on the canvas, telling Alex to keep still as he worked on his masterpiece. John returned from the kitchens with some tea and they all sat on the sofa - Alex still quite naked between the two men - and drank their tea. This made Alex chuckle a little with its patent absurdity and John caught on and laughed too.

Cranfield lit yet another cigarette and sipped his tea. He grinned at Alex and gestured towards John; "Now my darling, you are clearly interested in this young man and him with you, so you should fuck each other. I will sit upon that stool and watch with great interest and much enjoyment." Alex stared at him and then realised he meant it!

John smiled at her, and Alex slowly nodded; he was quite a handsome man, and she was certainly sexually aroused by the situation. "Oh, why not!" she said quietly, and the two men smiled. But when he stripped off - quite slowly - her eyes went to one part of him, and she smiled; really smiled. The bloody donkey had nothing on John the servant! Cranfield retired to his stool and watched with real interest as John removed Alex's flowers and wings. She stood in front of him and caressed his growing cock with both hands. "Use your mouth darling, all men do love that." Cranfield called out; it was obvious that he wanted to 'direct' this little performance himself. Alex went down on John as they retired to the sofa; both naked and aroused. She sucked and fondled his big cock which surprised her with its weight when fully erect. For his part, John's hand was between her legs rubbing her already wet vagina. She was clearly up for a good fucking and that made him smile.

Cranfield drew on his cigarette watching and after a few minutes told Alex to mount John - facing away from him - so he could watch the action without hindrance. Alex did as 'directed' and that pleased Cranfield; "Good girl, now up and down with some vigour please; I want to see those wonderful big breasts bouncing." John gripped her hips as she rode him with some 'vigour' and her big tits really did bounce. She fucked John for some minutes before Cranfield decided in another change. "Now darling, kneel on the sofa, hands on the back and let John mount you from behind. Plenty of slaps please John on that exquisite backside while you fuck her hard and fast. Don't hold anything back." As ordered, they changed position and Alex gripped the rear of the shaking sofa as the first little orgasms came under John's relentless pounding. John turned and shouted; "She's coming!" and Cranfield left the stool and Alex suddenly found his head next to her shaking legs; watching as her cum run down over John's cock and her thighs. Cranfield actually patted her head like she was an obedient dog.

"Now take this in your sweet mouth darling." He stood and pushed his modest erection into her mouth, and she sucked it hard - as directed - and Cranfield groaned and only lasted a few minutes before filling Alex's mouth with cum. "Swallow it down darling." He whispered with a hoarse voice. Cranfield was back on his stool and now wanted the pair to fuck on the rug in the missionary position which they did. John's stamina amazed Alex: he had been fucking her hard for almost half an hour and didn't show any signs of finishing yet. Cranfield was happy with their performance and praised them. Then told Alex to turn over onto all fours - which she did - and he ordered John to fuck her in the arse. John mounted her like a stallion mounts a mare and fucked her slowly; he was quite a considerate lover. He had only been poking her gaped bum hole for about ten minutes before Cranfield told him that he can cum now. Which he did right on cue and that trigged another orgasm for Alex. The pair lay on the floor panting and Cranfield gave a little round of applause. He walked over and knelt, examining John's cock still buried in Alex's arse. He fumbled in his pockets and produced a couple of gold sovereigns and pushed them into a surprised Alex's hand. "Now that performance should receive a little reward darling; Get me some damn whisky please John."

Alex groaned as John slowly pulled his big cock from her bum hole allowing his cum to run out. He jumped up and held out his hand which Alex accepted and pulled her up. He smiled and walked off to fetch Cranfield's whisky. Alex stood and watched as Cranfield returned to his easel and started to paint again." I won't need you until tomorrow darling, so off you go." He said without stopping and Alex walked slowly to the small dressing room, John's cum still leaking down her crotch and thighs. She gripped the two sovereigns and smiled a little - normally she would have thrown them in his face - but she didn't for the sake of the mission - and would give the coins to Freedom.

As she dressed, she could hear John talking with Cranfield about what was captured of the performance and intrigued, she pulled open the door and stared in amazement as Cranfield held up an 'Apple iPad' and both were watching it with some interest. it was clear that the whole 'performance' had been secretly filmed and it was also clear that Cranfield and/or John were time-travelers!

She slowly and quietly closed the door as the realisation that her porn film could find its way onto the modern internet; after all the girls had come from 2016 and porn was everywhere on the 'Net'. That didn't make her happy and she wondered how many films had been shot with various girls and what had happened to those movies? Alex finished dressing and joined the others who were heading for the village and the pub. She couldn't reveal what she had discovered because Jericho didn't know about her little sexual adventures and if he did; she wouldn't be on his team for much longer.

8. PHOTOGRAPHS DON'T LIE....DO THEY?

The team sat in the Kings Head pub that evening and enjoyed a good meal and some decent brandy, while Alex brought them up to date with what unfolded at Cranfield's house and studio. "I couldn't believe it at first, but young Florence just stripped naked in front of me, Cranfield, John the servant and Reynolds the photographer without batting an eyelid. There's more to that young lady than meets the eye. She certainly doesn't want to go home; she appears to detest her father but wouldn't say why. There's something not quite right about that 'happy' family all right. Her boyfriend is from another gypsy family who's camped near the old bridge outside of town. Apparently the two families are not that friendly to each other, which is unusual for Gypsies. She and the young man are headed for Rochester to start over together."

Jericho asked about Reynolds and ordered another round of drinks. He tipped the young barmaid a couple of pennies which delighted her.

Alex sipped her most welcome brandy and sighed; "I couldn't use my mirror on John Reynolds because I had nowhere to hide the bloody thing!" She said nothing the pair being time-travelers; if she explained how she knew all her secrets would pop out and she didn't want that; under any circumstances. Jericho must never discover her secret life.

Owen placed his glass down; "Does Cranfield know she's only fourteen? I mean, even in this time and place; it has to be wrong to paint a naked girl of that age?" Jericho just sighed; "It's a different age and children started work at thirteen or fourteen in these times. The law won't be too interested in some painter paying her to strip for his pictures." Wilson sadly nodded his agreement with that. "What did you find out about John and Reynolds?" He asked finishing his Shepherd's pie.

Alex shook her head; "Nothing really, he says little; he's a big man with real skill behind the camera; I can see why Cranfield gets him to photograph his models before he starts the paintings. He can then finish the job without the model being present. He doesn't have to keep paying for model sessions."

Now Alex smiled; "He wants me to pose for some 'naughty'

pictures at his studio. I've agreed because it means I can run my mirror over him and here's the real laugh; he wants Owen to pose!"

Owen didn't smile as he placed his brandy down; "Why is that funny? He obviously knows and see's talent when he comes across it!" Wilson laughed outright; "You are absolutely right baby brother; real talent, staring him in the face." Jericho just nodded; "Yes, but it means Owen can accompany Alex and that makes me happy." That's when Owen gestured towards the busy bar; "Isn't that the big copper we met earlier?" Alex was immediately interested and nodded; "It certainly is I wonder what the local police know about Reynolds and the servant John?" Jericho gave a wry smile; "That's a very good idea Alexandra, I'll invite the young man over and we can find out. I'll say we are concerned about you posing for him and is he trusted around women etc."

Jericho rose and headed for the bar to order another round and came upon the big policeman with some pleasant surprise apparently. He invited the young man over and soon as 'Jerry' saw Alex sitting there; he agreed and accepted a pint from Jericho. He joined the little group and was a most pleasant and congenial young man. Jericho skillfully 'interrogated' him without the policeman even noticing it. The team found that the police knew about his 'naughty' picture taking and did nothing. It appears that Reynolds had friends and protectors in high places. He also only called himself 'Reynolds' – and never offered any other name.

The young constable hadn't much to say about Cranfield except that everyone knew he was all ego and self-absorbed; but then he was a highly paid painter. But his friend Sir Thomas Edwin Crawly was a different matter. The constable lowered his voice and told Alex – quite bluntly – to watch out for him. Jerry looked about and spoke softly; Sir Thomas apparently really liked young women, whether they were willing or not! He had already had two serious allegations made against him which were both dropped. Jerry believed the girls and their families were paid off to drop the charges. "I wouldn't trust him with a dead cat, never mind a pretty young girl or beautiful woman." Jerry muttered – and meant it – finishing his free beer. He lightened the sombre mood by chuckling and pointing out that Sir Thomas had one good personality trait; he sometimes disappeared for weeks at a time. Apparently to his secluded house on the Kent coast, in some small village there; but Jerry said he often wondered what the dissolute bugger got up to there.

The team all exchanged a knowing glance; that was something few time-travelers could hide, disappearing for days and weeks at a time from their families and friends. The team would now look very carefully at Sir Thomas; very carefully.

Jerry was called away from the table by a couple of men; he was playing darts for the pub against a rival tavern; the 'House of Cards' from the neighbouring village. The team left the pub and headed back to the common. They found quite a surprise waiting for them.

The entire gypsy encampment was gone, including the team's caravans and horses! There was just dead fires and rubbish left behind. They all stood and stared until Owen finally shouted; "Fucking thieving bastards!" No-one could disagree with him. Jericho sighed; "Let's get back to the pub and book some rooms." Wilson folded his arms and almost smiled; "They [the gypsies] will be surprised when the caravans and horses are stolen back by Supplies. Old Joe won't let his precious stores come up short." Everyone chuckled a little at that and made their little at that and made their way back to the village.

Jericho walked hands in pockets and deep in thought, finally he said; "What really made them clear off? I mean they were about to make serious money from that bare knuckle fight, and they can only sell the caravans and horses to other gypsies, who won't pay that much for them. So why did they scarper?"

"Maybe they found out about Florence and her boyfriend running off to Rochester and went after them; taking our bloody stuff as a sort of bonus." Owen offered and kicked a can across the quiet road. Wilson nodded and wiped his face and neck; "Pity, I would have loved to see that Boxing match. I had ten shillings on Solomon." Owen sighed; "Yeah and I had the same. What a bugger!" Alex patted his arm and just smiled, then stopped outside the small tobacconists and waved the others over. She jabbed a finger at the small notice board outside. "Take a look, the fight is still on." They all gathered around and looked at the poster, complete with photographs of both boxer's and the date was tomorrow night at eight o'clock and the venue was Sir

Thomas Edwin Crawley's stables. The fight's purse was a staggering fifty pounds in gold sovereigns to the winner and fifteen for the loser. Owen tapped the poster and smiled; "Take a look at who's credited with the photographs; Reynolds."

Jericho rubbed his chin and smiled broadly; "Our gypsy friends will not let that sort of money go unclaimed. That's where they will be for sure." Wilson was staring hard at the boxer William Daniel Thatcher and pulled out his mirror. He scanned the picture and grunted with satisfaction and surprise. "I'm now not worried about my bet and yours Owen. Thatcher is really Jim Robinson who once fought the famous Mohamed Ali and has been missing since 1979. He was knocked down loads of times. No-one ever knew where he disappeared to and now, we know."

Owen tapped his mirror; "Hold on big man, if he was born in 1925 and disappeared in 1979, he would have been 54 when he vanished and he's certainly not that old in the photograph!" Wilson grunted again and stared at the photograph; "Do photographs lie?" he muttered, and Jericho tapped his arm; "No, I don't think so, but photographers can. Do you think that this photograph was taken in Robinson's youth and maybe borrowed?

Alex sighed; "Or Reynolds took the photograph at the time whilst he was in Miami in the 1960's. Either way one of them is a time traveler because Robinson's photograph cannot exist in this year of 1870 some 55 years before he was even born. So, it has to be one or the other travels in time." Everyone nodded at that clever deduction. Owen pushed his mirror away; "Do you think that the photograph is current, and Robinson jumped back with Reynolds when he was young to now, then jumped again in 1979 to some place he really wanted to live and probably retire in?"

Jericho held up a hand; "All good theories and if we attend the fight, we'll be able to find out for ourselves. Whatever the story is we pretty much now know that Reynolds could be the time-traveler. But is he actually involved in the abductions?"
Alex nodded; "And we must find those girls and return them. Their souls are in serious danger if anything happens to them whilst stuck here." Jericho agreed with that, and the team headed back to the pub looking for overnight accommodation. They were to have yet another surprise waiting for them.

John – Cranfield's man servant – was leaving the pub with a

giggling young lady on his arm who was hanging onto every word the quiet man said. He stopped and raised his hat to Alex and smiled but said nothing. The girl asked John to introduce her to his 'friends' and giggled again. She was quite a beauty with a good figure, but young. John slapped his hat back on and managed another smile. "This is Miss Caroline…. She's a model of Mister Sommers."

Alex asked him if he had seen Reynolds the photographer and he shook his head; "Probably working at his studios. He sometimes takes portraits in the evening." Alex thanked him and then asked where – exactly – Reynolds studio was. John jerked a thumb down the almost deserted street. "He has rooms behind the undertakers, but don't ring the wrong bell or you'll get a miserable old so and so trying to measure you up." The girl laughed and gripped John's arm, whispering into his ear. He grinned and said goodnight; the pair wandered off laughing and chatting.

 Owen discretely pushed his mirror back into his pocket and sighed; "Now that's a real turn up for the mission; John is from this time and place with nothing untoward known about him. He's legitimated for here." Wilson prodded him and asked; "So what's the big surprise then?" Owen almost grinned and pushed his flat cap back; "The girl is Caroline Hatfield who is one of the missing girls from 2016!"

 Everyone stood in silence for a second or two and Jericho folded his arms and said dourly; "Well, we can rule out abduction in her case then." They headed for the undertakers in Green Street a little subdued by the revelation that Miss Caroline appeared more than happy back in 1870. Owen checked her profile and sighed. He informed the other's that Caroline had left home at fifteen and was now nineteen and beyond the care of her parents – who she apparently hated – and social services. Soon as she turned
 eighteen, she started to appear in 'men's magazines' as a nude and sex model. She had also performed in several 'adult' films before disappearing. Jericho just grunted; "We'll deal with that later. She's heading back to 2016 whether she likes it or not. We are not about to lose her soul to the darkness."

 They arrived at the undertakers and Jericho rang the doorbell marked "Reynolds – The Photographer'. Owen thought it and so said it; "I wonder if the other two girls are just as happy to be here?" Wilson slapped his shoulder; "Well do profile checks and find out if they have sordid life stories too!" Owen didn't get his mirror out because the door opened. The team had their third surprise of the night, and it wasn't a pleasant one.

9. ANYONE CAN MAKE A MISTAKE!

Reynolds had his sleeves rolled up and both hands gripping his red braces. He grinned; "Good evening, Jericho and everyone of Team 74. I knew you would turn up all together and save me the trouble of picking you off one at a time." He dropped his hands, and they were gone. Kessel the demon laughed so much that it almost brought a tear to his eyes. He turned and went back inside; still laughing.

The cage swung wildly with even the gentlest movement of the persons inside. Jericho – gripping the wire that covered the metal bars – managed to crawl slowly to the edge and peer down, then up. The metal and wire box were suspended about twenty feet above the stone floor and some five or six feet from the vaulted ceiling. It was affixed with two chains to that grim stone ceiling. He turned and nodded to Wilson;" Alex and Owen are in a similar cage some yards away. Bloody stark naked like we are." He said quietly; any words seemed to echo around the chamber, which was cold, dark and smelling of damp.

Wilson sat back and ran a hand over his face; "How the fuck could we be as stupid and careless as to walk straight up to a demon's lair?" he sounded quite angry; mainly with himself.

Jericho took a deep breath and sat back against the wire without smiling; "Anyone can make a mistake. Kessel is a clever bastard. Had he killed us straight away our souls would have been registered as leaving and that meant Operations Control would have dispatched a Knight to find out why an entire team has disappeared from the timeline. So, keeping us alive – for the moment – allows him to continue with whatever evil plan he has going. But Operations may send another team immediately when they discover all four of us are away from our mirrors."

Wilson nodded and jerked a thumb towards the stone wall opposite them; "What concerns me apart from being locked in a metal cage, suspended some twenty feet above the floor of an evil smelling dungeon is that." Jericho stared at the beautifully

carved balcony set in the stone wall. It had several ornate and comfortable chairs with the walls covered with vivid red curtains. At the rear was a large piano black door with gold handles.
 Wilson folded his arms; "I wonder what sort of shows are watched from there?" Jericho nodded and then turned back to the other cage which was moving back and forth. Alex and Owen were awake. He whispered at them to keep still as much as possible and to keep their voices down; this place was like a sound chamber. They only had to talk just above a whisper for the words to sound around the place. They nodded and waved back. "I hope Owen – the little lucky shit – is enjoying the view in his cage." Wilson muttered with a glum smile.

Jericho pushed his hair back with both hands; "I think the acoustics are there to provide more enjoyment for the audience when the victims scream and plead." He said without emotion.

"They won't get that from me; the bastards." Wilson stated and meant it. That's when they realised that Alex was whispering to them and waving towards the floor. Jericho and Wilson carefully and slowly turned and peered down. She was right; there was a pile of clothes on the floor in a corner – their clothes. "I wonder if our mirrors are down there." Wilson said and sighed loudly. That echoed around the chamber like a steam whistle going off. He slammed a hand over his mouth and just shrugged his shoulders at the look Jericho gave him.

That's when they heard the slight rumbling noise below them and they saw a little dim light spreading across a corner of the dungeon; a door was opening. They watched in horror and fascination as several large apes crept in, grunting and sniffing. They both realised that the creatures were not apes, but ape men half walking upright and half crawling like chimps. They were making noises amongst themselves, occasionally growling and snarling at each other until the largest one – with silver streaks down his back – banged a solitary fist against his chest and the rest fell silent. They sat quietly on the floor; sniffing at the air and occasionally grunting at each other, almost like they were talking amongst themselves.

 "Now what the fuck is going on?" whispered Wilson as a trap door opened in the ceiling just yards from their cage. A small platform was being slowly lowered on four strong chains; it contained a goat that was bleating and shaking. They watched as the platform reached the floor and the ape men attacked. Wilson and Jericho heard Alex scream and then sob as the ape men tore the living goat to pieces with their hands and teeth. It was over in less than a minute.

 They sat around the blood-stained floor enjoying their meal in a little circle; apparently happily grunting at each other again. Finally, Jericho whispered; "I do hope that was their dinner and not just the appetizer."

Wilson stared at him and ran a hand over his face. "Sweet Jesus." Was all he managed to reply and eased himself down on the cage floor.

 "They were you humans at one stage of your development before his grandfather experimented on them and finally produced humans like yourselves." The voice made Jericho and Wilson jump a little and they turned – carefully – to see Kessel sitting on the balcony edge, both hands gripping his braces; he was smiling broadly. He continued; "They are developing fast, already have modern human traits; they have leadership, they love to kill and eat, they lust as strongly as any modern man. They are part of you; a part you try and hide, but it's there alright."

Kessel eased himself from the balcony edge and stood smiling, then fumbled in his pocket and pulled out something. He held them out with one hand and allowed the garment to fall to the floor of the dungeon. Everyone heard Alex shout; "That's my bloody knickers!" and they also heard Owen chuckling. His laughter stopped as they watched the silver back ape man grab them up and sniff them for some time before passing them around the other apes who squealed, jumping up and down in a mild, apparent sexual frenzy. The big ape screamed a couple of times and the others fell quiet.

"I do like to keep my boys happy. The last human female I gave them lasted two hours. They fucked her in some frenzy using every orifice they could find. Then when she was dead; they tore up the body and ate it. They don't waste much." Kessel laughed again and walked to the big door, half turning back; "They now have Alex's scent and so they can wait in anticipation of some pleasure before they eat again." He disappeared through the door; still laughing. The team sat in their cages in absolute silence until Alex managed to stand upright and grip the wire of the cage and whisper to Jericho. "Is it just me, but I think I know what the apes are saying!" she sounded quite shocked, but Jericho nodded; all temporal detectives had the ability to speak any human language there had ever been [the only exception was Welsh apparently!]. He asked her what she had in mind. She gestured to the silver back male and whispered; "He's taken my bloody panties off the others and is keeping them for himself and he hasn't taken his eyes off me since I stood up. Take a look; he's horny as a boat full of sailors."

Jericho and Wilson carefully peered down to see the big male – apart from the others – standing upright and watching every move Alex made. He was holding his big erection with one hand and her panties with the other! Jericho and Wilson stared at each other; a bloody horny, flesh-eating ape man really fancied their Alex! "That's some big ugly nasty moth that Alex's flame has attracted." Wilson muttered quietly.

Then they both heard Alex grunting in ape with little different squeaks and squeals which were different from the males. The big male started to grunt loudly and jump about. He was answering her. Jericho gripped Wilson's arm; "I can understand - I think – what he's saying but not what Alex is saying. As a male I can understand him, but not her. So, our language abilities have their limitations."

Wilson nodded; "From what I can make out; he's getting excited by what Alex is saying, really excited and for the first time in my life I wished I spoke monkey." He said and shook his head adding; "I wish I had my mirror to translate."

Jericho suddenly snapped his fingers which made Wilson jump a little; "Scent, bloody scent of a female will buy time if we're dumped on the floor. I think that evil bastard will lower Alex's and Owens's cage first; so, we can watch what happens to them before it's our turn. They will simply tear Owen apart as soon as they can unless they think he's another Alex."

Wilson nodded slowly; not quite sure what Jericho was on about.

Jericho whispered across to the other cage; "Alex, you need to pee on Owen as much as you can just before the cage is lowered. He needs to smell like you and that may buy some time!" Wilson sighed loudly; "The little pervert will love this." That echoed around the chamber and Owen gave Wilson the two fingered salute and mumbled something to himself: quietly. Whatever he said made Alex chuckle.

She whispered back that she had been enticing the big male with talk about sex with him and him only. She was sure that he had taken the bait and all it would need is for Owen to get to a mirror amongst the clothes and get them the hell out of here. She admitted it wasn't much of a plan, but what other choices did they have?

Jericho suddenly waved back at her; "Ask for a present! Ask him for a present. I understand that amongst the great apes, the males bring the females a little something; just like human males do." Alex nodded and gave the thumbs up and started squeaking and grunting back at the male who seemed to listen with some interest [between sniffing and licking her panties!]. "I'm no eavesdropper but I'd love to know what Alex is saying to her new boyfriend." Wilson grunted and watched carefully how the big ape was reacting.

That's when the big doors behind the balcony flew open with a crash and James - a knight of God – sauntered in followed by Inspector Harry Hadden and the members of Team 52. James was still manifested in his armour, with splashes of blood about his chest and leg; his sword was slung over his shoulder. He raised the visor and grinned; "I had no idea that Team 74 were practicing nudists!"

Harry and his sergeant – Tom Slurburger – found the ornate wooden box on the wall that contained the controls for the cages and operated the down levers for both. The two cages descended to the floor and the ape-men swarmed over them: screaming and grunting. Then there was silence; James had stopped time. Harry turned the switches and both cage doors came open. Team 74 dashed – almost as one – to their pile of clothes and started to dress. Alex's good friend Lisa Solomon shouted down from the balcony; "You best get your knickers from that big ape before he eats them!"

Alex just stuck a finger up and shouted back; "No thanks. I'll go commando until I can get some clean ones!"

James had transformed back into his ordinary clothes and leaned on the balcony; "Soon as all your mirrors went offline; the Duty Time Controller informed the Knight's Council and here I am. Harry and his mob came along because they say they owe you one."

Wilson waved a hand and shouted; "Thanks!" "I take it Kessel is back with his master." Jericho shouted up, pushing his mirror into his jacket pocket. James nodded and smiled; "It was close, but he's still inexperienced so I had the upper hand." Tom Slurburger jerked a thumb behind him, indicating the doors from the balcony. "They lead up into a photographers shop through a hidden door in a cupboard. There's a stark-naked girl posing on a sofa with a stuffed dog! I think she could be one of the girls you're looking for." He shouted down to Jericho who muttered; "One to go then."

10. THE PAINTING - PART 2.

"James will arrange for the mad ape-men to be transported back to their own time and Harry will escort that reluctant young lady back to 2016. Apparently, Kessel is quite the charmer in human form until he tires of the women and then he steals their soul. Alex and Owen will grab Miss Caroline Hatfield and return her to 2016 as well. So, we have just one girl to find. Who is she Owen?" Jericho was walking slowly and talking quietly, consulting his mirror, back towards the pub.

Owen tapped his mirror; "Its Ms Kylie McGovern aged nineteen and a student nurse." Wilson pushed his own mirror away; "So it appears that Sommers and his servant John didn't know about our little demon antic's; especially if the girls were all here at their own free will." Alex nodded; "The only thing that still concerns me is that Kessel said he had fed those bloody ape-men before; do you remember?" Everyone nodded; they certainly did remember those words. "Well, what if that poor woman was our third girl? Even if we check our mirrors, it will only show her as a missing soul because the mirrors cannot separate a soul that died out of its own time or one stolen by the Dark Side."

Jericho agreed with that deduction; "Well, if Sommer's painted her, then maybe he knows what happened to her." They reached the pub and managed to secure a couple of rooms for the night. Alex and Jericho would share one [they were supposed to be man and wife] and Wilson and Owen would share the other. They certainly enjoyed the bar and the young man who played the accordion and sang old folk songs. Tomorrow they would visit Sommers and, in the evening, attend the boxing match.

Old Joe from Supplies wasn't too happy about handing over another horse & buggy set to Owen. "I expect you to take better care of this one; Supplies aren't made of bloody horses and carriages you know." He said unsmiling and disappeared with his strange assistant who grinned a lot. Owen was convinced the little man was one of the Three Stooges!

The following morning the team made their way to Cranfield's house, they had good reason to visit; he was finishing Alex's painting, and everyone had to laugh at the sight of John – Cranfield's servant – trying to coax a donkey into the studio! Owen jumped from the buggy and walked over; he soon had the truculent donkey inside with little pushing and shoving. Wilson grunted; "You can't take it from him; he's a master when it comes to donkeys and mules." Alex, stepping down from the carriage added; "And horses don't forget. Maybe he should have been a vet and not a monk."

 John thanked Owen and offered them all tea which was gracefully accepted. He went off to the kitchens to fetch the cups. That's when Miss Caroline Hatfield strolled into the room and said 'Good Morning' to everyone. They just stared at her; she was stark naked apart from a pair of pink slippers. She sat on the sheet covered sofa and adjusted her hair and spoke to Alex; "Just through that door love. You can hang your clothes there and there's some robes too – if you bother with them – I don't see the point unless the bloody heating goes off."

Jericho smiled at Alex and Owen; "Over to your good selves, I think. An opportunity missed is an opportunity wasted." Alex sat next to Caroline and slowly pulled her mirror from her jacket's pocket. "Do you fancy a little trip?" she asked the puzzled girl, and they were gone with Owen following. "I hope they arrive back in 2016 and somewhere in doors." was all a dour Wilson remarked.

 Wilson and Jericho sat on the now empty sofa and waited for John and the anticipated tea. The doors swept open, and Cranfield appeared; he was dressed like a 19th century Russian peasant, complete with bare feet. "Ah my gypsy friends! The very people I was about to send for." He walked to the large easel and pulled the sheet from it and smiled at Wilson; "Can you strip down my big friend. In private fights the Roman boxers were naked and that much pleased the ladies I believe." Jericho and Wilson just stared at each other. Then Samson Cooper came through the doors; he was stark naked too!

Cranfield sighed a little; "I can't find Mr. Thatcher anywhere; he was scheduled to pose this morning with Samson, and I would have immortalized the pair as Roman fighters, but now you are here my big black friend; you will do nicely and there is five whole gold sovereigns in it for you." He gestured for Samson to stand before him in the classic pose that all boxers seemed to appear in. Jericho couldn't restrain from laughing as he slapped Wilson on the back; "My word Cousin Wilson, five whole gold sovereigns just to take your clothes off; that's easy money!"

The look Wilson gave him could have ignited ice cubes. He was about to decline the generous offer when Jericho shoved him towards the dressing room door and smiled broadly; "Don't keep the master painter waiting, as he said you'll be immortalized for eternity." Then sat back, grinning.

As Wilson walked slowly – and reluctantly – to the dressing room, the door opened, and Alex stepped out dressed in a red bath robe with matching slippers. Owen was just behind carrying a ladies bag which contained her clothes. Cranfield smiled; "My word, I'm so glad you gypsy families live up to your Bohemian reputations for all living together!" He clearly thought that Owen was in the dressing room when Alex stripped off. "I'm really impressed by your sexual freedoms and envy that." He added; also smiling broadly. Alex and Owen both nodded at Jericho in reply to his unsaid question about Caroline.

Alex stared at Samson who really smiled at her. "Jesus, he's a big man in all respects." She whispered to Owen who nodded his agreement; mouth open in amazement and it should be said, a little in jealousy too. John appeared and handed tea all round and didn't ask where Caroline was. He really smiled at Samson and gave him a huge mug. Both Alex and Owen noticed the look he gave Samson and were a little surprised. John clearly was either bisexual or…. they both shrugged their shoulders and sipped their tea; waiting for Wilson to appear.

Jericho appeared between Alex and Owen and whispered to Owen to use his mirror and conduct a 'body search' for McGovern to see if she's around the house or grounds. Owen nodded and slipped away. Wilson appeared and stood next to Samson; that made John smile even more and Alex had to smile herself; both at John and the two big men who were big men in every respect!

Cranfield grabbed up his pencils and asked the pair to pose as Classic boxers would. "I will prepare a rough draft then this very afternoon my darling Alex; I will paint you and the magnificent donkey in fairyland!" he was scribbling away on the canvas with great sweeps of his hand and Jericho watched with real interest; whatever he thought about Cranfield Sommers; he was a real talented artist.

Owen was surprised and a little puzzled that there was no one else in the house apparently. No maids, no footmen, no kitchen staff. He checked his mirror and smiled; it had located the body of Ms Kylie McGovern and he followed the signal up the grand staircase and across the upper hall. It was strong, emanating from a bedroom at the very end of the corridor. But the mirror showed no living humans inside, so he quietly and slowly opened the door; the room was indeed empty. But the signal persisted, and he followed it to the fireplace. He actually peered up the chimney and found nothing. He re-checked his mirror for other humans and stood back; five of them! They were obviously on the other side of the fire place, but this was the final room in the top corridor and that didn't make sense; unless…..He searched the ornate fireplace and mantle piece and found what he was looking for.

The switch was cleverly located beneath the top left-hand tile. He smiled; it was two buxom farm women bailing hay quite naked. "That figures." He murmured to himself and called Jericho on his mirror. It took a good couple of minutes before Jericho answered, he had to find somewhere discrete to operate his mirror.

"I'm on my way." Was all Jericho replied. Owen tapped at his mirror and identified the 'bodies' on the other side of the fireplace. He chuckled and shook his head. Jericho joined him and they both read Owen's mirror with interest. Ms Kylie McGovern had company, Sir Thomas Edwin Crawly, Noah Cooper, wife Freedom Cooper and a certain Constance Margret Crawly.

"I somehow suspect they are not playing bridge." Jericho muttered and stopped time whilst Owen pressed the switch and the fireplace slid to one side. The secret room was quite large and dominated by a huge – almost medieval – four poster bed. Everyone was naked on the bed; all entwined in various sexual positions and all smiling.

"Happy bunch of swingers." Owen said and gestured to the young woman astride Noah. "That's Miss Constance Crawly; she's Sir Thomas's younger sister would you believe." Jericho just nodded and lowered his mirror; "Let's untangle Ms Kylie from Sir Thomas and Freedom. We'll drop her off in 2016 and the job's done." With great care they managed to free the girl from the other two and Jericho operated his mirror, and they were gone. Time restarted and the 'swingers' all were wondering about what happened to Kylie and assumed she had left – for whatever reason – through the open fireplace door. So, they carried on with their orgy.

11. THE PAINTING - PART 3.

John escorted Alex to her dressing room and she stripped off - slowly - as he watched and when she was naked she bent right over and fussed over putting her clothes tidy. John came up behind her and ran his hands over her bottom and sighed; "I would really love to have this again, if I may." He said quietly, stroking her bum cheeks with some reverence. Alex turned and pushed his hands away; she wasn't happy and came straight out with it. "He didn't have to give me the bloody two sovereigns for having sex with you. I had already been paid for the modeling. the sex was my choice, I'm not some paid whore." She stood hands on hips and John smiled; "Forget about that Sabina, that's how he is. I didn't give you any bloody money and I would not insult you like that. So, you can forgive me...please."

Alex relaxed a little; he was right, it wasn't his doing, and she couldn't mention the secret filming otherwise he would catch on that she's not from this time and that would lead to some awkward questions and blow the mission.

Alex slowly smiled and allowed him to run his hands over her breasts and bum. He smiled and unbuttoned his flies, pulling out that big dick that she had enjoyed so much. She knelt and pushed it - still erecting - into her mouth and went to work. He didn't undress but stood and groaned a little at her expertise in cock sucking. Alex turned on the floor and pulled her cheeks apart; "I've already lubed my bum so I can enjoy that big cock of yours properly this time." John chucked, kneeling behind her, "What a woman!" He said and pushed his cock into that much desired brown hole and fucked her with some strength and determination. He gripped her shoulders and thrusted while she frantically rubbed her clitoris with her fingers - after spitting on them - and groaned with pleasure as the first little orgasm came quickly. John caressed her swinging breasts and kissed her neck and shoulders; bending right over her as he buried his cock deep in her back passage and she loved it.

They didn't notice the door open quietly and the figure slipped in and stood watching the couple fucking on the floor. John looked over his shoulder and smiled; "Hi Tom, I'm sorry but no photographs today, bloody Reynolds has gone missing, and no-one can find the bugger." He panted and leaned back, still poking Alex's gaping anus. She turned her head and saw the young man standing quite naked clutching a fair-sized erection with both hands. John patted her arse; "Tom was supposed to perform today for Reynolds but the bugger has disappeared without a word to anyone."

Alex seemed well surprised by that [she was certainly pretending obviously, but again; couldn't say how she knew he was gone] and John chuckled and whispered to her; "He's very good with women. Do you want to try him? He's fit and healthy, works on old man Chubb's farm." Alex groaned a little and nodded her head. John waved the young man over. "I'll turn her over and you can fuck her as you like while I'm staying firmly in her wonderful bum hole!" And he did and young 'Tom' – smiling broadly - climbed aboard. He couldn't keep his hands or mouth off Alex's big heaving tits as he fucked her hard and fast. He wasn't as big as John but certainly knew how to use his cock to make a woman happy. Alex soon felt the big one come and groaned loudly as her stomach tightened and her legs shook. It exploded from her vagina with some force, splattering down her thighs and onto Tom's cock and legs. The young man chuckled; "That's the fastest I've ever made a tart come!" And continued to fuck the quivering Alex with some force. They fucked for some minutes more before John emptied his load into Alex and - again - she felt every drop shooting up her back passage and she climaxed again. Tom carried on fucking her for another few minutes before he came too and the three lay on the floor panting and laughing. John waved a hand at Tom and laughed; "Sabina, this is Tom the farm hand and Tom this is Sabina; a very nice lady who absolutely loves cock!" Both the men laughed and withdrew from a trembling Alex who lay on the floor; recovering from her big orgasm and allowing the cum to leak from her gaped arse and fanny. John sat up and patted Alex's belly; "I think you'll be quite swollen with a baby in a few months' time my girl. Tom here has fathered at least four or five around these parts. All with married women of course; so no problems there. He was going to pose for Reynolds for some really kinky stuff." He turned to Tom who lay stretched out on the floor clutching his flaccid cock. "Did the bugger pay you already mate?"

Tom nodded and jerked his cock a couple of times; "Yeah, two gold sovereigns for the donkey job and today I was supposed to fuck some tart who the donkey was to fuck, also with my help."

Alex sat bolt upright and stared at the happy young man, finally she said; "What do you mean donkey job?" John answered her; "Tom is our animal expert. He fucked the donkey yesterday and I think it was a pig before that. The toff's in London pay a fortune for pictures like that and Reynolds always paid well, very well. That young tart Christine was going to perform with the donkey, but she hasn't turned up yet."

Alex rose from the floor and headed for her clothes; all she could think of was Tom fucking the donkey then fucking her. It made her feel sick, but - again - she restrained from saying what she really thought and said she that she needed the toilet. John talking with Tom didn't notice that she had taken her clothes.

Alex would soak in the bath for a long time tonight.

12. SAMSON AND BILL.

The team assembled outside the stables and watched the stream of men and some women heading into the place. Jericho stood hands on hips and spoke quietly; "I believe that Sir Thomas Edwin Crawly is a time travelling friend and we need to find his time portal and end his travelling days." He turned to Alex and smiled; "You can lure him to the hay loft above the where the fight will take place and Owen…. sorry Jackie can check him with her mirror and locate the portal if he has it on him." Alex slowly nodded; Owen had transformed into his 'alter-ego' Jacqueline so that he could accompany her; dirty Sir Edward would certainly not object to two beautiful young women in the same hay loft!

Wilson chuckled at the old pistol Jericho had stuffed down his trousers; it was part of his 'enraged husband' performance if needed. Should the girls need 'rescue' then he would burst in waving it about pretending to be shocked and enraged at finding his wife with another man. The damn thing wasn't even loaded.

They could hear music coming from the stables and recognized it; it was the excellent accordion player from the pub. "They certainly make a night of it." murmured Wilson as he watched Samson arrive with his grandmother and was surprised that none of the gypsy encampment had turned up. "I don't bloody believe it; his old Gran is his second!" he added with some amazement. The strange pair disappeared into the stable and they could hear cheers and applause.

"Now where's the other bleeding time traveller Mr. Jim Robinson aka Thatcher." Jericho said, discretely checking his mirror as Alex and Jackie headed for the stable to 'chat up' Sir Edward.

"I don't know who will be more disappointed me or the crowd if the bugger doesn't turn up." Wilson said and saw another carriage pull up. It was Cranfield and John; Wilson had to shake his head in mock despair; they were both dressed like a pair of Arabs with flowing robes and curved swords. "Do you think that John is more than a servant to Cranfield?" He asked Jericho who just smiled. "Each to their own." Was all he replied as the pair swept into the stables and received a round of applause too!

"Heads up, this could be him." Wilson tapped Jericho's arm and gestured to the two black carriages that had arrived. Four big men in expensive suits appeared from one and stood about trying to look tough and alert. One of them pulled open the door on the other carriage and helped a beautiful young woman step down. She was dressed like she was about to attend a ball at Buckingham Palace. Then her 'escort' jumped from the carriage and Wilson sighed in disappointment; it wasn't Robinson. He was over six feet tall and built like a brick outhouse [as Owen would say] and an African. He stopped momentarily and tipped his hat to Wilson with a big smile. Wilson raised his own hat in salute.

Then the entourage also swept into the stables to sudden great applause.

Jericho lowered his mirror and sighed; "He belongs in this time, born in 1848 in North Virginia, William Daniel Thatcher is a former slave who use to box for his plantation owner. He's killed over six men in the ring before he turned 'professional' after being freed. He's one mean son of a bitch and he's resemblance to Jim Robinson is uncanny but not surprising; they are related. His departure date is shown as 1902; he's killed in a fire at his boarding house in New Orleans. His soul will be collected and quarantined for over two hundred years for various murders. I can't find any reference to this fight in his Human Records File which is strange."

 "Shall we watch the fight?" Wilson said and it wasn't a request. Jericho smiled and slapped the big man on the shoulder; "Well, we have bugger all to do until Alex or Owen….sorry, Jackie calls." They headed into the packed stables and found a spot by the east corner of the ring. Wilson had to smile; two men had set up a bar and were doing quite a trade in bottled beer and spirits. They were both dressed in short white aprons and wore bowler hats; like you would find in a good London public house. Wilson fetched a couple of bottles and took a swig. "Not bad stuff this pale ale or whatever it's called. It would be better chilled of course, but you can't have everything can you?"

Jericho just chuckled and took a swig of his bottle. They both had to smile when the referee stepped into the ring with the young lady that carried the black small chalk board which would have the rounds written on it. She was wearing a black corset that barely restrained her ample breasts; black silk French knickers and stockings with knee length, laced up boots. She kept her small black hat on. The referee announced the fight over the noise of the crowd through a metal megaphone and the two boxers had arrived; each with their entourage; William Thatcher was first in the ring wearing gold silk shorts and lace up boots. He really did look magnificent. He waved both fists in the air; they looked big even from a distance. His four men encouraged the audience to cheer; not that they needed any.

Wilson wondered where the pretty lady was; maybe she didn't like to see the actual fight. Then Samson appeared in black silk shorts and boots, his grandmother carrying the bucket, towels and sponge. The referee brought the two men together in the middle and held up a red hankie. He shouted through the megaphone; "There's a purse of fifty gold sovereigns to the winner who will be the man still standing when the other cannot. The one on the floor will receive fifteen gold sovereigns for his troubles. May the best man win. Come out fighting when the red lady hits the ground. Each round will be five minutes and the bell will signal the start and end of each round. Good luck to you both!" He didn't have to explain any other rules; there wasn't any!

But he did whisper to the pair that if they disobeyed his rulings; he would have them locked up without bail for a few months and both men knew he could; he was the bloody local magistrate after all! He gestured to a weedy man on a stool by the north corner, who then rang an old school bell and yelled "ROUND ONE!"

The girl had chalked up a "ONE" on the board and was holding it up to the cheering crowd. The referee dropped the red hankie and ran for the corner, taking the girl with him. The two big men came together with some brutal determination; even Wilson had to wince at the sound of big fists crunching into faces and bodies. Bare knuckle boxing certainly wasn't for the squeamish and some 'matches' could go thirty rounds!

That's when Jericho's sharp eyes noticed the group of excited latecomers filing into the stables and gathering at the back; it was Noah and several men from the gypsy encampment. They didn't look happy at seeing him and Wilson looking back at them. Noah did raise his hat; unsmiling. Jericho returned the strained compliment but did smile; a little. "Now that's a turn up for the books." Wilson said and finished his bottle of beer.

"I told you the lure of all that money would bring them running." Jericho said and checked his mirror; there was nothing from Alex or Jackie and Sir Thomas certainly wasn't at the fight. That's when Jericho realised that Cranfield and John were also missing from the audience. "Oh fuck!" was all he said and gripped Wilson's arm, adding; "Come on! I think our girls could be in trouble."

They pushed through the crowd and headed for the back stairs that climbed up to the hay loft. They burst through the door and found the hay loft empty. Wilson looked around in desperation and then found a pair of ladies boots under some hay. He searched further and found a skirt and blouse. He held it up; "Wasn't Jackie wearing a gypsy blouse like this?" Jericho grimly nodded and checked his mirror for the two detectives and cussed loudly; "They are not shown with a body search but their mirrors are still on line and show them….." He rubbed his chin and tapped his mirror. "The mirrors are showing the year 2016 and a house on the Kent coast. That bastard Sir Thomas has a remote house there in this time and place and the other girls were all taken from 2016. Let's go!" He operated his mirror, and the pair was gone.

 The pretty young lady sat on the hay box in the corner and swigged her gin bottle; Bill wouldn't believe that she had seen two Arabs, one English gentleman and two gypsy girls disappear first, followed by another English gent and a very big and handsome black fella. Bloody strange place this England is, she thought and swigged her bottle again. Working as hooker in New York was strange sometimes, but it couldn't hold a candle to this bloody place she mused and took yet another swig. " Yep, the old country was weird; no wonder people flocked to bloody America!"

13. SIR THOMAS CRAWLY'S HOUSE OF DREAMS.

 Jericho slowly lowered his mirror and smiled; "There are people in the house and moving about." Wilson nodded and the pair walked up the path of the old house; there was smoke rising from a couple of the chimney stacks and the lower floor windows still had their shutters over them.

Jericho pulled the bell rope and could hear it ring inside. They waited for a minute or two and Alex pulled open the door – giggling – with a glass of champagne in her hand. "Come on in the party is great fun. Thomas knows how to throw a do!" she gestured for them to enter and John [Cranfield's servant] appeared behind her; drinking from a pint glass. "Come on in boys and enjoy yourself!" He exclaimed and Wilson shrugged his shoulders; why not?

Jericho just smiled and they wandered into the house which stank of booze, tobacco and perfume. The music was loud and mostly from the 1960's and 1970's. He smiled at that, and Wilson certainly did. "The best decades for real bloody music ever produced." He muttered. The place was packed with people in costumes; a very good Frankenstein wandered past with his arms around Tinkerbelle who blew a kiss at Wilson and winked. Jericho pulled Alex over to a quiet corner and asked about Owen/Jackie and the time portal. "She's working the bar at the moment and guess what we found in a locked cupboard in Thomas's study?" Jericho folded his arms and smiled again. Alex sipped her champagne and whispered in his ear; "A bloody Jerusalem mirror locked to 1870!" now that did make the Inspector of Temporal Detectives smile; he always knew that his 'girls' would come up trumps.

That's when he noticed Freedom Cooper dancing with Sir Thomas in just her underwear. "Novel costume, what's she come as?" He asked Alex who giggled again. "A real good time girl apparently and she's quite a card when Noah is not around, telling her what to do and when, despite apparently having an open marriage." Wilson tapped his shoulder and gestured to Cranfield Sommers dancing with his 'servant' John. "I was right about that pair." He muttered and accepted a bottle of beer from Jackie who had finished her turn behind the bar. Alex just smiled at that, she wanted to correct him about John; he was definitely bisexual!

"You've not heard the best bit yet Jericho, most of the guests here are bloody time travelers! Frankenstein is from 1982 and the gorilla dancing with the catholic schoolgirl is from 1790. You learn a lot about bloody people from behind a bar!" Jackie reported.

Alex stuck her smiling face between the two and said quietly. "Have you told him why they are having this bash?" Jackie grinned and spoke into Jericho's ear; "They are celebrating being free of Mister Reynolds influence! Apparently that bloody demon had dragged these time travelling folk into his evil plans, and they weren't happy about it. But James sorted him out and now they are free to get back to what they were doing." Jericho rubbed his chin and really did smile and mutter; "So they think."

A grinning monk grabbed Jackie by the hand and shouted; "Come on Jackie darling; you promised me a dance!" He dragged her off and Jericho spoke with Wilson; "There must be twenty people here and if just half is illicit time travelers, then this could be the biggest clean up and return in the Temporal

Department for ages. That will do your promotion prospects no end of good my friend." Wilson nodded; "Nice, but how do we get all these people to return to their own times AND remove their time portal devices at the same time?" Jericho sipped his champagne and said simply; "Well, I have a cunning plan."

Alex poured herself a refill and asked causally; "And how do we do all that?" Jericho patted her face gently and grinned; "We have a good old-fashioned orgy, that's how." Wilson stared at him and chuckled; "Just for a minute there Jericho I thought you said we would have an orgy!" Jericho raised his champagne class and said quietly; "There are few places to hide time portal devices when your stark naked." Now that did make Alex and Wilson laugh. "Come on let's start this bloody party!" Alex said to Jackie and pair headed to the centre of the room, giggling. Inspector Harry Hadden [team 52] really couldn't restrain from chuckling as he told his team to grab a body and return it to its original time and place. "Confirm with your mirrors before you jump." He called out as Lisa Solomon took hold of a very drunk young man who still had his gorilla mask on and nothing else.

Sergeant Tom Slurburger grabbed the half-naked penguin and checked his mirror; "1946 Chicago." He smiled and was gone.

Jericho and Alex were going through the clothes that had been piled up on the two sofas in the big reception room and handing various objects to Wilson who carefully placed them in a big canvas bag. Alex shook her head in disbelief, standing in just her skimpy underwear; "I have to hand it to you Jericho, when you have a cunning plan, it normally does turn out to be a cracker!"

Jericho held up a jeweled goblet and examined it with his mirror. "Unusual; a portable time portal locked to a specific place in 1794. Birmingham of all places. Who's was the 'Black & White' Minstrel?" Alex smiled; "Oh that was the man with the Cowboy; the one who offered to show me his big prairie while desperately trying to get my panties down. Thankfully you stopped time before my knee found his over eager testicles!" Wilson shuddered at that thought because he knew Alex would have carried it out with no qualms whatsoever.

Jackie had gripped a half-naked Monk and read her mirror; "I don't believe it! He's a real monk from an Austrian monastery in 1810. The dirty old sod asked if I would like some bum love!"

she sighed and operated her mirror, and the pair was gone. Harry called over to Jericho and gestured to Cranfield and John; "I'll drop this pair off together and on behalf of Team 52, I will accept your generous offer of dinner tonight. If the wonderful Mrs. Harris could knock up a curry, we would really appreciate that." He smiled and was gone with the pair who only had the boots of their Arab costumes left on.

Wilson peered into the bag and really did smile; "That's five confirmed time portals and all we have left to do is the Jerusalem Mirror in the cupboard. Now that's what I call a round up." He smiled as Suki [from Team 52] took hold of the cowboy who was only wearing his pistol belt, hat and holster and vanished, quietly laughing.

Jericho left Sir Thomas to last and took him back himself. Wilson and Alex checked the remaining party goers and satisfied they were all from this time and place; so, they left them where they were, and Wilson restarted time as the pair vanished. Back at the lighthouse Alex poured brandies and the pair enjoyed a well-earned drink. Alex still had the giggles remembering the happy faces on the party goers when she and Jackie stripped down to just their knickers [as told to do so by Jericho to kick the orgy off] shouting about having a REAL party!

They were quickly joined by Freedom who actually stripped stark naked and shouted; "All or nothing and I don't mind three at a time!" Freedom certainly lived up to her name and was clearly sexually liberated long before it became popular! More of the girls started to strip and very quickly so did the men. Wilson had carefully collected the clothes that were flying in all directions and smiled to himself; Jericho certainly knew human nature and the time-travelers had indeed kept their precious portals close to hand. He had then stopped time and summoned Harry and Team 52 to assist in transporting the now subdued and unhappy time-travelers back home.

The big dinner party at the lighthouse that night was quite a success and enjoyed by everyone from both teams; James put in an appearance and so did the team's old friend; Guardian Oscar le Farge. As Wilson put it; "You can have some great fun with your clothes still on!" Alex was about to change his mind about that!

NOTES:

[1] Old Joe and his strange assistant from Supplies 'stole' the horses and caravans back from the gypsy family they had been sold to. They woke up on the grass with all their possessions around them and the horses and caravans gone. You certainly didn't mess with Supplies!

[2] Apparently Alex's notorious sex tapes ARE floating around the internet porn sites of the early 21st century and are real collector items, with few realizing just how old they actually are; now amongst the first 'films' ever made! They can be found on 'vintage' and 'retro' porn sites with – obviously – few people recognizing the participants. What she didn't realise was that the dressing rooms had hidden cameras too……

[3] Jericho's 'cunning plan' produced a record equaling eleven illegal time-travelers returned and five portable time portals devices seized in one raid. Doc Underhill [whose record he equaled] was the first to congratulate Jericho!

The End

EPISODE 4: "ALEXANDRA AND THE PROFESSOR."

EPISODE PROLOGUE: "Dr. Xavier Tabbert opened his hospital for the chronically sick in the Autumn of 1849. It was supposed to be a place of final and peaceful rest for those facing certain death; in modern times it would be referred to as a 'Hospice'. Now in 1999, a team of paranormal students under Professor Alec Sweetman have arrived at the derelict hospital to investigate the many strange happenings that have occurred over the years - are they about to encounter some real evil? Alex finds that that the professor isn't just interested in dead people!"

60 Minutes approx. **Episode Warnings:**
Smoking – Alcohol – Strong language – Violence [including some Poltergeist action] – Strong graphic sexual references – Horror – References to death.

NOTES: This is the **ADULT version** of the original story which is published and appears in the **TEMPORAL DETECTIVES:** Series 3 – Episode 7 entitled: **"XAVIER TABBERT'S HOSPITAL FOR THE DEAD, THE DYING AND THE UNFORGIVEN."**

CAUTION: Recommended for **18+ only.**

1. THE FIELD TRIP; DAY ONE.

The University minibus turned from the road into Tabbert's Lane; "It may get bumpy so hold on!" 'Sibby' shouted [Ms Sylvia Fellows] and the other three occupants gripped seats and arm rests. Sibby kept a tight grip on the wheel and the minibus struggled up the gravel lane; sodden by weeks of rain. "Well, I'm not getting out and bloody pushing." Jen Phillips called out to no one in particular. She drew on her shaking cigarette. She was sitting right next to a large 'NO SMOKING' sign on the window and didn't give a fuck; like she did about most things "You would have thought that old 'Sweetie' [Professor Alec Sweetman] would have bloody warned us about the bloody road." She added and blew little smoke rings about.

Callan Carter just grimaced and waved the smoke away; he was sitting right behind Jen and had probably smoked three of her cigarettes with her. "For fuck sake Jen; couldn't you wait to light up when we stop?" He muttered and leaned back in his seat.

'Bloody selfish bitch.' He thought and stared out at the drizzle tumbling down the window. 'Why the fuck did 'iron pants' bother to come on this fucking field trip? She doesn't really belief in any of it.' He kept those thoughts to himself. Jen wasn't shy in expressing her opinion on what people thought about her and didn't care either - apparently - and for the sake of a peaceful trip, Callan would say silent, about what he really thought of her; a self opinionated, loud mouthed selfish bitch.

Little Morris Maxwell - sitting next to Sibby, smiled; "Should we erect a ring and let them fight it out?" Sibby chuckled and dropped a gear; "No Mouse; she'll bloody kill him." 'Mouse' did laugh quietly at that. He was always called 'Mouse' because he was so small; lots of people told him that he should have been a Jockey; others weren't so nice; they called him the 'dwarf'. 'Midget man' or 'mini man'. He pretended not to care and laugh along with the insensitive bastards; but sometimes the little pain inside wouldn't go away. He glanced at Sibby hanging onto the juddering wheel and sighed; he absolutely adored her. But she wouldn't - of course - look at him twice. Nearly all her previous boyfriends were sportsmen or academics or both. Sibby slowed the van and peered through the wet windscreen at the ornate big iron gates. They were heavily padlocked with a big yellow sign shouting "NO TRESSPASSING!"

The Tabbert hospital for incurables lay shrouded in rain. Sibby stopped the van and said quietly; "For Christ sake, they could make horror movies here." Mouse nodded and tapped her arm; he had seen the figure coming down the path, hunched up in a yellow raincoat with the hood up and walking slowly despite the rain. "Who the fuck is that?" He said softly. Jen tossed her cigarette on the carpets and stubbed it out with her boot. "Fucking Egor of course. He's just woke up Doctor Fucking Frankenstein and told him that his new laboratory mice have arrived. You had better be careful mouse; you'll be the first under his knife." Jen said, laughing at her own supposed humour. Mouse just smiled; "Yeah, very funny Jen." He really wanted to say something else; but couldn't bring himself to do so.

They watched as the hunched figure began to unlock the three heavy padlocks on the gates, with keys from a big iron key ring. He looked up at the van and the occupants, wiping rain from his face.

"Holy fuck! Old doctor Frankenstein must have experimented on him." Jen shouted, then laughed adding; "They must have hired the ugly bastard because his deformed mug matches this derelict dump." They could all see the scarred face and twisted lips on the man. He swung open the big gates with little effort and walked towards the van. "Stow any comments please Jen. He must be Gary the caretaker. We don't want to upset the bloody employee's and get thrown off site before we even start." Sibby turned, not smiling at her 'friend'. Jen just shrugged her shoulders.

Gary the caretaker walked up to the driver's side window and tried to smile. It just made his appearance worse. Sibby rolled the window halfway down and did smile at him. "You the party.... party...from York University...Profes...Profes..the Sweetman party?" He finally stuttered out. Sibby nodded; realising he was quite a young man; probably in his early twenties. Everyone noticed his stutter. "For fuck sake, course we are. York University is written down both side of the fucking van." Jen muttered quietly; for once.

Sibby explained that the Professor was following in his own car but should be here soon. She introduced herself and briefly, the others in the van. Gary nodded and gestured towards the old hospital; "The West wing.... on your...your right...is the only hab...hab.." He stopped talking and wiped his face; "The only...only part you can use." He stared at the ground and stepped aside as Sibby started the van and thanked him with a big smile.

The van pulled past the man and Jen laughed out loud; "For fuck sake, the place does have its own Egor and what a fucking dummy." Callan just sighed and stared back at figure watching them drive away, up the long driveway towards the old hospital. "Poor bastard, no wonder he lives and works in a place like this." Callan said and mouse agreed with him. Jen just laughed to herself. Sibby stopped outside the 'West Wing' and everyone stared at the building. This part looked alright. Well, the window's still had glass in and the roof above didn't appear to have gaping holes.

"According to Sweetie, this part of the building still has electricity, running water, heating, toilets and showers." Sibby said, leaning back in her seat. "I wonder where the caretaker stays?" Mouse asked.

"Probably got a fucking coffin in the cellars." Chuckled Jen and pulled out a cigarette and lighter from her big handbag. No one laughed and Sibby sighed; "We'll get the bags out first and set up the equipment later. We have maps of the place, so, we'll need to look around first. Pick the best places to set up." Mouse agreed with that and pulled on his coat, placing on a bright red woollen hat on his head. That made Jen laugh; "You now look like a fucking gnome." No one laughed at that either. "Come on." Was all Sibby said. The team decamped from the van, grabbing their bags,

Sibby turned and found Gary standing there; she wondered immediately how he got up the drive so fast! He gestured to the big black door and held up a couple of keys. "I'll unlock...unlock for you miss...everything is...on." He stuttered and unlocked the door. Sibby noticed one hand was badly scarred with the little finger missing. The other hand was big and quite normal. She immediately noticed the wedding ring on his finger. Christ, he's married. Then told herself off for being surprised at that. The little team strolled in and found themselves in some sort of reception area. There was big desk and chairs stacked all round. It looked like a hotel foyer that had definitely seen better days.

"There's a kitch...kitchen behind...and toilets." He stopped, staring at the floor again; "And a shower...plenty of...plenty of hot....hot water." He nodded at everyone and left without another word.

"Let's get settled in. Explore what we have and find a bloody kettle; I'm dying for a cup of tea." Sibby told the others and watched Gary the caretaker disappearing into the rain, under his awful yellow raincoat; he was quite a big man and definitely only in his twenties. She wondered if they would meet his wife during their stay; she really hoped so.

They set up their camp bed in two small rooms off the reception area. Sadly, Sibby would have to share with Jen; "Now that's a real bloody treat." She muttered to herself, throwing her sleeping bag and pillow on her wobbly, old ex-army camp bed. "Smile please." Mouse pointed the camera at her from the doorway and Sibby grinned and bowed a little. "Make sure you film all this. Show the bloody Dean that field trips are not holidays." She told Mouse, who nodded and disappeared, operating his camera with some skill, around the semi dark corridors and rooms.

The team met up for tea in the foyer and ate their packed lunches. They laughed and joked about the old hospital and the stories and legends about the place. Mouse lifted up on his chair and said - with a broad smile - "The boss is here." Sibby dropped her cheese sandwich back in her lunch box and went to the door. She didn't notice the amused look that passed between Callan and Mouse. She watched the professor jump from his old car - a classic Jaguar from the Fifties - collect his bags and walk to the door. He grinned and lifted his bags in greeting. Sibby opened the door and watched him walk up.

Professor Alistair (Alec) Sweetman was a tall, athletic, and very handsome man. He was employed to teach History, but the University allowed him to indulge in his hobby - that he was quite passionate about - the study of the paranormal and supernatural. He was thirty-eight years old and had been widowed for five. His wife Christina dying of breast cancer just a year after their marriage. Sibby watched him come through the door shouting; "Everyone here? Everyone OK?" and dump his bags on the floor. Mouse called back; "Yes boss, including Jen." rolling his eyes in mock despair. Sibby watched her 'boss' carefully; he only had to wag his finger at her again and....she pushed those delicious thoughts and memories away. She would have private words with him when the occasion arose.

He was dressed like some fashionable young man from the fifties. Three-piece suit, fob watch, classic brown shoes, 'Mackintosh' raincoat and Homburg hat. He openly admitted to being born in the wrong time. He loved the forties and fifties and lived the part; much to the amusement of his students and colleagues. But he was immensely popular with both. He stood hands on hips and looked about. "Well people, we are truly privileged to be here. There have only been two sets of paranormal teams allowed to study this place. So let's do a damn fine job." He removed his hat and joined the group. Sibby actually shifted her chair to sit next to him. Mouse finished his sandwich and asked the professor; "What did the other team discover? Is there a report available? I didn't think anyone else had been here. I can't find any of their reports."

The professor didn't smile - he sat, hat clasped in his hands - and looked around - He said softly; "They didn't make any reports, I'm afraid." Callan sipped his tea and asked; "Why not boss?" The professor almost smiled; "They didn't make out a report because they simply vanished, they were never seen or heard of again. That was in 1956 and all three simply disappeared from here." There was absolute silence until Jen said, "Well that's fucking terrific news." She actually felt herself shudder a little; if she had known that wonderful fucking fact; she wouldn't have come.

Alec smiled; "Let me settle in and we'll decide on the placement of cameras and microphones. You ok for the thermometers Jen?" She nodded; wishing she was at fucking home watching the TV.

It was quite a subdued team of paranormal investigators that placed their equipment around certain parts of the old hospital that afternoon. There were places they simply couldn't go; parts of the building were closed off because it was dangerous. They settled down and waited the night.

2. FIRST NIGHT.

It was just after seven in the evening and Sibby sat on the chair and watched the monitor; the screen was split into six channels. She adjusted the contrast on Number 4 - for the second time - and returned to her book; 'Pride & prejudice.' She was covering

6pm to 10pm. Mouse would take the 'witching hours'; ten to two in the morning.

The boss had volunteered to take the two to six slots. That allowed the other two to have - hopefully - an undisturbed night of sleep. She looked up from her book occasionally glancing at the flickering screen. She heard something behind her and turned slowly; it sounded like something hitting the floor.

There was no one there. Then she noticed the old leather-bound book on the floor; open. She eased from her seat and walked over. Sibby slowly picked the book up and stared at the open page.

"5th July 1956. Three people had signed the visitor's book: Mr. John Crabb, Mr. Malcom Sands and Miss Florence Hammond. Leeds University." She read out loud to herself and felt a shiver run up her spine. Sibby knew that these were the other team of paranormal investigators - the ones who had vanished here - and she looked around; there was nothing that could have disturbed the book or make it fall. "How the hell did it fall off the desk? It must have sat there for years; it's covered in dust. Why fall open at that page?" She was talking to herself for comfort. She jumped as Alec appeared in the doorway; two cups of tea in his big hands.

"Brew time." He said simply and saw the look on her face. He gestured to the chairs in front of the monitor. Sibby took her tea and joined him, explaining about the book. The professor had his notebook out in an instant, scribbling with a well chewed pencil. His tea placed on the dusty floor.

They were deep in conversation when Sibby noticed that the professor - on finishing his notes - reached down for his teacup and found it wasn't there. Nothing was said between the pair and they carefully and slowly looked around the room. Sibby actually let out a little yelp; the professor's teacup was on the desk! They both rose from their chairs. Sibby was now shaking a little with the hairs on her arms and neck standing. Alex slowly took her hand and gripped it; he was a picture of calmness. "Keep cool Sibby. I think something is trying to make contact."

Sibby could only manage to nod and gripped his big hand tightly. she wouldn't be letting go any time in the immediate future. They both noticed that the room was ice cold. Sibby could feel her big nipples standing up and visibly showing through her blouse. They both jumped and Sibby let out a scream; they hadn't noticed Mouse come through the door; also holding two cups of tea.

"Christ boss, you and I must have had the same idea. I think we should speak to Gary about the bloody heating in here. It's like a bloody morgue." Sibby sighed and felt the professor release her hand. She wished Mouse hadn't mentioned a bloody 'morgue'. Mouse grinned and held up the cups; "You can have mine. I'll brew another." That's when the cup on the desk flew across the room, smashing on the doorframe by the shocked Mouse's head.

Alec said quietly and with some real authority; "Get the hell out of here; it's a Poltergeist!" But he was very calm, and they ran for the door and into the corridor. Alec slammed the door behind them, and they stood in silence. He turned to his visibly shaken colleagues and shrugged his shoulders; "Well, we found out one thing about our supernatural visitor." Mouse - between gritted teeth - had to ask; "What's that boss?" Mumbling and rubbing his arms from the cold. Alec smiled a little; "It clearly doesn't like tea."

The three chuckled and Sibby felt a little better. "We now know that there must be substance to the supernatural stories about this place. We've just witnessed it." She said quietly. Alec was listening against the door and nodded; "I can hear a strange noise. I'm not sure but I think it's someone's crying; sobbing actually." Mouse pressed against the door and went a little pale; "Your bloody right boss. I can hear it too."

Sibby stood back, arms folded and wished she was a home in her own bed with Foster [her big tabby cat] laid on the pillows. Alec struggled to concentrate; "I think its saying something. Can you make it out Mouse?" Mouse pulled from the door and wiped his face; he looked terrified. "Yes, I can." He said and stepped well away from the door. Sibby said quietly; "What was it saying?" But actually didn't want to know! Mouse stared at both of them and folded his arms; he said softly; "Get the fuck out of here."

The professor stood - hands in pockets - looking like he was waiting for a bus; a total picture of calm. He sighed; "Well, all our equipment is in the foyer. So, we must go back in." The others exchanged a nervous glance; both saying the same thing without speaking a word: fuck the equipment. Callan joined them, yawning; "What's up people?" Then saw the looks on Sibby's and Mouse's faces. "Oh fucking shit." Was all he said. After a brief discussion, it was decided that Alec and Callan would go in. Sibby fetched two small radios's from her room - not disturbing the sleeping Jen - and returned with them. Both were set to Channel two and the professor tested his. Sibby standing down the corridor gave the thumbs up and answered Alec. He gave the thumbs up and she re-joined them.

Alec hesitated with his hand on the door handle. He turned and smiled; "Should I knock? It may appreciate the courtesy." Everyone chuckled; the boss was certainly the man to have in a tight situation. He slowly turned the handle and pushed quietly into the room. He noticed immediately the warmth in the room and sighed with a little relief; turning to the others, he said softly; "I think it's gone." They shuffled into the room and looked about. Sibby raised her hand and pointed to the old reception desk or rather the small door behind it marked; KEEP OUT. AUTHORISED STAFF ONLY. She knew full well that the door had been shut and locked. She whispered to Mouse; "Do you know where that goes?" Mouse nodded and really didn't smile; "To the bloody cellars."

Callan said what they were all thinking; "Is it an invitation? But to where or from who?" Alec gestured to the bags by the window; "There are torches in there. It would be quite rude not to accept." Everyone looked at each other - again - with the same thought. 'Who the hell is going with the boss?'

Everyone jumped again as someone knocked on the front door. They all stared at the door and jumped yet again at a second knocking; "Well, are you going to bloody answer it?" Jen slowly wandered in - wearing her 'Thomas the tank engine' pyjama's - and walked over and pulled it open. She spoke briefly and turned to Alec; "You aren't going to believe this boss. It's another bloody professor and his team from Edinburgh University. They're in the same game as us!" She stood aside and the visitors wandered in, burdened down with baggage and equipment.

The tall young man in the old raincoat held out his hand to Alec; "Jerry Tibbs. Edinburgh University. I normally teach history, but my little hobby is chasing the unknown. This is my team." Alec shook his hand - with some disbelief – thinking another bloody

164 | P a g e

team of paranormal investigators! "Mr. Prouse [a member of the Board of Trustee's for the old hospital] said that another group were already here. Which surprised me as we had this place booked a couple of months ago." Jerry spoke quietly looking around the foyer and nodded, addressing his team; "This is the last place that the team in '56 were seen alive. The caretaker at the time; a Mr. Ray Evan's reported that they were about to explore the cellars."

Alec's team all looked at each other - except Jen - she hadn't been present; she had been snoring in her bed. "Just in the fucking nick of time." Callan said and meant it.

Alec and Jerry sat and chatted while their teams talked quietly with each other. It was decided [by the two 'mad' professors' as Callan called 'Jerry' and Alec] to share the project. They had travelled all the way from bloody Scotland after all. Alex would bunk in with the girls and the boys would bed down in the corridor between the rooms.

"We'll be snug as bugs in a rug." exclaimed Owen. Sibby did stare at him closely; he did appear to have the traces of nail polish on one hand. Each to their own she thought. She took an immediate liking to Alex and helped her with her kit. She was amazed at her bed. Alex pulled a couple of levers and the bloody thing unfolded and inflated into a very comfortable looking cot. But it was Owen that really cheered everyone up; he pulled a couple of decent looking bottles of brandy from his old bag and held them up; "Brandy anyone?" He was nearly killed in the rush!

They sat about the old foyer and talked. Callan and Mouse really couldn't stop staring at Alex in her short skirt and business suit. Callan whispered; "That is one fucking gorgeous piece of skirt." Mouse, normally quiet about such matters, just had to agree. It was clear that the new girl liked the look of Professor Alec and that ruffled Sibby's feathers a little; but she wasn't surprised. Nearly every girl on campus fancied him, including her. Callan. Mouse and Wilson discussed both team's equipment and Callan was impressed with the big man's knowledge of the technology. Mouse showed off his new 'Sonny' cam-recorder which could play the video back through a small screen attached. He showed the pair the film he had shot earlier. He replayed Sibby making up her bed and nearly dropped the bloody thing on the floor in shock.

All three watched - Mouse & Callan a little horrified - as Sibby waved and bowed. The man standing on the other side of her camp bed was smiling too: a big fellow in an ill-fitting, old-fashioned three-piece suit. He folded his arms and faded. Mouse jumped up shouting and Alec calmed him down enough for him to run the video, through the big monitor. Everyone watched in absolute silence. Alec's team didn't notice the look passing between the other team. Jericho whispered; "Doctor Tabbert I presume." Wilson nodded; "Must have the time portal device in a pocket." Alex sighed; "He's got some balls appearing like that; must be checking out the new arrivals at this dreadful place." Owen was staring at his hand - cursing himself a little - having noticed the nail polish remains on his fingers from his recent manifestation as 'Jackie.'

Alec couldn't hide his delight at the capture of the 'spectre' on film. Jericho pulled his team into the corridor where their beds were and spoke softly, consulting his mirror; "There are three earth bound spirits in this place. If one can cause books and cups to move; they could prove dangerous to living humans. If it can harness telekinetic powers; then it's a poltergeist." Wilson scratched his chin; "Shall I put in a call for a Guardian?"

Jericho nodded; "It's time to put an end to their little games around here, especially the good doctor who should have died in 1861." Then Owen grunted; "How the fuck didn't Mouse, or Sibby see him? I mean he's a living human - a time traveller - how come the camera picked him up, but they couldn't see him at the time?" Jericho rubbed his chin and said quietly; "That Owen, is a bloody good question."

The two teams settled down for the remainder of the night. Owen joined Sibby at the monitor and pair chatted; Sibby really liked the quiet young man, who clearly had a sharp mind. Nothing happened and they were relieved By Mouse and Wilson. Sibby had to smile at the difference - physically - between the pair. But they certainly seemed to be getting on. Mouse didn't surprise her; he got on with anyone, even the bastards that took the piss out of the little fellow. She wandered off to find Alex. They could have a good gossip about the two 'mad professors' as Callan called them. She also wanted to know more about the clearly effeminate young Owen. What was his story? She wondered.

3. PROFESSOR SWEETMAN.

Sibby found Alex walking by the stable block and the pair chatted about the professor [Alec] and Owen. They wandered into the old stables and found Alec's big jaguar car parked there. Alex did admire the beautiful vintage car and Sibby pulled open the doors and the pair jumped in the rear seats and pretended to wave at crowds. They laughed together; "I bet these seats have seen some action over the years." Alex spoke softly to Sibby, who really did smile and sighed; "Yeah and I was one of them."

Now very interested, Alex asked Sibby for all the juicy details. Sibby explained how, on several occasions after lectures the pair would park up and fuck. She went into some graphic descriptions of their sexual exploits. Alex brushed Sibby's blond hair from her face and whispered; "Show me."

Sibby was laid on the leather seat, legs pulled up, gripping her small black panties in her hands and groaning a little. Alex was between her legs; lips tongue and fingers working the girl's vagina. Sibby moaned loudly as she had a couple of small orgasms under Alex's skilled hands and mouth. She pulled up from the seat and grabbed Alex, kissing passionately. Her hand reached under Alex's short skirt and was delighted to find that Alex was very wet, she pulled Alex's panties down, leaving them dangling from one ankle. It was Alex's turn to lay back and thoroughly enjoy Sibby's wonderful mouth feasting on her crotch. She was moaning and stroking Sibby's bobbing head. She opened her eyes to find Alec staring at the pair with a huge smile. She gestured for him to join them. He really didn't hesitate.

He fucked Alex first, while sibby watched from the front passenger seat, rubbing her dripping fanny vigorously with both hands. She was panting and groaning as loudly as Alex, who had her fanny filled with Alec's big cock. He was a skilled lover and Alex soon spurted and gripped his shoulders. His mouth found hers and their tongues crashed together. He was thrusting deep and hard; Sibby grabbed his head from between the front seats and they kissed passionately. He kissed Sibby and fucked Alex; hard. The two girls swapped over, and Alec now fucked Sibby with some passion. Alex leaned in through the rear passenger door and poked a couple of fingers into his heaving, sweaty arse and rimmed him with her darting, probing tongue. The effect was immediate; Alec groaned loudly and came deep in Sibby's pulsating fanny.

Alex dragged Sibby from the car and knelt between her legs as Sibby leaned back against the Jaguar, standing with her legs open. Alex cleaned her soaking vagina thoroughly; not missing a drop of Alec's cum that oozed from Sibby. He watched, sweating and jerking his cock. Both girls now squeezed into the rear seat with the horny professor and took turns sucking his cock back into an erection. He was soon hard and ready under their hot mouths. He lay on his back and Alex mounted him again, while Sibby fingered and licked her bum hole. Alec pulled Alex's big tits from her blouse and gripped them, squeezing and sucking hard on her big erect nipples. Alex was riding hard and fast; she had one hell of a climax and squirted equally hard. It splattered up Alec's chest and belly. She was panting and groaning loudly, her fingers digging into his shoulders.

The girls swapped over; Alex's legs were shaking, and she set about Sibby's jerking arse with fingers and tongue. It was Sibby's turn to have a monster orgasm. She actually screamed, cursing like a Liverpool docker. Alec was now soaking from the girls cum and loved it. The sexual frenzy now continued on the straw covered dirt floor. Alec was fucking Alex hard doggy style, while she ate Sibby's fanny. He groaned and cursed, pulling his cock out and presenting it to the girls, who scrambled to kneel in front of him, their heads together. He came again, shooting his hot cum over their smiling faces. He staggered back and watched the girls kissing passionately, swapping his cum from mouth to mouth. They licked and kissed each other until every drop was swallowed down. They sat grinning and kissing each other. "Now that's what I call fucking great sex!" He exclaimed and eased into the front passenger seat, gripping his flaccid cock.

The girls - unbelievably - were still horny and started to have hard lesbian sex on the dirty floor. The professor groaned loudly and knew he couldn't perform again without rest and almost staggered from the stables leaving the pair to it. The girls were in the '69' position when Sibby looked up and saw Owen staring at them. She grinned at him and shouted; "Get the fuck over here!"

He also didn't hesitate and joined the girls on the floor. Sibby grabbed his erection and sucked hard. Alex brushed straw from herself and smiled at Owen, mouthing; 'We've already had the fucking horny professor!' Owen just smiled - he knew Alex's sexual appetite - and the pair kissed with some real passion as Sibby caressed and sucked his cock.

He fucked Sibby on the floor in the 'Missionary Position' she groaned and gripped his arms, telling him to fuck her hard, with no 'fucking mercy!' Alex squatted over SIbby's face, and she set about Alex's cunt with some urgency, using her fingers and mouth. Alex soon rewarded her with a couple of spurts and Sibby enjoyed her hot cum with some relish. Sibby was now riding Owen furiously as Alex squatted over his face and he took up where Sibby left off.

Sibby had another monster orgasm and collapsed on him, moaning and swearing. She climbed off him and lay panting, gripping his cock with a shaking hand. Alex now mounted Owen and bounced up and down on his cock with some passion. Sibby knelt near the pair and sucked Alex's big swinging tits, squeezing hard and running her teeth over those big juicy nipples that were solid as stone.

Owen came in Alex, causing her to climax and it was her turn to collapse on him, panting and groaning. She pulled off him and Sibby was straight on her crotch to clean up. The three lay on the floor, quietly laughing and kissing. They were soon in the rear seats of the car, both girls sucking Owens's cock into another erection. But Sibby had to call it a day and staggered from the car, leaving Owen fucking Alex hard on her back. Sibby walked - a little awkwardly - back to the hospital with a huge smile on her face. She really admired Alex's sexual stamina and knew the pair would soon be at it with another cock or cocks; anyone's cock!

Alex and Owen left the car some half hour later, walking back to the hospital hand in hand. She really needed to pee and actually ran a little into the toilet and pissed like a horse. She had been well satisfied by both men - and Sibby of course - she also smiled broadly and wondered if they [Sibby and her] could get together again; preferably with another big cock!

4. THE FIELD TRIP; DAY TWO.

Everyone was pleasantly surprised by Alex and Sibby; they had knocked up a decent breakfast of porridge, bacon, eggs and beans on the small paraffin camping stove in the kitchen. Everyone was also surprised how well the two women were getting on; well, except Jen who only noticed the food. When Callan chided her about not helping the other girls; she just stuffed her face with an egg sandwich and muttered; "I'm a fucking lousy cook." No one disbelieved her. There was aloud rapping on the front door and Owen opened it and was surprised. A very pretty young woman stood there, clutching a casserole pot. Owen immediately took it from her and invited her in. Sibby looked delighted and quickly went to the door with Alex. "You must be Gary's wife. Lovely to meet you." She said as Charlotte told Owen that it could be easily reheated; it was vegetable casserole.

She didn't smile; "No I'm not Gary's wife; I'm his long-suffering sister. Someone has to look after him. My boyfriend Leon and he get on really well. They're both keen horse riders." Sibby apologised, but that was waved away. The three women sat and talked. It appears that Gary was a veteran of the Afghan war.

Charlotte [Lottie to her friends] explained that Gary's team had been caught by some Afghan fighters and two men were wounded. Gary had gone out to get them. He dragged one back under enemy fire and then returned to fetch the other man. But a homemade bomb had got them. He was badly wounded and rushed to a nearby Army Surgeon who saved his life. But he was scarred; the bomb had ripped up his face and tore off a finger. It had also damaged the nerves in his back and legs. But he had survived to come home to his wife and family.

That's when Lottie's attitude changed at the mention of his wife. "Caroline was beautiful on the outside [she gestured to Alex] a lot like you. But inside she was a festering bag of maggots. The very week Gary was discharged from the hospital she told him that she couldn't stand the thought of looking at him or letting him touch her. She packed her bags and fucked off. I believe she hooked up with some ponce that breeds really expensive dogs for a living." She spat the words out, adding with a smile; "Bloody appropriate that. Living with a pack of dogs. She's in good company." Lottie told the girls that Gary struggled to find a job. Prospective employers took one look at him and said the position was closed. But the Corps of Commissioners had found him this job; apparently no one else would take it.

Both Sibby and Alex were actually moved by the story; a very brave young man reduced to hiding away in a derelict hospital because the world really didn't want to face him. Lottie left, promising to bring back with some mash for the casserole near supper time. She was going to throw some chicken in but didn't know if anyone was vegetarian. Everyone thanked her for her unexpected generosity.

Alec's team now saw 'Egor' in a very different light - except Jen of course - who said simply; "So he's a brave ugly bugger." Sibby turned to her and said - with some restraint in her voice - "Just shut up Jen. Just shut up and keep you bloody filthy comments to yourself. No one wants to hear them." Now that did really surprise everyone else. Sibby normally tolerated Jen's nasty comments, but she didn't this time. Jen just shrugged and - wisely - didn't say anything else.

Later that afternoon, Jericho, Alec, Wilson and Callan disappeared down into the cellars. Sibby and Alex manned the small radio, drinking coffee and chatting quietly together. Jen apparently excluded from joining the other girls on 'radio watch' grabbed a reluctant Mouse and went exploring the safe parts of the old hospital. Mouse collected a radio from Sibby and followed, shaking his head in real despair.

The team in the cellars reported back nothing of interest. But near lunch time a quiet sounding Jen was calling on her radio; well, she was almost whispering actually. Finally, Mouse must have taken the radio from her. He spoke quite normally to Sibby; they had found several shallow graves, which looked a lot newer than the others, in the large cemetery that had serviced the hospital.

The cemetery was located at the rear of the old stables block. Their call was interrupted by Alec who said they were on the way back and everyone stay put.

Both teams walked around the derelict cemetery. There were graves dating right back to the 1850's, right through to the 1920's, when the hospital was closed down. Most of the small headstones were unreadable; they could make out the odd date or name, but little else. "They must have used cheap stone to save money and they haven't weathered well." Alec explained, but he couldn't explain the apparent 'modern' ones; buried at the rear of the cemetery, near the old stable block. There was some sort of memorial, but it was already too worn to be read properly. They could make out part of the date; 19--. Wilson whispered to Jericho; "That's not weathered. It's been deliberately defaced." Jericho nodded; he had already spotted that - but why? - What the fuck was going on?

"How the fuck were there burials after the bloody place closed. It had apparently been shut since the early 20's?" Mouse asked, filming the unusual graves. Alec tried his mobile phone -again - and still had no signal. Sibby wondered if the caretaker had a phone in the lodge. Alec nodded; he would contact Mr. Prouse on it and ask, if he knew the story of the 'modern' burials. They all walked back to the old hospital, talking quietly amongst themselves.

Alec's team disappeared inside, leaving Jericho and team 74 standing in the grounds. They were all staring at the young boy in ragged clothes and bare feet by the front doors of the building. Owen lifted his mirror and spoke quietly: "Charles Jobson; died aged 13 in 1882. His soul is listed as missing. He's one of the three earth bound spirits hiding here."

The boy was about to turn and go when Alex called out to him; "Charles or is it Charley? Which do you prefer?" She asked him. He wiped his nose on his jumper and said, "My mum always calls me Charles." He muttered and almost smiled at her. Alex walked slowly up to him and smiled; "Well Charles, my friends and I are here to help you. You don't have to be frightened of us." The boy smiled; "I ain't frightened. Gabriele looks after me."

That's when Herbie the Collector appeared. Jericho had summoned him with his mirror. Herbie was one of the best collector's, when it came to reluctant souls. He normally was able to 'scoop' them up. He and Alex stood talking to Charles.

Jericho, Wilson and Owen went back to the foyer and left it to them. "Herbie should really join the department. He's a real good man with the unhappy dead." Owen said and Wilson couldn't disagree; "So the other bugger, that can throw things about must be this 'Gabriele' he spoke about." Owen nodded and re-read his mirror and sighed; "There's no patient called 'Gabriele' that died here listed as a missing soul."

Wilson nodded; "So who the fuck is he?"

They found only Sibby sitting at the monitor. She explained that the others were checking the equipment for the coming night. Sibby was telling them that Alec had taken the group to the East

Wing which had burnt down in a mysterious fire, quite recently. "Bloody kids or arsonists." Sibby concluded and smiled at Owen, who sat with her and Wilson, whilst Jericho wandered off. They knew that Doctor Tabbert's time portal must be in the building somewhere. They could now use their mirrors freely, with the other group not around. They were joined by a smiling Alex; she told them that Herbie had worked his magic and the boy had gone with him. She also told them that 'Charles' had died of Type 1 Diabetes in 1882. It was incurable then and always resulted in death. Charles was from a poor family and that's why he was placed here: the hospital would bury the boy in its cemetery and the family could avoid a funeral bill they simply couldn't afford. He unfortunately, wouldn't talk about 'Gabriele' - except to say - he was a very unhappy man.

"Most poltergeists usually are unhappy ex-humans." muttered Wilson. Jericho rubbed his chin; "One down, this 'Gabriele to find and who the hell is the third one?" Wilson shrugged his shoulders.

The rear of the extensive building was the oldest - and originally part of the old manor house that stood here - and so they started there. Wilson found it. It was a carved medieval doorway on the ground floor. "Locked to 1472, June 3rd. Tabbert must have found it soon after the bloody place was built around the old Manor House. Shall we go and pay a visit?" He smiled at Jericho and Alex. Jericho nodded and the team operated their mirrors and where gone. Gary stepped from the curtains at the far end of the corridor and walked up to the doorway and wasn't happy. "The good doctor will not be impressed." He muttered and stepped through. The corridor was now empty.

5. DOCTOR TABBERT; I PRESUME?

They were in a medieval Chapel; the carved doorway had originally been the entrance. It was a hot summer day, and the sky was blue and cloudless. Jericho gestured to the Manor House and pointed out that it was quite beautiful. "If it was still standing now [1999] it would be worth a small fortune. But the bloody Victorians knocked it down and built the hospice....hospital all over it and the grounds."

Alex consulted her mirror and spoke quietly; "Currently [1472] the place is the family home of Sir Reginald Culpepper, his wife Margaret, daughter Elizabeth and son; John. He's a Knight of King Edward IV. The bloody War of the Roses was going on at this time."

"So where is our time travelling doctor hanging out?" Wilson asked and they walked up the old house. Outside the front door was a young boy - sweeping - and he just stared at them, apparently unfazed by their modern appearance. But he did look hard at Alex's long legs, then at Wilson; he had never seen a man with skin that colour. He leaned on his broom and grinned; he already had teeth missing. He jerked the broom towards a house some distance down the dusty road; "Your friend is there. He knows your coming. He gave me a apple to tell you." He pulled it from his ragged shirt and held it up; then quickly placed it back. Jericho nodded and thanked him, saying to the others; "Expecting us?" They walked down to the modest little cottage and Wilson banged on the door.

It was opened by a young girl who was lacing up her bodice and pulling down her skirts. She didn't smile or say anything but strode past them and headed for the Manor House. The team all looked at each other and Jericho shouted in; "Doctor Tabbert I presume?" The doctor was sitting at a rough table writing in a small notebook; he looked up and smiled; "I wondered how quickly you would find the portal. Please come in. That was young Lizzie; she's in early pregnancy. The baby's father is dead - killed in the bloody wars around here - but Lady Margaret is looking after her. The girl's mother was one of her maids. Loyalty runs deep in this time." He gestured to the equally rough chairs and added; "Please sit."

The team sat and looked about the cottage; it was stacked with books and bottles, bushes of herbs and a small bubbling cauldron. "In these times I'm called an 'Apothecary'. A man of medicine and science. As you can imagine, I have quite a few patients." The doctor smiled and loosened the medieval long coat; he was feeling the summer heat. Underneath he was wearing his Victorian suit. He closed his little notebook and pushed it into his pocket. He leaned back in the chair and clasped his hands in front of him; "I have no doubt you're on the trail of the missing paranormal investigators that are swarming about my old hospital?" Jericho nodded - he didn't smile - and said slowly; "Them and a certain time travelling doctor who should have passed over in 1861."

The doctor smiled; "Very commendable, I'm sure. You can snatch the investigators - they actually don't know they are dead and should pass over - but the doctor is far too busy to desert his patients in any time period." Jericho just nodded; "Quite so doctor, but our boss - Angel Margret - has her own ideas about that."

Wilson asked the Doctor about the paranormal investigators who were around the hospital in 1956. The doctor sat back and ran a hand over his chin; "Oh yes; those three." He muttered and leaned forward. "They must have been carrying something from the late medieval period - like I do - and they all disappeared through the portal." He held up a large Medieval Crucifix. "Must have come as quite a surprise." He chuckled.

"Do you know what become of them?" Alex asked. Doctor Tabbert nodded. "The older man - Crabb - I think. Didn't last long; he just couldn't handle the dark ages and went a little mad. He was last seen begging near the castle. But I think he didn't survive the harsh winter, living in the wilds."

Alex nodded and asked about the other two. The Doctor sighed; "The woman survived; she managed to get the local magistrate - an old widower - to marry her. She died some years ago; no children." He stared down at his hands and shook his head; "The young man was a bloody fool; he was a communist and an Atheist and practically preached it. The Church Inquisition got him. Screamed and struggled all the way to the flames. The idiot couldn't actually believe he was to be burnt alive for saying what he thinks."

Their conversations with the doctor were interrupted. The door swung open, and Gary stepped in; he had a very large piece of wood clenched in both hands. The team slowly rose from their seats and the doctor sighed, waving at Gary. "It's alright Gabriele, they are just leaving." The team all looked at each other and Alex whispered; "Of course; Gary is a modern version of the name Gabriele. He's our bloody poltergeist!" Gary lowered the stick and Doctor Tabbert said quietly; "As I said, loyalty runs deep around these parts. I gave Gabriele a job and a home in 1850, when the ungrateful British Government tossed him away like garbage. He was a very brave man, serving his country and paid a terrible price for that. But you do know his story?"

Alex nodded; "So Professor Sweetman's team think he was injured in the Afghan war that took place in the 1990's, not realising it was the bloody 1840's!" She then thought about his sister; how did she end up a ghost at the hospital?

Doctor Tabbert stood and shook his coat. "His sister worked at the hospital and looked after her brother, after the departure of his very unfaithful wife. She died in 1855, but couldn't bring herself to leave her brother, who she had cared for with so much love and attention." He gestured towards the door; "Goodbye my friends. Please do take those wretched paranormal investigators with you." He smiled and folded his arms. Jericho just sighed loudly and operated his mirror; time stood still. He walked to the door and stared at Gary/Gabriele and said softly; "You deserve a better fate than this. You need to jump and start a new life."

Alex jumped a little as Oscar appeared in the doorway - smiling and gripping his Staff of Moses - he was a Guardian of God and had the power to compel reluctant and unwilling souls to the light. Little Oscar was a good friend of the team, and they welcomed him with some affection. He gave Alex a big kiss and said, "What's up Jericho? I got the call you had a poltergeist running about?"

Jericho chuckled and pointed at Gary; "That's your man, he's all yours. The other is just a reluctant soul that needs to jump, whether he wants to or not." Oscar smiled and slapped his Staff onto his shoulder; "Sooner said than done." He was gone and so were Gary and the good doctor. Jericho consulted his mirror and smiled broadly; "Oscar is always on top of these things. He's already closed the time portal. Now that's what I call service from the Guardians Department." They all chuckled and Jericho operated his mirror, and the cottage was empty.

The small boy climbed down from the barrel under the window and scratched his lice ridden crotch. He thought the dwarf [Oscar] was funny, but he really liked Alex's long legs. He walked slowly back to the Manor House, tossing the apple in the air.

They walked down the corridor, heading back to the foyer, and Wilson stopped; "How did he appear in Sibby's room and get caught on Mouse's film, yet Mouse and Sibby didn't see him? He was a living human - just a time traveller - how the hell didn't they see him?" Jericho stood hands on hips and looked about the corridor; "I have a feeling the answer lies in those graves." Alex and Wilson just looked at each other; what was Jericho thinking now?

Alex volunteered to tell Lottie about her brother and the doctor. "Hopefully, she can now jump to another life. Her duty of love to her brother is now finally over." She said and left them. Both Jericho and Wilson agreed with that. They walked to the burnt-out East Wing and found Mouse and Callan there, filming. Jericho asked where Professor Sweetman was. "He's back with Sibby and Jen; they're setting up an external night camera on those graves. The professor thinks they could yield some interesting stuff."

Jericho nodded and tapped Wilson's arm; "I think the good professor is right." He whispered and the pair headed back to the foyer.

6. THE CARETAKERS LODGE - PART 1.

Alex knocked at the caretakers lodge and received no answer; she slowly opened the door and peered in. The place looked deserted and so she stepped in, calling out softly for Lottie. She noticed that the place was furnished like something from the Victorian era. She opened the back reception room door and found two people inside. But that didn't surprise her, what did was; Lottie in just stockings, bend over the big sofa, being fucked hard by Owen - also in just stockings - and the pair turned around and just smiled at her. Alex grinned and started to pull off her clothes. She joined them just wearing her stockings too!

Alex slipped next to the pair and smiled; Lottie had huge pert tits and Alex was soon on them. The girls mouths joined, and they kissed. Alex knew immediately that Lottie was up for it; and some. Owen grinned, thrusting hard and said, "She made me dress the part." He said, gripping Lottie's hips as she pushed back against him, he added; "And you know me and women's clothes; especially decent stockings." Alex just smiled and continued to explore Lottie's mouth and tongue. They were soon on the carpeted floor with Lottie on top of Owen and Alex squatting on his face. Lottie reached round and grabbed Alex's swinging tits and kissed her neck and shoulders with some passion.

Alex noticed something on the sofa and reached over and grabbed it; the 'something' was a large wooden dildo, with two heads; already smeared with grease. She handed it back to Lottie who didn't even have to ask what Alex wanted. Lottie carefully pushed it into Alex's willing and yielding bum hole, still bouncing on Owens's large cock. Alex groaned loudly; Lottie certainly knew how to use it. She thrusted gently at first until Alex's arse accepted more of the shaft into her back passage. Then she speeded up, thrusting deep and firmly. In just a few minutes Alex had a fantastic orgasm which filled Owen's mouth and dribbled down his happy face and chin. He loved every drop of her cum and ate her gaping fanny with some relish.

Alex staggered off Owen and took the dido from Lottie, who she pushed down onto Owen, and he held her with both arms. "Oh, fucking yes!" Lottie shouted as Alex slowly inserted the dildo into her open bum hole. She had clearly had the dam thing up there before. Alex positioned herself behind Lottie and inserted the other head into her gaping cunt. She fucked Lottie doggy style quite hard. Lottie was groaning and moaning with sexual frenzy; she loved being double penetrated. Alex held the dildo with one hand; the other gripped Lottie's shoulder and they both fucked hard. Lottie had a massive screaming climax that splattered all over Owen; it was like she was bloody pissing!

They changed positions quickly; Lottie - now in the reverse cowgirl position - with Owens's cock buried deep in her open arse hole. Alex was on top of her, the dildo inserted in Lottie's cunt and her own gaping vagina that was running with cum. The girls were kissing with some passion and determination. Both Alex and Lottie had another enormous orgasm which made Owen cum deep in Lottie's back passage. They all collapsed in a heap, panting and laughing.

Alex cleaned up Lotte's gaping anus, making sure she gathered up every drop of Owens's cum with her tongue. Lottie stood with shaking leg and grabbed a nearby empty plant pot; she crouched over it and pissed hard and fast - groaning with relief - and then offered it to Alex who squatted over the pot and pissed hard too.

Owen chuckled and stroked Lottie's face and hair.

"Anyone for a cup of tea?" Lottie finally said and headed for the kitchen, leaving Owen and Alex kissing passionately on the floor. Alex whispered to Owen that she needed to speak to Lottie - woman to woman - and Owen nodded. He wiped his dirty wet cock on a nearby curtain and dressed; carefully removing the stockings Lottie had lent him, leaving them on the sofa, next to the big dildo that had caused so much pleasure and fun. Alex eased onto the sofa and called for Lottie. She came from the kitchen and was a little surprised - and disappointed - that Owen had gone.

Alex patted the sofa and said she really needed to speak to her about her brother Gabriele. Lottie just nodded and dropped on the sofa next to her; she actually smiled. "He's finally gone, hasn't he?" Alex nodded. Lottie sighed with some relief. She stroked Alex's face and said softly; "He wasn't very good in bed. He came far too quickly for me to enjoy it. But I always had 'Mandingo' to rely on." She gestured to the discarded dildo at the end of the sofa. Very little shocked or surprised Alex; but that revelation bloody well did!

Alex was alone in the lodge after Lottie had disappeared with Herbie the collector. She walked to the door and then realised the lodge had changed; it had transformed into its true 1999 appearance. She nodded; "The ghosts had gone and so had the lodge's Victorian interior." She whispered to herself and was about to pull open the front door, when it opened, and Mr. Edwin Rush walked in - very surprised - to see Alex standing in his hallway. Alex sighed; she wasn't 'cloaked' and he could see her. She smiled at him; this would take some explaining.

7. THE CARETAKERS LODGE - PART 2.

Mr. Rush wasn't too happy about the young student walking into his house unannounced; especially when he wasn't there. He shouted at Alex, calling her Miss Fellow's. He had assumed she was Sibby. He grabbed the telephone that sat on the hall table and said he would be informing the police about this matter. It wasn't right that his home had been invaded by bloody students.

Alex kept smiling and touched his arm; "I am sorry Mr. Rush, But I thought you didn't hear me. I did knock and shout." He stood with the phone receiver in his hand and waved her apology away. He started to dial. She smiled at him; "Now, how can I make it up to you Sir?" And really did smile.

The bed was creaking under the hard fucking that Mr. Rush was giving Alex. She was again naked - apart from her stockings - which he had insisted she keep on. That didn't surprise her; but his bloody stamina did. She thought it would be quickly over, but she had really underestimated Mr. Rush. He was buried in her cunt, fucking her hard and fast in the 'Missionary position, his mouth on her big tits and her legs against his shoulders.

Alex pulled a pillow under head and tried to smile. He was quite rough with her and called her a dirty bitch several times. She lay back; hands gripping the sheets and stared at the ceiling. The dirty old bugger had made her suck his cock; which was really quite big and rock hard for a man of his age. Then he had fingered and licked her fanny and bum hole. He was really happy that her arse was open and yielded to his probing fingers.

He told her - with quite a smile on his old face - that he expected, no insisted - that she allow him to fuck her up the arse. His terms for not calling the police were quite explicit; she was to let him cum in her twice - at least - with no fucking condom as he politely put it. He was grinning as he trusted hard and slow; telling her what a dirty little whore she was.

Alex just turned her head and stared at the door, wondering when the dirty old pervert would shoot his first lot. He turned her over and mounted Alex in the doggy position; now fucking her much harder. She actually felt tightness in her stomach and really couldn't stop herself squirting; now that really made the old man laugh and slap her quivering buttocks - hard - and call her a dirty bitch again.

She was actually groaning a little under his hard fucking and was relieved when he came inside her; his language wasn't pleasant, especially about her. He climbed off her walked to the door; he turned and pointed to the bed side cabinet;" I'm going to get a cup of tea. There's a box of hankies in there and some 'KY' jelly. Get your bloody arse hole greased up for me. I'll be back when I've finished my tea." He was gone and Alex sat up, leaning against the pillows, with her legs open. She grabbed a couple of paper hankies and wiped his cum from her vagina and thighs. There were three tubes of the famous lubricant in the drawer, and she wondered about the old man.

He must have been gone for about fifteen minutes and Alex sat bored on the bed, staring out the window. Mr. Rush returned with a smile and big erection. He told Alex to kneel on the bed and push her arse into the air. She sighed and did as she was ordered. She had really lubricated her arse with the cream. He mounted her without a word. Pushing his big cock into her bum hole; he wasn't gentle about it and started to thrust deep and fast immediately. He reached around and grabbed her tits. He really tugged and squeezed her breasts and nipples. He called her some pretty nasty names and fucked her arse hard. She couldn't help herself and squirted a couple of times, cursing loudly. Now those made him slap her bum cheeks really hard. "Keep your fucking filthy mouth shut my dirty little whore. I don't want to hear another word!"

Alex actually had a hand over her mouth to stop herself cursing; but she really groaned and to her surprise; had a big wet orgasm with the dirty old sod right up her arse. He was treating her like a street whore, and she was coming because of that. He fucked her back passage hard and rough for some minutes before shooting his second load into her. He collapsed on Alex and groaned loudly. He slapped her bum a couple of times and pulled his cock from her. He grabbed hold of her head and turned her around, forcing his dirty cock into her mouth. "Now clean up the bloody mess you made." He said. Mr. Rush made her clean his cock for some minutes before he was satisfied that Alex had done a good job.

He slid off the bed - panting a little - and took Alex by the arm and frog marched her down the stairs, her clothes were scattered around the hallway floor - he had stripped her quite roughly in the passage earlier- "Pick them up and get out." Was all he said, and Alex scooped up her clothes and handbag. He pushed her out the front door and slammed it behind her. Alex stood on the step and dressed quickly - as best she could - and walked down the gravel path quite awkwardly; she could feel his cum oozing from her bum into her panties.

"Dirty old bastard didn't even offer me a cup of bloody tea." She muttered to herself and headed back to the hospital; she really needed the toilet and a good wash or a bloody shower. She knew that his hand marks would remain on her arse for some time. But she had a strange feeling about the encounter with the old caretaker; the wild little animal in her had been satisfied. Now that did surprise her. A smile grew upon her face as she headed back to the old hospital.

8. MIGHTY MOUSE.

Alex headed for the small shower room and pushed straight in; she stood and smiled. Mouse quickly covered his crotch with both hands and almost smiled; he apologised; "I thought I locked the bloody door!" He was stark naked under the running shower and looked a little embarrassed. Alex now grinned and asked if the water was hot. Mouse nodded and watched with much surprise and pleasure as Alex slowly stripped her clothes off. "It will take ages for the old heater to warm up more water, so we best share. Do you mind?"

Mouse shook his head; he certainly didn't bloody mind! Alex remembered to turn the key in the lock and stood naked. Mouse stared at her and slowly dropped his hands. Alex actually grinned and said quietly; "Christ! Mighty Mouse!" The little man was big in one special place; very big indeed and it was getting bigger by the second. Alex squeezed into the small cubicle and the warm water ran down her breasts and legs. She pressed up close and their naked wet bodies met under the tumbling water. Very slowly their lips came together, and Mouse took hold of her. "I know I'm bloody dreaming; I just pray I don't bloody wake up!" Mouse whispered as Alex took hold of his erection with both hands, she smiled; the water running down her face. "If you're dreaming then I must be asleep too." She giggled and slid down his hard body and knelt; she eased the monster into her mouth and Mouse groaned out loud; spitting water. "Oh fuck!" was all he said.

Mouse fucked her doggy style on the wet floor gripping her slippery hips with both hands. He pushed deep and hard and Alex loved it. The little man certainly knew his way around a woman's body. She had a couple of little orgasms and groaned loudly. The earlier sex with the old Mr. Rush had left her still horny and receptive to another fucking. They changed position and Alex climbed on Mouse; the bloody floor had been wet and cold on her hands and knees. Mouse didn't seem to mind lying on the floor – cold or otherwise – with Alex riding him; her magnificent big tits gripped in his hands and mouth. Alex pulled up a little and squatted on him; she was pushing up and down on his cock with some passion as he gripped her hips and moaned loudly with sheer pleasure. She felt the big orgasm coming; first in her stomach, then it crept down her thighs and finally spurted from her trembling cunt. She groaned loudly and her whole body shuddered with the sheer ecstasy of the powerful tremor that racked her heaving body.

Mouse also felt his own ejaculation come; he shouted something about the good lord and his son and spurted inside Alex with much moaning and panting. Alex collapsed on him, and the pair kissed passionately, lying on the flooded floor. It was a good minute or so before either could speak. Alex whispered; "Now that's what I call a huge fuck from a real big man." Mouse just grinned and pushed Alex's wet hair from her smiling face and asked quietly; "Do you fancy seconds?" Alex chuckled and nodded, gently kissing his face and lips.

'Well, you know what they say if you have a bad ride; get back on the bloody horse and ride it until your happy again!' She thought and eased herself down his trembling body and gripped his cock again. Her eager mouth worked the big stiff shaft with some passion and real skill. Mouse groaned in utter pleasure and stroked her hair and face. Alex really worked it for several minutes then turned and knelt on all fours and Mouse quickly mounted her from behind. He was fucking her so hard that she placed both hands flat against the door and groaned loudly. The bloody door was banging and rattling like it was caught in a hurricane. Neither of them cared about the noise.

They changed position again; now facing each other with their legs entwined in the scissors position and the fucking continued unabated with Alex and Mouse both pushing hard and fast. They quickly ended up in the good old fashioned missionary position with Mouse gripping her ankles with both hands as she played with her big tits and moaned loudly. Mouse was panting openly as he came again inside her which caused Alex to have quite a spurt herself. He lowered himself onto her and they kissed passionately again for some minutes. Lying naked on the cold wet floor they started to laugh softly.

Mouse pulled his cock from her and sat back against the door breathing deeply; "I can't tell anyone about this because they simply wouldn't believe me.... well, to be honest I don't believe it myself." He said quietly and Alex slipped across the floor and kissed him again. "You are a big man in every respect, and you really know how to treat a woman like a man should." Old Mr. Rush was now just a shitty sexual experience, probably one of many in a woman's life…..especially a woman like our Alex!

She slipped from the shower room; wrapped in Mouse's towel with her clothes under her arm. She tip toed past the foyer and headed for the small room she shared with Sibby and the obnoxious Jen. Mouse followed her out and stopped to squeeze water from his shirt and sneakers. Gallantly, he had allowed Alex to use his only towel and so had dressed still quite wet. But he couldn't care less.

Jen passed him carrying her shower items and gave the little man a strange look; "Is the bloody water hot?" She asked. Mouse just nodded and quickly walked off. Jen pushed open the door and swore loudly; "You fucking little git! What; did you wash a fucking elephant down in here! What a fucking mess!" But Mouse had gone; smiling broadly. Jen was even unhappier – if that's possible for her – when she discovered there was no hot water left. She only found that little fact out while standing under it!

Mouse – being Mouse – never said anything to the other men about his wonderful shower. He still thought it could be a dream!

9. SECOND NIGHT.

Sibby and Jen were watching the monitor as night was falling fast. They both wondered why Lottie hadn't appeared with the bloody mash she promised. Owen and Alex sat by the old desk and sipped their coffees. Alex had bought Owen up to date with the story of the caretaker and his loyal sister; especially the incestuous goings on between the pair that Lottie had confessed too. Strangely enough that didn't actually shock him.

Owen nodded and rubbed his chin; "So Gary actually died in 1845, probably from the injuries he suffered. He and Lottie must be buried in the old cemetery, but their graves are now lost with the headstones so unreadable." Alex sighed and finished her coffee; "She was actually quite happy to see Herbie the Collector I think she really wanted all this to end." Callan and Mouse [he needed it!] were catching up on some sleep, but Alex wondered where the gorgeous professor had disappeared too. Owen collected her cup and shouted to the other girls; "Anyone wants a refill?" They both smiled and held up their cups. He collected them and headed for the kitchen. Alex leaned back in her chair and stared about the foyer. She turned and picked up the old Visitors Book from the desk and blew off some dust and slowly flicked through the yellowing pages. She stopped and read the entry made by the paranormal investigators in 1956.

They certainly discovered something, and it had killed them - for good - they were in the darkness, lost souls. There were few other entries; all workmen, building Inspectors and visitors from the Board of Trustee's.

There was an entry from the fire inspection team, who dealt with the fire earlier this year. Alex looked at the date; 13th may, 1999.The last entry was also for this very year; Professor Sweetman had apparently filled out the details of his teams visit. She stared at the names and smiled.

Alex re-read the entry and realised that something was wrong. She read the entry again; but couldn't figure what was bothering her. Owen returned with more coffee and was chatting with the girls manning the monitor and radio. Alex placed the book on the floor and accepted her coffee from him. "Have a look at the Visitors Book. The last entry: can you spot anything wrong." Owen nodded and picked the book up and stared at it; "Everyone is there; Sibby, Jen, Mouse and Callan." He said and sipped his coffee. Both he and Alex slowly placed their cups down and rose from their seats. The same solution had appeared to both; the professor hadn't signed in the damn book at the same time.

Alex asked Sibby who had made out the entry in the book. She smiled and said, "Callan. The professor hadn't arrived when he did it. I'll tell him [the professor] to add his name." She smiled and went back to watching the monitor. Alex and Owen excused themselves and headed out, lighting the way with their mirrors. They could see the car headlights coming from the old stable block. They slipped through the broken doors and stood in front of the big Jaguar car. The professor was in the driver's seat, head in hands. Alex walked up and opened the door; "Do you want to talk about all those deaths Alec?" She walked around to the passenger door and slid in. Owen jumped in the back and checked his mirror.

It was quite a few minutes before Alec lowered his hands and breathed deeply; he was clearly suffering inside. He smiled at

Alex and wiped his face with a bright orange hankie. "I arrived late; you see this young student....I forget her name now....she stopped me just as I was leaving. Well. I couldn't...I mean I had no will power; she was very pretty."

Alex sighed; "You were having sex while your students burnt to death in an old hospital, unaware that they shouldn't have plugged anything in the East Wing sockets. But you knew it was not safe. They should have been in the West Wing; where they are now." Alec nodded and wiped his face again; "Yes, I was told that morning about the change of wings; except I was late, and the team had already left. I should have rushed down there, but the pretty little student distracted me."

"Who is in the graves Alec?" Owen asked, but he now already knew. The professor looked up; there were little tears on his face and in his eyes. "My team of very good young people; everyone felt it was proper to bury them here; where they worked and died doing something they loved."

Alex nodded; "Why did you deface the memorial date?" Alec sighed; "I hoped to change all that. I tried year after year and nothing changed. Then I realised something.... I realised..." He stopped talking and wiped his face.

"Mobile phone signals don't pick up round here; do they?" Owen asked him and he nodded. "I drove like a madman and arrived just as evening was falling. The East wing was already ablaze. They didn't get out." Alex gripped his arm; "You've carried this guilt for an awful long time Alec, it's time to put it behind you and move on." Alec nodded slowly; "Sibby had such a bright future. She was my best student by a long way. But all she wanted was a man to call her own and some children. I took all those little dreams from her...and the others ...all their dreams went up in smoke." He groaned and folded his arms, pushing back in the seat. He was in turmoil.

Alex gripped his hand and turned to Owen; "What have we got on him?" Owen checked his mirror and shook his head; "Nothing that would interest Jericho or the department. He's basically clean." Alex smiled; "I think you should head back to the University and take a few days to get around this. Every time you come back here Alec; they are unable to jump. They keep coming back and so they can't move on. They must meet their

Collector. It's your guilt holding them here and they really need to move on."

He stared at Alex and very slowly nodded. Alex slid from the car followed by Owen. They stood amongst the mud and straw, watching the big car pull away. Owen nodded as the dashing professor Alec Sweetman slowly changed back to his real appearance, an old broken man. The car disappeared down the hospital lane towards the main road and faded away.

"He's been coming back here on the anniversary of the fire for some twenty years and his team have been waiting that long; waiting for him to turn up and save their lives by warning them about being in the wrong wing. They don't even know they're dead." Alex whispered and Owen checked his mirror; the current date was 13th May 2019.

Alex took Owens's hand, and they walked back to the foyer; they both hoped Jericho and Wilson would soon join them. They had four lost souls to speak with.

Sibby stared at camera four - the night camera set up over the cemetery - and turned to Jen; "Does the caretaker or his sister have a car?" Jen shrugged her shoulders; "I don't know. I don't think so." Sibby called the professor on the radio and received nothing but static. She called again; nothing. Something told her that he had gone. She sighed and placed the little handset down. Jen was smoking again, standing by the open door. "I think he's gone; again." Was all she said.

"Well, we shall just wait until he returns." Muttered Sibby and shivered a little; not knowing why she felt so afraid.

Callan and Mouse wandered in, sipping coffee and looked about. "What's that slight smell? I could smell something earlier." Sibby chuckled, gesturing to Jen; "Battersea Power station is at it again." The boys smiled and dropped in front of the monitor. The ghosts were back in the East Wing and the timeline was replaying again with awful clarity and horror.

Sibby and Jen headed for their makeshift bedroom and Mouse put his feet up; he was knackered. Callan told him to doze and sat reading his book. The hours crept past, and Callan's head was nodding. He never smelt or saw the thin whips of grey smoke. He never felt death slip over him as the old hospital wing caught fire with some violence. The smoke had overcome the two boys as they slept.

The girls tried to get out the windowless room - screaming hysterically - but couldn't get past the wall of fire. They were burnt to death; mercifully, quite quickly. The fire consumed their bodies - curled up into balls - beneath their beds, where they sought refuge.

Jericho and Team 74 stood watching the blaze and Jericho checked his mirror; 13th may, 1999. They watched the big jaguar pull into the drive and the professor running up to the doors of the wing. He couldn't get past the flames and collapsed on his knees, screaming, cussing and sobbing. He had arrived too late. In the distance could be heard the sirens and bells of the police and fire brigade. The old caretaker: Mr. Edwin Rush had called them, and he ran over to the professor, dragging him away from the burning building. The screaming professor tried to crawl back on his hands and knees and was dragged back; twice.

"Where the hell are they?" Wilson said. Herbie the Collector shook his head; he didn't know. All four were in his Soul ledger for tonight. Jericho sighed and turned to the team; "He still won't let them go," He operated his mirror and the team disappeared.

Herbie shrugged and watched as the fire brigade arrived on scene. The old caretaker was shouting to them about the students. Two brave firemen crashed through the front door, under the protection of a spurting hose and wearing breathing apparatus; tired to find the students. Fire Officer Kevin Higgs fell under part of a crumbling blazing wall and didn't make it back out. The fire chief called off any further rescue attempts; he had lost one good man already; that was enough. Young Kevin Higgs and Herbie stood watching for a few minutes and then the pair disappeared.

10. THE FIELD TRIP; DAY ONE [AGAIN.]

The University minibus turned from the road into Tabbert's Lane; "It may get bumpy so hold on!" 'Sibby' shouted. [Sylvia Fellows] and the other three occupants gripped seats and arm rests. Sibby kept a tight grip on the wheel and the minibus struggled up the gravel lane; sodden by weeks of rain.

"Well, I'm not getting out and bloody pushing." Jen Phillips called out to no one in particular. She drew on her shaking cigarette. She was sitting right next to a large 'NO SMOKING' sign on the window and didn't give a fuck; like she did about most things "You would have thought that old 'Sweetie' [Professor Alec Sweetman] would have bloody warned us about the bloody road." She added and blew little smoke rings about...

Jericho sat in the front passenger seat of their van and turned to Wilson, who was driving the van that Supplies had given them. He checked his mirror; it was 13th may, 2020. "Right on bloody time; again." He muttered.

They had passed the professor's old Jaguar car parked in a gravel lay-by some minutes earlier. The old man had been sobbing into hands - again. Alex leaned on Jericho's seat and said quietly; "We'll have to confront him again. He must know that's he's holding them back." Owen tapped his mirror and looked up; "We have to do something. He won't be back next year. The cancer will finish him off next March. Then what will those poor buggers do?" Wilson grunted; "Ghosts waiting for a dead man who will never show up. How will that play out?"

Alex leaned forward and stared out the windscreen, the wipers pushing slowly across it. "Something is wrong. They appear to be stuck at the gates." She said softly. Jericho rubbed his chin; "Of course; we've changed things. There is no Gary the caretaker to open the gates for the other lost souls. He's moved on; willingly or not." Wilson chuckled a little; "If they can't get back in - as they always did - what will they do now?" Jericho smiled and pulled out his mirror; "A call to Herbie may be in order."

But Owen leaned across him and tapped his arm, shaking his head; "I would hold on that, take a look." They watched as the big Jaguar pulled up behind the van; professor Sweetman jumped from the car waving. He was his youthful self again.

Jericho stared at his mirror; "It's May 13th, 1999, for them." The team watched as he held up keys and walked to the gates, ignoring the tumbling rain and unlocked them. The van pulled away and the professor walked back to his car and followed the van in, locking the gates behind him. Wilson sighed; "Now that's a bloody turn up for the books. Now what do we do?"

Jericho's mirror buzzed and he answered it quickly. The call from the Senior Time Controller was not unexpected. Jericho spoke for a few minutes and when the call had finished, he turned to the team and sighed; "The current human timeline has changed. It appears that Alec has changed his and the students destiny. The wing still catches fire, and the young fireman dies at the scene. But the students had moved to the other wing - the safe one - and so they didn't die."

Alex asked; "How did the fire start if they didn't plug anything in?" Jericho almost smiled; "Apparently the professor set up a camera in there and that was enough for the dangerous wiring to start the blaze." Owen was already reading about the new timeline. He really did chuckle.

"You have to admire the fucker. He turned out to be one brave bastard." Owen said and smiled at his puzzled colleagues. "What happened Owen?" Alex asked gripping his arm with a growing smile. Owen stared at the big gates; "Alec turned up alright and moved everyone to the other wing. But he set up a camera in the old wing; knowing full well that it would start the fire. He was the only member of the team that was killed in the blaze. Sitting with the damn camera; the other's all escaped."

Alex flopped back in her seat and shook her head; "When we were talking in the car that night. He said he had realised something, but never finished what he was saying." She sighed; "He realised that only his bloody death would stop the team living that dreadful, terrible night over and over again."

Jericho nodded; "And it did. Professor Alec Sweetman defaced his own memorial. I bet if we take a look at that now; there's only one well kept grave there." Owen looked up and smiled; "Here we go." He said simply and the team watched the small convoy of cars approaching the gates, which were being opened by the caretaker, dressed in a bright yellow raincoat. It was a young ex-soldier called Dave Richards.

The cars passed through and Jericho patted Wilson's arm; "Shall we go?" Wilson nodded and started the van, following the last car through. Alex consulted her mirror; it was 13th May 2020. Some twenty-one years after the fatal fire. Owen tapped his mirror and spoke to her softly; "The firemen went in to save the professor and not the students - they were safe - and so fireman Higgs death, which was scheduled, could take place. That part of the timeline continues normally. He knew he was to die of cancer; an old and distraught man, living a terrible life of bad dreams and regret, this way he could die on his own terms and save his students. His terrible guilt was over."

They followed the other cars to the old cemetery and watched them empty out. Wilson stopped the van and the team quickly decamped, they headed for the graveyard in respectful silence.

11. A CEREMONY OF REMEMBRANCE.

They joined the mourners huddled around the little memorial and a strapping young man smiled at Alex; "Sorry, but this is a private service of Remembrance for my mum's old professor. May I ask who invited you please?" Jericho answered him, shaking his hand; "Professor Tibb's and the paranormal team from Edinburgh University. Being the 21st Anniversary of Professor Sweetman's tragic death, the University thought it would be appropriate for another team of investigators to show their respects."

The young man actually smiled and turned to the several other mourners; "Mum! You are going to love this. A flipping team of paranormal investigators from Edinburgh University have turned up to show their respects to dad." Everyone just stared at the young man; he was Alec's son!

They recognised 'Sibby' at once; she of course didn't recognise them but smiled and shook hands all round. She was still a very beautiful woman. She pushed her arm through her handsome son's arm and said quietly, about how nice it was; that the University had sent someone after all these years. She stared at Alex and really did smile, saying; "I'm sure we've met before. Maybe at a paranormal get together?" Alex just nodded and the two women chatted like old friends. A very small, but smiling Reverend joined them; the team recognised Mouse immediately. He was clutching his bible; "Shall we start Sibby?" He asked. The Reverend Maxwell stared at Alex and tried desperately to remember where he had met this beautiful woman before. He sighed: probably in his bloody dreams!

"I thought that was absolutely lovely." Alex grinned and settled back in her seat. The team were sitting in the van watching the cars depart. They had been invited to the small 'wake' at the local pub but knew they wouldn't attend. Owen folded his arms; "So Alec had more than one reason to save his students. Sibby was carrying his baby. I wondered where that pair had quietly isappeared to that first night. She had to tell him that she was pregnant. Little wonder her tragic death cut him up so much. He had killed his own child as well."

Wilson sighed; "He kept going back, each year and every year, trying to change things, then realised that only his death could do that; bloody human freewill and all that."

Callan's two daughters had represented their father at the ceremony: he had died two years ago, suffering from chronic heart disease. Ann and Sylvia had both liked the look of Owen and Wilson. Jen didn't bother to turn up and no one seemed to mind; that was Jen's way. Apparently, she was a very successful businesswoman - quite ruthless in her deals - she told Sibby that she couldn't find the time; but had sent some flowers; cheap ones.

Jericho's mirror buzzed and he really did sigh. The screen had lit up like Blackpool illuminations, everyone knew that was Angel Margret herself calling. He answered it slowly; unsmiling. It was a brief conversation and Jericho lowered his mirror and shrugged his shoulders. "I have an interview with Margret about this little mess. It appears that dirty old doctor Tabbert lied to us." He pushed his mirror into his jacket pocket and smiled at their inquisitive faces. "It appears that a certain young woman in 1473 gave birth to an unscheduled baby; the dirty doctor's child." Wilson sighed; "Young Lizzie I assume." Jericho nodded.

Owen chuckled; "Are we going to deal with that?" Jericho folded his arm; "Let's find a pub and have a drink. Not the pub with the bloody wake going on. We're in enough shit already." Then he smiled. Alex sighed - she didn't look happy - "I bloody hate medieval clothes and where can I get a maid? No woman of quality travels without one in those times. Ruth is on her Collector's course at the present." Jericho smiled; "Over to you, our Owen. How do you fancy resurrecting 'Jacqueline' again?" Owen laughed; "Why not." Wilson groaned; "I bloody knew it. I said he would go strange if he kept dressing in bloody women's clothes!" Everyone laughed at that including a smiling Owen. Wilson started the van and spoke with Jericho about the angel's interview as they headed for 'The Salty Dog' pub in the next village.

Alex gripped Owens's arm and really smiled, whispering; "I'm going to love sharing my medieval bedroom with my lovely maid who will have to bathe and dress me." Owen grinned and whispered back; "And one who performs some really dirty sex acts too." Alex nodded and leaned back in her seat, smiling in anticipation then caught Wilson staring at the interior mirror at her. She just smiled at him and he smiled back.

Jericho lowered his mirror and sighed loudly; "Well, there's a problem with Pharaoh Amenhotep the Fifth back in 1320BC. Apparently he's found a magic sodding mirror and it spells trouble for the Time Line with a capitol T."

The End

EPISODE 5: "ALEXANDRA AND THE DARK PHARAOH."

EPISODE PROLOGUE: "Pharaoh Amenhotep V's magician has been ordered to investigate a strange mirror that appears to show alternative versions of the future – apparently - the mirror was robbed from an ancient tomb which belonged to the legendary magician; Tha, who is said to have received it from the God Thoth himself. But the King is known as the 'Dark Pharaoh' and plans to use the device for his own benefit and alter the destiny of his ancient Empire. Mr. Tibbs is dispatched to protect the current Timeline from change. Alex finds out that he's also known as the 'Horny Pharaoh!'"

60 Minutes approx. **Episode Warnings:** Smoking – Alcohol – Strong language – Violence [including sexual violence & BDSM] – Strong graphic sexual references – Mild horror – References to death & torture.

NOTES: This is the **ADULT** version of the original story which is published and appears in the **TEMPORAL DETECTIVES:** Series 1 – Episode 9 entitled: **"PHARAOH AMENHOTEP V AND THE MIRROR OF TIME."** Names have been changed to protect the innocent!

CAUTION: Recommended for **18+ only.**

1. ROYAL COURT; THEBES (LUXOR) PERET (GROWING SEASON) 1320BC.

Simhenta-Kara carefully placed the brightly painted chest upon the stone floor and looked about the room that he and his master Sentus-Kasim had been provided by the Royal Chamberlain. He walked to the large open window, covered by two embroidered curtains and stared out. The city was sprawled out below the window; "Typical, we're at the back of the palace with no view of the river." He sighed and watched, as his master's two household slaves, started to unpack the personal luggage and set the room up.

The Royal magician; Sentus-Kasim would only allow his young assistant to move or handle the magic props. Lulha wandered in and also stared out of the window which dominates the room. "No bloody view of the river - great!" She muttered with some sarcasm in her voice. Simhenta watched her with envious eyes; the pretty young girl was the old Magicians slave of the bed chamber. Simhenta found it hard to stomach, that the old man bedded such a lovely young girl, just because he had paid gold for her.

He quickly averted his eyes when Sentus appeared and slumped in a newly placed chair and pulled the thick plaid wig from his head and cursed. He waved at Simhenta and groaned; "Some bloody emissaries have arrived from the Kadesh King and will receive audience with Pharaoh tonight - which means my performance will now be tomorrow night." Ghusan, the old magician's personal body slave, took the wig and placed it upon its stand and checked for new lice.

Lulha handed her master a cup of wine and said nothing. The old man ran his free hand up her thigh until it rested against her taught belly. "Still, it gives me more time to enjoy my new young bed slave." The old man grinned and sipped his wine, running a hand over the girls bum and between her legs; she didn't smile or react.

His gropes were ended by the arrival of the Pharaoh's personal secretary, who informed Sentus that the Pharaoh demanded his presence now. "It is not for performance, but council." The secretary reassured the near panicked magician.

Simhenta-Kara carefully placed the brightly painted chest upon the stone floor and looked about the room that he and his master Sentus-Kasim had been provided by the Royal Chamberlain. He walked to the large open window, covered by two embroidered curtains and stared out. The city was sprawled out below the window; "Typical, we're at the back of the palace with no view of the river." He sighed and watched, as his master's two household slaves, started to unpack the personal luggage and set the room up.

The Royal magician; Sentus-Kasim would only allow his young assistant to move or handle the magic props. Lulha wandered in and also stared out of the window which dominates the room. "No bloody view of the river - great!" She muttered with some sarcasm in her voice. Simhenta watched her with envious eyes; the pretty young girl was the old Magicians slave of the bed chamber. Simhenta found it hard to stomach, that the old man bedded such a lovely young girl, just because he had paid gold for her.

He quickly averted his eyes when Sentus appeared and slumped in a newly placed chair and pulled the thick plaid wig from his head and cursed. He waved at Simhenta and groaned; "Some bloody emissaries have arrived from the Kadesh King and will receive audience with Pharaoh tonight - which means my performance will now be tomorrow night." Ghusan, the old magician's personal body slave, took the wig and placed it upon its stand and checked for new lice.

Lulha handed her master a cup of wine and said nothing. The old man ran his free hand up her thigh until it rested against her taught belly. "Still, it gives me more time to enjoy my new young bed slave." The old man grinned and sipped his wine, running a hand over the girls bum and between her legs; she didn't smile or react.

His gropes were ended by the arrival of the Pharaoh's personal secretary, who informed Sentus that the Pharaoh demanded his presence now. "It is not for performance, but council." The secretary reassured the near panicked magician.

Thus, Sentus and Simhenta, suitably dressed to greet Pharaoh, made their way to the King's personal apartments; both were impressed by the King's bodyguard - Nubian soldiers dressed in silver and gold tunic's with vicious looking curved swords - they were known to be totally loyal to the King.

They knew something was up, when they were shown into the King's inner sanctuary and were greeted by two naked young girls, bearing cups of wine. Simhenta smiled broadly at the pair and received quite a smile back; they were wearing nothing, but thick decorated collars and lotus flowers entwined in their long dark hair. "The King will be here in minutes." Dushan, the King's secretary announced and took a cup from the girls, then shooed them away; with a wave of his hand.

Dushan looked about and pulled the pair close to him; "What the King is about to impart could get you both killed, if you unwisely speak of it, to the wrong person." He then bowed quite low, as a dark curtain was pulled aside by a particularly fierce looking Nubian. Simhenta whispered to his master; "That's Talin, the Pharaoh's personal bodyguard, he never leaves the King's side, he never speaks; except with his sword."

Old Sentus-Kasim gulped and nervously smiled as Pharaoh Amenhotep stood before them; everyone bowed quite low. Simhentra immediately noticed the physical difference between the new King and his late predecessor; Pharaoh Tutankhamen who had lain in his tomb, these past three years. Amenhotep was a powerfully build man with cold, cruel eyes of black. He was not known for his mercy. He had taken the throne of Egypt by marriage to the young king's widow, and none defied him; he had commanded the Egyptian Army [at the time] and was a great warrior. He was also pious to the old Gods and had overthrown Tutankhamen's father's change, to a single God; the Aten, reverting the Kingdom to the religion of the ancient Gods.

The 'heritic' Pharaoh Akhenaten's name and very existence in Egyptian History had been obliterated from monuments and court records. Even his new capital had been deserted and was turning to ruins in the Armana desert.

Simhentra knew one fact, well known to every Egyptian; you didn't fuck with this Pharaoh. The Pharaoh pointed directly at Simhentra and spoke to Sentus; "Can this young man be trusted with Pharaoh's secrets?" The old Magician bowed even lower, well. as much as his age and back allowed him; "Yes my Lord, Simhentra is my trusted assistant and apprentice. He only speaks of matters that I allow him: I would trust him with my life."

The Pharoah smiled and grunted; "If you're wrong in your trust Setus, then it will be your life." Simhentra saw the look of sheer fear upon his old master's face but said nothing. The King folded his arms adding; "And your life as well." He indicated to the nervous Simhentra with another evil smile.

A young naked girl brought a tray with cups of wine and Simhentra noticed that the King's goblet was solid gold, encrusted with jewels, while they received plain silver cups. The Pharaoh gripped old Sentus's shoulder and spoke quietly; "My Captain, who guards the old tombs upon the Giza, discovered that a local family had indulged in some grave robbing. He had them all thrown to the God Hapi and the good God's servants [Nile crocodiles] devoured them. No afterlife for such villains." He grinned broadly and clapped his hands. The pretty young girl disappeared with some haste; like her very life depended upon it.

"If anyone here speaks, writes or even whispers about what they see; the God Hapi will have more tasty morsels for his children." Pharaoh nodded to Talin, who walked to the dark curtain and pulled it aside.

Two large Nubian servants carried in a heavy chest and placed it before Pharaoh, standing to one side, when indicated to do so, by Talin. Pharaoh patted the box gently and Talin carefully unlocked the chest, which was entirely painted black with no writing or symbols. "A funeral chest." Sentus muttered and wiped his face with a very nervous hand.

The big Nubian slowly opened the chest which contained bundles of black cloth and Pharaoh pushed his hands inside and slowly lifted a small, square shaped object that easily fitted into one hand. It glinted and sparkled in the light of the rooms lamps; Setus and Simhentra gasped as they could clearly see their reflections upon its strange surface, which also contained hieroglyphs they did not recognise or understand.

"This was robbed from the tomb of a long dead Magician, who served a great Pharaoh some thousand years before." He turned the object in his hands slowly, almost with reverence. He smiled a little, adding; "I've had several of my best and most educated servants and priests examine it. Four are dead and two simply vanished - gone, no trace of them found. Now I want you to discover how the thing works and what purpose it serves."

He placed the object into Setus's trembling hands and patted the old man; "It's our little secret my new friend, after all, no pious Pharaoh wants to be accused of receiving goods that were robbed from a tomb; now does he?"

Sentus nodded and whispered; "Of course not my Lord." He carefully wrapped the strange, and apparently deadly, object up in the cloth. Pharaoh pointed to the exit; "Go now and see what you discover. But remember, you cannot leave the palace without my express permission; on pain of death. Everything you require will be provided by my secretary Dushan; food, wine, gold and silver, girls, just ask and it will be done."

Sentus and Simhentra bowed and backed slowly towards the door, they were almost outside the chamber when Pharaoh called after them; "Oh, and please don't fail me, as that could have quite unpleasant consequences for you." The King smiled broadly and walked away with Talin just steps behind him.

They both knew what Pharaoh meant by that: death; thrown to the crocodiles if they were lucky and if Pharaoh was merciful that day!

And that's if the strange device didn't kill them first.

2. THOTH'S MAGIC MIRROR OF TIME?

The pair sat in the gathering gloom of night and stared at the object, now placed upon a small table before them. They both sipped wine and for several minutes nothing passed between them, until the old magician sighed loudly and allowed a few tears to fall; "I know what it is." He said simply and gulped down his wine, allowing Simhentra to replenish his cup.

Simhentra could see fear - real fear - in the old man's face and hear it - in his trembling words. "You didn't tell Pharaoh what you knew because he would have killed us. Once we're of no use anymore, that will happen, and it will keep his dirty secret of receiving robbed tomb goods. I strongly suspect he kept all the gold and other precious items from those ransacked tombs, for himself." He whispered to the old man who nodded; yes.

Sentus pointed a shaking finger towards the object and spoke very quietly; "It was robbed from the tomb of the great and legendary magician; Tha. He died over a thousand years ago and his name and exploits are still known to this day. Whilst the many Pharaohs that have passed since then are mostly forgotten, with their temples gone and no one recalls their names. They have left history, but Tha lives on in people's memories and hearts; A good man, kind and generous to the poor and a magician who almost equalled Thoth in talent. It was said that he was able to part the Nile waters with simple words of power and Hapi didn't mind. He could cure blindness and leprosy with potions and magic. There is a story that he could even raise the newly dead - before the fucking undertakers and priests pulled everything from their bodies - and mummified the poor bastards." The old man sipped more wine and ran a hand over his face.

"Promise me Simhentra; that you will not allow them to disgrace my body in such as manner but bury me according to the instructions I have left for you. I have no family to object or prevent such a burial. You will inherit what little I have - as the son I never had. Do you promise me this?" The old man gripped Simhentra's arm with hidden strength.

The young man nodded his agreement; "Everything will be done as you say Master." That made the magician smile and he rose and walked slowly to his bedroom and rather strangely - to Simhentra's mind - he turned and said quietly; "May your God's bless you and let happiness into your life and love into your heart." The old magician retired for the night, leaving his apprentice to ponder his words.

Simhentra knew his master practiced a strange religion which declared just one God and grand stone tombs, mummification and offerings were not needed to enter paradise or gain its favour. He had also been an admirer of the heretic Pharaoh Akhenaten and often spoke about the religion that the Jewish slaves adhered to.

"A very complex old man, but he has always treated me well." Simhentra whispered to himself and knew that the real legacy, the old man had bequeathed to him, was the much-acclaimed art of magic. He was the royal magician, because in a land full of magicians; he was simply the best. His only rival in talent and fame was probably the young Menes; the great magician from the North.

The old man's words about Tha made him recall what every magician knew that part of the story kept from the adoring masses; that Tha had been visited by Thoth himself and given a mirror from the God's, which showed both the past and the present. The mirror also had the ability to carry its owner to the 'hereafter' or back to the distant past. Simhentra actually shuddered, despite the heat of the night. He had just imagined what Pharaoh would do with such a device.

Simhentra recalled the old man's story, spoken in whispers; "As a young magician, I heard some of the stories about Tha. It is said that he travelled to strange lands and encountered unbelievable beasts, people whose skins were of many colours and even birds made of metal that roared and swept through the sky, where only God's should go. Tha served three Kings, but was murdered by a black hearted Pharaoh, who heard his story about the fall of the Egyptian Empire and how the God's were replaced by a single entity, who demanded nothing from his people but love."

The old man had slumped in his chair, muttering curses upon the device that lay before him. "We should smash it and flee for our lives." He had whispered and stumbled towards his bed, calling for Ghusan to attend him. "Hide it well Simhentra, let no other person be infected by its presence." Simhentra did as his was told and wrapped the device up and carried it to his bed, where he lay sleepless for many hours, until he finally slept and suffered a horrendous nightmare.

But it was Lulha shouting that awoke him just before dawn. He scrambled from his bed and ran to his master's chamber to find Ghusan kneeling and weeping by the old magician's bed. Luitha gripped Simhentra by the arm and whispered; "He's dead.... but look at his face.....demons from the afterlife must have visited him!"

Simhentra approached the bed slowly and held a hand over his mouth; the old man lay face up and that face was contorted in pain and fear, the eyes and mouth wide open. "Fetch the physician." he spoke quietly to Ghusan and held Lutha tightly in his arms; it felt good.

The royal physician examined Sentus and pronounced that he had expired due to his heart suddenly stopping; "That would explain his contorted face and outstretched hands." The physician concluded and bowed to the Kings personal secretary, who nodded his agreement and acceptance of the good doctor's diagnosis.

Dushan stood by the bed and shook his head: "The Pharaoh will not be pleased by this turn of events." He sighed and told a servant to inform the king of the magician's untimely death. Dushan pulled Simhentra to one side and spoke quietly; "You will need to convince the Pharaoh, that you can finish the task assigned by him - despite the death of your master - and produce the results he wants. Do you understand me?"

Simhentra nodded; he understood all too well; what the King's Secretary meant.

"I understand that the old magician had no living family, so I will instruct the Priests at his local temple to find in your favour - you had served him for many years and was born a free man?" Simhentra nodded again. Thus, Dushan would arrange for the Chief Priest, at the old man's temple, to declare Simhentra as sole beneficiary to Sentus-Kasim. This would mean, the young man now owned slaves [including Gushan and Lulha] a house in Thebes and a small country estate in Edfu. - and of course; the magic act - if he stayed alive long enough to enjoy his new fortune!

The Pharaoh; was certainly not pleased at the death of the magician but was impressed enough with Simhentra to allow him to continue working on the strange mirror. As he walked from the King's private audience chamber, distant screams punctuated by wailing and crying, floated within his hearing. He stopped and stared towards the city wall that fronted the Nile.

He heard several splashes and more screaming, which continued for some minutes before silence. Well, not complete silence; the wailing of mourning women now replaced the screams of dying men: the children of Hapi had been fed again: several local thieves and a blasphemer had been thrown to the waiting crocodiles, torn apart and devoured in the frothy, reddish water of the special enclosure that had been constructed at the rear of the God Hapi's Nile side temple. There was some faint clapping, but the overwhelming sounds were of naked fear, terror, despair and mourning. Simhentra actually shuddered and lowered his head, almost running up the steps, back to his allocated rooms.

He slumped upon a chair in his rooms and stared out the window. There were now two Nubian guards posted to his quarters and they had orders never to leave the young magician alone. The King called them 'bodyguards' but Simhentra knew they were Wardens - looking after the prisoner before his execution.

He had arranged for Gushan and Lulha to be taken to the country estate, away from the King; out of sight - out of mind - well, that's what he hoped. Simhentra poured some wine and picked at the figs left out for him. Now he needed to apply his mind to the unusual funeral of his old master.

3. A COSTUME DRAMA?

Alex, at first, steadfastly refused to wear the outfit. She dug her heels in and said NO. But Jericho patiently pointed out that the clothes were totally appropriate, for a woman of high birth in ancient Egypt; particularly at the royal court of Pharaoh. They were very necessary to the mission and Jericho knew that Alex understood that and so pushed the point home. Finally, after some heated discussions, Alex reluctantly agreed - but still under protest! – to try on the damn outfit. Ruth followed her up the stairs; she loved playing a 'Ladies Maid' to Alex and hoped Jericho would let her accompany them on this mission back to ancient Egypt. She would be disappointed; the local Human Agent would take on that role.

Alex appeared in the study wearing a long dark trench coat, wrapped closely about herself, which drew some odd looks from the others. Jericho grinned and shook his head; "Come on Alex, we're in our costumes and I look a right twat in this skirt thing. You can't wear a trench coat in Ancient Egypt - besides you'll sweat to death!" He held up his hands, adding; "Best get it over with and you'll quickly get use to wearing next to nothing. - it may be very liberating - We are all good friends and total professionals here, you know."

Alex slowly unwrapped and dropped the coat to the floor, Young Ruth gathered it up and tried not to stare. She had never seen an outfit that high born women of Ancient Egypt wore - well, almost wore - it was very revealing and would cause a sensation, even in the 21st Century."I didn't know, that by becoming a Temporal Detective, a condition of service was that I had to show my fanny and bum to anyone who cared to look." Alex said, with her arms folded and then dropped them to her sides. "Well have a bloody good look and get it out of your system." She spoke softly and didn't smile. Jericho and Wilson chuckled and said, "Well done Alex." but Owen said nothing, He simply could not take his eyes off Alex. Wilson slapped Owen on the back and laughed; "Take a good look boy; that is a real woman in all her glory. Most men would happily murder their granny to possess such a beauty." Even the normally reticent Jericho had to agree with that statement; Alex was simply stunning in her costume.

Alex was dressed as high-born women of the Royal Egyptian Court dressed; with a full plaid black wig festooned with jewels, a long thin dress of the finest cotton which was almost transparent, and gold covered sandals. Her arms had amulets of gold and silver - she was completely naked beneath [as was the custom for such high-born women]. She placed both arms upon her slender hips and stared at Owen; "Would you like me to do a twirl, so that you can see everything?"

Owens's eyes fixed upon her magnificent breasts and dropped slowly to her thighs. He took a very deep breath and felt giddy; his life in the monastery hadn't equipped him to deal with such a sight. He actually couldn't say anything, and he simply couldn't look away - no matter how hard he tried to force himself.

She lifted her arms and turned around slowly. Poor Owen was already the colour of a tomato and he simply blurted out; "Sweet Jesus Alex! Your arse could drive demons mad!" But when he saw the look Alex gave him, he gulped and tried to apologise, but Alex actually smiled; "I'm joking Owen, I'm sure you didn't have many dealings with women in the Monastery, that your father dumped you in. I do know that you don't mean any offence by staring - fill your boots!" She did another little twirl and patted his shoulder, then walked to the table, picking up a glass of brandy - she really needed it - and no-one looked anywhere else but at her bum, moving from side to side with her little strides and Owen actually groaned quite loudly!

"Now you don't get an offer like that every day." Wilson chuckled and gripped Owen by the arm, adding; "Best put your eyeballs back in their sockets before they roll about the floor. But, by Christ, your right about our girls arse; it could easily drive dead men into a sexual frenzy."

Wilson turned to Alex, smiling; "Just one question baby girl - where the hell did you hide your mirror?" Alex grinned back and said softly; "Wouldn't you like to know!" she had recovered her humour, much to the relief of her colleagues. Owen kept looking at Alex and sipped his brandy with a strange look upon his young face. Wilson noticed it and whispered to Jericho; "I think our young apprentice detective has discovered what he missed; whilst he still breathed."

Jericho - still smiling broadly - clapped his hands and pointed to the door; "Let's go people and I hope you really like camels." The little group headed for the light room and jumped to Ancient Thebes in the year 1320BC.

Alex gripped Owen's arm outside the tent and smiled with real admiration; "For Christ sake Owen, you should win an Oscar for that bloody performance! For a second there, I even bloody believed it!" Owen just grinned; "Thank you my dear, just keeping our secrets our secret."

They had camped some kilometers from the city and sat about the fire, drinking brandy from silver cups and eating roast chicken and bowls of milky lentil's, garnished with herbs and a little spice. Angel Margret had provided servants and Nubian guards from the period, whilst Temporal Inspector Fabien Bisset had arranged for them to meet his human agent for this period.

Jericho recounted the brief he had received about the mission, they were now undertaking; "It was young Herbie the collector that reported what the old man had told him, to his boss. Who passed it onto Angel Margret and now we must investigate and recover the damn thing."

Alex - happily wrapped in a thin cloak - nodded; she had heard the rumours about the missing mirror. Apparently, it had gone missing from a member of Inspector Fabien's team, some thousand human years before this time. He had been discreetly investigating a breech in the Timeline [someone from 1935 had arrived in 2350BC] when it disappeared. According to Temporal regulations, Inspector Fabien would not be allowed to investigate an incident concerning a member of his team and so tracing the missing mirror had been passed to Jericho and his team.

Owen added to the discussion with his research on the incident: "It appears that whoever arrived from 1935 managed to steal the mirror and disappear. The suspect was an American called Russell Hudson who discovered a natural tear in the timeline and travelled back to 2350BC, where he attended the Pharaoh's court, using a magic act to fund his life here. He became a legend; still spoken about today [1320BC]. Unfortunately, he hadn't done much preparation about the period and upset a few powerful men by sleeping with their wives and daughters. He was murdered by a close friend of the third Pharaoh that he served, who covered up his friends crime. But his reputation forced the authorities to bury the magician with full honours. Inspector Fabien did search his tomb; but nothing was found."

"It was probably taken by thieves before the tomb was even sealed up - grave robbing was a full-time business for some families around here." Alex spoke quietly and finished her brandy.

Jericho nodded at that and said softly; "Our mirrors have a defence mechanism which does not allow living humans to operate them. Should one try, the mirror will freeze them and their time period. Then send a warning message back to the Control Centre, who would arrange for temporal detectives to attend. Since that did not happen, we can only deduce that the mirror is damaged; It has become a very dangerous object to leave around."

Wilson coughed and sipped his drink; "Herbie the collector was told by the old man - who was a magician himself at Pharaoh's court - about 'Thoth's Mirror' and realised it could be the missing mirror. It had resurfaced after nearly a thousand years. As Jericho said, the thing could be damaged, four people from here died trying to operate the damn mirror and worse; no souls were collected, and the mirror sent no SOS - very odd. Two managed to open the travel app and they ended up in Brazil in the year 875AD - local natives killed and ate them. The pair had stupidly or in ignorance, left the bloody mirror behind - they couldn't get back and being out of their own time; no souls were collected.

The Collector's called the finding of all these soulless bodies in. All the men were traced back to this period of history, but it was assumed that the group were playing around with yet another time portal, they had discovered locally. Only when Herbie the collector called the old man's story in, was it realised that the missing mirror could be the key to their soulless deaths." Wilson downed his drink and smiled a little.

"The old magician was murdered in his bed, by the slave girl that he raped on a regular basis; she suffocated him whilst he slept. It's a pretty good bet that the old man's apprentice knows where it is." Wilson added, refilling his cup. "He's, our target." Jericho said simply and allowed Wilson to refill his cup.

One of their guards shouted that a rider approached on a camel. "Our human agent, I do believe." Jericho smiled and they stood and awaited the arrival of Inspector Fabien's contact for this period and place.

Alex lay on her mat and stared at the ceiling of the tent and ran a hand between her legs; she was bloody horny and knew she needed a man – or woman – before she could settle down for the night. She sighed and then saw the shadow of the big guard pacing outside her tent. Supplies had provided the 'extra's' for the mission with care; they were all from this very era. She slipped from her mat – stark naked – and pulled the tent flap back slightly.

The big man stood leaning on his spear staring out into the darkness. He was a massive Nubian with visible scars upon his back and arms. He was only wearing the traditional Egyptian shendyt and sandals and didn't seem to mind the chill of the night. She coughed quietly and he turned and smiled; "Do you need anything my lady?" He asked and walked over, spear on his shoulder. She nodded and gestured him in. The big man made no comment that she was standing naked before him.

"Can you keep secrets, a lady's secret?" she said quietly, and he smiled slowly and nodded. "What secret does my lady wish me to keep?" Alex slowly sat on the mat and opened her legs a little so he could see what's on offer if he did keep secrets. He smiled again and dropped his spear; "For that my lady I would keep any and all secrets in this world."

"Good." Was all Alex said her voice full of anticipation and opened her legs wide. He dropped his shendyt and that made Alex really smile; he was a big man in all respects! There was no foreplay; she didn't need it and he certainly didn't. He became stiff immediately as he pushed her legs fully open and knelt between them. "Take me like a cheap whore." She whispered as he mounted her with some urgency. Little was said between the two strangers; their bodies did all the talking needed. He fucked her with little care or gentleness, and she loved it. The big man used her like she wished and almost brutally took her like a sex toy. She restrained from screaming with some difficulty as he thrusted deep inside her, his big hands abusing her breasts with a lot of assistance from his mouth and tongue. She had a couple of little squirts which made him chuckle and he set about fucking her as he liked.

She had a big orgasm under his rough handling and deep pumping which made her legs shake and a few tears appear. He fucked her for about twenty minutes, then roughly turned her over and fucked her hard 'doggy-style' for another ten minutes before finally pushing her down on the mat and filling her with his hot seed. They lay panting on the mat and Alex was happy. The big man fucked her again, this time for nearly an hour. They rolled around the mat, moaning and groaning with great restraint until he came again inside of her, as she squatted over him bouncing up and down on his big cock. She squirted again as she felt his cum shooting – like a fountain – inside her. They quickly collapsed together and lay quietly in each other's arms until they recovered.

He rose from the mat and picked up his shendyt and spear. "Thank you, my lady." Was all he said and resumed his patrol outside the tent. Alex rolled into a cotton sheet and slept soundly on the thick mat until the sun rose.

The following morning, a very grand camel train entered the ancient city of Thebes. Crowds of people watched the convoy passing through the great North Gate and whispered amongst themselves that the train contained Northern Egypt's Governor's daughter; the Lady Isis, who was rumoured to be the most beautiful woman in the Kingdom and a devotee of the Goddess, whose name she bore and whose powers she could enact at will. No man dared to try and possess such a woman [without her consent] because of the protection the Goddess bestowed upon her Priestess - few pious Egyptians would risk the wrath of the Goddess Isis.

Most agreed that it was appropriate, that she was accompanied by the North's greatest magician: Menes. The caravan reached the royal palace of Pharaoh Amenhotep V by mid morning and were greeted by the King's personal Secretary; Dushan.

4. MENES THE MAGICIAN.

Jericho bowed low and introduced his personal servant and travelling steward to Dushan; young Ossan. "Don't be fooled by his youth my lord, his mind is sharp and quick......" But the King's secretary stared beyond them both, at the large, imposing Nubian bodyguard who towered above everyone. "I take it that this man - if indeed he is a man - is the Priestess Isis's guard?" Jericho smiled and clapped his hands for the six litter bearers to lower their burden to the sand. "My lord, may I present the flower of the North, Goddess Isis's own Priestess who bears her name and enjoys the Goddess's blessings - the Lady Isis!"

Two slaves pulled the curtains of the litter apart and the Priestess stepped from it into the warm sunshine. There were loud gasps from the crowds, and many knelt down, Jericho heard several shout; "It must be herself!"

Alex walked slowly towards the King's Secretary, who simply stood with his mouth half open; the old man was transfixed. "By the God's Menes, she IS the Goddess in living form. No woman walking this earth could compare with her!" He actually bowed low himself and managed to mumble out an official greeting.

The crowds were cheering wildly; they knew that the priestess's visit would bring much luck to their city - and them. Alex thanked Dushan for his words and gave a small wave to the adoring crowds, some men in the throng were actually fighting to get a better look and city guards had to separate them, using their sticks.

Dushan escorted Lady Isis and the magician Menes into the state rooms of Pharaoh's palace where food and drink awaited them. Dushan whispered to a trusted servant to fetch the King - he knew that the King would wish to greet Lady Isis himself. Walking behind Alex, dressed a little more modestly, but still naked beneath her thin dress, was Thy, the Priestess's maid and the local human agent for this time. The difference in height between the two women was noted by all; Alex would be much taller than most grown females of this time because of human evolution - women had gained a little more height over the centuries and the difference was now pronounced. But it added to Alex's mystic; the God's were always depicted in art as much bigger than ordinary mortals [humans] and so that just confirmed her position, in the Goddess's blessings, to most citizens and palace staff. Owen and Wilson noted that the ladies of Pharaoh's court were dressed similar to Alex and there were some beautiful women amongst them - but none compared to Alex [they both agreed on that]. Owen smiled and whispered; "Best fill our boots as Alex says." Wilson chuckled and definitely enjoyed the views on offer.

Owen recognised that Thy was an attractive young woman in her own right and watched her swinging backside as she walked in front of him. Thy was the youngest daughter of the local magistrate and had received a good education for a woman of this period. Her father had signed a marriage contract with a certain captain in Pharaoh's army of occupation in Kush - the pair would formally marry upon his return in a year or so.

Alex was not surprised that Thy considered Wilson a very handsome man; her future husband was of Nubian descent himself and no one really cared about 'mixed marriages' around here - Thy was pale skinned with green eyes and that didn't matter to him either. "He's a good man and he calls me his 'Isis'." She had confided to Alex. Apparently, Inspector Fabian also admired the big man; he was Fabien's man in Kush!

Both Alex and Wilson admitted they would really like to meet this army captain, who had quite modern ideas about his forthcoming marriage. They were now in the centre of the magnificent State rooms and could see, it was filled with dignitaries of Pharaoh's court.

The High Priest of the temple of Amen-Ra [the father of the Gods and Egypt's Principal Deity] stood watching with his own secretary. Kumanine was also the pharaoh's Chief minister and the second most powerful man in the Kingdom. He drew a heavy breath and turned to his man with a worried look upon his face. "In forty years walking this earth, I have never seen such beauty bestowed upon a mortal woman. There will be trouble in the King's harem when he casts eyes upon her. We both know his appetite for women - beautiful women." He sighed loudly and added; "Then we have the most urgent question of the succession, so this lady may be the answer to all the king's problems." Then Kumanine hesitated and groaned a little; "Or be the cause of all the King's problems, if she refuses." The young secretary nodded; Pharaoh's Queen was a sickly young girl, who by marriage had bestowed the throne upon Amenhotep - she had no choice in the matter - her husband was dead, and she had produced no male heirs and still hadn't done so. The King's two chief Concubines had also failed to produce a boy, giving him three daughters: two of them already in their tombs. Infant mortality in the ancient world was common and affected rich and poor alike.

The King did have some twenty-one children by women in his harem - he had over a hundred women and girls - but none had the rank to be Queen or even produce a son that the Empire would accept as Pharaoh. The secretary stared at the Priestess and one thought passed through his mind; A real Queen; totally acceptable to all. But more importantly: able to have a son with a full claim to his father's throne.

The High Priest and his man exchanged glances, both knowing what the other was thinking; this woman had the sheer beauty to be Queen and her position as Priestess of Isis certainly gave her the rank to be Queen - there would be no argument about any son of her's sitting upon the Gold Throne - none whatsoever. But her position also created a real problem for the King; if she refused his offer of marriage and the throne - he could not just take her; that would be sacrilege and blaspheming in Egyptian law and could easily cause civil war amongst his nobility and Priests.

The High Priest wiped his face, terrified at his own thoughts. Such action would certainly incur the wrath of the Goddess and the people would not stand for that. The kingdom could be in bloody chaos and fighting in just weeks, in the event of such a disastrous decision by the King. Few Egyptians had forgotten the turmoil and trouble caused by the heretic Akhenaton, just several years ago. Egypt could not afford another religious civil war. "If our prince so desires her, then she must be persuaded to submit for Egypt's sake." He whispered and turned to the imposing grand entrance; Pharaoh was here.

The King desired to see the magician Menes about a certain little matter and thus came straight away. But all thoughts about the mirror simply faded when he was introduced to the Lady Isis. He eased himself onto a gilded chair and just sat staring at her; saying nothing. The Lord Chamberlain gave a nervous cough which broke the silence in the packed chamber; "Your majesty, maybe the great Northern magician will be allowed to entertain us?" The old man had to repeat his request twice before Pharaoh pulled his eyes away from Alex and mumbled a 'yes'.

Everyone in the chamber exchanged glances - but said nothing - they all knew their King was utterly captivated by the Priestess and each wondered if they were looking at their new Queen.

Menes stepped forward and bowed; "You Majesty, may I present a very humble performance called the 'empty chair?" The Pharaoh nodded and smiled broadly at Alex, who sipped wine with some grace from a golden cup. The King's eyes followed her body from its toes to her face [again] and felt his mouth dry. He actually muttered something which only Kumanine and the Lord Chamberlain heard, and both winced at his words; especially one of them: 'Queen'.

 A simple plain wooden chair was placed before Pharaoh and the audience shuffled a little forward to catch a better view. Menes unfurled a bright red sheet and showed it to everyone and then asked the Priestess to sit upon the chair, which she agreed and sat down. The magician carefully placed the sheet over the Lady Isis, covering her completely. She made the chamber laugh by complaining that the lamps had gone out. Pharaoh gulped down wine and leaned forward; "I trust the lady will come to no harm magician, for if she does, you may find yourself swimming in the Nile with some new friends." The King didn't smile.

But Menes did and clapped his hands; the bright red sheet slowly fluttered to the ground; the chair was empty. There was silence for a few seconds, then huge applause and shouts of praise rang around the chamber. Pharaoh rose and walked to the chair lifting it slightly; like everyone else, he was totally amazed; the great lady had simply vanished. Disappearing in a packed chamber with no hidden traps or mirrors, that could have been prepared in advance.

Simhentra could not believe what he had just seen [like everyone else - well, except Wilson and Owen, who smiled to themselves] the magician had performed an incredible disappearing act with just a chair and a sheet, whilst surrounded by a packed audience. "It's totally impossible!" he whispered and couldn't even begin to see how it was achieved.

The King slumped back in his chair; he had seen many magic performances in his time, but this simple little act was the most incredible thing he had ever witnessed. He stared at Menes, who was taking bows from the crowd, and knew this was the man to prise open the secrets of 'Thoth's Mirror'.

Menes placed the sheet carefully back over the chair and called upon Thoth to return the Priestess, then slowly lifted the sheet high above his head; revealing the chair was no longer empty; the Lady Isis sat drinking her wine and smiled at the crowd; "Have I missed anything exciting?" She said and laughed, to the delight of the audience and particularly Pharaoh, who had already made up his mind about both the magician and his new Queen.

Simhentra eased his way through the excited crowd and introduced himself to Menes, who appeared quite pleased to meet the young magician. But the chamber fell silent as Pharaoh arose and gripped Lady Isis by the hand and ran a soft finger across her lips; "My Lady you are truly beautiful, intelligent, pious, funny and graceful. You are already judged a Queen, just by those gifts that the God's have bestowed upon you. Now you WILL be Queen in truth." Alex was caught totally unprepared, as he simply gripped her and placed a kiss upon her lips. The King was most reluctant to release her, and Alex pulled away from him with some effort and stood back from the King; "I am no tavern whore to be handled and taken at will. I will retire for the night and hope your majesty will be in better condition come the 'morrow."

But the King grabbed her back with some force, causing her to yelp; "Yes, you retire for the night sweet lady and sleep well, for tomorrow you WILL become my Queen." He released the shaking woman, who was immediately attended by her maid; Thy. "No, I will not sir." Alex said with real defiance in her voice. The packed chamber was in absolute silence, and many stood quite shocked by what had just happened. The stand-off between the Priestess and the King continued for a few painful seconds and then wise

Kumanine, Dushan and the Lord Chamberlain diplomatically intervened. "This great matter must be discussed with your council your majesty, a Pharaoh cannot be seen to defy the laws of his brother and sister Gods. She IS the Priestess of Isis herself - she cannot be compelled to marry by threat or force - it will tear your kingdom apart - Remember the heretic Akhenaton and those troubled times my lord." Kumanine spoke in a whisper and the Lord Chamberlain agreed with him, adding; "Let us persuade the lady with reason and argument - she is a very intelligent woman my lord - she will see sense."

Pharaoh grunted his agreement with their words; "Make sure you succeed, for she will become my Queen - regardless of what happens I will have her." He turned to Talin and ordered; "Escort the lady to her chambers and see that she has anything she wants." The King's personal bodyguard obeyed; Alex and Thy said nothing but followed the soldiers. Alex glanced back at Jericho with a real expression of concern upon her face. Jericho nodded to her and found Wilson and Owen. "I think we may have over-egged the pudding this time. But I've made contact with the old magicians apprentice, and he does possess the mirror."

"To quote a very wise man Jericho, I think we should grab Alex and Thy, then the mirror and get the fuck outta of Dodge City!" Wilson shrugged his shoulders and smiled, but he - like Owen and Jericho - were now concerned for Alex's and Thy's safety. They had seen that; the 'Dark Pharaoh' was quite capable of anything.

5. THE ALL TOO HUMAN GOD.

Alex lay on the very comfortable couch and stretched her long legs out. She smiled to herself and sighed; the Pharaoh would be referred to in modern times as a 'very bad boy'. Strong, confidant and not afraid to get what he wants. She chuckled; "Probably in the 20th or 21st centuries, he would be a ruthless and very successful businessman or bloody Politian." Here, in this time and place, Pharaoh was regarded as divine; a human God and clearly got whatever he wanted by any means he employed. "A very bad boy and that makes him attractive to most women, even at his age." She told herself. But then, for this era he was actually a well built and reasonably handsome man. She wondered where Thy had disappeared to and was alone in the beautiful King's Chamber; but not for long. She sat up as she heard the strange noise - like stone gently grinding against stone - she looked about the semi dark rooms, lit only by flickering yellow lamps and watched with some amazement, as the large statute of Osiris [God of the Underworld] moved to one side. Alex jumped from the couch as Pharaoh Amenhotep stepped from behind the statue. He held up a hand and smiled; "Be not alarmed sweet lady. I come to express my sorrow at my behaviour. But you must understand that I am much used to obtaining what I want, especially with women. But in your case, I was wrong to behave so and I must beg for your forgiveness." He smiled and bowed. Pharaoh walked to a large ornate chair and sat down. He gestured for Alex to do the same, which she did.

Strangely enough Alex didn't feel frightened by his presence. He sat upright, with hands on his knees and confessed that he wanted her - permanently - as his new Queen. She could have anything she wished, desired or wanted, if she agreed. Alex sighed and explained they didn't really know each other, but he just smiled; "I know what I need and want my little dove and believe me that will be sufficient for both of us. You will grow to love and respect me as I will you. That I promise before the God's." Alex actually smiled; a girl didn't get an offer like that every day!

He rose and walked slowly over to her and held out his hand; "Please take my devoted heart by taking my hand and I swear that I will make you happy as you will make me. Be the lamp in the darkness of my life and I will worship and adore you whilst I have breath in my body." He smiled and Alex rose and touched the back of his outstretched hand. She was about to say just how impossible it would be for her, when he slowly gripped her hand. He gently pulled her to him and whispered; "May I have just one kiss before you answer?" Alex nodded and the pair embraced.

Alex was a little stunned; the kiss made her lips and face tingle, and he eased his tongue into her willing mouth. Alex lay back on the couch, still in his passionate embrace. They said nothing more as they pulled off each other's sparse outfits.

Alex groaned loudly as he kissed her breasts, working down her stomach until he reached her already wet vagina. He certainly knew what he was doing down there, and Alex gripped his shoulders as he feasted on her with some passion and skill. She lay back, legs open and moaning loudly as the first of her orgasms swept over her. He used his probing tongue and fingers to bring her off and when she was ready, mounted her. He was certainly a well-built Pharaoh! He filled her up with his throbbing erection and they made love with some urgency, on the couch and on the floor. They changed positions frequently and Alex gripped his thrusting arse as they enjoyed the 'Missionary' position, then turned and he fucked her in the 'Doggy' position.

Alex moaned and kicked her legs as she climaxed again. They were rolling about the floor like dogs in heat, their tongues urgently exploring each other's mouths.

She was panting like a Marathon Runner as he thrust hard and deep into her willing body. She pushed a breast into his mouth, and he sucked and licked her nipples, almost suckling like a child. She ran her fingers down his arched back and actually screamed a little. He was fucking her hard and suddenly, he shouted out and came inside of her. She felt the flood of the hot liquid and climaxed again. The pair fell into a heap upon the floor, still locked in a passionate embrace. They lay whispering with each other. The 'Dark Pharaoh' knew he had finally met the woman he had desired, dreamed and searched for all his adult life, a real woman and a real Queen.

He was very reluctant to pull out of her, but Alex needed to pee, and he finally let her go. She found the 'toilet' was a very beautifully carved and ornate pot behind a gold edged curtain and pissed hard and fast. She was squatting down over the pot and looked up; he was standing there; smiling. He chuckled; "You piss like a horse my darling."

Alex waved him away and continued to piss. She looked about; there was nothing to wipe herself on. She shrugged her slim shoulders and walked awkwardly back to the couch, where he lay, holding his cock. He sat up and held out his hand. "You will sleep in arms; I cannot let you go." Alex slid next to him, and they fell asleep in each other's arms. Alex woke an hour or so later, to find the Pharaoh had gone. She rose and collected her dress and cleaned her face as best she could. Alex - still naked - wiped her hands on a soft cloth and realised she was not alone in the room. She turned slowly and saw Talin with a tray. He placed it down and bowed a little. "Some food and wine My lady." Alex nodded and said 'thank you' quietly. She didn't cover herself. She stared at him; the Nubian was an incredible specimen for the times. He must have invented the 'workout' with that physic. She walked slowly across to the tray and picked up a date and slid it carefully between her lips.

Talin folded his arms and tried to hide his smile. "You're very loyal to Pharaoh, so you must know how to keep secrets?" Talin nodded; "If I'm told to forget. I forget." He said quietly. The pair stared at each other, and Alex picked up another date and slowly pushed it into his mouth. "You had better keep this one or take swimming lessons." The big Nubian really did smile.

She pulled off his flimsy loincloth and did gasp a little; his cock matched the rest of him - magnificent - and she knelt and eagerly pushed it into her mouth. She worked that big cock with mouth and fingers. Talin breathed deep and ran his fingers through Alex's loose hair. After several minutes of hard sucking and gentle caresses, Talin pulled her up and they kissed; tongues disappearing into each other's mouths. He walked her slowly to the bed and gently laid her down. Slowly, he knelt and eased open her legs. Alex lay back and gripped the soft pillows as Talin went down on her with lips and tongue. Alex groaned loudly with some passion; he certainly knew how to eat out a fanny.

He mounted her, pulling her long legs over his shoulders and pushing his cock into her dripping wet vagina. Alex really did groan as he filled her up with his massive dark cock. She gripped his arms and he started to thrust; slow and gentle at first, then hard and fast. Their mouths came together again and the love making got underway. The bed creaked and shook under the frenzied fucking by the pair and soon they were on the cold stone floor, fucking doggy style. Talin was gripping Alex's big swinging tits with both hands, thrusting deeply. Alex had a huge orgasm which splattered over the floor in little squirts. She moaned and pushed back on his cock with some passion. They were fucking with a real animal passion.

He easily picked her up and fucked her standing; she gripped his shoulders and pulled her legs around his thick waist. She had another mind-blowing climax, which dripped down his belly and thighs. He was throwing her up and down with some energy. She actually screamed a couple of times with sheer sexual ecstasy and covered his mouth with hers. They pressed against a wall and now Alex's perk pale arse was slapping against it with each thrust. At one point she actually bit his shoulder and he suddenly groaned and cursed. He flooded her with his hot seed and the pair slid down the wall and piled up on the floor. They lay kissing for some minutes before his big cock fell from her gaping cunt, Alex groaned as her fanny poured his cum down her thighs and legs. He gasped for breath and held her head and kissed her with some passion, whispering; "I will never forget this secret My Lady." He smiled and lay back on the floor; Alex held firmly in his big strong arms. They must have lay together for some minutes before he rose and gently pulled her up. They kissed again without a word said, he wrapped his loincloth about his sweating torso and with a little bow; left her alone.

Alex was breathing deeply, her legs shaking a little from the frenzied sex session and she needed a hot bath. She could smell his sweat and cum on her and smiled. She grabbed up her discarded dress and walked - awkwardly - to the water bowel and towels. "This will do until I can bath." She muttered to herself and set about washing her crotch, thighs and legs. She slipped into her gown and couldn't stop smiling; Talin was certainly the bodyguard to look after your body. She chuckled and shouted for Thy.

She could hear voices in the next room and wandered to the doorway. Thy was just waving away a couple of naked serving girls who had delivered wine and food, she smiled at Alex and pointed to the large wooden doors of the chambers. "He had to go. Urgent messengers from one of the provinces. It appears that the Syrians are on the march. It could mean another bloody war." Alex nodded and sat slowly down, she was about to speak when Thy raised a finger to her own lips and said quietly; "A loyal and loving ladies Maid never speaks about who her mistress takes pleasure from. Never, unless told to do so." She smiled and leaned forward; "What were they like my new Queen?" and giggled. Alex just smiled and pulled her close. They really had something to discuss; Pharaoh was an all too human God and Talin was a sexual God in human form.

6. RUNNING TO STAND STILL.

Alex and Thy sat quietly in their rooms, which were spacious and comfortable, drinking wine and nibbling at plump figs and dates provided by members of Pharaoh's harem. "I'd bloody murder for a coffee." Alex muttered, sipped her wine and stared about the rooms; for the period, they were the ultimate in luxury with tapestries and pieces of 'artwork' - nearly all connected with some God. Thy rolled her silver wine cup around in her hand and whispered;"I've tried coffee. It was really good, even if it was heated." Alex shook her head; "You can't have done Thy; it won't be around for another couple thousand years."

Thy leaned forward and grinned; "Mr. Fabien brought me some in a strange vase he called 'a flask' and let me try it." Alex did smile; "You like Mr. Fabien then Thy?" The young girl nodded and really did smile broadly. The pair were interrupted by the arrival of Menes the magician with Ossian and Lady Isis's guard close behind [that mean's Jericho, Owen and Wilson turned up] and Alex was really pleased to see them. She noticed immediately that Jericho was not a happy man and he explained that the old magicians young apprentice had fled into the night - taking the mirror with him. So Pharaoh was not a happy king; ordering Talin to take several men and go after Simhentra. He had decamped because he knew the Pharaoh would replace him with Menes; and that 'replacement' would mean death - for him.

Jericho informed Alex that several members of the King's council would soon arrive to 'persuade' her to marry Pharaoh; to save Egypt from further turmoil and possibly - civil war. Alex shrugged her shoulders; "I knew this bloody outfit would be trouble; you can't walk about in public, showing your bits without some sort of trouble." Everyone chuckled and Jericho rubbed his chin and asked Thy, if she had any idea where Simhentra could have run to.

Thy nodded; "The old magician left him a small estate in Edfu and I'm pretty sure that Pharaoh doesn't know about that - yet." Jericho sighed and pulled his mirror out; "Let's locate the estate of the late Sentus - Kasim in this time period." Alex noticed that young Owen was staring at her - again. She smiled; "I thought you would have seen enough Owen." with no censor in her voice and folded her arms. She almost laughed when he winked at her. Owen openly blushed and muttered several apologies and pretended to study a piece of 'artwork' on a pedestal near the windows. Wilson chuckled; "I think our boy has fallen in lust with you." Alex nodded and Thy even agreed; "He hasn't taken his eyes off you in that gown." She hesitated and added; "Mind you, neither have any of the males we have met so far." Both women laughed quietly.

Owen was now intently studying the little statuette and turned the piece around carefully in his hands. He pulled his mirror from the satchel he was carrying and for some minutes concentrated on both. Alex asked him what was so interesting about the little piece of stone; a small fat man sitting upon a chair.

Owen tapped the rear of the small statue and pointed out the few hieroglyphs scratched upon the back of the seat. "It says that this is an image of Tha - the magician. But according to human records on Ancient Egypt, this statue is on display in the Cairo Museum as being the only discovered representation of the Pharaoh Khufu; the King who is credited with building the great pyramid. That piece has no name marked upon it. Interesting little fact that." Alex accepted the piece and showed it to Thy, who nodded; "That's an image of the magician Tha - everyone knows that - well everyone living here now."

"Modern archaeologists must have the issue confused." Wilson muttered and wondered why his young friend - who was staring at Alex [yet again] - found it as interesting as he now found Alex!

Jericho called for everyone's attention and tapped his mirror; "We're off to Edfu and pay a visit to young mister Simhentra. it would be a lot easier if he could just turn the damn thing on and we could trace him in a second." Thy pulled a beautiful dark cloak about Alex and she was more than happy with it. The little group disappeared and arrived in the metropolis of Edfu, which was dominated by its famous temple to the God Horus.

"He now has a large house in the street of the Baker's." Thy informed Jericho, as the group made its way through the quiet streets as night gathered in. "He's probably still travelling down the river; that would be the quickest way from Thebes to here. So, we'll wait at his house." Jericho spoke quietly and smiled when Owen warned everyone to keep an eye on Lulha - she was a murderer - after all. They found the house after about half an hour: a large whitewashed villa with a roof garden. Thy quickly pointed out the name given to the place: 'House of illusions' [by its late owner] which was etched in hieroglyphics by the main entrance along with a pedestal holding up a small statue of 'Thoth the God of magicians'. Thy gestured to the figurine; "That's for people who can't read or write [that would be the majority of the population!] So they know a magician lives here."

She stopped by the entrance and shouted in that guests had arrived. Ghusan was a little surprised to see the famous magician Menes [and rival to his old master] at the door, and even greater surprise at finding the Priestess of Isis standing there too. Simhentra had not yet arrived and Ghusan felt compelled to allow the Priestess to rest in his new master's humble abode. Figs and wine were produced for the guests by Lulha, who bowed

really low to the Priestess and asked if she knew when, her new master would return. Before Alex could answer, Owen stepped back from the doorway and said quietly; "Pharaoh's soldiers are in the street: heading this way."

Jericho pointed to the back room - away from the servants - and everyone quietly made their way there. "Well, our magical friend won't be turning up here at any time in the near future. Not with Pharaoh's troops swarming over the city its back to the office for now." Jericho spoke softly, as there was loud banging on the door and shouting. He operated his mirror and suddenly the room was empty. Lulha stood in the doorway and allowed the tray of cups to fall slowly from her shocked fingers and smash upon the floor.

The villa was suddenly full of soldiers, shouting and searching. Talin gripped her arm and demanded where the bloody magician was. Lulha couldn't speak for a few seconds and Talin could see the look of horror upon her face. "They just disappeared - into thin air - I saw them with my own eyes." She whispered and came over faint. Talin heaved the girl up into his arms and carried her to a nearby chair.

One of his soldiers shouted that the magician wasn't here; but the magician Menes and the Priestess of Isis - with their servants - had been here just minutes ago. "That's impossible; we have the villa surrounded." He muttered, and then looked at the Lulha, who was drinking wine offered by Ghusan, and how she was shaking from fear. He wiped his face - Pharaoh will not be happy at this turn of events - especially now he has lost both the magic mirror and the beautiful Priestess. But he would definitely be interested in the Northern magician's latest incredible trick. Talin grunted and ordered his men out of the villa, after yet another search which yielded nothing, and headed back to their boat docked on the Nile. He would send a runner back to Pharaoh; especially informing him about the Northern magician Menes making five full grown adults simply disappear in a room without windows and the only door had a serving girl standing in it!

That made him turn back to Lulha, who was sitting on the small chair; smiling at him - her legs open and arms at her sides - she was offering sex for protection. Talin rubbed his chin and quickly reckoned that he would not hear from his master for some time. The big Nubian took hold of Lulha by the arm and marched her into the bedroom. The girl had only ever been with her old master and the 'big' Nubian came as quite a surprise; she screamed the whole time that he took her and when he left some one hour later; she lay half on the bed and half on the floor; wrapped in a blood stained sheet: sobbing.

Talin couldn't believe the girl was almost a virgin and smiled to himself, as he returned to the boat - her old master must have had a cock the size of a finger; he laughed out loud and was watched by Simhentra from a street corner - wrapped in a dark cloak - and full of hatred for the Nubian because of what he had done to Lulha. He clutched the mirror to his chest and headed for his boyhood friends house in the street of the sail-makers.

7. SMOKE AND MIRRORS IN STONE.

Pharaoh sat slumped in a little gilded chair with a gold cup in his hand, whilst a naked serving girl filled it with wine. He had received several messengers that night; the one from the Northern Governor made him throw goblets, overturn furniture and kick the Lord Chamberlain up the arse. He rubbed his face and stared at the floor, sipping his wine. The Northern Governor had informed Pharaoh that his daughter Isis was still at her Temple in Memphis - and the great Northern magician: Menes was performing at the very same temple - they had been nowhere.

"All fucking imposter's! But the magician was no fake." The King yelled at Dushan, who stood in silence; he knew how to handle the King's anger. Finally, Pharaoh had calmed down enough to think clearly and make decisions; the Lord Chamberlain had no answers, when the King asked him; "Who the fuck were those people and where is the woman?" He had already decided that the woman [when found] would be a royal concubine, regardless of her current rank amongst women - he really didn't care - even if she turned out to be the fucking illegitimate daughter of a camel dung salesman! Oh yes, Amenhotep had tasted what's available and wanted more: lot's more! Talin had kept the priestess's 'little secret' alright: he really didn't wish a mid-day swim in the Nile with Hapi's 'children'.

The runner from him made the King pace the floor; "Where is the little bastard with my mirror?" He yelled at Kumanine who also said nothing. The King announced a large reward of gold for Simhentra's whereabouts and an even greater amount for the woman posing as the priestess of Isis. Just for good measure, he had all Simhentra's property and land seized, handing the battered and abused Lulha over to her new 'master' - Talin. He kept Ghusan [who actually was a very good servant] for his own household.

With no family or Simhentra to bury him, the old magician's body lay in the Temple mortuary at Edfu; until the smell forced the priests there to bury him without ceremony or mummification [which was expensive]. They felt little sympathy for the old man, as he was placed in a sand-pit grave and covered up - strangely enough - just as the old man had wanted!

Pharaoh knew that the lure of so much gold would produce results - he especially hoped, that it would in the case of the missing beauty; he really did ache for the woman. She had fooled them all with her believable performance. That thought actually made the King smile; a beautiful, intelligent, cunning and resourceful rogue! What a Queen she could have made - in his dark heart - he had already forgiven her.

The little group of camels passed quietly across the sand, heading for the city of Memphis, as the coolness of night approached. Jericho consulted his mirror and stared up at the darkening sky which was full of stars. His thoughts were disturbed by Owen, who rode next to him. "We can get a visit to the Great Pyramid, can't we?" Owen asked, desperate to see the structure as it was meant to be seen; before the outer casing was stripped away some three thousand years later and used to build a mosque.

Jericho had to smile, and he nodded. That made Owens's day and he volunteered to cook for the group, when they camped that night just outside the city. Everyone chatted and ate, sitting around the campfire and Jericho briefed his team between mouthfuls of curry and sips of wine. "Thy tells me that a close friend of Simhentra has informed Talin that the young magician has fled to this city. He has managed to avoid capture for nearly a year despite the large reward offered in gold. The same informant also confirmed that he still has the mirror in his possession - and that's our priority; get the damn thing back - by any means."

Wilson chuckled and spoke directly to Alex; "You know that horny old Pharaoh has offered a massive reward if you give yourself up to him. I mean, Thy says its huge and all in gold. You would be the wealthiest woman in Egypt bar the Queen herself." Alex smiled and ate her curry slowly; "I think, I'll decline the dirty old sod's generous offer and stay with the team; thank you very much."

Owen coughed and held up the little statue of the fat man sitting on a chair, that he had 'borrowed' from Pharaoh's apartments; "I think I've worked out what the real story is about, despite the confusion that surrounds this." Jericho was now interested; he knew that Owen had a quite powerful deductive mind; that's why he picked the boy for his team.

Everyone sat in silence around the little fire and listened with real interest. "Thy tells us that this little statue is actually of Tha - the legendary magician - and NOT Pharaoh Khufu who is credited with building the Great Pyramid. Why the confusion? Tha WAS King Khufu's magician and so is known to everyone at the time and even now, is still known. So, here's something to ponder; Pharaoh wants a tomb that will not be robbed, so he builds a fucking massive structure right where everyone can see it and, most importantly, knows that the King's incredible fortune in gold and other precious stuff are sealed up inside. That's just plain crazy - every tomb robber then and now will try to get in and steal the stuff. It's staring them in the face!" Owen sipped his wine and pushed the statue back into the bag he was carrying and smiled.

Alex pulled the cloak about her shoulders and nodded; "Your right Owen; it doesn't actually make any sense; Pharaoh Khufu MUST have known about the robbery of the other royal tombs; even the ones that were hidden at the time. So why built a bleeding great tomb that everyone knows is full of treasure?"

Owen grinned broadly and said simply; "Tha."

Jericho started to chuckle and slapped Owen on the back; "Absolutely brilliant my young friend, fucking brilliant!" He looked quite amazed and shook his head in realisation of what young Owen had deduced. Alex actually clapped and stuck up a thumb; "That is just incredible; little wonder Tha is a legend."

Wilson looked quite puzzled, and Owen grabbed his arm; "What do magicians perform all the time; in nearly every trick big man?" Wilson shrugged his large shoulders; "Deception, distraction and illusion?" He ventured, then what Owen meant, struck home and he started to laugh.

"It's the greatest piece of deception ever performed - smoke and mirrors formed from ston - the whole world believed Pharaoh was buried, with all his treasure, in a fucking huge lump of stone that everyone knows about. But it was a bloody big deception thought up by Tha and it's simply brilliant. No-one would search for Khufu's tomb to rob, it was right there, staring them in the face. That's why it's never been found. Simply brilliant - no-one has ever looked for it - making it the safest tomb ever created for a Pharaoh." Owen Chuckled and sipped his wine.

"So the cunning old Pharaoh still lays undisturbed after three thousand years; simply protected by the fact; that no-one ever looked for him!" Alex gripped Owens's arm with real pride; "Brilliant." She repeated softly.

"Rider on a camel approaching." Wilson said and stood up; "Its Thy." He added and walked over to greet her. Alex was well pleased to meet up with her 'maid' again and handed Thy a cup of wine, as she joined the little group around the fire.

Thy sipped her wine and spoke softly; "I have really terrible news. Simhentra was betrayed by his childhood friend for the gold reward. Pharaoh tortured him but didn't find the mirror. They killed him just a few weeks ago."

Alex sighed; "A brave young man, I guess he knew what bloody Pharaoh would do if he regained the mirror and learnt how to operate it." Everyone nodded at that, and Owen asked; "I take it, they made him swim with crocodiles?" Thy shook her head and looked quite sad; "No, his death was worse than that."

Owen sipped his wine and asked; "What could be worse than eaten alive by really big reptiles?" Thy took a deep breath; "They buried him alive. Wrapped him up in bandages, placed him in an old sarcophagus and entombed in some hidden place. Probably at Saqqara, where there are lots of old empty tombs they could reseal and hide."

They sat in silence until Jericho spoke; "We really must recover the mirror before that bastard gets his hands back on it."

Everyone agreed with that.

8. ALEX & THY'S LITTLE PARTY.

Thy had arranged for the group to stay at her father's estate in Memphis for the time being. It was a beautiful two-story villa with a roof garden that backed onto the Nile. Alex was sharing Thy's rooms, and the pair had become quite close. Alex stood naked on the limestone slab in the small room and two maid servants poured warm water over her from big jugs: slowly. One girl then wiped her down with a soft cloth including wiping between her legs and bum cheeks! Alex knew that ancient Egyptians would bathe up to four times a day like this and there were public baths they could also use.

 Thy stood in the doorway and smiled; "They have heated plenty of water so I will join you." Alex smiled and Thy slipped from her thin cotton robe and now stark naked, joined Alex on the slab. She held up both arms as a signal for the girl to tip the first jug over her, but Alex took the jug from the smiling servant and poured it herself over the happy Thy. She then took a clean cloth and wiped Thy down. She knelt in front of Thy's completely shaved fanny [Egyptians - both men and women - removed most body hair to stop lice] and gently wiped between her legs.
Thy groaned a little and ran her hands down Alex's hair and face. Nothing was said between the girls as Alex's mouth and tongue set to work on Thy's clean vagina. With her skill and experience Alex quickly found her clitoris and Thy really did groan with pleasure as Alex worked it with fingers and tongue. The two young maid servants stood and watched without emotion or comment. The pair was soon on the floor in the sixty-nine-position enjoying each other's clean cunts. They were both experienced in pleasing another woman [that didn't actually surprise Alex about Thy]. They were soon kissing passionately

and rubbing each other's crotches with some vigour and urgency.

Thy told a maid servant to bring her chest and Alex was intrigued when it was placed next to them. Thy opened it quickly and tipped the contents onto the damp floor. Alex laughed outright; it was full of dildos and some strange looking sex toys. There was a coil of wooden beads on a thin rope and two wooden bricks with copper wires and holes.

Thy smiled and told Alex to bend over and she applied some oil from a small jug to her anus; pushing her fingers in to spread the soft oil. Alex turned her head and watched as Thy carefully rubbed oil on the beads and began to feed the string into her arsehole. She did it quickly and Alex knew that Thy had played this little game before. Thy chuckled as the last bead disappeared into Alex's back passage. "I see you have indulged in backward intercourse my dear. I do love that." The pair kissed again and Thy produced a double headed wooden dildo and oiled that too, then inserted it into Alex's willing fanny as she lay on her back with her legs open. Thy squatted over her and pushed the other end into her own fanny and the pair came together to fuck and kiss for some minutes.

Thy was riding Alex when a maid servant handed her one of the wooden bricks and she grinned at Alex, leaning over her and taking hold of her right tit. She pushed the big nipple into the hole and snapped the cloth covered copper wire over the breast. Alex squealed in pain but let Thy continue as she fixed the second brick to her other tit. Alex realised they were basically large 'mouse-traps' and when Thy let them go; she could feel the weight. Thy climbed off and made Alex stand with her legs apart, holding the dildo and thrusting it with both hands in Alex's vagina. "Swing your tits." she ordered her and Alex now felt real pain as the bricks swung on her breasts; pulling them down. The other maid now handed Thy a thick leather strap and she slapped Alex's arse with it a couple of times, then went back to thrusting the dildo in Alex's fanny. She alternated between the strap and the dildo for some minutes; leaving Alex with very red cheeks.

But Alex had orgasmed with the mixture of pain and pleasure; Thy clearly knew what she was doing. Alex - under the strap - was marched to the bedroom and Thy joined her on the bed, pulling off the 'mouse-traps' and gently extracting the beads from her arse. They then rolled about the bed fucking with the double dildo and Alex really did have a big orgasm under Thy's relentless use of the dildo and her mouth. They lay gasping and panting, held tightly in each other's arms until a tall Nubian woman appeared with huge milk filled breasts held up with a cotton sling; she was totally naked apart from that. "This is Anya, let's drink!" The big woman knelt on the bed and pulled the thin white cloth from her huge breasts revealing enormous dark nipples oozing milk. Thy and Alex was on them immediately, suckling hard, caressing the big firm mounds, squeezing and kneading them to let the sticky milk flow into their eager mouths. Thy kissed Alex between mouthfuls and soon they were swapping the milk with their tongues, starting the dirty passionate lovemaking all over again, with Anya joining in and Alex found that the Nubian knew her way around another woman's vagina; especially her 'little finger' as Thy called her clitoris.

Alex had another big orgasm with her new sex partner and now the threesome was rolling about, kissing, stroking, suckling and fingering with some ecstasy having unfettered orgasm's that caused screaming and laughter in equal measures. Anya entertained the pair further by tying the two bricks with string to her big swollen clitoris and with open legs, walked around the small room, swinging the bricks with an exquisite look of pain and satisfaction upon her face. Alex and Thy were soon back feeding on those big breasts and the girls fell asleep after their crazy sexual exertions; their naked bodies still mixed together in a heap, covered with sweat and cum.

Alex wiped her face and noticed that the sun was sinking outside the small curtained window, leaning up on her elbows she watched as Anya slipped from them, wrapping the cloth back around her magnificent breasts. She smiled at Alex and placed a finger against her lips whispering; "I must go my lady, for it's my turn and honour to service my master the living God Hapi-ankh, [Apis, the Bull God] at his temple." Alex stared at her for a full second, realizing just what the woman meant and ran a hand across her face; "You're going to ……I mean have sex…..with your master!" Alex knew that Apis was represented by a living bull who was mummified and buried like a bloody Pharaoh when it died: she had no idea that like the Pharaoh, he had his own Harem of women!

Anya smiled and slipped away leaving Alex actually a little speechless. She almost staggered as she left Thy sleeping; her bum cheeks and nipples were aching from the abuse they had received, but Alex was smiling; really smiling and looking forward to the next session with Thy despite Anya's revelations about the bloody horny bull!

9. IS HE DEAD OR ALIVE?

Jericho sat in the roof garden, enjoying the smells of the plants and the cool breeze coming off the river. He was consulting his mirror and looked up and smiled when Alex joined him - dressed far more modestly, now that she wasn't playing a high-born woman. She watched as Jericho expression changed to one of puzzlement, then real concern.

"What is it?" She asked and sat next to him, gripping his arm. Jericho tapped his mirror, and his face was grim; "No soul was collected from Simhentra, no Collector was sent because Dispatches have no record of his death - yet - and the missing mirror logged an attempt to use the Travel App."

Alex was slightly confused; "But Thy is certain that Pharaoh put him to death in that bloody awful way." Jericho nodded and rubbed his chin; "There can be a couple of explanations. The first is Simhentra was out of his time [a time traveller] but why couldn't the collector find a body? The second is, he's still alive - but he's been buried for almost four weeks now - that's simply impossible. It really doesn't make any sense with no soul and no body. There always has to be one or the other."

Alex leaned back and stared at the Nile; "So he appears to be alive - yet we know he must be dead. No one could be buried for four weeks without food or more importantly; water. So, what is he: dead or alive?" Jericho admitted he didn't know - it was one strange set of circumstances. Then he stared down at the new message just received from a Senior Time-Controller; he re-read the message a couple of times. "This gets stranger by the minute. Time control has reported that someone attempted to use the missing mirrors travel App and was successful - well almost - they logged to travel to Egypt in 1970 but didn't arrive. They never made it which is nearly impossible...." Jericho stopped speaking and drew a real full breath, adding; "The poor stupid bugger: he's trapped between the two." Alex asked Jericho, what he meant by trapped between two - two what?

Jericho folded his arms and said quietly; "He's trapped between the living and the dead - he's actually neither and there's no way we can help him. The bloody mirror is clearly defective, and his soul is still with his dead body, which cannot be located because Dispatch Records still show him as living!"

"Poor bloody sod." Muttered Alex and the pair were joined by Owen and Wilson - eating of course - they loved the local figs. Jericho bought them up to speed on the fate of Simhentra but added that Time Control had pinpointed where the mirror was operated from; and that's where they were headed.

"It was activated at Saqqara, where Thy believes they disposed of Simhentra just four weeks ago. He must have tried to escape by using it and the bloody defective mirror threw his soul into limbo and Pharaoh must have come across his lifeless body." Jericho looked quite puzzled and rubbed his chin; "If that's the case, why did Pharaoh bother to go through the whole 'let's bury the fucker alive' routine?" Everyone shrugged their shoulders - this case was becoming stranger by the minute.

Owen folded his arms and sighed; "How could he operate the mirror and end up apparently lifeless, when Pharaoh finds him and takes possession of the body - but no mirror is found on him?" Wilson whistled and ran a hand over his face; "Owen is right; Pharaoh should have found the mirror by the dead body - but we know he didn't, how could that happen?"

Alex wrapped her cloak about herself; "Someone else was there and witnessed the mirror apparently kill young Simhentra and cleared off with it, just before Pharaoh turned up. But who could Simhentra trust? Who could have been his accomplice?"

Jericho pushed his mirror back into his tunic and took a deep breath; "I asked Control to give me some details on what the defective mirror could have done to Simhentra and one possibility, may be the answer why Pharaoh still buried him alive - apparently. With his soul stuck between the living and dead, his body would appear just like a man in a coma. The Pharaoh probably tried a little torture to wake him, but with no success and so buried him 'alive'."

"The bloody mirror is still out there. Let's go people." Jericho added and pulled his mirror out again and tapped details into the

Travel App and the team was gone. "The city of the Dead." Alex said quietly, as they walked through some low stone walls and stared at the Step-Pyramid silhouetted by the moon, which was rising in the darkening night sky. "I thought that was bloody Hamunaptra." Owen whispered and smiled. Wilson murmured; "You watch too many movies." and pointed towards a small stone compound which had lights showing from within.

Jericho checked his mirror and nodded towards the building; "That's where our mirror may be." Keeping low, they made for the compound and found some statues of a dog headed god to hide behind. Owen gripped Jericho's arm and pointed near the wall of the compound; "Jericho; there's a dead soldier on the ground and it's so fresh, there's the bloody collector!"

Jericho waved Ali the Collector over - with the soul of the bewildered dead soldier in tow - They greeted Ali warmly and he bowed a little to Jericho, he gestured to the dead soldier's soul; "He said that tomb robbers are searching near the old temple wall, for some nobleman's burial. He was looking after the office, whilst his colleagues - six of them - have gone to the site, which is located on the other side of the complex. Then someone came up behind him and drove a dagger through his throat. He couldn't even scream, but he saw who killed him and he knew the man."

Jericho nodded and spoke to the soldier directly; "You say you know the man who killed you?" The soldier spoke softly; "Yes Sir, all soldiers know Pharaoh's personal bodyguard: Talin." Wilson drew a breath; "Do you think the so-called Tomb robbers are also Talin's men and thus, Pharaoh's men?" Alex folded her arms; "They think they know where the mirror is." She said simply.

"This soldiers death will be blamed on grave robbers and their supposed appearance here will also cover Pharaoh's activities in the cemetery, quite clever really." Jericho grunted and stared at the small building; how could Simhentra hide the mirror in a building constantly used by Pharaoh's troops? No, the young magician would hide the damn thing somewhere else; in plain sight? Jericho smiled at that thought. Owen pointed to the small, whitewashed building; "Someone is still inside; it must be Talin." Jericho told Ali to take the man's soul and depart, which he did. Jericho spoke quietly to his team; "If you were a magician and needed to hide something really well; where would you hide it?"

"Smoke and mirrors." Muttered Owen and Alex wrapped her cloak around tighter against the chill of night. "In plain sight." She volunteered and then Thy chuckled quietly; "In Pharaoh's palace?" Jericho really did smile at that remark; "No, the mirror was activated around here - somewhere."

Alex held up a hand; "But what about poor Simhentra, shouldn't we try and find him and his soul?" Owen grunted; "No can do, I checked my mirror, and he is not shown amongst the living anymore and worse; he's not shown amongst the dead either. We will not be able to locate his body or soul." Wilson waved a hand and said, "He's buried around here somewhere, and no-one will come digging for antiques and mummies for another four thousand years. The poor bastard."

10. HIDDEN IN PLAIN SIGHT.

Owen crept back from the compound's little office and re-joined the team by the low stone wall. "Talin is practically pulling the place to bits; he's even knocking holes in the bloody walls!" Jericho wiped his face and stared about the extensive cemetery of Saqqara; "Where would a magician hide the bloody mirror?" Alex and Thy were chatting quietly and Wilson was consulting his mirror.

Owen suddenly snapped his fingers and drew everyone's attention; "I know this sounds crazy, but what if Simhentra decided to be inspired by his hero; Tha. and like the Great Pyramid, come up with a wonderful distraction and hide the bloody thing in plain sight? or rather instruct his accomplice on where to hide the damn thing after he was dead?"

Wilson nodded, he liked that idea; "But where?" Owen grinned and jerked a thumb towards the North wall; "What about Tha's tomb, where it was originally stolen from?" Alex chuckled; "Now that would be really ironic if Pharaoh and his merry men are ripping the place apart and it's hidden in the last place they would even think of!" Thy folded her arm and smiled; "It's not such a crazy idea; remember they captured him in this place."

Jericho decided that since they had nothing else to run with, they would check out the old tomb of Tha the magician. The little group made their way quietly across the sand and stones of Saqqara. Some distance behind them they could see flaming torches; "Pharaoh and his men searching." Thy whispered, adding; "They can't be seen during daylight now they have Simhentra, they would have to explain why they're in the cemetery and what for. Pharaoh doesn't want anyone to know about the mirror, which was looted from a tomb."

Owen guided them to a quiet spot near a small ravine and the broken and derelict entrances to looted and abandoned tombs from the glorious 'Old Kingdom' of Egypt. "That's the one." He spoke quietly and the group disappeared into the dark recess, leaving Thy hiding in the entrance as lookout.

They followed the roughly cut tunnel, bent low because of the ceiling, into a three chambered burial area. It appeared empty apart from broken stones, pieces of dried wood and rags. Wilson was admiring the engravings upon the walls, now faded with age and smashed in many parts. "I take it that this magnificent looking fellow was Tha. They certainly used a lot of artistic license."

Owen chuckled; "He was small and plump in real life." He shone his mirror about; "Look for anything that appears newly disturbed." Alex and Jericho took one wall and started to search away from it - Owen and Wilson started from the opposite. They searched for several minutes without success until they met in the middle of the abandoned tomb. Jericho sighed; "Nothing."

Everyone stood in silence and stared about the room, then Owen grinned and shone his mirror against the wall opposite; "That figure of Tha is holding something. It looks like a square box." Everyone headed for the wall and Alex ran her soft hands over the engraving. "There's something under the paintwork." She said softly and Wilson produced his 'Swiss Army knife' and started to scrape about the paint and plaster. They stood back; "Well, he certainly lived up to his reputation as a bloody good magician, I have to admit that." Wilson eased the much sought-after mirror from the recess in the wall and handed it to Jericho. "I wonder who the hell Simhentrra's very loyal accomplice in all this was. I mean, they could have handed it over to Pharaoh and received a mass of gold - but they didn't. They probably carried out Simhentra's wishes - even after he was apparently dead. That's a real loyal friend."

Everyone smiled with relief at finally finding the mirror, then they heard Thy calling softly from the entrance. They made to the tomb opening and joined her, crouching low amongst the scattered stone blocks and mounds of sand.

"Tomb robbers." Thy whispered and they could see a group of men against the ravine wall opposite, emerging from a dark and shadowed clef in the ridge. They were carrying bags and boxes and worked in total silence, one old man carrying a wooden staff, appeared to be using hand signals to guide his fellow robbers. They disappeared into the darkness of the night without making a single sound. Thy leaned against the large stone and breathed deep a couple of times; Alex asked her what was wrong and Thy ran a hand across her face; "I know that old man and what I just saw could get me killed."

Jericho nodded and operated his mirror and the group found themselves back at Thy's fathers villa, where servants bought them wine and bread. Alex and Thy spoke together for some time before Jericho called everyone to order; it was time to return to the lighthouse and hand over the retrieved mirror to Angel Margret.

Everyone took their leave of young Thy and thanked her for all her assistance, especially Alex and the pair embraced like old friends. Then Thy was left alone in the house to contemplate what she had seen and the terrible consequences it could bring, if she ever revealed the identity of the old man who commanded the team of grave robbers.

Thy slumped upon her bed and sipped some wine, staring at the flickering lamps which illuminated her small bedroom. The scene she had witnessed earlier passed through her mind - yet again. She would have troubled sleep tonight and placed her wine goblet down and closed her tired eyes. Thy slept badly, turning frequently, wrapped in a single sheet.

Something made her wake suddenly and she sat up. Talin and three soldiers were standing at the base of her bed. She stifled a scream with a hand across her mouth and pulled the sheet around herself. Talin grinned broadly; "Well my little maid to a fake Priestess, the King would really like to speak to you."
He gestured to his soldiers, and they grabbed Thy, binding her arms and hands. She said nothing but breathed deeply as they dragged her from her father's house into the dark night.

11. SAME PLACE - NEW PROBLEM?

Jericho placed the file down upon the desk and rubbed his face with both hands. He looked up as Owen stuck his head around the door; "Alex and Wilson will be back from Human Records in a few minutes." He informed Jericho and sat in a chair opposite with hands upon his knees. The message 'little Ivan' had delivered was not good news. Thy, their human agent had been taken by the 'Dark Pharaoh' who wanted to find out where Alex had disappeared to. Luckily, he did not connect her or her companions to Simhentra's theft of 'his mirror' and it only concerned his desires for the woman [Alex] who had played the Priestess of Isis. Owen shook his head; "He's a persistent old pervert, I'll give him that." Jericho nodded and tapped the file; "This would never have happened to Thy in the original Time-Line. But because she assisted us and fell afoul of Pharaoh, the Timeline could now change, and Margret wants it sorted out."

"We just heard about Thy; what's the plan Jericho?" Wilson sauntered through the door and dropped into a nearby chair and after a few moments Alex swept in and eased herself into her favourite armchair. "I really don't fancy meeting that dirty old Pharaoh again, but we do need to rescue Thy from his clutches - thank heaven he doesn't associate her with that bloody mirror." Alex accepted a brandy from Mr. Harris and sipped it slowly, adding: "But how can we do that? - everyone in that time and place would recognise us."

"They would certainly remember you and that dress." Wilson chuckled and accepted the file from Jericho. "Alex has a really good point there Jericho; how can we return without being recognised?" Owen accepted a glass from Mr. Harris and sat back in his chair, looking quite concerned. Jericho sighed; "Well, we certainly have to do something, we've all seen what the 'Dark Pharaoh' is capable of and there's no way we're leaving Thy at his mercy." Everyone nodded their agreement at that.

Owen placed both hands upon his head and stared at the ceiling. He then sat up; "Simhentra never blabbed about our involvement in retrieving the mirror, we know that because Pharaoh didn't link Thy with the disappearance of his precious mirror - just with our little deception - he certainly admired you as a magician and that could be useful."

Wilson sighed; "You seem to forget that Pharaoh's soldiers came to Simhentra's villa while we were there; the servants are bound to have informed Talin about that and then it's no small leap to link us with him [Simhentra]. But I am puzzled why Pharaoh hasn't linked Thy to the mirror - she was Alex's maid after all, and he would know - that Alex was at the villa with her."

Owen had to agree with Wilson's deduction and sat back in silence. Everyone turned to the door as Mr. Harris appeared and whispered into Jericho ear, which made him smile. "It appears that Inspector Fabian has arrived to thank us for recovering his team members mirror and update us on young Thy. He's just returned from there."

Mr. Harris showed the Temporal Inspector in, and Jericho introduced Fabian Bissit to his team. He was a short plump man wearing a fine three-piece suit with shirt and tie - but everyone noticed the bright red training shoes that he wore. Fabian sported a black 'goatee' beard and a red beret. He was regarded as a 'little eccentric' or slightly crazy, according to Owen. He was delighted to be invited to dinner and the team made for the dining room, quietly chatting amongst themselves.

Wilson, with a little grin on his face, just had to ask Alex; "When Jericho did the trick with the empty chair that amazed everyone back there, Owen and I knew that you would simply operate your mirror and disappear; then return." Alex nodded; "Yes, quite simple really, so what bothers you about that?"

Wilson sighed; "Where the hell did you hide the mirror in that bloody skimpy outfit?"

Alex chuckled and pointed to her hair. Owen grinned; "Of course, you could get a dining table in that bloody wig, never mind a little mirror!" Alex rolled her eyes; "Some bloody detectives you two are!" They laughed quietly amongst themselves until dinner was started.

Fabian sat smiling, as he anticipated the famed cooking of Mrs. Harris and the conversation turned to young Thy - he certainly had some good news on that score. He slurped his soup and between spoonful's explained that Thy's fiancé - the big Nubian Captain - had returned to claim his young bride and wasn't happy about Pharaoh keeping her prisoner, until she told him about the whereabouts of 'Lady Isis'. So the brave young man broke into the palace one dark night and the pair escaped - after he killed a couple of guards. They fled to Kadesh, where the King there, granted them sanctuary and the captain became a Commander in the King's army. They are now married; quite happily it would appear.

Alex actually clapped at that statement and lifted her glass to the pair; Fabian and her teammates joined her for that toast. The relief amongst the Temporal Detectives was palatable and the atmosphere at the dinner table had changed completely. Fabian went on to explain, as the chicken in white wine was served, that Pharaoh's sickly young Queen had died, and he still had no son's by his two royal concubines. He was not a happy man by all accounts; prowling the palace at night and drinking to excess.

Alex asked if he had any news about poor Simhentra and Fabian sadly shook his head - nothing had been uncovered about the young magician's whereabouts, but he had some news about the slave girl Lulha. Apparently, she had run away from her master - which carried the death penalty - and was in hiding, in Kadesh. He didn't drop the bombshell about her until the pudding course arrived.

"The poor girl gave birth in that country and unfortunately died from complications of the birth. There would have been no one to care for the infant, since Lulha had no family living there. The child was, of course, Pharaoh's man Talin's baby. The little boy was clearly of Nubian ancestry and was taken in by a kind young couple, who raised him as one of their son's.

Fabian grinned and lifted his glass; "The little boy fitted in quite nicely with his new family despite being of mixed blood because the couple was Thy and her Nubian husband!" Alex nodded with real delight at that turn of events, then came the bombshell as the biscuits and cheese was served. "She may have bumped off her old master - I think she had pretty good cause to do so - but she must have felt something for her new master Simentra because after fleeing from Talin, the pair was on the run together for some time. She shared his poverty and fear, constantly on the move and hiding. She stayed loyal to him until death." Fabien helped himself to some blue Stilton Cheese and a couple of crackers, adding: "I take it you worked out that Lulha was the one, who hid the mirror in the old tomb, on Simhentra's final instructions before fleeing to Kadesh. You have to give her credit for that sort of loyalty."

Owen grinned and whispered to Alex; "How the hell did we miss that one?" But the Inspector had one lesser 'bombshell' to drop. The dinner party broke up and Fabian took his leave, but not before informing Alex that she was almost a legend in the Temporal Detectives Department. She was quite puzzled by that and asked why.

He now grinned; "Well, that incredible dress that you almost wore; someone lifted a picture of you from the life tape of that time and copies are appearing everywhere; I even have one!" He bowed, kissed her hand and left the slightly shocked Alex standing in the study. Owen and Wilson said a hasty good night to her and tried to head for their rooms - but she stood in the doorway; unsmiling and held out her hand: "Thank you boys, I will take them now."

Both sighed and very reluctantly handed the pictures over quite slowly, then sheepishly departed for their rooms in silence. Jericho sat by the study fire and allowed himself a small laugh. Alex bid him good night and ripped up the pictures; throwing them into the blazing fire and went to bed a little happier. Jericho sipped his brandy and smiled, he reached into his jacket pocket and pulled the picture out and studied it; "Very nice, but nothing on seeing the real thing." He whispered and laughed quietly - again. He sighed deeply and tossed the photo upon the fire, finished his drink and headed for bed.

He passed a happy Mr. Parker chasing a tennis ball down the stairs and stopped to pat the cat. "Alexandra and Elizabeth are much alike." He whispered and watched the cat disappear down the hall with his ball. Jericho undressed and slipped into bed and lay staring at the ceiling; he thought about Simhentra lost between the worlds of life and death. But he knew that he would be recovered – in a way – and would have some pretty crazy and interesting adventures in Edwardian London with a certain Miss Dorothy Hadden and her brother. That made Jericho smile a little and he fell asleep.

NOTES:
The young magician Simhenta-Kara is a major character in the **"MISS DOROTHY HADDEN"** Series of books by the same

author. Pharaoh Amenhotep V also appears in a single episode of that series.

EPISODE 6: "ALEXANDRA ENCOUNTERS THE OTHER NAPOLEON BONAPARTE."

EPISODE PROLOGUE: "Alexandra is with the team in 1814, investigating Napoleon's new mysterious mistress who has jumped back from 1864 and intends to change the great man's fate. The team hatches an audacious plan to trick the emperor and discover his new mistress's plans and thwart them. Which means Alexandra has to lure the emperor away from the scheming woman and she certainly has the talent to do that?"

60 Minutes approx. **Episode Warnings:**
Smoking – Alcohol – Strong language [including racial slurs] – Violence [including some sexual threats and BDSM] – Strong graphic sexual references – Horror – References to violence.

NOTES: This is the **ADULT** version of the original story which is published and appears in the **TEMPORAL DETECTIVES:** Series 3 – Episode 9 entitled: **"NAPOLEON'S CHINESE CABINET OF MAGIC – PART 1."**

CAUTION: Recommended for **18+ only.**

1. A GIFT FROM ONE GOD TO ANOTHER.

Captain Jean Pullaire stared at the crate which had been lowered with great care onto the polished wooden floor. He rubbed his chin in puzzlement and spoke quietly to the silent footmen standing next to him; "Fetch Colonel Le Grande and inform his majesty that the gift from the Chinese Emperor has arrived and get some labourers to open the damn crate."

He turned and smiled at the three strange little men with small feathers adorning their little black hats; he had to admit that he had never seen a real live Chinaman before and these three resembled exactly the drawings he had viewed in his youth. "I have sent for men to open the crate, Lord Yin." He nodded at the smallest of the trio, who bowed and in prefect French thanked the captain for his assistance.

From around his neck, Lord Yin produced a gold key fixed upon a gold chain and spoke directly to Captain Pullaire; "I need to place this key directly into your God's hand – it was placed directly into mine by my God Emperor Yongyan - and must be passed on in the same manner." The little Chinaman bowed yet again and smiled.

Several burly, rough labourer's had arrived with removed hats, accompanied by Monsieur Cission; the Emperors Chief Carpenter who viewed the heavy crate with an expert eye. "Use the bloody bars carefully you morons." He said, wiping his face with a clean polishing rag. The old man sighed; not more bloody pieces of expensive wood to maintain – the Palace of Fontainebleau was full of the stuff - and now bloody foreigners from the other side of the world were sending their gilded crap!

He stared at the three China amen and blew his nose hard into the polishing cloth; "We'll undress her gently Captain." Monsieur Cission smiled at Pullaire with a mouthful of yellow teeth and wiped snot from his heavy grey moustache, adding; "Will his majesty be present when we open her?"

That question was answered by the regulated stamp of army boots upon the shining wooden floor and through the doors, hurriedly opened by a sweaty Footman, came a dozen of the 'Old Guard'. With precision they took up positions around the room and snapped to attention at the command of their young

Lieutenant. Pullaire and Cissions exchanged glances; Lieutenant Vaccaro was not a popular officer or man, who apparently held his Commission directly because of who his father may be: The Emperor.

"I see the little poodle still hasn't found a hat small enough for his tiny brain." Cission whispered to the captain who wagged a disapproving finger at the far too blunt carpenter; but smiled broadly. The Lieutenant's hat was clearly too large and had been the subject of arguments between him and the Quartermaster of the Regiment; without success it appears.

Quartermaster Possini had informed the young man that Officer's supply their own uniform and that naturally; included the hat. But Vaccaro had been unable to find a decent Milliner to furnish such a small hat at a reasonable price – his ungenerous nature added to his unpopular character. So, in desperation, he had purchased the hat from another young Lieutenant who was dying in the local infirmary from wounds received in Prussia; the fact that he gave the young widow a handful of centimes for it, really did his popularity no good. To quote many; 'he was as unpopular as would be finding Wellington in the Emperors bathtub.'

Vaccaro gave Pullaire a clumsy salute and announced that Colonel Le Grande was attending the emperor and they would appear within minutes. Pullaire returned the salute but said nothing. The appearance of Marshal Nay in the chamber signalled the arrival of Napoleon. A large gaggle of Officers and Politian's poured into the small chamber, splitting into little groups and all staring at the strangers who stood quietly by the crate, which was being opened with great care under Cission's direction.

Napoleon sauntered into the room and all conversations stopped. Le Grande spoke directly to him and pointed at the Chinese group; "The small chink is called Lord Yin, he's apparently their Emperors Ambassador, I don't know about the other two, you're Majesty."

The three bowed low as Pullaire whispered to Le Grande; "He speaks perfect French." Le Grande shrugged his shoulders and grunted; "Thank you Pullaire, now get on with it – the emperor is a busy man." Le Grande was not marked out for a career in Diplomacy. But he was a damn good Officer on the field of battle and possessed a characteristic that Napoleon looked for in all his officers; he was lucky. Le Grande had been shot off his horse on no less than four occasions and walked away with just scratches, and then during one battle, his churning stomach forced him to find a quiet clump of trees to relieve the pain. Squatting down with liquid fire emerging from his bowels, he saw through the trees that the Austrians had left a gap in their right flank to bring up the supply wagons. Clutching his trousers, Le Grande reported the mistake to Marshal Nay. French troops poured through the gap and the Austrians fled the battlefield in disarray. Napoleon had thanked the captain himself and quickly promoted him to Headquarters' staff with the rank of Colonel.

Napoleon gestured approvingly to Lord Yin and the little China man approached bowing quite low: "Your brother Emperor Yongyan sends greetings of love and friendship and hopes you will be pleased with this little gift." He offered the gold key and chain with both hands and Napoleon took it slowly and smiled; "Please inform your Emperor that I will be most pleased to accept any gift from my dear brother and send him my warm regards."

There were little gasps of admiration from the crowd as the final pieces of the dull grey crate were stripped away; revealing a black and silver cabinet decorated with astronomical symbols and gold dragons; it was tall as a man, wide as a double wardrobe and deep as a card table – it was simply magnificent - a real masterpiece.

Napoleon nodded his approval to Lord Yin who spoke quietly to the Emperor, positioning his back to all others; "My Lord, with such a gift that can only be shared amongst God's comes a responsibility; a great responsibility. You must never open or enter the cabinet during the hours of darkness and keep her locked at all times. Please keep that key upon your person, no mere mortal must have access to her; only you."

The Emperor looked quite puzzled by his comments and studied the simple gold key; "What does the cabinet contain my Lord Yin?" He asked and the strange little man smiled and ran his long fingernails through his grey beard; "Darkness and light your majesty." Lord Yin bowed low, then walked over to the cabinet and opened the doors; a stunning white light shone from the interior making everyone step back, but Napoleon felt himself drawn to it and peered inside, shielding his eyes a little. The interior panels were decorated with glass and silver and Napoleon realised at once; that none of the 'mirrors' showed a reflection.

He turned slowly to Lord Yin and said quietly; "How old is she?" Lord Yin held up his hands and said, "We believe that four such cabinets were created by the God TAI-SUI-XING and given as presents to the early Emperors of the great Chin dynasty; they came into being at the start of human time." He smiled and added; "The interior panels have been re-housed many times over the Centuries, the present construction is only some four hundred years old and so should last; at least that again."

Lord Yin bowed again and gestured to his two silent colleagues, who shuffled gracefully into the cabinet, and both bowed low. He turned to Napoleon and spoke quietly; "We must now return home and report all is well between the great European God and our father who resides in the Heavens. Farewell my Lord and remember that light is darkness to devils and darkness is light to them." Lord Yin stepped into the cabinet of TAI-SUI-XING and slowly closed the doors.

Everyone stood in silence for a few moments until Le Grande tapped gently on the doors and called out; "Lord Yin, what the fuck are you doing?" The emperor smiled and told Le Grande to open the cabinet and help the crazy Chinamen out of his gift.

Everyone was laughing until the doors were opened; the three Chinese men had vanished – completely. There was total silence in the room for some time until Marshal Ney shouted for guards to search the Palace and grounds for the mysterious visitors.

Napoleon and the carpenter Cission examined the cabinet closely and found it solid. He ordered Cission to have it removed to his private study and locked the doors with the gold key, which he hung about his neck. He gripped Cission by the shoulder and said quietly; "I have a task for you my old friend and it must be kept between the two of us." Cission nodded his head; the skilled old carpenter had known the emperor since the days of the French Revolution and he had always played straight and fair with the old man.

But no trace of the three Chinese 'Magicians' were ever found, and no-one was allowed near the gift without Napoleon's express permission; but the Emperor had more pressing matters to contend with: his abdication.

2. A STAR FALLS FROM HEAVEN.

Napoleon quietly unlocked the rear study door and peered out into the corridor; two of his 'Old Guard' were posted at the far end. Napoleon relocked the door and sat down at his large ornate desk and held his head with both hands.

He must have sat for some minutes before he heard the gentle tap from the Chinese cabinet. He rose slowly and walked over to it; carefully unlocking the doors and stepping back. The doors opened and she stepped from the cabinet into his study. Lady Helena Covington smiled at her lover, and they embraced for some minutes. "I do love you in dresses of this time; they suit you much better than those damn tents you wear back there." Napoleon kissed the bare cleavage she was showing in her low cut 'Regency' dress. Her breasts had been pushed well up and if she sneezed; her nipples would escape; along with most of her breasts.

Tall and thin with dark Raven hair and soft brown eyes, Lady Helena was considered a beauty at the Royal Court of Queen Victoria in 1864. She had married the wealthy Lord Covington at just eighteen; he was forty-five, fat and failed to bath regally. But he owned a fabulous Chinese cabinet that, it was rumoured, had belonged to Emperor Napoleon I.

Lady Helena had only been married some six weeks and already had enough of her boring, lethargic husband and she avoided his company, as best she could; Covington House had some seventy rooms and she still felt that wasn't enough space to keep away from him. At least he left her alone in the bedroom; he was as impotent as he was smelly.

Then one day she found a fabulous Chinese cabinet hidden in the attic's and wondered why such a stunning piece of furniture wasn't on display in the house's main rooms. Her husband wouldn't explain anything; except that she was to keep away from it and he actually ordered her to do so. The very next morning, after Lord Covington had gone to the City of London, she was back in the attic and trying to open the cabinet. It was locked tight with no key apparent.

It took several days before Helena found that the key was kept in her husband's Library, inside a book about Napoleon and she rushed to the attic and triumphally opened the cabinet. She noticed immediately that there was no reflection showing from the mirrors it contained. Some strange force compelled her to step in and close the door. Lady Helena glanced down at the large book she was carrying; 'The life and times of Napoleon Bonaparte.' She chuckled to herself and tried to open the door - it was locked - but she still held the key!

Panicking a little at first, she struggled with the doors until she heard a voice outside; "Please, please help me. I can't get the doors open and strangely enough; there are no dam key-holes inside here." She shouted and heard the door locks being turned; they must have had a key too - but who was it?

She stepped from the cabinet and stared at the man who had rescued her; it was Napoleon Bonaparte, who had been dead some 43 years, but was very much alive. He took her hand and kissed it. He explained about the cabinet and what had happened to her for some minutes, and they drank wine together. A walk in the gardens, of Fontainebleau Palace, put her mind to rest about possibly going insane.

Two hours after arriving in 1814 France, Lady Helena Covington was 'cuckolding' her husband with the French Emperor [who had actually died before she was even born] they enjoyed passionate sex on the floor of the Imperial bedroom which included a sexual activity that was frowned upon by the Church and forbidden in law. Helena couldn't actually believe what Napoleon was doing to her bum and she cried softly throughout the ordeal; but made no effort to stop him.

He had told his new lover, that clothes from the 'hereafter' were bloody awful and ugly. So, he arranged for some dresses of the 'Regency' period to be made for her - with a particularly low cut bodice - and she utterly delighted in wearing the tighter, clinging dresses of his time, than the current fashion [of 1864] which she now considered shapeless, awkward and about sexually attractive as wearing a tent.

Now, almost four months into their 'time-travelling' romance, she had arrived to comfort her lover on a very important day; his abdication. But wrapped tightly in brown paper and string was a modest little book; it contained details of Emperor Napoleon's last 100 days as Emperor - including the all-important - world changing Battle of Waterloo. It was hidden in Lady Helena's travelling bag. A little present for her lover that didn't detail his death but could change his imminent future. She had, wisely, removed the pages that dealt with his final demise.

"I hate those dresses I'm forced to wear, as you say, it's like wearing a bloody tent my darling." She kissed him quite passionately and he pushed both hands up the back of her dress and gripped her bum. "I still think it strange that you are not even born yet my little dove." Napoleon muttered and they exchanged kisses again; his excited fingers, reluctantly, left her arse and he pulled at the back of her dress. She slowly began to strip off her clothes; "I want you naked." he whispered, and Lady Helena stepped from his arms and pulled her dress down. She was naked apart from her little pink shoes.

"Take me." Was all Lady Helena said - and Napoleon didn't need to be told twice. Their passion was satisfied some hours later and both lay on the bed, staring at each other. The emperor rose and threw a dressing gown about himself; "I have an unpleasant meeting with my ministers in a few minutes. I will be back in about an hour." Lady Helena grabbed a sheet and half covered herself, she leaned back on two pillows and closed her eyes. The little bedroom clock was chiming one o'clock. She sat upright and stared at the private doorway to the bedroom. The emperor, in uniform, stood smiling at her.

Lady Helena grinned and pulled the sheet from her naked body and lay back, opening her legs. She said nothing and neither did the emperor. They made love for another hour before the emperor, yet again, had to go. She lay breathing heavy for a few minutes and then heard the clock chiming above the fireplace. She stared at it for a few seconds; then realised it must be losing time. It was still only two o'clock, she was a little puzzled by that.

She lay in the bed and watched Napoleon dress and go. She leaned back and sat upright - again. This time surprised; The Emperor was in the doorway; why had he returned so quickly? She pushed her hair from her face and smiled a little. He was pulling off his jacket; "I told you I wouldn't be long, my darling." She just stared at him; utterly amazed at his stamina. But laid back on the covers and watched him undress.

That afternoon Napoleon finished his bath and dressed slowly.

The meeting with his Marshal's had not ended happily; every single one had demanded he abdicate to prevent the Allied armies swarming into Paris. He had been particularly hurt by the apparent betrayal of Marshall Nay. He stared at the colourful calendar hanging on his dressing room wall; April 11th, 1814. If only he had more time...a little more time, but time was so precious now and trickling through his fingers like beach sand. He had run out of that most vital commodity: time.

Napoleon had dressed without a servant and walked slowly to his study. He sat at his desk and stared at the single, large piece of paper that was the only item upon the large ornate table: The Abdication document. He rested his head on his hands and memories and thoughts clouded into his very troubled mind. He must have sat for some minutes like that and then slowly lifted his head; staring at the Chinese cabinet; the emperor smiled.

3. WHAT COULD BE?

Alex looked quite stunning; even Wilson and Owen had to admit that. She smiled at Jericho and nodded her head; "You really do carry a uniform well. I'm quite pleasantly surprised." She also grinned at Wilson who really did look resplendent in his servant's livery, but he didn't smile; "Why do I always have to play the bloody loyal black servant to his white master?" He groaned; then smiled.

Alex chuckled; "Because you do it so well!" Wilson shook his head and stuck up a single finger, then muttered; "Why can't I, just for once, play the master and Jericho the servant?" Alex patted the big man; "You know it really doesn't bother you; you don't have his enormous ego to please!" Jericho just sighed and finished checking his costume.

Owen looked himself up and down; he really didn't appreciate his young gentleman's outfit of the time. "The bleeding trousers are far too tight; no wonder they were always at war." He muttered and adjusted the crotch of his trousers - again. Wilson slapped his hand away; "Jesus, any excuse to play with yourself." Owen stuck up a single finger and pulled at his trousers yet again.

Everyone chuckled and Jericho placed his Colonel's hat upon his head; "Now, now children, we ALL look really good in our new play clothes. Let's get going, Supplies have everything ready." He smiled at Alex; "How's your French Madame?" Alex curtsied; "Mon français va bien, à toi?" Jericho just nodded and stared at himself in the mirror; "Not bad. Maybe I should have been a Military man - like my father wanted - and not a bloody lawyer." He said softly to no-one. They all headed for the light room and then had to wait - much to the amusement of Alex - for young Ruth to appear. She was to be Alex's Lady Maid. No woman of quality would dare travel without one, in the time period that the team was heading for.

Ruth arrived - apologising to everyone - and received a 'wolf whistle' from Owen. She too, looked quite beautiful in his eyes. "I love the clothes of this period!" She exclaimed and joined the team. Jericho just sighed and the little group departed for France in 1814.

The carriage moved quite slowly through the mud of the Fontainebleau Road and rocked steadily. Ruth had her head against Alex's shoulder - she was a little tired - Ruth wasn't used to jumping into the light and like many who weren't accustomed to travelling in that way, felt tiredness sweep over her. Alex patted her hand and smiled at Jericho and Owen, who sat opposite. "A few hours and she'll be fine. In the 20th century they would have called it 'jet-lag'." Owen nodded; "Yep, our young Ruthie has 'Time-lag'."

Wilson leaned through the small window above their heads - he was riding with the driver - and said quietly; "About another twenty minutes." Jericho waved his hand in acknowledgement and turned to Alex; "Napoleon has acquired a new young mistress who is a total mystery to everyone at the Palace. Even Marshall Nay doesn't have a clue who she is. The place has hundreds of servant's and Imperial staff, yet none has caught, as much as a glance of her. How she comes and goes is another mystery, considering the security around the emperor. "

Owen sighed; "We know she exists because Napoleon's boot maker mentions her in a letter to his brother in 1816. He was convinced she was an English spy and he mentioned, but didn't elaborate, about what happened to poor Colonel Durand. So, you had better watch yourself Jericho!" He smiled as Ruth roused herself and sat up; "Who's an English spy?" She asked. Owen said quietly; "Napoleon's mysterious mistress." Ruth nodded; "How many did he have; mysterious or not?"

Owen chuckled; "At this time and place, he had about nine." Ruth looked a little amazed and turned to Alex; "How did he find the bloody time to conquer Europe?" That did make Alex chuckle - she didn't know the answer to that.

"And I believe she could be the key to the strange changes that the current time-line is suffering. I've seen the alternative versions of history and they all directly start here at this time and place. The only difference IS the Emperor's new mistress. We need to find and identify her - urgently." Jericho said and checked his mirror for any mission updates. Alex adjusted her breasts and groaned; "The dresses are gorgeous, but don't suit women with ample breasts." She said to Ruth, who just grinned.

"Yeah, but you won't find a single male complaining about that." Owen muttered and looked out the window, adding; "The palace is bloody gorgeous too." The grand Palace of Fontainebleau had now appeared, and they were approaching - slowly because of the mud. Owen pointed out that mud had affected the outcome at Waterloo and exactly a century later, battles on the Western Front.

Wilson's head appeared and he smiled at Alex, fiddling with her bosom; "If either of those lovely big pups need a new home, I'm your man. By the way, we're entering the Palace through the South gate - apparently Jericho's not important enough - as a mere Colonel - to use the Grand Entrance." He wrapped his dark cloak about his big shoulders and chuckled. Jean Hessaine [the driver and a human agent of Jericho's for this time and place] laughed too.

"Steady there Wilson, I wouldn't mind taking both home myself; with Alex attached of course - She's about the most stunning woman I've ever seen, and I've seen some real crackers here and at Versailles. Old Boney [nickname of Emperor Napoleon] will be drooling in his soup at her; I can definitely tell you that." Jean smiled and slapped the reins; he didn't think much of Jericho's new team members - Owen and Alex - he had thoroughly enjoyed the company of Jericho's old team; Wilson, little Oscar - the crazy dwarf - and Jericho himself.

Jean recalled that the fourth member of Team 74 had been a real strange and moody bastard - he hardly said a word to Jean; or anybody else to be honest. But there was something about the bloody man that drew you to him, like a moth to a flame. [Jean is talking about Jericho's former Trainee Constable on Team 74: Conrad Bliss who was now the sergeant on Team 11 and is considered one of the finest detectives in the department.] Jean grunted; still Alex was a bonus - he would have fucked her at the drop of a hat; even if it damned his soul forever. That delicious thought was disturbed by Wilson pointing ahead; a small troop of cavalry was approaching.

"They check everyone and anything that gets within a few miles of old Boney." Jean nodded to Wilson, who learned through the window again and announced visitors. Jericho was handed an old leather document case by Owen who grinned at the girls; "Best behaviour now ladies - all smiles and bosom's - please!"

Alex stuck up a single finger and adjusted her dress - she was almost hanging out of it. "With those beauties staring at him, the young lieutenant won't be too interested in us or our travel papers." Owen chuckled and watched the cavalry troop approach.

Jericho flicked through the papers in his old briefcase and smiled to himself. The briefcase had travelled a few miles and many years with him now. He clearly remembered the first day - with the brand-new case under his arm - which he spent at Gray, Ogden & Davis - Solicitors. He was the new Junior partner of the famous old law firm. But his thoughts snapped back to here and now.

He smiled at Alex and Ruth; "Remember ladies, that if anyone will have information or knowledge of this mysterious woman, it will be the female staff and ladies of the court. I'm depending on you two and I know you'll come through." Both Alex and Ruth nodded as the carriage rolled to a stop and Wilson jumped down and opened the carriage door. Jericho stepped out and greeted the young Lieutenant, who dismounted with some grace from his sweating mare. Alex waved a fan over her face and stared at the strapping young man with dark hair and eyes. He was a very handsome man and moved with real strength and grace. He introduced himself as Lieutenant Henri Masion and smiled at Alex through the open coach door while speaking with Jericho. Alex couldn't help herself; she smiled back.

He insisted on escorting the carriage to the palace himself and rode next to the side that Alex sat, waving her fan over her face and occasionally sneaking a look at him astride his mare. She knew that she would enjoy being his other 'mare' and he certainly could ride her with the same skill. They arrived at the east entrance and were greeted by several footmen who removed the luggage. Apparently, they weren't important enough to use the grand entrance. A senior footman showed then to their suite which contained rooms for their servants. The Lieutenant accompanied them and said his goodbyes to the 'Colonel' and Alex, who allowed him to kiss her hand. No one saw the note she passed to him. He walked away smiling.

4. FONTAINEBLEAU PALACE.

Colonel Durand slapped his old briefcase down on the small ornate table and stared out the window at the rear grounds of the palace. He spoke in fluent French to his young Secretary; Monsieur Henri Le Gaurd. "Make sure you stick to old French - all the time - no slip up's. None." He cautioned Owen, who nodded and helped Wilson - now called Titus - to unpack the suitcases. "Alex and Ruth are just around the corner, in a beautiful suite decorated in the Chinese style. She always gets spoilt." Wilson muttered - in old French - and heaved the case upon the dark footlocker, at the bottom of the huge four poster bed.

Owen looked a little puzzled; "It's a strange tradition here that husbands and wives don't share the same rooms - why is that?" He asked Jericho, who chuckled; "So they could entertain their lovers without embarrassing each other. Fidelity was not a large concern in these decadent days."

"Well, Spoilt or not, she certainly got us noticed, even if we came through the tradesman entrance." Jericho smiled and added; "Apparently the Emperor rarely bothers to stick his head out and have a look at visitors arriving, but he did this morning." Wilson chuckled; "Those two footmen almost had a fist fight over who would carry her bloody bags."

Owen had slumped into a high back chair by the door and consulted his mirror. "Colonel Durand was tasked by General Charles Dulauloy to collate the possible numbers of new recruits that Napoleon could expect from the Northern Departments of France. Currently, history dictates that he arrived on the 13th of April 1814 - two days after the abdication. Still, it didn't matter, the news he carried would not have pleased the emperor."

Jericho sat on the bed and looked around the room; "We'll, we've arrived on the 9th of April with the same unwelcome message; very few recruits available. That won't change anything. But we only have a couple of days to discover how that damn woman changes history. I've seen the results of the possible changes to the current timeline and it's drastic, really drastic: Napoleon wins at Waterloo and Britain is forced to leave most of Europe under his boot."

Wilson pulled a bottle of brandy from the canvas bag he carried over his shoulder and smiled; "Well, a couple of these won't hurt." Owen jumped from his seat and fetched glasses from the ornate cabinet near the writing desk. They all heard the soft knock at the door. Wilson pulled it open and smiled at Alex and Ruth; "Jesus girl, you must have smelt me opening the damn brandy bottle!"

Alex just grinned and swept majestically into the room followed by her 'maid' and plonked herself down on the big bed next to Jericho. She accepted a glass from Owen and Wilson poured her a large one. "Well, we off to a good start, rather unusually - according to Napoleon's Personal secretary - you have been invited to dinner tonight with the emperor." Jericho nodded his approval at that and said softly; "I rather think you have been invited and he had to ask me to attend because I'm your husband."

Wilson chuckled at that; "You don't think he has mistress number ten in mind?" Owen offered Ruth a glass of brandy which she declined; "Any cold lemonade?" She asked and was slightly disappointed that there was none. Jericho lay back on the bed, arms folded, and stared at the canopy of the grand bed. "I want you to play up to him Alexandra but keep him at arm's length. He's used to having beautiful women fall at his feet and I think that one who doesn't play the game will really mess with his ego. Forbidden fruit and all that."

Alex smiled; "I certainly won't find it hard to play the faithful and dutiful wife; I did that for my entire life." Then sighed; "Most of the time!" Everyone laughed at that remark. Ruth eased herself down on the chair that Owen had pulled up for her and rubbed her ankles; "I don't like these high shoes; they rub my feet."

She then turned to Alex; "Don't forget your taking coffee and cake with Madame Nay and some ladies of the Court this afternoon. You'll need to change into an afternoon dress, you can't wear your travelling clothes to that." Jericho sat slowly up and smiled broadly; "Now that's what I call a good start. If anyone will know the court gossip about Napoleon's new mistress; it will be the ladies of the court. All girls together and all that." He was well pleased with that turn of events.

Madame Aglae - Duchess of Elchingen [Marshal Nay's wife] - watched Alex carefully over the rim of her delicate coffee cup. She certainly could appreciate the real beauty of another woman and Alex - to her - was something special. She smiled; "Your French is quite flawless my dear, but your Italian origins do appear in your voice." The other ladies all murmured their agreement with Madame Algae's deduction. Madame Margaret Du Loupe [Napoleon's current mistress - the official one!] placed her cup down and smiled; "I understand that you're from the Italian state of Cappanni?"

Alex nodded; "My father was Count there, but now my brother Philippe is Count." She sipped her coffee and wondered - strongly - about grabbing another piece of that gorgeous apple pie. She resisted that desire with some reluctance. Madame Margaret tapped her chin; "I am surprised that you are married to a mere Colonel. I mean you're a Lady of noble birth and the Colonel - a fine man, I'm sure - is from a family of bookkeepers or do I have that wrong?" The other ladies restrained their laughter quietly.

Alex smiled and dabbed her mouth with the lace napkin; "My husband is my best friend and my only lover. Other men would seem....well, inadequate compared to how he pleases me, and he really does please me." There were little gasps of mock shock and Madame Algae chuckled outright. "Oh, my dear, you will have us filled with envy with such a confession." Everyone laughed at that; but in a very ladylike manner!

Ruth sat in the quiet corner of the large stateroom and drank coffee and played cards with the other 'Ladies Maids'. They were all clearly intrigued with her Mistress, Lady Alex. They were all much older than Ruth and really queried how such a young girl could hold such a position. Ruth explained - with some sincerity in her voice - that her mother had been Lady Alex's childhood nanny and when she died, Alex had made her daughter - Ruth -

her maid despite her young age, so that she could stay with the family.

"It's good to see such loyalty running both ways." Madame Anna nodded her head and patted Ruth's hand. She was Madame Margaret's maid and knew nearly everything about her mistress's latest catch; the emperor himself. The discussion at the Maid's table was lively and quite coarse at times. Ruth actually found herself going a little red at some of the conversation's content. The other maids thought that was just wonderful and cute.

The little coffee and cake party broke up and the ladies retired to their rooms with their maids in tow, to dress for the Evening Dinner party. Alex and Ruth walked back to their suite in silence. There were staff and servants down every corridor and their discussion had only one topic: The Emperor's imminent abdication
.
An unsmiling young footman with a pock marked face opened the door to their rooms and bowed a little. He informed Ruth that Colonel Durand had been summoned by Marshal Nay to give his report on the Northern Departments. Ruth thanked him and both girls waited until he closed the door and left the corridor before speaking. Alex sprawled on the bed and chuckled; "That went well, but we learnt sod all about the new mistress." That's when she saw the smile on Ruth's face and sat up. "Go on, spill the beans; you're bursting to tell me!"

5. SURPRISES IN THE BATHROOM.

Alex had to smile at what Ruth disclosed and swept her hand across the bathtub and really looked forward to soaking before the evening entertainment. Ruth was sorting out the travel bags and laying out dresses for Alex's choice; she really loved having a real ladies maid again. She started to undress and was soon standing quite naked apart from her jewelry and shoes. That's when she watched in utter amazement, as the large portrait of some French King slid back, and Napoleon stepped into her bathroom. He was wearing gold-coloured slippers and a fur lined dressing gown with the Imperial eagle logo on the pocket.

He held a finger up to his lips and smiled. Alex folded her arms and just stared at him. He walked right up to her and rubbed his face; "Madame Durand, you are a real beauty. Normally, I wait some time before I take a woman I don't know. But in your case, I will definitely make an exception." He pulled off his robe and kicked the slippers away. The emperor was stark naked, and Alex glanced down and her eyes widened. A bloody stallion would be jealous of what hung between his legs, and it was moving and growing! That took Alex back a little; hadn't history been unkind to Napoleon with rumours about his 'small' organ? Someone actually stole the Emperor's penis at one point [thankfully after his bloody death!] but its size was never mentioned in any chapters of his many biographies apparently.

He gripped his cock with one hand and the other gestured to the carpet. "Please kneel young lady and give this some attention with that sweet mouth of yours." She slowly obeyed and accepted his big cock into her mouth. He groaned and smiled, patting her hair; "Good girl. You know you must obey your beloved Emperor in all matters and that includes cock sucking and fucking." He chuckled and clearly enjoyed the expert attention his erection was receiving.

As she was caressing and licking his cock, he pointed to his discarded robe; "In the left pocket is a small jar of pure clean cream. You will find that it will facilitate my friend entering your beautifully shaved honey pot. I find that your preparation of your fanny like a little girl's, quite exciting, though unusual." Alex managed to grab the robe and remove the jar and still please him. She smeared the cream over his cock and used plenty of it. She used the remainder to lubricate her own vagina. He knelt down and told her to turn around. "I will enjoy your charms like a stallion takes a mare."

Alex was bent over and without another word he mounted her, slowly and gently at first and very gently thrusted a few times. Alex groaned a little; his big cock had filled her vagina and she could feel practically every inch - or centimeter, since this was France! - "Try and stay still and quiet my dear. We don't want to distress your lovely maid by screaming and struggling." With those words, he started to thrust harder and harder. Alex actually clamped a hand over her mouth to stifle her little screams of pleasure. Alex couldn't believe how long he lasted, thrusting quick and hard; he was clearly a very experienced and skillful lover.

It had been quite a while and Alex was getting a little tender despite the very welcome lubricant. Finally, he groaned softy and called for God. Alex was relieved to feel his seed spurting into her. He lay over her, hands placed on the carpet and kissed her back and neck. But stayed inside her. One hand patted her trembling buttocks and whispered; "I am well pleased that, like your husband, you are a loyal servant of the emperor." and chuckled, wiping sweat from his face with the sleeve of his robe. They remained for a few minutes and Alex felt the big cock being pulled gently from her. A little trickle of cum ran down her thighs and dripped onto the carpet. He gave her bum a gentle slap and pointed to the small puddle. "Clean that up with your tongue my dear. It shouldn't be wasted."

He sat leaning against the bathtub and watched as Alex, still on all fours licked up his seed. He pulled her to him and cradled her in his arms, pushing his flaccid cock between the cheeks of her arse and holding her quite tightly. He caressed her big breasts and pulled gently at her erect nipple. Finally, he kissed her shoulders and neck and slowly stood, still keeping a firm grip on her. They stood and he ran his hands over her body. "I enjoyed that Madame Durand and I will enjoy you again. But I wouldn't tell 'old Boney' that I have fucked you before him. He gets a little upset at that." He laughed out loud and let the totally puzzled and shocked Alex go, she stared at him as he dressed and pulled his slippers on. "What the fuck do you mean?" She spluttered and then realised just who he was.

Monsignor Boucher [the emperor's incredible body double] grinned and placed a little kiss on her cheek. "Don't worry my dear; I won't ruin your chances of becoming the Imperial Whore. I will say nothing about this if you allow me to fuck you again." He headed for the secret door and smiled; "I'll arrange to have you sent for on a regular basis. There are a few tricks I wish to show you. When buried deep inside your cunt, I noticed your beautiful little bum hole. I'll be stretching that regularly. Goodbye my little slut until next time." He disappeared through the door and the painting slid back, leaving a stunned Alex standing alone in the bathroom.

Her head swimming with a mix of anger and disgust, she kicked off her shoes and jumped in the bath. She really did yelp; the water was stone cold. Ruth stuck her head around the door and asked what was wrong. Alex hid her tears from her and muttered about Ruth fetching some more hot water, which she did.

Alex decided that she would keep this little discovery to herself for now. The embarrassment of telling her colleagues how she found out that Napoleon had an exact 'body Double' didn't make her very happy. Ruth returned with a bucket of hot water and tipped it in. Alex lay in the bath and was a little ashamed that she had fallen for Monsignor Boucher's simple trick and wondered how many other woman had fallen for it. She grimaced as she remembered licking his cum from the bloody carpet, in front of his bloody grinning face. She would get revenge on him for treating her like a whore and the bastard certainly wouldn't be shoving that monster up her bum any time in the future.

Ruth's voice penetrated her dark thoughts, shouting about Alex getting out the damn bath before her skin resembled a prune. Alex sighed and stepped from the bath and dried herself. She stared at the carpet and noticed the small jar of cream laying there. She quickly picked it up and threw it into a nearby flowerpot. She strode into the bedroom and Ruth dressed her quietly, the girl knew Lady Alex well enough to know that she had some sort of mood on but didn't ask her about it. After brooding for an hour Alex returned to her bedroom and removed her clothes - except her shoes - and grabbed up the cream from the pot plant. She called Ruth to fetch her cloak and decided a walk in the gardens would help. Alex hoped the first man she met knew how to fuck a woman.

6. FONTAINEBLEAU PALACE'S GRAND GARDENS.

Alex needed to calm down and so Ruth threw her cloak about Alex's shoulders, and she walked in the grand gardens of Fontainebleau Palace. She ran a fan across her face and enjoyed the incredible, beautiful sight of the formal gardens; she turned and saw a gardener pushing a squeaking barrow filled with grass shavings and dead plants towards a small brick and glass building, discretely hidden amongst large bushes and small trees. Alex found herself smiling at the young man as he stopped and tipped his hat to her. He was about six feet tall with obvious muscles under his dirty thin cotton shirt. He didn't need to 'work out' he had been working hard - manually - in the gardens since he started his apprenticeship when he was thirteen. That was ten years ago.

Alex walked slowly down the terrace steps and joined him, waving him to walk on. He smiled and replaced his hat. She noticed that he smelt of earth, flowers and sweat. "And where are taking that Sir?" indicating the full wheelbarrow. He grinned and nodded towards the hidden building. "To the compost heap behind there Madame."

Alex waved her fan over her face and allowed her cloak to fall open a little and the young man wiped his face; strangely enough, not surprised that the 'lady' was stark naked underneath apart from her shoes!

The young man pushed the barrow with renewed interest and said quietly; "How may I be of assistance Madame?" Alex fluttered the fan in his smiling face, leaving her cloak open so that he could see what was on offer. "I'm sure you understand what I need....want young man. Do you have any objections to helping me out?"

The gardener almost laughed outright - but restrained himself - as he stared at her naked beauty under that cloak. "I have no objections whatsoever Madame." He replied quietly and the pair reached the outbuilding. He dropped the barrow and looking around, opening the old door which desperately needed a coat of paint. "After you Madame." Alex swept pass him, gently touching his weather worn face with her fan. He looked around again and smiling broadly, slammed the door behind him.

They stood looking at each other, amongst the broken and discarded pots, trays, racks, shovels and bundles of twine. Alex allowed her cloak to slip from her shoulders and whispered; "Take me like you would a tavern whore on a Saturday night in the town." He smiled at her naked body, especially those magnificent big tits with the large dark nipples and threw down his hat; "I certainly fucking will Madame." Pulling off his rough shirt and tugging down his trousers. His boots came off in seconds; he hadn't tied the laces because his feet had been playing him up.

Alex dropped her fan onto the discarded cloak and smiled; he was a common Adonis; his body was fine-tuned by years of hard labour. Then she saw his erecting manhood, growing and moving before her wide eyes. "Young man, you must be the best equipped gardener in Fontainebleau...no France!" She said with real anticipation in her voice. He chuckled and bowed; "I wish I had a Franc for every lady that said that Madame." They both laughed and he grabbed her. "My, you have rough hands young man." she whispered as his hands and mouth took possession of her heaving breasts.

Alex had instructed him to 'take her like tavern whore on a Saturday night in the town' and that's what exactly he did. When he had finished enjoying her big tits, he pushed her roughly onto the dirty floor and made her kneel before him. He pushed his cock straight into her mouth and told her to suck hard, which she did. Satisfied with her efforts; he pushed her onto her back and pulled her long legs apart. Alex managed to get the cream from her cloak pocket and spread some on and around her fanny before he mounted her. He wasn't gentle and fucked her with some barely restrained violence, pushing her legs up and thrusting like a road hammer. She groaned and gripped his thrusting arse with both hands. "Like it rough Madame? Then you get it rough." He whispered and slapped her bum several times with his big, calloused hands. Next, he dragged her onto all fours and mounted her like a stallion fucks a mare. His thrusts were relentless, and Alex had a couple of little orgasms which made him laugh and he slapped her arse some more.

They fucked against a big old store cupboard; Alex had her legs around his lower back, and he held her arse firmly. She was groaning and moaning under his assault and the cupboard door was banging like a drum. She held on tightly to his big shoulders as he jerked her up and down on his hard cock. Alex truly believed that it could have reached the top of her stomach with this fucking! They were soon back on the floor with Alex's ankles next to his head as he rammed his cock home. She felt the big one come, starting in her stomach and travelling down to her crotch and thighs. Her legs trembled and she actually screamed when it exploded from her vagina in big spurts of hot cum. He laughed and slapped her arse which was now quite red and clearly had hand marks showing. He fucked her hard for another five minutes and finally came. Alex lay back groaning as her cunt filled with cum. He lay on her for a few minutes, then pulled his cock out and walked over to his clothes and dressed. Alex stared down at the puddle that had formed from cum leaking from her fanny and groaned again, wiping tears from her face with a shaking hand.

She watched the young man disappear through the door and heard the squeaking of the barrow. Alex couldn't stop herself from laughing despite her arse hurting from his slaps; that had been the best rough sex she had endured in some time. The little animal in her stomach appeared satisfied with the first class fucking she had received. She rose slowly and picked up the cream and her cloak, then realised she needed to pee. There was a big plant pot by the door and so Alex squatted over it and pissed with some relief.

The door opened and the old man stepped in, sucking hard on his pipe and stared at Alex pissing in the plant pot. He placed his hands into his trousers pockets and watched, blowing smoke from his cob pipe. Alex just smiled at him; she couldn't stop pissing now she had started. He chuckled and removed the pipe; "Madame, that's the best thing I've seen in years. Thank you." He saluted her with his pipe and Alex just giggled. She stood and stepped over the pot and gestured to her cloak; "Could I have my cloak please sir?" and held out her hand. The old man picked it up and gestured to her beautiful - but marked - bum; "I see you visited Dante, most of his ladies get their buttocks spanked. Most seem to like that. "

Alex wrapped the cloak around herself and then realised; if the old man hadn't told her, she would have never known the young man's name who had just fucked her like a whore!

Monsieur Cission watched Alex slip away and had to laugh. His master certainly had grand taste in women and that one was an absolute peach. He settled down on an old wooden crate and waited for young Francis - the under gardener - to arrive. He puffed his pipe and thought that this modest Gardner's shed was the best brothel outside of Paris. He checked the coins in his pocket - payment for Francis's services - and waited with real anticipation.

7. THE LADY COMES OUT.

Jericho's meeting with Marshal Nay didn't go well; he was shouted at - several times - as he explained about the lack of potential new soldiers for the emperor's armies. Finally, Nay calmed down and muttered an apology for shooting the messenger. He slapped Jericho on the back and said he would [Jericho that is] enjoy tonight's dinner with the emperor and what a privilege that would be for the lowly Colonel. Jericho just smiled, bowed and left for his rooms. He found the team assembled in his rooms and Alex really did smile. He threw the Colonel's hat on the table - along with his old briefcase - and folded his arms. "I take it Alexandra that you have something to tell us?" Alex nodded.

Jericho sat deep in thought, rolling his empty brandy glass about in his fingers. He watched the fire in the grate and waited. Owen slumped on the chair opposite and yawned; "How long does it take one woman to dress another woman for bloody dinner?" That made Jericho smile a little; "Had you lived a bit longer, you would have learnt that men waiting for women to get ready, is a time-honoured custom between the sexes. But men; must never be late. Ever. Take my word for that." He chuckled at the blank look on young Owen's face.

Ruth opened the bedroom door with a flourish and grinned; "Madame Durand!" She announced with some pride. Jericho and Owen both rose from their chairs as Alex glided into the room and curtsied; she was utterly stunning in a very low-cut French Regency gown of white silk and lace. She wore a fabulous pearl necklace and a small, but exquisite, tiara in her hair that was piled up. Her long white gloves reached her elbows and her tiny white shoes had small, jeweled buckles adoring them. Jericho turned to Owen and said simply; "That's why men wait without any real complaint." Owen nodded his understanding without further comment.

Jericho looked Alex up and down, then placed a hand on his chin: "Alexandra, try not to sneeze, otherwise everyone will enjoy the escape of those." She just smiled demurely; "Apparently it's quite acceptable, at an Imperial ball for that to happen on occasion; almost required social etiquette for this time." Jericho nodded, then peered closer; "Alexandra, you've forgotten your bloody underwear I think." She shrugged her shoulders; "If you look as close as that, at the other women, you'll find they have all suffered the same lapse of memory. It's just something that the beloved Emperor likes, and what he likes, he gets. We poor ladies must obey our Emperor and our husband's commands in such matters."

Jericho muttered; "Obey? Like hell they obey men's orders. Perhaps when hell freezes...." Owen actually groaned a little and received a gentle slap from Wilson; "Steady boy or you might really split those trousers you complain so much about!" Even

Ruth chuckled at that. Then blushed a little, when she saw the look of disapproval on Owens's face.

Alex pushed her hand through Jericho's arm and grinned; "Shall we go to dinner my darling?" Jericho just smiled and the pair headed for the door, which Wilson opened and nodded to Jericho; "A big Imperial moth is going to head for the flames." He laughed softly and followed the pair, with Ruth and Owen walking behind - chatting quietly. Ruth told Owen what Napoleon's Mistress's maid had told her peers; that the mysterious woman would appear tonight - in disguise - simply because she had heard about the emperors apparent and sudden interest in Alex.

"Hence, the really low-cut bodice. Apparently, if a women is interested in the man, she'll have a little 'nipple slip' when they are together; it's quite acceptable in this Court. A sort of signal that the affair is on." Ruth explained and Owen didn't smile; "Bit of a bloody obvious signal, but I can see why it would work - especially; if Alex falls out of that damn dress in front of him."

Jericho whispered to Alex; "So, the mysterious lady is to make an appearance tonight in disguise, as Lady Guisse of Picardy. She will sit a few seats down from the emperor; to keep up the charade of not knowing each other?" Alex nodded; "Apparently Napoleon had his wife's dressmaker make her gown for tonight. His official mistress's maid believes that something really important will be announced at dinner. All four of his most powerful Marshals will be in attendance." Jericho grunted; "Time to unmask our quarry and find out what the hell is going on."

The little group wandered into the Grand Reception Room and were immediately served champagne by liveried footmen [unfortunately for Wilson and Ruth; that didn't include them!] Ruth joined a gaggle of Ladies Maids by the big bay window and Wilson stood a few feet behind his 'master'. He was actually surprised to see three other African personal servants in attendance.

One of the maids gripped Ruth by the arm and whispered; "I see your mistress has dressed to please him." Ruth just smiled; "Yes, she does love to dress well for her husband." The maid grimaced and released her arm and turned to another maid; "Thirty Franc's that her nipples are out before midnight." The other maid nodded her acceptance of the bet.

Alex and Jericho stood quietly by the doorway, sipping their drinks until Alex discretely touched Jericho's arm; "That has to be her." They both watched as the slim, blond woman swept into the room; she wasn't accompanied by a maid and that certainly drew looks from the women of the court. Her gold lace dress was gorgeous, and she gently waved a peacock fan across her face. Jericho nodded to Owen, who discretely operated his mirror. Lady Helena paused and threw a glance at Alex and then walked on, accepting champagne with a slight smile. She clearly was not happy. Madame Aglae - Duchess of Elchingen turned quietly to her friend and said softly; "I think we have all been fooled. There is no contest between the two, I suspect our Emperor has finally brought his real mysterious mistress to court and cleverly covered it with her husband's presence. Why else would a mere Colonel attend such an important dinner?" The other lady nodded her agreement, and the whispers ran around the assembled Court who exactly, the emperor's new mistress really was!

Napoleon stood in the doorway, until joined by Marshal Nay and then slowly made his entrance. The ladies curtsied and the men bowed; several men in uniform came to attention. A dozen of the emperor's 'Old Guard' followed him and took up positions around the room. Nay introduced him to several officers and Politicians [and their wives] then stopped in front of Colonel Durand, who bowed again. "Well Durand." was all the emperor said and Jericho gestured to Alex; "May I introduce my wife Alexandra, your Majesty." Alex curtsied quite low, and her nipples popped above her bodice- she made no attempt to cover them.

A little, quiet gasp rolled around the room. The lady maid slapped thirty Francs' into her friends hand; well disappointed. Alex modestly held her fan over her breasts and half smiled at the emperor but said nothing. The emperor actually smiled; well, no, it was a grin, and he bowed a little; "Madame, your husband is a very, very lucky man and I always reward men of luck." He took her hand and kissed it, pushing the fan up, getting another look at her heaving breasts. "I will have the honour of a dance with you Madame." Alex smiled; "No your Majesty; the honour will be all mine." She curtsied again, revealing more of her ample bosom. Napoleon nodded and stepped a little back, staring at her dress or rather through it. He really did smile and walked away - a little awkwardly, it must be said!

Wilson restrained his smile but muttered to himself; "Straight into the bloody flames." Owen slowly joined Jericho and Alex and they found a quiet corner. He folded his arms and spoke softly; "Lady Helena Covington, who is from Victorian Times. By her age and knowing her birth date, we can work out that she travelled here from 1864." Wilson nodded and asked; "The big question, of course, is how?"

Owen grinned; "Her husband is Lord Covington and guess what piece of furniture he owns that once belonged to Napoleon?" Wilson sighed; "A Chinese cabinet?" Owen nodded; "A gift from the Chinese Emperor in 1814. The story or legend is that the Chinese ambassadors simply vanished from inside it. But we know that the damn thing contains a time portal. It must be in his study, which is next to his bedroom."

Jericho nodded and smiled; "So we need to get into the study, which is only available from his bedroom. So, a distraction is in order. One which allows us into his bedroom and then the study." He then noticed Alex was struggling with her magnificent breasts; "I need some safety pins." She muttered to Owen.

"And I know how we can do that." Jericho rubbed his chin and glanced across the ballroom to see the emperor talking to 'Lady Guisse of Picardy.' You could have frozen peas with the cold atmosphere between the two. "He's official mistress will jump at the chance to get back in his favour now and I think we can give her an offer she simply won't refuse." Jericho actually chuckled; Alex will go nuts at this one, he thought.

"We need to get into the emperors study and put that particular time portal out of commission. We can return Lady Helena to her own time, and she won't be able to return, because if the cabinet's time travelling ability is removed here and now, the cabinet won't possess the ability in 1864."

Jericho rubbed his face; "I think the emperor should be diverted by an irate and betrayed husband, whilst another gets to work on the cabinet and Lady Helena. I think it's time to use our very reliable honey-trap." They all looked at Alex, who just sighed; "Playing the bloody tart again." was all she said.

8. THE WRONG RENDERVOUS.

Ruth and Owen slipped from the dining room as the first course was served to the guests, now all seating and enjoying light, polite conversation. Alex and Jericho had been seated just a few chairs down from the emperor himself; that really did cause some quite lively conversation amongst the guests. With Jericho's rank, he should have been at the far end of the table.

Apparently, Napoleon had told his butler to make the changes; but the man was not surprised after seeing the Colonel's wife. Owen waited in the corridor outside the door to Madame Margaret Du Loupe's rooms; her ladies maid opened it and waved Ruth in, shutting the door firmly on Owen; this was for women only. He stood outside, arms folded and a little bored. Several staff members and servants passed him; none said a word or even acknowledged that he was there. He straightened up as the door opened and Ruth appeared; a little smile of satisfaction on her face.

"Well?" Was all Owen whispered and Ruth slowly nodded, then smiled broadly. She pushed her arm through his and the happy couple headed for the Ball Room; the plan was now in action. They stood by the door and Ruth opened the palm of her hand and said quietly; "I now just have some words with Alex and everything is underway. Oh, and make sure these are fitted correctly; that's really important." She showed Owen her hand, who just rubbed his chin in puzzlement; "Safety pins?" He asked. Ruth nodded; "I'll fix my lady's bodice so that her nipples don't pop out whilst she's dancing. They've done their job." she grinned.

Owen sighed and muttered; "Pity about that. But what about that bloody see-through dress? Do you have anything to fix that?" Ruth shook her head; "There are no strong lights in the ball room; she'll be fine." Owen nodded his head, now he knew why Alex greeted the emperor in front of the fireplace; it was like placing a lamp behind her. "I now realise, what Jericho's been saying about you bloody women and the way you operate is quite true. I shall listen very carefully to him in the future." He grunted; Ruth just shook her head, but still smiled.

The guests were now starting to fill the Ball Room and Alex, with Ruth, disappeared to a side room. Jericho smiled at Owen, who simply nodded; indicating the plan was on. Wilson joined them and informed him that Marshall Nay will make up some excuse, to pull Jericho [Colonel Durand] from the dancing; leaving the field open for his majesty to go after Alex. Jericho really smiled at that; "Good luck to the poor twat." Was all he said - much to Wilson's and Owen's amusement.

"What was the important announcement he made at dinner about?" Wilson quietly asked Jericho - who did not smile - and looked about before answering; "He's not going to resign. His time travelling mistress must have supplied him with information that he believes, can change his destiny. We really must put an end to this - by any means." He glanced back at the doorway; Ruth signaled that Alex was ready and that meant that Madame Margaret Du Loupe was also ready.

The Emperor swept into the ball room; he didn't hide that he was looking for someone and appeared a little disappointed when his official mistress; Madame Du Loupe came up to him. After a few minutes of conversation; the emperor really did smile and kissed her on the cheek. They strode out and danced the first dance together. The 'Lady of Guisse' stood by the fireplace and sipped her drink; the look on her face betrayed a very unhappy woman.

"Now for my walk on part." Jericho muttered and approached the unhappy lady and wondered if she would care to dance. She smiled and took his arm. "He does actually have the charm and looks that women go after." Owen muttered - a little surprised - but Wilson just chuckled; "Come on baby brother; time to perform for our pay." Owen sighed and then rubbed his chin; "Yeah, but we don't actually get bloody paid." He muttered and followed the big man out.

They nodded and smiled at Alex, as she walked gracefully into the ball room and waved away a glass of champagne offered by an attentive footman. She stood arms on hips and stared at the dancers; she did not appear happy. Despite the dancing, everyone had their eyes on Alex, as she strode across the crowded room and walked straight up to her 'husband' and slapped him hard across the face. He staggered and released the 'lady Guisse, who screamed in shock.

The ball room went silent - apart from a few stunned gasps from the ladies present, oh, and the Count du Moranle, who was known to be quite squeamish - and the pair [Jericho and Alex] had a shouting match in front of everyone. Alex stormed from the ball room, throwing her fan at the feet of the shocked

Emperor with Jericho following her, protesting his 'innocence'.

The 'Lady of Guisse' also fled the chamber by a different door. There were just murmurs of shocked conversation about what just happened. The emperor leaned down and picked up Alex's fan. He smiled at Madame Margaret Du Loupe and pushed the fan into his pocket. "Beauty and passion are quite a heady mix." He said to her and indicated that the ball should continue - which it did.

The Emperor waved aside demands that the pair should arrested or something. He stood in a quiet corner with just Marshal Nay beside him and pulled the fan from his pocket and read the few lines scrawled on it. He smiled and nodded his head; "Now that is lady worthy of a crown." He muttered and spoke closely in Nay's ear. The Marshall wasn't happy about his instructions; but he would carry them out. Napoleon then nodded at his mistress and the pair began the dancing again, as if nothing had happened.

Marshal Nay danced with his inquisitive wife and whispered to her; "I think this little rendezvous was not made in heaven; but hell." She just smiled and he explained what she had to do. She left the ball some minutes later; her maid trailing behind; totally intrigued.

They were allowed into the emperor's private suite without question and Madame Aglae - Duchess of Elchingen [Marshal Nay's wife] helped her maid uncover the huge bed. She whispered to her loyal maid; "Our beloved Emperor is going to celebrate staying on the throne, in right royal style with a little party of three. He will be the guest of honour of course." The maid smiled and said softly; "Who are the lucky ladies, my lady?" The Duchess grinned; "Well, Madame Du Loupe and that little firebrand; Lady Alexandra, of course!"

The maid chuckled; "I think Colonel Durand will get his wish and don a general's uniform after this." Madame Aglae smiled; "Lady Alexandra is a loving, loyal and obedient wife who will do her husband's bidding. She will open her proud legs and earn her husband's Generals hat on her back; as many women have done!"

They both laughed and straightened the bed clothes. The maid lifted up Napoleon's night shirt, laid out in anticipation of its owner's arrival. Madame Algae took it from her and threw it on the floor. "I don't think his majesty will want that." Both women laughed again and finished what they needed to do and left.

Margaret and Alex walked slowly down the corridor to the emperor's private suite; giggling together in apparent sexual anticipation of what the evening will bring. "He really loved your little performance tonight, to throw the rabid ladies of the court off the scent. Your husband will probably get the Pay Core: no fighting and lots of money. I think he will look quite splendid in his general's uniform and of course, the Title that will go with it. A general will need a title and so will his loyal wife. He will make you a Duchess when you're sadly widowed." Margaret chuckled and the pair swept in the Imperial bedroom.

There was a tray of champagne and wild strawberries placed on the bedroom table. The candles had all been lit and the fire raised into a proper blaze. Madame Du Loupe gripped Alex by the arm and pulled her close, running a finger down her lips; "We'll, enjoy each other first, he really likes that; foreplay that he can enjoy without exerting himself too much." Her finger ran down Alex's chin, then her neck and finally between her breasts; the rest of her fingers on that hand, soon joined it. "Let me undress you first: slowly." She whispered but was interrupted by the Emperor Napoleon standing in the doorway; jacket unbuttoned and a glass of brandy in his hand.

"Let the party begin." He said softly and placed the brandy glass down on the small table by the door. He pulled off his jacket and threw it down. "You two can play after I've enjoyed my new Lady's arse." He added and really did smile and started to pull at his shirt.

9. THAT WASN'T IN THE PLAN!

Napoleon came up behind Alex; he was now shirtless and ran both hands down her back until they reached her bum. He whispered into her ear; "I will take you naked and sitting backwards on a chair with your arse in the air..." He gripped the cheeks of her arse quite firmly as Margaret pulled at Alex's dress and loosed the small silver clasps that held her bodice in place. "These are mine for now." She whispered and pulled Alex's heaving breasts out with both hands. She ran her mouth and tongue over one and smiled.

Alex was wondering where the hell was Jericho and Wilson; she was feeling really vulnerable now; Napoleon had showed up way too early and Margaret was enjoying her breasts far too much; for it to be just play for the emperor. Where were the boys? She wondered again. What has happened?

That's when; they all heard the noise in the study next door. "Thank heaven for that." Alex whispered to herself; Jericho and Wilson were now on scene, so she thought. Where the bloody hell have they been?

The emperor stopped licking Alex's neck and stared, as the study door swung open. The nearest English translation to what he shouted was; "What the fuck!" Lady Helena Covington stood in the doorway, her face streaked and red from crying, but it was what she held in both hands that really caught everyone's attention.

An 186o's revolver and she looked like she would use it.

"You fucking betray me... after I gave you all the information about Your future...how to change your bloody failure into victory...then you fuck these whores in preference to me! You fucking bastard!" She clicked the safety off and visibly trembling, took aim. Napoleon pushed Alex to the floor and told her to stay down; Madame Du Loupe was backing away and clutching at her dress with both hands; pleading not to die.

"You wanted to change fucking history! Well, this will do it!" Lady Helena shouted and waved the gun up and down, as if not knowing, who to shoot first, Napoleon or Alexandra. The shot came from the balcony door and slapped into Lady Helena's right shoulder; her pistol went off and fell to the floor. The soldier on guard, on the balcony, had defied orders to keep well away from the glass doors, whilst the emperor entertained his ladies. But simply couldn't resist taking a peek. Napoleon was bloody glad he did and promoted the man to corporal for using his 'initiative'. Lady Helena fell backwards, screaming in pain and surprise, blood starting to spread over the floor. Alex leapt forward, ripping the hem of her dress off, and set to work on the now quiet woman. "Get Jericho….get my husband for Christ sake!" She yelled and tried to stem the blood, or she would lose the young woman and because she wasn't from this time; her soul.

Jericho and Wilson appeared in the doorway; their plan had gone horribly wrong, and Jericho told the emperor to leave for his own safety. Quite numb from shock, he did so without argument and Madame Du Loupe ran screaming out behind him. Jericho and Alex exchanged a look and Jericho said quietly; "1864 now." He operated his mirror and Alex, with Lady Helena cradled in her arms; disappeared.

Wilson waved the balcony guard away; he was standing with his mouth open and staring at the empty space, where Alex and the girl - he had just shot - once were. Wilson closed the bedroom door and locked it, pulling his mirror from a jacket pocket; "I'll call Owen and Ruth, tell them to get the fuck out of here." Jericho nodded and stared at the study door; "She must have come from there."

There was now shouting outside, and muskets were being slammed against the door. Jericho headed for the study, followed by Wilson, who stopped to scoop up the revolver. They ran into the study and stopped; the doors on the Chinese cabinet were open and Jericho's mirror was buzzing - Alex had got Helena back and she would make it - Wilson slammed the study door, as the bedroom door was finally breached by several soldiers. "Into the cabinet!" Jericho yelled and they piled in, slamming the doors behind them. The soldiers of Napoleon's 'Old Guard' crashed through the study door and fired their muskets straight at the cabinet. Wood, glass and silver flew about the room and gun smoke filled the place.

Finally, the Corporal forced open the doors, now riddled with musket fire and to his - and his men's - great surprise, found the damn thing empty; except for broken mirrors. Apparently, no-one would be jumping through time in that big Chinese box of magic anymore.

The Corporal lowered his musket and said to the man nearest him; "You best fetch Marshal Nay. Those bastards have done what the Chinese ambassadors did. Vanished into thin air." The soldier nodded and disappeared himself.

Captain Jean Pullaire stared at the cabinet and with a gloved hand, lifted a large piece of glass from the wreckage; he looked at his face in the reflection and dropped it back onto the floor. He turned and saw Colonel Le Grande standing behind him, quietly surveying the damage. "Did anyone ever meet Colonel Durand before he appeared here or more importantly; that wife of his?" He asked the grim looking Colonel. Le Grande shook his head; "He was just a Colonel from a small district; never been in battle, as far as I know."

"Yes, but with a wife like that; a noble lady with such beauty, you would have thought she would have been noticed and gossiped about. But no-one appears to know anything about her. Strange that; especially after the emperor's mysterious new mistress tried to put a pistol ball through his head." Pullaire sighed and the pair walked from the room. That's when Le Grande saw the small brown paper package on the floor. He picked it up; "It's addressed personally to the emperor. I'll give it to Marshal Nay." He muttered and followed Pullaire out.

10. FINAL DAYS AND STRANGE PLANS.

Napoleon sat in Marshal Nay's study and stared at the fireplace; he gripped a glass of brandy. It was all quite in the room, but outside was chaos and noise. Madame Du Loupe sat at his feet and gripped his leg, her head against his knee.

Nay stood in the doorway, arms folded and unsmiling. "There is no trace whatsoever of Durand, his wife or servants. They have vanished completely, along with the so called 'Lady of Guisse'. All that was found, was this package; addressed to you sire." He handed Napoleon the brown little parcel. Napoleon took it without saying a word. "Like those bloody chinks, they got away without anyone seeing them. The palace was crawling with guards - inside and out - yet they simply disappeared." Napoleon dismissed him with a wave of his hand.

Finally Madame Du Loupe whispered; "What's in the package my dear. What has that insane bitch left you?" Napoleon lifted the little parcel and shook his head; "If it's from her, then it's just more lies and fairy stories." He threw the parcel into the flames and watched it burn. "Just lies and falsehoods my dear." He said and sipped his brandy. The real disappointment he felt, was missing out on having Madame Alexandra's arse. He had run his hands over it, and it was a real beauty; like the rest of her. He sighed; his abdication was now a certainty; he had run out of time here and his precious cabinet was destroyed by his overzealous men.

He smiled at the fire burning in the grate; Young Helena had been an obedient and submissive fuck who had tried to help him survive on the throne of France. But he knew all was lost now; the odds were stacked against him. The Allies could mass troops and replacements despite how many victories he won; they were out to destroy him; not France. But in another time and place, with another big war, everything would be different.

But he couldn't understand Colonel Durand - if that's who he really was? - If he was an assassin; as Nay advocates, then why did Durant tell him to go? He had him there with just one guard, who now had an empty musket - nothing to protect him? It didn't make sense. He patted Madame Du Loupe's head; "Let's get some rest my love. I have a busy day tomorrow." He rose and placed the glass down and took one last look at the burning package. What a narrow escape he just had. The woman was clearly insane with passion for him; but obviously matched the Chinese in the skill of magic or was that bloody Durand and his crew?

Napoleon ran a hand over sweaty face; there was something strange about 'Durand' - almost if he knew about Lady Helena and her visits from the 'hereafter' - and had appeared to stop him [the emperor] from gaining such knowledge of future events. Napoleon nodded to himself; he had an uneasy feeling that he would meet the mysterious - and clever - fellow again.

The pair made their way to the emperor's private suite; surrounded by his faithful and loyal 'Old Guard'. He stopped and spoke to Colonel Le Grande; he was to inform Marshall Nay, that the emperor would abdicate and accept the Allies offer of exile on Elba. He stopped momentarily outside the door, to the suite of rooms next to his and almost smiled. By the sounds coming from inside, Monsignor Boucher was entertaining another lady of the court. He sighed; something will have to be done about him.

That's when a thought crossed his mind; Monsignor Boucher could do him a final service; a very final service. The emperor smiled and walked to his public office, which was unlocked and slipped in, checking that the chest still stood beneath the window. He nodded with satisfaction and actually rubbed his hands together and knew that his plan would work. "One door closes, but there are always windows." He muttered, now smiling slightly which puzzled the guards following the great man.

11. ALEX RETURNS TO THE TEAM AFTER A SLIGHT DIVERSION.

Satisfied that lady Helena would be fine and leaving her sleeping in her bed after treatment, Alex operated her mirror and jumped back to 1814 and the found herself outside the entrance to the servants quarters. She hid in the shadows of the doorway and waited for him. He didn't disappoint her and appeared with a big smile. They talked for a few minutes, and he took Alex's hand and led her to the huge stable complex. Alex was a little disappointed that all he could think of was a roll in the hay. But she was pleasantly surprised when they slipped through a small backdoor and appeared in the 'Coach' Room.

There were four magnificent carriages that the emperor used, and the young Lieutenant gestured to them - holding her hand - and told her to pick one. He smiled at her choice of the large State carriage which was gilded with real gold and took four horses to pull it. "That would have been my choice; it's upholstered with the most choice and comfortable fabrics and the seating is wide." He whispered and pulled open the door and helped Alex in. They sat opposite each other and undressed.

Alex slipped off her cloak and waited for him to help unlace her dress which he did with some speed. They didn't stop looking at each other as they quickly removed their clothes and sat naked. Alex slowly opened her legs and showed him what he was about to receive, and he smiled broadly and joined her on the seat, taking her hand and placing it upon his erection. His cock wasn't the biggest she had ever seen, but as she gripped it, she realised that it had a formidable girth. She jerked it gently and their mouths met with some urgency. That simple act seemed to explode intense passion between the two. Alex managed to remember the small pot of cream and it certainly came in useful. Alex sat with her back against the sumptuously upholstered carriage wall with her legs open and the young Lieutenant's cock buried in her vagina. He clearly wasn't one for foreplay, but he was fucking her hard, deep and fast with real animal strength. She threw her arms around his big shoulders and pulled him close, and their mouths came together again. He pushed her legs right up and drove his cock deep with each powerful thrust. She had a little orgasm and knew more would follow with the excellent fucking she was receiving from this young Lieutenant of Calvary.

They were kissing passionately, and Alex wasn't surprised that he suddenly cussed and moaned, ejaculating deep inside her. She ran a hand down his neck and shoulders whispering; "I'll soon get you hard and ready again darling." The young man pulled his cock from her and staggered back and sat on the seat opposite. Alex rose from the carriage seat slowly, feeling his cum trickling down her thighs and knelt in front of him and gripped his thick cock and pushed it into her hot wet mouth. He stroked her hair as she caressed it with tongue and fingers.

His other hand reached for his jacket and pulled the big fob watch up to his sweating face and cussed; "Fuck" I didn't think I would last that long first time. I had anticipated having you twice before the guards arrived. Bollocks!" Alex dropped his flaccid cock and jumped backwards, slowly sitting down and grabbing her handbag. The Lieutenant didn't smile; "Sorry Madame Durand, but I have to arrest you in the name of the Emperor and France!" He grabbed up his trousers as Alex heard the door to the Coach Room opening with raised voices and the sound of heavy boots. "The emperor will certainly promote me for capturing you Madame; I suggest you inform me where the rest of your traitorous friends are and maybe the emperor will be merciful and keep you from Madame Guillotine because that is where you are headed." He now smiled.

Alexandra also smiled, reaching into her handbag and operated her mirror; "I am sorry to deny you that final pleasure, but I have studied the Chinese art of magic and need no fancy cabinet to return home," In an instant she was gone; vanished right before his eyes. He sat in a state of shock until Captain Jean Pullaire jerked open the door – pistol in hand – and stared at the young Lieutenant sitting naked holding his watch in his hand with a very vacant look on his face. The captain stared at the women's clothes scattered about the carriage and lowered his pistol. "Fuck!" he said softly and poked the young man with the pistol, who continued to stare at the seat opposite. Captain Pullaire turned to the corporal of the 'Old Guard' and said quietly; "Get him out and dressed, the emperor will want to speak to him. It appears the Durant's practice the ancient art of Chinese magic without the bloody need for cabinets or anything else." He stepped back and the corporal pulled the still stunned officer from the carriage, chuckling to himself; this young officer would need a fantastic imagination to explain this one.

Alex arrived back at the lighthouse, stark naked apart from her handbag and walked nonchalantly past Mr. Harris, saying; "I'll join the others when I have cleaned up a bit." He watched her pass without comment, but a smile crept across his normally dour face, and he headed for the kitchens. Mrs. Harris will love this one, he thought.

12. JERICHO HAS TROUBLED THOUGHTS.

Now back at the lighthouse, Jericho stood by the fireplace in his study and watched Alex pour some well-earned brandies for the team. She gave him a glass and smiled, dropping into her favourite armchair by the fire. "If the cabinet was destroyed by musket fire, then Lady Covington - or anyone else - will not be dropping in on Napoleon." She raised her glass, and everyone did the same. "Napoleon." was all she said.

"Well, Lady Helena will have scar on her shoulder for life, but Alex certainly saved her soul. Here's to you girl." Wilson raised his glass, and everyone agreed with him. "I'd love to know how she explained to her old man, how she got shot with a musket ball?" Owen chuckled and sipped his brandy. "It was quite a good plan; we just didn't count for the wrath of a women scorned or Napoleon being so desperate to have Alex, that he left the ball early and un-noticed. But Lady Helena; now that came out the blue."

Alex sipped her brandy and said nothing about Napoleon's randy doppelganger; she didn't wish to explain to her colleagues how she knew he existed. Jericho was a clever man; he would work that one out for himself. Jericho sighed; "I was looking forward to my big outraged and betrayed husband bit with old 'boney', whilst Wilson took care of that bloody cabinet and dragged Lady Covington back to her own time. In a way, our plan did sort of work; Lady Helena is back in her own time and Napoleon won't be able to use the damn cabinet to find out about his future, then change it."

"If she hadn't turned up with big pistol, I may not have been able to sit properly for a few days. That was a close-run thing." Alex sipped her brandy and didn't smile. Jericho took a sip from his glass and rubbed his cheek; "By the way Alexandra; did you have to slap me so hard? We were only play acting you know." Alex now grinned; "I had to make it look authentic, besides, it was poor old me that had her bum felt up by a horny old man and her breasts fondled by a bisexual nymphomaniac!" Everyone chuckled at that. Then Owen tapped Wilson on the arm and asked quietly; "What's a nymphomaniac?" Wilson groaned and said to Alex; "It's about women, so you can bloody tell him!"

Alex had to chuckle as she smiled at Owen, he played his role as the 'innocent' former novice monk really well.

But Jericho sat deep in thought, rolling his brandy glass in his hands; he stared at the fire; he was troubled. Ruth and Owen were almost sure; they didn't see the emperor leave the ball so early. Lady Helena had been his mistress for some time before that faithful night; if she had told Napoleon anything important about his future; why didn't he act upon it? The current timeline is unaltered, apart from a few, acceptable minor changes. The great Napoleon fails at Waterloo and is exiled; just as history recorded it. Then his suspicious death in 1821.

Jericho sighed; a nagging little thought kept pestering him. Why didn't he [Napoleon] really try and change his fate in 1814?

EPISODE PROLOGUE: "Britain is basking in an unprecedented heat wave with a drought declared, but a small group of students at Oxford University have other matters on their minds. This group consists of students - who are studying various degrees - that have formed a very special out of Study club; 'The Spirit Chasers'. While they do like the 'hard stuff', the spirits they chase don't come in bottles! But it's when they decide to play with an old Ouija board, found in an attic that things start to go wrong. Mr. Tibbs is sent to investigate, and Alex meets a hunky professor and his team..."

60 Minutes approx. **Episode Warnings:**
Smoking – Alcohol – Strong language – Paranormal Violence – Strong graphic sexual references [including a sexual assault] – Mild horror – References to death & Demonic activities.

NOTES: This is the **ADULT** version of the original story which is published and appears in the **TEMPORAL DETECTIVES**: Series 4 – Episode 8 entitled: **"THE OXFORD OUIJA BOARD SESSIONS."**

CAUTION: Recommended for **18+ only**.

1. THE OLD PUB: 'THE DEVIL & THE PIT', OXFORD, ENGLAND. Friday 13th August 1976

"It was last open for business in 1969 when the owner died, and the place closed and was simply never re-opened. His heir, a nephew didn't want it and put it up for sale. It never sold obviously. Little money has been spent on its upkeep as you can see." John Morris waved a hand at the derelict building and wiped his face. This evening was unbelievably warm; the summer of '76 would go into the history books all right. There were reports on TV about road tarmac actually melting and a severe drought across the country. Still, he had persuaded Ellen – his live-in girlfriend – that sharing the bath water was in the nation's best interests! He fumbled in the small canvas bag that was slung over his shoulder and found the key's that the Estate Agents had handed him.

The owner was more than happy to co-operate with the team of 'Paranormal investigators' from Oxford University; no-one had gone near the pub or made an offer since it fell empty in 1969. It had quite a reputation for strange and almost demonic activity which would not have crowds flooding back into it. Thus, the little group had arrived to investigate and record what was happening in the old building.

Dave Clay slung the heavy camera over his shoulder and stared at the old tavern; "If I owned the boozer, I would certainly change the bloody name!" he said quietly to Maggie who smiled and heaved a couple of bags from the back of the Austin Morris estate car. "I think your right Dave; the 'Devil and the pit' won't attract too many punters in for a good time!" Dave chuckled and cussed the camera again. He was a second-year student in Media Studies and had borrowed the damn thing from the University Film productions Unit. He was becoming quite proficient with it and now believed he could actually get a job as a cameraman on one of the TV stations. He smiled at Maggie bending over the bags in her shorts. He harboured some delicious thoughts about his fellow 'Ghost Hunter' and they weren't all fraternal. But she was under the spell of 'JP' Bonaparte – the Professor of African Studies – at the university. Like a lot of young female students. He hid his disappointment well and Maggie never realised.

But John speaking to him snapped his attention away from her delicious backside and he grabbed a bag up. "Come on, let's

get in. I've been told we can have the run of the place and there is still electricity and water on, but no beer apparently. It's been broken into more times than I've had a bag of chips."
He waved the keys and they waited until they were joined by William Kent, who eased himself from the car.

Willy was a big man and played Rugby for the university and a local team. He had already been sought out by several Rugby league teams who would sign him as soon as he finished his degree in Physics. He was intelligent as he was big.

Everyone in the 'Oxford Spirit Chaser's Club' always felt a little safer with the big man around. He also had some real experience of ghostly activity and had been involved in the almost infamous 'Portsmouth Poltergeist' incident last year. He became a legend – apparently – when confronted by a chair throwing entity; he slung the bloody chairs back at it! He and 'JP' had dealt with that one. They were close friends and 'JP' also played rugby for the university. Willy was in his last year – like John – and was quite a character.

John was reading Archaeology and Ancient History. Everyone he met soon formed the same opinion of the quiet man; he was going places. He already possessed the demeanour and personality of a professor, and his knowledge of his subjects could only be matched by the 'Don's at the University. Oh yes, he was destined for the top in his chosen profession. He and 'JP' were really close and good friends.

"When is the man himself joining us?" Willy asked John who was sorting through the keys as they approached the front door. John grinned; "JP has a little matter of a gorgeous young air hostess to deal with first. He met her when he flew back from Nairobi a couple of weeks ago. They are probably deep in conversation about the early African civilizations as we speak!" Willy laughed out loud and waited for John to open the reluctant door.

Maggie didn't smile at hearing about the air hostess and Dave noticed that with a small smile. JP was never short of female company that was for sure. The dashing new professor of African studies was big as Willy and was of mixed European and African heritage. His father was a Surgeon in France and his mother a journalist in Kenya. He spent his time between the three countries that he loved: France, Kenya and England. Only in his early thirties he was already a professor. Like John, he had the talent to go far in his profession. He was also very attractive to women; very attractive. JP was handsome, charming and intelligent. He also really knew about the supernatural and paranormal, which didn't surprise anyone; his maternal grandfather had been a very famous Witch Doctor! Well, that was the rumour and JP encouraged it without actually confirming it.

Maggie really missed the other team member tonight, Rose McGovern. They were good friends, but Rose was at a dinner dance at the local police station; she was 'seeing' a clever detective police sergeant who was divorced and about ten years older than her. But they seemed to get along really well. Maggie suspected that Rose was a lot more taken by the Sergeant than she would ever admit to her friend, at the moment. Rose also had a real sense of humour and could make anyone laugh. She was straight off a Belfast housing estate on a scholarship paid by some big Irish Whisky company. She [Rose] always said that she was just getting back some of the money that her father and Uncles had given the distillery!

They gathered in the old main bar which was dominated by the original pub sign – taken down to avoid theft – that showed the devil standing before a pit filled with flame and screaming souls. Maggie found the kitchens and brewed a huge pot of tea which was welcomed by everyone. They sat at one of the tables by a boarded-up window and John briefed the team.

"Apparently there has been a tavern on this site since the fourteenth century. It was a coaching Inn in the 17th and 18th centuries. It has changed hands many times and been called by several names; but the name 'The Devil and the Pit' is the original fourteenth century name; resurrected by the owner's in 1866 for some insane reason only known to them!" John sipped his mug of dark tea and turned the page of his notebook.

"There have been all sorts of incidents recorded here over the years, ghostly apparitions and poltergeist activity. The most well-known one was a stag party in 1952 which came to an abrupt end when a demon appeared and attacked the two strippers in the middle of their act! Apparently the two girls ran up the road in just their stockings, followed by the men. That appeared in several papers at the time." He chuckled to himself and looked about the place adding; "Maybe if Maggie or Rose took off their clothes on the bar, we may get some action." He grinned at the two fingers stuck up by Maggie. He knew that Rose would have retorted with some humour; but Maggie wasn't Rose. John actually grinned to himself; Rose probably would have taken off her clothes if it would conjure up a poltergeist or two!

"So apart from Rose or Maggie stripping what else can we do to attract the spirits that apparently infest this dump?" Dave asked and finished his tea; he could murder a cold beer. John smiled and heaved up his old black satchel that he always carried and slowly pulled the old cardboard box out. Everyone stared at it. The box was old and faded but everyone knew what it held: a Ouija Board. "It's late Victorian and was found in the attic's here when the place was closed down, by one of the workmen clearing the place. I brought it from that little Curiosities shop in the city. Apparently, the storekeeper said that the workman gave it to him and ran out the shop!" He carefully opened the fragile box and removed the wooden board and placed it on the table. "I should have paid about five or six pounds for it, but when I explained that I was from the university and our little club, he gave it to me for a pound. Actually, I think he would have given it to me; he seemed more than happy for me to take it."

John looked about the table and asked quietly; "I take it everyone has used one of these before?" Willy folded his arms and nodded; "Yeah, a couple of times and nothing bleeding happened." He smiled as Dave grunted; "Little wonder, the spirit didn't want a bloody chair broken over its head." That broke the sombre mood, except for Maggie who kept looking at the old pub sign. She would find something to cover that before they started. So, it was decided to try the board before the summer evening descended into darkness. Maggie made more tea and handed out the sandwiches she had made and several bags of 'Chipmunk' crisps. Everyone ate in relative silence and Maggie found a bright red tablecloth and threw it over the pub sign. As she did, she suddenly realized that her nipples were standing up and she shivered a little. The closed pub was oppressively hot, and the men were openly sweating. But a cold sensation had swept over her. She really wanted to get out the place but stopped herself thinking about that and returned to the table, where John had set up the board and Dave the camera and tape recorder, which he was announcing place, date and time into, with a solemn voice.

Maggie had her large notebook, clock and pencils. She wouldn't touch the board; just record the session. Only Willy and John would actually use the board. Two battery powered lamps were the table and the lights dimmed. John spoke carefully and quietly as he and Willy placed their hands upon the Planchette. Maggie noted the time 6.46pm and date; Friday August 13th, 1976. She wiped her face, Friday the thirteenth!

John called several times if anyone was there; nothing.
Willy now took over and called out if anyone was there. The pub lights flicker a couple of times, and everyone looked at each other. Maggie noticed that her hand shook a little as she wrote that down. Willy called out again and the lights dimmed and went out. Dave quickly switched on the two lamps, and everyone sat in silence. Willy called out again and suddenly the Planchette moved slowly to 'Yes'. Both John and Willy whispered – quite nervously – that they weren't pushing the bloody thing! John wiped his face and spoke softly; "Who wishes to make contact?" he repeated it and watched as the Planchette moved to each letter in turn.

Maggie – with a real shaking hand – wrote down the reply and noted the time; 6.50pm. She whispered the word to the others; "Norman." Everyone stared at each other, and Dave almost smiled; "A bloody spirit called Norman?" John drew a deep breath and asked; "What do you want to say Norman?"

The Planchette moved again, and Maggie wrote down the answer. "Get out now my friends. Now! Now! Now!" John wiped his face again and said quietly; "Why Norman, are we in danger?" The Planchette moved quickly around the board with Willy and John shouting that they couldn't take their fingers off the damn thing! Maggie kept her head and wrote down the words spelled out. "Get out now! Get out now! He's coming!"

Suddenly the Planchette flew from the board and spun around like a top and fell from the table onto the floor. Willy and John were holding their fingers and cursing; "It feels like my fingers are fucking alight!" John shouted and jumped up. Willy stuck his fingers into his mug of cold tea and cursed soundly. No one noticed the strange smile on his face.

Everyone calmed down a little and Dave slowly lifted the camera and managed to gasp; "For fuck sake! Look at the pub sign!" The red tablecloth that covered the picture was being consumed by little red and yellow flames; the burning cloth fell to the floor leaving the picture untouched apparently. That's when everyone stared in utter horror as the Devil raised his pitchfork and gestured to the damned souls in the pit; they were screaming and pleading as the flames consumed them.

The little group went through the front door almost as one.

Everyone sat in the car in absolute silence and took a swig from Dave's hipflask of whisky. Finally, John whispered; "We best find a phone box and ring JP." No one argued with that.

2. JEAN-PAUL BONAPARTE; PROFESSOR OF AFRICAN STUDIES.

JP slowly replaced the receiver and sighed. He turned and smiled at the small blond woman asleep next to him. He eased from the bed and headed for the bathroom, showered quickly and dressed in silence, He grabbed up his old 'Gladstone' bag and headed for his car; a little convertible Triumph Herald and pulled the top back; the evening was hot and sticky. He headed out the city onto the Marsh Road and towards the old pub.

He didn't notice the black Bedford J4 Van join him some yards behind. Wilson gripped the wheel and cursed a little; "Is this heap the best Supplies could come up with?" he directed the question to Owen who just shrugged his shoulders and muttered that he wasn't responsible for the bloody van supplied. Alex leaned over and smiled; "The 1970's was not the best time for decent vans big man." Wilson grunted; "You don't have to drive the bloody thing. It has a mind of its own I swear."

Jericho looked up from his mirror and gestured to the speeding little car in front; "Keep behind him Wilson, we know where he's going, so no need to rush." Wilson nodded and the gear box groaned as he changed up. Alex tapped Jericho's shoulder and asked quietly; "Has Demon Ingress identified who has flipping appeared?" Jericho shook his head; "As soon as we or they do; they'll send a Knight or Guardian as appropriate."

Owen rubbed his face; "The last demon to make an appearance at the old pub was Jessel – a Tier 2 – in 1952. Apparently, he likes females and had a go at a couple of pub strippers at a stag party there. According to Operations, Big Frank the Guardian kicked his arse back to the Dark Prince, but not before he nicked a couple of souls. Apparently, a couple of drunken blokes from the party jumped into their car and drove like nutters until a tree stopped them. He got the dumb pair before the bloody Collector appeared to scoop them up."

Jericho sighed and lowered his mirror; "Well, it appears some idiots have used a Ouija Board in the old place and didn't like who appeared from the other side. Apparently, a bloody demon – unknown at the present – and guess who else?" he grinned as they all shook their heads. "Bloody Norman Tanner again!" Everyone laughed at that revelation by Jericho.

Alex groaned and sat back; "Bloody Norman again. I thought he had given that nonsense up and decided to stay at that big castle in York?" Jericho smiled; "Well, he's certainly now put in an appearance here and give him his due; tried to warn the silly buggers before the demon turned up." Owen laughed; "I like Norman; he's really just a naughty poltergeist who doesn't hurt anyone; just scares the shit out of them!"

"It wasn't his cold bleeding hands up the back of your panties, wasn't it? You might change your tune then." Alex said and settled back in her seat. Owen smiled at her, and the pair laughed. He whispered; "It might have been, if I was Jackie at the time." Now that did put a smile back on Alex's face. "Well, that would have certainly surprised the pervert poltergeist." She said quietly.

Jericho ignored the banter between the two and gestured to the small car turning left ahead. "His grandfather was a real 'Passer' who could see and communicate with lost souls. I wonder if Jean-Paul has inherited that skill." Alex leaned forward and smiled; "Well, his grandson could certainly talk to this lost soul. He's a very handsome man all round." Owen chuckled and consulted his mirror again; "Blimey, his grandfather had seven wives and thirty-one children. Where did the find the bloody time to talk with the dead?" He tapped his mirror; "Did you know that the old boy is now a Collector?"

The conversation ceased as the small car pulled up in the pub car park, next to a battered old Austin Morris estate car. Wilson parked the van up at the entrance to the pub drive and sat back. Owen consulted his mirror; "No activity recorded at the moment. I wonder what they will do now." The team watched JP as he was joined by his relieved looking team. They stood talking in the deserted car park for some minutes before heading back in the pub. Jericho slapped a hand over his face; "Sweet Lord, what are they doing? They have balls to go back in there." Wilson was staring at the little group as they disappeared back into the pub. He tapped the steering wheel with his fingers and spoke quietly; "Do you know that the big white fellow seems familiar to me. I think I've seen him before, somewhere." Owen leaned over and laughed softly; "You're getting old my friend and your memory is going." Wilson just nodded and sat back; "I'd swear that I've dealt with him before."

Jericho sighed with relief as the little group appeared with their baggage and headed back to the car's. "They collected their kit and locked the place up. Thank heaven for that." Wilson moved the van back up the road and the team watched as the two cars departed the pub and headed for the Oxford Road. "At least he had the sense to call it a day." Jericho muttered and instructed Wilson to head for the pub car park.

They parked by the side of the pub, where the brewery would normally deliver, and Owen said quietly; "We have company." They watched as the Ford Cortina pulled into the derelict pub car park. A young couple sat in the car smoking; the smoke pouring out the open windows. The team started to chuckle as the pair threw their cigarettes out and started to kiss. "A bloody courting couple; that's all we need." muttered Jericho who went back to consulting his mirror.

Alex leaned between Wilson and Jericho and grinned; "They are not wasting much time, are they?" The seats in the car were down and one of the girl's legs was hanging out the window; her pink panties hanging around the ankle. The young man was on top, and his big, bare hairy arse was clearly seen. Owen chuckled; "Now that might attract our demon if it's Jessel. He really loves human females." Wilson nodded and realised his mirror was buzzing.

Jericho's mirror also started to buzz – loudly – and flash. All their mirrors had gone into alarm. He looked up and saw the hooded figure coming through the pub wall; the van turned over with glass smashing and rolled again ending up on its roof. There was no one inside; Jericho had managed to operate the Emergency Travel app despite hanging upside down. He would be grateful that he kept his seat belt on. They brushed themselves down outside the lighthouse and Jericho consulted his mirror. "Demon Ingress reports that a Tier 1 Demon called Sol has appeared at the pub. A knight is on the way. Everyone OK?"

Owen picked glass from his hair and didn't smile; "Thank the bastards for the early warning." Alex shook glass from her blouse and short skirt. Then grabbed Jericho by the arm and shouted; "The bloody courting couple! We have to go back now!" Jericho nodded and checked his mirror; "Come on, James is on scene." He operated his mirror and the team disappeared.

They joined James by the Ford Cortina; he wasn't alone. Suki the Collector was there, and she and Alex exchanged a kiss. They all could see the body of the young man inside the overturned car. His head had been crushed like a rotten apple and his trousers were still around his ankles. There was no sign of the girl. Jericho slammed his hand down on a spinning tyre and cursed. This had turned bad; really bad. A demon had abducted a living human right under a team's nose; not that they could have done much about it against a Tier 1 demon.

Suki stated that the young man was due to die tonight and that's why she was there. But there was no soul to collect. It had been taken. He was Colin Folds from Oxford, and he should have been killed tonight by his lover's jealous husband who would turn up in his works van and catch the pair. He would have killed Colin with a large spanner from his toolbox. He was a railway engineer with serious anger and jealousy problems.

"I should have called for a Knight earlier." Jericho said and cursed again. James patted his arm; "Operations would have not sent one until there was a confirmation, you know that my friend."

Alex walked towards the pub front and then stopped; she bent down and picked up the pair of pink panties. "He has her." Was all she said and sighed. This was now quite serious, and the team knew it. Jericho's mirror buzzed and he answered it slowly. He nodded and lowered his mirror; "One human soul has gone missing from the current Human Timeline. A Mrs. Ellen Tate aged twenty-four from Oxford. Her scheduled departure date was 2008. Her boyfriend Colin is now a missing soul as well."

Jericho folded his arms; "This changes the Human Timeline and not in a good way people. Mrs. Tate would have remarried in 1983 and have three children. One of her grandchildren is important to the Human Timeline due to what she does in 2041. The shit has hit the fan alright. It also means that her husband Jerry doesn't go to prison and murders three young girls over the next seven years before being caught and finally jailed."

He continued; "Angel Margret has ordered us to restore the Timeline and do it quickly. The time controller has said that the new Timeline will start to take effect in 72 human hours."

"He's a nasty bastard – Sol I mean – I hope that poor woman dies quickly, but her soul now belongs to the dark side. There's not much we can do about that unless we can undo what happened here. Who called the bloody bastard up in the first place? Tier one's normally appear when followers of the Dark Prince call for them." James spoke with real anger in his voice and stared back at the body of the late Colin Folds.

Owen coughed for attention and held up his mirror; "This place, the pub I mean has seen no less than thirteen missing souls over the centuries and one missing living human before the woman tonight. A certain Jeremiah Cornerstone in 1772 disappeared from the Human Timeline and is still registered as a missing soul. This place has provided rich pickings for the Dark Side."

Jericho nodded his thanks for update and operated his mirror. They returned to the lighthouse with James following a few minutes later. Everyone gathered in the study and was served drinks by Mr. Harris, who was more than happy to serve Mr. James, a Knight of God. To him it was like serving royalty!
Jericho sipped his most welcome brandy and tapped the glass; "I think we need to go back and find out about the Ouija Board use in that old pub. Check out Mr. Bonaparte and his team and change the bloody outcome of their stupid interference with time and people's lives." James sat and smiled at Alex but answered Jericho; "I will accompany you Jericho with a Tier 1 on scene. But it's still your case my friend."

Jericho nodded and finished his drink. "So, it's back to 1976 with a decent cover story and try and sort this bloody mess out."

3. SATURDAY 14th AUGUST 1976; OXFORD ENGLAND.

JP lowered his newspaper and picked up the coffee cup; the paper was full of the story about the happenings at the old pub; the terrible 'accident' with the young man's body trapped in the crushed car for almost three hours and the total disappearance of his lover; Mrs. Ellen Tate. He sighed and sipped his coffee and wondered if his team would be happy to return to their mission at the place now. But he knew that something was happening at the old pub; something supernatural and possibly dangerous. He wondered if the terrible incident with the lover's was linked with the pub reputation for paranormal happenings. Someone had disappeared totally there before. He lowered his coffee cup and stared at the picture of his grandfather on the wall opposite and smiled. "Thanks gramps, you would have gone for it regardless and so will I." He would call the group together and hit the pub that very night, but first he would contact the local police to ensure they had no objections to his team appearing at the site of the tragic 'accident'. But they [the police] insisted that they could only allow the students back on site the next afternoon.

With the arrangement made for another visit the following afternoon, JP headed for his car and pulled the top down. This summer of '76 would go in the history books with the weather creating more headlines every day. There was an official drought in place and tarmac on the roads had taken to melting.

JP slipped into the little car and started the engine. He looked back at the old house where he had an apartment and wondered about its history. One of his live-in girlfriends [at the time] swore blind she saw a woman walk through a wall in the upper hallway. The big house was split into six apartments. JP's rooms would have been the old servant's quarters in Victorian and Edwardian times. With a big smile he pulled away and headed for the university. He had resided there for three years and had seen and heard nothing. Maybe they [his team] should try the old Ouija Board there.

Just after the mini-roundabout and the turning for the city road, JP slowed his car and stared at the little mini parked against the edge of the country road, but it wasn't the car that caught his eye despite the obvious flat tyre. It was the woman kneeling by the deflated wheel. He came to halt a few yards behind the mini and whistled to himself. You didn't see a woman like this every day. She was absolutely stunning, and she rose and smiled at him. He gripped the wheel and actually swallowed hard. He was already getting an erection!

JP took a deep breath and tried to push the picture of her naked from his mind. Now that was difficult, but he jumped from the car and smiling broadly walked up to her and offered his assistance. The closer he got; the more beautiful he realized she was. He thanked his lucky stars and fate for this fantastic chance encounter. He introduced himself and was surprised – and really pleased – when he found out that she was a doctor. A woman on his intellectual level: [he did have an ego!] Brains and beauty in one gorgeous package he told himself and immediately offered to change the tyre.

That's when he saw the other lady sitting in the passenger seat, a dark-haired beauty with a long pair of legs in a short skirt. "That's my friend Jackie. We just don't have the strength between us to turn the little nuts!" Alex smiled at him, and he gulped; this pair could turn the nuts on any man with just a smile. He watched as 'Jackie' eased from the car, giving him a glimpse of pink thighs and damp white panties. He groaned under his breath as he pulled the spare wheel from the boot. The two women stood by the front of the car and watched as JP wrestled with the jack and wheel brace. Alex bent right over him, and he stared down her half open blouse and groaned again. Her breasts matched her legs in magnificence. She asked if they could do anything for him.

He eased the flat tyre off and smiled; he knew bloody well what they could do for him! But he smiled and suggested a drink or a pub lunch. He knew a very nice pub near the university and would buy the ladies lunch. Alex smiled and insisted that she and Jackie would buy him lunch. He nodded and didn't protest anymore. He had the tyre changed and wiped his hands on a cloth from his glove compartment. The ladies would follow him to the pub and they did.

JP grinned broadly as they walked into the Kings Arms and every male - and some women – turned to watch the girls enter. They were quickly shown a table and given menus. They enjoyed chicken salad and JP was surprised that both ladies enjoyed a half pint of cask ale with their lunch. He was further surprised to find that both ladies were rugby fan's and Jackie was particularly knowledgeable about the game. He grew more and more impressed with the pair as the lunch went on. Finally, he told them about his passion for the paranormal and supernatural. Normally, most women were totally uninterested in his hobby. But Jackie squeaked with delight and gripped his hand; telling him that her older brother was a professor of History at Rutland University and that was his all-consuming hobby too! They were in the city to meet him; he was on some case with his associate; an American writer from New York. Now JP was really interested and wondered about the 'case' they were working on. He told them about his latest case at the old derelict pub, The Devil and the Pit. Both ladies were really keen to hear all about that.

He explained that he had been asked by the current owner to check out the stories and legends about the pub and maybe, put the stories to rest. "I think he [the pub owner] hopes that such a report will help sell the damn place." Alex leaned across the table and smiled; "We would love to help with such a task. Jackie's bother would be absolutely delighted to assist, especially a fellow colleague in the same endeavours." She also gave his hand a little squeeze. He simply couldn't refuse!

Jackie wrote a phone number on a beer mat and pushed it – with a big smile – into his hand. He took it quickly and they left the pub, agreeing to meet up that evening at his rooms in the University. He watched them walk to their car with swinging hips and big smiles; they waved and drove away. He slumped into his car and thanked God – which he didn't do often – and drove to the University with a huge grin. He knew that Willy and John wouldn't mind about the girls appearing on the case. Nor would Dave – especially not Dave – and the only problem might be Maggie; she was jealous of any woman who came near him and would flip when she saw these two stunners.

Now that made him smile even more. Rose wouldn't give a toss; that's the way she is. He had real respect for her; she certainly didn't chase him, but then she seemed quite taken by her police sergeant friend these days. He believed that relationship could easy turn quite serious. JP spent the day in anticipation of meeting the girls again. He also looked forward to meeting Jackie's brother and his friend from New York. This could prove to be a very interesting evening he told himself. That's when he picked up the evening paper and he's smile vanished. It was full with the death of Colin Folds and the apparent disappearance of the railway engineer's wife – all from the very pub car park that he and his team were in earlier – linking the tragic incident to the ghostly tales and history of the pub. He groaned aloud; that's all he bloody needed; crowds of on-lookers turning up!

But he would be disappointed over the girls visit because the caretaker at his Apartment building called asking – no insisting – that he speak with him tonight at his apartment; he wouldn't discuss the matter over the phone. It was with some reluctance that JP drove home that afternoon and waited in his rooms. He dozed on the sofa, and he actually jumped a little when his door buzzer sounded. He opened the door slowly; it was Mister Hamish McTabb – the building caretaker – who stood grim faced and looking concerned. "I wonder if I may have a word with your Sir; about what occurred here last night?" JP was now puzzled and asked the old man in. Some twenty minutes later – after some whisky – Mister McTabb left in a far better mood; he could tell the two elderly spinsters in Flat Nine that the professor was on the case.

JP sat on the couch and rolled the whisky glass about in his hands and actually smiled at the story the old caretaker had recounted. The two sisters – both in their sixties – had a close encounter in their sitting room with a ghost! Well, technically it was a poltergeist since it moved two chairs about and pulled up both the ladies nice new summer dresses and slapped their bums. JP chuckled and picked up the phone. He called Rose and she told him that her 'friend' Danny had been placed on the team investigating the death and disappearance in the pub car park and he was on his way to meet JP and would also have to speak the others, who were there that night.

JP agreed and told Rose about meeting the two women from Yorkshire and that a fellow professor and his associate would also be in attendance. He told her about the appearance of the naughty poltergeist in Flat Nine and she agreed that they should investigate; immediately. "I can get the caretaker to let us in; the two old ladies have gone to stay with their married brother for tonight and so the place is available." JP told her and Rose would call the other's and see who could assist at short notice.

He replaced the receiver and was actually quite happy that Rose and her friend would be there. But he wondered what the two girls [Alex & Jackie] would be doing this evening. He pulled the beer mat from his pocket and smiled; maybe he should give the pair a call and see if they would be interested in a little ghost hunting.

4. THE PROFESSOR LOVES THE UNEXPECTED!

JP climbed from the bath and wrapped a towel around, then picked up the small transistor radio he had been listening to and headed for his bedroom to dress. The news on the radio was all about the bleeding weather; he grunted and switched it off. Then the doorbell went, and he went to the front door and asked who it was. A big smile crept across his face as Alex answered, quietly apologizing if she and Jackie were early. He told them he had just stepped from the bath; both girls said they didn't mind!

He pulled open the door and the pair wandered in, smiling broadly at the big man standing in just a small towel. Unusually – it was one of the hottest summers on record – they were both wearing long summer coats. He was about to ask when they both pulled their coats off, grinning. JP stared in disbelief as they tossed the coats on the nearby small table and stood – hands on hips – in just their underwear. Both were wearing black stockings and suspenders with little black panties and see-through black lace bodices. Their 'outfits' were finished with black high heels.

JP managed to say; "I see you dressed for the weather….and for me!" Both girls laughed and nodded. Alex walked straight up to him and kissed him; "And I see you dressed just for us!" and took hold of his towel and he smiled as she pulled it away and threw it on the floor. Alex ran her hands down his torso and took hold of his stiffening cock which was wonderfully big and erecting at her touch. Without a word she knelt and pushed it into her moist warm mouth and her tongue went to work.

Jackie joined the pair and JP grabbed her to him and their tongues explored each other's mouths with some urgency. He ran his hands over her small perk breasts and down to her bum. "You have a fucking stunning arse my darling." He whispered and groaned as Alex was now really hitting the spot. "Then you'll enjoy using it then." Jackie whispered back and the girls then swapped over; with Jackie now working his shaft with her expert mouth.

Alex took his hands and placed them around her back, and he skillfully had her flimsy bodice off in a second or two. His big hands took possession of her magnificent tits, and his mouth found a rock-hard nipple to enjoy. Both his hands slid down her slender body and slowly eased down her little black panties until they fell around her ankles. She kicked them away. He sucked her breasts hard, working her nipples with his tongue and teeth while Jackie did the same with his throbbing cock.

Finally, JP pulled off her tits and gestured to the big sofa; "On your back there and I will fuck you hard. While your friend watches, then it's her turn." Alex submissively nodded and he watched in delight and anticipation as she walked to sofa; her gorgeous arse swinging with her hips. She sat on the sofa and slowly pulled open her legs. "Nice and wide for a big man like you." She said quietly. JP patted Jackie's head and grabbed her hand; they walked over to Alex and Jackie kissed his cheek; "I'll get her ready for you." She knelt between Alex's legs and really worked her crotch with tongue and fingers. All JP could do was watch – wide-eyed – and jerk his cock in anticipation.

He couldn't wait any longer and told Jackie to step aside and pushed between Alex's legs and mounted her with some urgency. He kept his promise and fucked her hard; like a bloody road hammer thought Jackie, a little jealous of the fucking Alex was receiving. Alex was pushed back against the sofa as JP leaned over her; gripping the back of the sofa as he fucked her deep and fast. She groaned and gripped his arse with both hands to encourage the fucking. He stopped fucking suddenly and groaned; Jackie had knelt behind him and was rimming his bum hole with her tongue; she included his big balls hanging between his legs. He groaned out loud and Alex pulled his head down and they 'French' kissed with some real passion. The arse licking did the job and JP managed a few more hard thrusts and exploded inside Alex; moaning and cussing. He staggered back and watched in utter delight as Jackie cleaned up Alex's gaped fanny with her tongue and Alex gestured him over and took hold of his cock and cleaned it with her tongue and mouth.

"I've fucking died and gone to heaven." He whispered and slumped on the sofa with the girls either side of him, sharing his cock with their mouths and skilful tongues. His new erection appeared pretty quickly under such a delicious assault. Jackie bent over in front of him, and he groaned with sheer joy as he slid her panties down and Alex reached around her and pulled open her bum cheeks to reveal a well lubricated delightful anus.

JP didn't hesitate and pushed his cock in gently at first and then started thrust. Jackie was on all fours and JP dominated her, fucking her arse with some real pleasure and satisfaction. He and Alex kissed some more; their tongues exploring each other's mouths. He carefully moved Jackie to the sofa, and she knelt on it, head down and arse in the air. He really fucked her now, pushing down hard and fast. Jackie was groaning and gasping with each thrust. He lifted her around and sat on the sofa with Jackie on his lap and continued to fuck her, thrusting upwards. Alex was rubbing her fanny vigorously at the sight of Jackie getting arse fucked by JP. She joined them and sucked Jackie's cock, but JP thought she was licking and fingering Jackie's fanny and shouted encouragement; not that Alex needed it!

Jackie was bouncing up and down with Alex sucking her cock and she came in Alex's mouth, gasping and cussing: that made JP chuckle and he couldn't stop coming himself and filled Jackie's back passage. He laid back gasping and panting. Jackie put her arm around him pulled his head to her mouth and they French kissed for some time. Alex fetched a towel from the bathroom and gave it to JP who was really reluctant to withdrawn from Jackie's bum. Jackie slowly lifted herself off his cock and held her cheeks together and walked slowly to the bathroom. Alex cleaned JP's dirty cock with the towel while they kissed.

Alex left JP on the couch and joined Jackie in the bathroom. JP lay quietly on the sofa and smiled; what a fucking pair of incredible tarts he thought. He already wanted them again, especially Alex's big breasts and Jackie's incredible little arse. He could hear the talking and laughing in the bathroom and he breathed deep and lay staring at the ceiling and then glanced at the clock on the mantelpiece. He leapt up - Jesus Christ! - The team would be arriving any minute!

"Girls, sorry Girls, but my paranormal team will arrive in a few minutes, and I really need the bathroom." He shouted, standing naked by the door, which was opened by a smiling Jackie who took hold of his hand and pulled him in. "Oh God!" he muttered and smiled broadly.

5. THE OLD SOLDIERS.

The girls sat in the little mini and laughed, their long coats wrapped around their flimsy underwear. "You realise that he has no idea that he just fucked a young man." Alex said to Jackie who gave her hand a little slap; "I'm a lady when I'm my other self; you know that you naughty girl." Alex apologised and the pair laughed some more. They watched JP's team [who could attend] arrive and disappear into the building. Jackie shifted in her seat and consulted her mirror; "Nothing known about any of them. All belong to this era, and all are clean." Alex started the engine and pulled away, heading for the city road and their hotel. They didn't get far; it made some strange whistling noises, backfired and rolled to a halt.

They both stood by the car and Jackie sighed; "I have no bloody idea why it's conked out. I'll put a call into Supplies, and they can collect the heap. It will be dark soon and we don't want to be standing around here in just our underwear." Alex chuckled and then saw the headlights as the old van came to a stop; they couldn't see the two men for the glare of the headlamps. Then they appeared; both wearing the same blue jacket and red berets. They were both in their late fifties and looked quite smart. "Can we be of assistance ladies?" The bigger one of the two asked. For his age, Alex reckoned his was in good condition and must have been quite a handsome man in his youth. That also applied to his friend. They all stood and chatted; the two men were heading into Oxford for a Regimental reunion - hence the matching outfits - it turned out that Graham Case and George Babette had landed on the Normandy beaches as young soldiers and managed to survive that and the rest of the war.

Both girls stared at each other: Babette! Alex had to ask, if he had a grandfather called Frederick Babette who worked in service before the First World War. The old soldier smiled but shook his head. Then he tapped his chin; "I seem to remember my old Gran saying something about one of her brothers- in-laws [her husband's brothers: Eric Babette, had three brothers] simply disappearing back before the Great War. I believe he worked in service in some big house in London. Sorry, I don't know much else, not even his name." Jackie gripped Alex's hand: Eric was the name of Freddie's brother, whose little apartment Alex and he had practically wrecked on their honeymoon, by their sexual activities. [See episode: 'Alexandra: the reluctant French Maid'.] Graham offered the ladies a lift into Oxford provided they didn't mind the smell of the gym mats in the back of the van. The pair now ran a gym in the city and Alex realised that the two men were in good shape for their age: very good shape. She glanced at Jackie who smiled at the pair and then at Alex. Both girls smiled and gracefully accepted the offer of a lift. Alex hoped to find out more about George's ancestor who 'vanished'.

Jackie whispered: "I've always had bit of a 'daddy complex' for really good-looking older men." Alex – smiling – agreed: the two charming and dashing old soldiers were in for a treat.

The old van was rocking as George fucked Jackie on the front seat; he had seen that Jackie was a 'special lady' and didn't care; he made up his mind to fuck her when she pulled off that long raincoat. The sight of stockings and suspenders was enough for him; then the blow job that made him squeal with pleasure before she knelt - awkwardly - on the front seat and allowed him to fuck her arse. He was fucking her hard and slapping her bum with some force. He looked into the back of the van and saw Freddie fucking Alex in the Missionary position. "You have to try this arse Graham, its fucking heaven!"

Graham looked up and smiled; "I fucking will, this one is a fucking sex monster, she licked my God damn arse before I fucked her!"

George panted, thrusting deep into the soft arse under him and prayed to God that he could get another erection so he could fuck the big titted tart after Graham. Clearly, they had fucked girls together before this and the pair could recount some real ripe stories about their time in France during 1945 and 1946. One included a French mother and daughter they fucked in the back of a derelict furniture shop in a quiet Paris back alley. He couldn't hold it much longer and after fifteen minutes he pulled out his dick and told Jackie to turn quickly, she grabbed his throbbing cock and pushed it into her mouth. He came, groaning and cussing, watching Jackie swallow every drop. "Thank God you do ATM." He whispered and that puzzled Jackie as she wiped her mouth. She thought that was a cash machine and he chuckled as he explained that it meant "Arse to Mouth". They laughed and Jackie's head was in his lap; sucking his cock with some determination again; she didn't want Alex to be disappointed. Graham also finished coming in Alex with some force and lay back gripping his cock as she edged down to his cock and began to suck; she didn't want to disappoint Jackie. The two men - luckily - responded to the urgent sucking of their cocks and equipped with fresh erections, they swapped over.

George was delighted to fuck a woman like Alex, and he fucked her - also in the missionary position - hard and fast whilst enjoying those big titties with his mouth and hands. Meanwhile in the front seat, Jackie had both hands on the dash, sitting on Graham's cock while watching out the windscreen as she rode him with some skill. He gripped her pert tits and groaned with sheer pleasure; George was right, her arse was heaven itself. The foursome fucked for another twenty minutes, and the men were done. So, Jackie and Alex entertained each other while they rested. It was almost two hours before the van pulled up outside the Team's hotel and the girls gave the men a cheeky little kiss and said their goodbyes. The men were wise enough not to offer the girls money for their entertainment despite believing they were a pair of high-class hookers! Graham drove to the reunion - somewhat late - and then realised that they didn't even know the girls name's and worse; they hadn't even taken a bloody phone number!

They heaved the gym mats from the van and Graham smiled; "It was like that time in Paris in '45, those two sisters who lived above that café. Christ, you would never have guessed that the tall one was her bleeding brother!" George nodded, smiling at the memory. "It didn't stop us fucking the pair!" They both laughed and George added; "Then that mother and daughter in Saxony. Now, if the daughter didn't have such a big dick, I would have sworn on my mother's life, it was a woman." Graham locked the van and sighed; "I really took to the little dark haired one, she was fucking incredible." He hesitated then added ruefully; "We have to find them again mate, I really have a thing for Jackie and I don't give us toss about her cock. You can't get choosy at our age, and she was fucking special. Really special."

George smiled at his friend and shook his head; It appears that Graham wanted more than just great sex with the young 'lady'. The pair carried the mats in the gym laughing together.

Alex now wondered what had happened to Freddie Babette: had he really disappeared before the Great War? Had he jumped in time? She lay in the bath with her head full of outcomes and idea's about Freddie. Finally, she decided to do something she swore she wouldn't: she checked Freddie's Human Record and just stared at her mirror. According to the current timeline Frederick Babette was a missing soul! Either he had sold his soul to the Dark Side or jumped through time! She shouted with delight to Jackie, who stood in the doorway, sipping a brandy, and smiling. "Does it say what age he disappeared at?" she asked, and Alex really smiled; "He was exactly thirty when he jumped, so that's the age he is now."

Jackie now smiled; "A young breeding bull if we can find him." Alex splashed the bathwater and chuckled: "Oh bleeding yes we will find him!" And the pair both laughed.

6. STILL SATURDAY 14th AUGUST 1976; APARTMENT NINE, KENNEDY BUILDINGS, OXFORD, ENGLAND.

Danny and Rose were the first to arrive and JP poured them some whisky. Rose wanted to know about the women JP had met and JP just smiled and didn't elaborate much more than he had already divulged about them. Their conversation was interrupted by Maggie arriving with John Morris. Dave Clay and Willy Kent couldn't make it. John had the old Ouija board in his satchel which he placed on the table. JP gave them a whisky too and briefed everyone on the strange happenings in Apartment number nine.

Suitably fortified with whisky, the team headed for apartment number nine and JP unlocked the door and they wandered in. John pointed to the large Dining table by the big bay window. "That's perfect to set up the board." And walked over, slapping his satchel on it. "Even has a bloody candle." He added and was joined by Rose who lit the candles and really wanted a cigarette but wouldn't smoke in the old ladies dining room. John set up the board and explained to Danny how it worked. Maggie would again take notes and sit away from the others. Rose sniffed a couple of times and asked JP if the old ladies had male visitors. JP chuckled; "No they are proper old spinster aunts, why do you ask?" Rose shrugged her shoulders; "I would swear that I could smell traces of aftershave. That stuff Henry Cooper advertises on the goggle box; two of my uncle's used to bath in the stuff."

JP chuckled again and told everyone to take their places around the table. He wanted to start right away and checked his watch; it was just before nine o'clock. They settled in around the table, with JP and John placing their fingers on the Planchette. JP called out for any spirits to manifest themselves with no reaction. He called a couple of times, and they waited in anticipation and silence, looking about the gloomy room lit only by the flickering candles. Rose had a big torch in her lap, and she gripped it tightly.

Maggie sat bolt upright in her chair and whispered to the others, pointing to the fireplace with her trembling felt tip pen. "The bloody mantelpiece clock's second hand is running bloody backwards." Everyone turned to the fireplace and saw that she was right. She composed herself and wrote the time down with a brief description of what was occurring. Danny whispered that the room had gone strangely cold, and JP nodded his agreement and called out once more for the sprit to make contact. The Planchette began to move slowly, and JP called the letters out to Maggie and realised that he was sweating despite the chill in the room. After a few minutes the Planchette stopped moving and everyone turned to Maggie who lifted her note pad and said softly; "He knows. He will come. The Devil is already with you. Beware of the Devil with the mask." she lowered the notebook and coughed; her throat had suddenly become quite dry, and she really needed a Coke or Fanta or anything really.

"What does that mean; 'the Devil with a mask is amongst us'. I don't understand that." Danny said quietly. Everyone glanced at each other, and JP sighed; "Let's ask them to clarify who the Devil is." He called out again asking the spirit to clarify what it meant. He repeated his question twice before the Planchette began to move again. He called the letters out to Maggie who nervously scribbled them down. The Planchette stopped moving and Maggie lifted up her note pad and read out what she had written. "He is. He is. They are here for him. Seek their help." She lowered the pad and asked what it meant. No-one knew. JP wiped sweat from his face with his free hand and asked the spirit its name. The Planchette set off again around the board and JP called the letters out.

"Norman." Maggie said and John groaned; "That's the bugger we made contact with at the old pub and then all hell broke loose. I think he's a poltergeist." JP nodded and decided to shut down the séance and get professional assistance for this case, perhaps old Professor Lightfoot immediately came to mind and JP would call him in the morning. That's when her realised with some horror that he couldn't move his finger from the Planchette and he whispered to John, who cussed and said that his finger was stuck too. The Planchette started to move again. His voice now a little hoarse, JP called out the letters to Maggie. It suddenly stopped and Maggie - her voice now trembled a little - read out what was said. "Too late. Too late. He's here. Run. Run. Run."

Everyone rose from the table as one and stood in silence, looking at each other. Danny whispered; "For Christ what have you done?" JP and John jumped back as their fingers were released from the Planchette. The board started to turn slowly, becoming faster and faster. Everyone stepped slowly back from the spinning board. It flew from the table - just missing Maggie - and landed in the fireplace. The little flames appeared, and the board was consumed with fire until it was ashes. That's when Maggie screamed the house down. Her baggy bright coloured shorts had been ripped off her and she stood in her white panties. She screamed hysterically as she appeared to be thrown to the floor. Everyone rushed forward but was thrown back with some force. Maggie's T-shirt was torn from her back and thrown to one side. Her bra followed and despite their attempts they couldn't get near her; some powerful force was keeping them at bay. Rose was now screaming hysterically for someone to do something; anything.

They watched in utter horror as the screaming and struggling Maggie had her panties torn from her and her legs pulled open with such force that bruises started to appear on her thighs. She suddenly lay still; she had fainted with her legs open and standing straight up like invisible hands were holding her ankles. Danny fumbled in jacket pocket and pulled the wooden crucifix out and ran forward, holding it high. He stumbled and fell forward, landing next to the still Maggie. Everyone else rushed forward and Rose grabbed hold of Maggie; "She's still alive thank God!" Danny wrapped his jacket around Maggie and then picked her up and everyone ran to JP apartment. As JP dialled for an ambulance, he noticed the time on his watch; they had started the séance just before nine. His watch was showing eight o'clock. He asked John the time as they watched Rose trying to bring Maggie around with some brandy. John stared at his brand-new LCD watch as said quietly; "It's over an hour out. It's showing eight o'clock and it should be well past nine o'clock."

After contacting the emergency operator on '999' JP asked Danny the time. He tapped his watch; it was over an hour out. It was showing eight o'clock. JP nodded and told the very concerned Rose that the ambulance was on its way. Rose had made Maggie as comfortable as possible and stood physically shaking and had to compose herself with some real hidden strength. Finally, she took a deep breath and confided what she had discovered. Everyone just stared at her until John finally said; "She can't...I mean there was no-one there.... we all saw nobody. Are you fucking sure Rose?" Danny eased himself down on the edge of the sofa on which Maggie lay and asked Rose if she was right. Rose nodded slowly and said quietly; "I think she's been raped." Everyone stood in silence until they heard the sirens growing louder. JP headed to the front door saying he would greet the ambulance and Danny called his station on the phone asking for a WPC trained in sexual assault cases: a specialist female officer for sexual assault cases.

John grabbed up the whisky bottle off the coffee table and took a long swig, then handed it to Rose saying; "I think we are all going to need this." Rose took the bottle and stared down at Maggie, then took a swig, coughing, she said; "You are bloody right there John. How the fuck do we explain all this without sounding like total nutters?" He shook his head with great sadness and a little fear; he bloody didn't know.

7. STILL SATURDAY 14th AUGUST 1976; THE OXFORD ROYAL INFIRMARY.

They sat in the quiet waiting room and there was very little conversation. Danny was in the corridor speaking to the female detective sergeant from his station with two uniform constables standing by. Rose walked to the glass door and watched for a couple of minutes and returned to John and JP sitting cradling plastic cups of really bad coffee. She sighed; "Boy's, I think we're in deep shit. Who the hell is going to believe that a fucking poltergeist raped our Maggie?" JP shook his head; "I think it was a demon that the spirit 'Norman' was trying to warn us about: 'The Devil who wears a mask' that's the only bloody clue we have." They all managed a smile as Dave Clay appeared in the corridor and spoke to Danny before coming - grim faced - into the room. Rose gave him a hug and asked where Willy was; but Dave didn't know but he seemed to remember that Willy might be at a piss up at the Rugby Club.

They all stopped talking as Danny came in the room and just stood staring at the floor. Rose went to him and gripped his hand. He nodded and took a little breath. "Maggie is in a coma. The doctors say that her brain has closed down due to shock, but she may come round at any time." He took a deep breath this time and continued, speaking slowly; "They, the doctors confirm that she was sexually assaulted. Roughly violated but they can't find any trace of semen in her, but her thighs are badly bruised as is her.... her vagina. She was violated quite violently and they say it has all the signs of a violent rape. Both her ankles have finger marks - bruises - on them." Rose eased into a hard plastic chair and sobbed openly. Danny sat next to Rose and cuddled her, stroking her hair and talking quietly.

John and JP crushed their plastic coffee cups and threw them into the bin by the window. They both stood by the window with their arms folded. John sighed; "No-one is going to believe our story until Maggie pulls out the coma and bloody tells them what happened to her. Until then, I think, we are the number one suspects for this." JP rubbed his face; "I think I'll call Professor Lightfoot...." He stopped in mid-sentence and almost smiled; "But I do know another professor who is actually here right now and is a paranormal investigator of some note. I met some friends of his and they said he would assist us with the old pub job. I have his sister's number and I'll give her a ring. He has a team with him apparently."

John nodded; "What's his name? Have I heard of him?" JP pulled the beer mat from his pocket and said quietly; "Tibbs, Professor Tibbs." The female Police sergeant came through the door - unsmiling - with the two uniform police officers. She gripped her handbag with both hands; "Alright everyone listen up. You are all going down the station to make full statements about what happened tonight. You are the only witnesses to what happened to that poor girl so I know I can expect your full co-operation in this matter. Come on, let's go." JP asked if he could make one phone call and got a very unsympathetic look from the sergeant. "I'll tell you when you can call your lawyer." was all she said and gestured for everybody to leave. They filed out in silence and found a police van waiting for them in the hospital carpark. John and JP were placed in the van, whilst Rose and Danny travelled to the station in the back of the sergeant's car. Dave was told to make his own way to the police station - if he wanted - since he wasn't an actual witness or suspect.

Dave watched the little convoy depart and clutched the beer mat. JP had said the mad professor's sister was a stunner. He went back into the hospital and found a public telephone that wasn't occupied by a hospital visitor. The phone rang for a few seconds and was answered by Jackie who thought it was JP until Dave stopped her in mid-sentence and explained who he was and what had happened. Jackie went silent for a second or two and then told him that her brother would be on the way soon with her and the other two members of the team; her good friends; Alexandra and Mister Wilson. She reassured Dave that Professor Tibbs could certainly help JP in this matter. Dave replaced the receiver and thought about poor Maggie.

8. STILL SATURDAY 14th AUGUST 1976; THE 'DEVIL & THE PIT' PUBLIC HOUSE, OXFORD, ENGLAND.

"The police think the car was hit by something like a tractor or Bulldozer; after all, what else could have done that sort of damage? The police had the car lifted and taken away on the back of a lorry. They searched the surrounding woods and found nothing. They think Mrs. Tate ran off in shock and fear; her husband is a very jealous and apparently, violent man. They're making appeals for her to come forward and offering her protection. She hasn't appeared yet." Jackie informed them. "I can sense a minor demon, but the signals are quite strong." James whispered to Jericho.

Switching on their mirror's lights the team slipped under the police incident tapes and headed into the old pub. Wilson soon had the door open without having any keys, which never ceased to amaze Jackie; "I always said there was something dodgy about you. How many New York detectives know how to burgle?" Jericho stared at the old pub sign and picked up the undamaged red tablecloth from the floor. It appeared unchanged despite the 'fire'. Wilson was discretely checking his mirror in a dark corner as James and Jericho discussed what actually could have happened. The girls sat at the table by the window and Jackie went through the notes, that Maggie made on the night they used the Ouija board. Dave had been more than happy to hand over the papers when he had met Alex and Jackie in the Kennedy Building car park earlier. They had managed to talk him out of joining the team and he headed to the hospital.

Wilson and Jericho were now behind the bar, lifting the trap door to the cellar. Wilson shone a small torch down and grunted; "That is one huge beer cellar, come on we'll take a better look." He and Jericho descended the stairs and were gone.

James was joined by Jackie who was pushing her mirror back into her handbag. "Norman was definitely here; I've picked up his presence almost everywhere, but strangely enough very little traces of a demonic presence. Maybe a Tier 3, but the bastard turned over our van and the lover's car and would indicate a demon." She whispered and James heard Wilson calling from the hatchway behind the main bar. He and Jackie walked over, and James smiled at Wilson staring up from the dark cellar hatchway.
"It's like a rabbit's warren down here but there's a very old door - looks like something you would find in a medieval castle – it was hidden behind some old shelves, but I was drawn straight to it and according to my mirror; it's a portal." Wilson said quietly and James smiled, he had already picked up on its presence; Knights of God didn't need mirrors to discover such things!

James helped the girls down the hatchway with Alex cursing her short skirt. "I'm always showing off my damn bits." She muttered as James held her quite close and easily lifted her down from the hatchway. He smiled; "You won't find me complaining." Then Wilson pulled Jackie down not so gently. "I see you got the real gentleman again." She moaned to Alex, pulling down her equally short skirt.

The team made their way to the old doorway using their mirrors to light the way and Jericho shone his over the magnificent archway and ancient door. "Anyone recognize the strange writing running about the mantle of the archway?" It was rhetorical; he knew the origin of the writing. Jackie sighed; "Aramaic I believe my mirror can translate it…" she never finished as James read out what it said. [Again, Knights of God really don't need mirrors].

"It states that the door leads to God's world of the hereafter, an underworld for the unholy dead who can't enter heaven or hell." He shrugged his shoulders adding; "Come on, let's find out where it really leads." He simply walked through and vanished. The team had to operate their mirrors and the dark pub cellar was empty.

9. SUNDAY 15th AUGUST 1976; St. ALDATES POLICE STATION, OXFORD ENGLAND.

They sat waiting in the corridor outside the CID offices after their strenuous and lengthy interviews. JP picked up a paper that was a couple of days old from the table by the drinks machine. He had drunk four cups of really shitty coffee from plastic cups and really needed a shower, some breakfast and hopefully Alex and Jackie. He just stared at the print and really didn't actually read; he couldn't stop thinking about poor Maggie and the dreadful scene he had witnessed in the old ladies apartment. He blamed himself for poor Maggie and wondered what he could have done to stop it happening. He sighed loudly and slapped the paper back on the table. Rose - sitting next to him - patted his hand and smiled; "It wasn't your fault JP so don't blame yourself. We all knew the risks and so did Maggie; she would be first to tell you that it wasn't your fault." JP now smiled; Rose was bloody marvelous and how the hell did she know what he was thinking! John stood and paced the floor - for the tenth time - he folded his arms and yawned. He needed a drink and his bed. "Is there any update from the hospital about Maggie?" he asked no-one in particular. Rose shook her head; "Danny said he would tell us as soon as they know." John nodded, then asked her; "Is he ok with all this? I mean with his bosses?" Rose nodded; "They know he's a good copper and a honest decent man, so he's ok I suppose." JP stood and stretched his legs by pacing the corridor with John. "An hour and a bloody half and the same bloody questions over and over again. That woman sergeant is bloody something else." John moaned to JP who just nodded his agreement. That's when he saw Danny walking towards them.

Rose jumped up and really smiled; "Anything new Danny?" she asked cautiously and tided up her hair. She thought Danny must be thinking how rough she looks after a night of questioning in the CID offices. They gathered around him and he smiled; really smiled. "Just had words with Inspector Dawes and the Hospital just called to say that Maggie came round about an hour ago and told the detective sitting by her bed who attacked her; we are well and truly off the hook and so you three can go." The sense of sheer relief was obvious; the four all hugged and finally Rose, looking well puzzled, asked Danny; "How could she tell the detective who attacked her when there was nobody there, we all witnessed it for ourselves and there was nobody there." Danny's smile disappeared and he looked about and lowered his voice before answering. He took a deep breath and spoke quietly; "Maggie knows - for certain apparently - who her attacker was. He is known to her and she has known him for some time." He took another breath and whispered; "She's named big Willy Kent as the man who raped her."

The three stood in absolute, shocked silence at Danny's strange revelation. Then they all stated to talk at once; loudly. Danny waved his hands in the air for quiet. "I know, I know, but that's what's she saying. She's absolutely convinced that Willy raped her. She said that he laughed as he did it and threatened to kill her if she didn't submit. From what I managed to gleam from the WDC who took her bedside statement she painted a really convincing picture of what he did to her. It's so convincing that he will be arrested and questioned over the alleged attack. Even though we all stated that there was no-one there and Willy wasn't with us at any time during the night." He looked around again; "They have asked a psychiatrist to examine her."

Rose wiped a tear away and whispered to JP; "Poor bloody Maggie. She's gone off the rails, but why pick on poor Willy. He wasn't even bloody there!" JP shook his head; he certainly didn't know. John nodded his agreement; "Didn't Dave say that Willy was at some rugby piss-up, so there will be loads of witnesses and they will say he was with them, and they go on until one or two in the morning and this all took place at about nine o'clock." JP rubbed his chin; "Except all our watches showed eight o'clock which is also impossible because we all knew the correct time was nine o'clock." Danny held up his wristwatch and didn't smile; "My watch is now showing the correct time.... even though I didn't have time to set it correctly. It sorts of changed itself which is impossible. I only noticed this morning."

The other three all checked their timepieces and there was silence again for a few seconds then John nodded; "Mine's telling the correct time as well and I never touched it." He gestured to the big clock above the table. JP sighed; his watch was correct too. Rose stared at her delicate little wristwatch and nodded too; "Mine's back to normal and like Danny; I haven't fiddled with it." JP spoke quietly; "I strongly suspect that all our watches losing an hour is important, but I don't have a bloody idea why." The woman detective sergeant stuck her head out of her office door; "You lot can go home, and Thames Police thank you for your co-operation in this matter. Now off you go." The head disappeared back inside, and the door closed. They all trooped from the Police Station and stood on the pavement enjoying the beautiful, warm early morning sunshine and their freedom.

JP gathered them together; "Let's go home and rest up. We'll all meet again this afternoon and go visit Maggie. Bring flowers and chocolates, she'll like that." Rose smiled; "I'll get her some things she will need in hospital; pajama's and girls stuff." John chuckled at that; "Thank heaven you're around. None of us dumb blokes would have thought of that."

He stuck his arm up to wave down a city taxi; "Come on JP, the cabbie won't mind two fares. He can drop me off then run out to your place. I take it Danny you'll run Rose home." Danny nodded, smiling with his arm around Rose. The Nissan Bluebird 1800 pulled into the kerb and John and JP jumped in; shouting their goodbyes to Rose and Danny.

They walked to the police parking bays and climbed into Danny's Ford Escort and didn't see the big man entering the police station; it was Willy Kent and he was smiling broadly.

10. THE LAIR.

They gathered in front of the magnificent fireplace, but it was the huge portrait that hung above it, that caught their unanimous attention. Wilson chuckled; "Well, he certainly posses' with some style for his portraits; mounted on a black horse with a blazing halo around his head." The portrait of the 'Dark Prince' confirmed what James had stated; it was the demon's hidden lair. He looked around the huge room which was furnished in the Gothic style, complete with tapestries and suits of armour. James grunted; "I always suspected that Sol was a medieval nut, he was a Professor of Ancient History at a New England College when still a human. He's a clever bastard and has hidden his lair well."

Alex called everyone over to the big oak feasting table that dominated the room with thirteen equally impressive chairs set around it. They joined her and Alex picked up the little bundle of women's clothes that had been thrown onto the table. She lifted a blouse up and gestured to the other items; "Basically it's a woman's summer outfit, from the mid 1970's I would guess. It's all here except a pair of panties. I wonder if it's missing these." She rummaged in her big handbag and pulled the little pink panties that Mrs. Tate had dropped whilst being abducted by Sol the demon. Jericho rubbed his face; "I think we should have a careful and thorough look around Sol's little lair. He's known to like female company; particularly when their forced to keep him company."

Jackie was already onto it, tapping away at her mirror when James placed his hand on hers; "Don't bother Owen...Sorry Jackie. I can sense her soul and it's still in her flesh suit. Come on." They followed the Knight back to the fireplace and he climbed over the cold dead fire basket and gestured for them to follow; there was a descending staircase hidden in the dark recess of the fireplaces rear. They followed it down and found a big black door, which was reinforced with steel bands blocking their way. There was a large gold handle and keyhole, which Alex bent down and peered through. That caused the boys to chuckle, and Jericho said without censor in his voice; "For Christ sake Alex, could you wear a shorter skirt? We've just enjoyed your bum and little white panties thank you." She ignored him and jerked a thumb at the door, but before she could say anything James smiled; "Mrs. Ellen Tate I believe."

Alex nodded slowly muttering; "I was going to bloody say that." James told them to step back a few feet and simply pressed one hand against the mighty door and pushed. Little bits of wood flew about, and the hinges snapped as the door was pushed open, hanging to one side. Wilson rubbed his chin and whispered to Alex; "He did that without any real effort." Alex nodded and smiled; now that was man a girl could feel safe with. They climbed around the shattered door and entered the demon's dungeon. The strange big reptile with a gold collar and chain remained sitting in the corner with his bed and bowl. It may not have been the brightest of creations, but it knew what Knights of God were capable off.

Jackie stared at it and said with real bewilderment in her voice; "The bloody collar says it's called 'Marmaduke' - who calls a scaly dinosaur wannabee - bloody Marmaduke!" James chuckled; "I always said Sol had a strange sense of humour for a bloody demon." Alex shouted over to them standing by a wire cage which contained a very distraught and naked Mrs. Ellen Tate. James simply pulled open the thick wire until a reasonable hole appeared and Alex helped the poor woman out. She had bruises on her back and legs with several nasty love bites on her neck and shoulders. Jericho nodded to Alex and Jackie; "Look after her girls." James stared about the place; "At least the bastard keeps his dungeon clean. I've seen some you wouldn't keep a dead rat in." Wilson handed his jacket to Alex, who wrapped Ellen up with with it. "Yeah, but where is the bastard now and what's he up too?"

Jericho grunted; "That's a very good question big man."
Jackie whispered to Alex as they sat Ellen down and gave her some brandy from Alex's hipflask; "That's a strange scent she's wearing. Smells like something bloody Jericho would wear." Alex took a deep breath; "I've smelt it before when we've visited the seventies or eighties of this century. It must be popular." Wilson stood next to Jackie and asked Alex how the woman was. Alex shook her head; "In some shock I'm afraid." She dropped her voice to a whisper; "She's clearly been raped, probably several times by the bastard." Wilson nodded and then sniffed the air. "Sweet Jesus, why would she be wearing bloody 'Brut', I use to wear that when alive back in the seventies. It's certainly a man's deodorant."

Jericho folded his arms; "That must be what our demon wears when in human form. It's rubbed off onto her when he...." he didn't finish the sentence because Ellen was coming out of shock. She screamed and cried and became quite hysterical until James simply waved his hand over her, and she slumped into Alex's and Jackie's arms and slept soundly. "I've wiped her memory of all this and she will sleep until we get her home; can you manage her Wilson?" who nodded and gently scooped the woman up.

Jericho finished checking his mirror and was satisfied there weren't any other humans around the dismal place. "Let's go people." was all he said, and they vanished back to the pub cellars.

11. STILL SUNDAY 15th AUGUST 1976; OXFORD, ENGLAND - PART 1.

 They stood outside the old doorway and James closed the portal; Sol would need to find another home, office and dungeon. Upstairs in the bar they shared their hipflasks whilst Jericho used his mirror to connect with the current telephone system. He smiled as Alex and Jackie dressed Mrs. Ellen Tate in her clothes that they recovered from the demon's lair. They made her comfortable on the bar using several chair cushions that were in a relatively good condition.

Jericho made the anonymous call to the emergency operator who was very surprised that she couldn't trace the number he was calling from! They sat in the van and waited until they could hear the sirens and Wilson pulled from the car park and headed for the crossroads that would take them to Oxford City and their hotel. Jericho dispatched the girls to visit JP and check up on Maggie. They would now start the search for the demon 'Sol' in earnest.

Alex drove their replacement car - a Vauxhall Viva SL - and quite liked it because it was bigger that the damn Mini. The hospital Receptionist informed them that Miss Margret Sellers had been discharged; her mother and father had taken her home. So, they drove to JP's apartment and arrived outside his door. Jackie was about to press the door buzzer when Alex quickly grabbed her hand and without a word held up her mirror to Jackie. There were three people in the apartment: JP Bonaparte, John Morris, and William 'Willy' Kent. But Alex's mirror was flashing a big red warning signal that a Demon was close by; very close by and the girl's mirrors had automatically 'cloaked' them for safety.

They backed away from the door and Alex called Jericho immediately. "We've found him; he's JP, John Morris or Willy Weaver!" she whispered into her mirror. A very concerned Jackie said softly; "I hope to God it's not JP."

Alex nodded at that. If discovered that it was JP, that would mean the end of their careers as Temporal Detectives. They waited by the lift at the end of the corridor with real frantic apprehension. They both jumped a little as the lift doors came open and James stepped out with Jericho and Wilson following. He smiled at the girls; "Well done Ladies." That sentiment was echoed by Jericho and Wilson. "It's William Kent; he's Sol." was all James said and Jericho folded his arms; "We need to separate him from the other two. Alex, I want you to connect with the phone system and ring the flat, get JP and this John fellow to meet you somewhere. Promise them sex or something, just get them out of that apartment." He smiled at Jackie; "And take Jackie with you. So, they'll think it just a friendly get together."

Alex operated her mirror and JP handed another can to John before picking up the receiver; he was most impressed to hear from the girls. He was a little surprised at Alex's forthright offer and really smiled to himself. He replaced the receiver and pulled John to one side; "Do you fancy having a drink with those two ladies I told you about? They want to meet up and apparently the little dark haired one - Jackie - wants to meet you. She's an absolute stunner in her own right. But I'm afraid that whilst four is a happy number; five is not." They both looked at Willy sitting, slurping his beer on the sofa. John slowly smiled; "He won't mind. Let's go." The team waited in the cleaners cupboard until they saw JP and John dive into the lift with big smiles on their face and Willy walked down the stairs; unsmiling. James followed him, transforming into his silver armour with his big sword over his shoulder. They came together in the rear garden with Willy/Sol also transforming into his armour; black of course. James had stopped time for living humans but didn't affect the team running back to their van, past the frozen JP and John. "Sorry boys!" Alex shouted as they dashed past them in reception.

They sat in the van in relative silence; a fight between a Knight of God and a powerful Tier 1 demon could last some time or be over quickly, if either one got really lucky. No living humans would have been able to watch the contest because time had stopped for them.

Jericho sat in the front passenger seat, his attention never moving from his mirror. Finally, he sighed loudly with some relief; "James has sent Sol back to his master and his lair below the old pub will vanish with him; leaving just a carved medieval doorway." He sat back; clearly relieved. Wilson slapped the wheel and cussed; "God damn it! The big man – Willy – I know where I've met him before. I was in detective Constable on Stella's team [Temporal Detective Stella Longstreet] and we jumped back to 1970 because two souls had gone missing from a boy's boarding school. He was one on the missing souls and must have been fifteen at the time. I remember him from the photograph we were shown by the headmaster. Then suddenly the mission was over; the two boys had turned up. It was believed that they had stumbled through a rouge time portal somewhere in the old school grounds and then managed to return. That was the end of the matter for temporal detectives."

Jackie leaned over and asked who the other boy was involved; Wilson just shrugged his shoulders; he had long forgotten and now couldn't recall the other boy. Jericho rubbed his chin; "Check with Operations and find out who that other boy was; if one came back as a Demon then the other one probably did too." Jackie was always impressed how Jericho's sharp mind worked and worked her mirror with real interest.

"It's a Terrence John Downes and again like Willy Weaver showed no signs. Nothing is known......" Jackie spoke quietly then stopped in mid-sentence, adding; "He lives and works in the City of Oxford as a minibus driver, which could mean that - if he is another bloody demon - the pair could be working together!" Jericho turned to the girls; "Keep that date with JP and his friend. This case is not over yet. I'll get Operational Control to contact the Knight's Council for assistance; we may need another knight."

12. STILL SUNDAY 15th AUGUST 1976; OXFORD, ENGLAND - PART 2.

 They met up in 'Wong's' Chinese restaurant in the city centre with Alex and Jackie and enjoyed the lunchtime menu. The men were impressed that the girls ate their meals with chopsticks. John was absolutely taken by Jackie, and it showed which made JP and Alex chuckle. The conversation was all about Maggie and the sudden recovery of Mrs. Ellen Tate who apparently had suffered 'amnesia shock' and couldn't recall anything about the 'accident' or what happened to her afterwards. Police concluded that she must have wandered about and then - for whatever reason - returned to the old pub. Maggie was now convinced that Willy didn't rape her; logic and rationality dictated that it was impossible, and the witnesses were her best friends; so, she had accepted that she had a bad accident during the Ouija board session.

After a very good lunch they separated into their cars and Alex drove the Vauxhall Viva to JP's apartment [with JP] and John Dove JP's car [with Jackie] also returning for further 'drinks'. JP and Alex disappeared into his bedroom and John and Jackie remained on the sofa in the big lounge room. After a few minutes John started to laugh, and Jackie giggled; they could hear clearly what was going on in JP's bedroom. John didn't hang about and soon the pair were kissing and caressing on the sofa. Jackie told him - in no uncertain terms that she was special lady - and to her surprise [and delight] John just smiled and whispered; "Well, no-one's perfect." That was a signal for the relationship to turn serious; sexually.

 John was delighted to find Jackie was wearing stockings and was quite aroused by that fact alone. He was further delighted when he received oral sex that he described later to JP as 'the best fucking blow job I've ever had'. He had no qualms or reservations about fucking someone he called a 'tranny' because he was so turned on by her. He didn't hesitate to push his adequate cock into her welcoming bum hole and fucking her hard. They ended up on the floor, lying next to each other with Jackie's arm around his neck and his tongue buried in her mouth. He fucked her for about fifteen minutes before he groaned loudly and shot his load into her back passage with immense pleasure and satisfaction. They lay kissing and talking quietly together on the rug; both stark naked - except Jackie who still had her stockings and suspenders on at his insistence - until Alex, also stark naked apart from her black stockings and suspender belt - stepped over them to reach the drinks cabinet.

With a broad smile, she handed the pair some bottled beers and returned to the bedroom, stopping in the doorway, and gesturing in; "Come on, let's really make this an interesting party." She said provocatively and John whispered to Jackie that he wanted to fuck Alex. Jackie just nodded; not really surprised by that revelation! He slipped from her, and they made their into the bedroom where Alex was sucking JP's cock as he lay back on the bed and sipped his beer. JP grinned at the pair and waved at the bed; "You can fuck Alex and I'll take little Jackie. They really are a game couple of birds." John nodded at that and was soon fucking Alex 'doggy-style' while she sucked Jackie's cock. JP had mounted her from behind and she was on his lap being fucked in her arse as Alex dealt with her erection. John asked JP if this was an orgy or a foursome. JP thrusting hard upwards moaned and said quietly; "It's a foursome, I think you need five or more for a bloody orgy!"

John gripped Alex's hips, thrusting hard and deep. He asked out loud if the girls would be interested in an orgy with Danny and Rose. Now that shocked JP a little when John revealed he and Dave had both fucked Rose while Danny watched and took pictures! The boys were delighted when both girls agreed. It was arranged for Monday night after a discrete call to Rose by John. It would be three girls; Alex, Rose and Jackie with four boys; JP, John, Dave and Danny. The little 'foursome' broke up late in the afternoon and the girls left the men sleeping, JP on the bed and John on the sofa. They both left giggling and very satisfied with Jackie declaring that she loved group sex!

Both the girls were really looking forward to Monday night. John and JP knew better than to ask Maggie; she was still recovering from her strange 'accident' and wouldn't be interested because she was after JP for herself. But JP now had no interest in cultivating Maggie as one of his girls. He only wanted Alex and Jackie now, with young Rose as a big bonus.

Alex drove the Vauxhall Viva back to the hotel; laughing and chatting with Jackie and the pair were totally disappointed to find the team would be jumping back to the lighthouse immediately to prepare for another assignment. They would return if the circumstances of the case changed and something else quickly occurred in this time and place. The pair reluctantly and with some disappointment said nothing about what had happened - obviously - to Jericho and Wilson.

They would be recalled to Oxford in 1976 within a few days in tragic circumstances.

13. WEDNESDAY 18th AUGUST 1976; THE DEMONS REVENGE.

 JP finally convinced his team after several drinks in the University student's bar. No one had heard from Willy or knew of his whereabouts. But JP had talked them around; they would return to the old pub and continue their investigations; especially about the doorway. JP convinced Rose to bring Danny along; knowing full well that Danny wouldn't let Rose go back there on her own without him. So, they planned to return that night and try and make contact; again.

 "We're going to have some powerful protection in that I've asked old professor Lightfoot to come along. He knows how to handle demons and other nastier spirits." JP raised his glass and saluted his team. They all knew the reputation of the old professor, but Maggie still needed further assurances and Rose told her that Danny was routinely armed; he was part of a squad that went after armed robbers. Maggie finally agreed and everyone would meet up in the professor's rooms; he had managed to convince the Dean, to allow them to use one of the Universities minibuses.

 They set off just after seven in the evening; with Danny and Rose following the minibus in Danny's nondescript police car. The two professors sat at the rear discussing the case. The old man nodded several times and scribbled in his notebook. Dave sat by the side door and checked his camera equipment, whilst Maggie and John sat behind the driver and shared a bag of sweets. The young driver adjusted the radio and picked up BBC Radio 1, he grunted and turned into Shakespeare Road which was fully surrounded by woodland on both sides.

 It was Dave that noticed the strange behaviour of the young mini-bus driver first; he seemed quite odd and kept laughing to himself; like he was talking to someone that no-one could see. John leaned over his seat that gestured down the road; there was a car on fire at the side of the road. There appeared no-one standing near it and suddenly Dave shouted; "What the fuck is our driver doing? What the fuck is he doing?" The driver was laughing as he slammed the minibus into the blazing Estate car which he had soaked in petrol. The two vehicles came together with an evil crunching sound, glass shattering and metal tearing open; then a little spark ignited the inferno.

Terrence John Downes or Lucius the demon ran – almost skipping – with joy back through the woods; the dead schoolboy's now adult body had, over the years, provided him with no less than fourteen souls and given the 'Light side' a headache of another five unscheduled departures. He laughed and leapt into the cold dark lake and would soon be back with his master. He anticipated promotion to a Tier 2 now. He knew that his friend and mentor 'Sol' would be happy that their revenge was successful.

 Danny managed to avoid the vehicle spinning across the road and skidded to a halt some yards down the road; he was shouting into the vehicles radiotelephone for assistance when he watched the small fireball light up the sky. Rose managed to pull open the door and stagger onto the roadway. Danny jumped from the car and held her close. Slowly they walked towards the wreckage and the pair just stared at the burning vehicles. Rose managed to whisper; "No one made it out." and buried her head against Danny who held her tight.

 That's when Danny shouted; "Look there!" They both started to run towards the rear of the burning wreckage as they watched JP dragging the old professor across the tarmac and then collapsed on the roadway. He stared at Rose and managed to shout; "What the fuck happened?" he repeated himself several times before sprawling on the cold tarmac. Danny wrapped him in his jacket and prayed hard for the ambulances to arrive.

 Rose cradled JP in her arms and watched Danny check the old man; he shook his head and looked quite grim. "He's dead." Was all he said and turned back to the blaze and hung his head in sorrow and shock. Rose stroked JP's face and sobbed openly. All her close university friends were now gone.

 Heather the Collector – somewhat surprised by so many unscheduled deaths - was shepherding the confused souls to the side of the road and immediately noticed that one body had produced no soul: Terrence John Downes. She called it into Operations and was told that a team of temporal detectives were already at that time and place. Team 74 would be assigned to the missing soul and investigate the unscheduled departures. She thanked the Operations Controller and gathered the souls around her; they followed her into the light.

 It took the fire people several hours to recover all the bodies from the wreckage and get the vehicles removed before the road could re-open. The terrible accident made both local and national news, both on the radio and TV. Tributes were paid to the two professors and their students. There was little mention of how the accident actually happened. But young Terrence John Downes body was found to contain four times the legal limit for driving. That was good enough for the authorities to close the case. The other vehicles involved belonged to a missing person of police interest; William 'Willy' Kent. They concluded it was 'co-incidence' that and accepted that Willy had burnt to death in the vehicle before it was hit by the drunk driving the University Minibus. Sol had - of course - abandoned the body after it was no use anymore; well, except to extract some revenge of course.
 Both Danny and Rose had not seen the actual accident from behind and they couldn't argue with the coroner's verdict of death by a drunken driver and a further tragedy in that Kent's car was set on fire and killed him. JP sat in his wheelchair and said nothing to the reporters that gathered around him. How he had survived the dreadful accident was still a mystery. Rose and Danny wheeled him to the waiting car and helped him in.

 JP gripped both their hands and promised he would be up and about in weeks, certainly in time for the memorial service for the old professor, his students, and the driver. He made no comment about big Willy, his good friend who had died in his blazing car and was driven back to his rooms in silence. The coroner had attributed his survival to simply being sat in the rear of the minibus. His elderly colleague – Professor Lightfoot – had been an old man and the autopsy proved he hadn't suffered life threatening injuries; but the shock to his old heart had done the trick.

Convalescing at home for some weeks, Professor Jean-Paul Bonaparte brooded over the death of his friends which he blamed himself and his stupid passion for the paranormal on. He received two special visitors. Alex and Jackie brought him up to date on the paranormal investigations at the old pub and he was really pleased to see them. Alex informed him that the "Medieval" doorway was of historical significance and would be preserved [she obviously didn't mention that James had removed the time portal from it] but the old pub had been scheduled for demolition. Its owner in desperation had sold the place – quite cheaply – to a local property developer who had planning permission to build a luxury block of flats on the site. The doorway would be removed and placed on display in the local museum. Workman removing it would find that it was just for decoration and built against solid rock. Its true purpose would never be known to current living humans.

Alex and Jackie obviously made no mention of the lair that existed on the other side of the portal or the demon's activities. They both could see the difference in the young professor, and he made no attempt to replay their previous sexual encounters, so they left him alone, sitting in his apartment mourning the deaths of his close friends.

Sitting in their car Alex and Jackie was silent for a while then Alex tapped the steering wheel with her fingers and slowly smiled, turning to Jackie who was consulting her mirror; "Sweetie, do you fancy – whilst we're back here – a little reunion with a couple of old soldiers?"

Jackie lowered her mirror and smiled; "I bet the local veterans association will know where they live, but we would have to be discrete; not call on them at home or work...." She didn't finish because Alex held up a hand and said quietly; "I think a visit to the gym they use – after closing hours – would prove fruitful." Jackie now grinned and crossed her long legs; pulling up the waist band of her already short summer pleated skirt so that it hung well above her knees. Alex grinned; "That's a good idea, let's go!" She pulled away with the pair laughing in anticipation of some more sexual antics in the 'swinging seventies' but this time demon free!

EPISODE 8: "ALEXANDRA AND THE SCHOOL FOR SCANDAL."

EPISODE PROLOGUE: "In the spring 0f 1961 at a very expensive and exclusive girls school there are some very strange happenings occurring and Jericho Tibbs is ordered to investigate after a soul goes missing. So, team 74 must jump back and Alexandra finds herself playing the role of A school Matron, whilst young Owen must appear as his alto ego: 'Jacqueline' and go undercover as a Schoolgirl. They find some very naughty girls and a chef who is better at sex than cooking and some gardeners who look after more than the school grounds!"

75 Minutes approx. Episode Warnings:
Smoking – Alcohol – Strong language – Violence [including a murder] – Strong graphic sexual references – Horror – References to death, Prostitution & Pornography.

NOTES: This is the **ADULT** version of the original story which is published and appears in the **TEMPORAL DETECTIVES:** Series 5 – Episode 3 entitled: **"QUEEN CHARLOTTE'S ACADEMY HOSTS THE DEVIL."** This is a special **EXTENDED** episode of the original story.

CAUTION: Recommended for **18+ only.**

1. FRIDAY 5th MAY 1961. QUEEN CHARLOTTE'S ACADEMY; KENT, ENGLAND.

"I think it's going to piss down." Katherine Gapp pulled the cloak around herself and held her hood. Kath's friend Susan Toller nodded and stared up at the darkening sky; "Come on we still have a good hour before anyone will notice we've gone." She said and giggled a little gripping her friend's hand under her cloak. Both girls disliked the old-fashioned cloak they had to wear and wished the school would update its dress code and include a proper coat; preferably like the ones they saw in 'Seventeen' magazine which one of the American girls smuggled into school on a regular basis and charged the other girls two pennies for a damn read! As Kath said, "She's going to be a bleeding million-pound heiress when she leaves next year the tight cow." Susan had agreed totally, but still paid up to read last month's edition.

Both girls were in the final year at the select and exclusive 'ladies Academy' but were still bound by the strict dress coat that the school applied regardless of age. So, despite both being seventeen they had to continue wearing the same uniform that the younger girls wore, a one-piece summer dress, stiff hat, sensible black shoes and white knee length socks. Even their panties were regulation, plain white cotton. The older girls [the sixteen- to eighteen-year-olds] rebelled a bit by wearing stockings and suspenders, complete with 'naughty' knickers in the dormitory at night when unsupervised.

The girls complained about the winter uniform too; a knee-length black pleated skirt, white blouse and school tie with a black school jacket and black socks. They referred to this uniform as the 'funeral suit'. But it was Friday afternoon, and it was their turn to visit Mister Jerome Hobbs; the dashing and charming Under-Gardner who lived next door to the big glasshouse at the bottom of the south playing field. He was quite good looking with dark features; he told people his mother was Italian, and his English father had met her during the war in Italy, when he drove tanks. To the girls he was better looking than Clark Gable and of course was actually available and not just an image on the silver screen.

They now hurried and pushed open the side door to the big glasshouse and almost ran through the numerous wooden shelves' holding hundreds of pots and trays with young plants growing. At the very end was apparently a big wooden cupboard which was always locked. Only certain people knew it wasn't a cupboard and the girls knocked on the worn and weathered doors so hard that the thing rattled and creaked, as if objecting to the abuse.

The pair giggled, making sure their hair was tidy and they each checked each other's sparse make-up and waited. After ten minutes both girls were angry and disappointed at Jerome's failure to appear. Reluctantly they walked slowly back through the glasshouse shouting their disappointment at each other. That's when Kath stopped and just stared. Susan tugged at her arm and reminded her that it would 'piss down' soon and they best get back for afternoon tea. Then she saw the look on Kath's face and followed her staring eyes to the floor. It was a foot sticking out from one of the big wood shelving units that held the bedding plants. Susan slowly knelt and peered under the shelf; she screamed and Kath joined her and the pair ran from the glasshouse; still screaming as the late spring rain started to fall.

Jerome Hobbs would not be entertaining any more young girls in his hidden boudoir behind the big cupboard. The young man was stone dead beneath the plants he loved as much as young girls. His face was contorted in agony and his right hand – clenched into a fist – was gripping a page ripped from a magazine; a very naughty 'under the counter' magazine. Someone had driven a very large knife between his ribs with some force, yet there was little blood lying around his stiff body. His trousers pockets hung outside; empty. Jerome's wristwatch was gone and the small solid gold ring that he wore on his right thumb was also missing. He normally carried an old leather wallet in his back trouser pocket that could be button up for security; that was gone too and the pocket had been pulled open with such force that the button was missing.

The local police concluded that someone had murdered and robbed the young gardener; especially when they searched his little cottage and found it in utter chaos. The sofa had been slashed open, the carpets pulled up and there was not a single drawer or cupboard that hadn't been opened and left. In his bedroom they found the same scene; the mattress had even been cut open and his clothes were strewn about the floor. The kitchen and bathroom didn't escape the apparently frenzied search: the porcelain cistern lay smashed with a small trickle of water running from it and all the kitchen cupboards were open. Even the small oven door had been left open. The police now concluded that the murder must have been frantically looking for something!

But it was when the officer in charge [Detective Inspector Gerald Harper of Kent Police CID] finally managed to prise the magazine page from the dead man's fingers that things took a turn for the worse. It had been ripped from an 'Adult' magazine and was a page of advertisements with one advertisement circled in red ink. A company in Soho, London would pay 'decent' money for films or photographs [colour or monochrome] featuring very young models in sexual poses. That didn't please the Inspector; he would now have to inform Scotland Yard and get them to check out the Post Office Box Number shown on the magazine advertisement. He wasn't the very best detective in the world, and he certainly didn't want the much-acclaimed Scotland Yard detectives pushing into his investigation and taking all the credit for solving it.

His two principal witnesses [Kath & Susan] were very quickly removed from the school by their concerned parents after making brief statements about finding the body. Their excuse for visiting the glasshouse [which both girls stuck too] was to ask Mister Hobbs about some strange plants they had seen growing by the Hockey field. They both stated that he would know what they were, and they could impress the Biology Mistress with their newly acquired knowledge. Neither girl revealed the true motive for their visit, nor certainly made no mention of what lay behind the old cupboard.

Police officers searching where the body was found, saw that the cupboard was locked with a padlock and hasp and didn't even bother to have it opened. Their interview with the Headmistress didn't provide much to go on; she simply read them the details from Jerome Hobbs personal file. He was 22 years old and came from Yorkshire [though he didn't have any trace of a Yorkshire accent] was obviously unmarried and had produced very good references from York City Council where he had served his Gardening Apprenticeship. She mentioned that the school's head Gardener; Mr. Harold Fields thought the world of him and often praised his gardening skill and happy character. She added that he was quite upset by Hobb's sudden and shocking death.

Detective Inspector Harper was a little surprised that the head Gardener was only 32 and like Hobb's, lived on the school grounds. He had a two-bedroom cottage at the rear of the school pavilion, which contained the showers and changing rooms. He was married but had no children and his wife; Janet worked in the school kitchens as a 'Diner Lady'. The pair didn't have anything criminal known about them and had produced good references from Maidstone City Council where the pair had worked previously.

Inspector Harper's team checked with York City Council and received quite a shock: they had never heard of him! [Hobbs] It appears his references were false and that put the cat amongst the pigeons with Miss Evelyn Scott-Harris [the Headmistress] ordering her admin to check and confirm all references supplied by the current teaching staff; rather strangely, she didn't include 'ancillary' staff and another member of the workforce breathed a huge sigh of relief……..

The police now had an 'unknown' man [they couldn't find any relatives or friends] who may not actually be Jerome Hobbs! That didn't help their inquiries. A month flew by and Detective Inspector Harper didn't even have a suspect and enquiries in London by the metropolitan Police had drawn a blank. The 'film' company had never heard of Hobb's. The savage murder of the mysterious school Gardner was to disappear from the public's interest. But it drew the interest of another more tenacious 'Detective Inspector' and that was Jericho Tibbs of the temporal detectives department.

 Jericho was reading the report from Demon Ingress about a minor demon [Rul] who had appeared in the area no less than six times in the spring of 1961. Now that interested Jericho because nothing was reported on his movements or actions while there. As the Senior Agent [Louise Joskia] from that department stated, "He just appears to visit, never does anything and the timeline is unchanged. Quite odd really, but he certainly has an interest in that school you mentioned." Jericho left the busy office and headed back to the Lighthouse pushing the strange problem to the back of his busy mind. Then, as if by chance, a report of a 'Missing Soul' landed on Jericho's desk from the very same place and time. A body had produced no soul and the Collector had called it in. That body was a certain Jerome Hobbs and Jericho checked his mirror and found that Jerome Hobbs last visit to the Human Life Cycle was 1962 to 2014 and that, not only had he died too early, but was a Time-traveller and now lost his soul to the darkness of real death because he had died out of his ordained time.

He gathered team 74 together and briefed them on their latest mission, jumping back to Queen Charlottes Academy for Girls in the spring of 1961. Because a minor demon was known to frequent the area at this time, they were accompanied by a Guardian of God, Preston Sutton. Preston was a slightly built Jamaican fellow who normally introduced himself as the man named after two towns. He was certainly a colourful character with a good sense of humour and the team liked him at once.

Alex and Owen both chuckled at their characters for this assignment; Alex would play a School Matron and young Owen would transmogrify into Jacqueline and play a schoolgirl! Jericho and Wilson would play Insurance Inspectors from the Royal Liverpool checking the schools safety procedures and equipment for their insurance renewal. Preston Sutton was delighted to play a temporary cook at the school. He was well suited to the role, when alive he had been a Chef for a Kingstown hotel chain. Jericho had decided to run this investigation from before Hobbs was killed and lost his soul. So, the team jumped back to 1961; before the dreadful murder and strange happenings that occurred at the posh school.

2. MONDAY 1st MAY 1961. QUEEN CHARLOTTE'S ACADEMY, KENT, ENGLAND.

Alex loved her costume; a wonderful summer dress with three layers of petticoat [all frilly and white lace] stockings and white heels, with a gorgeous small hat, little white gloves and neat blue jacket. She really looked the part of a well-educated young lady of the period. Jericho nodded his approval; "It was easy getting you a temporary placement as a matron. In this time and place, posh girls schools were struggling to attract the right staff and so temporary staff were common. They have been given all your qualifications and references by the staff recruitment bureau in Canterbury; the woman who run's it is a local human agent for Stella. [Temporal Inspector Stella Longstreet] So your covered should they make any enquires."

He turned to Owen and really had to smile. He had changed into his 'alter-ego' Jacqueline Jones and was dressed for the part. He had to agree with Wilson and Alex; he certainly looked the part and could fool his own mother dressed up as the young schoolgirl who would be staying at the school – temporally – until she sat her 'A' Levels for university; she was studying History and hoped to become a teacher. "The Headmistress has agreed to have you while you cram for your 'A' Levels. Your family has just returned from Australia so that you can attend a top English university and money is not a problem. The Headmistress has been paid for the full year, even though – for the cover story – you will only be here one term, so she will be really pleased to see you!" Jericho briefed Owen and had to smile again; Sweet Jesus, he really did look and act the part!

"The same recruitment Agency has supplied them with my details and they [the school] were happy to take me. The woman on the phone actually said they don't mind coloured's as long as they are Christian and know their place!" Preston rolled his eyes and chuckled, adding; "Yes Ma'am, this boy knows his place around decent white folk!" That made everyone laugh and the van pulled up some yards from the school gates and saw old Joe from Supplies waiting with Inspector Longstreet [she was playing a very brief role as Jacqueline's mother] and he handed out the other vehicles required. A Rolls Royce Phantom V for Stella and Jacqueline to arrive in; he would play the chauffer himself. An Austin Healy 300; a two-seat sports car for Alexandra to create the expression she was from a wealthy family too and Alex loved the little car and would be sad to hand it back. Wilson and Jericho would use the dark blue Ford Thames 300E van they had driven up in. It was already sign written as "Royal Liverpool Insurance".

Preston slapped old Joe on the back and asked about his transport and Joe just smiled; from the behind the superb big Roll-Royce Joe wheeled a Vespa Scooter and handed Preston the key; "That's why Operations told you pack everything in a backpack." He chuckled and with his strange young assistant in tow; disappeared into the front of the Rolls-Royce and placed his chauffer cap on. Everyone laughed including Preston, who looked around and realised that there was no crash helmet. "You didn't need one at this time under the traffic laws in place." Jericho reminded him. Preston jumped on and quickly disappeared through the gates, a guitar case wobbling on his back and his small pack on the rack. The bloody thing backfired several times and that made everyone laugh again.

Jacqueline asked Jericho; "Where the hell is his Staff of Mosses?" Jericho smiled; "Mind your language young lady and for your information it's in the guitar case; I thought that was quite clever." Jacqueline nodded and slipped into the back of the Rolls-Royce with her 'mother' Stella who expressed – a couple of times- just how authentic and convincing Owen looked like a girl. Alex and Wilson exchanged a glance and laughed again. "You should see her in stockings and suspenders!" Alex whispered to Wilson who grunted and rolled his eyes.

Jacqueline smoothed down her summer uniform dress and pulled the socks up, then adjusted her stiff little hat with the school badge on. Stella chuckled; "Jesus Owen, if I didn't know it was you, I would have thought you were a young woman in her last years at school. I am amazed; just don't let the boy's get too friendly!" Jackie just smiled and replied; "I'm safe on that part; this is an exclusive girl's school with definitely no boys allowed." Later, she would laugh about that comment......

The big car swept up the gravel drive and stopped outside the grand entrance to the school where Miss Evelyn Scott-Harris [the Headmistress] waited with Miss Helen Ward [who would be Jackie's dormitory mistress]. They greeted Stella with some warmth and Miss Ward took immediate charge of Jackie who was handed her case and bag by old Joe who looked resplendent in his chauffeur's uniform. Stella played a wonderful part as Jackie's mum and said goodbye to her daughter with some unrestrained emotion. Jackie wanted to laugh but restrained herself and played her part well too.

Miss ward escorted the 'new girl' to her dormitory and Miss Evelyn Scott-Harris waved goodbye to Jackie's mum and watched as the sports car powered up the drive and came to a stop. Several girls watching from the edge of the Hockey field were immediately interested and fascinated as they watched Alex slip with some grace from the car and greet their Headmistress, who had quite a surprised look on her face. As they stood chatting, Alex caught sight of their quarry, pushing a wheelbarrow towards the Hockey Field and noticed that all the girls there waved and greeted him with some affection. She watched discretely as two of the older girls walked with him; the three talking and laughing together.

Miss Evelyn Scott-Harris showed Alex to her modest quarters

which actually surprised and pleased Alex. She had a small sitting room, bedroom and bathroom with a toilet. Her little window overlooked the small basketball court. She dumped her suitcase on the bed and called Jericho on her mirror; he was waiting in the lane that ran past the school gates until he and Wilson made their appearance. There was a knock on the door, and she quickly hid her mirror in her handbag; it was another teacher who lived next door [there were only two rooms on this part of the fourth floor] and she introduced herself as Candice Fuller [Biology & Chemistry]. Alex liked her and the pair sat chatting in Alex's small sitting room, until a gong could be heard.

Candice leapt up; "Come on Alex that means it teatime with muffins. The pair made their way to the Dining room and Alex sat with Candice at the very end of the big table [which was placed on the hall's stage] as staff and pupils filed in. Alex spotted the new 'girl' and smiled; it appears that Jackie had already made friends with a couple of girls from her Dormitory and sat with them at the Senior Girls table. "I'll be mother." Candice said and poured the tea as Alex enjoyed her muffin. Candice discretely whispered; "Afternoon tea isn't much. The bloody dinners are really good, you have to be careful, or you'll blow up like a balloon scoffing it."

The young woman who served them overheard and laughed; "Hopefully our new cook keeps up that standard." Alex noticed her name tag, pinned above her large bosom; 'Miss C. Pickles'. She was very pretty girl, but her voice was quite common; she smiled at them and slipped the pair another muffin and more jam. Candice thanked her quietly, then turned to Alex and mouthed; "Her and the under gardener have a thing going, so it's rumoured." Alex nodded and set about her second muffin with relish.

After tea Alex 'bumped' into the new girl and her new friends, Alex really smiled; it was Kath and Susan. Jackie was certainly not hanging about with this case. Alex explained to the girls that she was the new – temporary – Matron. Alex really had to restrain from laughing as she and Candice walked to the school's small infirmary and Candice commented on what a little beauty the new girl was.

The infirmary held six beds and was actually well equipped to deal with minor injuries and illness. Alex checked the medicine cabinet – she had been given the infirmary's keys by Miss Scott-Harris – and was satisfied with her stock of equipment and drugs. Candice disappeared saying she had an afternoon class but would meet up with Alex before the diner gong sounded. She was really friendly, and Alex wondered about that. Alex now walked to the infirmary's big window and stared out; she could see the large glasshouse and smoke rising from behind it; from Jerome's little cottage. That's when she saw a scruffily dressed young man on a bicycle disappear behind the glasshouse and didn't appear from the other side; so he was either in the glasshouse or visiting Jerome. Alex sat at her desk in the corner and went through the drawers; they were empty except various medical forms and medical magazines. The desk was clean otherwise, too clean for her liking.

 That's when she realised that she had a customer or rather patient. It was a senior girl called Rachel Jukes who nervously sat at her desk and complained about a persistent headache. Alex gave her some aspirin and they pair chatted; Rachel unaware that she was actually being questioned by the clever temporal detective. It became apparent that the senior girls all liked Jerome and his boss, Harold Field and his wife Janet. Some of the girls even had taken dinner and lunch with the nice couple. Alex asked her about the scruffy youth who visited Jerome on his bike.

 "Oh that's Ronnie Rabbit, or that's what we call him. He's lives in the village above the Baker's. He's really funny and always brings us stuff that we…..." She stopped in mid-sentence, realizing who she was talking too. "You know sweets and papers from the village and stuff like that." She stopped talking again and took her aspirin. Alex watched her go and knew that she was hiding what 'Ronnie the bloody Rabbit' actually brought the senior girls.

Alex stood by the window and caught sight of Harold Fields walking to the glasshouse and he disappeared from view. "Talk of the devil. I wonder if he's visiting Jerome and his scruffy friend." She called Jericho and asked him to take a look at who lived lives over the Baker's in the village. He said they would call her back.

Alex then dealt with two twelve-year-olds who had small cuts on their knees from playing hockey with far too much enthusiasm and she had to smile; from the mouths of the innocent always comes the truth. They were laughing together about the senior girls and their secret club, 'The Lawrence Club'. Alex, applying iodine and plasters, asked them about it. "Oh, it's named after Sir Lawrence Oliver and it's all about acting and plays and stuff like that. Old bathroom knows about it I suspect and so does the drama teacher, Miss Flowers. They meet up in the old glasshouse and practice their performances. Kath Gapp runs it with Susan Toller, and you have to be invited to join. They won't have us because we're snots." The bigger girl was a real talker and her friend the opposite; she said very little. "What's a snot?" Alex asked smiling. The girl sighed; "Any girl not turned sixteen Miss." Sighing as if everyone knew that. Patched up they departed laughing and chatting together.

Alex had found out that the Headmistresses' nickname was 'bathroom' after an incident with Mr. Pickles [School-Caretaker] who surprised her by cleaning the windows while she was taking one. She wondered if he and young Kitchen Assistant were related, Father and Daughter possibly.

She sat at her desk and wondered what the girls had said about Kath & Susan; about the co-incidence of that: the very two girls that would find Jerome's body were regular visitors to the glasshouse [or Jerome himself?] for secret club meetings about bloody acting. Alex recalled what Jericho always said about co-incidences and decided to investigate the glasshouse and the secret club more closely. That's when her mirror buzzed; it was Jackie with some news.

3. NIGHT MANOEUVRES – PART 1.

They met up in the infirmary just before the dinner gong was sounded and Jackie had some news to impart. "Miss Evelyn Scott-Harris has called in Paranormal Investigators because of what's been happening around the old school. She's thinks she has kept a lid on matters, but most of the girls and staff know about it." Alex was now intrigued, and the pair sat chatting about the ghost called 'Pungent Pam' who has been seen about the place and just vanishes from rooms without using the windows or doors, leaving a pungent odour behind.

"Apparently a young woman in a white dress – of course – who is the ghost of a murdered daughter of the old house that the school has become. It's said that her father murdered her because she was about to run off with the bloody gardener in the

1790's." Jackie said, consulting her mirror and nodded with some surprise, adding; "Sweet Jesus, there was a girl bloody murdered here in 1794! A certain Miss Pamela Hobbs who is another missing soul; her departure date was March 1794, and the body produced no soul. There have been no temporal detectives assigned the case because it was believed she sold her soul to the Dark Side. According to Human Records she was a practicing witch – like her mother and grandmother was – and that's the real reason her father killed her; he caught her red-handed it would appear. He [the father] didn't even stand trial because the family doctor said the girl had killed herself over her lover; the gardener who the report doesn't name, but I can search newspaper records for the time and maybe find out."

Alex sat back, somewhat impressed with her young colleague; "I wonder if Jericho wants to appear tomorrow as himself – an investigator of the paranormal – and not a bloody Insurance Inspector?" Jackie grinned; "Now that Alex is a cracking idea."

Alex called Jericho immediately and he agreed. He told her that the scruffy young man on the bicycle was a certain John Victor Newcomb - nothing known and from this time period – who worked in the local Boots the chemist. He developed all the films handed in for processing and sometimes helped the gardeners and maintenance staff when required.

Jackie leaned over the desk and tapped her mirror; "Now that's a real strange co-incidence. The ghost's name is Hobbs and reportedly wanted to run off with the Gardener in 1794 – if she actually wasn't a witch – and the Gardner today is called Jerome Hobbs."

She looked down at her mirror and didn't smile; "Her father Harold Hobbs died in 1813 and guess what?" Alex shrugged her shoulders. "He received no quarantine; he obviously didn't murder anyone, let alone his daughter." Alex folded her arms; "That story is worth an investigation in itself, so the original house – that's now part of this school – was owned by the Hobbs family and the current gardener is called Hobbs and he died, like Miss Hobbs in 1794 without a soul to be collected. Interesting; so what's the pungent smell that the ghost is supposed to leave behind? Roses? Lavender? Dead body or what?" Jackie didn't know and pushed her mirror into her dress pocket.

"I think we need to have a real close look at the glasshouse." Alex said quietly and both heard the dinner gong go. "Thank heaven for that, I'm bloody starving." Jackie said jumping up and Alex chuckled; "You always are." They headed for the dining room, separating on the stairs so that they arrived at different times.

Alex noticed that Jerome helped out at evening meals, cleaning the tables, removing crockery and washing the kitchen floor when necessary. Despite being in conversation with Candice, She watched the interaction between young Jerome Hobbs and Miss Caroline Pickles [who was serving tables] their affection for each other seemed well apparent. Alex wondered what her father – the caretaker – thought of their blossoming relationship.

 It was just after midnight that Alex woke, startled by the noises from the floor below – Jackie's Dormitory was immediately below her – there was screaming, shouting and raised voices. She grabbed her dressing gown and ran out the door. Bumping into Candice and they both ran down the stairs to find Miss Ward comforting one of the girls. Whilst Candice spoke with Miss Ward and the distraught girl, Alex pulled Jackie to one side and asked what happened. Jackie whispered back; "Clare went to the toilet – which is across the hall – and walked into the bloody ghost! A young woman all in white with a sad horrid skeletal face; Clare screamed and ran back in here and that woke us all up. Everyone else was in their beds, I saw that for myself."

 The three women sorted the girls out and everyone was ordered back to their beds by Miss Scott-Harris who appeared in a vivid pink dressing gown and matching slippers with her hair in curlers. Alex heard her tell Miss Ward that the investigators should arrive tomorrow from the University. That made Alex smile and she was joined in the corridor by Candice, banging her torch; "I think the bloody batteries have gone." She told Alex who was sniffing deeply. "What do you smell?" Candice asked and Alex said; "Oh, flowers I think." But what Alex had smelt wasn't flowers; she knew exactly what the strange odour was; the naughty 'ghost' had been smoking bloody cannabis!"

 Alex returned to her rooms and locked the door, grabbing up her handbag and mirror. She operated it and found herself outside the huge glasshouse and quietly pushed through the door and felt the warmth of the place immediately. She switched her mirror on to show a dim light and walked carefully between the packed shelves. It took her at least ten minutes to find what she wanted; a much smaller shed located at the far end behind a metal grill which was locked. It was totally enclosed with no glass anywhere, which was a little unusual to say the least.

Alex ran her mirror over it and smiled; it was hotter than the Sahara Desert and had the same moisture rating as the Amazon rain forest. There was only one plant growing inside: the well known 'Cannabis sativa' or better known as the cannabis plant. Alex looked about and her mirror caught a cardboard box from a plastics company that was new and in good condition. It was open and so Alex peered inside, then pulled a handful of small plastic bags out. "Perfect for selling dope in." she muttered to herself and tossed them back. That's when she also noticed the big cupboard with its huge staple and hasp lock on. She lowered her mirror and was about to head for the main door when she heard a noise from the cupboard. She quickly hid beneath the shelf, switching off the light on her mirror and watched – a little surprised - as the side of the cupboard was pulled inwards revealing an entrance and someone was emerging.

It was the scruffy youth [Newcomb] who called softly behind him; "Tell Harry I'll have the pictures for him tomorrow but the film will not be ready until Wednesday. Soon as I finish it, I'll drop it round. I think it's one of his best." A voice answered him, but Alex couldn't make out what was said or who was talking. John Newcomb quickly walked away, and Alex watched the panel slide back and it really did look just like an ordinary side panel. She eased herself from under the shelf and brushed her long coat down and headed for the main door. She was almost through the door when she heard the footsteps and muffled voices. She – again – dived under a nearby shelf and mid behind a couple of big pots that were stored there. Two figures came through the door so she pulled her mirror out and scanned them as they passed.

She stared at her mirror and sighed; it was Harold Field and his wife Janet. Human records had nothing on them except their scheduled dispatch dates: 1981 for Harold and 1991 for Janet. Harold's departure date caught Alex's attention; he would be stabbed to death outside a pub in Canterbury. She sighed and struggled to climb out from under the dirty shelving and outside operated her mirror and returned to her rooms where she compiled a brief report for Jericho and sent it. She climbed into bed and tried to sleep but suddenly realised that she could hear very low voices from next door: Candice's Room and one was definitely a man's. Alex sat up and tried to listen but couldn't make anything out. She managed a smile; Candice was breaking all the rules by having a man in her rooms in the middle of the night; she could be sacked out of hand for that. She had to stifle a giggle as she clearly heard the bed springs going!

Alex lay listening to the love-making next door and wondered who the lucky man was and that intrigued her; whoever he was, he knew how to slip into a locked school and pass undetected to reach Candice's room. Thinking about the mystery man, Alex slipped off to sleep until she heard soft knocking at her door. She eased from the bed and opened it. Candice slipped in quietly and Alex was surprised, no, a little shocked, to see that Candice was naked under her open dressing gown and wearing a black strap on dildo that had was long with a thick girth!

Alex couldn't hold the giggles back and Candice joined her, gripping the big plastic cock. "I can't get the fucking strap open! The bloody clasp is stuck firm, and I knew you wouldn't betray me," Alex nodded and Candice pulled off her dressing gown and stood naked. She had a massive pair of tits, but with small nipples and she had discrete tattoos on both [really unusual for this time and place for a woman]. Alex turned her around and tugged at the strap. "I may need to cut the strap; it appears stuck fast." She told Candice then sat back; "Candice, I heard a man's voice, so what are you wearing this bloody monster for?"

Candice smiled and gave the dildo a slap; "That's what he likes, dressing up as a school-girl and getting fucked in the arse with a big black plastic cock!" She shrugged her shoulders and Alex asked who 'he' was. Candice really smiled and held a finger to her lips; "Can't say; unless you want to meet him, but he would probably expect to fuck the pair of us or fuck you whilst I fuck him; again." She chuckled and waved the dildo under Alex's amused face.

Alex sighed and thought, 'Oh, well it is for the sake of the mission.' She smiled at Candice and gave her bum a little slap. "Go on darling." She whispered.

Candice was gone only for a few seconds and returned with the scruffy youth; John Newcomb who really grinned at Alex. He was stark naked and gripping a substantial erection with one hand. He was tattooed over his chest, upper arms and thighs. Alex was to find that he had a magnificent full Golden eagle tattooed on his back, an absolute masterpiece. Candice introduced them as Alex slipped from her nightdress and now was totally naked as the other two. "Give his cock a good sucking while I lube his arse and this bloody thing again." Candice whispered as she quickly rummaged in her dressing gown and produced some lubricant. Alex sat on the bed and pushed his big cock into her mouth and went to work. The young man groaned; "Christ Candy, she sucks as good as you. It's like someone stuck a vacuum cleaner on my cock!" Candice just smiled and bent down behind him, pushing her fingers up his arse, covered in lubricant. When she finished, she came from behind and knelt next to Alex whispering; "Open your legs darling and I'll give your fanny a good going over and then lube it with this stuff."

Alex opened her legs and Candice's head was soon between them, licking and fingering. She certainly had played this game before. She expertly spread the cream around Alex's cunt and patted her arse. "Now the fun can really begin." She said softly; and it did.

Alex lay on the floor with a pillow under head, on her back with her legs up and open [they couldn't use the bed; it would creak and groan with three of them on it performing midnight sexual gymnastics] while John fucked her hard and fast with Candice squatting closely over him; pushing the big dildo into his arse with some skill and appeared well experienced in doing it. John groaned a couple of times and whispered to Candy; "Oh fuck, for the want of a fucking camera. This is the best we've had in some time."

That comment was noted by the moaning Alex who was really aroused by this scene and produced a couple of small orgasms. They swopped around with Candy mounting Alex's bum with the monster [after more careful lubricating] while Alex squatted over John and rode him closely as he enjoyed handling her big swinging tits. Now this unusual 'double penetration' produced in Alex a big orgasm and she had to cover her mouth with a hand as it exploded from her and down John's hard thrusting cock, splattering his belly and thighs. John groaned and squeezed her tit into his mouth and sucked hard, squeezing the other one with his soft hand. He came in Alex with some restrained groaning and panting. Finally, he muttered; "You two get at it and I'll watch."

John lay against the bed, tugging at his flaccid penis as candy fucked Alex in the bum, doggy-style. After a few minutes, she pulled from Alex and slapped the dildo. Alex caught her meaning and grabbed the scissors from the bedside cabinet and cut the straps. Candy groaned with relief and tossed the thing to one side and crawled onto Alex. They had passionate lesbian sex; first in the sixty-nine position, then 'scissor' together for some time. They ended up rolling around the floor, kissing and fingering each other with some unrestrained passion. John interrupted the pair and pulled Alex onto all fours and pushed his fresh erection straight into her back passage, Candy quickly slid underneath her and went to work on her already soaking wet fanny with skilled fingers. Alex couldn't believe it as another big climax racked her body and she almost collapsed on top of the chuckling Candy. "Christ darling, I could take a shower under that lot." Candy whispered and lay back watching John fucking hard and fast. She crept round to him, and the pair kissed and caressed, while Alex had her head resting on her arms and head turned; watched John fucking her bum while Candy held the cheeks of her arse open for him. He came pretty quickly for the third erection of the night. They collapsed on the floor, panting and talking in whispers.

John had to go; he thanked Alex and kissed her, then did the same to candy and slipped away and the two girls climbed into bed and lay in each other's arms. Alex was well satisfied by the night manoeuvres and Candice giggled; "Do you know what's funny about the fruit bowels in the Dining Hall?" Alex kissed her face and neck; "No I don't know what's funny about them darling." Candice kissed her back – with some passion it should be noted – and giggled again, with Alex feeling Candy's hand between her legs. "The bloody bananas disappear as soon as they are put out by the kitchen staff; especially the really big ones!" they both chuckled and started to kiss and caress again.

But Alex kept on the job and casually asked Candy how John slipped in and out the school without being seen or heard. Candy kissed her breasts and smiled; "Easy darling, like everyone else who knows about them. He uses the secret passages." Now Alex was really interested and kissed Candy's neck and shoulders as she caressed Alex's big tits with her mouth and hands. "Tell me about them darling." She whispered and Candy did with Alex smiling about the effectiveness of good old fashioned 'Pillow talk'.

4. TUESDAY 2nd MAY 1961. QUEEN CHARLOTTE'S ACADEMY, KENT, ENGLAND.

Alex just made breakfast and joined Candice on the staff table. The conversations around the table cantered on two topics: yet another visit by 'Pungent Pam' and the arrival of the paranormal investigators. You could say the Wilson was third topic of conversation and Alex overheard the dour mathematics teacher telling her friends; "They will take over the place. First one appears in the damn kitchens' and now another has turned up to supposedly investigates the bloody ghost." All the teachers agreed; except Miss Evelyn Scott-Harris – who told her to keep her voice down – and Miss Flowers [the art & drama teacher] who said it was wonderful to have such diversity in England these days. That clearly wasn't a popular statement and the rest of the ladies said so with some unkind words directed towards her. The conversations faded away as the food was served.

Alex and Candice said nothing and finished their breakfast. Candice had early lessons in the Chemistry lab and Alex needed to open the infirmary for the morning sick list. She walked up the grand staircase towards the infirmary and found Jericho and Wilson standing beneath a large portrait of a medieval knight on horseback. They both had big satchels and notebooks. Alex joined them and reported all that she had discovered with her 'night manoeuvres'. Jericho rubbed his chin and said quietly; "Apparently the ghost hasn't made an appearance for years, the last recorded event was in 1915 when this place was a temporary military hospital for soldiers wounded in the Great War. But the really interesting thing that we discovered; is there are no earth-bound souls around the damn place. So, our ghost is definitely human and is being manifested for some reason."

Wilson stared about the place and said, "From what Alex says about young Newcomb, he may be organizing some very naughty film and photograph sessions here. The 'Harry' he mentioned could be Harold Field the Head gardener and they could be using those secret passages that she heard about, to move around the place unseen and undetected. Then you have the bloody cannabis industry in the glass house; who are they selling it too?"

Jericho shook his head, thinking; "It doesn't make sense, with all that illegal activity going on in this place, why draw attention to the school? I mean, if you are working, making illegal films and growing illegal plants, would you want the place crawling with ghost hunters and getting the place noticed?

Wilson and Alex had to agree with that conclusion, so why the supposed haunting? It certainly wasn't in the best interests of the naughty film makers and drug dealers. It would be like throwing stones in a glasshouse!

"I think we may two sets of characters about the place. Working against each other's interests I suspect. First, we unmask the bloody ghost and then we may start to get some answers." Jericho told them and Alex had to get to work; she left them scribbling down notes and pretending to investigate a ghost that didn't actually exist. But they were on the trail of the human who liked to play at ghosts around the school; but the why?

Alex had no patients this morning and was soon bored sitting in the empty infirmary and decided to walk the grounds. Carrying her old 'Gladstone bag' she watched the junior hockey match for a few minutes and shook her head in mock despair; the girls went for each ball with absolute determination and no fear. "Bloody Amazon warriors would be proud of them." She murmured and noticed some older girls on the touchlines; cheering 'the snots' on. She grinned; Jackie was amongst them – again with Kath and Susan – she certainly was working hard to cultivate their friendship and find out why they really were in the glasshouse on the Friday that Jerome Hobbs was murdered.
She walked slowly towards the staff cottages that lined the drive and found a cheerful Preston with his guitar case over his shoulder heading back to the kitchens. They stopped and she started to bring him up to date with the mission. But he smiled; "Jericho has already done that. I understand you know where there is a secret passage. I'm not due back in the kitchen until dinner tonight. Shall we explore?"

Alex nodded at that, and they returned to the school, and he followed her up the grand staircase to the third floor [the seniors dormitory was one half of the east wing] and found the cleaner's cupboard. Alex briefly looked around and tried the door; it was unlocked, and they slipped in. It was the size of a box room and lined with shelves, except one wall contained just a big cupboard marked; 'CHEMICALS' and she pulled the door open and with Preston's help, shifted some cans and big glass bottles. She felt round the top of the rear panel and grinned; "Got it, just as Candy said."

They stepped over the cans and bottles and pushed into the dark entrance that had revealed itself. Alex lit the way with her mirror, and they followed the dusty dark panelled tunnel – sloping downwards – until Preston tapped her arm and gestured to the dirty floor. "What is that?" he asked. Alex bent down and picked up the object. They both stared at it in the light of her mirror and Alex yelped and threw it down: "Christ! A bloody used condom!"

Preston chuckled; "At least we know what the damn passages are used for." They were about to walk on and Alex waved her mirror over it; "That's pretty thin for a condom from the 1960's." she muttered and then smiled; "Bingo, it was manufactured in Birmingham in 2023. That mean's Jerome has been up to something naughty around here. He's our resident time-traveller." Preston nodded, then said; "Did your mirror say who the semen belonged to?" Alex acknowledged that was a very good suggestion and tapped at her mirror, she didn't smile; "A certain Samuel Collins who belongs in this era. Temporal Operations has nothing on file about him; he appears clean." Preston chuckled; "I've never met him, but I bet he's a white boy." Alex smiled; "And how did you work that out, may I ask?" Preston shrugged his shoulders; "It's too small to be a brother's." They both laughed at that. "That's some boast; can you back it up with any evidence?" Alex coyly asked him, and Preston grinned; "If you want I can." She folded her arms; "I want you to." She whispered. Preston unzipped his flies and pulled out his swelling cock saying softly; "Alex, you are real erection material."

Alex stared at his big member, which was growing and twitching in his hand and sighed a little; "Oh dear look at what I've done. I had better make it better." Preston pulled down his pants and trousers whispering; "Amen to that." Alex knelt and gripped the cock with both hands and guided it to her welcoming mouth. She sucked, licked and caressed to Preston's delight. He groaned; "I always wanted to fuck a nurse in uniform." Alex murmured; "Matron Sweetie." And set to work on his cock. Preston pressed back against the wall and watched with some delight. After some minutes he said, "I want you now." Alex stood and hitched up

the hem on her uniform, revealing her stocking tops and white panties. Preston had her knickers down in seconds, then really laughed when Alex whispered; "I lubricated before I came."
He fucked her with real energy and skill against the wall; her arms around his shoulders, she was groaning and tossing her head about as she felt every inch of his boner [as he called it] filling her up. He gripped her arse and pushed his cock hard into her.

Alex now moaned and pulled his face to hers and they kissed with some passion; all moist and sticky, with tongues exploring deep. He lifted both her legs from the floor and now bounced her up and down on his large rampant cock. He clearly was much stronger than he physically looked and Alex was groaning with sexual pleasure. He lay in the dirt and Alex climbed on him and rode like a rodeo star. She had her first small orgasm which was quickly followed by another, riding him with some determination, making sure every inch of that big dick was buried inside of her. He groaned and gripped her big titties with some joy and real skill. Alex loved that and responded by thrusting down quickly. Preston pulled her down to him and they french kissed with some unbridled passion. She was having another, more intense, fiery climax when the torch light fell upon the pair of lovers. They both stared up and the torch was lowered; they saw who was holding it. John Newcomb smiled; "Hi Preston and Alex, see you later people." Susan Toller giggled and whispered; "Hello Miss and you Sir!" They carefully stepped over the pair on the floor and Alex and Preston saw that the 6th Former had no panties on; she was holding them and John's hand. They disappeared down the dark little corridor, whispering and chuckling.

Alex suddenly felt Preston cum in her and he groaned; "Bloody women in uniform."Alex sighed; "It's like Liverpool Street station around here, come on, let's go." Preston agreed with that, muttering; "I wonder if the bloody ghost has to wait her turn to use them." They adjusted their clothes and Alex pulled her panties back on; they would need changing and Preston brushed Alex down with his hands. They kissed again and headed up the corridor with Alex thinking about Susan Toller and just how deep her involvement was with Newcomb and Hobbs. Then, did Candice know about Newcomb's other girls?

Alex shone her mirror down and gestured to Preston; "Come on, there's another entrance." They stood in front of the recessed panel and Alex peered through the peep hole and sighed; "It opens into the girl's toilets and shower room. They are empty so come on." She pressed against the little lever on the side and the panel opened quietly and they stepped through. They walked through the long room and came out on the ground floor, just yards from the kitchens.

Preston grinned; "Oh well, I could get an early start on the bloody chips." He headed for the kitchen door but stopped and turned; "Tell Jericho there is no trace of demonic activity around the place. None at all, so Rul isn't around here and hasn't been here for someone time; if he ever was." He gave Alex a kiss on the cheek and disappeared through the door and Alex headed back to the infirmary; so, if there is no demonic activity, then Jerome's soul would be lost to the darkness of real death since he was out of his ordained time. She sat in the quiet infirmary and consulted her mirror, reading about the previous owners of the school buildings and especially the Hobbs family who had owned the house from when it was founded in May 1714 to its end in July 1952, when the last survivor of the family died, and the estate was sold. She read that Queen Charlotte's Academy had moved here in 1955 after the buildings and grounds had been altered to accept its use as a school. Queen Charlotte's original building complex had been located on the other side of Canterbury but had to close down due to serious building faults and the place was eventually demolished in 1959 after lying derelict for some years. Apparently, a council housing estate now stood on the grounds in the 2020's.

The Hobb's family had been shipping owners and rather disturbingly, owned large swathes of the American colonies which they shipped thousands of Africans to, for working the cotton plantations and had grown very rich doing it. She quickly hid her mirror; she had a visitor. It was Jerome Hobbs. He wandered in and sat down without invitation and smiled at her, leaning on her desk. "What can I do for you Mister Hobbs?" Alex asked politely studying the big man's powerful hands resting on her desk. Close up, she realised that he was a very handsome man with really incredible green eyes; they were like emeralds. He certainly had no accent and Alex was surprised by that since he was born in 1998 in East London.

He ran a big hand through his sandy blond hair and lowered his voice; "Well Alex, Candy and John tell me you are quite a woman who likes to partake in some pretty dirty sex. I'm told you like anal, oral, double penetration and lesbian. That makes me very interested in you." Alex was a little shocked that Candy had betrayed her but wasn't surprised. "Go on Mister Hobbs." Was all she replied, and he chuckled; "I knew Candy was right about you. We'll get together tonight, and I have a very rewarding proposition for you. Very rewarding indeed."

They both looked around and saw Miss Flowers helping one of the hockey girls in, moaning about her ankle. "One for you Miss Cappanni," Miss Flowers smiled at her and Jerome, who leaned over the desk and asked her if she wanted to go the 'Empire Theatre' cinema in the town and perhaps a drink in the Kings Head afterwards to discuss a very good offer. She agreed and he walked away smiling with the date set for tonight. That should uncover more about our time-travelling friend, she told herself. As she attended the girl, Miss Flowers praised the under gardener: "He's become quite a leading light in our modest amateur productions. He acts so well and it's almost like he was a professional, a proper thespian. He was superb in our last Christmas production of 'Twelfth Night'. He was so utterly convincing and very funny. His comic timing was wonderful." Alex checked the girl's ankle and wondered if that revelation was important; that Jerome Hobbs was a very good actor as most that travelled in time actually were! She also wasn't surprised by the other fact she learnt from Miss Flowers; that the Drama & Art teacher was clearly smitten by him.

5. NIGHT MANOEUVRES – PART 2.

With Jackie primed about her 'date' with Jerome [she would cover Alex's absence and call Alex on her mirror if she needed to return, which Alex could do in an instant using her own mirror.] Alex headed for the little car park to fetch her car, then realised that people might realise it was gone and that could cause some awkward questions. She jumped a little as Jerome emerged from the shadows and spoke quietly; "We can't use your car; people will notice it's gone. Come on." He gestured for her to follow him, and she did. They walked to his cottage, and he disappeared down the side and Alex heard an engine star. She watched with real curiosity at what would emerge then laughed, as the big motorcycle and side car appeared. He pulled up the cover on the side car and grinned; "Get in, your hair won't be blown about and it's quite comfortable; so I've been told."

Alex admired the red and blue 'Matchless' combination and held her dress up and slipped in; giving the smiling Jerome a good look at her stocking tops and frilly white panties. He leaned over and whispered; "Was that an invitation for me?" Alex smoothed down her dress and just smiled. He pulled away, switching on the headlamp and headed for the village at speed. He parked in the road opposite the cinema and joined the small queue. Alex read the neon sign and didn't smile; another bloody war film was all she thought. The cinema was showing one of the big hits of May 1961; 'The Guns of Naverone'. Jerome bought decent tickets at two shillings and four pence for two and the usherette showed them to their seats. The screen was showing a 'British Pathe' News reel, all about the American astronaut Alan Bartlett Shepard Jr's forthcoming space flight.

They sat by themselves in the rear and the lights dimmed. The major feature started, and Jerome whispered in her ear; "Now be a good girl and let me have a taste of you." Alex turned to say something and found Jerome's' mouth over hers and his tongue exploring with some determination. He had his arm around her shoulders and held her tight; he certainly knew how to French kiss and Alex responded. His other hand disappeared under her skirt, and she opened her legs slightly, so that his hand was on her crotch. He gently rubbed and fingered her fanny through her little cotton panties. Her hand was in his trousers and gripping something big.

Within a few minutes she had gone down on him, with her head in his lap and sucking hard. She could just about fit it in her mouth. She jerked it with some strength and skill, using her teeth and tongue on the monster; he stifled his groans and stoked her hair and fanny with real dexterity. Luckily enough, Alex was swallowing a serious amount of cum by the time intermission lights came on. He eased from his seat and kissed Alex on the head, as she wiped her mouth with a hanky; "I'll get you an Orange Kia-Ora to wash that down." Jerome smiled and joined the queue with the nice lady standing in the front of the screen, holding a tray of goodies. She noticed how the young usherette and Jerome talked together; maybe she was another of his girls and could understand why; after experiencing his big cock in her mouth. She imagined it buried in her vagina and bum. That made her really smile.

Alex enjoyed sucking her orange cordial through a straw and

Jerome pointed out that she sucked beautifully, and the pair giggled. They were soon back at it as the lights went down. They were so engrossed in foreplay that neither noticed the usherette slip into the seat next to them. Jerome only removed his tongue from Alex's mouth to introduce 'Ellen' to her. Alex managed to nod and was well surprised when the young girl's hand joined Jerome's under her skirt! Her fingers disappeared under Alex's moist panties and Alex had to groan; she knew how to work a clitoris and Alex soon had a little squirt which made 'Ellen' laugh softly.

Jerome sat back and watched 'Ellen' explore Alex's mouth and fanny with some passion. After a few minutes, 'Ellen' rose and kissed both of them and headed for the front office; the lights were about to come on and she would be needed to help clear the cinema and close up for the night.

Jerome and Alex left arm in arm and neither had actually seen the bloody film! They sat in the Kings' head and Jerome brought her a brandy and himself a pint of cider. She sat with uncrossed legs since her panties were wet from his and Ellen's caresses. They had really aroused her with their expert and passionate kisses and their hand and fingers knew exactly how to please a woman through her panties. Their hands around her shoulder had managed to explore her ample breasts - they had one each - and work the nipples through her thin summer dress; she wasn't wearing a bra, which absolutely delighted the young man and woman.

He leaned over table and pushed the ashtray to one side. "You can make more money in a single month than you could working a whole year at the school, are you interested in that?" Alex sipped her brandy and nodded. He smiled and took a sip of his cider and continued in a low voice. "I make adult films with some associates of mine; you have already met two of them; intimately. Now you're just the sort of girl we need to really make films that would sell. Just say the word and I can set it up. You'll be paid a hundred pounds in cash for the first film, and you can approve the script, change it about if you don't like certain bits of sex. I'm thinking about six or seven films a month. They will run for about twenty minutes or half hour. Are you alright with that?" Alex knew that a schoolteacher in these times earns about £3,600 per year or £300 per month. Just making six or seven twenty minute 'blue' films would mean that she could double her money each month for far less 'work'.

"That is some rate of pay, almost double what I would earn playing Matron or teaching." She said quietly and Jerome smiled; "Speak to Candy; she'll tell you that I always keep my word and pay up front each and every time. She's earned enough to buy a little house on the Kent coast already. You can secure your future and enjoy yourself at the same time." He swallowed down some more cider and asked if she knew about the 'casting couch'. She nodded and finished her brandy. "Good, I won't have to explain that and are you willing to audition for me?"

 Alex took a little breath and placed her glass on the table; "Alright, where and when?" he nodded with satisfaction; "Does tonight suit?" and Alex said 'Yes' quietly. They quickly left the pub but didn't walk back to the motorcycle but walked down the quiet High Street to a closed-up Taylor's shop and Jerome pulled pulled some keys from his pocket and unlocked the front door. Alex noticed a sign that declared the shop had closed down in March 1959 after the death of the proprietor Mr. Joseph Pickles. Christ: this place is full of Pickles! Alex thought. To her surprise, Jerome shouted; "Harry it's me and the new girl Alex. The film is on. Are the others here?" He locked the door behind him, and they walked up the small rear staircase in silence. Alex could hear music and voices. He pushed open a door and stepped into a big room with tripod lights and two cameras' set up. The bay window was covered with a 'blackout' curtain and sealed around the edges to stop the powerful lights leaking light out. The centre piece was a large dark sofa with several scatter cushions thrown about it. The film would be shot in monochrome and without sound, which was typical and normal for 'Blue' films in this time and place. The pornography industry would embrace colour later in the decade, adding sound when the technology became cheaper with Japanese imports.

 Alex wasn't shocked to see Janet sitting naked on the sofa, drinking a cup of tea, while Harry her husband - just in his underpants - fussed with a camera. Janet put the cup and jumped up, kissing Alex on the lips: "I think it will be great working with a beauty like you. I'm really going to enjoy your fanny and I hope you enjoy mine." She kissed Alex again and pulled her over to the sofa and they sat down. She was all over Alex like an adolescent sex starved boy; her hand up Alex's dress and her tongue buried in her mouth. "'I'll undress you but keep on your stockings and panties for now." Janet whispered; her hand rubbing the front of Alex's panties and kissing her mouth with some unrestrained sexual desire and passion.

"Your wonderfully wet already my darling!" Janet sounded quite pleased by that discovery. The door opened and Alex couldn't actually believe who came through it. Miss Edna Flowers was dressed in red stockings and panties, with a big, spiked collar around her neck and a dog chain attached to it. Holding the other end of the dog chain was a big rough looking man with scars on his face. He was naked apart from a matching spiked collar and Alex's eyes opened wide at the size of his erect cock; It stood proud and must have been ten inches long or more and thick as a jam jar! It swung like a gate in the wind as he walked. Alex found she couldn't take her eyes off it. She was mesmerised by it; it was like a snake shifting and moving.

Jerome clapped his hands; "OK people; we'll shoot Alex and Janet on the sofa first. Then Percy and Edna will appear, and Percy will whip Edna with the dog collar. Then Janet and Alex, you join them and Percy fucks Edna first on the floor then takes you Alex, bent over the sofa. I join in and fuck Janet in the same position. Edna, you get behind us and do your special. We'll see how that goes. Are you ready Harry?"

Harry gave the thumbs up and Alex, now just in her stockings and panties watched as Jerome pulled on the black mask and started to pull off his clothes. "ACTION! Please Janet and Alex!" Jerome shouted and pulled off his underpants. Alex could feel Janet pulling her back on the sofa but couldn't take her eyes of Jerome's swollen cock; it easily matched Percy's monster. Janet grabbed a pot cream from the small table by the couch and tossed it to Edna chuckling; "You are going to need this. But save some for Alex, she'll need it too!" Both women laughed and Janet went back to fondling Alex with some real joy. Harry worked the cameras with some skill; he certainly knew what he was doing behind the lens and his wife knew her way around another woman's body.

Alex lay on the sofa on her back, with Janet between her legs, slowly tugging down her panties. She discarded them and went to work on Alex's fanny with some skill, using her fingers and mouth. Harry moved in for the close up of that. Meanwhile Percy and Edna had started their performance with Jerome operating the second camera. Percy was slapping Edna's quivering buttocks with the dog chain. Alex groaned and then realised her bloody handbag – under the table – was buzzing; only she could hear her mirror calling, then realised it was an alarm that it was sounding. She reached under and grabbed it; sitting up and telling Janet and Jerome that she needed to piss. "That's great, just piss in Janet's mouth darling, she'll love it and it will make great cinema!"

The door came open and a tall, very handsome dark haired young man wandered in, smoking a cigar. He shook hands with Jerome and didn't notice Alex slip from the disappointed Janet who pointed to the green door for the toilet. Alex closed the door behind her and checked her mirror; the Minor demon alarm was sounding and showing that a Tier 3 demon called Rul was close by. "Oh fuck!" she exclaimed and knew she had to get the hell out of here. If the demon saw her, he would instinctively know she was a temporal detective. He hadn't noticed her on the sofa, whilst greeting and talking with Jerome.

Alex had no bloody choice; she operated her mirror and returned to the school's infirmary.

Jackie was dozing, sitting at Alex's desk and looked up and smiled, gesturing to Alex's lack of clothes; "Looks like you had a better evening than I did." But Alex didn't smile, she was already calling Preston on her mirror and gave him details of the flat above the disused Baker's in the High Street and that he would find his quarry there; Rul the demon. She lowered the mirror and grabbed one of the Infirmary gowns [which didn't cover much because the infirmary's guests were usually much smaller!] and wrapped it around. "You won't believe what I discovered. But disappearing like that from a toilet with just an A4 sized window will be hard to explain. I think I've fucked up the mission, well, the bit regarding recovering Jerome's lost soul." She sat on the chair; not very happy and consulted her mirror adding, "Jericho won't be pleased with this."

Jackie sat back and smiled; "Have you forgotten that By Preston tackling the demon; time will stop. When he's vanquished the bastard, you can return, and it will be like the demon never bloody turned up; time will restart, and no-one will even notice you had disappeared; for them that time never occurred." Jackie chuckled and Alex leaned over and kissed her; she knew that

Jackie was right. They sat waiting for Preston's call and Jackie pointed to the clock on the wall; the second hand had stopped, and Alex consulted her mirror and found that time had indeed ceased to move forward for living humans in this time and place. Alex's mirror buzzed; it was Jericho calling to congratulate her on discovering where the demon Rul was hiding and to say that Preston had sent the bastard back to his master and was about to restart time for living humans. Alex asked Jericho to tell Preston not to restart time until she called him. Jericho agreed to that and ceased transmission. Alex grinned and said, "You can come with me and help for a few minutes. No-one will arrive here; they are all frozen in time." The pair chuckled and disappeared.

6. THE FILM: 'THREE WOMEN AND A SOFA'.

Jackie really chuckled at the figures frozen in time, especially Jerome who was in the middle of saying something and smiling broadly. Janet was leaned against the sofa; the look of sad disappointment that Alex didn't piss in her mouth, still on her face. Edna was kneeling on the carpet with the dog chain hanging in mid-air just above her arse; big Percy smiling and gripping his huge cock with the other hand. Harry working the camera was the only one who almost looked normal; though he was in just his underpants; which were bulging.

Alex slowly opened the film canister on the Paillard Bolex 8mm Movie Camera and pulled the reel from it and placed it on the table then did the same with Jerome's camera. She gave the sticky reels to Jackie who checked they were 'fogged' and replaced them in the cameras. Jackie kissed her and disappeared with the tapes, which were headed for the school's furnace. Alex lay on the sofa and pulled her panties back on, then called Preston to re-start time some two minutes before he received her call about the bloody demon. He readily agreed and Alex hurriedly pushed her mirror back into her handbag and dropped it under the table. Everyone was suddenly animated again; "ACTION! Please Janet and Alex!" Jerome shouted.

Alex lay on the sofa on her back, with Janet between her legs, slowly tugging down her panties. She discarded them and went to work on Alex's fanny with some skill, using her fingers and mouth. Harry moved in for the close up of that. Meanwhile Percy and Edna had started their performance with Jerome operating the second camera. Percy was slapping Edna's quivering buttocks with the dog chain. Alex groaned and ran a hand over Janet's head while the other caressed her big heaving tits.

 The pair had hard lesbian sex on the big sofa for a few minutes before Janet posed Alex bending over the sofa and quickly rubbed lubricant in and on her vagina. Janet did the same with Percy's cock and he mounted her quickly. Alex really groaned as the big man with the big cock fucked her brains out. He gripped her hips and thrusted without mercy. Her body was getting such a fucking that it didn't bother with the normal little orgasm's first; it went straight to the big one and Alex really gripped the back of the sofa and enjoyed it fully. Her legs were shaking as she squirted three times and she actually felt sick from sheer pleasure. "Pump your load into me!" she shouted at the amused Percy, and he did. Alex's eyes actually rolled; it was like someone had stuck a garden hose up there and turned the tap on full. She slumped on the sofa and felt the big man withdrawing the now empty monster. Janet was straight on her gaping and wet fanny to clean up using her tongue and mouth.

 Jerome shouted for the action to continue and hastily rubbing the cream on his cock; stood over Janet who was between Alex's shaking legs and pushed his cock into Alex's arse without even asking and fucked her, leaning right over so that Harry could capture the superb action. Edna sat cross legged on the floor, twirling the dog chain, wondering when she would get one of the big dicks. Percy certainly wouldn't disappoint her, and he stuck his cock in her mouth and she worked it up to a fresh erection.
 Alex simply couldn't believe it; another big orgasm swept her body as Jerome pumped her gaping bum hole with some power. She squirted again and Janet was delighted as it filled her mouth and ran down her chin and onto her heaving tits. Percy was now fucking Edna in the Missionary mission and Harry was cussing and moaning as he operated both cameras, jumping between the two with real skill. He would have John edit the takes and the young man certainly knew how to create a cracking 'blue' film from all this top class action being recorded.

Jerome was gripping Alex's big tits and pumping her arse with his well lubricated cock when he groaned loudly and cussed; he shot his load into her back passage and the pair slumped on the sofa; panting. Jerome managed to shout; "CUT! That's a wrap!" and started laughing. Alex wiped a tear and joined in the laughter. That had been the best fucking sex session she had taken part in for some time! But she still felt a little hunger inside for more cock or fanny. Her appetite was had been seriously aroused. Maybe another session with Jerome when they returned to the school would help.

They walked back to the motorbike in the dark; Alex had her arm through Jerome's, and he was clearly very happy. He turned and kissed her with some passion and whispered; "We are going to make a small fortune together!" then helped her into the side car. He buttoned up his jacket and wrapped a scarf around his neck. He leaned over and kissed her again; "I think I'll market it under the title; 'Three women and a sofa' or simply 'The sofa'. I'll decide when I see the final cut. Come around tomorrow night and we'll show you one we shot last week called 'The Naughty Schoolgirls'. You'll love that and recognize where we filmed it."

Alex nodded and restrained from laughing; the bloody film will never need a title now. She had a pretty good idea who the stars of that other little gem could turn out to be;sadly, the corrupted young girls, Kath and Susan.

Jerome went to start the bike, then stopped; "I'm surprised that Max never turned up tonight like he promised. He's normally spot on time with the money." Alex tapped his arm; "What money?" Jerome sighed; "He pays for everything and would have paid you for tonight. Still. He's good for it. We'll get it off him next time he calls." He stamped down on the kick start and pulled away. Alex smiled to herself; no-one will be getting paid now that Preston has kicked 'Max's' arse back to his master; the Dark Prince.

Alex and Jerome kissed outside his cottage for some time – in the dark shadows of the doorway – before Alex pulled away and headed for the side door which she had a key too. She turned and watched the lights go in his cottage and took another couple of steps, then stopped and turned. She could see there were two shadows behind the net curtains; someone had been waiting for Jerome to return, sitting in his front room without the lights on. A figure pulled the curtains together and Alex walked on. Surely, he won't be serving another girl after all the sex above the Taylor's shop? Christ, he must have the stamina of a breeding beef bull!

She stopped again and realised someone was in the doorway

already and unlocking the door; the light streamed out and Alex saw it was the caretaker; Mr. Norman Pickles in his raincoat and hat. He turned and lifted his hat to her, speaking quietly. "Good evening, Miss, did you have a good time tonight at the pictures with young Hobbs? I saw the 'The Guns of Naverone' myself. A very good picture, but a young lady like yourself would probably have preferred a Romantic Comedy." He stepped aside and gestured her in, closing the door behind them and locking it.
 "No, it wasn't bad; we went to the Kings head and had a drink before coming home." She said and smiling Mr. Pickles nodded, chuckling; "I know, I popped in and had a couple of whiskies before heading home myself." He stopped at the foot of the small staircase and rubbed his chin; "Had a little party at the old Taylors did you Miss?"

Alex didn't smile and just shrugged her shoulders. He removed his hat and stared at the floor, then pulled a bunch of keys from his pocket and smiled; "Did you notice the name of the Taylors Miss?" Alex gripped her handbag; she certainly did; it was Joseph Pickles!

 He tossed the keys and caught them; "I wonder how you could persuade me not to report what went on in the flat above my late brother's shop that I now own. I allow young Hobbs to borrow it occasionally to entertain his girlfriends: keeps the headmistress happy having all that off site. But she wouldn't be too pleased with you and the gardener getting it together. I think you'll be jumping into your nice little sports car and driving away with no references. Shame that. But what can I do; I must be loyal to people who pay me, don't I?"

 Alex smiled; she knew that she couldn't be dismissed because the mission would have to end if her cover was blown. This was a major problem that was totally unforeseen. "I'm sure we can work something out Mr. Pickles, we're both reasonable adults." He smiled and pocketed the keys; "I knew you were a clever woman Miss. Would you like a night cap in my rooms?" Alex sighed and nodded.

 She pulled the pillow behind her head and stared up at the ceiling. She was on her back in the caretaker's bed; just in her stockings and he was on top of her panting and groaning, his modest cock inside of her. He lowered his head and sucked her tits; he wasn't gentle and used his teeth and mouth with little care. She turned her head slightly and saw the time; it was almost midnight and the dirty old sod had been fucking her for fifteen minutes already. He pulled up on his hands, thrusting hard and fast – well, as best he could at his age! – And suddenly he cussed and shook his head; he had shot his load into her. He patted her face and sighed; "Twenty years ago I would have lasted twice that. Never mind sweetheart, you certainly won't object to a cup of tea and a quick sucking of my cock and when I'm hard again, we'll do it French style. I really like that." Alex looked back at the ceiling; she knew that 'French Style' meant having up her bum. She slowly nodded as he pulled from her saying; "I'll put the kettle on. How do you take yours?"

She lay back and sighed; "The bloody things I have to endure in the line of duty." then giggled. Mr. Pickles returned with the tea and an erection. They sat on the bed leaned against the pillows and drank their tea. Alex used her free hand to jerk his cock and when both had finished their brew; Mr. Pickles set about Alex's bum hole with real pleasure and anticipation. She was on all fours, gripping a couple of pillows beneath herself and wondering how long he would take; she was looking forward to her bed.
"Hold still sweetheart and thank you." He pushed his cock in and started to thrust; Alex checked the clock and lowered her head as he really began to fuck her, hard and fast. This went on for some time and Alex had to look around at the old man to ensure it was still him! His hand rubbed her fanny and found her clitoris in an instant and worked with some skill. Alex groaned as the first little orgasm came and she was now backing up against his cock. "Good girl, you make me feel a million pounds and twenty years old again." He said softly but didn't slow down and now was buried up to his balls in her back passage and she could feel every inch.

Alex gripped the pillows and cussed as two or three orgasms' swept over her; she really pushed back, moaning; "Fuck me! For God sake fuck me!" and he did. She had a big orgasm which made her legs shake and the tears to fall. Then she felt old Mr. Pickles pumping his cum into her, in big spurts of the hot liquid. She managed to raise her head and stared at the clock; he had fucked her arse and fanny like a steam engine for nearly forty minutes!

Alex walked slowly and awkwardly back to her rooms, a little stunned by the great sex she had with old Mr. Pickles. He had invited her to take more 'tea' with him and now seriously considered that she would!

7. WEDNESDAY 3rd MAY 1961. QUEEN CHARLOTTE'S ACADEMY, KENT, ENGLAND.

Jericho and Wilson joined them in the infirmary and Jackie made tea. "Well done, Alex, your date with our time-travelling friend produced the goods alright. Rul is back with his master and the finance for their contribution to the porn industry has been ended. Now, we need to discover Jerome's time travelling device or where the fixed time portal is located. I strongly suspect It's around the school buildings or grounds." He accepted his tea from Jackie and took a sip before continuing; "Jerome's very presence here is changing the current Timeline, though in a minor way and we're tasked to recover him and sent him home; permanently. Then close the time portal he has been using. When that's done, we can go home." Jericho smiled and sipped his tea again, adding; "You brew a cracking cup of tea Jackie!"

Wilson raised his cup to Jackie and said, "Ditto. We have only to Friday to return Jerome to his own time and save him from being a lost soul, so we need to get our skates on. Regarding the porn and drugs set up; that is really not our concern since that entails human criminal behaviour."

Jericho grinned and tapped Wilson on the shoulder; "Spoken like a future Temporal Inspector!"

Everyone chuckled and Alex placed down her cup; "He wants me to watch a bloody film they made last week. I assume that John Newcomb uses the chemist's he works for, to process the films and pictures. So, they must set up and watch them somewhere and my money is on the closed-up Taylor's shop. The bloody film is called; The Naughty Schoolgirls" and I suspect it stars Jackie's new friends Katherine Gapp and Susan Toller. Sadly, I think Jerome has already corrupted those two."

Jackie finished her tea and tapped the cup with a finger; "Those two tarts applied and received a pass for tonight to see '101 Dalmatians' at the Victory cinema. I understand Miss Flowers will be taking them. I could plead with her and get taken along; the seats are only a shilling currently for school children and I have hardly touched the allowance my generous mother gave me."

Alex chuckled; "You really are in character." and agreed with that plan, voicing her suspicions about Miss Flowers and Jerome. Jericho didn't smile; "If this Miss Flowers is under Jerome's influence and those three are really going to the premiere of their porn film, then she'll refuse you. If she does, call us because it mean's Alex is right about the woman." Jericho placed his cup down and sighed; "Now, back to ghost hunting. What a way to make a living….well, death actually." Everyone chuckled at that.

On that amusing note the team broke up with Alex running her morning 'sick parade', Jackie attending a lecture on the English Civil War and the 'Ghostbusters' heading for the attic's as part of their ongoing performance. It would also start their search for the elusive time portal [if it was located in the school buildings] and they would sweep each room using their mirrors which could detect time portals or time devices.

"This could take for bloody ever. The school's huge and so are the bloody grounds and outbuildings." Wilson moaned as they walked down the attic stairs to start on the fourth floor. Jericho patted his shoulder; "Calm down big man. Hopefully our Alex will discover something at the porn film premiere tonight and we can all go home." Wilson nodded his agreement with that.

Alex walked to the staff rest room and found Candice there, smoking and reading a magazine. She greeted Alex with some warmth and real affection, getting up and pouring her a cup of tea and snatching a couple of biscuits from the staff biscuit tin. They sat together talking small talk until Miss Ward finished her tea and left. Alone in the staff room Candice suddenly planted a big kiss on a surprised Alex's lips. "John tells me you were great, and Jerome is well taken by you. You will come to the viewing tonight?"

Alex sipped her tea and nodded. Candice ran her hand up Alex's uniform skirt [she was dressed as a school Matron obviously!] and caressed her thigh with some strength. "Afterwards we could get together with John again. What do you say?" The excitement in her voice obvious. Alex smiled; "Maybe, it depends on what Jerome wants me to do." Candice nodded – a little disappointed, but still hopeful – she snatched her hand away as the staff room door opened and rather splendid fellow in Chef's whites stood in the doorway.

"I'm looking for Miss Evelyn Scott-Harris, could you ladies help me please? I'm the temporary chef sent by the Recruitment Agency." Both women rose from their seats and invited the big man in. Alex noticed immediately that he had a wonderful smile and was extremely well built; he certainly knew what a gym was for. Candice offered him tea which he declined, and Alex told him that Miss Evelyn Scott-Harris – if not in her office – could be lecturing the Senior Girl's on social etiquette in the big lecture room on the second floor. He asked where that was, and Alex offered to show him. He thanked her and the pair left, walking slowly together, and chatting; he was an ex-navel chef now looking for a permanent position and was working temporary jobs to earn some money. He wasn't a shy or reserved man and told Alex without any reservations that she was a 'stunner'. Alex thanked him for his compliment. She had now realised with the demon vanquished, Preston Sutton [the Guardian of God] had to move on. Apparently, the school received a phone call saying that his old mother was desperately ill in Jamaica. Preston explained to Miss Evelyn Scott-Harris that he would need to catch a boat quickly and she agreed that he should go straight to his poor sick mother. It was all bollocks of course; but it worked! So, Steve Prince had been sent to cover until the position was filled permanently.

As they reached the big lecture Room; Steve thanked Alex and told her she should pop into the kitchens for anything that was on offer. She smiled cheekily at that, and John held up his hands chuckling; "Come on Alexandra, you know what I meant." She patted his face and whispered; "Oh, I know what a man like you means by that, and I might just take you up on that generous offer." He grinned and lowered his voice; "Oh boy, do I love a woman in uniform who knows her own mind. I will be baking French tarts this afternoon, come and try one." Alex stared at him – smiling – as he stared back at her. There was silence between them for a few seconds and Alex whispered; "If you are lucky, I might come dressed as French tart myself." And walked away, looking over her shoulder and smiling. She enjoyed flirting with the handsome chef and actually giggled to herself about it. Steve Prince watched her hips swinging with her gentle small steps and smiled; really smiled. He knocked on the door and stuck his head around; "I'm looking for Miss Evelyn Scott-Harris." The woman on the small stage gestured him in.

Jackie admitted that Alex was probably right about Miss Flowers;

she had turned her request down flat and Kath and Susan giggled about it. So, Jackie informed Jericho who told Alex that she best attend the film show and find out what she could. With no patients, Alex sat in the empty infirmary and read a couple of medical journals about the advances made in plastic surgery, when Susan Toller stuck her head around the door and smiled; "Miss, I have a message from Mister Hobbs, he says that the show starts at eight tonight and popcorn will be provided. I have to run; Miss Aspen is giving a talk on the Amazon natives who eat people." The girl was gone, and Alex sat back and then decided she might fancy a French Tart and a cup of tea with the new hunky chef. She now headed for the kitchens with real anticipation in her walk. Alex certainly wouldn't be disappointed! She arrived just as the morning shift was departing; they would be back to serve the evening meal - like most catering staff they worked 'split shifts' – and that left Alex and the Chef alone. He explained quietly as he poured the tea, that he had a room in the village, so it wasn't worth going home between the shifts. It was above the ladies dress shop in the High Street, between Boots the Chemist and an empty Taylors shop. Alex said she knew that part of the High Street well.

 They didn't even have tea, never mind a bloody French tart. He locked the Vegetable store door behind them, and they pulled off their uniforms in quite a frenzy; though he pleaded with Alex to keep her stockings and sensible flat shoes on and, of course, her Matron's hat. She insisted he keep his big chef's hat on and laughing they fell together. They sat on sacks of potatoes and kissed quite passionately, both with a hand down each other's pants. Alex murmured; "Jesus, at least I can say I had King Edward between my cheeks!" Then she really grinned as she took hold of a monster that moved, stiffened and grew between her fingers. "Christ Steve, you could beat a dinosaur into submission with this." His hand gently rubbed her already moist vagina under her little black panties, and he whispered; "Well, my hand tells me that you can certainly handle it sweetheart." Their mouths came together again and they French kissed; Alex would swear that she could see and feel sparks and Steve thought she had wired her lips and mouth to the mains electric!

 That was the cue that their bodies wanted to meet properly, and Steve was soon kneeling between her legs, slowly pulling her panties down, He went to work and Alex was to discover that some men really did know how to please a woman. For the first time for quite a while; Alex had a little orgasm just with oral sex performed on her. She gripped his head and shoulders and groaned as he ate her out with real skill. The feelings in her crotch and stomach were intense and she told him to fuck her good and hard; NOW! He did as instructed and mounted her on the dusty potato sacks. She gripped his arse with both hands as he pushed his cock into her welcoming cunt and started to fuck her; slow and gentle at first, then when she slapped his buttocks, he got the signal and fucked her hard, deep and fast.

Their mouths came together, and Alex held onto his big neck and broad shoulders with some determination as she groaned and cussed a little as two more orgasm's swept over her. With legs high in the air, next to his head; Steve fucked her with real passion and commitment to please and it paid off; Alex was gripping his shoulders; unusually she couldn't stop herself from digging her nails in, but a big climax was building. She felt it first beneath her heaving breasts and it moved down to her stomach, where she didn't have butterflies flying around; they had turned into Eagles. It moved like a wave down to her crotch and legs causing a massive series of spurts. Her fanny ran like tap water through a colander and her legs shook so much that her sensible shoes flew off!

Just for a few seconds Alex actually thought she was about to faint and held onto Steve as he kissed her mouth and breasts; "Are you OK darling? Do you want me to continue?" he hoarsely whispered, a little concerned at Alex's reactions to his fucking. She spoke, but nothing came out and he repeated his question, one hand stoking her face and hair. Finally, Alex only managed to whisper a very quiet YES and he continued to fuck her until he couldn't hold out anymore. He whispered; "Where do you want me to cum darling?" Alex passionately kissed him and whispered again; "Breed me darling, let it go, I want your juice in me, NOW." Steve groaned and took a couple of deep breaths and praised God as he filled Alex up and he really did fill her. It felt like someone had thrown a bucket of hot paste into her fanny. They lay together just kissing and caressing for some minutes before the chef pulled gently from her and handed her a clean tea-towel from a nearby shelf.

She gripped the tea-towel and pushed it slowly between her legs which were still shaking, and she noticed that her hands had joined them in trembling. He lay on the floor and wiped his face with his hat. He said nothing for a good minute, then sat up on his elbows and watched Alex wiping her crotch with the towel and her face with the other hand. He had fucked her to tears. "I think….No, I know that I feel….I mean I think I…." He tossed his head back and cussed; "This can't just be it darling. I want; no, I must see you again. That was something special and we both know it. I want you in my life. I don't want to lose you, ever." He spoke quietly and Alex could only nod; she had felt it too. The passion had been so intense they both couldn't deny what had happened. He rose slowly and helped her off the sacks of King Edwards and they embraced; just standing and holding each other; they didn't have to say a word.

Alex sat in the quiet infirmary and rolled the cup around in her hands; the tea inside was cold now. The French tart lay uneaten on the small plate next to the saucer. After some minutes she placed the cup down and folded her arms. She was desperately trying to come to terms with what happened between her and the Chef, or Steve, as she now thought of him. Her Steve…she quickly dismissed that thought. She was a temporal detective, only resurrected to service God and police the Timeline. Romance wasn't part of their duties, but when back in Human form they could suffer the entire spectrum of human emotions and love was certainly one of them. She argued with herself that it had just been really great sex. But her heart said otherwise.

She confided in Jackie who listened with real interest. Jackie pointed out that Steve the chef was nearly thirty and Alex counted her birthdays in centuries. They were born over 60 years apart and should never have met as lovers, never mind feel so much passion for each other. She also pointed out the fact that Alex died in 1901 and Steve is still alive. "Summing up; it's a truly impossible relationship that neither of you will survive. When the mission here is finished, you will be gone, and he will live out his ordained life here. I won't tell you what Human Records say about him, and I know you won't look them up. But you two could never be together; ever. That's the hard awful truth of all this. Please accept that for the sake of your sanity and pass that damn tart over." She then ate the 'damn' French Tart! That made the really sad Alex smile and they heard the Diner Gong sounding.

"Come on, they say the new chef can really cook chicken stew and dumplings…." Jackie stopped, seeing the look on Alex's face, then said; "Come on, I'm starving, let's go to diner." They both headed to the Dining Room in silence.

8. THE FILM SHOWS INTERUPTED.

Alex waited behind the sports pavilion and checked her mirror. Wilson and Jericho had to call the time portal search off at five o'clock because that was the time Miss Evelyn Scott-Harris had deemed they would vacate the school for the day. They had taken rooms in the Beckett Arms pub in the High Street and would probably be in the bar, waiting for the evening meals to be served. Her thoughts were disturbed by the sound of Jerome's motorcycle arriving. He waved and smiled, pulling the cover back on the sidecar and Alex stepped in with lady like grace. He seemed disappointed; "No flash of the silk and cotton then?" He asked chuckling and leaned over and kissed her. He slowly pulled away and didn't smile adding; "You all right sweetheart?" Alex forced a smile and nodded.

He started the bike and headed away, scarf flying and drove slowly until he reached the school gates and turned into the road to the village, then he opened the 'Matchless' up. They arrived just before eight o'clock outside the old Taylor's shop and Alex stared down the quiet High Street to the Ladies dress shop and sighed a little, then gathered her thoughts together; she had an assignment to complete and the others were depending on her. Jerome was moaning about Harry and how on earth he could have failed to notice that the bloody films had 'fogged' in the cameras. "We'll have to shoot it all again; you don't mind, do you?" Alex said she didn't mind and restrained from smiling.

John Newcomb pulled open the door and gestured them inside; "Everyone is here except Max. He doesn't usually miss the big premieres, so I expect he'll show." He kissed Alex on the cheek, and she thought; you'll wait a long time for that bastard my friend.

The big room had a large white screen set up and a 'Bell & Howell' projector was sitting on a table, facing it with two canisters of film next to it. Harry was busy feeding a film through it and fixing the accepting reel. It was ready in a couple of minutes. Alex sat on the sofa next to Janet and Candice who ran her hand over Alex's thigh. Janet was drinking a glass of wine and handed the pair a glass each and produced the bottle from

the floor. "I've brought us girls three bottle of decent plonk. The boys have a bottle of whisky to kill." Alex accepted her glass of wine and noticed Candy was opening some bottles of coke and pushing a straw in each. "For Sue and Kath." She said smiling.
 Alex nodded and knew she had been right about those two. They been corrupted by Jerome and his pornography; she felt quite sad about that. John Newcomb sat cross legged on the floor next to Candice and the pair talked incessantly together. Jerome kept checking his watch; "Where the hell are Flowers and my two little stars? She said they had been given pass out's by old Bathroom." he asked Harry, who shrugged his shoulders.

Jerome disappeared downstairs and checked the street. He came back unsmiling; "Let's start without them." and switched off the lights.

 Harry turned the noisy projector on, and the opening credits appeared; the title was 'THE NAUGHTY SCHOOLGIRLS' directed by Max Cummings, produced by Ivor Biggun and photographed by Fanny Gapp. Alex really shook her head at those dire attempts at humour, but the others all laughed. Alex recognized the female teacher who was only wearing black stockings, mortar board hat with tassel and a black graduation gown with flapping batwings; it was Candice. Everyone cheered [Alex just grunted] and Candice stood and bowed, sipping her wine. The two young schoolgirls – not wearing Queen Charlotte Academy uniforms – appeared and soon the lesbian action started.

 They were quickly joined by the 'school Janitor' who quickly lost all his clothes apart from his boots; it was John Newcomb. The audience all cheered at his appearance and applauded. Alex sat arms folded; she didn't drink the wine - it was cheap and nasty – like the film and her present company. That's when there was a firm knock at the door and Jerome smiled; "At fucking last, come on girls you are missing it."

The door flew open, and the lights were switched on; Detective Inspector Harper and several uniform constables poured into the room followed by two men in long mackintosh's and hats; CID obviously. The Inspector took hold of Jerome's arm and said quietly; "Jerome Hobbs, I am arresting you for suspicion of distributing pornographic material, outraging public morals, corruption of minors and possession of controlled drugs with intent to supply; You don't have to say anything, but what you do say will be taken down in writing and may be given in evidence; do you understand?" Jerome, looking quite shocked, could only nod.

A big constable had turned off the projector and was taking possession of it and the films. Two constables grabbed hold of Harry and John, marching them down the stairs to a big black police van and shoving them in. There were two other police cars parked in the street and quite a crowd had gathered to watch. A CID officer stood over Alex and waved her up; "Come on love, your career as a movie star is over."

Alex grabbed her handbag and stood as the big man took her arm quite firmly and took her down the stairs without trouble. But the screaming Candice had to be manhandled and dragged down the stairs to the van by a CID officer and a uniform constable. She had become hysterical and had to physically dragged into the van and handcuffed.

Janet just walked with her police officer and said nothing except to nod at Jerome who was actually handcuffed. Alex climbed into the back of the police van and threw a glance at the really interested crowd that had formed on the pavement. She saw Steve standing there in his old raincoat, staring at her. The shock made her stagger a little and she slumped on the bench and ran a hand over her face. She wanted to call out to him, but he stared at the pavement and turned away. She watched as he wiped his face and shook his head. He was gone.

Alex sat with her head in her hands and took several deep breaths until one of the CID officers whispered into her ear; "Are you Miss Cappanni?" she nodded, and he pulled her from the van and placed her in the CID car. "The station Superintendent wants to deal with you himself." he muttered, and car pulled away; the bell sounding.

Everyone was bundled into the van and with siren sounding, taken to the local police station. In the back of the big black CID car sat Miss Flowers with Katherine Gapp and Susan Toller; all unsmiling. They had been picked up as they left the cinema and the big car pulled away. Jerome was pushed into the rear of the Inspectors car and Harper sat next to him, lighting up a smelly cigarette. Finally, as the car pulled away, Jerome said quietly; "How did you find out?" The Inspector drew on his cigarette and smiled; "We received information from an informant. Your school is currently being raided by our colleagues from the city. They are assisting us on this one. When you are found guilty or plead guilty because we caught you bang to rights; you'll probably get five to seven years at her Majesty's pleasure. The others will probably get slightly less; though I think the teachers will get at least three years apiece and never work in education again. They will be lucky if they get jobs working in a dockyard café. "He chuckled and finished his cigarette and threw it out the window, rubbing his hands together.

Jerome had to ask; "Who informed on us?" the Inspector smiled at him. "I can't give you her name, that is confidential and protected and if required, she will give evidence in court simply known as MISS X. The Superintendent has given her immunity from prosecution because of her co-operation in this sordid matter."

Jerome sat back and wondered who had betrayed him and more importantly why? He was taken from the police car, searched and charged and placed in a separate cell from John and Harry. The two schoolgirls sat in the lost property office with a large and fearsome WPC. It appears that the police viewed them as 'Victims' because of their young age and Jerome as a corrupt evil predator. They were probably right!

Candice, Janet and Miss Flowers ended up in the same cell after being searched and charged with obscenity and pornography. But Miss Alexandra Cappanni sat in the Superintendent's office and sipped a very welcome cup of tea. The Superintendent was a huge man with no hair and a rough manner about him. He sat reading her statement, nodding and sipping his tea. "Excellent statement Miss, are you sure you've had no legal training? This could have been written by one of my CID officers – one of my better one's as well – It covers all we and the court will need."

Alex whispered, 'thank you sir' and finished her tea. He sat back and shook his head; "I know you fell by the wayside for a short time, but good Morales will always come through. You have done the right thing here, for yourself, for young women everyone and for society. Well done. You can go whenever you want." He stood as she did and opened the door for her, offering a lift back to the school which she declined. She was heading for Beckets Arms pub and some serious brandies with Jericho and Wilson. She pushed her way through the crowds outside the police station and found a quiet doorway to operate her mirror. She appeared in the small alley way next to the 'Empire' cinema and walked to the pub, passing the Taylor's shop which had a bored constable standing in the doorway and she stopped outside the Ladies Dress shop and could see the light on in the flat above. Steve the Chef was at home. The temptation was overwhelming to ring his bell, but she sighed and walked on.

The Beckett Arms was quite busy, and Alex found Wilson & Jericho sitting at a table clutching brandies and reading the local paper. They both looked up and smiled; Wilson gave her his brandy glass and she downed it in one. "I think I best make a report about what just happened."

Jericho leaned back, sipping his brandy and nodded. "Please do." Was all he said.

9. THURSDAY 4th MAY 1961. QUEEN CHARLOTTE'S ACADEMY, KENT, ENGLAND.

Miss Evelyn Scott-Harris peered over her glasses at Alex and re-read the report from the Superintendent and then picked up her teacup and took a sip. "Regardless of the praise Derek….the police Superintendent heaps upon you Miss Cappanni, I am of the opinion that you are not suitable for this school which will soon be mired in enough scandal. Therefore, I am letting you go. Please be off site by lunch time. I will of course, give a reasonable reference to any future employer who may contact us. I feel obliged to do that at least for you exposing this nest of vipers." She lowered the teacup and piece of paper. "Thank you, Miss Cappanni and goodbye." She gestured to the door.

The interview was over, and Alex headed back to her rooms and stared out the small window occasionally as she packed what few items, she had bought with her for this mission. She was glad to be going, especially after the incident with Steve the Chef.

Jackie appeared in the doorway, eating an apple; "Christ Alex, you certainly know how to escape from a boring film!" she smiled and waltzed in and sat on the bed. "The papers are full of the story; they are calling this place the 'School for scandal' and there's lots of pictures [in the tabloids] of stills from those old comedy films; St. Trinian's and the glasshouse is taped off with a nice-looking young constable standing there. The girls have taken him down lots of tea and sandwiches."

Alex stood by the window, arms folded and unsmiling; "We still need to find Jerome's time controlling device. Jericho and Wilson have swept the school and outbuildings and found sod all. So, he must have it hidden somewhere else. The mission's not really over until we find that. We have changed his destiny and he certainly won't be stabbed here tomorrow. But we still need to return him to his own time; now that could be the difficult part with him on remand in bloody Canterbury prison. Finally, there's still the bloody 'lady in white ghost' to figure out; there are no earth-bound spirits recorded here."

Jackie finished her apple and grinned; "Oh, the ghost is sorted. I hid in the toilets and shower room after lights out last night and sure enough; the secret panel came open and out she popped, putting on her skeleton mask and gloves. It was Miss Ward and was she surprised to see me sitting there! We had a nice chat and I found out the Miss ward was very angry about being passed over for the headmistresses post – again – and hoped her activities would have Scott-Harris shown up. But it worked better than she ever expected; with some of the girl's parents complaining. So, Scott-Harris had to be seen to do something! So, she called in paranormal investigators. I said I would say sod all, being only temporary here and she was really nice and grateful for that."

Alex laughed and shook her head; "That's a bleeding cracker. You've cheered me up with that." Alex stared out the window and saw the caretaker cleaning up the basketball court. She had to smile. "I'll be staying at the Beckett Arms with Jericho and Wilson for now. Apparently your 'mum' will collect you when we've found the bloody time portal device."

Jackie nodded and threw her apple core into the waste bin with some skill; it was the other side of the room. "My basketball skills have improved considerably. It's a popular sport with old Pickles, the ex-gardeners and Mister Collins coming to watch most of the time. I think they really like watching young girls in really short skirts and loose tops throwing a ball about; dirty old sods."

Alex nodded, then asked; "Who's Mister Collins' when he's at home?" Jackie jumped from the bed; "I'll help carrying your stuff to the car. Oh, Mister Collins is the school engineer, he's the maintenance man; he runs the boilers, so nobody really sees him. Doesn't turn up for meals and is only seen when needed. He's a big hockey, basketball and sports fan. Especially if it involves young girls in skimpy outfits I think." Jackie grabbed Alex's case and headed for the door; "He was a friend of Hobbs apparently." She added.

 Alex rubbed her chin; "Have you checked him with Human Records?" Jackie shook her head; "I haven't, because he doesn't seem to be involved in any of this." Alex picked up her handbag and 'Gladstone' bag; "I think we'll stop by the boiler house after we've packed the car." She said softly.

 They were stopped by one of Jackie's friends, young Adelaide who waved a paper about; "Take a look at this Jack! He was a bloody Houdini, wasn't he?" Jackie took the paper and they both stared at the front page of the local paper. They both looked at each other; "Forget the boiler house, I need to see Jericho!" Alex said.

 Jackie thanked Adelaide and the pair walked off together; the bell for assembly was sounding. Alex sat in her car and just stared at the headlines; "He must have had the bloody time controller on him." She muttered and shook her head. "Mister Jerome Hobbs had simply vanished from his prison cell after lights out last night and no trace of him has been found. A nationwide police search has been launched. He is not considered dangerous and the public are encouraged to contact their local police station if they have a sighting of him." Alex read quietly to herself, then sat back and gripped the steering wheel.

 "Something doesn't make sense here, the police and then the prison staff would have searched him thoroughly before he was placed in the cell. He would have been given prison uniform and all his possessions taken. So where did he hide the damn time controller?" she was speaking with Jericho on her mirror; he and Wilson were on their way to the school. Alex stared across the playing field at the big boiler house with its two tanks some yards away surrounded by their own bund. They were kept well away from the main school buildings in case of explosion or fire. She recalled what Jackie had just said; "A friend of Hobbs apparently."

Alex slapped the wheel; Hobbs didn't have the time controller hidden on him; the police and prison searches proved that and since he's disappeared from a locked cell in the middle of the night, there is only one explanation; he had an accomplice who knew how to operate the time device. He simply jumped to the cell and they both jumped back. But who was the other time-traveller and his accomplice? Hobbs had worked at the school for about a year before he was murdered [in the original time lime, now changed of course] so who else is a new starter around here? She started the car and drove to the gates and turned into the road that ran down to the village. She reached the Beckets Arms just as the pub was opening up and found Jericho and Wilson outside; they were reading the local paper.

Alex eased from the car and smiled; "I see you don't need to be told about Jerome 'Houdini' Hobbs. But I think we have two-time travellers here; otherwise, how the hell did he get out of prison?" She explained her thoughts about that. He had to have had assistance.

Wilson agreed with her; the police and prison authorities would have thoroughly searched him and removed everything. He had to have an accomplice to carry out his impossible escape. Jericho rubbed his chin; "Jackie informs me that there was indeed a breach of the timeline last night for this time and place. Two people left for 2022 and two returned." Wilson leaned against the window ledge and watched two early morning drinkers rush into the pub. "That means his accomplice saved his skin and they returned here, but who the hell was it?"

They walked into the pub and ordered coffee's, sitting at a quiet table by the door. Wilson sipped his coffee and leaned back; "Why was Jerome here in the first place? He was born in 1962 and we know that this school closed down in 1991 and the buildings became a luxury hotel and golf course. So, Jerome must have a personal connection with the place. But what could that be? Then why jump back to 1961 to make bloody porn films and grow a little cannabis? It really doesn't make sense."

"Amen to that; all we have achieved is finding out who the fake ghost was and scaring off Jerome to travel somewhere else in time unless….." Jericho slowly placed his cup down. He managed a smile; "Alex, do some research; find out whom Jerome's mum and dad were or his grandparents. They would have been born around the 1930's or 1940's. He must have a connection with the school somewhere in his past." Alex finished her excellent cup of coffee and discretely operated her mirror behind the local paper.

"According to Human Records, his grandfather was a vehicle mechanic in Southend-on-sea, Essex and was born in 1935. His grandmother worked as a hairdresser until she started a family and was born in 1940. There doesn't really appear to be any connection with the school for them. But Jerome's father is shown as Jerome Hobbs and his mother worked as Kitchen Assistant until she had the baby." Alex lowered her mirror and shrugged her shoulders.

Jericho sighed; "Any relatives shown as time travellers? We're getting desperate now!" and chuckled, finishing his coffee. Alex tapped at her mirror thinking; Owen is far better at this or rather Jacqueline at the present.

"Nothing yet....Blah, Blah, Blah....nothing. Wait, there's one entry about a Norman Pickles vanishing from the Human Timeline in 1961 when he was 42 and is a missing soul; he missed his departure date in 1982. He was Jerome's Mum's, older brother. Team 34 investigated and closed the case because they couldn't discover if he travelled in time or fell foul to a demon. He was working as a Taylor in the village, but that went bankrupt in 1960 and all he had left was his shop and the flat above. But the Bank repossessed that in 1962."

Alex stared at her mirror, then added in a quiet voice; "The current school caretaker is called Pickles who said his brother owned the Taylor's Shop in the village. Now that's some co-incidence!"

Jericho sat up; "Co-incidence my backside. I think we should run a mirror over Pickles the caretaker. When did he join Queen Charlotte's Academy in that position?"

Alex checked Human records and said quietly; "Just last year, within a few days of Jerome becoming Under Gardener! They must have arrived together." Wilson leaned forward; "I think this Pickles character is the original Time traveller who travelled from 1961 with his nephew and together they travelled back for some really important reason to this school."

Jericho pushed his cold coffee cup away and clasped his hands; "Why would someone stab Jerome to death? Find the murderer who would have struck tomorrow, and we may discover what the hell this is all about." Alex folded her arms; "I've just had an unpleasant thought; what if it was Jerome's accomplice that killed him for whatever reason. If he was planning to kill Jerome tomorrow and suddenly Jerome is nicked and banged up; he would have to rescue him to ensure his plan – whatever it is – stays on track. He could have sprung Jerome so that he can kill him tomorrow, so Friday 5th of May 1961 must be really important for either or both of the time travellers, but why?"

Wilson tapped the table; "Check Jerome's date of birth; he was born in 1962 and who exactly was his mother who gave birth to him; she had to have conceived in 1961." Alex operated her mirror; "According to Human Records Jerome Hobbs was born February 1962 which means his mother conceived in or around May 1961." They all looked at each other.

"Who was his mother, Alex?" Jericho asked and Alex stared at her mirror and didn't smile; "Sweet Jesus; She was a Caroline Pickles who worked as kitchen assistant here from 1959 to 1961. She died in childbirth and her soul was collected and processed. Another Pickles connection: her brother was a time traveller!"

Jericho smiled broadly; "I think I have worked this cracker out. Come on, let's speak to Pickles." Alex wasn't happy about that but didn't have any choice. She then remembered she couldn't go back on school grounds and told Jericho so. He just nodded and muttered about 'sit in your car.' They headed back to the school.

The van was just turning into the driveway when Jericho's mirror buzzed, and he answered it; he spoke with Mr. Albian who was the Senior Time Controller on duty. Jericho said yes, a few times and a couple of thank you's. He lowered the mirror. "The bloody timeline has just changed; some nine descendants of a certain Jerome Hobbs have been erased from history and the Timeline is adjusting itself. That included Jerome Hobbs who now has never existed because someone killed him on May 4th, 1961, before he was even sodding born, at the back of the glasshouse at Queen Charlotte's Academy!"

Jericho gestured up the drive; "Get to the boiler house quick!" he shouted, and Wilson put his foot down and they arrived a minute or so later. They decamped from the van and ran around the back of the old boiler house.

They found the old caretaker standing by the rear door, searching a big wallet and stuffing some of its contents into his pockets. He smiled at the Temporal Detectives and placed the wallet in the big canvas bag hanging from his shoulder. They stared down at the gravel path; the body of Jerome Hobbs lay sprawled with a large puddle of blood surrounding it.

Alex didn't need to take Jerome's pulse; he was clearly dead. Norman Pickles smiled at Alex and said, "Hello darling, bought your friends with you I see." Jericho lowered his mirror; "He has a time portal in a medieval dagger concealed under his coat. It's free ranging so he could jump anywhere as long as he has an object from the time period, he wants to visit."

"Why?" Alex asked quietly and Norman smiled and gestured to the dead Jerome; "He would take my baby sister to the pictures on Saturday night [6th May 1961] and seduce her and then abandon her after finding out that she was pregnant. Not a pleasant thing to happen to a young girl in 1961. It would have ruined her life, but the poor girl died having the baby. I had planned to stop that tomorrow by killing the bastard. But you messed that up darling by informing on him. So, I had to rescue him and kill him when I could; today. I'm no scientist but if your father dies before your born, you certainly can't travel back and impregnate your mother. You see Jerome here changed time by seducing his own mother without knowing it. I found out he was going to meet her on Saturday, and I put an end to it before it even started. The perfect murder I would suggest; Jerome now was never born because his father was never conceived. So, no murder; you can't kill someone who never existed."

Norman sighed; "I accidently found the time portal dagger in the small museum here at the school, I was cleaning it and suddenly found myself in 1912. I finally worked it out that the time portal – as your friend pointed out – would take you wherever the other object you hold was from. I had my father's Edwardian watch in my pocket, made in 1912. The rest I worked out. I knew the story of my poor sister and persuaded my descendant Jerome to accompany me, travelling back here. Except I didn't know he was a sexual predator and opportunist, but he convinced me that

I could save my shop and flat by making lots of money-making porn films and growing dope. The Bank was about to repossess my home and shop, so I agreed. I didn't know then; he would be the man who ruined my baby sister and that he was his own father because I brought him back here. I slowly realised what I had done. So, I put it all right, I searched his shithole and found hidden in the kitchen several small films; two contained my poor sister being used by that bastard. They will never see light of day."

Only the Temporal detectives could see the time wave sweeping through, adjusting the current timeline. The body of Jerome Hobbs disappeared; he had never been born. All his actions in 1961 were also removed. There was now no seduction of Kath & Susan, no pornographic movies and the cannabis plant farm was gone. Harry & Janet Field never became his partners in the blue film business and Candice, Miss Flowers and John Newcomb would never meet the man who ruined their lives.

Norman smiled at Alex and blew a kiss; he was gone. Jericho checked his mirror and sighed; "Norman appears to have landed back in 1912 – he still must have his father's watch handy – Unknown to him, he has returned the Human Timeline to its original state; before Jerome was born. The existing timeline was actually the altered one. That's why the Senior Time Controller called me; to thank us for a job well done!" He shook his head and pushed his mirror away.

Wilson folded his arms and smiled at Alex. "A job well done my girl." Then really smiled and Alex thought about him fucking her again and it was her turn to smile.

"I think you should call Stella and tell her to collect her daughter and we can all go home." Alex said to Jericho, and they walked back to the van.

Wilson chuckled; "Do you realise that if we hadn't jumped back here, the original timeline would have been restored anyway, with Norman killing Jerome before he could father his own father!" Alex sighed; "Still, we did fix it just by bloody turning up!" They sat in the van and watched a string of girls streaming onto the hockey field with Candice blowing her whistle and shouting. Alex smiled to herself and wondered how Candice's life would now evolve. She stared down the drive to see a taxi pulling

Up and a big ex-navel Chef stepping out to start his career as a school cook and Alex really smiled at that. If he was as good at cooking as he was as fucking; the school meals would certainly take a turn for the better.

It was followed by a Rolls-Royce driven by old Joe from Supplies. Stella had arrived to collect Jackie and with that, all traces of the temporal detectives visit would be gone. The van drove down to the gates and parked up; they would wait until Stella collected Jackie and then the whole team would jump back to the lighthouse for a well-earned dinner and some very lively conversations.

Jericho admitted that the team would probably receive a mission file to go after the elusive Mr. Pickles which didn't make Alex very happy and she confided to Owen who just smiled and said they would deal with that problem when it arose. Him saying 'they' made Alex smile and she gripped her friends hand under the table.

Mr. Collins – the boiler man – lit a cigarette and watched the girls playing hockey with some interest. He smiled as a young John Newcomb cycled down the drive; he was here to apply for the Under-gardeners position which had been vacant for some time. Mr. Collins knew he worked in the chemists developing films and photographs. He was friends with Harry who was an excellent cameraman and the pair would soon get together. The boiler man had a few good idea's how he.... sorry, they could make some decent money with all these young, horny women around the damn place and that included some of the teachers!

Mr. Collins threw down his cigarette butt and would put his proposition to them all tonight. It could make them a lot of money. Katherine Gapp and Susan Toller walked past him and waved, smiling and giggling. Then blew him a kiss; they both looked about then hitched up their skirts, showing him their regulation white cotton panties. Susan made an obscene gesture with her hand and mouth and that did really make him smile; they were clearly looking forward to their visit tomorrow afternoon in his secret playroom in the big glass house. He would have to replenish his stock of condoms with a quick visit to the chemist and could have a little chat with John at the same time.

He headed to Harry's cottage, where Janet would certainly

welcome him; he had told her that he would drop by after breakfast and he smiled at the thought of her naked on the couch; waiting to be fucked and her husband would only be upset because he missed the show!

Oh yes, as Harold MacMillan [the Prime Minister] told the British people back in 1957; 'You've never had it so good!'

The End

EPISODE PROLOGUE: "Alexandra is under investigation after a saucy picture of her appears in a newspaper in 1985. It appears that she's been on a date with David; the Dark Prince. They apparently attended the famous 'Black Ball' World Snooker Championship Final and Alex was caught flashing her stocking tops and panties to the TV cameras! But Alex gets the opportunity to visit someone she really wanted to see."

 60 Minutes approx. **Episode Warnings:**
Smoking – Alcohol – Strong language – Violence [including a sexual assault] – Strong graphic sexual references – Horror – References to a Demonic presence.

 **NOTES:** This is the **ADULT** version of the original story which is published and appears in the **TEMPORAL DETECTIVES:** Series 3 – Episode 10 entitled: **"SNOOKER, STOCKINGS & DEVILISH DECEIT."**

 CAUTION: Recommended for **18+ only.**

1. 'DOC' SILAS UNDERHILL AND TEAM 13.

Old Doc checked his fob watch and watched through the window of his cabin; his sergeant, Isabella Pugg and their Constable, Skyrise Young Mountain was due back from horse riding at any minute. He eased himself back into his rocking chair and picked up the file that young Ivan - the messenger - had delivered from Angel Margret's office. It was the team's latest mission, and it was a strange one. He sighed and re-read the summary. He tapped the enclosed pictures and smiled at one. "Sweet saints, she does have some pair of legs." He muttered, looking up as 'Crabby' appeared through the door.

Crabby stood arms folded and didn't smile; "Doc, Ma Washington wants to know when those two white folk are getting back; she wants to dish up supper." Crabby was a big African male, who had been a house slave to a white family for about thirty years; he had been born and died a slave. He and the Doc had real history and had been together for years - when alive - and were still friends now, many years after passing over. Doc just sighed; "Crabby, do you have to refer to Issy and Skyrise as white folk? You know you like the both of them; just use their damn names once and again." But there was no admonishment in his voice. Crabby just grunted and gestured to the file; "Where you off to now? Anywhere interesting?"

Doc held the file up and showed him the picture and old Crabby grinned from ear to ear. "Now, that's the kind of white folk I like. Long legs and don't mind showing her drawers." He chuckled and ran a hand over his face. "Ain't that the nice white lady who doesn't mind coloured folk and is some kind of doctor?"

Doc nodded; "Alexandra Cappanni from team 74; she's the mission." Crabby smiled and scratched his arse. "What she been up to? Who's she been showing her crotch off to?" Doc sighed; "This picture was taken from a television still, apparently in 1985, she appears to have attended a big sporting event and was caught on camera, flashing her stocking tops and white panties to a television audience of about 18 million people. But that's not the real problem."

Crabby stared at the picture again and smiled - again. "What's wrong with that Doc? No one could surely object to seeing them legs and knickers. That damn girl is a real beauty. She could show me her parts any time of day...or night!" He laughed and Doc just shook his head; "Crabby, you are a dirty old man; you're old enough to be her grand daddy." Crabby just grinned; "Yeah, but I ain't. So, it's fine to stare." He shuffled to the door and turned back; "I'll tell Ma that the white folk ain't back yet, so what's the problem with her showing her crotch on that television thing?" Doc eased back in his chair and just smiled. Despite being dead for nearly 200 years, Crabby hadn't changed a bit. "It's the man sitting next to her, that's the real problem." Crabby stared back at the picture; "Who's that then?" He asked.

Doc didn't smile and tapped the photograph; "It's the bloody Dark Prince himself." Crabby scratched his arse again and sighed; "That's bad ain't it?" Doc nodded and closed the file, saying quietly; "It sure is Crabby. It sure is." He could hear horse's and voices outside and Crabby smiled; "I'll tell Ma to dish up, since the white folk are back." He disappeared through the door and Doc shouted after him; "Just call them by their names for heaven's sake!" But he knew that Crabby wouldn't change.

He and Crabby had been born slaves together; Crabby was a house servant and had quite an easy life on the plantation, good food and no hard labour. He really loved his 'posh' servant's livery, even if, it was just dark trousers and frilly white shirt. But Doc had worked the fields under the overseer's whip. Everyone called him 'Doc' because he had a real aptitude for fixing up people; especially after a good whipping or beating. He had gone on the run after the family had sold the young girl he was madly in love with.

Doc had discovered that young Delphi had been sold to a sugar plantation some two hundred miles downriver. He went after her and it was almost a year before he found what had happened to her. She had died in childbirth, giving birth to a daughter by her new owner. She was fifteen. Doc spent the next few months on the run and finally ended up in the North before the civil war and was taken in by a Methodist Reverend and his wife. They paid for his education, and he became a doctor, in all but title. But then, he could only 'practice' on fellow coloured people, Chinese, Mexican or Native Americans.

He had real fond memories of Reverend Joshua Gates and his wife Margaret. "Good people. damn good people." He muttered to himself. He and Skyrise got on really well, both had become

'Doctors' under extreme circumstances, and both were not from privileged white families. He didn't realise, just how much Skyrise admired the old man; both as his Inspector and as his friend.

Jericho could have told him, just what a decent man old Doc was; Jericho valued his opinion above all others and that says a great deal about the elderly, quiet thoughtful man.

Like all team Inspectors, he had the choice of where to place his home and office in any time or place. Doc had chosen a small cabin in the woodlands of North Virginia. The cabin was like Jericho's lighthouse - suspended in time and place - the current date here was August 8th, 1869, and it was 6.25pm on a warm and pleasant summer night. The inside also defied space and time. Everyone in the cabin had their own suite of rooms. The household staff consisted of old Crabby - who didn't like being called a 'Butler' - Ma Washington, a lovely lady in her forties, who could cook anything, but loved dishing up Cajun food. The other member of the staff was young Rosemary Dogwood.

Rose was the maid of all duties, and she loved her new life working for Doc. She had died at just twenty from smallpox in 1791. She really didn't fancy another slice of life, as a living human and so joined Doc's staff. She had been a maid to some rich white people in Boston. But they had treated her really well and actually did mourn the young girl death, when she quickly and unexpectedly passed over. Doc could hear her laughing with Crabby in the dining room, setting the places for dinner. But his attention was drawn back to the front door.

Skyrise came through the door and slapped his hat down on the hallway table. He jerked a thumb behind him; "Sweet Jesus Doc, she is impossible!" and headed for the dining room without another word. [For the history of Skyrise Young Mountain: See the episode: 'Alexandra: an angel of mercy.'] Doc just chuckled to himself; young Issy was one hell of a woman. She was NEVER wrong and would NEVER admit it, even if she was!

But she was a fine Temporal Detective Sergeant. Not quite up to the standard of young Jericho, when he was Doc's Sergeant, but then, who could follow that young man? Doc cleaned his glasses and waited for Issy to storm through the door. He certainly wasn't disappointed; she pushed in and said loudly; "That bloody Indian can never be wrong, can he?" and threw her riding helmet and whip on the same little hallway table. "Like someone else I can mention." Doc muttered, adding: "What has he done now?" Not really wishing to know about the latest disagreement between the two. Issy stood, hands on hips, and sighed loudly [she did very little quietly!] "I try and tell him, about just how damn lucky his people were to be given the gift of real decent civilization, by the settlers to his land and he throws a fit. He simply can't listen to facts. Oh no; he's always bloody right; just another typical, domineering oppressive man!" She walked past the smiling Doc and into the dining room.

Doc sighed; the dinner conversation could be lively tonight and grinned. Still, his trainee, Leon Murphy would bring some sanity to the chat around the dinner table; he always did. His real name - in full - was Napoleon Wellington Patrick Murphy! He had been a history teacher in a small Irish village. His father: Patrick had worked the roads, laying tarmac, but was a model war games enthusiast and only played the Napoleonic Period. He had a total fascination with Napoleon Bonaparte and the Duke of Wellington. The attic rooms had no less than four massive layouts of famous battles; Waterloo, Battle of the Pyramids, Marengo and the Battle of Austerlitz.

Little wonder that the boy, who played for ages with his dotting father, became a history teacher. Leon was soft spoken and gentle in his ways; he saw good in everyone; even the rotten bastards, like those that had ended his life at just 27. He was caught up in a Belfast bombing, while shopping with his fiancé, Grace McCurry. She survived the bomb with minor injuries, and he was killed outright. He had worked as a collector for a few human years and had been recommended for Temporal Detective Training because of his sharp mind and dedication to detail. Angel Margret very rarely got her recommendations wrong and even old Doc - who had high standards - was already well satisfied with Leon.

He was the only current member of Doc's team, that Crabby called by his name. That spoke volumes! Doc would outline their latest mission over dinner. Issy would be happy going after Alex and her apparent failings; she couldn't stand her. Alex was everything that Issy detested in another woman. She [Issy] thought she [Alex] was a disgrace to the feminist agenda; with her expensive clothes, letting men fawn over her, wearing makeup and acting the 'little woman'. She didn't even admit that

Alex was quite a beautiful and intelligent woman in her own right.

But no, Alex was practically a traitor to the cause of feminist change. She would enjoy exposing her and maybe, even getting her thrown out the Department. She ate her meal with a much revived appetite and that made Doc sigh.

2. ALEX HAS AN AFTERNOON OUT.

Returning from the mission early left Alex with time on her hands so, she decided that a night out may be a good idea. But realised that there was a briefing tonight, so, since she was still wearing her business suit, Alex headed for a wine bar in Sheffield in the year 1985. 'Dominic's' was a busy little bar and bistro, typical of the Thatcher 'Yuppie' years. But it actually did serve good food at lunchtimes and the bar staff really did know how to mix American style cocktails. Alex pushed her way through the noisy crowds and reached the bar. The young girl quickly served her with a 'Manhattan' and Alex stood sipping her cocktail and enjoying the music and atmosphere of the place. That's when her eyes fell upon the man standing by the French doors, which opened out onto the street, and gave access to the tables outside.

"Now that's a bit of a hunk." She whispered to herself and immediately noticed that he wasn't wearing a suit - like most of the males in the place - and was dressed in just a tight white t-shirt and casual dark trousers. Alex wondered how he got in without being challenged by door security over not wearing a shirt and tie. The short dark-haired woman next to her grinned and leaned towards Alex and said; "Wondering how David got past security?"

Alex nodded and smiled. The woman sipped her Italian beer and gestured to the young man. "That's easy. He bloody owns the place." Alex chuckled; "So it's do as I say and not do as I do." The woman chuckled; "Something like that. But he is actually a real cool guy. I'm Gay by the way." She said casually Alex sipped her cocktail and really did smile; "That's...nice. Your quite brave just telling strangers in a bar that." The woman gave her a funny look and then burst out laughing; "That's my name! I'm Gay Willis by the way." and offered her hand.

Alex really did laugh and tried to apologise. Gay waved that aside; "My fault. It's happened before." She gestured back to

'David' and finished her beer. "Do you want an introduction? He's the best equipped bar owner in the city." She giggled at that, as Alex shook her hand. She had one firm grip. "Yeah, why not." Alex said and finished her cocktail. Gay kept hold of her hand and the pair walked over to David, now apparently flicking through his 'File-O-Fax', and Gay whispered; "What's your name?"

Alex whispered it back and Gay waved at David and yelled 'Hello!' He looked up from his little book and really did smile at Alex, who smiled straight back. The three stood talking quietly by the old-fashioned Jukebox until David offered the girls some champagne, in his flat above the bar. Gay said 'Yes' straight away, and Alex shrugged her shoulders; "Why not. It's nice to have a bar owner buy one, now and again." They disappeared through a door marked 'Staff Only', then walked quickly through the kitchens, to another door marked' Private' in big red letters.

David opened it with a key, and they ran up the stairs. The apartment looked like it had been built for a 'James Bond' film. Alex was truly impressed. David went to a gorgeous bar by a set of ornate double doors and pulled a bottle of Champagne from the fridge; complete with three glasses. Now that did catch her eye. She wondered how well Gay knew the bar owner. She soon found out that Gay really did know him well.

They sipped champagne, sprawled across the beautiful white leather sofas in the Reception Room. They made small talk and Alex sat next to Gay, while David sprawled on the big chair opposite. The bottle was quickly finished, and they started to drink shorts. Alex, of course, had brandy. They drank together for a while and Alex wasn't actually surprised when Gay started to give David a blowjob; right in front of her. His strong hands soon had Gay stripped down to just her panties. She had quite pert, but small breasts, with a taunt body; she certainly knew her way around a gym. Alex was also well impressed with the man himself; Gay had certainly not exaggerated, he WAS the best equipped bar owner, anywhere, never mind just this city!

Alex placed down her brandy and walked across to the pair; David smiled and pulled her close to him and the pair kissed passionately as Gay sucked his cock and jerked it gently with both hands. She slapped Alex gently on the lag and said, "Come on Alex, help me out with this bloody monster!" But David told

Alex to strip down to her panties and she obeyed. He was clearly delighted that Alex was wearing stockings. He ran a hand between her legs and his fingers probed her vagina under her little, white frilly panties. He was also delighted that she was wet, quite wet. In between pleasing that big cock, Gay giggled; "Don't worry Alex. He has the stamina of a bloody bull. You won't be disappointed." She certainly wasn't!

The three had sex for over two hours. At one point, David sat watching, sipping more champagne, as Gay had quite strong - and a little brutal - lesbian sex with Alex on the floor. Both girls had loud orgasms and lay on the floor panting and kissing. David re-joined them and fucked the pair to even more orgasms. At one point, Alex held open Gay's bum cheeks and David fucked the girl hard up the arse. That actually made the young woman sob but didn't tell him to stop. He finally, pulled the pair together and held their heads close to each other. He came over their faces. The girls then cleaned each other up; swapping cum with their tongues until they finally swallowed the entire load. The three sat on the floor gasping and panting from their exertions.

As Gay collected her discarded clothes, David and Alex passionately embraced. He whispered to her, that he desperately wanted to see her again. This time it would be just her. To her real surprise, she agreed. He had tickets to the World Snooker final being held that very evening. Gay stood naked by the bathroom door and asked if Alex wanted to share a bath. David was very reluctant to let her go. But the girls cleaned themselves up in the deep, hot tub. But it was when David kissed Alex goodbye - really passionately - that's when Alex received the shock of her life. She asked him his real name and he just smiled; "It is David. David Willis." He murmured as they embraced after Gay had left.

Alex just stared at him; "You're married to Gay?" She whispered, the surprise in her voice apparent. He nodded and shrugged his shoulders; "We have quite an open marriage." Then chuckled; "Well, you know that now."

Alex stumbled down the stairs and made her way through the quiet kitchens and into the bar, where the staff were clearing up. They all stopped and smiled at her; they knew full well what had gone on in their Bosses apartment. Gay was behind the bar and waved at Alex, blowing her a little kiss and grinning. Alex almost fell into the cold, snowy street and wiped the tears from her face and operated her mirror without any thought to any living humans around. She just wanted to get away. She walked slowly back to the lighthouse, knowing full well that she had been seduced by an expert pair. Little wonder Gay made the first move and was so friendly; the pair probably played the same game with any young unattached woman who showed an interest in David. She sat - alone - in the study, waiting for the briefing to start and vowed to keep this little incident to herself.

Alex couldn't believe how easily she had been seduced into the threesome. She leaned back in her favourite armchair and sipped a much-needed brandy. No matter how she felt about her actions; she couldn't hide the disturbing fact that she had thoroughly enjoyed the sex session with the pair; especially with David, he was a very skilled lover.

"Little bloody wonder." She muttered to herself and looked up as Owen and Wilson came through the door and headed for the drinks tray. She accepted a re-fill from Owen who remarked; "Christ Alex. You look like the cat who found his bowl full of cream."

Alex just smiled a little and said nothing. After the briefing, the team jumped to Egypt in 1922 for their latest mission. Alex kept the details of her afternoon out to herself.

3. A MATTER BETWEEN TWO GOOD FRIENDS.

The reliable Mr. Harris had met the team at the door [as usual] and immediately spoke to Jericho; "You have a visitor Sir; I have placed them in the study." He informed Jericho, as he took coats and hats from the team. "Who is it?" asked Jericho - not actually expecting anyone this evening for dinner - and headed for the study. "Why, it's Inspector Underhill. He is quite anxious to speak with you in private Sir." At that, Wilson ushered Alex and Owen into the Dining Room, where young Ruth was laying down warm plates.

Jericho greeted his old 'Boss' with some warmth and poured the pair a large whisky each. He, of course, invited 'Doc' Underhill to dinner. But the Inspector had to refuse; he was expected elsewhere. "I'll come straight to the point Jericho; how much do you trust Detective Constable Alexandra Cappanni?"

Jericho gestured for him to seat and joined him; the pair sat in the armchairs by the fire and 'Doc' pulled a brown file from under his white linen jacket. He tapped the file gently; "My team has christened this mission; 'Snooker, Stockings and the time cop.' My human agent recognized the girl in the picture; he had met Alex when she was temporarily attached to me. You remember when she was stood down over that damn Shakespeare play, that was apparently written about her? You got 'Jumbo' in replacement." Doc sipped his whisky and opened the file. [That was a **TEMPORAL DETECTIVES** mission entitled; **'William Shakespeare's lost play: The lady of Cappanni.'**]

Jericho remembered that mission well; James 'Jumbo' Jolly had replaced Alexandra for part of that mission. He had been genuinely pleased, when he heard that 'Jumbo' had been promoted to Temporal Detective Sergeant on Inspector Stella Longstreet's Team 35. But he had also heard that Doc's new sergeant was a real pistol!

He accepted the file slowly and Doc continued; "That's a newspaper cutting from 1985 - the day after an incredible final of the World Snooker Championship - which is still talked about even now. But the papers also ran a story about a young lady who - by accident apparently - flashed her stocking tops and gave everyone a glimpse of her panties on TV. She was in the audience and crossed her legs just as the camera ran over the crowd. This newspaper was famous for topless women and sex scandals. They offered thousands of pounds, if she would come forward and does topless lingerie shoot for them. She never showed up. Take a look at the picture taken from the evening's television coverage."

Jericho stared at the photograph; it was apparently Alexandra! He handed the file back, but held on to the photograph and studied it carefully; was it really Alexandra? He stared long and hard at the photograph and felt a little knot in his stomach; surely it couldn't be her? and sipped his whisky, slowly.

Doc finished his whisky; "What the bloody hell was Alex doing in Sheffield, in 1985 flashing her knickers to the world? And guess who's the man, sitting next to her with her hand firmly gripping his knee?" Jericho sat staring at the newspaper clipping and then rubbed his chin. "Your mission wasn't in Sheffield in 1985 then?" He mumbled.

Doc shook his head and smiled a little; "We were working on a case during the Miners' strike in 1984. That's how my human agent met Alex. She was temporally on my team." He placed down his glass and dropped the file upon the coffee table and straightened his jacket; "You're a friend Jericho and I think you deserve the first pass over this one."

Doc refilled his own glass; "No one would really care if Alex flashed her underwear. Most men would bloody enjoy that, but it's the man sitting next to her that is the real problem." Jericho stared at the handsome young man and grunted; "Who is he?" Doc sipped his whisky; "The reason for the mission; Operations Control confirm that man is one of the human forms that the Dark Prince uses." Jericho ran a hand over his face. What the fuck was going on?

Doc finished his drink and walked to the door; "I can sit on the mission for a human day or so, then I will have to act. But I'll wait to see what you uncover about it." He smiled and Jericho shook his hand. They walked to the front door together and Mr. Harris showed Doc out. Jericho returned to the study and sat back in the armchair and stared at the picture again. If it wasn't Alexandra; then it was her twin sister. The word 'sister' produced some bad memories for him. He grunted and pushed the file into his jacket pocket and stood, as Mr. Harris stuck his head through the door and announced dinner.

"Thank you Mr. Harris. I'm just coming." He muttered and headed for the Dining Room. Dinner conversation could be quite lively tonight and smiled to himself, he could soon sort this matter out, by simply checking Alex's mirror. All he needed to do was enter his Inspectors Code and he could check where his Detective Constable had been and more importantly; when.

But that little matter could wait - for now - Jericho had other problems to contend with; the whole team was summoned to appear before Angel Margret in the morning. He knew that Alex's resurrection by the Dark Prince would be the major topic of conversation. Despite the incident in the Devil's Garden, the Prince had basically saved her soul from the darkness of real death. The young prince still had a real passion for Alex and clearly had forgiven her insults against him. [See **TEMPORAL DETECTIVES** mission entitled; **'Ghosts in the Devil's garden of the damned.'**]

Jericho sighed; was it co-incidence that such a story [about the snooker final] appears after the prince had basically saved her soul? He stood outside the dining room door and thought about the changing seasons of a woman's heart. He had suffered that at the hands of Elizabeth; it could always go the other way. On that disturbing thought, he pushed open the door and smiled. Suddenly Jericho had a terrible and clear feeling of Déjà vu. It stopped him in his tracks, and he actually shivered. Something was wrong - but what? - He knew that such a strong feeling could indicate that time itself had changed. He leaned against the hall wall with one hand and took a couple of deep breaths; the feeling was almost over whelming. Something had changed with the near past and had altered the future.

Something in the past that involved him. [Jericho was close: but it actually concerned Alexandra.] He called the Duty Time Controller on his mirror and was reassured that little changes were happening all the time, but none concerned him yet. He pulled the file from his pocket and stared at the picture again. Had it altered? He sighed; he couldn't tell. Replacing the file and his mirror, he headed for the dining room. Mr. Parker rushed past him from the stairs and quickly disappeared into the kitchens; something must have bugged him, or it was dinner time for the big cat. He shrugged his shoulders.

Jericho joined the others in the dining room and Mr. Harris served the soup course. He asked for everyone's attention and the table fell silent as he produced the file and passed it to Wilson. "Who do you think the woman is in the picture?" He asked and Wilson snapped open the file and really did grin. "Sweet lord Alex, I think I'll keep a copy on my bedroom wall; what the hell were you up too!" He handed the file to Owen who smiled broadly; "That is definitely a keeper; stocking tops and little white panties. I'm in heaven!"

Alex snatched the file and stared at the picture. Jericho watched the expression change on her face. She said nothing for a few seconds, then exploded in denial and a little horror. Jericho calmed her down and asked, quite plainly, if it was her. She slammed the file on the table; "No it's bloody not! Why the hell would I be watching bloody snooker back in 1985 and showing my underwear to bloody TV cameras? I don't even like ruddy snooker!" Everyone chuckled at that; a little relieved.

"Well, it's really easy to sort out Alexandra; I simply check your mirror and if you were never back in Sheffield, England in 1985. That's the end of the matter." Jericho smiled as Alex quickly dragged her mirror out and pushed it into his hands. "Check away, I've never been there. The nearest I got was the bloody Miners' strike: the year before." She managed a smile and sat back, folding her arms. Wilson chuckled; "That's right, we had to swap you for bloody 'Jumbo' on that case with William - I'm a piss head - Shakespeare." Owen nodded; "I do remember that one, the old boy threw tantrums because Alex wouldn't be his bloody muse; dirty old drunken fucker!"

Jericho accepted her mirror and tapped in his Inspectors Code; "A quick look and we can all enjoy dinner." He smiled at Alex and sat reading her mirror. Alex held up the file and didn't smile; "You don't think old 'Doc' Underhill is pulling a fast one on his old pupil, I mean this is quite funny, I suppose. I wonder who he got to produce the bloody picture...." She stopped in mid-sentence, when she saw that Wilson and Owen were staring at Jericho. The expression on his face was priceless. He slowly handed the mirror back to Alex and said softly; "It confirms that you were in Sheffield, England in 1985."

4. IS THE ACCUSATION PROVED?

There was absolute silence at the table. Needless to say Alex exploded again. It took a couple of minutes for her to calm down. She jumped up from the table and paced the room; no one had ever seen her so angry, and it should be said; confused. Mr. Harris brought everyone a large tray of brandies and Alex downed her first one straight away. No was now thinking of food. That's when Owen picked up the file and opened it. "I wonder if anyone has checked the young man next to the Alex look-a-like." He muttered and ran his mirror over the photograph. Jericho already knew who was in the picture but remained silent for now.

He wanted someone else to make that announcement and was actually pleased that young Owen was on the ball; he really could become a good detective if he matured a bit more. But all the early signs were excellent.

Wilson had managed to calm Alex down enough for her to sit back down at the table. Owen looked up from his mirror and ran a hand over his face; "Everyone, Human Records confirm that the woman is Alexandra Mary Cappanni - nee Featherstone - and the man, whose knee she has hold of is....." He hesitated and held up his mirror; "You can see the Warning its flashing - the man is known and is on record - as one of the Human forms that the Dark Prince uses. It's him."

Jericho actually jumped a little as his mirror buzzed and he answered it slowly. It was the Duty Controller with a grim message. Jericho muttered 'yes' a few times and placed his mirror on the table. He was not smiling; "Doc Underhill has been given the official go ahead to investigate this. We're all stood down until it's resolved. Basically, Alexandra, you are under house arrest. I must take your mirror." He held out his hand and Alex just sat staring at him. "I must take it now Alexandra." He said simply and Alex handed him her mirror very slowly.

"Thank fuck they allocated it to old Doc Underhill. He's fair and thorough." Wilson said quietly; everyone's appetite for the excellent cooking of Mrs. Harris was gone. Jericho pushed Alex's mirror into his jacket and clasped his hands together, he spoke softly; "Normally, a Knight would be dispatched to oversee the investigation. But because who may be involved in this, The BOSS [he glanced up at the ceiling to reinforce his words] has decided that someone from the family will babysit Alex - just in case her supposed boyfriend turns up - and that's his sister, Princess Isis. She'll be here asap." He turned to Mr. Harris, who was actually gripping the back of Jericho's seat in mild shock. "The guest suite is up to your usual excellent standards?"

Mr. Harris managed to nod and mumble quietly; "Yes Sir, I'll inform Mrs. Harris of our guest." He walked away very slowly and headed for the kitchens. They all heard the normally reserved man yell; "Yes! Fucking Yes!" and then there was silence for a few seconds, and everyone started to laugh, even Alex had to chuckle as she brushed tears away. "I dread to think what awful waistcoat he'll have on for this one." Wilson said and everyone knew exactly what he meant.

Jericho leaned back in his chair; "I don't even have to ask that everyone WILL be on their best behaviour until this is over." Wilson chuckled; "You know that her grandfather – when designing the new female form for humans* - imagined a female like her. You would have certainly met your better with this one Alex." Owen just grunted and sat in silence. Wilson slapped him on the back adding; "Best behaviour baby brother!" and laughed some more.

*The 'original' female form was the Neanderthal female, which was replaced by the modern form and the same applied to the males. Then the Neanderthals were made extinct. That fate could easily apply to the modern humans one day.

Alex sighed loudly and sat up in her chair; "I want to see the actual film, the part where I supposedly expose my crotch to millions on TV whilst groping the bloody devil!" She turned to Jericho; "I take it we have the bloody game on record?" He nodded and rose from his chair; everyone followed, and the team headed for the study, past a confused looking Ruth holding a silver soup tureen.

"We'll be back." Owen smiled at her, and they all disappeared into the study. He whispered to Wilson; "Even if it's a bloody look-a-like, I'm still going to enjoy this!" Wilson just shook his head in mock despair and muttered; "There is no bloody IF."

Wilson served everyone large brandies and they settled in front of the big ornate mirror above the fireplace and Jericho said quietly; "The world snooker championship final in 1985, just the final frame please." The mirror flickered into life, and they sat watching, with very little conversation. After a few minutes Jericho grunted; "The broadcast Director plays the camera upon the crowd to create more atmosphere. It was a male dominated sport and men were clearly the majority and target audience, so any pretty young ladies would have the camera pointed at them."

Owen rubbed his chin; "I don't see many in that lot - pretty women I mean - no wonder he zoomed in on Alex...well, the look-a-like I mean."

"That's if he actually did; at the time." Jericho said softly.

5. CHESS WITH BRIGHTLY COLOURED BALLS.

They were disturbed by a beaming Mr. Harris who stood in the doorway and rubbed his hands together; "She is here Sir." Everyone rose from their seats, and all groaned a little inside; their normally exquisitely attired Butler was sporting a bright gold waistcoat, embossed with black and silver....kangaroos! He stepped aside and bowed quite low. Her Highness Princess Isis swept into the room; they really did all stare; she was stunning despite wearing a loose-fitting white jumper and black jeans with tears about the knees!

"Jericho my man, how are you?" She gripped his arm and smiled, broadly. He managed to bow and mumble; "I'm fine your Grace." Wilson and Owen bowed, well they tried, but it didn't turn out too well. Alex curtsied with some elegance and Isis walked straight up to her and placed a kiss on her cheek. "Hi Alex or do you prefer Alexandra?" Alex whispered that 'Alex' was fine.

Princess Isis turned to Wilson; "Mister Wilson, how are you?" Wilson nodded and said softly; "Very well, thank you, your Grace." Owen just stood with his mouth open. She nodded at him; "Owen, isn't it? I understand you were a monk at some stage." Owen just stood with his mouth open. Wilson smiled; "Yes, that's right you're Grace. He was a novice monk in his last lifetime." She smiled and stared at the paused screen.

"So you're watching snooker, my brother David loves the game, he says its Chess, only its played with bright coloured balls!"

Jericho gestured to the big armchair that he normally relaxed in; "Would you like to sit your Grace...and maybe Mr. Harris could fetch you a drink?" She nodded; "Thank you Jericho; I'll have a large brandy please." And plonked herself down in the chair and smiled at Alex. "Everyone, please sit down." She added and accepted a giant glass of brandy from the shaking hand of Mr. Harris.

"Well, let's see what the fuss is all about. Please play the naughty bit." She grinned and downed the entire glass of brandy in one go. She offered her glass to Mr. Harris for a refill. He poured her another large one and actually wondered if there were enough decent bottles of brandy in the bar stockroom for this visit!

Everyone sat in silence as the screen played on; the camera swept across the audience and stopped suddenly at a very pretty young woman in a stunning business suit with a very short skirt. She was in conversation with the young man next to her and she slowly crossed her legs. Owen actually groaned a little, as her black stocking tops were revealed, and everyone received a view of her tiny white, frilly panties. The camera moved on and the commentator chuckled that she'll be in the news papers tomorrow.

Wilson and Jericho exchanged a concerned look, both thinking the same thing: If that's not Alex, then they are a pair of monkeys. Everyone was now staring at Alex - well, the Princess wasn't - Mr. Harris was pouring her another refill. "Oh, that's definitely David. He often uses that form when visiting humanity. He goes by the wonderful name of 'Adam Anderson'. He says that form is quite popular with human females, and we know how much he likes them!" She actually giggled a little and relaxed back in the chair, cradling her brandy glass with both hands - warming the contents in the traditional way.

She sipped her brandy and peered over the rim of her glass at Alex, whose cheeks had gone a little reddish, "Now Alex, don't be embarrassed, I'm sure a lot of women have a revealed a little too much, when crossing their legs. Just they didn't have a camera peering up their skirt!" She placed the glass down and leaned forward in her seat. "I take it you now realise that it IS YOU in the film. David told me he had quite a date; he was impressed that you love snooker too. Oh yes, he was really impressed with you - really impressed."

Everyone sat in absolute silence until Alex pushed a tear from her cheek; "That can't be me. I think, I would remember going on a date with the 'Dark Prince' and showing my crotch on TV." She whispered and swallowed down her brandy.

Jericho rubbed his face - something wasn't right here. He knew that Alexandra had no real interest in the game of snooker; no interest whatsoever - she would prefer Chess any day of the week. He sighed and picked up his glass. Something was definitely not right here; but that was Alexandra in the film, and she was with the Dark Prince. He sipped his brandy and thought hard about what the hell was going on. He glanced at Alex sipping her brandy and wondered if Alex was actually telling the whole truth here. Had she been up to something she really didn't want found out by her colleges? Had it all gone horribly wrong? Then the awful feeling of Déjà vu that had swept over him; had the Timeline changed in a way that affected the team? Was Alex's behavior behind any such changes?

In the quietness of the late evening, Jericho was walking alone in the grounds of the lighthouse; the only real noise was the sound of his boots on the gravel. He stood and watched the sea for some time and then headed back. Jericho sat in the study and re-watched the scene on the big mirror; he had already decided that it was indeed Alexandra. But he truly believed that she was being totally honest in her denial that she was out with the 'Dark Prince', but her mirror definitely put her in Sheffield at that time. That thought made Jericho sit straight up and he thought about the last encounter the team had with the Dark Prince in person.

Boston, 1959 in the car park of the North Boston College of Art and the Dark Prince had intervened with his own minions, to ensure that Alexandra's soul wasn't lost after the demon Phara had killed her. It would have been lost because she was out of her own allocated time period. It was a danger all temporal detectives faced whilst on duty in a time period that was not their own pre-ordained time. [See episode from the **TEMPORAL DETECTIVES** series entitled; **'Sister Sarah dreams of demons.'**]

"Why did he do that?" That was the question Wilson had asked Jericho after the incident. Jericho stood staring at the now dead fireplace and ran a hand through his hair. "Why did he do that?" He repeated to himself; they had a Knight of God there; James, who could have easily recalled Alex's soul. Jericho sighed, time was running out; Archangel Michael had convened a special disciplinary hearing against Alex tomorrow and it certainly didn't look good for her - despite her vehement denials - If only he had more time.

It was like a light being switched on his head; Time. He actually laughed out loud and headed up the stairs to Wilson's room and knocked gently upon the door. He could see the lights were on and so the big man was still up. Some very quiet music was playing; probably soul music from the 1970's.

Wilson opened the door and Jericho stepped in. On the small table by the window was a very old-fashioned typewriter. There were sheets of paper scattered around the table and on the floor. Jericho smiled; "Writing your memoirs big man?" and was definitely surprised when Wilson nodded; "I put together stuff about the missions we get lumbered with, just an interest, well, hobby really and the latest one is a cracker; first the Dark Prince turns up and saves Alex's soul, then his bloody sister appears and practically condemns Alex's soul for the disciplinary hearing tomorrow."

Jericho nodded and then grinned; "Do you fancy doing something naughty and help Alexandra?" Wilson smiled and picked up his jacket; "I hope by naughty you don't expect me to flash my wedding tackle on prime-time TV?" Jericho chuckled; "No, we would need a special wildlife permit to let that bloody thing escape!" Wilson stopped; "The team is stood down; the bloody light room won't allow us to travel and; besides, our mirrors are offline." He grimaced and sat back down on the end of the bed. But Jericho smiled; "We don't need either of them, if we have a Knight of God." Wilson nodded and grinned; "And boy, do we know one that will do anything for our girl." they both now smiled as the same name came to them; James.

As they sneaked down the stairs, they passed the darkened Guest Suite and stopped suddenly - they really struggled to stop laughing out loud - at the noises coming from the room, which caught their attention. "Sweet Jesus, she snores louder than a pig on bloody steroids!" Whispered Wilson and they crept down the stairs holding back some terrible fits of giggles. They made the study and let it go; both laughed for a few minutes then calmed down. "Oh bollocks! How can we call him without our fucking mirrors?" Groaned Wilson and slumped into his favourite armchair.

But Jericho pulled on his coat and jerked a thumb towards the door; "I think a little visit to our resident recluse will solve that one." Wilson jumped up; "You clever fucker; John of course!" They slipped quietly through the front door and headed for the small cottage at the end of the Island, as they closed the door behind them, Mr. Harris stood in the doorway of the kitchen and sipped his glass of milk and grinned; Mr. Jericho Tibbs could be accused of many things and loyalty was certainly one of them. He made his way to his suite, smiling, Mrs. Harris would love this latest twist in the 'Cappanni panties case!' as she described it.

They were pleased to see that the lights were still on in John's small cottage. Jericho tapped on the door, and it was opened by John, who smiled; "Let me guess gentlemen; a very naughty, unauthorized little mission to Sheffield in 1985 to save the reputation and career of our much respected and loved Lady

Alexandra?" Jericho and Wilson exchanged a knowing glance. John may be a reclusive bugger, but he certainly had knowledge about the human condition - and rather strangely for a recluse - human friendship.

Jericho just nodded and was about to ask about James, when John picked up his coat and hat, then grinned; "Let's not get a good Knight into trouble with his Arch-Angel. I can help and no-one will call me into question. Let's go." The three disappeared and found themselves standing outside the Crucible Theatre, in Sheffield on the afternoon of April 28th, 1985.

6. THE GAME IS ON!

"Fuck!" Exclaimed Wilson as little snowflakes, tossed by the breeze, fell about his face and shoulders, then added; "I should have grabbed my bloody coat." Jericho pulled his jacket around himself and just had to smile at John, in his heavy black coat and woolen hat. "How the hell did he know what the weather would be doing?" Wilson muttered. Jericho didn't answer and checked his mirror; it was still offline. Then wondered if the Duty Time Controller had picked up their naughty and unauthorized, little time breach?

John rubbed his hands together and seemed quite excited; "I'm a great fan of snooker and this was simply, one of the greatest matches ever played. It went right down to the final ball in the final frame - fantastic!" They watched the crowds forming outside the doors and Wilson stopped smiling; "How the fuck can we get in with no working mirrors and more importantly; no fucking tickets!"

John just smiled and rummaged in his old black coat; he pulled three pieces of paper from his pocket and tapped them; "Three tickets for the final session of the World Snooker Championship Final and we'll be sitting just three rows behind where Alex and her unwanted date will apparently be." Wilson just stared at them, but Jericho chuckled; "He is the BOSSES son, he can do things like that. Come on, let's get our seats." They joined the happy queue and John said quietly; "My uncle told me once, that snooker was basically Chess played with brightly coloured balls. That's a good analogy, isn't it?"

Wilson gave Jericho a strange glance and Jericho held a finger to his lips; "Not the best time to mention how much we dislike his uncle." Wilson just nodded; he had his own thoughts about Prince John but would keep them to himself for now. "Does this place have a decent bloody bar?" He said and pulled his jacket tighter.

The Principle Time Controller: Estelle Lagarde walked slowly into the Duty Time Controllers suite and stared at the mirrors full of flickering images. There were nearly a hundred Controllers working this shift under her Senior Assistant Theodore Rhodes, who greeted Lagarde at the door. He gestured to the Special Operations section. Located in its own space, in the corner of the room and almost smiled; "First trip he's taken in some time and he's not alone; that's why I called you in."

They walked slowly to the busy room and Lagarde asked quietly; "All the other family members are located and where they should be?" Theo nodded; "Prince David is still cloaked - as usual - Princess Isis is at that bloody lighthouse of Jericho Tibbs - you know - dealing with that classified matter and now Prince John has suddenly stopped being a recluse and jumped to Sheffield, England in 1985. The Heir is still sitting on that bloody mountain in Canada and Prince Alexander has cloaked himself but was last reported in Scotland in 1746. The Princess Mary is...fishing in an Arctic Lake back in 1844 with that useless boyfriend of hers." He saw the look on Lagarde's face and added; "Sorry, with her current best friend." but she just smiled, as a rebuke for his disrespect to a family member.

Princess Mary's latest 'boyfriend' was a Knight who was as useful as a snowball in space. He owed his current position entirely to his 'friendship' with the BOSSES' daughter. He made the 'Three Stooges' look like a trio of Einstein's or Gavel's*. Still, the princess must see some good in him, even if no one else could.

*Bernard Kelvin Gravel [2048 – 2112] was a Jamaican scientist who won the Nobel Prize for inventing a human like cyborg that could have human memory and consciousness downloaded into it. Basically he had created immortality for the wealthy!

Lagarde folded her arms and stared at the screen before her. She sighed; "In the company of Inspector Tibbs and his sergeant – Wilson... isn't it? - looks like they are all snooker fans." Theo smiled at that; Lagarde leaned on the desk and stared at the screen; "The two Detectives are not cleared to be there. The prince can be where he likes and with whoever he likes. But inform Angel Margret about her snooker loving, currently suspended Detectives, who apparently, are taking a little sightseeing trip; I don't think." She then chuckled; "I have a pretty good idea what Tibbs is up to there; clever bugger, getting John's help. That is really clever. Best inform Family Liaison and get some directions about what action we should take; if any is necessary."

Theo nodded and watched the screen; "Well, the cold weather surprised the detectives, but not Prince John." He leaned forward and pointed to the corner of the screen; "Ma'am, isn't that him, in that human form he's so fond of?"

Lagarde ran a hand over her face and nodded; "Yes and I know who the pretty human female is. He has her under control. Inform Family Liaison at once about this." Then she stepped back; "No, inform the Queen directly. She may be needed on this one and get a message to Princess Isis. Then Inform Demon Ingress to get some Knights on standby; if he's there, then he's bound to have some very senior Minions hanging around him. Those two brave, but naïve detectives would be in real danger; if Prince John wasn't with them."

Theo agreed and Lagarde returned to her office, leaving explicit instructions that she would be kept up to date regularly. She was smiling broadly to herself; that young woman certainly has a pair of good friends in those two crazy detectives - they were simply risking everything for her: including their souls!

Jericho eased his way past several people already sitting and joined John and Wilson. He was impressed; they had a good view of the table and the final, evening session was about to start. John tapped his arm; "That's the seats they'll be sitting in." Jericho rubbed his chin; "There are three empty seats, why three seats?" He whispered and Wilson said softly; "I just mentioned that, but we never caught sight of the people sitting next to them, with the bloody camera pointing at Alex's underwear."

Jericho sighed; "And we don't have any bloody mirrors to check now." Wilson shifted his big frame about in the chair - getting comfortable - and stared down towards the aisle which contained the empty seats they were very interested in. He wiped his face; "They're here." The trio all leaned forward at the same time and saw the Dark Prince - aka 'Adam Anderson' - with 'Alex' on his arm. They took their seats with no conversation. "The dirty bastard has his hand up her fucking skirt!" Wilson said with real anger in his voice. They all noticed that Alex's face was expressionless, and she appeared to make no comment.

Jericho rubbed his chin; "There's something very wrong here." John agreed and Jericho could see he had formed his right hand into a fist, with the other hand clutching it. "I really don't like the way he's taking advantage of his position with that young woman. He clearly has her under control...he's removed her Free-will, just like he would with every human; if given the opportunity."

The game was now underway and the seat next to the pair remained empty; "No-one will be allowed in now the match is underway." Wilson muttered with real anger growing inside of him, as he watched the Dark Prince push his other hand into Alex's blouse; still without any reaction from her. "Dirty bastard." Was all he managed to add.

John turned to Jericho with a real determined look; "I now see for myself why my...why he must never inherit the throne after his brother. I see and understand it as clear as day." They watched as the Dark Prince stopped molesting the silent Alex and sat back in his seat, he simply waved his hand and Alex started talking and placed her hand upon his knee. "This is it." Jericho said quietly and they watched, as Alex now opened her legs as the ceiling camera passed over the pair. The Dark Prince was actually laughing, and Wilson really wanted to punch him straight in his grinning face.

Jericho stared hard; the outfit Alex had on, was the very one she was wearing on the Boston Mission, where the dark prince had recalled her soul. He wondered about the significance of that. He ran a hand over his face and stared at the couple; how the hell did the Dark prince get control of Alex; he would have to physically touch her to gain that sort of control...He groaned as remembered the Boston incident. He turned to Wilson and was about to speak, but that's when he noticed that everyone was silent, there was no noise from the crowd and the players were like mannequins in a shop window. The three friends rose from their seats and could see the Dark Prince also slowly standing.

John smiled at Jericho and Wilson. "I've stopped time. Let's have a word with the ..." He pushed both hands through his long hair and finished his sentence slowly; "Rat." Was all he said and meant it.

Jericho and Wilson followed John down the aisle stairs and saw the expression on the Dark Prince's Face; He was grinning. He had recognized John, his nephew.

7. NOW A DIFFERNET GAME.

Theo stepped back from the screen with a real serious and grim look upon his face and gripped the shoulder of the senior Controller sitting before the mirror, who also was unsmiling, "Get me the Palace; urgently; the Queen herself - NOW!" The second controller was already calling Lagarde; he didn't have to be told. John stood in front of David [The Dark Prince] and gestured towards Alex, still sitting with her legs open, having no further orders to move. She stared ahead with no expression. "Sorry Uncle David, but we're here to collect young Alex and take her home. I'm sure you'll find another little plaything to amuse yourself with." He folded his arms.

David nodded at Jericho and Wilson; "You really are a clever little human Jericho. You knew that you couldn't come up against me without some real heavy protection. I really have underestimated you. I won't do that again, believe me." Jericho just stood unsmiling and said nothing.

John simply waved his hand across Alex, and she slowly came round; she looked totally confused and jumped from the chair and grabbed John with both arms and gripped him really tightly; she was crying. John put both arms around her and whispered in her ear. He turned to Jericho and Wilson, with a smile; "Take her home please." Alex, Jericho and Wilson disappeared.

They were outside the lighthouse and Wilson had Alex firmly cradled in his arms; She was now sobbing. She wiped her face with both hands and smoothed her clothes; "That bloody demon Phara, [back in Boston in 1959] had hold of me and there was darkness, I was in total darkness, I could feel nothing....see nothing. There WAS nothing except darkness. I was dead and my soul was...lost." Wilson embraced her tightly and stroked her hair. "The Dark Prince had you in his clutches, but you're safe now." He whispered and noticed that Mr. Harris had appeared in the doorway, gesturing for them to come.

Jericho wiped his face and muttered; "Now what?" The team made their way into the lighthouse and Mr. Harris opened the study door; "You have a serious visitor Sir and herself has gone [Princess Isis]." He stared at Alex and looked quite relieved; "I was also about to inform you that Lady Alexandra had also disappeared." Jericho smiled; "John dealt with little problem; we can't have two Alexandra's here, can we?"

Jericho just sighed and said to Wilson; "Take Alex into the kitchens. Get Mrs. Harris to look after her." Wilson nodded and took Alex to the kitchens with Mr. Harris following, saying there was a decent bottle of brandy next to the Utility Room door. "Good because we need a big one." Wilson said and guided Alex through the door. Jericho took a deep breath and stepped into the study. He knew immediately who was sitting on his sofa, legs crossed and holding a large Vodka - neat. It was Adam; yes, that Adam - the First human ever made by the present BOSSES Grandfather - He was himself's personal Servant and Private Secretary. Adam was simply the most important - and powerful - human that existed. He has close up and personal dealings with all members of THE FAMILY each and every day. It was said that Adam was totally trusted by the hierarchy and carried real power in the organisation. Jericho was a little stunned; Adam didn't usually make house calls!

Adam rose and held out his hand; "Hello Jericho, I hope I'm not intruding on your leisure time." Jericho shook his very firm hand and mumbled; "No Sir." Adam gestured for him to sit and dropped back on the sofa. He smiled. "I trust that Miss Alexandra will recover from her ordeal. Queen Mary is quite concerned about what befell the girl. The matter will be taken up by Himself, you can trust me on that." Adam finished his vodka and placed the glass down. He leaned forward and the smile was gone. Jericho had a strange feeling that he really didn't want to know, what Adam was about to tell him.

"Prince John has told me that you can be trusted - completely - I was also told that by Queen Mary. That means, I know I can also trust you and your judgments." He sat back and Jericho refilled his glass from the bottle that Mr. Harris had left. "Excuse me Sir; I think I may need one of these." Jericho said and filled the second glass [left on the tray with the spirit bottles] with brandy.

Adam chuckled; "You and your team have a well-earned reputation for hard work, hard playing and total commitment to your assigned roles, that is how it should be. That's the sort of endeavour that I need."

"What happened to Alexandra would just be the tip of the iceberg should Prince David [The Dark Prince] inherit his brother's throne. Currently, his plans for his grandfather's creation – us humans- do not look good. The Heir appears to have made it quite clear, that's he wants nothing to do with his father or humanity. His brother Prince John displayed no interest in anything to do with humanity and had also refused to take the throne, when the time comes. But that was until the little adventure with yourself. He now understands what will happen to humanity, should his uncle be placed upon the throne. Those feelings will be encouraged Jericho and I'm sure you can clearly understand why?" Adam ran a hand over his face; "They MUST be encouraged - Yes?"

Jericho swallowed his brandy in one hit and nodded; "I do understand Sir." But thought; what fucking shit have I landed myself in? Adam rose and walked to the door; "I'll be in touch Jericho." He hesitated and turned, unsmiling; "Watch your back Jericho. There are some very powerful forces that would see the Dark Prince on the throne, and they will stop at nothing to see that happen." On that unhappy note, he departed.

Jericho held his head with both hands and muttered; "What the fuck have I got myself into?" He looked up and saw Wilson standing in the doorway; almost smiling; "You mean what the fuck have WE got into." He dropped into his favourite armchair and clasped his big hands together; "Mrs. Harris has sorted our Alex out - she's quite a knowledgeable and caring woman - and now our girl is just plain angry. A bit like our Owen, who is sulking over being left behind; despite me telling him why we did that."

They both turned to the door and watched Alex march in and pour herself a large brandy with some real determination. She took a couple of mouthfuls and placed one hand on her hip; "I going to shove the bastards balls so far up his arse, he'll think he has bloody tonsillitis!" and finished her drink, then poured another one. She took a couple of deep breaths and tried to subdue her anger.

"Feel me up will he, the bloody creep!" and sipped at her brandy, adding; "What did our Adam want Jericho - if you don't mind letting us into the little secret." She slumped into her armchair by the fire and very slowly and ladylike, crossed her legs. Wilson started to clap, and Jericho joined in; that did surprise Alex, then she realised why they were applauding. She raised her glass; "See, the lady can seat herself comfortably without displaying her panties and stocking tops to the entire world." Then she actually chuckled.

Wilson stood up and fetched himself a large one from the drinks tray and refilled Jericho's glass, whilst he was at it, he poured a large one for Owen, who he knew wouldn't sulk for long, if there was brandy about. He pretended to grimace; "Tonsillitis!" was all he said and sat back down.

Everyone looked back at the doorway. Owen stood there - arms folded - looking a little angry. He walked over and sat down on the sofa. Wilson passed him the brandy he had poured. Owen took a sip and nodded; "I do understand why you had to leave me behind. New to the Department, a novice, my career as a Temporal Detective would have been over before it really started. But I still feel that I should have made that decision for myself. Nevertheless, I do understand why you made the call Jericho." He raised his glass to his silent colleagues; "I apologise for acting like a spoilt brat. I'm sorry."

Wilson and Jericho exchanged a really surprised look, until finally Wilson smiled and raised his glass too; "I think our boy has finally turned into a young man." Alex nodded; "Bloody amen to that." Jericho just smiled.

8. REVALATIONS.

"Room for one more?" Everyone turned again to the study door and John wandered in and dropped on the sofa next to Owen. Since they all knew, who John was now; they started to stand, but he waved them down; "I normally like a red wine, but a bloody brandy will do me nicely." Alex stood and fetched him a glass and pushed it into his hand, she bent over him and placed a real smacker on his lips. "Thank you so much." Was all she said.

He really did grin at that and to everyone's real surprise knocked the brandy back in one hit. "I suppose you all want to know what happened with my arsehole of an uncle." He walked over to the drinks tray and refilled his glass; "Re-fills anyone?" Everyone was utterly amazed that such a powerful entity would actually perform a service for their minions. But he did and with a big smile.

"What did happen Sir. With the Dark Prince?" Jericho said quietly. John smiled; "It's still John my friend. Uncle Arsehole is not happy. In fact, to quote that wonderful and colourful human expression; His strawberries had been well and truly pissed on." John raised his glass, then took a sip. He grinned and relaxed back on the sofa and patted Owens's arm in friendship.

There was a silence for a few seconds, then a dour faced Wilson asked; "So, officially, we can call him Uncle Arsehole now?" Everyone stared at Wilson in amazement and a little horror. That was some serious breach of protocol. But John just started to laugh, and everyone joined in. Jericho held his hand up; "Come on people, stick to the rules. Prince John can refer to his uncle how he likes, but we'll keep the required respect for a senior family member."

That made everyone laugh even more.

Alex grinned; "Spoken like a true diplomat Jericho." and downed her brandy in one hit. John finished his drink and stood. Everyone rose too and John sighed; "Stop that - please." He smiled and headed for the door, then stopped; "Oh, and by the way, that Discipline Hearing called for tomorrow over our Alex's unwilling dating of Uncle Arsehole, will not go ahead. Mother has put a stop to that. But Mickey will probably want to see her." He disappeared and everyone really did relax. Owen scratched his chin in wonderment and muttered; "He calls the Archangel Michael 'Mickey!"

Owen refilled all their glasses, and the conversation was quite lively. The team went to bed a great deal happier. But Jericho remained in the study, sitting by the dying fire and deep in thought. He had checked his mirror - it was back online. He sighed and stared at the smoldering embers of the fire; something still troubled him, and he couldn't fathom out what that was. Had the Timeline changed slightly because of the Dark

Prince's interference? Both teams sat outside the Arch-Angel's grand office in relative silence. Only Doc Underhill and Jericho were really chatting. Owen tapped Wilson and nodded towards Isabella [Issy] Pugg; "If Alex gets away with this, without a warning or official caution, they will have to shoot her with a tranquilizer gun." Wilson chuckled and glanced at the miserable looking Sergeant. "By the look on her face, she already knows the result." It was Owen's turn to chuckle. Skyrise sat arms folded and stared at the floor; even he didn't like to hold a conversation with 'Issy' unless he had too. Being a doctor; he had informed his friends on team 74 that she clearly had suffered a 'personality and humour bypass' at some point. Even old Doc had smiled at that, though he did 'tut tut' a couple of times and wag a disapproving finger.

Everyone stood as Prince John appeared from the office with Madame Eleanor [the angel's private secretary]. He grinned and slapped his hands together; "Mickey wants to see you two for a moment." He gestured to Doc and Jericho and still smiling, walked off down the corridor. Everyone turned to Issy as she groaned and slumped back on the seat and folded her arms; she was not a happy Temporal Detective Sergeant. Now that did make everyone smile.

Madame Eleanor showed Doc and Jericho into the angel's office and everyone sat back down, a lot happier now. Issy couldn't believe that Alex had 'got away with it' again. She stared at Skyrise, Wilson and Owen. "Bloody men; always fools for a pretty face and pair of long legs." She muttered to herself and searched in her handbag for some mints she had there; she didn't offer them around.

Doc and Jericho emerged from the office - unsmiling - and Doc patted Jericho's arm and smiled. He gestured for his team to follow him, and Team 74 watched their colleagues depart in silence. Jericho jerked a thumb towards the office door and said quietly; "The Arch-Angel will see Team 74 now." They followed him into the room without comment. Jericho stopped Alex briefly and said softly; "Keep your lips firmly together. I will do all the talking." Alex nodded and refrained from smiling. They lined up in front of the Angel's ornate desk and everyone stared at the sole object upon the beautiful marble desk; it was a miniature gold guillotine!

The Archangel sat in his chair with both hands clasped in front of him. He nodded to Alex; "Officer Cappanni, you will be pleased to know that no discipline action will be taken against you. The matter is closed and will not appear upon your Personal File."

Alex almost smiled but restrained herself; "Thank you Sir." was all she said. He gestured to Owen; "You took no part in this matter and; thus, your record remains clean - as it should for a novice Detective - and I suspect you have your Inspector and Sergeant to thank for that." Owen just nodded and also didn't smile. He folded his arms and still unsmiling spoke to Jericho and Wilson; "But you two broke several rules; and you know the very ones I am talking about. You admit that?" Jericho and Wilson nodded.

The Angel tapped his desk gently and said quietly; "I'm afraid that Sergeant Wilson Franklyn is reduced in rank to Constable for an indefinite period. He must receive a disciplinary sanction for what he did. I trust you can all understand that?" No one nodded at that revelation. The Angel continued; "Inspector Tibbs is suspended from duty forthwith for an indefinite period." There was absolute silence from the team; no one expected such a hard punishment. Alex wanted to speak, but the caught the look on Jericho's face and remained silent. Owen just stood with his mouth open. But Jericho and Wilson said nothing; they had actually expected far worse, for breaking some very serious rules of the Temporal Detectives Department, they had illegally time travelled whilst stood down and interfered with another Teams investigation into a fellow team members Discipline case. They should have been thrown out of the department for that alone; never mind the unauthorised time trip!

Archangel Michael slowly pulled a small fob watch from his pocket and flipped open the lid. He stared at the watch face for a minute or so and looked up at the silent and dour Team 74. He grunted and snapped the lid shut; "Now that the indefinite time period is over. You're restored to the rank of Sergeant, Wilson. Your suspension, Inspector Tibbs is lifted. Now take a seat all of you." He smiled and leaned back in his chair. The Archangel had done his job; dished out some serious enough punishments to his naughty staff - even if it was for only two minutes! - Temporal Department protocols had been satisfied.

Everyone slowly sat on the marble bench and a little ripple of laughter passed between them, The Angel clasped his hands together; "Now onto more serious matters." The smile was gone, and everyone sat upright as the angel explained the 'serious matters' happening around them.

It was some minutes later that Team 74 trooped from his office in absolute silence and remained so until they returned to the lighthouse. They gathered in the study and Jericho closed the door and actually turned the key in the lock; no one had ever seen that happen before. He stood in front of the fireplace; grim faced and arms folded. "Well, you heard what the Arch-Angel said. Certain parties within - and outside - the Palace are making moves to have Prince David declared his brother's heir. I certainly don't have to explain what that would mean for us humans. Alex has already had a taste of that. But equally powerful parties are determined to stop that and have Prince John declared the heir. For good or bad; we have chosen to support Prince John and that will put us directly at odds with the Dark Prince and his supporters. To quote Archangel Michael; 'the bloody gloves are off'. We are now in the firing line from some pretty powerful parties."

He walked to the drinks tray and smiled; "Brandies all round, I think." No one argued against that! Owen cradled his brandy glass and said softly; "I think we're really in the shit." No one argued with that too.

Jericho sat alone in his study and using his Inspectors code, watched a portion of a 'Life tape' which Control had recorded. He sat expressionless as the tape was replayed. He watched Alex in the bar and the subsequent threesome. He grunted to himself; "Little wonder she said nothing about why she had really been in 1985." He stopped the tape and stared at 'David Willis' with a little anger. The flashing red warning indicated that the Dark Prince was in human form. Little wonder he had such control over Alex. He [Jericho] had kept to himself what Prince John had confided to him about the conversation - a little heated - at times with his uncle.

Alex had no recollection of the 'Snooker Incident' because the Dark Prince had wiped her memory. The third seat had been for one of his 'Little Princesses' who was more than happy to join in the sex games with her master; but hadn't accompanied him because the Dark Prince wanted Alex to himself. He would have probably stopped time in the Crucible Theatre and enjoyed sex. Right there and then, with Alex. The Dark Prince knew full well that Alex would have been thrown out the Department and that would make her easy prey for him to snatch up. Jericho knew that Prince David would not forgive him for thwarting his plans. The Dark Prince had certainly lived up to reputation as a cunning clever, evil bastard.

Little wonder Jericho had felt strange, that night, that old Doc had visited. The Timeline had changed. The Dark Prince had returned Alex back to the lighthouse after the seduction. Jericho sighed; the bastard had finally got his way with her - even if only by devilish deceit - and rather disturbingly, Prince John had told Jericho that his uncle - having finally experienced Alex sexually - now really did want her for his Queen. Jericho leaned back in his armchair and stared at the dying fire; should he let Alex know what really befell her?

9. ALEX GETS LEAVE.

Alex was delighted to receive some leave from Angel Margret to recover fully from the incident. So, she visited her 'friend' Mr. Albian [A Senior Time Controller] and he was more than happy to assist her. [See episode: **'Alexandra and the Aztecs'.**] So, she jumped back to Victorian London in the summer of 1861 and booked herself into the fairly new Claridge's Hotel which had been opened in 1854. She had her loyal 'maid' for company; Jackie, who Jericho insisted accompany her and arranged leave for her too. Thus, the two ladies arrived in London and Alex had one simple goal; to find a young Mr. Frederick Babette! See episode: **'Alexandra: the reluctant French maid.'**

"According to my calculations Freddie would be twenty-five years old in this year and worked for Sir John Coleville as a Footman. We won't have any problems with Edward or Harold this time because they are boys in this year." Alex spoke to Jackie as they walked to the cab rank and caught the first cab in line.

Tentatively she told the rough looking driver to take them to Sir John Coleville's house. She was relieved when he just nodded and grunted as the two ladies boarded and settled back for the journey. Alex sighed; "These dresses are like wearing a bloody tent and are about as sexually attractive as a sewage farm. I hate them." Jackie chuckled; "Yeah, but your sick, perverted friend Mr. Albian would probably find the shit farm attractive!" Alex had to smile at that and leaned over, whispering; "The dirty bastard only agreed after I took a dump in his lap. He really needs to see someone about his sexual habits." Jackie really grimaced; "You must really want Mr. Babette badly my girl!" Alex now grinned; "Bloody right I do!"

The cab stopped out the impressive house which would later become a rescue centre for 'fallen' women with alcohol and prostitution problems. But for now, it was the family home of a very eminent Victorian archeologist and adventurer. Alex paid the cabby and the pair headed for the tradesman entrance. A burly man was unloading a wooden grate filled with fresh vegetables and walking down the alley at the side of the house. "I bet he's about to deliver, so let's follow him." Jackie said and they walked behind him. He stopped at a brown door and pulled the rope by the doorframe and a middle-aged woman opened it and didn't smile; "Your bleeding late again Mr. Combs. I expected these an hour ago. The cook is not happy." The big man just nodded and walked past her as she stood wiping her hands on her apron. She stared at Alex and Jackie and again; didn't smile. "Can I help?" she said and Alex smiled; "We're here to see my cousin; Mr. Frederick Babette, is he in?" The woman placed her arms on her hips and now did smile. "You want to see Freddie?" Both girls nodded. She turned and shouted down the hallway; "Lucy! Go fetch Freddie; there are a couple of tarts to see him!"

Both Alex and Jackie stared at each other; "Tarts!" they both thought but restrained any angry reply and waited. The woman shook her head and rubbed her face; "Which of you two has he knocked up now? Or is it both of you!" she chuckled and told them to wait here and wandered back inside; still laughing to herself. Jackie folded her arms; "It appears your man has quite a reputation already." Alex nodded; "Don't care, I know how he turns out, so what are a few youthful indiscretions considering how he becomes a sexual God!" Jackie laughed at that and then a young man appeared at the door with a cup in his hand. Alex really smiled; she was right about Mr. Frederick Babette; he had been a very good looking, rugged young man in his day with a handsome face. She had only known him previously as a middle aged man during the mission to 1880's London. He sipped his tea and smiled; "Which of you beautiful young ladies is my supposed cousin?"

Alex said quietly; "I am Freddie." He really smiled, but shook his head; "I certainly don't have a cousin that looks like you darling. The two I do have look like pigs wearing wigs and lipstick." He chuckled and closed the door behind him and gestured for them to follow him; "The gardeners big shed is a discrete place to talk, otherwise bleeding Mrs. Reynolds the housekeeper will be taking notes for Sir John. You just met her, so you'll understand." Both girls nodded and followed.

The gardeners 'hut' was a big brick built, one story place with small windows and Freddie pushed open the shabby door and walked in. It smelt of flowers, compost, and tobacco. He closed the door and placed his cup down. "Now, how can I help you ladies?" Alex smiled and ran her hand softly over his face; "Oh, Freddie you won't believe my story, so I won't tell it, but you and I are true soul mates and we actually ended up getting married. I have come back for you, risking everything including my bloody life to be with you. We should be together, no, destined to be together. Do you understand?"

Freddie looked quiet puzzled; "Blimey darling that's some bleeding story and I can't make head nor tail of anything about it. But does that mean you want me to fuck you and maybe, your pretty friend too?" Alex sighed; "You catch on fast Mister Adonis and Casanova rolled into one." Freddie nodded; "OK darling, when and where?" Alex told him she was booked into Claridge's Hotel, and he should visit there. He nodded and said, "Who do I ask for?" Alex stroked his face; "Lady Alex Cappanni." He grunted; "And when; I get Thursday afternoon off but can wrangle a whole night or two if I pay the other footman to cover for me, but that's bloody expensive." Alex nodded and opened her purse; "How much to bribe them for a whole weekend? This weekend."

Freddie grinned; "Five bob each, but I'll need cab fare and that, so call it fifteen bob." Alex handed him a sovereign coin which would more than cover his 'expenses' for the weekend. He took the money and kissed it; "Lady, you've booked me for the weekend, I'll see you about nine o'clock Saturday morning then." He pocketed the coin and walked to the door. "Oh, I take it that includes her as well." indicating Jackie and chuckled; heading back to the big house. Jackie folded her arms and sighed; "Is he that good in the sack?" Alex gently tapped her arm; "Bloody unfortunately, he bleeding isn't just good, but utterly fucking phenomenal!" Jackie smiled; "I can't wait." Was all she said.

The girls sat around in anticipation of Saturday morning, but the clock seemed to drag the hours and minutes and the tension and wanting grew with the passing hours. Finally, Saturday morning arrived and both girls shared a bath and then dressed for his arrival. Well, dressed meant they both just wore stockings, panties and a Basque that barely covered their breasts. They practically prowled the rooms of their hotel suite like lionesses awaiting their prey.

Finally, there was a knock at the door and Alex rushed to and opened it slightly and stared at the young man standing there. "Miss Alex Cappanni?" he asked and removed his hat. She nodded, keeping her body behind the door. He smiled and handed her a folded piece of paper. "The gentleman said to deliver this, and you would give me sixpence for my troubles." Alex slowly took the note and called to Jackie to bring her purse. She gave the young man his money and he smiled and walked off. They both stood by the fireplace and Alex opened the note. It said: *"Sorry ladies, but I've had to leave due to circumstances beyond my control. Thank you for the money. Take care of yourselves. I'm so sorry as I was looking forward to having some fun with you girls. Ta-Ta and see you sometime. Freddie."*

Alex read aloud getting a little angry. The girls were bitterly disappointed and then wondered why he had to leave so quickly. "Come on, we're going back to that damn house and find out what happened." Alex said, folding the note up. She went back to the door and stuck her head out, the young man had reached the top of the staircase, at the end of the long corridor, when she called him back. He took off his hat – again – and smiled, "How can I help Miss?"

Alex asked him how old he was and smiled at the reply: 18. She gently ran a hand down his face and asked if he was experienced with women [she was horny and needed cock: urgently!] He shrugged his shoulders, "Some would say I was and other's I wasn't. But mum and Rose – me sister – are both on the game, so I would say I know about women!"

She chuckled, "Well, that's good enough for us, do come in!" and also pulled him through the door. He stared at both of them, dressed in their underwear and especially at Alex's magnificent big tits, barely restrained by her bodice. He wiped a hand across his face, "Sorry darling, but all I have is the bleeding tanner [slang for sixpenny piece] you gave me, sorry!" She started unbuttoning his jacket, "It's free dear because we need a bloody cock!" He then stared at Jackie, standing smiling at him, with an erection in her flimsy panties. He wiped his sweaty face with his dirty cap and swallowed hard muttering "Oh fuck!" under his breath and sort of smiled back. Young Albert Springs only had sexual experiences with an elderly prostitute called Mavis [a friend of his mother: it was a 'treat' for his 15th birthday!] and a drunk fishwife [who gutted fresh fish for sale at Billingsgate Fish Market] behind the 'Queen Victoria' Tavern in Whitechapel Road last Christmas Eve. It was part of his Christmas present that year: he received a new pair of boots from his mother and sister and a nasty dose of lice and crabs [Definitely not the kind you eat…..] from Fanny the fishwife. Albert knew instinctively what he had to do.

Alex and Jackie stood with arms folded as the damn door slammed shut and they could hear him disappearing down the corridor at speed, shouting "Fuck this for a game of darts! Not again!"

Jackie just sighed and headed for the bedroom to dress saying, "I think that has to be the first man who turned down free sex with two horny ladies this side of hell freezing over!" Alex followed, cussing a little and determined to find out what transpired to make Freddie depart so quickly. They took a cab to Sir John Coleville's house and banged on the tradesmen's door. Mrs. Reynolds opened the door and folded her arms; she was actually smiling which surprised the girls. Before they could speak; she chuckled; "You're out of luck. He's long-suffering wife has dragged him off; she's found him another job away from women and especially women like you two trollops. So, piss off before I call a constable." Laughing, she slammed the door.

They stared at each other and both said together; "A fucking wife!" They walked slowly from the door in a state of utter bewilderment and some bitter disappointment. "He had a wife?" Alex repeated, still a little stunned by that revelation and Jackie just sighed loudly; "Now what the hell do we do?" Alex stopped and opened the gate; "I'm not giving him up." Jackie nodded and the pair walked to the corner and stood outside the busy little newsagent shop. "We'll tack him down…." Alex was interrupted by her mirror buzzing in her handbag. Jackie's was now also activated. It was Jericho calling informing them to return; they had a mission in 1860's America. Both sighed and Alex stood hands on hips and said defiantly; "We'll find him Jackie; we do have all the time in the world."

The End

EPISODE 10: "ALEXANDRA AND THE BUFFALO SOLDIERS."

EPISODE PROLOGUE: "In 1864 a small company of African-American soldiers – soon to be known to the Arapahos Indians as 'Buffalo Soldiers' because of their bravery and courage - are trekking through the wilds of South Kansas on the North Oklahoma border, heading for the strange town of 'Devil's Dyke' and come upon a band of Arapahos under war Chief Youngblood. What happened when the two groups meet brings Jericho Tibbs on the scene because the time line is threatened with change. Alex meets some interesting young men who really want to get to know her!"

75 Minutes approx. **Episode Warnings:** Smoking – Alcohol – Strong language [including racial slurs] – Violence [including a knife fight] – Strong graphic sexual references – Mild Horror – References to prostitution and a orgy.

NOTES: This is the **ADULT** version of the original story which is published and appears in the **TEMPORAL DETECTIVES:** Series 4 – Episode 7 entitled: **"YOUNGBLOOD AND THE BUFFALO SOLDIERS."** This is a special **EXTENDED** episode of the original story.

CAUTION: Recommended for **18+ only.**

1. FORT CALEB: KANSAS/OKLAHOMA BORDER MAY 1864.

Captain Dwight Russell slowly folded the letter and nodded at the dust covered messenger; "Thank you corporal, get yourself some food from the canteen and the Sergeant will find you somewhere to bed down. The stables will take care of your horse. But when you're rested I'll need you to ride back to Fort Jackson." The corporal saluted and left as the Company Adjutant stood in the doorway, adjusting his glasses. The captain sighed; "Get me Lt. Graham please Arthur." The Adjutant didn't smile and headed back into the outer office, shouting at old Trooper Byles to fetch the young lieutenant.

Dwight reread the communication from the Fort again and slowly smiled; at last the company was going to see some action in this bloody war. He walked to the big window and stared across the dusty parade ground. Sergeant Mosses Mckay was taking 2nd and 3rd Sections through mounts and dismounts on the wooden horses. It was going well; the men were keen and willing to learn, now that had surprised him about his coloured troops, who were 'C' Company of the 27th Coloured Regiment of the Kansas Volunteers and had been holding the small outpost on the border with the Indian Territory for the last few months. They had relieved the previous company – all white – so they could fight in the Civil war between the states. They were certainly not expected to see any kind of action since the Indian nation had been quiet for a few years, following the unexpected death of their War Chief 'Little Bull' in a bad winter.

There had been rumours about 'Youngblood' who apparently was filling his place and that could mean real trouble; the young brave would have to prove himself before the other braves and would mean fighting the 'white dogs'. Dwight wondered what the Indians would make of the coloured soldiers. Maybe they would call them 'Black dogs'. Either way, the captain knew that trouble was on the horizon. The Arapahos had been resident in Kansas for centuries and they weren't about to give that up.

There was a knock at the door and he shouted enter. Lt. Foster Graham strode in and saluted; he was smiling. The Captain gestured for him to join him at the big map pinned to the office wall. The pair stood discussing the letter and Lt. Graham was clearly happy about being assigned this patrol. "Foster, I want you take sections 2 and 3, a supply wagon and some mules and head out to Devil's Dyke. It's a small town that borders the Indian territory about here." He tapped the map and they both had to stare at the tiny dot that indicated the town. It appeared right in the middle of nowhere. "For some God forsaken reason; Lee has send a small detachment of cavalry to the place. Intelligence doesn't know why and we're the only Union troops for hundreds of miles and so it's landed in our laps. I do suppose they know we're a coloured Regiment. "

The lieutenant grinned and pushed back his hat; "Our boys are spoiling for a fight Sir. No mistake about that." The captain grunted and walked back to his desk; "Take McKay as your sergeant, He's been in action and was a scout for General Reynolds before he re-joined the colours." He hesitated and sighed a little, continuing; "And do listen to his advice Foster; it may stop too many boys being killed." Foster didn't smile and just nodded.

The captain watched the young Lieutenant stride from his office with a little sadness; the boy had arrived just three weeks ago and wasn't – frankly – much use. But Dwight couldn't send the other – and much experienced - Lieutenant; Harvey Banks because he was still laid up with the fever. So it was down to the untested new boy. He sat behind his desk and puzzled over why the Rebel Commander would be interested in a small town, sandwiched between basically nothing and the Indian nation.   He had commanded this area since the sudden death of Colonel Jarvis some months ago. They had found him stone dead in bed. Old Doc Hamilton reckons it was his heart and the heat. The young squaw that normally shared his bed had also disappeared off post. That may have explained the money missing from the late Colonel's wallet: he smiled at that.

He rose and walked back to the map; in his six months here, he hadn't even heard the place mentioned. Shouting and activity from the parade ground drew his attention back to the window and he watched the preparations for the extended patrol to be undertaken by Lt. Graham. That's when the Sergeant Major knocked and brought in the Captain's afternoon coffee; Dwight asked him about Devils Dyke. The old soldier rubbed his chin; "That's odd sir, just a few days ago I was in town and Isaac the saloon owner told me that a wagon had stopped overnight and the young man with it asked about Devil's Dyke. Isaac said he had a young boy with him and a huge Negro servant. But what caught everyone's eyes was the young woman with them; an absolute peach apparently. They purchased some supplies and headed off; didn't really mix with anyone."

The captain sipped his hot black sweet coffee and wondered if that was a co-incidence. He told the sergeant major to let the young Lieutenant know about the story. He looked again at the map; why the hell hadn't he heard about the damn little town before this? He stared at the dot on the map; 'Devil's Dyke' the long abandoned town appeared to be placed in the middle of nothing with just one dirt trail in and out. There was no mines [for gold or silver] no forests [for lumber] and no grassy plains [for cattle] so how the hell did it appear and disappear in just forty odd years and what was it established for?

The patrol left that afternoon; Lt. Graham commanded thirty troopers and a supply wagon with Alphas the old Negro cook and his young assistant; Troy. They were civilians because army cooks were hard to get hold of around here. The patrol was accompanied by two mules loaded down with ammunition and water. At least he had a good sergeant with him; Mosses Mckay knew his way around real fighting. He had fought in the early Indian wars and scouted for the general. He had re-joined the colours in 1861 and had seen action at Fredericksburg and later at Gettysburg. He had been transferred to a frontier post after being wounded at 'Little Round Top' there. Mosses also thought the coloured troops had potential and treated 'his boy's' well. Very firm but fair and they seemed to respect him.

But Lieutenant Graham was a different matter; he used the 'N' word openly to the men and showed them little respect for volunteering to fight for their freedom. He could be a real problem unless seeing action changed his ways. But Captain Russell wondered how many of the 'boy's' would die during that change? Then there was the mysterious wagon; probably whisky and gun peddlers to the Indians. Little wonder they kept themselves to themselves. He wasn't surprised that the town Sheriff – Phil Bates – did nothing about them; he was a fat useless man with a yellow streak. He was only sheriff because he was married to the mayor's ugly sister!

The captain thought about the Confederate cavalry; what possible interest could the derelict small town be to General Robert E. Lee? Now that really did get his mind racing. Could the wagon be heading for a meeting with them for some reason? He finished his coffee and picked up the Post Order's and signed them. He would take a small bottle of decent whisky and visit Harvey in the infirmary: maybe with Doc Davis they could play some cards.

2. JERICHO TIBBS AND THE ARAPAHOS.

The wagon trundled through the dust with Wilson at the reins and Owen sitting next to him. Alex was just behind; sprawled across a pile of colourful blankets; moaning about the heat and being over dressed. Jericho rode a small pony some yards in front, constantly lifting his hat and wiping his face and neck. Owen was consulting his mirror; "In the original human time line, the Battle of Devil's Dyke never took place and then suddenly; there are thirteen unscheduled souls. Something or someone changed this little piece of history and the time line alters badly some 101 years later. Apparently Jericho had an assignment back here in the late 1840's and he knows the local Native American's well. Except, of course he hasn't aged a day: so he's here as his own son!"

Alex stirred and ran a beautiful big fan over her face; "It's hard to imagine our Jericho as an Indian fighter." She stared through the rear flap of the wagon and found herself smiling at the extra member of the team; added just for this mission from Doc Silas Underhill's team 13. 'Skyrise' was a Native American and had helped team 74 previously. He was also mounted on a pony and really did look magnificent to Alex. She wouldn't admit to her colleagues but she found him very attractive; very attractive indeed. [See the episode**: 'Alexandra: An angel of mercy?'**]

Jericho turned his pony about and joined the wagon – as did Skyrise – and they stopped. "Several Indians skirting the ridge on ponies; they will make contact because we're on their lands now." He gestured to the stick tied against the side of the wagon; it was an Arapahos signal meaning peace and friendship; he had acquired it from his old friend 'Little Bull' many years ago. "They will certainly be curious about that and wish to find out how we obtained it. I hope it still works." He smiled and wiped his face again. Alex leaned forward, a little concerned; "Will Skyrise be OK? I mean he's Apache; aren't they enemies or something?" Jericho smiled again; "He'll be fine; the Indians are now fighting a common enemy; white people." Everyone watched carefully as the group of warriors approached slowly and Jericho noted that only two had rifles; the rest were armed with spears and had bows strapped across their backs. "Gun runners must be in short supply around here." He said quietly and held up his right hand. He greeted the natives in their own tongue, which made them stop and stare.

Youngblood rode forward and stared at Jericho really hard; then the sign hanging from the pole. "How did you come by this white stranger and how do you speak our tongue?" he said simply with no emotion or curiosity in his voice. Jericho nodded and gestured to himself; "Jericho Tibbs, son of Jericho Tibbs the father. Big Chief Little Bull and he had friendship pact and I have come to pay my respects to great chief and tell him that my father has passed into the land of the spirits. I bring gifts for my father's friend and his people." Youngblood sat up in his saddle and really did look surprised now. "You are son of Tibbs?" Jericho nodded and asked if he was Youngblood; the old chief's nephew .

Youngblood and the other braves all looked at each other; Tibbs – this man's father – had saved Little Bull from certain death and carried him on his back through the desert to his village. He had been made a friend of the tribe and good friend of the old Chief. Youngblood nodded and indicated beyond the ridge; "The camp lays by the river Tibbs. You do indeed look like your father. I was only a small boy, but I remember your father and what he did." He indicated for the wagon to follow him and the warriors turned their ponies and headed back towards the ridge with the wagon following.

Jericho could have won an Oscar for his performance when Youngblood told him that the old chief had died. He knew the chief had – of course – but played the sadness of the declaration well. He had liked the old chief and so that part wasn't hard to fake. They made the encampment just before dusk and Jericho realised that it was a warrior's camp. There were no women or children about the place. That fact alone made him curious; what were Young blood and about thirty braves doing so far away from their villages? The conclusion wasn't pleasant; they had to be a raiding party. But who were they raiding? There were few settlements or farmers around here and the nearest town was Devil's Dyke and that had been abandoned years ago. Jericho knew that Union troops were headed for the old town because of the approaching Rebel Calvary. None of this was in the original time line and that's why Team 74 was there and of course; the thirteen unscheduled deaths that should never have taken place here and now.

Jericho cautioned Alex to stay close to the wagon and him. A beautiful white woman would be considered fair game to the warriors who would easily fight over her. He told the team to pretend not to understand the language; that would be nearly impossible to explain and would raise too many awkward questions. It was accepted that Skyrise would know some of the language and indeed three of the braves could speak some Apache. Jericho was a little surprised that the Arapahos accepted him readily into their camp and that did concern him too.

Only Jericho was invited to sit by the big fire with Youngblood and his senior warriors. Owen brewed coffee and cooked beans for supper with some cold ham and biscuits. Wilson was the centre of attraction to the braves – after Alex of course! – They had never seen a black man before and appeared fascinated by him. Some asked to touch his face and arms to see if the 'black' came off. Youngblood impressed Jericho by asking him to keep Alex away from the men; he didn't want to lose a single warrior fighting over a woman. Not even one that beautiful. He confided to Jericho that Chief Little Raven would pay at least 20 ponies for such a woman and most of his braves knew that.

Youngblood knew that the whites were after land and even the poor land they occupied would be taken; eventually. He passed Jericho some 'prairie chicken' and lamented his lack of modern weapons; he needed rifles and pistols that shot more than just one bullet. But his land produced very little gold and gold was what the white gun traders only wanted. He shrugged his shoulders; "Much has changed since the time of your father and a young Little Bull my friend; except the lies, stealing and killing by the whites." Jericho could only nod and enjoy his meal and then re-join his team by the wagon. The Indians sat around their camp fires and sang mournful songs about the glories of their past.

The team sat around their fire and quietly talked amongst themselves. Owen reminded everyone about the events which would unfold around this time and place come autumn; "The Arapaho and the Cheyenne join together to fight the whites and it all ends up with the Sand Creek Massacre in November of this year. A Union force killed hundreds of Indians including a lot of women and children who were camped and peaceful. A real dark day for humanity."

After supper they bedded down for the night; Alex slept in the wagon, with Owen and Wilson beneath in their blankets while Skyrise found his own place to sleep. Jericho made himself comfortable on the wagons seat and discretely consulted his mirror. Their peaceful night was interrupted by the arrival of a single stranger with a pack mule. The team recognised him at once; it was Sage Columbine and he clearly recognised them; but made no reference to their previous encounter which Jericho found strange and disturbing. [See the episode; **'Alexandra's midnight(s) at Gettysburg.'**]

The Arapahos also knew him and he made his camp away from the wagon and the Indian encampment, sitting around a small fire, smoking a cigar and swigging from a hipflask. He clearly felt safe amongst the Indians and Jericho wondered what his actual involvement with the Arapahos was.

Jericho joined Wilson and Owen and they discussed the arrival of Sage; they knew he had been a scout for the Confederate Army at Gettysburg and Jericho believed he must be involved with the Confederate Calvary troop that was heading this way. "He's dangerous and we know he's from 1925, so he would clearly know what should happen here. Is he trying to change the fate of someone alive now? Or maybe the fate of the Indians, but whatever he's up too, we need to find out and make sure nothing changes."

They were joined by Skyrise and Jericho gave him some specific instructions which he was more than happy to follow. Everyone settled back down for the night. Well except Alex.

3. SKYRISE AND ALEX.

Alex found where Skyrise had made his camp - in a small crevice - and handed him a plate of dinner as he squatted down making his bed from a blanket and his saddle bag. He took it and smiled with nothing being said. The pair stared at each other for a minute or two before Alex whispered; "I want you to take me like you would a squaw you've just been given to fuck." Skyrise carefully put the plate down and just nodded. He walked over and said softly; "A squaw wouldn't wear a tent to cover her beauty; strip naked - now." Alex nodded and it took a minute or so to get the dress she hated off. She had already removed her bloomers and corset. She whispered; "I best keep on the boots; it would take ages to get them off." Skyrise nodded and simply pulled off his calf skin breeches and Alex really did smile; the Apache was a big man in all respects.

The pair lay together on the blanket and Skyrise ran his hands over her body. "I'll fuck you like a squaw, and I won't be gentle about it. Is that what you want?" Alex nodded and lay on her back with real anticipation. Skyrise fumbled in his saddle bag and to Alex's real surprise produced a short wooden stick which he carefully pushed into her mouth, saying softly; "To bite off the screams. Sounds travel in the desert at night." Alex nodded and held the smooth stick between her teeth, watching as Skyrise's head disappeared between her open legs and his mouth found her already wet vagina. Alex rolled her eyes and cussed - as best she could - with the stick in her mouth. Skyrise's lips and tongue certainly knew their way around a fanny, and he quickly found her clitoris and set to work. Alex gripped her big heaving tits with both hands and fondled them, groaning and moaning as Skyrise worked his Apache magic on her.

She had a couple of small, but intense, orgasms as he buried his tongue deep in her and his fingers worked her clitoris with great skill. He pulled himself up and gripped his big cock; "I'm now going to fuck you hard. Yes?" Alex nodded vigorously and he smiled as he pushed his big cock into her soaking wet vagina. Well, Alex certainly found out how Apache's fucked their women; hard, rough and without mercy. She compared his fucking to a great ship's piston; he simply hammered her, thrusting hard, deep and fast. He didn't stop and soon Alex was thankful for the damn stick otherwise she would be screaming so loud she could be heard in Washington. The only respite she received was when he roughly pulled from her and made her kneel on all fours and remounted her like a stallion would a mare. He gripped her big tits and squeezed so hard that she almost spat the stick out. He was pumping her so hard that her head and shoulders were on the blanket, and she was grabbing handfuls of it. His hands were now on her shoulders, keeping her head down and her arse up in the air.

Skyrise rammed her so hard that she had an enormous orgasm

that started in her chest, ran down to her stomach and exploded from her stuffed fanny like a soda syphon squirting. If she didn't have the stick in her mouth, Alex would have screamed so loud that if noise was light; the prairie would have lit up like Blackpool Tower. She was being fucked so hard and roughly that she cried with real sobs and buried her face in the blanket. Her tears didn't stop Skyrise and he continued to fuck her for some minutes and Alex had another explosion between her legs and she almost fainted. Then she felt him cum; it was like someone had shoved a garden hose up her snatch and turned it on full. Her eyes rolled and she gasped for breath; finally spitting out the damn stick. The pair collapsed on the blanket - still locked together - and lay breathing deeply in silence.

It was a good couple of minutes before Alex managed to gasp; "For fuck sake you fucked me like a dog-whore you bastard!" and wiped her tearful face. Skyrise – smiling - just chuckled and softy whispered; "Just like you asked for and really wanted. If you were my squaw you would have to get use to that. You would obey me and be submissive to everything I say and love it. Now clean my cock with your mouth while I eat my dinner." He pulled from her and picked up the now cold plate of stew and began to eat with his fingers. Alex crawled down to his cock and cleaned it with her tongue, calling him a bastard again. He patted her bobbing head and between mouthfuls of stew muttered; "Now if you really were my squaw, I would make you suck until I was erect and I would fuck you again. But I think you need to rest, not being used to a real man having you." Alex sat back, wiping her mouth and nodded slowly but he had satisfied her like no man had done so in a long time. She slowly gathered her clothes up and dressed quietly as he finished his late supper and pulled on his breeches.

"Goodnight Alex. I know you will want to please me again so until then goodnight." Skyrise settled down to sleep and Alex walked slowly back to the wagon, she could feel his cum running down her thighs and really smiled.

4. JOHN NORTON – CORPORAL: 'C' COMPANY of the 27th COLOURED REGIMENT of the KANSAS VOLUNTEERS.

Alex noticed immediately that Skyrise had gone and that Sage Columbine had also left early; both before sunrise. She handed Jericho a hot cup of coffee and he smiled; "Skyrise is back doing what he loves; tracking. He'll follow Sage discretely and report on his movements. We need to know what he's up too and Skyrise can shadow him and keep us informed." Wilson accepted a cup and smiled too; "He [Skyrise] couldn't wait to brush up on his tracking skills and I hope he's good at it because two Arapaho braves left with Sage. I know because I counted them yesterday and there were thirty; this morning there's only twenty eight." Jericho nodded; "There is something going on because Owen overheard two braves at the well filling their water sacks. They obviously thought he wouldn't understand Arapaho and they know all about Sage and the 'white dogs in grey'. That must mean the Confederate Calvary." He finished his coffee and gestured to the wagon; "Come on people, we're heading for the ghost town of Devil's Dyke this morning and should get there by tomorrow afternoon."

Owen and Wilson walked the horses to the wagon's yoke and soon the team was heading south; the warriors in single file some distance in front. The day was hot and humid and Alex swore she was melting in her dress and wasn't comfortable. "A pair of shorts and a t-shirt would be better." She moaned to Owen who handed her his water bottle. "You dressed up like that would cause quite a stir amongst the Indians; they probably have never seen a white woman dressed like a squaw." Alex just shrugged; "It would be better than bleeding melting!" She had pulled open her blouse and was removing the tight bodice, allowing her magnificent breasts freedom. She could now breathe without struggling; "Bloody men oppressing woman." She added, making Wilson and Owen chuckle.

Corporal John Norton wiped his face several times and replaced his hat, staring at the barren horizon. His companion – Isaiah Smith – slumped in the saddle and cussed; "Why the fuck did whitely pick us for point duty? I wouldn't know a fucking red man if one stole my fucking horse from under me!" John smiled; "Don't let the lieutenant hear you call him whitey; he'll have you digging latrines again." Isaiah just grunted and followed John towards the small ridge. "Does this fucking town have a saloon that serves us black boys?" He asked for the third time and John sighed; "No, like I told you, McKay says the bloody place was abandoned years ago. There ain't no beer or a cat house; just bloody ghosts and dust." Isaiah groaned loudly and wiped his face. "No beer or women? What the fuck do those Southern white boys want with a dump like that?" John chuckled; "If I knew that, we could all have stayed at the Fort and I would have been promoted to sergeant!" They rode for several minutes and made the ridge; both dismounted and John left Isaiah holding the horses. He climbed the ridge quickly and lay staring out at the shimmering horizon. There was nothing and he wiped sweat from his eyes several times and gripped his rifle. He was about to start the climb back to his friend when something caught his eye. Covering them with a hand, he stared really hard and slowly smiled, then quickly descended and ran back to his companion. "Single horseman with a pack mule and his headed south east; towards the old town I would guess." Isaiah finally smiled; "Does that mean we can join the fucking column again?" John nodded; "I think the lieutenant will be very interested in this and McKay will have a good idea what's going on; he knows the meaning of stuff like this." They both mounted and turned east, back towards the column and straight into the Arapaho scouting party.

Rain Cloud stared at the two black troopers and they stared back at the braves. Isaiah was struggling to get his carbine from its holster hanging at his side. John slowly pushed his hand away and said quietly; "Keep calm. I don't think they've ever seen a black man before." He held up his hand and smiled slowly, introducing himself and Isaiah who was physically shaking in his saddle. The five braves all exchanged glances and Rain Cloud rode forward – spear at the ready – and shouted at the pair [in Arapaho of course] making John shake his head and gesture that he didn't understand. Rain Cloud patted his pony and sent Dog Face back to Youngblood; TIbbs would understand what the black men were saying.

Sage lay on the ridge top and lowered his little brass telescope and cussed a couple of times; if there were two Union troopers way out here from Fort Caleb; then there must be others. Probably a couple of dozen under a white officer or experienced sergeant and he guessed that they could only be heading for Devil's Dyke. He cussed again; someone had betrayed them, it was too much of a co-incidence otherwise. He lay on his back and stared at the clear blue sky; now what? He struggled to his feet and quickly climbed down and remounted his horse. He examined the horizon behind him and wondered where that damn Apache of Tibb's was. Still, he would deal with him later; he needed to get to Devil's Dyke.

Youngblood stood arms folded and listened to Jericho without any expression. John and Isaiah were squatting in the dirt; arms tied behind their backs and two Indian spears at their heaving chests. Their horses had been stripped of their saddles and lead away by a young brave. The horses had value to the Indians; but they didn't use saddles. The trooper's carbines were now the prizes of Rain Cloud and Dog Face who swore that they would treat them better than their squaws. That didn't please Alex who grabbed a water bottle and took it over to John and Isaiah; the braves didn't stop her; it was the white's water after all.

John asked nervously about what was happening. Alex didn't smile; "Jericho is trying to convince Youngblood not to stake you out over an ant hill. He's explaining that you are slave soldiers who are made to fight by the white dogs who own you. You better pray that he's making a good case." That's when Isaiah spotted Wilson and called out to him for help. Wilson just raised his hands in a hopeless gesture and shrugged his shoulders; he couldn't do anything to help.

Owen joined Jericho as Youngblood stood talking quietly with his senior braves about the fate of the black men. Owen whispered into his ear about what he had discovered about the two troopers from Human Records. "The one called Isaiah Smith is of no real importance to the Human Time Line; he's killed in a couple of years in Kansas City over an unpaid gambling debt. The line would change little if he's dispatched early. But John Norton is a different matter entirely." The pair walked a little further back and were joined by Alex and Wilson who was particularly concerned about the fate of the two 'brothers'. He would find it hard to watch the pair murdered and just stand by, doing nothing. Owen continued; "John Norton – a former slave – is really important to the current Human Time Line and if he doesn't survive and marry Lilly Washington then the line changes a hundred years from now. You see, John is the Maternal Great Grandfather of el-Hajj Malik el-Shabazz; a very important figure in the Civil Rights movement of the early 1960's."

Wilson rubbed his chin; "I've never heard of him." Owen smiled; "He was better known as Malcolm X big brother and if he doesn't get born, then things change and not for the better apparently." Wilson now nodded and whispered; "Shit! That's a major problem baby brother – a real major problem." Jericho slapped Owen on the back and smiled; "Excellent research Owen; as usual. Here comes Youngblood."

Youngblood didn't smile; "The black soldiers are fighting for their freedom like we are. But they wear the colours of the dogs that kill braves, women and children. So if they want freedom they must fight for it; to the death. That is our decision; if they win they go and are free. If they die, then it was their fate never to be free." Jericho nodded and took a deep breath; "Wilson you better tell the pair they are about to fight to the death. Make sure they know that they must kill their opponent otherwise the other braves will kill them for their weakness." Wilson sighed and walked over to the pair and explained quietly. Owen anxiously whispered to Jericho; "We can't let John Norton die Jericho!"

Jericho nodded, grim faced; "We'll cross that bridge when we come to it."

Two braves were picked and stripped everything off; keeping only a knife. Wilson told John and Isaiah to do the same and Youngblood gave both a knife; throwing them into the dirt at their feet. John pulled off his tunic and spat on his hands slowly picking up the knife; he had been in the Indian lands long enough to know the score here. But Isaiah was having none of it and screamed in fear and panic; he ran for the wagon and a brave simply shot an arrow through his back. Alex actually hid her face as another brave jumped on the screaming man and slit his throat in one swift movement. Only the Team saw 'Little Rajiv' the Collector appear and walk the confused soul towards the light. Everyone's attention turned to John and the brave; Big Bear. They were circling each other knives at the ready. Alex forced herself to watch and gripped Wilson's arm tightly who muttered; "Come on brother, you know you have to kill him; just fucking get it done!" Alex just hung her head – a little ashamed – at what was happening. All she could think of was Ancient Rome and the gladiatorial contests. Now she was witnessing one for real and close up. It made her feel a little sick.

Big Bear shouted in Arapaho and kicked dirt at John who jumped to one side and swapped the knife to his right hand. Jericho almost smiled at that; John was clearly left handed but would the brave fall for that. The two came together and rolled about in the dirt grunting and shouting at each other. Big Bear drew first blood cutting John across the chest, but it wasn't deep enough and John rolled from under him and staggered back. Big Bear leapt on him and caught his shoulder with the blade and blood ran out but didn't spurt; again it wasn't deep enough to inflect real damage. John and Big Bear rolled in the dirt again; Jericho noticed with a little smile that the knife was now in John's left hand. Then a sickening scream filled the air and the Indian staggered to his feet, clutching his belly. John certainly had gone deep enough with his knife. "You have to fucking kill him!" Wilson shouted with real emotion.

John jumped to his feet and crashed down on the brave and drove his knife through the screaming man's throat. There was no sound after that. John rose to his feet and stared at the now quiet braves; he threw the knife down and staggered a few feet then sat down. Alex grabbed her 'Gladstone bag' from the wagon and rushed over; she skilfully attended his wounds while the braves quietly carried off the body of their fallen comrade. Youngblood nodded and turned to Jericho; "He has won his freedom Tibbs. He can travel with you without fear as a warrior should."

Youngblood walked away to oversee the burial of Big Bear. Wilson and Owen would bury Isaiah Smith whilst Alex and Jericho helped the shocked – and relieved – John Norton to the wagon. "He'll need stitches but they are not dangerous. Infection could be the only worry, in this heat the wounds could suppurate." Jericho handed John a water bottle; "Keep him in the wagon in the shade. There's a bottle of brandy in my satchel; you may need that." John managed a smile; "I think I need it more than her." That made Jericho and Alex chuckle.

John swallowed down plenty of water and stared through the wagon flap at Owen and Wilson digging. "All he ever wanted was women, beer and poker. Not too much to ask was it." He murmured and drank more water. Alex smiled; "This may hurt, I have to sew you up and I can't give you anything for the pain John." He just smiled; "Be my guest pretty lady, to me you are an angel of mercy." He winced as she threaded a big needle after dosing it in brandy. "You may not think that when I've finished." She said quietly and set about stitching him up. He just chuckled and took a swig from Jericho's brandy bottle.

Jericho had to ask; "Where did you learn to fight like that John?" The big man didn't smile; "Being a slave taught you many things Mister Tibbs; some of them not very pleasant." Then he stared out the tent flap at the burial of Isaiah and sighed. "My master had a great fascination and love of Ancient Rome. Once a month he organised games for his friends; if you won you were given beer and a woman. Nothing has changed much." He gestured to the brandy bottle and Alex and then smiled a little. "See what I mean." Jericho just nodded and dropped from the wagon; Youngblood had returned and told him that they were moving out. The wagon could follow at its own pace and the braves mounted up and departed in small cloud of dust. Owen and Wilson returned – shovels slung over their shoulders – and grabbed the water bottle from Alex who had finished stitching up John Norton. Jericho was reading his mirror and called the others over; "Skyrise tells us the Sage Columbine is definitely heading for the old ghost town and he asks what happened to the Buffalo soldiers." Alex sat on the wagon step, wiping her hands; "What the hell is a buffalo soldier?" Wilson smiled and jerked a thumb towards John Norton resting in the shade of the wagon; "He is."

5. ALEX LOOKS AFTER JOHN.....

That evening Alex found herself alone with John in the wagon. Everyone else was at the Indian encampment and the pair sat talking. John was interested in how Alex knew so much about wounds and she explained that both her father and brother were surgeons and she had watched their work real closely. John smiled and admitted he was glad - and impressed - that she had paid such close attention. They chatted and he laughed about his two friends at the fort; old Alphas the cook and young Troy who was desperate for a woman. He smiled; "Alphas is the best equipped cook in the US Calvary and he really can knock up some great grub. Young Troy is a good lad but shy around women. He needs a good and generous woman to look after him properly the first time."

They sat in silence for a few minutes, then Alex leaned over him to check his bandages; smiling. John grunted and took hold of her chin and gently pulled her mouth to his and they kissed, slowly and gently, then with some passion. Kissing John, Alex tugged down his trousers and found an adequate erected cock. "I best go on top. I don't want you to exert yourself too much and open your wounds." she whispered gripping his cock. He nodded and fumbled under her dress and petticoats and was delighted to find that she had already removed her long panties. His hand soon found her fanny as was further delighted to find it wet and ready. But Alex's mouth was now on his cock, caressing and licking. He really groaned with pleasure as she sucked and gently jerked his cock with some skill.

Alex - holding her dress and petticoats up - squatted over him and lowered herself down, guiding his twitching cock into her willing fanny. She rode him like a Grand National winner and John loved it; groaning and gasping with pleasure as she bounced up and down. She leaned over him and they gripped hands, John tried to thrust upwards and Alex admonished him between gritted teeth to keep still; she didn't want to have re-stich his bloody wounds! She would do the fucking and he agreed with a big smile; groaning and cussing a little. he pulled open her blouse and was surprised to find no corset and overjoyed as her big breasts spilled into his eager hands. He pulled her down by them and his mouth went to work; sucking, licking and squeezing them. He particularly enjoyed her big nipples which were hard and delicious.

Alex was moving up and down and back and forth with some energy as John enjoyed her big soft tits. She had a couple of small orgasms which trickled down her thighs and she groaned a little. John suddenly cussed quite loudly and Alex felt his seed spurt into her but she continued to ride him for a few more minutes before his flaccid cock slipped from her wet vagina. She slowly climbed off him and took hold of it and sucked hard, licking and cleaning. John gasped and ran a hand over her hair and face. He lay back and breathed deep as Alex attempted to get him hard again. For all her skill, his cock didn't respond and so she gave up and the pair sat talking quietly. John asked her if she would be 'as generous' to young Troy and Alex agreed [believing it wouldn't happen] as she wiped her thighs and fanny with a damp cloth. John admitted his only regret was not seeing her naked! She then jumped from the wagon to find a place to pee.

She found a small crevice by some rocks and squatted down with her dress and petticoats pulled up. She groaned with relief as she pissed hard into the dirt. Then she looked up and saw the young brave standing watching her. In the moonlight he looked like the statue of King David; the young man was all taunt muscles and could easily have been mistaken for a body builder in more modern times. She couldn't stop and so just smiled at him. He thrust his spear into the dirt and walked slowly towards her;

pulling off his loincloth. Alex just stared at the size of his manhood as it swung from side to side; growing bigger and stiffer with each soft step he took. "Oh fuck." was all she whispered and slowly stood as he reached her and without a word, started to push her gently to the ground. Her legs kicked a little as he mounted her in the Missionary position. He certainly wasn't gentle and didn't attempt to kiss her.

She gripped the dirt with both hands as he fucked her hard and fast, pushing up her legs and gripping the ankles. He simply didn't stop and Alex felt each hard, deep thrust. She groaned and gasped as he fucked her roughly, then pulled from her and turned her over onto all fours. The young brave pushed his cock back in and continued to fuck her hard; thrusting deep, hard and fast. His hands holding down her shoulders as he fucked her like a dog in heat. Alex felt her stomach tighten and her legs were shaking as the big orgasm exploded from her fanny, running down her thighs and dripping into the dirt. She could hear the young brave laugh softly as he gripped her waist and drove his cock into her. Alex was breathing deeply and cussing as the hard fucking continued for some minutes. Finally the young man groaned a little and she felt every drop of his cum as it poured into her. He stayed in her for a couple of minutes breathing deep and then pulled his cock from her and she collapsed into the dirt. He wiped his cock on her soft petticoats and stood. He smiled at her as she lay in the dirt panting and gasping. He walked away, snatching up his discarded loin cloth and spear; disappearing into the dark gloom of the night.

Alex sat and wiped her fanny and thighs with her petticoats, breathing deeply. She cussed the young brave for not fucking her some more! Finally she slowly walked back to the wagon and climbed in to find John sleeping soundly. She sat and sipped brandy from Owens's hip-flask and slowly smiled, thinking that Apache's and Arapaho's certainly knew how to treat women like her. Their bloody squaws must walk around with big smiles on their faces!

6. THE CONFEDERACY NEEDS GOLD.

Captain Jerome Sommerville halted the small column and wiped his face and neck before pulling out his small brass telescope and scanning the bare horizon. He turned to Master Sergeant Amos Yallu and lowered his telescope, gesturing towards the sole blackened and dead tree that dominated the horizon because it was the only thing standing there. "That's the rendezvous point Sergeant. The lightening tree is where we meet Sage and he'll guide us the rest of the way." The sergeant spat with some relish; he loved chewing tobacco. "Can what he say be trusted captain?" Jerome sighed and wiped his face again; pushing the telescope into his small sack that hung from his saddle. "Well, I don't know Sergeant, but old Granny Lee can't afford not to check the story out. We need money and fast; Spanish Gold will buy a lot of supplies that we need. A damn lot of stuff that we must have to win this damn war, so we must check it out."

The sergeant eased in the saddle and stared at the old burnt tree and spat again. "Is it true that the nearest Yankee troops are all useless, cowardly n****rs?" The captain threw a sideways glance at his sergeant and nodded; "A black man with a rifle can kill you just as good as a white one." The sergeant missed the sarcasm in his voice. Captain Jerome was a Confederate Officer who hated slavery, but loved his State; Virginia and he didn't want his home state bullied by some damn Northerners who wanted to dictate what they could do and say. He believed that the evils of slavery would die of "natural causes" over time. But the war was here and now and he had rushed to defend his home state from invasion and occupation. Before the war he was a Lawyer with a modest practice in Richmond; that made him think of Julia and Katherine; his wife and infant daughter.

He patted his mounts neck and gestured the column forward. "We'll camp by the tree and if this Sage fellow doesn't appear by noon tomorrow; we'll head home." Now that did make the old sergeant smile; he was gasping for a beer and a proper bed to sleep in. The little column headed up the gentle slope and Jerome watched carefully as two riders appeared; both waving a hat in the air. His scouts were signalling that it was clear ahead. He looked back at his command; twenty troopers, a supply wagon and two mules. He actually chuckled as he thought about what Julia would say about his ragged little command. She had pleaded with him not to go; but she knew that he must and like thousands of other men; he had joined the colours to defend his state. Most had never owned a slave in their lives and really didn't care about slavery; that was for the rich folks. But they cared enough for their state and their 'rights' to fight and die for them; something old Lincoln couldn't quite get his head around. With the pickets posted Jerome sat on his ground sheet and studied the two pages of his written order – direct from general

Jim Longstreet himself – and shook his head; a little in disbelief. He had been ordered to check out the story that a certain scout had imparted to old granny Lee [General Robert E. Lee] about a large amount of buried Spanish Gold Coins in or near the ghost town of Devil's Dyke. The scout had produced a small bag of old coins – all Spanish Gold Doubloons – as an example of what was buried there. Just that little bag would buy rifles and ammunition for half a Regiment; and they did. General Lee had no choice but to check the story out. Hence Jerome was sitting deep in enemy [and Indian] territory. He sighed deeply and took a swig from his canteen and watched the rations being handed around by large Corporal Swiggers. They were on cold rations for now; a fire could be seen for miles around these flat bare plains and would bring either hostile Indians or federal troops down on them. He replaced his canteen and pulled the last letter he had received from Julia out and re-read it with some pleasure.

Night had now fallen and the moon was full and clear. Everyone was wrapped in their blankets and cussing; most would happily shoot someone just for a cup of hot coffee; the days were hot and uncomfortable and the nights cold, but dry. The troops smoked their pipes and cigarettes under their blankets; any light could be seen for miles at night here.

The captain was dozing under his hat and blanket when Sergeant Amos woke him with a couple of pushes and whispered; "That man sage is here captain." Jerome rolled from the blanket and jumped to his feet, adjusting his hat. Sage stood arms folded in the moonlight and Jerome looked the big man up and down; Sage looked exactly how General Longstreet had described him. He walked over and the pair shook hands.

The two men squatted down and spoke quietly with the sergeant standing a few yards behind. Sage told him about the coloured troops and where they were; just a couple of days ride away. He told the captain about the band of Arapaho's under their war chief Youngblood who were even closer; maybe a day's ride away. Sage mentioned Tibbs and his small party; saying they could be gun or whisky peddlers. But they were definitely heading for Devil's Dyke as well. He chuckled as he spoke quietly about the Apache that had trailed him so skillfully. "Now he's the real mystery here captain; the Arapaho's are allowing an Apache to cross their land without killing him. "

The captain nodded and the pair agreed to reach Devil's Dyke by nightfall tomorrow which would mean hard riding with only fifteen minute intervals to rest the mounts. The men could smoke and eat on horseback if necessary. A plan of action agreed; the pair separated and Sage found himself a snug crop of rocks to settle down behind. He watched the Confederate soldiers settling back down for the night. He rubbed his chin and pulled his blanket around his big shoulders; he was concerned - really concerned - about Captain Sommerville; he had not once asked about the gold! Sage checked his pistol and slept lightly with it close to his chest. The captain's apparent lack of interest in the gold worried him until he fell asleep. He did smile about the two braves going after the damn apache that could wreck everything: he hoped they would be successful.

John Norton finished off the last of his beans and bread with a long swig of the water canteen and watched through the canvas flap of the wagon as the dry barren plains passed behind him. He gently touched his bandaged chest and nodded; that woman knew her stuff. John thought again about young Isaiah and shook his head with sadness. Young Owen leaned back from the driver's board and shouted if he needed anything. John raised a hand shook his head again. "No thanks Owen, I'm doing just fine back here." Owen grinned and returned to face front. Alex leaned across him and reminded John to shout for her if any signs of blood appeared around the bandages. He again nodded and thanked her again. She just smiled and turned back to speak with Owen.

Jericho and Wilson were riding with Youngblood in silence. Indians didn't make small talk and Jericho was quite happy about that and wondered how Skyrise was getting on. That's when Youngblood dropped the bombshell that put a smile on Jericho's face. He slowly gestured to some thick brush that was growing up the walls of the ridge they were by passing to reach Devil's Dyke. "That's where we go; it will take a day off our journey. The little gap cuts through the ridge and so, we don't have to go all around." He held up a hand and signalled for the group to head for the dark and deep brush. "Will the wagon fit?" Jericho asked and Youngblood nodded.

Jericho threw a glance at Wilson and the pair smiled. They both wondered if Sage knew about the short cut. Wilson turned his horse saying; "I'll tell Owen and Alex." and rode to the rear of the slow moving group. A thoughtful Jericho finally asked the quiet Youngblood if he knew anything about what happened for the settlers to abandon the town. Youngblood shrugged his shoulders and didn't smile; "The whites all moved away many moons ago; they all left for somewhere better except for the dead man who walks their resting grounds." Jericho stared at him and realised he could mean a ghost!

When asked to elaborate about the 'dead walking man walking the resting grounds' Youngblood just shrugged his shoulders again; "The spirit walks the place where he should rest and is a fearsome spirit who can move things and is filled with much anger." Jericho sat back in the saddle and whispered; "A bloody poltergeist!" he rubbed his chin and thought they may have to call a Guardian for such an aggrieved soul; if it won't go with any collector they may call.

Two braves rode ahead and started to pull the brush back and sure enough; there was a gap in the ridge. The convoy passed into the ravine and the wagon did fit; but only just. Jericho was a little amazed at Owens's skill in handling the wagon and horses. As they appeared from the small ravine onto an open plain, Alex slapped Owens's shoulder and praised him. John slept soundly in the back and didn't even know they had passed through the tight gap until told by Alex when she checked his bandages. They would reach the deserted town by the afternoon. But they weren't the only ones to reach the town before the soldiers. Jericho and Wilson joined Rain Cloud and Youngblood as they went ahead to scout the town. That's when they saw the smoke rising from what would have been the saloon. Someone had a fire burning in the derelict saloon! As they slowly rode down the main street, they saw a horse and pack mule tied up outside the saloon called the "Golden Nugget". Jericho quietly advised Youngblood that he should make contact first; some white folks had an itchy trigger finger around Indians. Youngblood just nodded his agreement and Jericho and Wilson dismounted and shouting out that they were coming in; headed into the saloon. They carefully stepped over the broken wooden swing doors and walked in.

The little man was sitting at a dusty table; his boots slapped upon it and gently rocking a little in the chair. He pushed back his hat to reveal a full white beard and deep dark eyes. He made no effort to pick up the colt pistol laid upon the table next to his boots. He almost smiled and ran a hand through his long beard; "Howdy strangers; what brings you strange pair to Devil's Dyke on this fine warm day?" he had a strange accent which neither Wilson nor Jericho could identify.

Jericho raised his hat to him and said they were passing through with some Indians that they were friendly with. The little man dropped his boots from the table and scratched his beard; "Local Arapaho's or that damn Apache that's been creeping about these parts?" Jericho and Wilson exchanged a glance thinking; how the hell did he know about Skyrise? The little man really chuckled when Youngblood and Rain Cloud walked in. "That answers that my friends." He raised a hand to Youngblood and in Arapaho asked who the strange white man was and what was he doing here with his servant. Youngblood actually smiled and gestured to Jericho; saying he was son of good friend to Arapaho's old chief Little Bull.

The little man eased himself the wobbly chair and stared hard at Jericho, then slapped his thigh and laughed; "Sweet Jesus and mother Mary! He's a dead ringer for his pa!" He walked over and shook Jericho by the hand and slapped his shoulder; "Me and your pa had some good times before the damn war. Did you bring me what the bastard owed me from back then?" Jericho shrugged his shoulders and said he didn't understand what he was saying. But Jericho had recongnised Walter Carlton, though he had aged badly from their last meeting almost twenty five years ago!

Walter had been running guns, whisky and whores to both settlers and the Indians and Chief Little Bull didn't like his braves getting drunk and knocking their wives and children about. He would have taken Walter and buried him in the desert with just his head showing, but Jericho talked him [the Chief] out of that and Walter ended up fleeing the Indian village in nothing but his long-johns after Jericho cheated him out of all his belongings paying bent poker when Walter was drunk! Jericho was a little surprised that Walter had not only managed to survive with nothing, but ended up continuing his 'career' with a new wagon, more guns, fresh whisky barrels but the same tired old whores.

It appears Walter wanted restoration and compensation for what Jericho's 'father' had done to him. The old man shook his head and grunted; "Well, let's have a drink and discuss this." He muttered quietly and picked up his big canvas bag from the floor. "I got a good bottle of sipping whisky in here my friends." Jericho turned to Wilson and whispered; "I've never met him before!" and shrugged his shoulders again. The old man produced some 'frontier' whisky and slapped the bottle on the table. He walked slowly over to the bar and pulled up a handful of whisky glasses and handed them around. Wilson wiped the dusty glass on his shirt and the old man filled the glasses; still chuckling to himself. He raised his glass and said; "Here's to old friendships and debts that have to be paid." He knocked the whisky back in one hit; coughed violently and re-filled his glass. He clutched his glass with both hands and spoke quietly; "Well, young Tibbs, in payment of your pappy's debt to me I'll take the Negro servant and sell him. I will also take your wagon and horses' and sell them too. You can keep the dumb looking boy and Youngblood can have the beauty to sell for plenty of ponies' and rifles. I think that's fair aren't all round don't you think Youngblood?"

Jericho lowered his glass and shook his head; "I don't think so old man…." He didn't finish because Youngblood's spear was at his throat. "I think that satisfactory deal Tibbs. We get rifles and horse's and you stay alive." Rain Cloud was already shouting out the door for the braves to grab the wagon and horses and the white woman; but not harm her. She would fetch many rifles and horses. The old man now had his pistol on the pair and he slowly grinned; "Youngblood and me have a sort of agreement. I supply what he needs and he gives me what I want."

Jericho just stared at Youngblood who finally smiled; "The man who owed you his life is dead. I owe you nothing and we need rifles and horses to kill more of you whites. You understand that my no longer friend?" Jericho just nodded slowly.

Rain Cloud returned angry and shouting; the white woman, the boy and the black soldier had gone from the wagon without anyone seeing them. The old man cursed loudly and told Youngblood to search for her; they could do what they like with the black and the boy. Rain Cloud disappeared back out the door; shouting orders.

Wilson and Jericho managed to refrain from smiling as they were tied to chairs by the bar. The old man sat at the table and re-filled his glass; he wasn't a happy soul. Finally he shouted at Jericho; "What the fuck are all these soldiers heading here for?"

He finished his whisky and poured another one. He repeated his question and finally – unsmiling – Jericho answered him. He told the old man about Sage Columbine and the old Spanish Gold that had been found here. Both Youngblood and the old man exchanged a glance and both nodded. The old man coughed; "Well, I know that's the truth God damn it Tibbs. Like fuck I do!" The old man rose from his chair and spat on the floor, he turned to Youngblood; "Let's find that damn woman; she's worth real money and not imaginary Spanish fucking gold!" A young brave was assigned to watch the pair after the old man and Youngblood disappeared to search.

Jericho and Wilson spoke quietly together; in French. They both wondered how Alex and Owen knew it was time to disappear. Skyrise had called Jericho just half hour ago to say that he had lost the two braves following him and they certainly were working for Sage; so the rest of the Arapaho's must be also. Jericho whispered that there was more double crossing going on than in some crime novels! The brave waved his spear at them and shouted for silence. He stood back and stared at the pair, gripping his spear with both hands; he was very young, not much older than Owen. Jericho smiled at Wilson and managed to push some fingers into his rear trousers pocket.

7. THE DEAD ARE DAMN RESTLESS IN DEVIL'S DYKE.

Alex crouched low behind the big tombstone which declared that "Ambrose Cuttings was resting in heaven with his favourite horse; Judd. May 1842." and watched the braves spreading out in the old town. She turned back to John and whispered; "Thank you John, you were right about that old bastard. Good job you recognized his horse and mule." John just nodded and said quietly; "He's a know gun runner to the Indians and his description was circulated at the fort several times. You can't miss that damn horse of his. It looks like one of them Zebra's that you see in books about the old country. If that bastard Indian was heading here too then something wasn't right. You being worth so many guns and horses I guessed that's why he allowed you and your friends to travel here with him."

Owen lay behind a small mound that actually looked quite fresh. The grave was unmarked apart from a stick driven into one end with a pair of boots hanging from it. Owen pulled the boots down and turned them in his hands. He whispered across to Alex;

"Unless I'm mistaken these are army boots." Alex rolled her eyes in mock despair; "Terrific, but does knowing that really help?" Owen placed them down;"I don't know but my mirror tells me they were made in 1971, in France."

Alex glanced at John and sighed with relief; he had been too busy watching the Indians to hear about the mirror or the strange boots. She crawled over to Owen and picked them up. Carefully she checked her mirror; he was right. The boots had been made in Paris in 1971. Discretely she ran her mirror over the grave and sat back; "Jean-Paul Duvance; born in 1949 in Marseille and is a missing soul. Little bleeding wonder since he obviously died out of his time." Owen nodded; "Yeah, but what the hell was he doing here and how did he get to this time and place?" Alex stuck the boots back on the pole; that little mystery would have to wait. They had more immediate problems to worry about; like freeing Wilson and Jericho and getting out of this ghost town that was crawling with now hostile Indians.

John gestured to his left and both stared at where he was pointing; it was a half filled drainage ditch and it ran to the rear of the cemetery. Alex and Owen followed him slowly and carefully into it. They made their along the ditch on their hands and knees. They crawled for a couple of minutes and the ditch suddenly dog-legged left and sloped down. They crawled on in silence until both Alex and Owen suddenly stopped; staring up. John couldn't see anything and whispered for them to move on: after a few seconds they continued crawling; both throwing concerned glances at each other. The ditch ended by a broken down fence and an empty horse trough. They were outside the derelict undertaker's shop which declared that Finagle McCafferty also pulled teeth!

John whispered he would take a look and crawled into the abandoned shop and yard. They both turned and stared at the figure that had followed them. He was wearing a shabby suit with a holster hanging from his right hip. He slowly pushed back his dark black hat, revealing sandy blond hair and deep green eyes. He was about six foot and aged in his mid twenties; he was a big man. A silver badge was hanging from his jacket collar. He folded his arms and stared down at the pair. "Just what the fuck are you doing? Why did you bring all those damn Indians here?"

 Alex managed a smile and introduced herself and Owen to him

and said that John was checking out the undertakers. He pushed his hat back and nodded; "So you can damn see me! First people that have in many a year. Now what are you doing in my damn town?" Alex explained about the Spanish Gold, the two opposing Calvary troops and the Indians. She explained that they were holding two good friends of theirs in the saloon. He stood hands on hips and finally smiled; "Well, I'm the damn sheriff of Devil's Dyke and I don't allow that sort of behaviour in my bloody town. The two damn Spanish fellows who hang about the saloon won't be happy about this."

Alex asked for his help with a big smile, but was interrupted by John telling them it was safe to come in. The sheriff jerked a thumb towards the old undertaker's; "You best get. Them damn savages won't go near the coffin shop when I've finished with them. Hold tight missy, Sheriff John Hammond is on the case." He disappeared and they crawled into the "coffin shop" and found John reading a very old newspaper with some interest. He held it up and tapped the headlines of the "Devil's Dyke Courier" which was dated May 1842. "Towns folk moving out!" it shouted. John sighed; "The water dried up and so they couldn't stay. Apparently people had been killing each other and stealing water whenever they could. Finally the Mayor called it a day and they have arranged a wagon train and everyone is leaving. The paper says this was the last edition. It says they would go on May 20th and head north; apparently about one hundred and fifty people." He lowered the paper and wiped his face. Owen took the paper [it was a single, double printed sheet] and read for himself about the coming evacuation. But what caught his skilled eyes was the small column on the back page; next to the obituaries.

"Listen to this; three kids playing near the dried river bed pulled a strange helmet from the dirt and they dug around and found a sword hilt and two gold coins. Miss Edna Weemes the local school teacher identified the coins as gold Spanish Doubloon's from the 16th century and the helmet was Spanish too; from the same century. This – she said – gave credence to the legend about Spanish Conquistadors having passed through the area some three hundred years ago who were killed by natives in a big battle. Says here that a chest of the coins is supposed to be buried around Devil's Dyke, but no one has any details of where it may lay. It finishes by saying that some town's folk have vowed to return and find it." Owen stopped reading and placed the paper down. "Do you think bloody Sage found it?"

Alex shrugged her shoulders; she didn't know. The discussions were ended by the noise of gunfire; lots of it. Crouching low they gathered around the big window and could see horsemen in the main street; all in grey uniforms. They were having a brisk running gunfight with the Indians. "The cavalry have arrived." Owen said with a grin. John just grunted with some anger; "Yeah, but they are wearing the wrong uniform. If they find me I'll be returned to slavery or killed." Alex patted his arm; "Not while we're around John." That's when they heard the big bang and dark smoke arose from the east part of the town. John crouched down; "That's bloody dynamite! Who the hell is throwing dynamite about!" he shouted as another big explosion was heard and more black smoke rose into the air. Owen gestured to the far end of town as yet another huge explosion was heard and a big, thick cloud of black smoke and dust rose into the air.

Alex shouted; "The Indians are running for it! They think the rebels have brought artillery with them I bet!" That's when she could feel her mirror vibrating under her dress. She tapped Owen on the arm and he understood what she wasn't saying and he distracted John by talking about the rebels and returning coloured soldiers to slavery, while Alex disappeared out the door to answer her mirror.

Owen and John watched the band of Indians disappearing onto the plans; the Confederate troops didn't follow. "I think they are setting up HQ in the saloon, where Jericho and Wilson are." Owen said quietly but Alex, standing in the doorway, chuckled and jerked a thumb behind her; "Not any more they are!" Wilson and Jericho followed her in and Owen jumped up with happiness; "Come on, how did you do that?" Wilson grinned; "Which do you mean? The explosions or the escape?"

John – for the first time in hours – actually smiled; "It was you two throwing the damn dynamite about weren't it?" Jericho and Wilson nodded, with Jericho patting his shoulder; "Now we need to deal with the gold hungry rebels. They won't be taking you anywhere." He smiled broadly and added; "Just follow me people."

The old man lay on the saloon bar with little Jim the corpsman wrapping a bandage around his leg. "It went clean through old timer. You're lucky." The old man cussed him out and groaned loudly again, he wanted to throw a punch at the grinning young man but both his hands were tied. He would have difficulty explaining about the ten rifles and case of whisky found on his mule.

Captain Sommerville stood by the broken door watching a burial party carry two dead troopers up to the cemetery; the three wounded men weren't seriously wounded though one could lose an arm without some proper medical help. Sage was telling him to search for the Tibbs party; the woman was skilled in medicine and would certainly help if asked. The captain wiped his face and stared out the door. "Just find us the gold Sage; that's what the boys died for; that damn gold to help the cause." He slapped dust from his trousers and turned to the old man; "Well Walter, your whisky and gun running days are at an end. We're going leave you and your illicit stock for the Yankee's to find. I understand they're hanging fellows who trade such items with the Indians now days. You know; because of the war." He chuckled and waved to sergeant Amos; "You and I will assist Sage in procuring the gold."

The sergeant just stared at him and the captain sighed; "You and I will help Sage find the gold." The sergeant grinned and grabbed up his hat and rifle. The captain turned to Corporal Swiggers; "Take some boys and find them strangers who like throwing dynamite about and find that coloured soldier; I need to talk with him." The Corporal nodded and grinned; "You gonna hang the black bastard sir?" The captain wiped his face and told him to get on with it. He watched the corporal and two men go with some sadness. "I really don't know where all this hate comes from." He whispered to himself and followed Sage through the saloon doors with sergeant Amos close behind, chewing some tobacco and spitting.

The captain wasn't there when everyone ran – some screaming – from the saloon just minutes later. Even old 'Walter' had jumped from the bar and hobbled at speed through the door; shouting and cussing. He hadn't seen anything like it before in his sixty-one years. He hid himself in the ladies dress shop opposite and breathed deep, wiping his face with a shaking hand.

Two figures had simply walked through a wall dressed up like a couple of soldiers from hundreds of years before. They had swords, big helmets and were wearing long boots. Old Walter thought they were shouting in Spanish; some of the old Indians around here still knew some Spanish words. But it was when two rebels fired their muskets at them and the bullets passed straight through, making neat holes in the wall behind them that did the trick. Everyone in the saloon was gone some seconds later. The two ghosts exchanged an amused look and faded away.

The team reached the ruined church at the far end of the town and managed to climb over the big door that lay to one side. The interior was surprisingly cool and that made Alex happy – who was still moaning about the 'tent' she had to wear – ladies fashions in the 1860's were layers of petticoats and skirts built over a hoop. It was actually like dragging a tent around and she hated it. She had enough of that and pulled her skirt off and a layer of long petticoats; the corset came next and basically she was in her underwear [for the time] had it been the 1920's or 1960's she would have looked quite fashionable!

John was quite surprised that her male companions said nothing about her stripping down to her underwear in front of them. They just carried on if such an outrageous performance [in his eyes] was perfectly normal. Owen showed Jericho the newspaper that John had found and he read it quickly with some interest. Alex checked John's bandages and he certainly felt a lot better as she leaned over him; the removal of her corset had allowed her magnificent breasts some freedom and John was more than happy to enjoy the view on offer.

Wilson had to smile at that; she's one hell of a distraction he thought as he sat on the far pew and checked his mirror. That's when he called Jericho over – quietly and calmly – and showed him the mirror. Jericho rubbed his chin in thought; there was a powerful machine operating nearby – really powerful – powered by nuclear fusion. Now that certainly didn't exist in the 1860's! "Can you locate it?" Jericho asked and Wilson nodded, tapping at his mirror and sat back; "Apparently it's coming from just outside the town, from that ridge we passed through. Now let's try…." He tapped at his mirror again and smiled; "Got it. The ridge slopes down on the west side and there's an old silver mine there. It was abandoned even before the town was: that's where the energy signal is emanating from."

Jericho nodded and looked at John having his bandages changed. He had to smile at the happy expression on John's face. "I'm sure Alex and Owen can keep John distracted while we take a look at that old mine." Wilson pushed his mirror into his shirt pocket and smiled; "None better for distractions." He murmured and they called Owen over quietly and explained what was happening. Owen nodded and watched as the pair disappeared out the side door to operate their mirrors. He returned to Alex and John and whispered in her ear.

8. THE OLD SILVER MINE AND ALEX MAKES A DISCOVERY.

Jericho and Wilson walked the edge of the ridge carefully as Wilson consulted his mirror. He stopped and pointed to a thick clump of scrawny trees and bushes that seemed to climb up the ridge. "They seem to be well watered for a place where there's supposedly no water anywhere." He said and the pair headed for them. They both jumped back a little as the big mountain lion broke from the bushes; roaring and growling. It lowered itself as if to pounce. Wilson actually smiled and held up his mirror; "It's bloody good, but it's just a hologram, probably being generated by the power source as some sort of defense mechanism."

Jericho nodded and checked his mirror; "Yeah, but what is it protecting? The power readings are off the scale. I wonder what's being generated by all that power; it can't just be holograms like this." They walked towards the growling lion and it simply vanished. They pushed into the thick foliage and found what it was hiding after a couple of minutes; an old cave entrance. There was wood scattered about and the remains of a small, wheeled carriage that would have been pulled by a mule or pushed by a couple of men. They stood in the dark entrance and shone their mirrors in. It twisted and turned, going downwards; they noticed a small gauge rail track and decided to follow that.

They walked constantly descending for about ten minutes. Jericho stopped and ran his fingers over the dark walls; "These walls are damp, there must be water under the ridge." That's when they heard the rumbling noise. Wilson held up his mirror and shouted; "Another illusion I think!" the wall of water came rushing around the bend and crashed over the pair and faded away. Jericho folded his arms; "Someone or something really doesn't want any visitors; do they?" Wilson nodded and they walked on; still descending.

The tunnel seemed endless with no conclusion and so they stopped at a junction; two tunnels now. Wilson grunted; "Which one do we take?" Jericho shrugged his shoulders; "The mirrors cannot give an accurate location of the power source now. We are too damn close to it." Wilson stabbed a finger downwards; "Only one has the little rail track. Follow that?" he asked and Jericho nodded. It was that or toss a bloody coin!

They continued to follow the rail tracks and found another carriage on its side and the tunnel now seemed to narrow. That's when Wilson sighed loudly as he peered into the open carriage; "Take a look Jericho. We have a visitor." Jericho looked over the side and wiped his face: it was skeletal remains with the hat and boots still in good condition, but the checked shirt and trousers had almost disappeared. Wilson ran his mirror over the bones. "Phillip Renior, born 1946 in Perpignan southern France with a scheduled dispatch date of 2010, but he never made that; he's a missing soul and now we know why. Strange that no temporal detectives were allocated the case."

"Another bloody missing soul from France with army boots. Alex and Owen found one in the cemetery." Jericho rubbed his chin; "Now that's very interesting." He muttered and the pair walked on; still descending. They turned yet another corner and Wilson grabbed Jericho by the arm and gestured downwards; the little rail track stopped in mid air, below some sixty or seventy feet lay a cavern. It was huge with a small waterfall running down one wall into a small dark pond. Their mirrors showed that the floor of the cavern was strewn with bits of mining equipment and two ramshackle huts; one much larger than the other. There were two dark entrances on the opposite wall, right on the cavern floor. There was a pale white light showing from the smaller of the two.

Jericho patted Wilson's arm; "Thanks for that my old friend. I think that's the next tunnel we want." He gestured to the tunnel with the light emitting from it. Then added; "I hope the mirrors can do small jumps." He tapped his mirror and the pair was gone.

Owen sat by the window and watched the rebel activity in the town. "Sage, the rebel captain and sergeant have just gone into the old school house. Some more men appear to searching each house in turn, the rest must be in the saloon." He told Alex who left John resting on a pew and joined him by the door. Owen chuckled; "You know if you stand in strong light, those petticoats will be transparent?" Alex sighed and asked; "How long have they been in the school house?"

"About ten or fifteen minutes, why?" Owen replied and Alex sat down and leaned against the wall. "Just in that newspaper it was the school teacher that made the statement about the legend of Spanish Gold, confirmed the authenticity of the coins, helmet and sword hilt as being Spanish. Consult your mirror while John is asleep and find out if that story appears anywhere else." Owen tapped his mirror for a couple of minutes and shook his head; "There's no mention of the story anywhere. But then; how many copies of the 'Devil's Dyke Courier' would exist? I mean how many would have reached the Newspaper archives?"

Alex almost smiled; "So if there are no records of the story available for historians; how did Sage know about the story? We know he's from the 1920's and not from this time and place, so how the hell did he know about the story?" Owen rubbed his chin; he knew that was a bloody good question. He pulled the old newspaper from his back pocket and ran his mirror over it. The look on his face was priceless. Alex gave him a gentle shove and said "Well?" with some frustration. Owen slowly smiled; "You clever girl; this paper was made from tree's felled in 1957 and the ink was manufactured in 1961!"

"I smell a large rat and its called Sage Columbine. Do you think he showed that fake newspaper to General Longstreet and set this whole thing up for some reason we haven't discovered yet? All he had to do was have a bag of Spanish Gold doubloons that he could have acquired from anywhere; he's a damn time-traveller after all! Then add the newspaper and he has Longstreet hooked. Such a quantity of gold would be irresistible to the rebel cause; they are desperate for money to pay for equipment and keep the war going. But why is he doing all this? If he was a true supporter of the rebel cause; why not just give them the damn coins?" Alex spoke quietly and Owen leaned back and looked at his mirror; "Because the coin hoard doesn't actually exist; but that don't make sense, as you say, why then, all this crap?"

Alex sighed again; "The original mission was to undo minor changes to the current time line caused by the rebels and federal troops fighting here: thirteen unscheduled deaths that never happened in the original time line. Then we discover that John Norton's great grandson is important to the time line in the 1960's...." She stopped talking and then said quietly; "The paper was made in 1957 and the ink in 1961. Sage is from the 1920's but would have lived through the 1960's had he not discovered time-travel. There's a definite connection there; but what the hell is it!"

Owen lowered his mirror; "Sage changed the original time line with this fake gold scam. He engineered the fight between the rebel and Federal troops by convincing General Longstreet that there was gold in this old ghost town, but as you say; why?"

Alex tapped his shoulders; "Who were the soldiers that died? Check each one against Sage's human genealogy and see if anything comes up." Owen tapped his mirror again; "If I remember the mission briefing; it was five federal troopers and seven confederate soldiers." Alex grabbed his hand and almost smiled; "That's only twelve men; who was the thirteenth victim?"

"Good spot." Owen murmured and held up his mirror; "A certain Walter Carlton who died of blood poisoning from a wound to his leg. Probably Sepsis." Alex now grinned; "That's the name of that mean old whisky and gun peddler that was dealing with Youngblood and the Indians. What changes to the original time line did that cause?" Owen consulted his mirror and didn't smile; "His great grandson was a civil rights lawyer in the 1960's and defended several top civil rights activists at the time. But that's weird, I mean Walter is sixty-one in this year with no record of any children born before this date. That can't be right can it? He fathered a child in his sixties?"

Alex was checking her mirror and grunted; a little angry. "In the original time line dear old Walter is hung in Silver City in 1865 for the rape of a minor; a seventeen year old girl. She had a child; a boy in 1866 that was given up for adoption. That's how he had descendants. The fucking animal." Owen pushed his mirror back into his jacket; "I bet the prestigious layers family won't shout about an ancestor like that or they don't know. That sort of family history wouldn't be passed down if the boy was adopted."

Alex eased herself up; "Well, we've discovered why the original time line changed in the 1960's. But if we restore it now, then that fucking beast rapes the girl and the child is born right on schedule. That means we have to stop Walter getting Sepsis and dying. Now that's really going to get up my nose." Owen nodded; "I'll inform Jericho."

Alex stood arms folded; "Do you know I think Sage was aiming to kill someone else; not bloody Walter Carlton, to change the 1960's but we turned up and changed all that. Youngblood would have killed the two coloured boys if Jericho hadn't convinced him to allow them to fight for their freedom. That threw a spanner into Sage's plan. I think he hoped that John would be killed in the fighting and if not, kill him himself and history would have put the death down to the battle, but we messed all that up. I don't think he even knew about old Walter's descendant. Nobody in the 1960's would have done. But he would have certainly known about that civil rights leader's family history." "Come on, we need to stash John somewhere safe and find that sick old bastard and save his wretched life." Alex walked over to the sleeping John and didn't look happy. She placed a hand upon his forehead and sighed again;"No wonder he's so sleepy; he's burning up. He has an infection and we need to deal with it urgently." Owen nodded and held up his mirror; "I'll watch him and you jump to the lighthouse and grab your bag. Does he need penicillin?" Alex nodded and pulled out her mirror; that's when a bullet smashed what's left of the window and another thudded into the wall. "They have found us!" Owen yelled and Alex said; "No shit Sherlock." she operated her mirror; the temporal detectives were gone and John with them.

Corporal Swiggers came through the door, bayonet at the ready and cussed loudly; "Where the fuck have they gone?" the two soldiers following said nothing; they certainly didn't know.

9. THE MACHINE.

Jericho and Wilson shone their mirrors at the tunnel with the faint light and made their way down the much smaller tunnel; Wilson had to bend a little and moaned a couple of times about that. Both could feel the vibrations in the walls and floor and it was becoming louder with each step; almost to the point they covered their ears. "De-materialize!" Jericho shouted over the intense and painful noise. They both stood and sighed with relief; they were now basically holograms or ghosts for want of a better description and the physical noise didn't bother them now.

"Now that's one clever fucking defense mechanism against humans and animals." Wilson said as they walked on for several minutes. The tunnel suddenly opened up into small cave with smooth walls and ceiling. It looked 'man made' and they stood before a stone door covered with strange hieroglyphs. Wilson lowered his mirror; "No translation possible. They are totally unknown." Jericho grunted and ran his hand over the surface of the door. "It appears to be stone but I bet it is not." That's when they both realised they were not alone standing before the impressive door. They both turned and stared at the women standing there. She was dressed in a short white skirt and blouse. Her dark hair tied with a black ribbon; around her neck was a collar that looked like gold. She would easily be called beautiful. Jericho noticed a gold ring on her big toe; she was barefoot.

Jericho held up a hand and introduced Wilson and himself. Wilson lowered his mirror and whispered; "She's a real strong hologram, probably made from hard light, like they discovered in 2205." Jericho nodded; "Agreed, but I don't think she's from that age. I think she could be much older than that. Probably even before modern humans."

The woman said nothing but gestured towards the door. Jericho and Wilson turned to see the door slide back revealing a brightly lit room. The floor and ceiling appeared to be made from light itself. The hologram swept past them and gestured for them to follow. They did. The big door closed silently behind them. They walked slowly down the passage and stared at the 'mirrors' on the walls. One each every seven feet and as they passed each, several human faces appeared in the mirrors and they eyes watched the pair pass. Jericho stopped at one and studied the faces that were studying him. "They appear human – like we were when alive – but I don't think they are now." He looked closely at a couple who smiled at him; did he know them? A strange sensation passed over Jericho and he wondered why the faces were there. But the woman urged them on and so they walked until the lady hologram stopped by a large round mirror that protruded from the wall by four or five inches. She bowed and was gone.

An old man's face appeared; he looked ancient and neither Jericho nor Wilson could even guess his age. He smiled slowly and spoke; the language made no sense to the pair and they both consulted their mirrors which – unusually – couldn't translate it. Jericho quietly explained they couldn't understand. The face smiled again and said; "Colloquial English, in use from the fourteen hundreds until the end. I welcome you to Omega. It has been a long time in human years since I had visitors. Please state you business here."

Jericho explained who he and Wilson actually were and – briefly – the case they were on. The face nodded; "Jericho Tibbs; a human who existed organically between 28 human years from birth to death. Wilson Franklyn; a human who existed organically between 35 human years from birth to death. Now both existing in the secondary plane of existence and serving a higher species. Your current endeavours please me. You are still basically animals but are struggling to evolve further; to assimilate with your creators. What do you wish to know?"

Jericho and Wilson glanced at each other; the holy family [God] is just a 'higher species' to this face? Jericho had to ask; "Who created you?" The face smiled; "I have been in existence since before this planet was newly formed. I was created to watch and wait for humans such as you. My creator was myself; I came together by my own means. I existed because I wanted to exist. Everything on this planet apart from you humans I called into existence. I created the garden and your creators filled it. I am existence; I am time past, time present and time to come. I am rock and water; night and day. I cannot die because I was never born. I am light and dark without me there would be nothing; a great void of non-existence. I am everything including nothing. I am the dream without a sleeper. I exist in everything and everything exists in me. I am the why to all the questions you could ask. That is I. I am I. Do you understand?"

Jericho rubbed his chin; "So you created yourself; how was that possible? I mean creating yourself from nothing?" The face smiled; "I have existed before humans could even understand what time is and will exist long after they have gone. There is no time; just me. Humans have no understanding of true existence because they are organic with a limited time restrained by their fragile creation. Even your higher species will succumb to the passing of organic decomposition eventually. But I will still be here. Nothing can exist outside me; even nothingness itself. There is a void because I exist; without me even non-existence would not exist."

The face slowly faded and was gone. The woman was back and gestured them to follow her. They did in silence and found themselves back outside the door and it closed silently behind them. They stood in silence for a second or two, then Wilson said softly; "Is it only me or did he have a huge ego?" Jericho started to laugh; "I don't think he is a he. I think it's a very, very old machine that's been around for millions of years and it has no idea who created it; so it's worked out that it created itself; logical really. But for what actual purpose it was created for; God only knows."

Wilson grunted; "And I can't see him telling us that anytime soon." He stopped and held up his mirror; "My mirror tells me that no time has passed since we entered the tunnels from outside the ridge. Like that hour didn't happen." Jericho checked his mirror and agreed.

Now standing outside; below the ridge, they both stood for a minute or two without speaking, just staring at each other. Wilson looked about and ran a hand over his face; "Well, that was a waste of time. There is no energy source around here. My mirror is showing nothing. Come on let's go, this was a waste of time." Jericho nodded; "Must have been some sort of surge that the mirrors picked up. But your right; there's nothing here to investigate. Let's get back." He operated his mirror and they were gone.

The face smiled and all the faces in the wall mirrors smiled with him.

10. SAVING CORPORAL NORTON.

 The old house was still in fair condition despite being abandoned in 1842 and was located on the edge of the equally deserted town. "This was the town's doctor's house; it has a small surgery room with a big table and a large window for light. Apparently the doctor was called Thaddeus Ambrose and he left with the wagon train. It will do nicely." Alex placed her 'Gladstone' bag down and rolled up her sleeves. She watched as Wilson and Owen gently lowered the mumbling John Norton onto the table. He was a little delirious and talking about angels; at one point he sat up and cursed God for having no mercy, then slumped back and continued to mumble.

Alex carefully removed the chest bandage and sighed; "The wounds infected. The Indians knife probably hadn't been cleaned for ages. It could have been contained with old blood or dirt. I'll start with some penicillin shots and then clean and redress the wound with fresh sterile bandages." Jericho nodded, standing in the doorway, checking his mirror. He told Owen to watch for anyone coming up the dirt street. Owen didn't say anything and sat in the large front room on a clean chair and watched the street. Alex set to work, watched by an interested Jericho and Wilson. What did make Wilson chuckle was Alex's wonderful pink rubber gloves! She prepared her needle and carefully injected John's thigh. Then set about cleaning the wound. "How long before we can move him?" Jericho asked; still a little puzzled about his mirror; the local time shown seemed to be about an hour out. Alex checked John's temperature and didn't smile; "I'd say about a couple of hours. He's young and fit which helps a great deal." Jericho nodded his thanks and then answered an incoming call on his mirror; it was Skyrise. He smiled and thanked Skyrise and lowered his mirror. "Skyrise is now trailing a detachment of Federal Calvary, a young white officer, but all the troopers are coloured. They will here by morning. So that will give us time to thwart Sage's gold trick. I think he will supply the coins himself to cover their arrival in this time and place. History will record it as a convenient find for the rebel cause. But it never happened in the original time line and so we need to stop him. Such an amount can buy many extra weapons and horses and that could have serious effects later."

Alex reminded him that they had to save – reluctantly – that old bastard Walter or the time line would also change. Wilson chuckled; "We get all the good jobs don't we?" and helped cover the sleeping John with a blanket. "We can leave him for his own side to care for, once Alex says it's ok." Jericho rubbed his chin and consulted his mirror again. But Owen interrupted them; "There's something going on in the town. The troopers are mounting up and the officer, with Sage and a couple of troopers are loading something into their supply wagon; covered with a blanket."

Jericho cursed; he knew that Sage had already probably pulled the switch and the confederates were about to leave with a huge quantity of gold that could change the time line a great deal. "I could stop time, but that would only give us fifteen minutes to grab the box and dispose of it. Then the story of the chest's disappearance could be repeated; there would be a lot of witnesses to a totally unexplainable event. So this is a tricky one." Jericho folded his arms and didn't smile. Wilson slowly did smile; "I can think of a way to do it which will cause very little change and the confederates won't shout too much about being conned and history won't be too bothered to note it; considering there's a huge war going on."

Jericho slapped his back; "Over to you prospective Temporal Detective Inspector!" Leaving Alex to watch over John, the rest of the team disappeared.

Jericho was crouched low beneath the window ledge of the big bedroom on the second floor of the now deserted saloon; watching the activity in the street below. He checked his mirror for Wilson's signal that they were ready to do their own little bit of switching. His mirror beeped and he ran from the room, down the back stairs and in to the alley which opened directly on the street. He stopped time; he had already informed the Senior Time Controller on duty. Wilson drove the wagon quickly from the back of the saloon and pulled up just behind the Rebel's wagon. Owen leapt from the back and threw the canvas flap up. Wilson and Jericho ran past the still figures of Sage and the captain and grabbed the blanket covered chest from the two troopers.

It certainly was heavy and they lowered it to the ground. Owen appeared with a large metal box; he was struggling to carry it. Jericho pulled open the lid on the confederate chest and they all stared in. "Sweet Jesus, that's a lot of coin." Muttered Wilson and waited for Jericho to appear from their wagon carrying a big metal box that was empty. They carefully tipped the gold into the metal box. Jericho – panting – said quietly; "Six minutes to go." Owen opened his metal box and tipped the washers into the chest. Everyone grabbed a couple of handfuls of coins and covered the washers. Then the lid was slammed down and the blanket replaced; the chest was carefully placed back into the arms of the two troopers. They almost dragged the metal box back to their wagon and hoisted it aboard. "Three minutes to go." Jericho shouted and Wilson drove the wagon behind the saloon and Jericho operated his mirror and re-started time. He then – again – operated his mirror and the wagon and horses, with them aboard disappeared. They had done it with just one minute remaining.

The two troopers pushed the chest into the wagon and climbed aboard; Captain Sommerville gave strict instructions that only he and Sage were allowed near the box. He shouted to the sergeant for the men to mount up and the little convoy headed out of the town. The three wounded men in the wagon shouted they didn't mind squashing up for the box and passed a canteen of water amongst themselves. "Granny lee will hand out whisky for what we did!" The youngest shouted and the other agreed with him. They would be heroes.

Alex checked John and pulled his blanket up, that's when she heard the noise in the doorway and turned expecting the team back. She was disappointed; it was old Walter, limping badly and holding a scatter gun on her. [In the UK, that's a shotgun]. He smiled and cussed at his leg, then at Alex; "Get away from that black bastard you white whore and get over by that old sofa!" He yelled and held the gun up. Alex realised that her mirror was in her 'Gladstone' bag; sitting next to John's head. She raised her arms and walked slowly to the old sofa under the big window. "I need to look at your leg Walter; see if it's infected…inflamed. That could be dangerous." She said quietly, smiling a little.

Walter just grunted; "Fucking standing there in just your shirt and drawers with that black bastard, I can see what's been going on you slut! Now the only fucking thing you can help me with is this!" his free hand tugged at the buttons on his trousers and he pulled out his cock and tugged at it. "Now fucking strip naked and bend over that dam sofa, I'm gonna fuck you then kill him!" He weaved the gun at her and pulled the safety catches back on both barrels. "Come on! Get them fucking clothes off!" Alex slowly pulled off her blouse and Walters eyes opened with delight and lust. "What a fucking pair of tit's, God damn it whore, I'm really gonna enjoy this. Now get those drawers off and bend over that God damn sofa before I cum in my own hand!"

Alex slowly pushed the petticoats down and stood naked apart from her little boots; she covered her herself with two hands. But Walter screamed for her to drop her hands; which she did. He was almost raving; shouting for to bend over the sofa with her knees on it and her hands on the back of it. She did as she was told and could hear the old man frantically trying to get his trousers down with one hand.

That's when she heard the loud thud and turned slowly to see

Walter stretched out on the floor, with John carefully pulling the scatter gun away from his hand. Her Gladstone bag lay next to Walter's head; broken open and the contents spilled out.
John smiled; "The old idiot should have killed me first." Was all he said and threw Alex the blanket he had laid under. She wrapped herself up and walked over; kissing him, which really surprised John. He smiled again; "Thanks for that, but just seeing you naked was thanks enough!"

Alex leaned over Walter and checked his pulse, then his eyes. "Fucking shit! He's dead!" She exclaimed. That's when she saw little Yuri the collector in the corner with a protesting Walter. Yuri just raised his soul ledger and smiled. The pair was gone soon as the light appeared. John just shrugged his shoulders; "Must have had a weak head or your bag is more lethal than anyone could imagine."
That's when Jericho and the team returned, walking through the door, laughing amongst themselves until they saw Alex in just the blanket and Walter dead on the floor clutching his cock. Owen shifted the body with his foot and said quietly; "Now that may fuck up things."

John was telling Jericho and Wilson what happened as Alex grabbed up her discarded clothing and dressed under the blanket. Jericho patted John arm and thanked him, telling John that his comrades would be here in the morning and he would travel back to the fort with them.

Alex discretely ran her mirror over Walter and nodded to herself; the old man had suffered myocardial infarction [heart attack] and must have suffered heart failure for some years and in this time and place there was practically no treatment. John clobbering him with the bag must have triggered the fatal failure. But when she spoke to Wilson about it; he just chuckled and muttered; "Or seeing a woman like you stark naked, bent over in front of him, could be the real cause!" She just sighed in reply and didn't even bother telling Owen why the old man had died. But she was happy that the old bastard died before he could get hold of that young girl. She now knew he would have been quite capable of such a terrible act; despite his age.

That's when Jericho's mirror buzzed and John looked around; puzzled. Wilson pulled John to one side and asked about the dead old man again. Jericho wandered into the hallway and answered his mirror. It was Skyrise.

11. ANOTHER BATTLE OF DEVIL'S DYKE?

Jericho stood – arms on hips – and sighed loudly. This was not good news from Skyrise. Youngblood's renegade band of Arapaho's was on course to cross paths with the Federal cavalry unless one or both changed course; and soon. If they clashed, then the time line would change drastically with the unscheduled deaths, as it did in the altered time line. He cursed Sage and his plan to supply the confederacy with Spanish gold.

There had been minor – and acceptable – changes with the deaths of the few Indians and Confederates during the fighting in the town. But this would be different; a serious number of deaths will alter things and not in the best interest of the current time line. He stared down at his mirror and thought hard; then saw the wagon and horse's through the broken down door, standing quietly in the deserted street. He managed a smile; "Sod it, must be worth a try." And when John was sleeping off his penicillin and pain killers; he called the team together and outlined his plan. The wagon trundled slowly through the clouds of dust and dirt being whipped up by the unusually strong winds that were now running across the prairie. Owen slapped the reins and adjusted the scarf tied about his face. He glanced back at John sitting up in the rear, with Alex checking his bandages; they were laughing quietly together. Owen smiled and called out to Wilson, who was riding next to the wagon. "I take it the Indians now have the rifles and whisky that old Walter had on his mule?" Wilson tugged at the scarf over his mouth and shouted back; "Yeah, Skyrise said they half of them now had rifles and they were passing bottles amongst themselves!"

Owen shook his head; "Not a good mixture; guns and whisky and Indians not use to either." Wilson nodded and looked behind to see Jericho reading his mirror as he rode. They should cross the path of the Federal cavalry in a couple of hours. What concerned Wilson was that they [the team] should soon see scouts from the cavalry or as Jericho had commented; they should have seen them already. Wilson stared at the horizon; it didn't look good, there was a storm coming. Jericho spurred his horse and joined Wilson, pulling down his scarf; "My mirror tells me there was quite a storm in these parts about this time. We may need to find shelter and sit it out!" Wilson nodded his agreement with that.

Then both shouted about the lack of scouts from the cavalry column and Jericho called up Skyrise and asked where the Indians were. The reply made him laugh out loud and then cough as the dust got up his nose. He shouted over to Wilson; "The Arapaho's have stopped in a small ravine about twenty miles east of us. Skyrise says they are firing their rifles and staggering about; they must have finished that case of whisky!"

Wilson laughed and coughed too; "I think we should call it a day. Maybe the bloody Indians will be too drunk to ride through the storm!" Jericho nodded and gestured to a big clump of trees and bushes ahead. "We'll stop there; at the least we'll have some protection. I've told Skyrise to take no chances and get some shelter!" He turned to Owen who raised a hand; he had been listening and drove the wagon towards the thick trees and bushes. He managed to get the wagon and horses several feet into foliage before he had to stop; the wind was now really driving the dust and dirt, so much so that the sky had actually darkened.

With the horses secured; everyone crowded into the wagon and the canvas sides and back flap were tied down with extra rope. Owen passed his hipflask around and everyone had a sip; except John. Alex wouldn't allow him because he had been shot full of antibiotics! He didn't understand that but refused the alcohol because Alex said so.

The canvas flapped and the wind could be heard above anything else. "I think it's getting bloody worse." Muttered Jericho and moved up the behind the driver's seat and discretely consulted his mirror. Alex was handing out the rations; salt beef, biscuits, cheese and apples. The water canteens were greatly welcomed. The talking soon died away as the storm now raged around them. John was asleep with Owen leaned against him; snoring quietly and moving slightly in his sleep. Wilson was dozing, his head nodding gently up and down. Jericho lowered his mirror; now concerned. The storm they were enduring was far stronger than was reported in the original time line. He wondered just how significant that could be. Still, there was absolutely nothing they could do nothing about anything until the damn storm cleared. Bored; he checked his mirror and read about the two French men from the 1970's. Jericho had little doubt that Operations would probably lumber Team 74 with that one. That's when he thought he could hear something above the storm; strange deep, weird noises that he couldn't place or recognize. He adjusted his mirror and did a body search for five square miles. He had to look twice; there were five living humans not a hundred yards from his position!

Covering his head with the scarf; he peered out the driver's front flap; but could only see flying dirt and moving trees and bushes. That's when he caught a glimpse of something. He stared hard and between gust of howling wind and dirt; he saw what it was for just a second or so. He ducked back inside and shook his head. Alex moved carefully over the others and joined him; "I can hear it too over the storm. Do you know what it is?" Jericho slowly nodded and whispered in her ear; "A bloody American armoured car from the Second World war by the looks about it. It has EC-417 pained on the side. I think the crew of five is still with it!"

He tapped at his mirror while Alex sat back and said quietly; "Oh fuck." Jericho looked up from his mirror; "It's from the 7th Calvary, it should be in the Libyan Desert in 1943 fighting the German 'Afrika Corps'. What the fuck is it doing here?"

Alex suddenly sat up and tapped his arm; "Listen. I can only hear the storm." Jericho quickly re-checked his mirror and rubbed his chin; "Nothing. No humans for miles. They have gone." He said quietly. Alex leaned back; "Rouge time portal?" she whispered and Jericho agreed. There was something definitely strange about Devil's Dyke and he couldn't put his finger on it; yet.

Darkness was starting to fall when the storm finally cleared up and the decision was made to stay where they were. The Federal Calvary wouldn't travel at night with no moon. Alex and Owen managed to brew some coffee and cook beans to go with the remaining salt beef and everyone appreciated their efforts. That's when Owen slipped up to Jericho as he relieved himself behind a tree. "I couldn't say anything to you or the others in front of John, but check your mirror and see what the local time is." Jericho buttoned up his flies and pulled out his mirror and really wasn't happy. The local time was April 8th 1551. Jericho lowered his mirror and cussed; they [him and Alex] had been right about the rouge time portal.

Owen looked grim; "That's not the best of it. Check your mirror for where Devil's Dyke will be located; there's a column of Spanish soldiers, cannon, Calvary and wagons camped there. But it gets worse; Coming from behind that ridge is a huge band of Arapaho's and I don't think they'll welcome the Spanish in a friendly manner."

Jericho called Skyrise who confirmed that his band of Indians was still laid around; trying to recover from some serious hangovers. Jericho told Skyrise to use his mirror and jump to where the town is and report if there were any Spanish troops there. Skyrise did laugh at that assignment, but did as he was asked. He buzzed Jericho back to say the place was deserted with no humans in sight. Jericho grunted his thanks and called the Senior Time Controller; he needed to know if this totally unknown conflict was in the original time line. The answer came back; yes it was, just human history had never recorded it!

Owen scratched his chin; "That could mean that the gold is genuine and Sage must have stumbled on the story somehow and that's why he had that old newspaper printed. He may have jumped back to 1551 and saw that the Spanish were really here; then came up with his plan. What happens to Devil's Dyke in the modern area I wonder?" Jericho told him to look that up and tell him later; for the immediate future they need to travel back to the civil war era.

Jericho operated his mirror and they returned; it was just in time [pun intended!] for the Federal cavalry passed their position just an hour later. Corporal John Norton had a very happy reunion with his colleagues, but some were sad over the killing of Isaiah. Sergeant McKay thanked the team for looking after John; the officer was more concerned about where the confederates were. He also tried to 'chat' up Alex at the same time! He wasn't successful in that endeavour. But some of his men were.

12. THE BACK OF THE SUPPLY WAGON.

John spoke softly to young Troy who almost giggled and wiped his face nervously; "Old Alphas will kill me 'cos I didn't tell him about this. But I'll shift the stuff about and put down some blankets." he rubbed his hands together and asked John for the fourth time that the white lady really would let him fuck her. John slapped his shoulder and told him to rearrange the wagon. He then signalled to Alex that everything was ready. It was a tight squeeze in the supply wagon for the two men and Alex; but no-one seemed to mind.

Troy seemed utterly fascinated by Alex's big tits and insisted on sucking them for some minutes while John mounted her from behind. Alex groaned quietly as the big cock pushed up inside of her and turned her head to John and their mouths found each other urgently. Troy squeezed and sucked each tit hard and with some happiness. He tugged at his cock and was quite patient about waiting his turn with the nice white lady that certainly didn't mind coloured folk. Alex was in the reverse cow-girl position with John on his back, slowly pushing herself up and down on his cock whilst Troy enjoyed her magnificent tits. John groaned loudly and slapped a hand over his face to keep the sound down; he had cum inside Alex with some joy.

Alex slipped off him and he pulled himself up and sat back, clutching his empty cock. Troy had his trousers down in an instant and Alex - now on her back, with her legs up and open - helped him insert his cock into her fanny. He didn't care about 'sloppy seconds' and fucked her hard and fast. She gripped his shoulders as he thrusted with some determination. John chuckled; "For Christ sake boy; pace yourself or you'll come too quick. Take your time and enjoy what the lady is giving you." But Troy wasn't listening to such good advice and suddenly found that he had emptied into Alex who just smiled; but was certainly unsatisfied.

Troy staggered from the wagon, straightening his trousers and pulling up his braces and walked straight into Alphas who folded his arms and said nothing. Troy also said nothing and Alphas pulled open the wagon flap and stared in to find a naked white woman sucking hard on John's flaccid cock. He grunted and heaved himself up and into the wagon. John stroked Alex's bobbing head and whispered; "Sorry about not telling you that we needed to use your wagon Alphas; but you can see why my old friend." Alphas nodded and pulled down his braces, saying quietly; "I'm sure the white girl won't mind paying a little fee for its use." Alex turned her head - mouth full of cock - and nodded. Her eyes widened as Alphas tugged down his dirty trousers. John had said he was the best equipped cook in the US Calvary and she could see why!

Alphas fucked Alex hard and slow as she knelt over John; sucking and caressing his stiffening cock. She had to pull it from her mouth several times to groan; Alphas' huge cock was certainly bringing on little orgasm's and he gripped her tits with both hands and squeezed hard; especially on her rock hard nipples. As the old cook buried his big cock deeper with each thrust, Alex felt her stomach tighten and her legs shake a little as the big orgasm swept over her. The cum ran down her thighs and Alphas chuckled; "The young white lady certainly loves the black cock." Alex nodded and sucked hard on Johns cock; this was one spit roasting that she was really enjoying.

They changed position with Alex on top of Alphas and John pushed his cock into her willing anus and the fucking started in earnest. Alphas gently took hold of Alex's hair and pulled her face close to his his; "Do you mind a little kiss?" was all he whispered. She smiled and their mouth joined with the tongues meeting; it surprised Alex that she responded with such passion to the old man's kisses. She sucked and caressed his darting tongue and he did the same. John, thrusting hard into Alex's bum, watched with growing interest at the unbridled passion unfolding under him between the two. Sweet Jesus, who would have thought that an old black man and a young white woman could get it together with so much fire, he thought and then groaned as he emptied his load into Alex's back passage.

He sat back and watched the pair fucking with some real passion and then felt that he should leave them alone and slipped from the wagon to find somewhere to pee. Alex was now on her back with a hand clutched over her mouth as she came again. Alphas had her ankles around his head and was ramming his big cock home with some passion. Alex compared him to a bloody road drill and had to stifle some real screams of passion. But the fire really flared up when their mouths met again. Her arms wrapped around his shoulders and pushing her arse up; Alex had one hell of an orgasm. It was so powerful that she cried - something she hadn't done during sex for some time - and lay back, panting, crying and groaning as Alphas continued to fuck her until he whispered; "Can I cum in you girl?" She nodded vigorously and pulled him down on her; Alex's tongue was in his mouth as he came inside of her and she felt every spurt. The old man groaned and passionately kissed her; running his hands over her quivering body.

They lay together for some minutes; kissing passionately, until

John tapped on the wagon saying it was almost midnight. They parted - really reluctantly - and Alex headed back to the Team's wagon; walking awkwardly it should be noted. Alex hadn't been so well satisfied by a man like since Skyrise fucked her. "This mission has turned out alright." she laughed to herself and wiped her eyes and knew that she would have to wash thoroughly in the morning; in this heat she would soon smell of all the cum that she had taken in. She slept well and to her surprise thought of old Alphas with some affection and some real longing.

Dawn was not due for a hour or so, so Alex slipped back to the supply wagon and smiled at young Troy sleeping underneath and slipped into the back of the wagon. She found Alphas asleep in just in 'long-johns' and she whispered into his ear; pulling off her travelling cloak to reveal she was stark naked underneath.

Alphas just smiled and pulled off his dirty underwear. Alex's mouth was on his big cock in an instant; her mouth soon had it stiff and ready. She rode the old man frantically as he gripped her swinging big tits. Then she leaned down and their eager mouths met with some unbridled passion. They held onto to each other's hands as she bounced up and down; pushing herself deeper onto his magnificent cock each time until she was full with it.

Alphas groaned a little and insisted she moved under him; they changed into the missionary position and he fucked her really powerfully; thrusting hard and fast until she had a huge climax under his skilful pounding. One hand gripped his neck and the other covered her mouth; she wanted to scream with absolute sexual ecstasy and had to silence herself. Alphas had her legs folded right back and Alex now gripped her ankles as he fucked her without mercy. He stopped and stroked her hair and face with a shaking hand; "I'd love to try your arse girl, can I?" he whispered and Alex nodded; she had already lubricated her bum with 'KY' jelly from her 'Gladstone' bag. She never travelled through time without a handy tube!

Alex was on all fours as Alphas pulled apart her bum cheeks and gently inserted his cock into her willing back passage. It was a tight fit and Alex had to cover her mouth again. He pushed it slowly in until Alex held up a hand and then, he started to fuck her with more speed and determination. Gripping her big tits with both hands he fucked her with great pleasure and determination.

Alex actually had a few tears in her eyes when she felt the old cook finally unload a massive amount of cum into her arse. They collapsed on the wagon's floor and kissed passionately. Finally Alex managed to whisper; "Jesus Alphas, you could bottle your cum by the quart!" the old man just grinned and ran a hand over her taunt stomach; "All good stuff girl, I fathered seven children by five women when I was on the master's plantation and I've had another two by the young squaw I keep at the fort. You'll swell up soon with a black baby after all this fucking with black boys." He patted her belly and smiled adding; "Drop me a letter to say what you had or better still tell me in person. You and Running Deer would certainly get on and it would make the hard winter nights damn easier."

Alex pushed her arm around his neck and pulled his mouth to hers and whispered; "Now that's a generous offer Alphas." He kept his cock buried in her gaping back passage while they French kissed for some minutes, then very reluctantly, he had to pull from her and the pair lay back, savouring the afterglow of the hard sex session. Alex was actually really sad that this was the last time the pair could come together; but she smiled at her pun: they had certainly 'cum' together alright! She just made it back before sunrise and cleaned herself up with tepid water and a soft cloth. She chuckled to herself that she would be sitting awkwardly for a few days after that sex session!

The Calvary troop left at dawn the following morning and Alex was sad to see the supply wagon disappearing down the dirt track. Alphas did raise his hat to her and Troy waved frantically as they departed. Alphas and Alex really did smile at each other which only Owen noticed; but he wouldn't comment on that to anyone except Alex.

John said his goodbyes to Team 74; especially Alex. Jericho watched the column leave; heading back to Fort Caleb and when they were out of sight operated his mirror and everyone was gone. Supplies arrived and cleared up everything and returned with the wagon and horses. There would be no trace of the temporal detectives visit. The team joined up with Skyrise outside the lighthouse and the dinner conversation that night would definitely be lively! But that would not be the end of Team 74's mission to Devil's Dyke. [See episode**: 'Alexandra and the Devil's Dyke showdown'**.]

The End

EPISODE PROLOGUE: "April 1912 - the ill-fated RMS Titanic is sinking: But when Mrs. Lucy Crawford gives up her place in the lifeboat, the services of Mr. Tibbs and his team are required to protect the Time-Line - she should have survived the sinking, but for some reason she abandons her seat to a strange young man and this gesture will change the future - and possibly not for the best! Our Alex gets something to remember when the heating in her cabin goes wrong...."

60 Minutes approx. **Episode Warnings:**
Smoking – Alcohol – Strong language – Violence [including a violent domestic murder] – Strong graphic sexual references – Horror – References to a Demonic presence.

NOTES: This is the **ADULT** version of the original story which is published and appears in the **TEMPORAL DETECTIVES:** Series 2 – Episode 10 entitled: **"MRS. LUCY CRAWFORD LEAVES LIFEBOAT No.13."**

CAUTION: Recommended for **18+ only.**

1. 'A' DECK CABIN No.3 [First Class]

The first act for Alexandra in her allocated cabin was to bounce on the bed. She was impressed; it was firm but yielding. She could smell the faint odour of fresh paint, but it was only a background smell. She pulled her small perfume bottle from her handbag and gave a little spray into the air. She smiled, that solved the slight smell of paint problem. She could feel the great ship moving but didn't feel seasick by any measure.

Alex then sat at the small writing desk and picked up some writing paper and envelopes; all with the 'White Star' insignia on. "Bloody worth a fortune after she goes down." Alex muttered and dropped the papers back on the desk. She stood and paced the cabin, measuring the space. It was more than adequate for the short time that she and the team would be on board. Alex did smile at the thought of Wilson stuck in his cabin with Owen until she ship goes down. A big African wandering about the damn ship would generate a lot of interest and would certainly be reported by survivors. So, he had to sit in the cabin until the actual sinking. It had been decided that her and Jericho would tackle the strangely behaved Mrs. Lucy Crawford, until everyone was in the lifeboats. Alex sighed and pulled off her coat and hat. She felt the cold immediately. The bloody cabin heating was off. Alex grunted and jabbed the Stewards bell push.

It was some minutes before the Steward answered her call. She was wrapped in her coat again, when there was a hard knock at her door; she jumped up and pulled it open. The young man smiled and asked how he could be of service. Alex also smiled and gestured for him to enter. He was in his early twenties and built like a rugby player, with big hands and gorgeous green eyes. She explained about the cold, and he checked the heating and nodded; "I'll get Frankie, one of the maintenance men up here straight away madam." He said and rubbed his hands together; "Your right madam, its well parky in here."

Alex further explained that she was travelling without her husband and so would have to deal with it herself. The handsome young man nodded and stated that he would look out for her personally on this trip and smiled.

Alex sat on the bed and crossed her legs slowly and very lady like. She smiled at the young man and he actually grinned. "I do like the idea of being taken care of personally, by a nice young man like yourself." She said very softy and slowly unbuttoned her coat, adding; "I really need to get warm quickly; do you have any idea's?" He nodded and pulled open the buttons on his neat white jacket. "I was just going off duty ma'am, so I can give you my undivided attention, in the matter of warming you up." Alex really grinned at that.

They were both stark naked under the bed covers with Alex on her back and the young man on top. He was thrusting with some determination and the bed groaned and shifted under his efforts. Alex had both arms about his broad shoulders and her tongue buried in his mouth. He had a wonderful large cock with a good girth and clearly knew how to use it. He had filled her up with it and was fucking her hard and fast. She loved it and groaned a little under his sustained pumping. They changed position and Alex lay on her side with him behind, both his big hands on her breasts. He now fucked her deep and slow and Alex had a couple of little orgasms under his skilful lovemaking.

Pulling the sheets about them, they fucked doggy style, and he caressed her neck and shoulders with his hands and mouth. Alex was groaning with pleasure; the young man was a good lover. His head came close to hers and he whispered if it was ok to cum in her. She nodded vigorously and the young man thrusted for a few more minutes before groaning loudly and poured his seed into her. They collapsed together; kissing and whispering, with their hands gently exploring each other.

Alex sat up in bed, the sheets pulled about her, leaning against the pillows behind her back. She smiled, watching him throw on his uniform. He leaned over and kissed her slowly; he was off to get Frankie, who could fix the bloody heating for her. He left quietly and Alex relaxed in the bed and smiled; not a bad start to a sea voyage, even if the bloody ship sinks!

She must have dozed for a few minutes and heard the soft knock at her door and the young man's voice. He pushed open the door and stepped in, followed by a big man with a toolbox. "I told Frankie that you needed warming up and he'll soon get the heating on." Alex smiled and pulled the covers back a little, revealing her magnificent bare breasts. "Best you get in here before you freeze darlings." She said softly. The young steward his clothes off - again - in seconds and dived under the covers. Frankie fixed the heating as he pulled off his clothes too. Alex really did smile; the maintenance man was hung like a small horse. The bed really did protest under the weight of its heaving occupants.

Alex sucked the young man's cock as Frankie fucked her hard in the missionary position. He gripped her swaying tits and squeezed hard, sucking the hard nipples with some force. The bed was creaking and moving violently under the threesome and the lovers decided to move to the floor - despite the cabin not being thoroughly warmed yet - but no one seemed to notice! Alex was now on top of Frankie, her arse in the air and the steward buried in her yielding bum hole. Both men held her tightly and fucked hard. She groaned and cursed, spurting with shaking legs. Frankie pulled her head down and stuck his tongue in her mouth with some force. He practically cleaned her tonsils with it!

He came inside of her and cursed loudly. They lay kissing passionately as the young man emptied his balls into Alex's arsehole with some loud cussing too. They all lay panting and laughing on the cabin floor. They dressed [the men] and quietly left Alex dozing in her bed. She certainly had no complaints about the service she was receiving from the shipping line! That's when she heard a soft knock at the door, and she sat up in bed and pulled the covers around her. "Who is it? I'm in bed." She said and stared at her small fob watch on the bedside cabinet. It showed eight thirty. The door creaked open, and a head appeared around the door. It was a young man with a tray apparently; "Your steward said you missed dinner ma'am and told me to bring you some." He grinned and offered the laden tray as proof.

Alex smiled and gestured for him to place it on the writing desk. She sighed; he was a good-looking boy of about eighteen or nineteen. He stood nervously in the room and smiled; asking if he could be of further service. She just smiled and threw the covers back. He stared at her naked body and didn't need a further invitation.

2. ALEX'S NIGHT TO REMEMBER.

Alex was a little disappointed with his performance – but quickly accepted that he was young and inexperienced with women - and so made no comment about it. He had fucked her in the missionary position only for about fifteen minutes before coming quickly inside her. She caressed his face and kissed him gently, then used her experienced mouth to raise his flaccid cock. She struggled for a few minutes, but hard sucking didn't work, and he left some minutes later; thanking her profusely.

She sat in bed and enjoyed the dinner; which like the cabin earlier; was a little cold. But the bottle of wine was excellent. There was yet another knock at the door and Alex heard a woman's voice asking if she could use her [Alex's] steward's bell push because hers wasn't working and the cabin was cold. Alex sighed and shouted that she could. A short young woman with a long coat and her hair tied up, wandered in. She smiled and apologised for the inconvenience. Alex waved that away and offered her some wine. The young woman almost giggled and produced a bottle of brandy from her coat pocket. She admitted that she believed Alex' was having quite a party; she could hear everything from her cabin next door.

Alex laughed and held up her empty wine glass. The woman called over her shoulder; "You were right hubby darling; she really has been enjoying the service that the shipping line offers." Both women laughed and Alex smiled as the tall young man - also in a long coat - sprang into the room and closed the door. Alex sipped her most welcome brandy and watched - a little fascinated - as the pair pulled off their coats, to reveal they had nothing on underneath except their shoes! Alex grinned and pulled the covers back. "I think it must be the bloody sea air." She whispered to herself as the pair climbed into bed. The young woman was between Alex's legs; her nibble fingers and tongue buried deep in her gaping wet fanny. She was enjoying all the cum that remained inside from Alex's other lovers. Alex - on her back - was sucking and caressing the man's adequate stiff cock. He groped her big tits with some passion. They changed position, with Alex now treating the woman to her expert tongue and fingers; the woman came like a burst tap and covered Alex's face and lips with cum. Her husband was fucking Alex hard and fast, doggy style.

He slapped Alex's arse a couple of times and shouted; "Yee-haw!" and gripping her trembling bum came deep inside of her. His young wife cleaned that mess up as Alex cleaned his cock.

The happy threesome snuggled down under the covers, laughing and chatting, sharing the brandy bottle. Alex came up with a cover story; she was travelling to New York to meet her estranged husband over their divorce. The young couple admitted they had indulged in group sex before, with the wife's older sister and husband! Keeping it in the family - like the money - was definitely an English trait.

The two women went at it again, giggling and whispering under the sheets, while the young man jerked his flaccid cock and watched with happy interest. The girls were in the 'sixty-nine' position and enjoying the feast on offer. The young wife particularly loved Alex's skilful tongue in her bum hole. She groaned and rubbed her crotch vigorously, but didn't forsake thoroughly licking and fingering the open, wet cunt under her mouth. Finally, the husband had raised his game - well, his cock - and joined in. He mounted Alex from behind, as she lay on her side, firmly embraced by his moaning wife. She was the 'meat' in a very satisfying human sandwich and loved it.

They changed position after just a few minutes and he fucked Alex on her back, with his wife squatting over Alex's face. She had to grip the headboard as she spurted, groaning and cussing like a drunken sailor. He came inside Alex again and the three collapsed on the bed and lay gasping and panting. Alex did smile, as the wife didn't neglect her cum filled fanny and cleaned it with her tongue and fingers.

They all finished the brandy bottle and said their goodbyes; with a promise to meet up in New York. Alex lay back and pulled the cover over, watching the young couple replace their shoes and coats and then leave quietly.

Alex lay - almost dozing - when she sat up a little; she could hear voices from the couple's cabin; she laughed outright. 'Frankie' the maintenance man was serving more than the bloody cabin's heating system! Then her mirror buzzed; it was Jericho informing her that they should meet in the First-Class bar. He had seen that Owen and Wilson received drinks and meals in their cabin. They only had an hour before the damn iceberg made a deadly appearance. Alex sighed and jumped from her bed and quickly headed for the small bathroom to clean up. She dressed quietly, grinning broadly at the noises coming from next door. The young couple were clearly enjoying the First-Class service that the shipping line provided. The heating man's deep voice could clearly be heard: groaning and cussing.

Wrapped in her coat, scarf and lovely big hat, Alex slowly opened the cabin door and checked; there was no one in the small corridor. That's when she heard the thud behind her. She turned and saw the much-abused bed in pieces. She shrugged her shoulder; "Well, no one will know. The bloody ship will be at the bottom of the Atlantic in a couple of hours." She muttered and still grinning, left to meet Jericho in the bar.

3. OLD NIGHTMARES.

Mrs. Lucy Crawford woke with a jerk and covered her face with both hands, she sighed as she wiped the tears from her cheeks and groaned a little about her neck – she had fallen asleep in the damn chair again and dreamt about him – yet again. It had been over a year since Robert's death, and she still cried at dreams in which he appeared; smiling and pushing back his dark curly hair with a real exaggerated sweep of the hand; then the broad grin and gentle touch upon her hands.

She rose slowly from the chair and stretched; glancing at the wall clock which displayed 10.05 PM - she must have slept for about a half hour which was good for her. She poured water from the pitcher and opened her embroidered pillbox, removing two little white tablets and dropped them into her mouth and sipped the water slowly. Lucy could feel the movement of the ship and so she wrapped her coat about herself, adding a hat and scarf, for extra warmth. "I'm on a damn ship in the middle of the ocean, so i will follow Doctor Harker's recommendation and get some sea air!" She muttered and unlocked her cabin door and made for the Deck stairs – the chill of the air made her draw shallow breath's - as she opened the sea door and stepped upon the deck.

Lucy was surprised to see several couples walking the deck and a polite 'Good Evening' was passed between them. She wandered along the deck until she noticed the young man smoking a small pipe by the Dining Room doorway; he was wearing evening dress and checking his pocket watch – a very handsome man with black curly hair and dark eyes. He watched her approach and raised his pipe in salute; "Good evening, Madam." Lucy quickly concluded that his accent was American, probably from the Southern States.

She nodded her greeting and walked on; she resisted looking back for a few seconds, then glanced over her shoulder and for the first time in many years; blushed. He was smiling at her and he raised his hand a little, and then disappeared into the Dining Room. Strangely enough, she didn't feel any shame; after all, married women should not send such signals to unknown handsome young men; but she didn't really care!

In reality, her marriage had been over for some years before Robert's death, but divorce was no option for a woman like her; in England. But not so in America and so her husband; John Crawford was waiting in New York. The Lawyer's had been carefully selected and now all that was required was a five-minute court case before a sympathetic Judge and it would be finished. Lucy noticed the lights coming from the bar and decided upon a large brandy for a nightcap and a shield against the cold of the North Atlantic. A very smart looking Steward opened the door, and she was greeted with a smile. He helped remove her coat and scarf, but Lucy kept her hat firmly on and sat at the table by the fireplace, ordering her desired brandy.

"Will you be joined Ma'am?" The Steward asked, placing the large Brandy upon the table. Lucy was about to say no when the Sea Door opened, and the handsome young man stepped in; rubbing his hands against the cold – he smiled at Lucy, and she turned to the Steward and ordered a second Brandy. He dropped into the seat next to her and pushed his hand through his dark hair; "I'm David Gray and I do believe you are Mrs. Lucy Crawford, of the Crawford's of Liverpool, am I correct?"

Lucy smiled and nodded; "How did you acquire such knowledge?" She asked sipping her Brandy, watching his dark eyes which never left hers. He grinned and held up both hands; "I asked the damn Steward!" They both laughed and began to chat, all small talk and Brandy. They left the bar just after Eleven o'clock and walked slowly to her cabin and David opened the door with the key offered. Lucy hesitated in the doorway for a few seconds then strode into the room, removing her hat and gloves. They stood before each other for about a minute without saying a word; then David slowly gripped her and they kissed very passionately.

At 11.40 pm the pair was disturbed by a large shudder which interrupted their lovemaking and made the lovers laugh as Lucy admitted it was the first time she felt 'the earth move!' The interruption didn't last long as they immediately continued their embrace, oblivious of the chaos that was starting around them.

4. THE NEW NIGHTMARE.

They were woken by hard banging on the door and a voice shouting; "Mrs. Crawford, Mrs. Crawford, the Captain has ordered all passengers to their Life-boat stations at once – please dress warmly and wear your life-jacket!" They could hear the same message for their neighbours and so both slipped from the bed and David helped Lucy dress. They kissed passionately and made their way to the deck. The corridor was packed with people walking slowly, talking and smoking, with many carrying their lifejackets. When on deck the couple joined a group gathered around a lifeboat which was being swung out by a couple of sailors. A young Officer stood close by with both hands in the air and shouting; "Women and children only! Captains orders! Women and Children only!" Lucy and David exchanged looks and gripped each other's hands.

They quietly argued about the situation and David won; Lucy would board this boat and he would find one that was allowing men to go. The Officer helped Lucy climb in and she joined about fifteen other ladies and several children. She watched David standing upon the deck; talking with several of the other men and lighting his pipe – she could make out the small white sparks and little yellow flames. He grinned and waved; like she was catching just a train and not saving her life by going.

Their eyes met, and Lucy knew what she had to do. David was a young man with all his life before him – her life was over, and she knew it. She signalled the Officer and spoke to him quickly and quietly; he reluctantly agreed that the pair could trade places. David refused at first, but Lucy convinced him that she had a far better chance of gaining a seat in another lifeboat than he could. Much to the shock and embarrassment of the waiting passengers, the pair embraced with some passion and swapped places, with Lucy striding down the deck, this time not looking back, heading for the bar.

Lucy gripped the doorway to the bar and breathed deep; she had already decided not to bother seeking out another life-boat and made her way inside and sat at the very same table the pair had enjoyed earlier – except there was a very striking young couple, sitting and drinking brandy, in two of the chairs. Lucy sat down without introduction or inquiry about the empty seats and ordered a Brandy from the Steward.

The pair smiled at her and the very beautiful young woman raised her glass and said quietly; "To family, friends and loved one's – and a damn space on a little wooden boat!" They both chuckled and sipped their drinks, Lucy smiled and raised her glass; "To love and the stupid, but wonderful things it does to you!"

The pair agreed with that sentiment and the three sat chatting, strangely enough they made little negative comment about Lucy giving up her seat for someone, who was a total stranger yesterday. Lucy discreetly omitted the part concerning their lovemaking - they were strangers after all!

Through the door came an Officer with two Stewards who were carrying blankets; he glanced across to their table and walked over. With a grim face, he leaned over the table and spoke quietly; "You ladies need to get to a boat at once, this ship is sinking and will go under. There are too few lifeboats for everyone, so go now. The captain has ordered only women and children first, but the boat I am to command will take young men, make for number nine and do it now; do you understand, you must go now; she will sink in less than an hour, get to a boat now." He straightened up and without further comment walked away followed by the two Stewards struggling with their pile of blankets.

There was silence at the table until the young man slapped his top hat on and smiled; "Well, Mrs. Crawford, I think it's time to find that little wooden boat and take our leave from this wonderful but dying ship." The young Lady arose and adjusted her hat and coat; "Come on Lucy, let's find our future."

At first Lucy refused, but the pair was very persuasive, and she slowly agreed to join them and the little group headed for the deck and all three could feel the strange new movements of the ship. "She'll break up and with the sea temperature near freezing anyone in the water won't last for more than fifteen or twenty minutes at the most. Only those in the lifeboats have any realistic chance of survival." Jericho said quietly and pulled his coat tight around him. They passed a mum and daughter, gripping their lifejackets and walking quickly up the deck, the young girl stopped and threw a bottle over the side shouting; "I promised I would write!" She actually grinned, but a couple of men standing opposite shook their heads and also threw something over the side; several deckchairs tied together, forming a fragile raft. They watched as it broke up upon hitting the water; such was the distance from the deck to the sea. They appeared unmoved and started to search for material made of sterner stuff to fashion their own 'lifeboat'. Other people were just rushing about in a panic. Real fear was starting to appear.

5. THE UNTHINKABLE HAPPENS TO THE UNSINKABLE.

Bright white flares punctuated the dark night sky and illuminated the dreadful sight of people rushing about the decks; some crying and screaming, some standing with arms folded and grim faces. "The ship is going under." The young man commented with no emotion in his voice, and they made their way through the throngs of desperate people until they reached boat number nine. Lucy glanced at her watch and saw 1.25 AM; the boat was starting to be lowered. It was the young lady who called across to the Officer; "Have you room for this Lady?"

He nodded, and the young man gripped Lucy by the arm and almost frog marched her to the boat, where the officer helped her board for the second time that night. "Aren't you coming?" Lucy spluttered in amazement as the two started to walk away from the boat, which now jerked gently and started the long descent to the quiet ocean surface.

The young woman called back; "See you in New York Lucy!" and the pair disappeared into the crowds heading for the boats. Lucy gripped the side of the boat and watched until she couldn't make them out anymore. The boat dipped into the sea and cold water splashed nearly everyone in the small boat. Lucy pulled her coat about herself and brushed off the freezing spray, then realised that the water was so cold few people would be pulled from it alive. She slumped back and gripped her seat as the lifeboat rolled with the waves and started to head away from the ship. The woman next to her wiped her wet face and sighed; "I can't see him anymore, I can't see him."

Lucy and the woman gripped hands and she stared up at the ship and felt her heart stop; by the rails where number nine was launched stood David, looking about and puffing hard on his pipe. Lucy sat in cold fear and with some growing anger, tried to stand shouting; "You idiot! You had a place in a bloody boat, what are you doing there!" She was screaming and the other passengers shouted for her to calm down – the sailor at the helm pushed her hard into the seat shouting; "You'll capsize us you stupid cow!"

The boat was rowed away with some effort as several of the women sobbed loudly; including Lucy, but the little boat fell almost silent as the terrific noise of escaping steam and breaking metal filled the night air. They watched in utter horror as the ship plunged into darkness and they could make out her silhouette splitting into two and slowly [so it seemed] the great ship disappeared from view. For a few long seconds there was a kind of silence, then the screaming and pitiful crying of those thrown into the icy water floated across the sea's surface.

With a shaking hand, Lucy held her watch up to her face and could just make out the time: 02.20 AM. It had been just over three hours since David and she had found each other. They had been together for just three hours and now that was all gone. Lucy bowed her head and sobbed.

"Why don't we go back and help them?" One elderly lady shouted at the sailor holding the tiller, He said nothing, and she repeated the question, being joined by another couple of women who demanded they return to help those in the water.

"No." He said simply and wiped his face with a dirty rag, he looked about the little boat and added; "They will swamp the boat and sink us – they are desperate and won't care a fig about drowning us – so we'll wait until it gets a bit quieter, then we'll try." He coughed loudly and blew his nose. The Lady sitting opposite Lucy also wiped her face and said with a very firm and clear voice; "You mean go back when most of them are dead?" There was a little murmur amongst the women, but several agreed with the sailor and the discussion seemed to fade away in the shivering, bitter cold as the little boat rose and fell with the soft waves.

Lucy sobbed quietly for some minutes and then felt something in her coat pocket and fumbling about, pulling it out – to her utter Amazement it was a large hipflask. She had no idea how it came to be there and she slowly unscrewed the cap and sniffed the contents; Brandy!

She ran her fingers over the metal body and found it was etched with the name; JERICHO TIBBS, Esq. she had never heard of him, but Lucy took a little sip – it tasted like nectar – then she offered the Lady next to her and the woman gulped some down and smiled at her benefactor. "I couldn't see him, you know, I just couldn't see him." Lucy gently lowered the woman's head upon her shoulder and wrapped her coat tightly.

"I couldn't see my husband, David; I never saw him to say goodbye." The woman gripped Lucy's hand and Lucy whispered; "What was his name?"

The woman lifted her head and wiped her face again; "David Gray. My husband is called David Gray, We're from Richmond in Virginia. Some people are surprised.... or even shocked because he is so much younger than I. But we don't care about that." Lucy realised that the woman must be similar in age to herself and noticed that her tears had stopped. The woman introduced herself as Mrs. Elizabeth Gray and had been visiting London for the funeral of her English grandmother; she was also showing off her new, young husband to relatives.

Lucy found out that Elizabeth had been widowed a couple of years, her first husband had been a very wealthy man involved in the textile business and cotton production. He was found dead in the toilet of his Richmond factory; a vicious heart attack had taken him quickly and with little fuss. It made Elizabeth a very wealthy widow, but she was sad that her and Henry [her late husband] never had the blessing of children - she was apparently barren and every doctor the pair consulted reached the same diagnosis. She had met David shortly afterwards, but the pair had to wait a 'respectable' time before marrying due to the period of mourning expected or rather; required by polite society.

Elizabeth wiped a couple of more tears from her face and confessed that David and her had fought over the revelation that she was in fact, barren. She had only confessed after they married, and he was quite angry about it. But why on earth did it matter - he knew she was an 'older' woman - when they wed, and the prospect of children was already gone!

Lucy spoke about the loss of her young son; Robert to influenza and the enduring pain that she carried regarding his death. Her only comfort was her two grown daughters; both due to marry next year. She slumped back on the hard wooden seat and realised that she would have given her life up for an apparently worthless, cheating seducer. She shuddered and sipped some more brandy, thanking her lucky stars that she had encountered that strange couple – but what had become of them - she wondered?

She stared out into the darkness and could make out another lifeboat some yards away; everyone waved and shouted; the sailor at the tiller turned towards the other boat and shouted to pull hard at the oars. The two little boats headed for each other in the icy blackness.

6. SO MANY DEAD; SO MANY SOULS.

The white galleon slid across the sea's surface with great ease, dipping gently and rolling very little with the waves. On the fore deck, Captain Alfonzo Stark consulted his mirror with great interest, doing the maths in his head, he turned to Alex and smiled; "We've recovered some 1, 496 souls from the water. but we have nine souls still missing which is rather strange, wouldn't you say?" he gestured to the vast empty ocean and added; "Where the hell could they go out here?"

Alex was also reading her mirror and shook her head in puzzlement; "The total taken by the sea is given at 1,503, so how do we have nine missing souls; that's two to many by my calculations." Jericho chuckled and pushed his mirror back into the folds of his long, dark frock coat and folded his arms; "There were two stowaways amongst the steerage passengers, they came aboard when the ship stopped at Queenstown [now called Cobh]. They pretended to be part of the crew working the PS America - the tender that carried passengers and cargo to the Titanic - they then slipped aboard."

He looked down at the lower deck, watching countless souls being greeted by the ten collectors assigned to the case. Little flashes of light gave notice of individual souls commencing their journey to the 'hereafter'. He smiled at Alex; "Angel Margret is going to be busy processing this lot. I understand that Angel Francis is lending a hand [he was Duty Death Angel before

Margret took over the position] He knows what he's doing," Wilson and Owen joined the little group upon the fore deck and confirmed the figure of 1,496 souls being processed - they had the figure on good authority; Raj Bakshi, the Senior Collector present, had told them. Wilson also informed Jericho that the two stowaways were amongst the missing souls. Jericho rubbed his chin, deep in thought until Owen said; "Maybe they were hiding deep in the ship and simply couldn't escape to the upper decks in time."

"Maybe, but that wouldn't explain why their souls are missing." Jericho muttered and his thoughts were interrupted again, this time by Alex, who tapped her mirror; "The two stowaways were local men whose families reported them missing some weeks after the disaster. Of course, no-one knew what had actually happened to them and so there was never any link to the Titanic."

"We need to look very carefully at the missing souls. Owen, get me all the information Records has on them. I think the answer may lay with one of the missing souls." Jericho thrust both hands into his pockets and one hand emerged with a strange little glass orb. They all gathered around him and watched as soft red streaks started to appear around its circumference.

"Fuck." Muttered Captain Stark as he realised that those little streaks indicated a Minion of the 'Dark One' was about - possibly in human form. The group stood in silence until Jericho sighed loudly; "There is only one place the bastard could be hiding in this vast nothing." Everyone followed his gaze towards the huddle of lifeboats some distance away.

"We must have been too quick on scene for it to escape with its prizes." Captain Stark spoke directly to Jericho, who nodded his agreement; "Yes, you would have seen the dark light appear quite clearly and could have called for a Guardian. So, the bugger hid where it thinks it's nice and safe - amongst the still living."

"Which means we must go amongst them and find it before the rescue ship arrives [RMS Carpathia] in a couple of hours. We are now really up against the clock and it's not in our favour." Jericho stared at the little boats as they tried to gather together in the rolling waves. "I've put a call in for a Guardian." Wilson said simply, then chuckled; "It's quite a swim to reach them." Jericho allowed himself a little smile and pointed to an empty and damaged lifeboat floating some yards away; "Can you get that for us captain?" Stark shouted; "Yes!" as he made way down the stairs nearby to arrange its retrieval.

"History records that 705 people survived this disaster, which means our little friend, must be one of them. If we take him or her, we change history and we can't do that, so we need a changeling. Alex, pick one of the dead who has not yet been processed and keep them on standby - I'm pretty sure they will be happy with that!"

Not surprisingly Alex objected to being an arbiter of life and death, but nevertheless, reluctantly agreed. To no-one's surprise, she selected a young child; but remained unhappy about her allocated task.

But everyone was happy when the Guardian appeared; it was their old friend and former colleague; Oscar. He was greeted with much warmth and friendship, even receiving a little kiss upon the cheek from Alex. "O.K. you motley crew of old sea dogs, let's go demon hunting!" Jericho shouted and they made their way to the now resurrected lifeboat and headed towards the other boats.

7. HIDING IN PLAIN SIGHT.

Lucy watched the other lifeboat approach with great interest and a little relief; the odd young couple were safe and sound after all. But the other three characters in the boat caught her eye and she was both puzzled and a little amazed; a strapping big African man, a well-dressed dwarf and a strange young boy with a peculiar grin!

She certainly couldn't recall seeing a big black man about the ship and Lucy would have noticed a dwarf amongst the passengers - he and the black man would have been the talk of the voyage. She wondered about their connection with the strange young couple and believed they must have kept to their cabins to avoid being objects of fascination, whilst at sea.

"Oh my God a black man!" Elizabeth Gray almost spat the words out and added; "I hope he doesn't expect to share this little boat with decent white people." Her words didn't shock Lucy, but they but they did surprise her. Mrs. Gray clearly didn't like or value people, but she was from Richmond, Virginia and that may go a little way, to explain her unpalatable hatred, Lucy reasoned to herself.

That bought her thoughts back to David and they weren't pleasant ones - she really was disgusted and ashamed with herself, at what had passed between the two, especially now; sharing this lifeboat with his wronged wife - and she was the other half to that awful, cheating infidelity and deception. Lucy wondered how many other stupid, desperate women had fallen for his obvious fake charm. She glanced at Elizabeth, who was adjusting her hat against the sea spray and felt a little sympathy for her. She pulled her coat about and shivered in the cold night air and she realised that it would be good to speak to the strange couple again - they had a quiet, reassuring manner about them - and they had certainly saved her life.

Jericho's lifeboat came aside and the sailor at the tiller of Lucy's boat shouted out in welcome; he was clearly relieved to see other men had escaped the terrible calamity - but wondered why the boat only carried five persons. Mr. Andrews [the Titanic's designer and architect who had sailed with her from Liverpool] had told the lifeboat crews; that the little boats were built to carry seventy full grown men.

The sailor also knew that many had been launched only half full, under officer's orders to fill with women and children only. He looked about his little boat and deduced that nearly everyone here was a first- or second-class passenger. What happened to all those women and children in steerage? He pushed the thoughts from his mind, but had his wife and children been on board, they would probably be at the bottom of the sea now. He shuddered at that thought and tried to focus on the job in hand; keeping his passengers safe and sound until rescue.

Oscar leaned forward and, in a voice, just above a whisper said; "It's not here, there's nothing showing on my orb." He pushed the little glass ball back into his pocket and relaxed back in his seat. Jericho nodded his agreement and also replaced his orb into a coat pocket. That's when Alex spotted Lucy, waving and smiling at her. Alex turned to Jericho; "Its Lucy Crawford!"

They both exchanged a quizzical look and Jericho rubbed his chin; thinking hard on the significance of this co-incidence. He turned to Owen, who was on the tiller, and ordered the boat away; to try another craft.

"Wait, hold on!" Alex suddenly exclaimed, as she realised that Lucy was moving quickly, but carefully, through her boat towards them. She could hear Lucy telling people that her friends were in that boat, and she was going to join them. The sailor at the tiller made no objection to that; it was one less damn woman to worry about!

Lucy was gently eased into the lifeboat and hugged Alex with some feeling and settled next to her. Alex noticed the look upon Jericho's face and shrugged her shoulders in reply. There wasn't much they could do about this unexpected turn of events - and Jericho understood that; he sighed loudly and ordered Owen to guide the boat towards another two lifeboats nearby.

"That must be some sort of record for any disaster; a place in three lifeboats in one night!" Owen grinned and guided the boat away. As Alex introduced Owen, Wilson and Oscar to Lucy, Oscar suddenly pushed a hand into his pocket and pulled out his orb - tiny little red streaks had suddenly appeared. He peered hard at the little glass ball and grabbed Jericho by the arm; "I have a very weak presence coming from our new lady friend here!" Jericho confirmed the weak signal with his orb and the little boat went silent with everyone staring at a very confused Lucy.

The team of temporal Detectives all knew what a tiny, weak signal like that indicated; a dark Angel in the making - one in human form and born to a human mother would mean that the dark Angel could survive in the world of humans. It would be a very dangerous adversary when it grew to adulthood and that must be prevented.

But there was the dilemma that Jericho faced; if Lucy perished in the disaster that would prevent the birth of the dark Angel but would change the current Human timeline as she should have survived the sinking! Jericho wasn't very subtle with his questing of the very reluctant Mrs. Crawford, he asked her directly; "Who did you sleep with in the last few hours?"

8. BETWEEN A ROCK AND A HARD PLACE.

It was Alex that finally squeezed the information that Jericho required from a tearful and embarrassed Lucy, the name of her lover.

"There's a David Gray from this era who died at 26 years of age, at Lexington USA. He's a missing soul. Doc Underhill investigated and discovered that the body had been removed from the scene of departure as well, but the fucker was a Satan worshipper." Owen lowered his mirror and Jericho nodded; "The demon has possessed the empty body and re-animated it. If Lucy is right in what his wife has told her, the bastard must have realised he couldn't produce a child with her; hence the seduction of a grieving, separated and vulnerable woman."

They all gazed at the weeping Lucy and Oscar coughed; "If the demon survived the sinking, we'll find the animated corpse of David Gray sitting in one of these little boats. If it couldn't get off the ship, it would abandon the body and make a run for home with its prize of nine souls and the possibility of a dark Angel in future times - all in all - a good day's work for the dark bastard."

"Let's check these boats!" Jericho stated and looked back at Lucy; with her the team was between a rock and a hard place. The young dark Angel that she carried must be destroyed and that would mean leaving Lucy to die in the freezing water apparently just another victim of the disaster. But that would change the current human timeline and they can't allow that to happen! Then, there was the small matter of nine missing souls that needed to be recovered.

Alex nodded her head and folded her arms; "A bloody big rock and hard place!" she muttered and sat back down next to the distraught Lucy. Jericho would have to make a decision - and soon: the rescue ship was less than a hour away.

But first, they must ascertain if the demon or the possessed body of the late David Gray was lurking around the survivors and so they made for the next little gaggle of lifeboats, some metres away. Nothing there and so Jericho and the team moved on to the last few lifeboats, floating together in the soft currents, and again found nothing. But they did get some information about David Gray; the young officer in command of the last lifeboat remembered him and stated that an older woman had given up her seat for him.

"It was really odd Sir." The Officer spoke to Jericho as the two boats bumped gently together; "No sooner than the lady had left, he leapt from the lifeboat and went after her. But that wasn't the last time I saw him."

Jericho asked the young officer to explain about the final view of David Gray. The officer wiped spray from his face and sadly shook his head; "Just before the ship went under, I saw him standing by the staircase to the bridge, just standing there, smoking a bloody pipe like he was on Blackpool promenade! Then she split, with her arse hanging in the air and I watched in horror as he fell into the open decks, smashing off this and that, as he plunged into the interior of the ship. I watched that poor bastard die a terrible death and I will never forget that."

Jericho thanked him and sat back in the lifeboat, pulling his mirror from the folds of his long frock coat; it was gently buzzing and vibrating. He flipped open the device and read the report with some astonishment; the nine missing souls had been recovered and were now aboard the Galleon with Captain Stark!

The second report; from the Records Department was both disturbing and interesting - Jericho kept that one to himself - for the moment. Wilson and Owen were totally puzzled by this turn of events; "Why the hell did the demon abandon such a prize?" Wilson pulled his jacket tightly around and stared at Lucy. Both he and Jericho exchanged a smile, which Alex caught and realised what they were thinking. Jericho turned to Alex and Owen; "Help Lucy into this boat. "He said simply and Lucy was gently transferred to yet another lifeboat, after Jericho had retrieved his hip-flask. Owen grinned broadly and whispered; "Number Four!"

With Lucy safely transferred back to the original lifeboat that she should have been in; Jericho and the team rowed from the scene in silence. Alex broke the quiet; "The bloody demon had no idea that Lucy would end up in our lifeboat and when it saw that temporal detectives were on the case of the missing souls, it made a cold, calculated decision."

Jericho nodded with a little smile; "Yes, it was caught between a rock and hard place too - Had it attempted to call the dark light and escape with the souls, we would have seen, and Oscar would have dealt with it - so losing the souls anyway. So, our clever little demon gambled that we didn't know, what had happened to Lucy, and released the souls to throw us off its case - giving a great chance for the survival of the unborn dark Angel. But it had no idea that Lucy would suddenly climb into our bloody boat and give the game away!"

"Well, its gamble seems to have paid off. We've let Lucy survive the sinking and she'll soon be on the rescue ship and heading for New York, complete with the young dark Angel. Swapping nine souls for a future dark Knight is a pretty good result for the dark bastard." Oscar spoke softly, unsmiling. Jericho gripped his arm and smiled; "Nothing is over until the fat lady sings, my friend." Everyone exchanged confused glances as Jericho sat back in the bow and grinned broadly. The galleon: 'The River Styx' had appeared to pick the team up and they climbed aboard with some relief.

The three bodies that had been originally found in the lifeboat were carefully replaced and the little boat was cast adrift for the final time. It would be found a month later by RMS Oceanic, complete with rotting corpses and of course, no traces of the temporal detectives were ever discovered. Mrs. Lucy Crawford woke with a start in the lifeboat and found two elderly ladies wrapping her with a rugged blanket. "You were calling out in your sleep; we think you may have passed out." One had a posh English ascent and smiled broadly. Lucy felt in her pockets but could not find the hip-flask - she asked the ladies about the strange couple, the big black man and the little dwarf from the other lifeboat.

The two ladies chuckled and told Lucy that she must have dreamt the strange story up; she had gone nowhere since the lifeboat was lowered! That's when Lucy realised, she was in lifeboat No.13 and there was no Elizabeth Gray. She asked the younger of the two ladies, about the young man who was with her, when she entered the boat. Had they seen him in another boat? Had they seen him at all?

Mrs. Alice Cassiter wiped spray from her tired face and told Lucy that she saw the young man disappear into the crowds. Both elderly women exchanged knowing glances; but said nothing. Such things were known to happen on romantic sea voyages, and both had witnessed the passionate embrace of the pair, before Lucy stepped into the little boat. Lucy stared across the dark sea and wondered about the strange dream, as thoughts of young David plagued her mind and she started to doze again.

But the shouting and movement in the small boat stopped her from sleeping. She stared at the horizon and could see the silhouette of a small steamer approaching. The loud voice of the sailor at the stern ended the movements, but the not the happy conversations. He was yelling at everyone to keep still, or they would have the damn thing over.

Lucy watched with real joy, then realised that so many people had not made it; they were at the bottom of the North Atlantic simply because the big steamer didn't carry enough lifeboats. "The bloody Human Hubris strikes again." She thought to herself. Humans though they were invincible and masters of this world. Their ship was unsinkable; nothing could sink it so why bother with lifeboats? Humanity's ego had taken a battering tonight, but would the stupid fools learn from it? Lucy slumped on her seat and pulled her coat around herself. She already knew the answer to her question; no, it bloody wouldn't!

They would create other monsters and worship their own genius until it slaps them in the face. Such was the Human Hubris.

9. NEW YORK; AUGUST 7th, 1912.

Lucy sat in the drawing room of her husband's New York apartment and sipped her tea; she ran a protective hand over her slightly swollen belly and smiled to herself. She had forgiven David for his cheating and lying, for her easy seduction and decided that his death, on that wretched ship, had wiped the slate clean between them. The baby was now Lucy's, and she would love it.

John Crawford had reluctantly taken Lucy back into his house; her condition demanded that - the scandal that could have surrounded his good name and family honour over her infidelity and subsequent pregnancy would have ruined him and his business. Lucy had almost taken delight; informing her cuckold husband, about her condition - she certainly could not have passed the child off as John Crawford's - they've had no sexual relations for almost a year!

She had decided to call the child David, if it was a boy and

Elizabeth if born a girl. Lucy had read about Mrs. Elizabeth Gray becoming a widow for the second time and felt a little sorry for her. But they had never actually met - and she relished the idea of a new baby, despite her age. But her doctors had assured that the child appears normal and healthy for an 'older mother.'
Lucy still thought it was strange, that a woman she had dreamt about was an actual person and she had been on the Titanic. Thoughts about the strange young couple disturbed her sleep - they appeared so real to her - She wondered what had happened to them.

Another woman, Mrs. Doris Edgeware [a widow for six years] was not happy; in fact, she was deeply angry and upset that Lucy had thwarted her plans and future with John Crawford. She had been his mistress for some three years now and even birthed him a son; John had promised marriage as soon as he could divorce Lucy - that dream was now ashes; and the taste was heavy and bitter for her.

John had pleaded with Doris to stay his mistress, but with little pride or future left, Doris had simply left him and returned home to Washington, taking his precious son with her and married a retired sea captain, who was delighted to have a young wife and son to dote on. John Crawford was a very angry and disappointed man - Lucy had simply destroyed his future and appeared to have taken great delight in doing so.

John Crawford brooded on his miserable life and after drinking for some hours, walked into the drawing room that afternoon, confronting Lucy with all his anger and heartache. She simply laughed and patted her stomach; "My child will know all about his real father, when he's old enough." She placed her teacup down and smiled at John.

He said nothing more but stepped back and picked up the heavy poker from the fireplace and beat his unfaithful wife to death. He walked slowly from the room and slumped in the big, high-backed chair in his study. After several minutes he could hear Lucy's lady-maid screaming and pulled open the bottom drawer of his desk and removed the little, pearl handed pistol from it. The already distraught maid heard the single gunshot and ran screaming into the road, where a passing police officer rushed to her aid. She almost fainted into his arms; still screaming "Bloody murder!"

10. THE FAT LADY SINGS.

Alex eased herself into the big, comfortable armchair by the fireplace and picked up her latest book; **'The wreck of the Titan.'** [also known as **'Futility'**] by Morgan Robertson. She was on the last few pages and sipped her brandy with some pleasure.

"I can't believe he wrote these some fourteen years before the Titanic actually sank - it's totally fascinating that he could have made such a prediction." She spoke to Owen, who was playing chess by himself, copying moves from a book on the subject of great Chess games. He looked up and grinned; "I knew you would love that, especially after that little adventure on the Titanic."

Owen moved a couple of pieces and decided now was the time to broach the subject of the Internal Affairs inquiry outcome; "Alex, can I ask you something?"

Alex nodded; "Of course Owen." He chuckled and held up both hands; "How the hell did Jericho get you and Skyrise off the bloody hook; that Chief Inspector Samoski had you dead to rights!" She smiled and shook her head; "I honestly don't really know Owen, all we received was a strong caution, when we both should have been demoted - that's what we were expecting."

"Wilson believes he [Jericho] got Angel Margret to pull a few strings with the Archangel himself. But little Oscar said he heard 'himself' [God] had made his opinion known and that was that. Wilson also understands that 'himself' had a visit from James the Knight [who had quite a thing about Alex!] just before he made that opinion known. Strange that eh?" Owen stated quietly and grinned.

Alex just smiled and settled back to finish her read but was interrupted by Mr. Harris announcing Dinner and that Mr. Tibbs had returned to the lighthouse, straight from his meeting with Angel Margret. "Where's Wilson?" Owen asked; it was unlike Wilson to miss dinner!

"Mr. Wilson is at the Inspectors Training Course and tonight is one of his study groups - Mrs. Harris will keep him something warm." Mr. Harris allowed a small smile to cross his face and departed for the Dining Room. Owen chuckled and jumped up;

"Come on Alex, let's grab some grub." Alex sighed and closed her book, placing it upon the coffee table and looked up as Jericho sauntered into the room and warmed his backside by the fire. "I saw Oscar today; he had some interesting news regarding that little adventure we had on the Titanic." Jericho said quietly and poured himself a whisky, sipping it very slowly. Owen and Alex stopped in the doorway and Alex folded her arms in anticipation of bad tidings.

But Jericho smiled; "That little dark Angel won't bother any humans or us. It's dead." He swallowed down his whisky and rubbed his hands together, adding; "Let's get to dinner, its roast chicken with all the trimmings."

"I can't wait to hear the rest of Oscar's news." Owen followed Alex and Jericho into the Dining Room, where over an excellent chicken dinner, Jericho imparted the news that Oscar had passed on to him. Alex admitted to being sad over the manner of Lucy's death, but glad that the little dark Angel was gone. She asked Jericho if he knew her fate when he allowed her to re-join the lifeboat. He nodded.

"I received an interesting message from Records, when the call came in about the return of the lost souls. It appeared that Lucy's estranged husband would kill her less than four months after she reached New York, in a fit of drunken anger." He picked up his wine glass, adding: "You see if Lucy died on the Titanic, then her husband would not have committed suicide, but would have married his long-time mistress and raised their son together. The boy was the problem, under his father's influence and with his inherited wealth, he entered politics and would have ran for President in 1960 instead of Jack Kennedy and he would have won!"

"Bugger!" exclaimed Owen and swigged his wine; "What did happen to the boy?"

"In the current Timeline, he fell out with both his mother and Stepfather. He left home at sixteen without finishing school or college and joined the Navy. He was killed at Pearl Harbour." Jericho sipped his wine and smiled a little at Alex; "Angel Margret was really quite pleased with the outcome, considering the assignment took a couple of shitty twists!"

Owen shrugged his shoulders and raised his glass; "To the fat lady singing."

BOOKS AVAILABLE IN THE "ADVENTURES OF ALEXANDRA" SERIES.

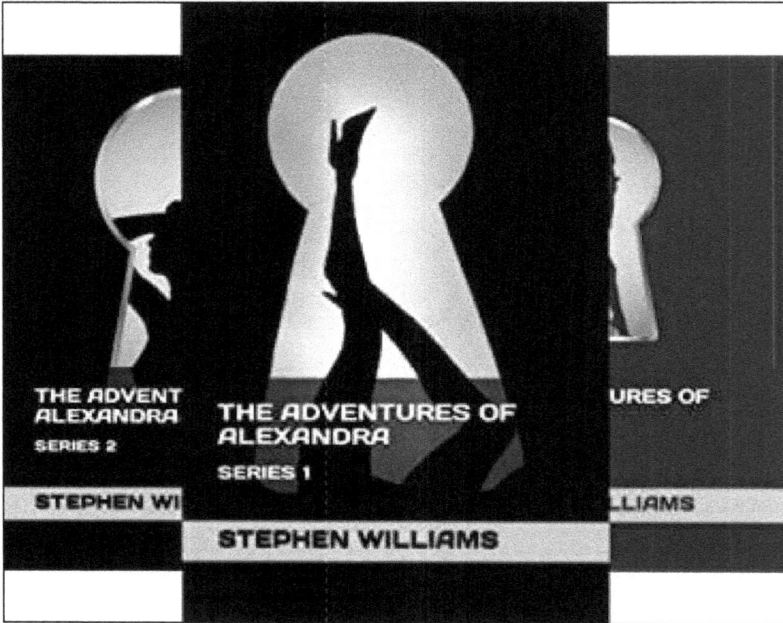

"The naughty adventures of ALEXANDRA - A character from The Temporal Detective series of books - follow Alexandra and her sexy & naughty adventures through time!
Warning: Contains content suitable for ADULTS ONLY with open and mature minds! These stories contain erotic scenes and graphic sexual descriptions, mixed with adventure, action, supernatural & paranormal activities: Not to mention time-travel!

These are the ALTERNATIVE ADULT VERSIONS of stores appearing in the series: 'THE TEMPORAL DETECTIVES' by the same author. This series is also available on AMAZON and good bookshops everywhere."

BOOKS AVAILABLE IN THE "TEMPORAL DETECTIVES" SERIES.

"THE TEMPORAL DETECTIVES!"

"Welcome to the amazing adventures of Mister Jericho Tibbs!" Jericho lives in Stark Island's Lighthouse on Heaven's Edge Bay, in the North of Scotland. A wild and desolate place, the now disused lighthouse is his home and office. You see, Jericho actually works for God - well, his direct Boss is, for now - Angel Margret who is the current Duty Death Angel and runs the Temporal Detectives Department. The Temporal Detectives police the current Timeline of Humanity on the lookout for people who, for whatever reason, have appeared in the wrong time and place in human history. Their mission is protecting the current human Timeline from unwanted changes."

AVAILABLE FROM 'AMAZON.COM' and all good bookshops!

9 781738 487578